No Need
to Know

D1558884

Mark A. Hewitt

Black❀Rose
writing™

ISBN: 978-1-61296-578-9

PUBLISHED BY BLACK ROSE WRITING

www.blackrosewriting.com

Printed in the United States of America

Suggested retail price $23.95

No Need to Know is printed in Adobe Caslon Pro

The principle of "**need to know**" is applied when safeguarding confidential or secret information. Access to highly classified information is restricted to those who need to know the information while pursuing their official duties.

No Need
to Know

I have too much admiration for those who fight evil, whether
their choice of ends and means be right or wrong.
~Czeslaw Milosz, *The Captive Mind*

PROLOGUE

April 9, 1945

Pierre's eyes fell to the dark satchel as four jackbooted Nazis abruptly entered the smoke-filled nightclub. A lengthy loop of chrome chain swayed from a sleeve, suggesting the bag was shackled to the wrist of the man in the suit. The German officers' intentionally clicked their stacked leather heels with every step on the wooden floor, the sound was intentional and intimidating. Slow-motion eddies followed the old patrons as they moved through the Jovian-like atmosphere, retreating from their perches at the bar to hunt for a table or to leave. The room hushed as a fever of dread and friction spread. The suited man emerged from the protective cocoon of black uniforms of *Obersturmführers* and *Sturmbannführers* of the Gestapo and placed the briefcase atop the bar. Long links of chain spilled over the side of the bag. Even in the dull light from kerosene lamps the polished links sparkled. The security detail of officers moved as remora to surround the man in grey, two on each side. Their eyes scanned the clientele for threats.

The bartender hid his fear well as he poured drinks for the men at the bar, relieved he hadn't spilled a drop. That might have elicited a nasty response from one of the younger officers who would have to prove he was more captious and evil than his counterparts. Such a response had happened in the past; the bartender had learned his lesson days earlier when a short-barreled Luger was raked across his face. As one of the many defeated and patriotic Frenchmen, he would mind his manners and be very careful as he served the snakes that slithered into his nightclub.

Nearly every Frenchman and woman unconsciously lowered their heads in submission as the Germans went through their boisterous and domineering routine. The lone exception, Pierre Oliver, broke his fixation on the satchel when the chained Nazi raised a stein of beer toward his colleagues in toast and damned the American President, Franklin Roosevelt. The unusual toast quietly angered him but it also stirred his curiosity. He raised his eyes from the briefcase to the Nazis just as the impolite and arrogant man in the grey suit raised his beer and damned the United States of America. Oliver frowned and pinched his lips; his temples bulged from his conscious attempt to prevent grinding his teeth together. Under sharp black hats adorned with silver braid, eagles clutching a wreath, and a silver skull, a *totenkopf* or death's head, framed penetrating iceberg blue eyes which telegraphed evil and malice. The four uniformed men panned the room for trouble while demanding compliance and submission without uttering a word; they placed their hands over polished black leather holsters to emphasize their superiority. The nightclub patrons hurriedly raised their glasses and responded in kind to the men with red armbands, black swastikas, and the electrified SSs on their collars.

Five against one. Four weapons. Fair odds. Oliver crushed his cigarette under his boot and began to excuse himself and leave the building when the shackled Nazi raised a drink and loudly damned the United States Marine Corps. Pierre sensed the Gladstone was likely a trap as the Germans were well aware an American Marine was operating in the immediate area. *Damning the Marine Corps?* A handful of Marines were in the European theater but only one stood out. Their interest in him made him smile. Captain Ortiz often stood in uniform on a horizon, his captain bars gleaming in the sun, his hat cocked, arms akimbo, brazenly taunting disorganized Germans after an attack. No longer considered just a nuisance, the Nazis redoubled their efforts to find and kill the American leader of the Resistance. If the bag was bait, Ortiz stalked his prey. He hurried out of the back of the club and into the rain.

. . .

United States Marine Corps Captain Peter Ortiz, attached to the Office of Strategic Services, had parachuted into the forest near Lyon to help organize and lead elements of the French underground forces. As war broke out in Europe, Ortiz had enlisted in the French Foreign Legion to fight Nazis, and rose through the ranks from private to lieutenant. After three years of fighting and killing Nazis, he was wounded and captured, spending over a year as a prisoner of war. After a number of failed escape attempts, he finally succeeded and returned to his home in the United States. The only son of an American father and a French mother, he was eager to get back into the fight in Europe. With France occupied and the French Foreign Legion a fragment of what it used to be, he enlisted in the Marine Corps where, as a lowly boot camp private, he stood out from the rest of the recruits of his platoon. He wore the medals he had received as a Legionnaire—for valor under combat—multiple *Croix de Guerre,* the *Croix des Combattants,* the *Ouissam Alaouite,* and the *Medaille Militaire.* The decorations created significant interest with his Drill Instructors and the senior officers at Parris Island. His medals and service with the Legion explained much about the remarkably quiet and fearless man. A Marine colonel recommend Ortiz for a commission. Based on Ortiz's unique experiences in France, he suggested another private going off to war in the Pacific wasn't in the best interests of the Marine Corps or the Nation. However, a French-speaking Marine Corps *Lieutenant* would be of exceptional value to American units in North Africa or France. Promoted directly to Captain from Second Lieutenant, Ortiz was assigned to the newly formed and secretive Office of Strategic Services and was immediately thrust back into the worst of the fighting. General Wild Bill Donovan, the head of the OSS, welcomed the fluent French speaker and assigned Ortiz to lead Free French *Maquisards* against the Germans. Ortiz picked up where he left off as a Legionnaire and killed Germans by the score. And, he left calling cards.

When leading *Maquis* groups, Captain Peter Ortiz wore his dark green Marine uniform during raids on German positions or when ambushing Nazi troop movements. Having an Allied officer leading bands of *Maquis* bolstered the Frenchmen's morale immensely, especially when the Marine's uniform bore the combat decorations of the French Foreign Legion. Ortiz and his small band of French patriots left great numbers of Germans dead and wounded in their wake. Taking a few non-lethal injuries, not a single *Maquis* was ever captured or lost under his leadership. While the German High Command was furious at their inability to capture or kill the maverick Marine; Adolf Hitler took a personal interest in the American troublemaker and placed a bounty on the unnamed man.

• • •

In his role as a spy, Ortiz donned the garb of an effeminate Parisian and the persona of Pierre Oliver who frequented a nightclub which often catered to transiting German officers. The cover enabled him to gain much needed intelligence regarding Hun activities in the area, which he turned to good use against the Germans. This blatant *demarche* of an apparent Nazi civilian surrounded by Gestapo bringing a tethered and chained satchel into the nightclub was too much for Ortiz to ignore.

He raced into his apartment and changed from the rutty garb of a gay Frenchman into the uniform of a U.S. Marine; a black leather Sam Brown belt passed diagonally over his right shoulder, a black holster at his right side with a service .45 caliber pistol tucked firmly inside, loaded, locked and cocked. He shrugged into a raincoat and returned to the club.

A rain-soaked man shook off the wetness at the door and stomped his boots before he sidled up to the bar next to the German officers and ordered a round of drinks "for the house." Under the curious eye of the man with the briefcase and the Gestapo, the barkeep served refreshments to the Nazis at the bar first. As the Germans acknowledged their host with a truncated toast and a click of their heels, Ortiz dramatically tossed aside his raincoat and stood brandishing the .45 pistol and pointing it at the older German in the middle of the group. The Nazis in black were shocked, the patrons stunned; the only sound was the Nazi civilian's sudden asthmatic wheezing as he attempted to say, "Teufelhund." In German it meant "Devil Dog." That was what the German soldiers yelled when they encountered U.S. Marines on the field of battle.

Resplendent in his fully tailored green uniform with a chest full of Legionnaire decorations, Ortiz demanded another round of toasts. He waved the dull grey Colt toward the Germans and shouted, "To the

President of the United States!" His pistol moved from Nazi to Nazi as they toasted the President Roosevelt and quickly emptied their glasses. The semi-automatic rarely left the chest of the hyperventilating older man in the suit. When it did the Colt was pointed at the foreheads of the other blonde haired, blue-eyed men. The Marine ordered another round of drinks and then offered a toast to the United States of America. The Nazis reluctantly toasted the United States with encouragement from the big bore pistol. The Germans emptied their glasses. The other patrons in the bar cheered inside but remained outwardly quiet. All were curious to see how the drama would end.

"Hands on the bar, gentlemen," said Ortiz coolly.

The Nazis had concluded the American Marine before them was insane, and they anticipated a final toast before their death. Their weapons remained tightly holstered. With their hands on the bar they knew they hadn't a chance to escape or put up a fight. The nightclub was eerily silent. All eyes were transfixed on the man brandishing the pistol as he plucked the strings of the taut and terrified Germans like a virtuoso cellist.

"One more, gentlemen," said the Marine, his voice menacing yet firm. Without taking his eyes off the men in black, Ortiz ordered another round of drinks. The bartender quickly complied, and then backed away to a safe corner. The big pistol was more intimidating as he moved incrementally closer to the Nazis. Ortiz then stepped back and loudly offered a toast to the United States Marine Corps. The Germans were transfixed, afraid they would be shot if they refused to comply.

"*I can't hear you!* It is very simple...if you want to live. To the United States Marine Corps!" He thrust the .45 into the face of each tremulous German officer and demanded, "All together now, to the United States Marine Corps!"

In heavily accented Bavarian, the five men shouted, "To the United States Marine Corps!" The wide-eyed Germans struggled to drink as beer splashed from the sides of their trembling mugs. Before the men could return their glass to the bar, Ortiz shot the four uniformed Nazis in the knees. The Colt erupting in the confined space of the club was deafening. Smoke from the barrel mixed with cigarette smoke; spent cartridges arced through the haze. The man in the grey suit jumped with every round fired.

Ortiz assessed the damage. Four screaming and bleeding Gestapo writhed on the floor clutching four shattered knees. He grabbed the shocked Nazi civilian by the neck and drove him aggressively backwards into a chair. All eyes in the club darted from Nazis to the Marine. The chained bag flew from the bar top, through the air, and onto the floor. Ortiz jammed the smoldering pistol into the open mouth of the terrified man and slammed his knee deep into the crotch of the German. The old Nazi's eyes bulged, his face turned crimson as he cringed and wept.

"Key, *mien Herr,*" ordered Ortiz.

The old Nazi reeked of fear; he shook his head violently. The barrel of the weapon crashed into and chipped his teeth with every terrified shake of his head. The Gestapo officers screamed in a growing pool of blood on the floor, in such agony as to be unable to think about protecting their general. The pain from their shattered knees was so severe they were unable to flee the maniac or draw a weapon to kill their assailant. The club clientele leaned forward to get a better look, silently encouraged retribution as they watched the Marine officer viciously slap the man with a gun in his mouth.

"Last chance. *Key! Schlüssel!*" Ortiz was out of patience.

The German refused; his eyes ballooned from their sockets like a surprised Peter Lorre as more pressure from an insistent knee was applied to the old man's genitals. The American wouldn't be denied. Ortiz yanked a length of chain from the man's wrist and draped it over the German's knee. As he extricated the weapon from the man's mouth, the Nazi followed the barrel cross-eyed. The withdrawal of the weapon from his mouth provided immediate relief which turned to instant horror when the Marine placed the pistol's barrel against the links of the chain. The immediate emotional reversal drained all color from the Nazi's lips and face, and the man passed out. A pull of the trigger severed the chain in a burst of metal, bone, and blood and nearly separated the unconscious man's lower leg.

Ortiz grabbed the freed satchel by the handle and backed away from the whimpering and blood-soaked Nazis. He took a moment to assess the damage to the Germans on the floor. Each man was defeated, their nearly severed legs were askew at odd angles. They sobbed in shock and pain. Satisfied none of them could recover sufficiently to be a threat, Ortiz retrieved and casually draped his raincoat over his uniform. With the briefcase in one hand, he saluted the astonished patrons with the pistol in the other bidding, *"Adieu. Vive la France!"*

. . .

There were spies everywhere and soon the word spread of the American who again ambushed the Germans. The Nazis would never let him escape with the bag, and the French would pay dearly for their treachery. Within an hour of his attack on the Nazis in the nightclub, the German High Command flooded Lyon with Nazi stormtroopers. They were told to find the Marine and to be especially vicious to the French who helped him orchestrate his attack and facilitated his escape. Ortiz fled to the forest overlooking Roman ruins at the base of the French Alps, back into the arms of the *Maquis*. The leather satchel never left his hand.

"I must leave you, my friends," he said to a standing dozen Free Frenchmen. "I must go to Geneva by all haste. You must leave too. These woods will soon be crawling with Germans."

"We will take you," offered several freedom fighters.

Ortiz half-bowed. *"Merci beaucoup.* I am honored. I accept your assistance. But we must move quickly."

Seven days and 85 miles later, a weary band of Frenchmen and an American entered the outskirts of Geneva, Switzerland. A three-hour train to Bern and a forty-five minute walk placed Captain Peter Ortiz at the doorstep of an apartment at Herrengasse 23. The Swiss Director of the U.S. Office of Strategic Services, Allen Dulles, received the weary Marine officer and took possession of the dark brown leather satchel, still encumbered with two feet of heavy chain. After he sent Ortiz to bathe and rest, Dulles retired to his study, sliced open the thick leather, and removed the contents of the bag of SS General Stephan Hinkle.

Dulles would never again see a more diverse set of important documents. A green, clothbound logbook detailed descriptions of artwork removed from museums and residences with annotations for artist, condition, and dimensions. He opened the book to a random page and read the names of the great masters: Duccio, Perugino, and Botticelli. Another page listed Leonardo da Vinci, Raphael, and Correggio. He sighed at the entries of Rubens, Delacroix, and Rembrandt van Rijn. "All in German hands; a pity." He glanced over his shoulder to ensure he was alone. He repositioned his pipe and thought, *"I doubt that ruffian Ortiz would know the difference between a Raphael, a Rubens, or a Rembrandt."*

Dulles put down the logbook and retrieved a gold-embossed, dyed-blue leather diary. He mulled over the book and wondered whose thoughts were contained within. He was shocked to find he was holding the diary of Admiral Wilhelm Canaris. Dulles held the book with trembling hands and reflected that the head of the dreaded *Abwehr*, German military intelligence, was suspected of treason and had been jailed by Hitler for an assassination attempt. Canaris' incarceration had been a poor secret for the better part of a year, but the proof of his treachery had yet to be found. Dulles was cognizant of reports that Canaris' recent execution likely occurred on the day Ortiz acquired the satchel. The realization suddenly shamed Dulles. The man upstairs in the bathtub might not have had a classical education in the arts but was probably the smartest man in Europe to have recognized the satchel for what secrets it might have inside. Ortiz was undeniably courageous for getting the bag out of France and into the hands of the OSS.

Intelligence sources—Nazi, American, British, and Russian—had been in a mad dash for over a year to find the Canaris diary which they believed contained countless Nazi secrets and detailed mass atrocities, as well as the names of key people who had participated in the plots on Hitler's life. Dulles thumbed through the book and quickly ascertained the intelligence analysts were more than correct. In Nazi hands, the diary signed Canaris' death warrant and those of his friends. He allowed the diary to fall gently across the logbook of stolen art. "Explosive," whispered Dulles.

A set of blueprints opened up to reveal an airplane design. Very long wings with a canopy atop a fuselage with an extended nose and no propeller marked the aircraft as unusual and odd. To the uninitiated OSS man, the design was perplexing. "*Outré*," uttered Dulles. He tossed the blueprints to the side.

A small black leather bag lay before him. It tinkled inside when he lifted it to inspect it. Dulles was confused by the contents of sixteen penny-nails with a seventeenth embedded into the center of a small block of wood. A manila file was attached to the pouch with a clip. With the thick red rubric *Siebzehn Nagel*, 17 Nails, dozens of loose-leaf, lime-green sheets—from an engineering tablet—listed names, addresses, occupations, and time. *"Time?"* thought Dulles. He dropped the file and left the nails to rest atop the pouch.

The final group of documents contained individual sheets of lines of letters, numbers, and symbols. "Gibberish," he spat. Hand-printed letters, numbers, and symbols spilled across engineering paper, each character inked into the tiny squares of the graph paper. Two groups of eight to a line, aligned in groups of four, twenty lines to a sheet. Five sheets printed on a single side. Dulles became more frustrated as he recognized the work of a cryptologist. He searched the inside of the satchel and the outside pockets thoroughly. No one-time pad. No key to break the code. No other scraps of paper. "Another mystery," he sighed without letting his pipe fall from his lips. "Probably need an Enigma machine to crack the code."

"Pardon?" asked a freshly bathed, shaved, and combed Captain Ortiz. In stockinged feet, he padded into the study to find the OSS Director staring dreamily out of a window. Dulles was grateful the previously odiferous man had the sense to use cologne before he changed into a freshly laundered shirt.

Without breaking his gaze, Dulles gestured in the direction of the satchel and its contents, and said, "Not sure what you have here, my man. But it's a bloody gold mine. A catalog of artwork—likely stolen by the Nazis. Every major impressionist and painter from the middle ages to…ah, Leonardo da Vinci. The long lost Admiral Canaris diary. But the other contents, I'm at a loss as to what they are and what they may mean. By my calculations, Canaris was executed on the day you picked these up. General Donovan will be interested in your treasure trove. You've done exceedingly well. You deserve a medal."

Ortiz's curiosity was piqued. He diverted his attention to the bag and flipped through the logbook, the diary, the file, and the loose documents. The names and titles in the art logbook meant little to him; some were vaguely familiar. He shook his head to reconcile why five German officers would protect such a bizarre set of items. The diary of the head of military intelligence, was its discovery the tipping point in Canaris' death? Did it contain the names of his co-conspirators? The identification and location of stolen artwork—it'd make some sense to protect that information. Blueprints for an airplane? A bag of nails and a folder? That was more than strange; it was bizarre. Ortiz picked up a single nail and inspected it. Dulles heard the dull rustling of metal against metal and turned from the window, looking over his shoulder to see what the Marine was doing with the nails.

Ortiz placed the block of wood with the nail impaled upright on the table and scrutinized the vertical nail with the one in his hand. He rubbed the nail between his fingers to get a sense of what material made up the nail. Convinced the nail was a standard penny-nail, he placed the loose nail atop the other, until it balanced perfectly on the flat nail head. "It's a test of some kind," he said. Ortiz's demeanor instantly changed as he assessed the challenge, like a detective who realized he had just found the first murky clue surrounding a murder investigation.

"Are you sure?" asked Dulles, spinning from the window to the table. He wasn't convinced the nails represented anything important and remained wary of the man's outburst.

"Quite. The folder has a column to record times. It must be a test. Intelligence. Aptitude. Likely complex problem solving. Something. For it to be in the satchel, it must be very important. At least it was to someone."

"What does it mean? Can you solve it?"

"I'm not sure. It seems the most improbable task would be to balance all of the nails on the head of the other." Ortiz banged two nails together. "They're not made of a special metal nor are they magnetized." He then tried to hang them, one on each side, from their large flat heads on the nail suspended atop the other.

"But...*that's impossible!*" objected Dulles as he scrutinized the man in uniform as he tinkered with individual nails.

He tried to hang two nails over a third but they wouldn't hold. Ortiz watched intently as the two nails swung in opposite directions and slipped off the balanced nail, sending all three loose nails crashing onto the table. As Dulles barked, "See—impossible!" Ortiz subconsciously rocked on his heels. He saw something. Something very subtle in the movement of the opposite nails swinging...unbalancing the top balanced nail before falling. His mind raced at the possibilities, juggling options and discarding the obviously wrong solutions. Once he discerned the proper sequence, he broke out into a broad smile. Ortiz's hands flew over the table as he arranged nails left and right on top of one nail. Then he put another nail on top of them, then lifted, and gently placed, and balanced sixteen nails on the head of the seventeenth. He turned and smirked at the OSS man.

"My God!" whispered Dulles once he composed himself, "I never could have done that. My man, that was...*brilliant*."

He dismissed the compliment and flipped open the file folder. "Obviously, not impossible. But why? Who are these people? What does it mean?"

Dulles searched to find words after the quick display of the man's brilliance and acumen. "I do...not know. I know I must get these—all of these—to General Donovan immediately." He continued to stare at the sixteen balanced nails which looked like an impaled fourteen-legged crab.

Ortiz offered his hand to Dulles. "And, I must get back to the war. The French need me." The two men shook hands firmly. "Thank you for your hospitality, Mister Dulles. May the next time we meet it will be under better circumstances." Captain Ortiz donned his uniform coat and stepped outside the apartment in freshly shined boots. He smiled and offered, "There are many more Nazis to kill before this war is over." He informally saluted the OSS man with a touch of his brow, then turned and walked away.

CHAPTER ONE

October 31, 1969

U. S. Air Force Technical Sergeant Lincoln Hunter stepped through the doorway of the apartment expecting to find his three boys running around getting ready for Halloween. He was unprepared for what he saw in the middle of the small living room—slabs of cardboard were scattered about the sofa and chairs. On the floor, his wife and children were handling dozens of yellow and chrome metal pieces. A small but wildly bright yellow frame and two black tires—one small and the other even smaller—suggested the contents was some kind of bicycle. "What the hell is that?" he inquired, tossing questioning hands up in the air.

"Duncan won a comic book contest. We're trying to put this bicycle together," said Jackie Hunter. Her dark eyes and smile flashed pride just as jet-black hair cascaded over her face. She tossed her head just enough to reposition her unbundled tresses. She read curiosity on her husband's face. She smiled. She winked. "We need help."

It took an hour to assemble the fork, to screw pedals into the chrome crank, install yellow handgrips, mount a speedometer and a headlight on high handlebars, tighten the banana seat to the tall seat post, and inflate the disparate tires. Once finished, the family went downstairs to watch the oldest of the boys take to the street on the yellow Schwinn Lemon Peeler. Duncan begged his mother to let him go out to the woods, where he and his friends would ride their bicycles. "You have to be back before it gets dark to take your brothers Trick or

19

Treating," she replied. Jackie smiled at Lincoln. He hadn't anticipated being alone with his wife.

On the flashiest American bike in Europe, with the 16-inch balloon tire in the front, Duncan Hunter rode the yellow Sting-Ray out of the apartment complex that was base housing of Ramstein Air Base, West Germany. He took the sidewalk past the gymnasium and bowling alley, around the fishpond, and past the swan's nest. He continued a circuitous route to the other side of the air base to a well-hidden location in the woods where Duncan could enjoy his first passion—watching the big Phantom jets take off and land. As he made his way around to the perimeter road and past the runway threshold, he was surprised that he couldn't hear any jets landing or taking off or flying overhead.

The Phantom II looked and played the part of a rhino—it was a brute with a longish nose which some claimed resembled the massive horn of rhinoceros and it always signaled its presence with a thunderous roar. When it'd take off the two huge General Electric turbojet engines in afterburner were deafening. Burning jet fuel at eight gallons a second, the supersonic shockwaves from the engines shook the ground until well after the aircraft departed the runway. Duncan would grin and press his hands to the earth to feel the power of the thundering jet. He would crawl on his belly to get as close as he dared. He worried that pilots, military police, or even air traffic controllers would see him and send a security truck out after him. Sometimes he would get so close he could feel the heat of the engine exhaust as the jet took off. During landing, the jet screamed in an unbelievably high-pitched mechanical wail. Duncan would jam his pinky fingers into his ears until the jet landed. With no roaring or screaming coming from the runway, Duncan embarked on his second favorite passion, riding a bicycle as fast as he dared along animal trails through the woods.

He raced up one trail and sped over tiny hillocks. Faster and more daring, he rode with all the zeal of a kid with a brand new bike. Hunter checked the speedometer from time to time to see how fast he could get the sturdy bike to go. He was in new territory, further in the woods than he had ever dared.

Through leafless trees and piles of leaves he saw a small hill that looked like it'd be immensely fun to race down. Maybe he could get the bike to go even faster than before. He pedaled like a petite Tour de France racer as he climbed the gradual hill and stopped at the top to set up for the big event, to speed down what looked to him like a near vertical decline. Anxiety shook him; the hill was steeper than he expected and riding down it was going to be more than a little scary. He kicked caution to the curb. He had a speedometer and he was determined to see how fast he could make the new Schwinn go. He told himself that after he conquered the hill, he'd head back home. Duncan summoned up courage and with the yell of a soccer announcer, pushed off like an Olympic bobsled racer and pedaled like a crazy person, his legs pumped wildly. He shifted the tall gearshift lever between his legs through most its gears—first, second, third! As he crossed the apex of the hill and tore through a mound of leaves, the earth collapsed out from under him.

Duncan and the Sting-Ray collided with something hard, bounced back and then tumbled straight down. At first, he couldn't let go of the handlebars but self-preservation took over and he pushed away from the bike. He anticipated pain and fear while he fell, kicking and clawing in midair; he knew it was going to hurt at the sudden stoppage. When he landed in a thick pile of leaves, he immediately took stock that he was unhurt. He thrashed through loose leaves to find out what happened to his new bike. When he found the Schwinn he checked it for damage. He ran his hands over the frame and checked the tires. He whooped with joy that the Sting-Ray wasn't damaged. He adjusted the headlight to its proper position. A blast of cold air from behind him shocked his senses and scared him, as if some evil monster had suddenly crept up behind him and exhaled on his neck. Fear spiked as he looked over his shoulder.

The dark maw of a cave beckoned. Adrenaline shot through his veins. He shook slightly as he slowly looked away from the darkness of the cave and toward the hill from where he fell, wondering how far he had fallen, when he saw it. He stared and couldn't move. Frigid air enveloped him as if a malevolent spirit surrounded him.

High above the cave opening drilled into the rock face was an eagle with elongated wings clutching a wreath. Inside the wreath, a swastika. The eye of the eagle looked back at him. Duncan's eyes darted back and forth from the emblem of the Nazis to the cold darkness of the cave. He looked around him and saw a wall of camouflage netting, heavy with decades of leaves that he could use to get out, get away. The chill of solid concrete behind him propelled him to move. The eye of the eagle didn't leave him.

He'd seen the remnants of Nazi bunkers—his father called them pillboxes—along intermittent stretches of the autobahn when the Hunters had first come to Germany in the early 1960s. The huge concrete structures usually had small openings; every bunker Duncan had previously seen had been shattered from aerial bombings. He could hear his father's voice warning him, "You can't go inside—they're very dangerous." He also learned a new word—booby-trap. Dad said the pillboxes had been booby-trapped when the Nazis left.

"This isn't a pillbox," Duncan whispered. Two inner voices punctured his fear—the monsters inside the cave and the wrath of his mother if he was late. He could face the monsters or he could flee and tell his mother what he found. His curiosity was winning the tug of war. He noticed the chain of his bike hadn't even fallen off of the crank during the fall, but the light generator had gotten bumped and the friction wheel of the dynamo now rested against the racing slick tire. Hunter lifted the rear of the banana seat and spun the crank—light from the headlamp increased its intensity as the tire rotated.

With the heavy yellow bicycle on his shoulder, and with knees trembling slightly, Duncan Hunter spun a pedal on the crank and slowly entered the cave, aiming the anemic light at his feet. The illumination from the bike lamp wasn't very bright, but he could see rows and rows of large tall boxes, not unlike the containers he'd seen in his father's supply warehouse. He hadn't taken twenty tiny cautious steps into the cave when the bike light reflected off something small and shiny. In the otherwise pitch-black area, he neared the source of the reflections and saw several stacks of cloth bags. With much trepidation, Duncan reached out and lifted one of the bags. It was heavy and he heard the soft tinkle of metal. *That's enough* he thought and slid the bag into his jacket pocket as he backtracked out of the cave. He spun the crank and hoped some sleeping monster from Hell didn't awaken from boxy shadows and surprise him during his escape.

After a nightmarish five minutes of climbing around the thick camouflage netting and over years of leaf debris, Duncan was back in the saddle of his yellow banana seat and was about to push off and head home. He reached into his pocket and withdrew the cloth bag. Sometime between putting the bag in his pocket and removing it, the physical structure of the old cloth failed and the contents of the bag spilled out. A number of dull yellow coins scattered on the ground. Duncan hurriedly reached down and retrieved every one and returned them to his pocket. With some concern that he had become a thief, he pulled a coin out of his pocket and gazed at the face of it.

On the obverse of the heavy yellow coin, a crude Nazi emblem— eagle and swastika—was embossed. The coin was as big around as his mother's silver dollar necklace but twice as thick. Below the emblem was stamped 1943. The reverse was center-stamped with letters and numbers. He sucked cold air and quickly looked all around him. He kicked his kickstand and ran to the top of the hill. He gathered branches and placed them across the hole he had punctured in the camouflage netting between the two stones. Armfuls of leaves completed the work and covered the bunker entrance.

Duncan made it home with little time to spare and never told his mom or anyone else of his discovery. He had escaped the monsters and the eagle's eye once, he never returned to the cave although he thought about it every day. He hid the fifty coins in a sock in the corner of a toy box for several years, and when he was old enough to carry a wallet, he carried within it a single gold coin as a memento of his first great adventure.

CHAPTER TWO

0200 May 5, 2013

As the little black airplane turned toward the East African coastline, turbulence bounced the pilot around in his seat; his helmet banged into the side of the canopy. After ten minutes of fighting the buffeting tailwinds, the aircraft streamed over the beach and dense jungle of Somalia. The night air calmed down as the Jubba River came into view. Moonlight reflected off a long uninterrupted stretch of waterway.

The pilot retarded the throttle and allowed the aircraft to slow naturally and slip into its quiet flight profile. He lowered the turret housing the FLIR—forward looking infrared—into the airstream under the aircraft. A couple of clicks of elevator trim and the aircraft's flight controls accommodated for the additional drag of the thermal imaging sensor.

He choreographed the intercept perfectly. The pilot slewed the FLIR to view the middle of the river and acquired the little skiff; the heat from the engine was ablaze in white thermal energy as the long wooden boat raced up and away from the Jubba tributary, turning north into a long straight waterway. Two miles behind the skiff, three silent rubber Zodiacs followed, each with the heat signatures of eight men. The pilot flipped on night vision goggles and looked to the left of the huge bubble canopy. In shades of green he could see six surviving pirates in a long wooden skiff. From their lackadaisical actions, they didn't know they were being followed.

• • •

Two hours earlier, the pilot had located and tracked the band of pirates as they steered toward a Chinese fishing vessel. He monitored the three small boats filled with reed-thin men and AK-47 assault rifles as they headed directly toward the slow moving fishing trawler; its nets dragged in the water as they trolled the fishing area with impunity. The pilot attempted to hail the fishing vessel on the international maritime guard frequency; his Chinese was nonexistent but the aircraft was equipped with a satellite data link. A few clicks from switches on his throttle and control stick, and he accessed the internet from a satellite and searched for the Chinese word for "warning" and its phonetic spelling. Not knowing if the crew would be monitoring the radio or not, he barked into his microphone the word on one of his three multi-function displays, "Jǐnggào! Jǐnggào! Jǐnggào!" He watched to see if he had been able to alert the ship's crew that trouble was on the way. "Come on, sound the alarm!"

In the FLIR, the pilot watched several men pour from hatches and race around the deck. Some moved to the gunnels just abaft of the foremast and scanned the horizon. By the men's rapid gesticulations, the thermal image confirmed someone had located the threat bearing down on them. Once the crew verified the threat they sprang into action to defend their ship.

The pirates mounted a three-pronged attack as each fast wooden skiff probed the ship's defenses. Men from one skiff tried hard to gain an advantage at the bow to board the vessel. They threw a grappling hook over the gunnel and pulled it taut just as the ship's small security team fired machine guns and assault weapons at the front of the fishing boat. The ship's crew repelled the boarders with ferocity, knowing they could be fighting for their lives. They braced for another assault, for pirates were usually successful when they were able to split and separate smaller crews. Numbers were usually on the side of the pirates.

As the Somalis retreated from the side of the fishing boat, some men on the ship noticed tiny fireballs in the near-total darkness of the sky. After several of the mysterious streaks of light angled high from the night sky and landed in the sea or close to some of the pirate's boats, they looked at each other quizzically. They had seen meteors race across clear night skies, but these streaks of light were different from meteors and they questioned what they saw. As their eyes returned to the sea surface battle, a spout of flame shot upwards from one skiff, engulfing the entire vessel while another skiff broke apart and quickly sank, spilling a half-dozen pirates into the water.

The fishing crew sensed their fortunes had reversed and vigorously attacked the remaining pirate boat, firing for effect and riddling the Somalis in the water with a burst of bullets. In less than a minute the remaining pirate boat commander assessed they were now disadvantaged and retreated quickly, leaving the area around the fishing trawler littered with bodies. The skiff's helmsman ignored the desperate cries of men flailing in the water; his boat was already heavy with wounded men and he sped back to the beach. The men on the fishing vessel erupted in cheer and celebrated their victory over the attackers. Shortly after the pirate attack terminated, the crew surveyed their ship for damage then went back to fishing.

What had once been a lucrative enterprise—hijacking ships on the high seas and holding the cargo and crew for ransom—was now a remnant of its former glory. Nearly every ship that plied the waters off the coasts of East Africa and the Arabian Peninsula now had heavily armed security forces, making attacking a ship at sea, if not a suicidal event, then at least a losing proposition. While most pirates were being put out of the hijacking business, a few groups still held ship's crew from several countries.

Shipping companies and their insurance agents continually tried to secure the release of the hostages through whatever means were available. The most famous insurance company in the world went to extraordinary lengths to pay the ransoms demanded by the pirates while the Somalis went to extraordinary lengths to maintain the secrecy of their hideouts. Russian-speaking aircrews flying decrepit Ilyushin Il-76s—smuggled out of country after the fall of the Soviet

Union—were hired by the insurance firms to make the ransom drops. The aircrews were instructed to follow a series of navigational directions taking the aircraft over Kenyan wildlife preserves and Ethiopian deserts before being directed out over the water off the coast of Somalia. A small fleet of boats would speed across deep ocean swells to catch the money bundle that was tossed from the low flying jet. Unfortunately, the pirates would keep the money and the hostages, slink back into their hideouts, threaten more shipping vessels, demand more ransom, and continue to abuse their captives.

Months of satellite imagery analysis and high altitude surveillance and reconnaissance flights yielded nothing significant; no clues and no trace of the missing hostages, and worse, no hint of where the hostages could be. Ambassadors from a dozen nations beseeched the U.S. Secretary of State for assistance. The Secretary of Defense reluctantly acknowledged his airborne ISR—intelligence, surveillance, and reconnaissance—assets had failed to locate the hostages after numerous attempts.

Then a brazen attack on a Nairobi shopping mall spilled into the consciousness of the world as Muslim terrorists of al-Shabaab executed non-Muslim patrons and allowed Muslims to go free. The Presidents of the United States and Kenya discussed the situation, and asked the Director of Central Intelligence to look into the matter and use "all means necessary" to find the killers. A contractor who specialized in executing high-risk missions was contracted to perform the work. It took a week to get the special purpose aircraft and crew into position.

During the Special Operations Command mission brief special emphasis was placed on finding and exfiltrating two women, if they were still alive. They had been missing for over two years. Everyone in the briefing room knew what was unsaid. If the hostages and particularly the women were alive, they were surviving in what had to be unspeakable conditions.

After only three hours in the Lockheed YO-3A flying at several hundred feet over the Somali rivers, Duncan Hunter found both the jungle prison and the command center of the al-Qaeda affiliate

27

terrorist organization, al-Shabaab. Using some of the tricks of the trade of tracking, he located the faint ground scars where skiffs had been pulled up and out of the river, across muddy banks and into the jungle. Hunter assumed native fishermen working the river wouldn't move their boats out of the water; there were no imperatives to hide a fishing boat. Families living along a stretch of the river would've beached their boats and the fishermen would've carried poles or nets and their catches, not AK-47s.

He had picked up some of the tracking skills from his days in the U.S. Border Patrol. Agents in Super Cubs would fly low and slow over the southern border of the U.S. "cutting sign" from the air, discerning the small telltale indicators of illegal aliens moving across scrublands and desert—something that couldn't be done at 35,000 feet from an unmanned aerial vehicle or a satellite. Border Patrol pilots flying at a few hundred feet over the ground would find hints of tracks and would follow them—then "work the trail." They might find a shoe with a body attached hiding under a bush or spot a flash of clothing or an empty water jug in an otherwise empty or monochromatic green environment. Trained eyes close to the ground could find the faintest of clues.

Al-Shabaab expected surveillance of high-flying airplanes or satellites and took appropriate countermeasures. However, they had no strategy to counter a low-flying, quiet airplane with a pilot trained to find traces of human activity to locate their hideouts.

The two compounds were in close proximity—walking distance— in a very remote part of western Somalia. Twenty-four hours after locating the confined crewmembers and the terrorist outposts, Hunter became the "eye in the sky" coordinating teams of U.S. Navy SEALs dispatched from a submarine to ambush the murderous terrorists and rescue the hostages.

Now, after sinking the pirate skiffs, he depressed a combination of switches on his control stick, and the laser-designated, single-shot, .70- caliber gun folded back into the fuselage of the aircraft. A light on the instrument panel went out indicating the weapon was fully retracted and the gun bay doors were closed.

The gun had been precision-machined by the CIA's Science and Technology laboratory; the "black" program developed the very long-range sniper rifle using state-of-the-art, albeit experimental ammunition. The weapon was very effective; using its electronic targeting system, it boasted a probability of kill of 98% at three miles. Hybrid propellants within the ammunition—a combination of black powder and a tiny solid rocket motor—reduced the severity of the G-load on the electronics in the head of the massive bullet. Once the .70 caliber bullet left the muzzle, a solid rocket booster, much like a microminiaturized Space Shuttle's rocket motor would light off and supersonically accelerate the projectile to its target. The only drawback of the new and disruptive technology weapon was the fire from the tiny chemical rocket motor was visible at night. The aircraft was old school—it was one of the first and nearly the last of a short line of acoustically stealthy airplanes.

The airplane had been the epitome of ingenuity and engineering in 1969 when Lockheed Aircraft Company built eleven YO-3As for the U.S. Army for low-altitude night reconnaissance. The prototypes were derived from the top-secret "Quiet Thruster" designs. They were modified gliders with heavily muffled engines and a huge slow-turning propeller. In Vietnam, the quiet little airplanes easily found the enemy under jungle canopies—all under the cover of darkness. Flying at low altitudes allowed the aircrews to look between the layers of jungle canopies, sometimes at significant slant ranges, to find and observe the enemy.

Armed with the intelligence from the YO-3As, affectionately called Yo-Yos in the field, U.S. Army soldiers consistently ambushed and routed the Viet Cong at night. The Yo-Yos were never heard, never seen, and never shot at. Except for a NASA test airplane Hunter had the last flyable aircraft.

He placed the throttle in the QUIET detent. The reduction gearing immediately slowed the wide six-bladed propeller until it provided just enough thrust for the *Wraith* to maintain level flight.

The YO-3A's FLIR's video recorder caught the white images of pirates banking the surviving skiff as injured men tumbled from the boat and struggled toward the collection of huts in the well-hidden jungle hamlet. A handful of uninjured men retrieved their weapons from the boat and walked single-file through the jungle; some helped their injured comrades. Four men worked to get the skiff out of the water and into a reed-woven shelter. Hunter relayed the location and the placement of the huts to the SEAL Team.

Skimming at high speed up the river and closing fast, the SEAL's three rubber boats were as silent on the water as Hunter's airplane was in the air. Hundreds of laptop computer batteries drove powerful electric motors which turned two high-speed screws and enabled the helmsmen to maneuver against the steady but weak river current. Ten minutes after the pirates landed at their camp, Navy SEALs set foot in Somali mud. The third Zodiac proceeded up the river at a crawl.

Hunter's FLIR traced ten heavily armed men as they ran down a path; they slowed as they approached a set of reed huts and a large mud structure. He transmitted, "All targets are in their huts." The SEAL Team leader raised his hand to the sky with a "thumbs up." M-4 assault carbines with foot-long silencers were at the ready. Over each SEAL's eyes, night vision goggles were down and locked in position. With no guards to slow them down or raise the alarm, eight SEALs entered eight huts simultaneously. Flashes of white-hot energy escaped between the cracks of the reed panels and flashed in the aircraft's FLIR. As he kept the aircraft in a 30° right turn, the FLIR recorded the SEALs movements, entering and leaving the huts before moving to the large structure. Hunter radioed, "No other activity in the area." The SEAL Team leader responded, "Threats all neutralized and the prize is in safe hands." Hunter clicked the microphone switch on his control stick—twice—in response.

Hunter continued to scan the river and the jungle as the first images walked out of the jungle toward the SEAL team's Zodiacs. He counted thirty-four ambulatory images in the FLIR. He paused to reflect from the Director of Central Intelligence's brief the number of hostages. Two hostages were missing. He sighed and acknowledged that sometimes pirates would kill a hostage if their home country refused to pay the ransom. It disappointed him that they were unable to rescue them all.

He gently zoomed to a higher altitude, careful not to create any whistling of a deflected flight control. There was still another location to investigate, and now was not the time to announce the aircraft's or the SEALs' presence or their egress from the country. Hunter cross-checked the aircraft's GPS coordinates with the FLIR's symbology. He pressed a combination of switches on the instrument panel's multifunction display which selected a series of communications commands and terminated the transmission of video to a satellite. The challenge now was to get the hostages safely down the river. Hunter made an encrypted radio call. As two Zodiacs pushed off from the beach and headed downriver, the other rubber boat steered away from mangroves and slowly proceeded upriver to the al-Shabaab command post.

The YO-3A flew lazy "S" turns in front of the overloaded rubber boats. Tension was high in the aircraft cockpit as Hunter scanned the FLIR for any possible heat signature, any possible threat that would upend the rescue mission. He was looking north out of the canopy when the radio crackled. A U.S. Marine Corps MV-22 *Osprey* popped up on the classified communication net, as well as in his night vision goggles when he turned his head to the south. Hunter responded, "I've a tally on you…probably five miles. The LZ is clear. Package is about five minutes out."

Hunter remained overhead in a tight orbit, keeping watch for any threat from the ocean or the patches of jungle as the rescued captives crawled from the Zodiacs and left their rescuers; some exchanged hugs and handshakes before they boarded through the aft cargo door of the Marine tilt-rotor.

As the last hostage was helped aboard the *Osprey*, the aircraft's crew chief turned to the SEAL Team leader and saluted. The SEAL returned the honor with a tap of his fingers to his brow. The man spun around and returned to the nearest rubber boat. In seconds, SEALs in two Zodiacs splashed across the waves of the Indian Ocean in search of their submarine as Marines in the *Osprey* flew to Mombasa where their aircraft carrier was anchored.

Hunter's overhead work for phase one of the operation was complete so he jammed the throttle to the firewall and hard-turned the YO-3A to head back up the river to assist the other SEAL Team. The little airplane rushed across the night sky and closed the distance inside of three minutes. He let them know he was on station. Images were bright in the FLIR. "Back with you; target ten o'clock, three hundred meters. One guard on the pier and one roving patrol on the far side of the compound."

A distorted electronic voice in Hunter's helmet said, "Tally ho." The SEAL Team commander was using a special waterproof keypad on his forearm to transmit computer-generated verbal communications; a satellite antenna and a cellphone-sized battery was embedded in the carbon fiber casing. Hand and arm signals were the preferred method to communicate because at night, voices could be heard at long distances especially over the flat, slow-flowing river. A pair of SEALs slipped into the parasite-infested waters and swam underneath the rickety pier. Hunter sat transfixed as he stared into the FLIR scope. One of the SEALs came silently out of the water and sneaked up behind the guard while the SEAL in the water tossed a fish onto the pier. The guard was startled at the sight of a fish flopping a few feet in front of him, and he ran to capture it. The distraction was enough for the other SEAL to chase the distracted man and drive his dive knife into the man's upper back severing his spinal cord and killing him instantly. The Zodiac silently motored to the compound as the body of the guard was lowered over the side of the pier and the corpse floated downriver.

Hunter provided a situation report. "Still no movement; the other guard has stopped to take a piss—he's on the other side of the compound maybe a hundred meters." Hunter's anxiety was high as eight SEALs disembarked from their rubber boat and fanned out, silenced M-4s were jammed into their shoulders, their eyes fixed behind their night vision scopes as they scanned for threats and targets of opportunity.

A man stumbled out of a hut carrying an AK-47 and saw men in rubber scuba suits; the lead SEAL popped the man in the head with a single shot. As the dead man fell to the ground, his trigger finger became lodged in the trigger guard of the Kalashnikov and a string of bullets flew off into the jungle. The sudden outburst set the compound alive as pirates poured from huts with guns pointing and blazing. The SEALs anticipating the response, dropped to the ground and shot every man that came out of a hut.

In the FLIR scope white-hot lines of bullets streaked from the huts and SEALs. Hunter watched a man at the far end of the compound break out of the back of a hut away from the action. He struggled to drag a nude woman with him. She appeared to be resisting and fighting the man as he struck her and jerked at her; he had her by the hair and dragged her unwillingly into the jungle. Hunter transmitted, "A single target popped out of the back of a hut dragging a woman—she might be a hostage. He's heading north-northwest. My dot."

More men of all sizes continued to rush out of huts and makeshift thatched buildings into the precision fire of the SEALs. In the FLIR thick white lines traced the automatic fire from the AK-47s and M-4s; the SEALs were fully engaged in a minor firefight while the al-Shabaab fired indiscriminately into the jungle.

Hunter's thumb and fingers depressed the switches on his throttle and control stick; he powered up the .70 caliber gun and lowered it into the airstream. More white hot lines traced bullet paths in the FLIR as al-Shabaab and Navy SEALs fought to the death. Pirates dropped like targets at a shooting gallery.

He slewed the FLIR to the escaping man pulling the terrified naked woman. He used the coolie hat on the control stick to move a cursor to the white ghostly image in the FLIR and pressed another switch to lase the target with the laser designator. He double clicked another switch on his throttle to engage the software to track the target. Electronic symbology boxed the target and a blinking cursor pinpointed the laser's designated position. Hunter pulled the trigger on his control stick to fire the gun. The hybrid slug left the YO-3A in a flash—momentarily disrupting the FLIR image—and followed the laser beam to the man's chest.

At 2,000 feet of slant range the projectile was still accelerating supersonically when it punctured the man's sternum; white-hot ejecta spurted from the man's back. The man instantly went limp, he released his grip on the screaming woman, and fell dead. The woman, highlighted in shades of whites and greys in the thermal sensor, collapsed in a heap and wrapped her arms around herself. In the pitch-blackness of the jungle, she had nowhere to go so she sobbed in place. Hunter stared at the FLIR screen and sighed heavily; the ravaged thermal visage was now free but needed rescued.

He slewed the FLIR back to the main compound to find SEALs clearing the huts. Bodies littered the compound, but Hunter couldn't discern if any SEALs were injured. He transmitted, "Bogey down. You've an unarmed woman due west of your position—fifty meters. The west guard is running away from the compound. I confirm I will not intercept him." Hunter heard two clicks in his headset, the universal signal for "message received." In the FLIR scope he watched a pair of SEALs move cautiously through the jungle until they located the dead terrorist and the woman.

In the FLIR, Hunter watched as one SEAL located and talked to the woman. The SEAL flipped his NVGs up, reached down, and picked her up. He cradled her in his arms as she wrapped her arms around his neck and buried her head in his chest. SEALs led another white ghostly image of a partially clothed woman from one of huts.

Eight men had disembarked from the Zodiac. Ten human images entered the rubber boat and pushed off into the river. Hunter smiled. All the hostages were accounted for and rescued. As the SEALs sped downriver with the current the commander typed into his keypad; the eerie electronic voice broke the silence in Duncan's helmet. "Thanks for the help, Skipper. Semper Fi GI dog."

As the Zodiac and SEALs shot out of the estuary and into the Indian Ocean Hunter programmed the aircraft to expedite his departure away from Somalia. He touched the center multifunction panel to activate the autonomous flight software to energize the automatic takeoff and landing system, essentially turning the YO-3A into a robot. He programmed the autopilot to return to his initial take off point. With his hands and feet off the flight controls Hunter pulled his BlackBerry from his lower flight suit pocket. He sat back and checked his email, casually looking out over the blackness of Somalia and Kenya, and monitored the little airplane's progress as it headed for a small dirt strip near the little town of Garissa. As always during the programmed "hands-off" landing profile, he was a little nervous. As the airplane made a smooth landing he feigned terror until touchdown. The ATLS program had again worked as designed and, after rolling out on the grass strip and shutting down the engine, Hunter jumped out of the cockpit. In less than four minutes the YO-3A crew disassembled and rolled the fuselage into its container in the idling Air Force Special Operations Command MC-130. Once airborne Hunter and his ground crew crawled into sleeping bags for the ride home.

CHAPTER THREE

Five men and five women sat around the conference table to monitor the U.S. Navy SEAL Team operation in Somalia. They anticipated one of the National Reconnaissance Office's polar-orbiting satellites would soon emerge from its southward trajectory and train its cameras over the area of interest. Days before, satellite controllers had adjusted the orbit of their upgraded KH-10, one of the most secret assets in the NRO's stable of assets.

Publically cancelled in 1969 and reportedly never launched, the KH-10 satellite was secretly held in reserve for national emergencies or special operations, quietly circumnavigating the globe on its polar orbit for years until it was called on to monitor activities in the Islamic Republic of Iran. The camera system was codenamed *Dorian Gray.* Hidden deep in the intelligence budgets the KH-10 was continually upgraded over the years with cutting-edge technologies. During the third year of the Space Transportation System, the satellite was captured and returned to Vandenberg for upgrades, repairs, and refurbishment before being blasted back into space. Then every three years a Space Shuttle would chase down and intercept the spacecraft, and astronauts would install new electronics, sensors, and optics, as well as refuel the unique aerodynamically shaped satellite. *Dorian Gray* cameras could see in the visible, infrared, and ultraviolet. Its controls allowed it to descend from the exosphere through the thermosphere and into a smooth layer of the atmosphere above the mesospause, some 62 miles above the layer where weather and clouds are generated. Its engine enabled it to climb back through the layers of the upper atmosphere and return to orbit. With new cameras and optics installed but unchecked, it was time for an operational check of the America's first-generation and only *waverider* satellite.

Tucked away in some sub-basement operations center at the NRO complex, the electronic voice of the KH-10 controller sizzled through speakers in the restricted access conference room, "Penetration successful, minor turbulence. Approaching the Kármán barrier and the target." The controller continually monitored the ancient satellite's operational parameters for signs of trouble. The *waverider* has been de-orbited seven times since it was launched. An assessment by the last group of astronauts to service the spacecraft found the old satellite was showing her age and fragility. Several brittle thermal tiles ground against one another during the *waverider's* most recent deorbit. A crack between a pair of thermal tiles, similar to the Space Shuttle's external heat-resistant black tiles, opened up from underneath the spacecraft and allowed a microscopically-thin and high-pressure stream of superhot gas into its superstructure. At first an infinitesimal hole punctured the titanium hull. Seconds later the hole widened to the width of a pencil lead.

As the satellite settled in on its assigned altitude, bouncing along the boundary between space and the atmosphere, the controller continually monitored her instruments. She noticed a spike in internal temperature and began to troubleshoot the possible problem through crosschecking other performance instruments. When the internal temperature readings stabilized and rapidly decreased in conjunction with the cooler and more stable demarcation of the stratospheric barrier, she dismissed the fluctuating temperatures to an anomaly to be investigated later. They had a mission to fly. With no secondary indications that there was a major problem with the KH-10 and knowing she was on a timeline she announced, "Sir, you have live video."

The tall, Asian-American U.S. Air Force colonel had burst through the heavy SCIF door and strode to a workstation. He shouted, "Roger!" as he pounded keys and inserted his blue-badge into a slot of the computer. Moments later a clear and sharp thermal image of a Zodiac boat with eight men on a river came into view. Those around the conference table were impressed with the clarity of the picture being replicated on several very large flat-panel screens at the front of the room. They watched in rapt attention through the changing visual aspect as the streamlined stubby-winged satellite sailed high overhead and headed for the North Pole. They saw two SEALs slip over the side of their boat and disappear into the river.

The colonel smiled smugly and he crossed his arms in satisfaction at the success of the flight test when the silhouette of a very long-winged black airplane emerged from one side of the image, crossed over the river, flew directly over the SEAL's position, and then departed the picture just as the visual lock was broken on the signal transmission. The video feed ceased when the satellite reached the limits of the camera's gimbals.

Colonel Bong and the audience were shocked at the image of the glider-like aircraft. Bong turned to the group, threw his arms wide, and shouted as he pointed at the newly black screen, "What the hell was that?"

A man in a suit offered, "Obviously, Colonel, we don't have a need to know."

Furrowed brows and angry eyes turned on the funny man. You weren't supposed to question the unknown in the intelligence community, but Bong couldn't get the airplane out of his mind. He spun around to the blank screens and shook his head as the team departed the conference room.

• • •

The television monitor captured the usually enthusiastic blonde correspondent with the iceberg blue eyes in earnest seriousness. She focused on the camera in front of her, as if she was hiding a growing fear. Her demeanor and black suit seemed to presage that something malevolent was slithering behind her. In the background a large mosque was silhouetted by the moonlight; a black shadow, foreboding, barely visible. The structure's minaret was topped with azure tile and was ablaze from powerful floodlights. She moved toward the camera as if she sought the safe arms of an old lover. Dozens of diamonds flashed from her earlobes as she stared directly into the camera. Without blinking, she recited from memory, "Good evening, I'm Holly Holmes and this is Special Report. Tonight we'll present an updated report from the highly successful documentary, '*Is Your Neighborhood Mosque a Sleeper Cell?*' Our Middle East correspondent, Demetrius Eastwood, will describe how the Muslim Brotherhood and al-Qaeda have infiltrated the U.S. Government. These terrorist organizations are growing in North Africa and the Middle East and are now here at home. When we first broadcast this special last year we didn't know what kind of reaction we'd receive. The original story was one of the most watched in cable TV history. You asked for more. Here is, updated and expanded, *Is Your Neighborhood Mosque a Sleeper Cell?* Part Two."

After several commercials and a wild rapid-fire graphics presentation which featured short snapshots and file footage marking the exploits of the war correspondent, Lieutenant Colonel Demetrius "Dory" Eastwood, the camera slowly zoomed in on him in front of the U.S. Embassy in Algiers. He stood erect and wore his trademark baggy cargo pants, combat boots, and a white long-sleeve denim shirt.

The former Marine Corps officer had once been a household name and an icon of hate from the political left. The Time magazine cover of Eastwood standing before a congressional committee in his uniform was indelibly smeared on the American psyche. He found his place in life as an imbedded correspondent in war zones, reporting from makeshift camps and military bases. He interviewed young Marines, soldiers, airmen, and sailors in Afghanistan, Iraq, the Middle East, and Africa. He reported the news without liberal spin and garnered the respect of men and women in uniform everywhere. Liberals and Democrats hated him. Osama bin Laden had personally threatened him. Civil libertarians, liberal and Muslim groups hectored his network for years demanding the Islamophobic Eastwood be fired for misrepresenting peace-loving Muslims as terrorists.

Eastwood smiled into the camera. The man of over a hundred reports from the battlefields of Afghanistan and Iraq had changed little in ten years of war and hadn't strayed very far from his Marine Corps' roots. With his cropped silver-gray hair he looked the part of a grizzled old Marine infantry officer. A boom microphone hovered over his head; when the camera stopped moving, Eastwood, the epitome of confidence, began speaking.

"Thank you for joining us tonight, I'm Dory Eastwood. When we last reported, we asked a question, 'Is Your Neighborhood Mosque a Sleeper Cell?' We provided a forensic case, with many examples of circumstantial evidence, which suggested your neighborhood mosque might not be a place of worship but rather a fortress and possibly even an extremist training center. We reported the unpublicized FBI sting operations at a few dozen mosques around the country. Those operations have been shut down. When those programs were active the FBI disrupted hundreds of jihadist terror plots which were percolating within every one of those neighborhood mosques. These mosques are now completely 'hands off' to any FBI surveillance or undercover sting operation. As extremists were led into courtrooms across the country, civil liberties groups sued the FBI for entrapment and violation of the civil rights of these homegrown terrorists. Under withering pressure from Muslim groups, the media, and certain members of Congress, the FBI surveillance program was terminated."

Eastwood walked easily toward the camera until he received the signal that his headshot had filled the director's monitor. He continued, "Imams across the country shouted that it was peace-loving Muslims who were being unfairly charged or entrapped; that all these men were somehow innocent and were illegally set up or surveilled by the FBI. Tonight we're going to visit with an FBI agent as well as with a group of imams. Imams that…*defected*. Imams that have left Islam." He paused for effect and with a distinct Mephistophelean and ominous quality said, "And, they have an interesting story to tell you." His demeanor was stiff and cold. "But first, Agent X."

The interview began with the FBI agent in silhouette, his voice altered by an electronic scrambler. He confirmed that every mosque under surveillance shared one common trait—the imams were likely engaged in a host of illegal and terroristic activities.

After Agent X's story and a lengthy commercial break, Eastwood introduced three former imams who had similar stories. They had escaped from the dregs of the Middle East when they were children. Their parents had fled with them to a new country, a safe country to raise a family because, in their words, it didn't have too many Muslim immigrants. They had attended public schools and were often the only immigrant in their class. The imams articulated they had every chance in the world to adapt, to become assimilated, and to become a normal citizen of their new country. But when they reached their teens they were drawn to others like them. They became interested in Muslim circles. Bored and impressionable, they became infatuated with a liberal interpretation of the Qur'an and embraced a murderous politic that the West called Islamic extremism.

"As an imam I told kids a lot of dubious things just like my imam told me. I would tell them. You cannot find a job. They hate you and they discriminate against you. The police are bad. I would tell them these things to bring them closer to Allah."

The imams related they had learned to detest democracy and free speech, books and women. They also indicated they would preach, "books are prohibited" and charged their acolytes to destroy them. Books of all kinds—poetry, philosophy, children's stories, culture, history, and science. "I would say, 'Books promoted infidelity and encouraged disobedience to Allah.' Those books cannot be permitted to exist," said one imam. "So they would be burned. The only books that remained were Islamic texts. Allah, the teachings of Mohammad, and life after death would become their only concern."

At different stages of their lives, the three men encountered what they called "the lies and deceit of Islam," but while questions burned in their heads, they confessed they still believed in the Qur'an and Islamic ideology. "After all, you are to submit, not to question," said one former imam. They rationalized the problem as they saw it in the early days. At first they believed people did not interpret Islam in the right way. Then they began to question everything. Over time, they each found a safe place to be alone and began to read the proscribed books. One imam read the world's most important religious volumes. Another read the philosophers of the Enlightenment. The other imam read world history. The three men realized there was so much they didn't know, that the world was a much larger stage for laws and civilizations, as well as the great religions. As an epiphany, each came to realize that Islam was unique, different, and deadly. A turning point in their education was the acknowledgement that Islam completely prevented any free speech and freedom of thought. "You are to submit, not to question. If you question, you can no longer be trusted to carry the Muslim faith, and you'll be killed," said one imam. The imams all acknowledged this fear of being unworthy... and being killed.

The imams embarked on the processes that led to their escape, their conversion, their rebirth. The imams went from being hardened and fierce Islamists—murderers who would dispatch murderers—to being kind, thoughtful, and remorseful. They reported their transformations were remarkable as if a great weight had been lifted from their shoulders. To their surprise they found there was a purpose to their being. They were filled with love for life and love for their fellow man as well as being filled with gratitude to be living in a free country. They shaved and secretly converted to Christianity, but they were afraid to tell their stories. They worried the acolytes of Islam would never let them leave.

Toward the end of the telecast, the camera opened to a wide view of several scenic, multi-story buildings, and then it zoomed in on Eastwood. The camera followed him as he walked up a narrow cobblestone street lined with dull antiquated structures. Viewers would correctly assume Eastwood was somewhere in Old Europe. Along the alley corroded green bars covering tight shutters suggested the area was off-limits to thieves and other undesirables. Brass numbers over street-level doors were electronically blurred to obscure their true location.

He stopped at a nondescript door. After several seconds it opened noiselessly and he stepped inside.

Long-time watchers of "the Colonel" could tell that the man was very concerned. He had seen his share of traps before and the path he was on had all the hallmarks of being an ambush.

After a commercial break, Eastwood sat in the small studio apartment of one imam as they shared a cup of coffee. The man had been the victim of several recent assassination attempts in Europe. His crime, offending the prophet. He commented he had gotten pretty good at spotting an ambush. He looked for the wild-eyed men who would unconsciously stare at him and tremble with rage before they attacked. He knew what to look for. He had been one himself. He had trained many to kill the unbelievers that had walked away from Islam.

The two men raised their coffee mugs; the image of a cartoon of Mohammed with a bomb in his turban was lacquered on the outside of the steaming cups. Eastwood sipped the strong coffee. He began his interview of the imam whose head and shoulders were in silhouette. "I call you one of the imams that defected. Is that an adequate characterization?"

"I say I escaped. You Americans have a term. I wised up—before they killed me; before Islam killed my spirit and my soul."

"How should we react to the Islamization of our countries? In America and the United Kingdom the prevailing wisdom is that most mosques are run by peace loving imams." Eastwood stared into the imam's eyes, not into the camera.

The man thought for a second and said, "A devout Muslim is at war with infidels always. Every devout Muslim is an Islamist. The truth is that there isn't a single mosque in Norway or Sweden or in all of Europe that isn't run by or isn't under the control of what you in the West call Islamists." With a wave of his free hand the former imam said, "It's that way in America and England also. You enter the house of the believers; you're met with Islamism whether you want it or not. You go to mosque for that purpose. I would preach that the mosques are our barracks and the domes are our helmets. We're always at war with the infidel and we cannot be defeated. As soon as you cross this imaginary line and become a devoted Muslim, you're pushed toward more hate and anger. You're encouraged to fight Christians. Kill Jews. You learn Islam is the only, the one true religion. You could not begin to believe what occurs in the office of an imam or in the basement of a mosque."

"How did you leave Islam?" asked Eastwood.

"It's not as simple as going to an embassy and knocking on the door and saying, 'I'm a Soviet general and I want to defect to the United States,' and they open the door and you're welcomed inside. In Islam, it is fatal to declare your desire to leave. Defection is a death sentence. There's no place to go. You've no money. There's no one to welcome you, no one to roll out a red carpet, and declare, 'Welcome to America. You're now a free man.' What do you do? You stop going to mosque and run away, preferably to another country where you aren't known." The man raised a finger for emphasis, "But they know you cannot go far because every imam has his contacts and his hands have been drenched in blood at some time. I know this; I trained many to find and kill unbelievers. These hands have spilled much blood for the Prophet. I now know my actions were wrong, sinful. I fully expect this interview will lead to my death. I know because I would've been one of the first to send true believers out to find those who turned their back on Islam and to kill them. And you must kill them in the most gruesome manner to send a signal, to submit and to not ever think about leaving Islam."

In the final scene of the broadcast, Eastwood stood in front of a brightly lit mosque. "We end our investigation with this last quote from imam number two: 'America's media...very gullible. Whatever you have to say, they come running to you. They're very supportive of Muslims. I would preach we must take advantage of them!'"

Eastwood pointed at the mosque in the background. "Al-Qaeda has come a long way since its early days, when groups of fanatical jihadi fighters hatched plots to attack the West. These days, al-Qaeda has developed into a truly global brand, a multinational terror force with chapters across the globe. The Muslim Brotherhood and al-Qaeda are just as capable of drawing recruits from socialist Europe and the prosperous Midwest of the U.S. as they do from the slums of Nigeria."

"After 9/11, we've been told 'if you see something wrong, report it. However, Americans are finding out *it's perilous* to ask questions or investigate questionable behaviors of Muslims. Submit; don't question or you'll lose your job. Or your life."

"Tonight we reported on the links between mosques and terrorism. We attempted to outline, without conjecture, the scope of the radical Islamic conspiracy against the U.S. Government and the American people. The United States intelligence community and the FBI should be leading the charge on this, but they're not. They cannot. It's too perilous to question the curious activities and behaviors of certain Muslims or to investigate Islamists. The evidence is clear that al-Qaeda and the Muslim Brotherhood are here in America, and their messages are shouted from *minbars* from coast to coast. Our attempt to raise awareness will undoubtedly invite the charge of Islamophobia or race-baiter. We'll be accused of witch-hunting."

"Since 9/11 there have been over 22,000 Islamic attacks in the United States and Great Britain, each one with the imprimatur of a Muslim cleric, each one tied to a mosque, each one funded by Saudi elites. Your local mosque may be a sleeper cell. Our research indicates it probably is. Thank you for tuning in with us. Take great care, good night, and God Bless America." Eastwood signed off, as was his custom, with a gentle salute from his brow to his viewers. The spotlight on him quickly faded to black.

"That's a wrap!" shouted the director. "Now let's get the hell out of here." The camera operator and Eastwood quickly followed the tall thin director into the sport utility vehicle. As the driver, Khalid al-Alawaki, drove them away at high speed the director broke the tension in the truck. "I don't know, Dory. That may have been too much. The coffee mugs with the Mohammad cartoons were a little over the top. I'll probably get fired for this."

"The imams' testimonies were powerful. America is under assault by a clandestine force hiding under a *keffiyeh*. Khalid has attended thirty mosques, and within an hour after prayers he's brought into the fold as they tried to recruit him. He knows they're up to something—isn't that right, Khalid?"

As the driver nodded vigorously, Eastwood continued, "The bottom line is they're probing our defenses, planning an attack. This should be police work but the FBI isn't interested, or there's no political will to investigate them. If we don't raise the alarm, who will?" Eastwood sighed as Khalid continued to nod his agreement and smiled into the rear view mirror. Eastwood spread his arms across the back seat. The video was complete, in the hands of the director and the producer, and who knew what the final product would look like once it emerged from the cutting room. Eastwood's mind raced to his next project. The director seemed to be reading his thoughts.

"Off to Texas….? You're interviewing…."

"Duncan Hunter. Former Marine. He's running a business with wounded soldiers."

"Good news story?" asked the camera operator.

"The best!" Eastwood returned a smile in the rearview mirror, suddenly enthusiastic.

"Okay—one bad news story and one good news story. Fair and balanced. That's us!"

Looking out into the darkness of the night Eastwood said, "Yes, that's us. The sane network."

· · ·

The nurse in clean blue scrubs and matching-color *hijab* had thought she'd seen it all, but the man in the bed refused to die. A congregation of specialized life-support machines was hooked up to his appendages. No system failure alarms had been triggered, just steady beeping or flashing lights indicated the devices in the white plastic casings were doing their part to keep the man alive and monitor his vitals.

Two men in white *dishdashas* and black and white *keffiyehs* had arrived with the patient at the Amman Surgical Hospital emergency room, and waited countless hours during surgery and recovery. They didn't move from their chairs when the nurse entered the room to change the patient's bandages. Their eyes scanned her body from headscarf to shoes.

The patient was barely alive, at the tipping point of death but was kept alive by a continuous supply of drugs and fluids pumping into his body faster than what leaked out. A normal human would've succumbed to the injuries from the bomb blast. He had hundreds of various non-fatal shrapnel injuries and cracked ribs, but the loss of an arm and an eye should have been too much trauma for even a professional athlete to withstand. Blood leaked into a catheter bag, fragments of metal, glass, and wood continually oozed up through the man's taught white skin. Trails of fresh blood marked the latest eruption of the foreign bodies which hid underneath bandages. The nurse used forceps to remove and drop puss-coated scraps, splinters, and shards into a kidney-shaped bedpan. After cleaning the wounds and refreshing the bandages, she looked around the room to see if she had missed anything.

The two men continued to stare at her. She never made eye contact with them but focused on her work. She hoped to get out of the room without one of them molesting her. On her way out the door, one man grunted, the other asked, "Why is he not awake?"

The nurse turned; keeping her head and eyes facing the floor. "He's in an artificial coma so he may rest and heal."

It wasn't a sufficient answer for the man, but he didn't know what else to ask. The other man barked, "Go!"

The nurse spun and quietly left the room. She nearly collapsed when she entered the nurse's station. Another nurse patted the woman's hand. Both turned to look at the door of the severely injured patient and hoped the evil fat men would stay in the room or leave altogether.

CHAPTER FOUR

Duncan Hunter crosschecked the YO-3A's multi-function displays for aircraft performance and navigational data. He was on the planned course and touched several buttons, which outlined the MFDs, to activate and deploy the suite of sensors to irradiate the next set of coca fields in the mountains of Colombia. Systems status indicated the large multisystem gyroscopically stabilized ball turret was in transit from the belly of the airplane as it deployed into the airstream. The additional drag required a trim change—Hunter clicked the coolie hat atop his control stick—and moved the throttle imperceptibly to add a hundred engine RPMs to maintain straight and level flight. Once the FLIR was deployed, the computer software program lowered the *Weedbusters* system.

The nighttime air was calm and the outside air temperature was cool; perfect flying weather for the aerial eradication of Colombia's main cash crop. The YO-3A was the perfect combination of airframe, engine, and propeller to employ the suite of sensors. The oversized prop provided plenty of thrust, the seventy-five foot wingspan provided plenty of lift, and the big engine provided plenty of power to drive the reduction gearbox as well as drive twin alternators that powered the electronic systems of the FLIR, the laser, and the hyperspectral analyzer.

The YO-3A approached a mountainside hiding a coca field among other jungle plants. Spectrally similar materials were distinguished and sub-pixel scale information was extracted using the hyperspectral data. The system was tuned to extract the coca from the other "leafy" plants; coca appeared as orange against the other green spectral elements. He drew a circle on the MFD within the amorphous orange patch and depressed a button on his control stick to "target" the spectrally dissimilar plants.

With the *Weedbusters* system armed, Hunter mashed the trigger switch on the control stick—to fire the laser at the side of the mountain—and lased the targeted patch of coca, apparently the species *Erythroxylum novogranatense*. As the aircraft orbited and the high intensity laser eradiated the mountainside plants, the hyperspectral imagery in the MFD turned bright orange and then deep red to indicate dead coca.

Hunter repeated the process several dozen times throughout the night—find the coca with the hyperspectral system, clear the area of humans with the FLIR, and fire the *Weedbusters* laser. Check that the plants were dead and fly to the next target. He was happy with the results. He checked the GPS, set the autopilot to take him back to the army base, and engaged the ATLS.

As he approached the field, Hunter flipped the helmet-mounted NVGs over his eyes to monitor his surroundings during the landing. He held onto the canopy rails through the approach to the completely dark—no runway lights—runway, and half-heartedly screamed for the software to work as the airplane executed a very controlled descent and touched down perfectly on the runway centerline. "Nothing to it," he said as he taxied the Yo-Yo to the far end of the runway. Mission Complete.

Eradicating illegal crops using an unseen laser beam was a novel idea but the suggestion to use a manned platform for the risky counter-narcoterrorism missions forced the leadership at the CIA to nix the concept from the beginning, especially after the U-2 debacle involving Francis Gary Powers. The CIA had a long history of putting men at risk in airplanes in the most dangerous or austere environments. CIA Directors vowed to "never again" put a man in a single engine aircraft over hostile territory where he could be shot down.

As the Chief Air Branch, Greg Lynche worked tirelessly to

develop an unmanned "system of systems," to develop sufficiently capable unmanned aircraft to forever get the "man out of the cockpit" in order to safely collect the Agency's most sensitive intelligence. However, Lynche soon discovered the reality and economics of the state of technology in unmanned systems. The little airborne robots would ultimately "go stupid" at the worst possible moment or lose their data link after a few minutes of flight or crash in the worst possible locations. Several dozen ignominious failures—at one point destroying the CIA's entire unmanned fleet—left CIA leaders with few choices. Either throw more money at the problem and hope that the technology would catch up to the point where unmanned systems wouldn't crash after a few hours of operation, or put a man in an airplane and get on with the risky counterdrug and counterintelligence work.

The YO-3A, under the Special Access Program *Wraith,* proved to be very reliable in its first mission, but moreover, it proved to be a spectacularly effective drug war fighting capability. The aircraft never left any traces behind. After fifteen years of moving the *Wraith* and her crew into and out of high-risk locations with the orchestration of the U.S. Air Force Special Operations Command, AFSOC, and if available, the CIA's own aviation cargo assets, the missions were refined to a fine art. The addition of *Weedbusters,* killing thousands of plants with radiation in one night, made the *Wraith* one of the greatest counternarcotics successes in the Agency. Few knew of its existence, and the President and the CIA Director wanted to keep it that way.

The effort to fly the YO-3A at the most effective altitude and airspeed was surprisingly Herculean. A former world-class athlete, Hunter found out the hard way that seven days of intense flying at night, using night vision goggles, was too taxing on his system. It was exhausting work. Once, on a solo return trip to the airfield, he had fallen asleep at the controls. When his ground crew called him on the radio Hunter awoke to find himself heading out over the Pacific Ocean. Subsequent *Weedbusters* missions were limited to no more than four nights of flying. Hunter needed to scramble for a sensor operator to replace his flying partner, the retired Greg Lynche—now the Director of Central Intelligence. His boss.

When Hunter finally shut off the engine and the propeller chugged to a stop, his ground crew and four members from the AFSOC aircrew sprinted to disassemble the YO-3A. They removed the long glider wings, and a tow cable winched the fuselage into its shipping container inside the Special Operations MC-130.

As the AFSOC pilot and copilot expedited their start, taxi, and takeoff checklists, the ground crew—Bob and Bob—spread out on the troop seats and crawled into sleeping bags. After the Hercules took off and retracted its landing gear, Hunter drove the support vehicle off the airport property and headed to downtown Bogotá to one of the best five-star hotels in South America.

· · ·

The woman adjusted her airport security uniform before she settled in front of her assigned X-ray machine. She checked her watch and made one final adjustment of her headscarf. She was ready. She nodded to the Transportation Security Administration supervisor of the concourse that she was, indeed, ready. He snapped an order to another TSA agent at the entrance of the passenger screening rat-maze to lift the barrier-tape and open another line for travelers to screen their baggage.

Passengers at the international terminal of JFK International Airport lined up by the hundreds, removed their shoes, coats and laptops, and "anything metal," and placed them into plastic tubs for screening. The woman focused intently on her X-ray monitor as handbags, electronics, shoes, luggage, and myriad other items passed through her machine.

Everything and anything to be carried through the checkpoint had to be subject to either a physical or an electronic search. Hundreds of items were screened every minute. The X-ray machine operator processed a continuous uninterrupted stream of belongings from passengers. When there was a break in the action—usually when aircraft were boarding their passengers—concourse vendors would send their goods through the X-ray machine. Paperbacks, magazines, clothing, souvenirs, candy, gum, sodas—everything was screened.

Nothing was exempt from the scrutiny of the TSA agents operating the X-ray machine.

.   .   .

The Automatic Kalashnikov model 47 rested against a backdrop of two hanging black flags. The white script announced these were the flags of al-Qaeda and depicted the *shehada*, the profession of faith. "There is no God but God, and Muhammad is His messenger." Had a man been kneeling and facing away from the flags, viewers would've known the scene was the beginning of a beheading video. There was no bound or blindfolded kneeling man. There was only an old wooden chair in front of the flags. The empty chair suggested something ominous was in the works.

A young bearded man in traditional robe and black *keffiyeh* entered the dark room and took the empty seat. Fat in face and chunky in stature, he raised his head menacingly and looked directly into the camera. Then he began to speak.

He wailed about American crimes against Islam, the killing of Muslim children, the invasion and pollution of the holy lands, the American manipulation of the world's climate, and the continued blasphemy of the Prophet. Then the man said, in perfect English, "The brothers and sisters of Islam will no longer endure the obscenities or the affront to Allah and Islam's holy places." The man lowered his head for effect. Evil burned from his eyes, his words filled with venom and vitriol. This cosmopolitan version of "Islamic rage boy" spoke in the King's English outlining his case against the infidel, Demetrius Eastwood, for despoiling mosques, falsely accusing Muslims of crimes, and blaspheming the Prophet by drinking from a cup with the image of the Prophet.

The man leaped toward the video camera and shouted, "Reject the lies! Muslims are peaceful, honorable, and most holy! Reject the lies! Muslims wish to live in peace and harmony with their neighbors! Reject the lies! Kill the liar!" The man grabbed the AK-47 from the wall and thrust it into the camera. He spat, "My brothers! Smite the infidel Eastwood and his family and friends! Slay his babies while they sleep! Rape and kill his women! Stab his friends and then cut off the head of the snake! No movies against the Prophet and his holy places! I sentence this Eastwood to death! I urge my brothers to find this infidel and kill him."

The furious man returned to the chair, took a deep breath and spat, "*Kill him!*"

. . .

The bright yellow and red DHL delivery truck came to a quick stop in front of the multi-story Bank of Arabia building. Every day, before afternoon prayers, trucks from all of the domestic and international delivery services screeched to a halt, offloaded packages and parcels, loaded a bevy of outgoing boxes and letters, and roared off to their next stop. Within the large bank building the receptionists at the offices of start-up and established companies were busy at work, collecting the mail from the mail carriers, processing the parcels from the delivery services, and making the rounds to the different offices to distribute the morning's mail and parcel deliveries.

In a small sterile office without the typical framed photographs of His Royal Highness, the King of Jordan, adorning the walls, a short and chubby receptionist took the package from the counter and inspected it. Her dark brown eyes and thick brows were framed in a light blue *abaya*. Her finger underlined the words, her lips moved as she read the address. She checked her clothes for modesty as she stood and walked down a dimly lit hall. She rapped on the doorframe to announce her presence; she didn't want to embarrass him again by finding him asleep at his desk. She handed the packet to the man in the smoke-saturated office.

He cut open the wrapping and slipped the VHS tape into a player next to an ancient TV monitor. For Ali Tolani, the Al-Jazeera associate editor, receiving packages from across the globe was normal. Most of the time the videotapes in the packages were anything but usual.

Four scarf-wearing Africans, holding Kalashnikovs and heavy bandoleers came into view on the monitor. Standing on what appeared to be a dirt road in a jungle setting they served as a backdrop for two other men, one white and one black. A heavy-set man in minister's raiment sat in an old wooden chair. Suspended from his neck was a large gold cross; a black blindfold covered his eyes. The other man brandished a sword with one hand while he read from a paper in the other. A pair of khaki-colored flags with white Arabic script indicated these were the flags of the Boko Haram, an al-Qaeda terrorist offshoot from Nigeria.

A dozen times in the span of seconds, Tolani nearly dislodged the long thin cigarette from the edge of his lips as he settled in to watch the tape. His expression flipped from concern to frown to surprise. Nearly every day he received tapes from other al-Qaeda affiliates. The quality of the video was always poor when they came from Africa. The audio was barely decipherable, but the background scene was dramatic so he anticipated the ending. Somehow the cigarette between his lips stopped flying about like a conductor's baton as he focused on the image on the screen. He puffed like a steam locomotive as the man with the sword, obviously one of the leaders if not the head man, performed before the camera. The Nigerian leader had done this before. Tolani had the tapes.

The bearded African man railed against Christians and white men and their crimes against Islam. He railed against the teaching of Western values to children and women—that was blasphemy to the Prophet Mohammad. The leader of Boko Haram had worked himself up into a frenzy and uttered the oft-repeated message of al-Qaeda, "The brothers of Islam will no longer endure the obscenities or the affront to Allah and Islam's holy places." He tossed the paper away, re-

54

gripped the hilt of the sword with both hands, and swung at the white man's neck. The men in the background didn't flinch or watch but stood impassively as their leader lopped off the head of the white priest. The leader held up the severed head as a trophy, another taunt to the Nigerian army.

The bloodletting gave the wide-eyed Tolani an erection. He relished receiving beheading videos, especially those of infidels. With the excitement still fresh in his mind Tolani's index fingers poked at the computer keyboard as he converted the rough analog video to digital and uploaded the Boko Haram message onto the company's intranet for the African and Middle East markets. The corporate office of Al-Jazeera received their copy of the Nigerian beheading video for top-level review of content, context, and quality. Ali Tolani would look for it once it was approved to air exclusively on their African network.

. . .

A Marine Corps colonel in a khaki short sleeve shirt and green trousers approached the lectern in the middle of the dais and asked the standing assembly of officers to take their seats. He made a few comments regarding the topic of the lecture—interagency intelligence gathering and analysis—and confirmed, "This lecture is classified SECRET—NOFORN. I'd like to introduce Miss C. We can't tell you her real name; if we did we'd have to kill you." The old joke still generated hearty laughter from the audience.

"Miss C's been with the Central Intelligence Agency since 2003 serving in positions from field agent to Chief of Station. She's currently the deputy director of counter terrorism at the National Counter Terrorism Center and is a member of the Senior Intelligence Service. She has a juris doctor degree from Oxford and is a PhD candidate at Georgetown University where she is studying international affairs. I have to tell you there are very strong rumors within the intelligence community that it was Miss C's analysis that found the mastermind of 9/11, Osama bin Laden. You're in for a real treat. Ladies and gentlemen, please give Miss C a great Marine Corps War College welcome."

As the raven-haired woman stood and shook hands with the Marine that had introduced her, a lone Marine officer in the middle of the auditorium shot to his feet and began to clap. In seconds the complete assembly, students and faculty, were on their feet clapping and roaring their approval. Nazy gripped the lectern, swallowed hard, and collected her thoughts. It was easy to get emotional from such a welcome, and she didn't want to be distracted. She broke out in a broad smile and said into the microphone, "Thank you." She made little gestures with her hands encouraging the group to stop. Nazy was humbled, and she knew if they kept clapping she would cry.

On the surface she looked like the perfect guest speaker as she took the podium. Picturesque, a wide toothy grin, conservative business suit and a warm, approachable demeanor. Hers was an American success story; the trajectory and character arc from "rags to riches" would've made a riveting television special, and now she had a cause to which she devoted her life. But she also had secrets; a past life as an unrepentant Muslim sympathizer, a battered wife, one who rejected the Qur'an and teachings of the pedophile and warmongering Mohammad for the embrace of Christianity and the Bible. In the service to her country she had been wounded in action. Her scars, both internal and external, were hidden under her blouse.

The pain from Algiers would never be a distant memory and any outburst of appreciation seemed to crumble the defenses she worked so hard to build and maintain. She worked every day to keep the memory of her kidnapping, rape, and disfigurement by Islamic terrorists in the farthest corner of her mind. As she looked down and mindlessly arranged her notes, she was relieved when the audience stopped their applause as they began to sit.

Nazy's hair was pulled back into a ponytail and held in place with a gold clip. Platinum-green eyes were offset by a hint of smoky shadow. Her diamond-stud earrings sparkled in the light from the single spotlight high overhead. A form-fitting black suit and a white silk blouse telegraphed that she was all business. She continued beaming her disarming smile and nearly shouted into the microphone, "Thank you! You certainly know how to make a girl feel welcome! Thank you, Colonel Riggs, and thank you, Marine War College for that warm welcome."

Her distinct estuary British accent came through the audio system clearly, causing many in the auditorium to wonder if the incredibly striking woman on stage was actually from England. The lecture was briefed "no foreign nationals." If her accent caused a little confusion for some in the audience, her beauty created the greatest stir. The men and women in the audience were shocked and surprised that anyone could be that beautiful and intelligent and be in federal service.

Early in their relationship, Duncan Hunter had teased her that she was the "perfect woman" and that he had a picture and the scientific community to prove it. Some magazine survey took a thousand men's and women's thoughts about which celebrities' "body parts" were "perfect." The magazine compiled the answers, assembled the individual pieces, and constructed the "perfect woman." The results for the perfect woman from a man's perspective was a pouty buxom blonde. The perfect woman from a woman's perspective was Nazy. She had only spoken a few words but already had become the fantasy of a significant number of the men and women in the auditorium.

She spoke for several minutes describing the basics of the intelligence gathering process, the challenges of acquiring and developing intel, and the goals of the CIA with respect to the collection of intelligence from those captured on the battlefield. As she spoke about the difficulty of interrogating a hostile prisoner her face showed the strain and concern. She became conscious that she'd sped up her delivery so she took a few seconds to settle down and speak more slowly.

"I cannot speak for the other services represented here today, but I think I'm on safe ground to say that if you're a Marine you likely have been to Afghanistan or Iraq, or maybe some other places we can't talk about. I would surmise that several of you have probably deployed many times." Many heads in the auditorium bobbed in unison.

"What was that all about? A reaction to 9/11 for sure, but is that all we're doing? Have we been at war with parts of the Islamic world for a decade or for centuries? The first verse from your Marine Corps Hymn provides the answer. 'From the Halls of Montezuma…to the Shores of Tripoli….' Marines have been fighting bands of Muslims for over two hundred years. Some of you may know there are sailors and Marines from the Barbary Wars buried in Tripoli, Libya from that war. You've likely lost friends and family on Middle East battlefields. Several Marines come to the CIA every year and continue the fight against Islamic extremism. Yet few Americans will fathom, much less admit, we've been at war with the most extreme elements of Islam for more than two centuries."

The audience, initially upbeat and excited with the strikingly beautiful intelligence officer commanding the podium, had grown somber and reflective. The trajectory of the woman's message looked to be negative.

"I'd like to ask you a few questions. I would be surprised if these questions haven't been running through your heads. It's the answers that are the problem. Are Islamic extremists a threat? Are they winning? And, are they here?"

After an hour-long lecture and a lengthy standing ovation, Nazy answered a few questions and received a Marine Corps sweatshirt as a token gift from the Commandant. She drove off the Quantico Marine Corps Base and followed the GPS to Dulles International Airport. She reveled in the success of her lecture and remembered the pleasant surprise of the Marines' warm greeting. She glanced at the big red sweatshirt in the seat and imagined wearing it on cool Texas evenings. Her sense of duty to her adopted country was strong. Nazy knew the evil strain of militant Islam better than most everyone else in the CIA and was fighting it with everything she had. She was grateful her post-traumatic stress disorder hadn't flared up while she was on the dais. She caught herself readjusting her damaged breast unconsciously as she moved her Mercedes into the left lane of Interstate 95. The underwire irritated the thick scar and she planned to remove her bra before she boarded the airplane.

Nazy put Quantico and Islamists out of her mind and focused on her Marine. She accelerated into the northbound restricted lanes and raced to the Dulles Airport. She was reluctant to travel on her tourist passport instead of using the protection of her diplomatic passport, but this was a pleasure trip. She was so excited about spending time with Duncan in an exotic locale that she knew sleep wouldn't rush in but would come in a slow tidal wave of relaxation after she got on the airplane. She hoped she would dream of love and passion and not of Algeria.

CHAPTER FIVE

The two men on the motorcycle slowly weaved in and out of traffic until they found a huge opening, then they rocketed off toward the airport. In a city where every other vehicle is a motorcycle or a motor scooter the event should have been one of countless others, like another grain of salt in a shaker. Yet people who witnessed the riders in their drab windbreakers watched them with astonishment—and great concern. They were openly violating one of Bogotá's most stringent counterterrorism laws. Not wearing the required high-visibility numbered vests and helmets was a sure sign they were affiliated with the narco-terrorist group the *Fuerzas Armadas Revolucionarias de Colombia,* the Revolutionary Armed Forces of Colombia. The FARC's hit-and-run assassins had seemingly left the security of their mountain sanctuaries and come into town to shoot American contractors and other gringos on vacation. For the FARC to be out in the open, openly flaunting the counterterrorism law, meant someone was about to be killed. It was time for cautious Colombians to move indoors or at least take cover until the threat passed.

Those that witnessed the unmarked motorcyclists weaving between vehicles had assumed that the FARC would never take such a risk. They might as well have been riding with a large red flag attached to the rear of the motorcycle to announce their presence to law enforcement or the army. Lawmakers assumed the counterterrorism measure would stop the FARC's murderous and terroristic approach of killing foreigners. However, police officers on motorcycles who came across suspected FARC motorcyclists were so intimidated by them that they wouldn't attempt to follow or chase the heavily armed narcoterrorists for fear of winding up on the wrong side of a bullet or having their families killed. The FARC had a way of finding out who fingered or confronted them. For years senior police officers, military leaders, and countless attorneys general with large protection details were hunted down and their families were murdered. For the public, if significant reinforcements weren't immediately forthcoming, it was best to turn away and pretend what they had seen had never happened.

•   •   •

Hunter received an email confirming that "Bob" and "Bob," his septuagenarian YO-3A support crew, and the forty-four year old Yo-Yo were safe "on deck" in the Lone Star State. The special purpose aircraft always received special handling as well as the highest movement priorities for her counter-narcoterrorism missions. There wasn't anything like Hunter's YO-3A.

In the war against narco-terrorists, the quiet airplane only came out at night and unlike the NASA aircraft, could be quickly disassembled and put away in minutes. Hunter had found a dozen fairly well-hidden drug labs, four new FARC campsites, and several possible locations where cocaine-smuggling submarines were being built. Satellites and high-flying aircraft with the latest thermal and camera technologies couldn't penetrate the jungle canopies, but the secret low-altitude airplane could. Video recordings and GPS coordinates of the locations of suspected illegal activity were downloaded for dissemination to the Colombian intelligence and law enforcement communities. No questions were asked about how the intelligence was acquired. Videographic evidence, thermal and infrared—sharp, clear, and obviously gyroscopically stabilized—was shot at a highly depressed angle with unfathomable clarity. The video clearly marked the hot spots. Analysts and their supervisors understood that whatever aircraft had taken the stunning high-definition video it had to have been very low and very close to the action on the ground to be able to peer between layers of the jungle trees.

Instead of following Bob and Bob back to Texas after completing their last mission, Hunter remained behind in Bogotá for a little rest and relaxation. He was violating one of the most ironclad protocols of the special access program. The rules of engagement were that immediately after the mission was complete the aircrew was to depart the country by the most expeditious means available. The purpose of the protocol was to ensure that *Wraith* activities couldn't be discerned by the Colombian intelligence services or the narcoterrorists. Flights at night into and out of remote fields ensured the aircrew and aircraft wouldn't be discovered. During the early days of the contract when Hunter flew with the former CIA executive, Greg Lynche, they would usually depart via the first commercial flight out of the country— American Airlines to Miami. When Hunter acquired a Gulfstream G-IVSP business jet through a drug forfeiture program administered by the Drug Enforcement Agency, the American Airlines flights were rarely used. American businessmen flying in a corporate jet was better cover and the masquerade became the preferred method of travel from Texas to Bogotá and back.

For fifteen years the *Wraith* team executed the protocol to the letter of the contract. The aircraft, mechanics, and aircrew departed as soon as practicable after the final flight was complete. Hunter or Lynche, before he claimed he was "getting too old for this shit," would debrief the final mission with the embassy's Chief of Station in a safe room at the Hotel Sofitel Victoria Regia. After the COS departed and Hunter snagged a few hours of sleep, he would head to the airport.

He and Nazy had always played it straight. Mission was always first. Life took a back seat. With very few exceptions, they hadn't even shared with each other what they were doing for the Agency. Nazy didn't know exactly what Duncan was doing for the CIA, and Duncan rarely acquired tangential information on what Nazy was working on in the Near East Division. Maintain the protocol and you maintain your clearances, your access, and your cover. Don't share classified information with someone not authorized to receive it and you passed the polygraphs. Follow the rules and you kept your job.

Their professional rules of engagement completely changed when Nazy and Hunter nearly died during an assignment in Algeria. He had been shot out of the sky by a shoulder-launched anti-aircraft missile and she had been kidnapped, beaten, gang raped, and nearly dissected before a pair of retired Navy SEALs, assigned to the U.S. Embassy rescued her. The near-death events changed both of them.

Nazy had run away from an abusive husband and Islam, and given a new lease on life as an intelligence analyst for the Central Intelligence Agency, courtesy of Duncan Hunter. But the horrors of Algiers weren't far away. She could never fully escape the trauma of being dragged away from an embassy under siege and ravaged. Nor could she believe Duncan could continue to want her and love her after she had been so fiercely violated. Work was the great healer and distractor, a way to recover through being busy. She consciously and continuously stuffed intelligence and other information into her head, as if the damage could be smothered with words, books, and studies. The horrific dreams had largely ceased, but Nazy rarely slept well without Duncan by her side.

For the man who thought he had found the woman of his dreams only to almost lose her, Hunter sought strategies to keep Nazy away from the edge of the abyss of pain and fear. He helped her transition to some level of normalcy. He wanted her pain to go away forever, for them to return to happier times, and doing what they did best when they were together. Evenings, when the lights were dimmed, they'd dance close while the Moody Blues played softly in the background; those were their favorite times. Out of a desire to be part of her continued therapy he sought ways to gradually introduce fun, exciting, and safe things they had always done when they were together. They kept each other from dwelling on the destructive Algerian past.

On his ubiquitous BlackBerry, Hunter had exchanged several emails with Nazy and spontaneously invited her to come to Bogotá. He shunted aside the mission safety protocols. The city was huge and they should be able to move around incognito. If she could get away and make the trip they would spend some time at the hotel. At night they could go up into the mountains for a little dinner, or take a walk away from the lights and gaze at the Milky Way, or maybe even do a little dancing. When Nazy emailed her response Hunter was elated and counted the hours until she arrived. Now that she was inbound he drove to the airport without concern, buoyed by the thoughts of seeing her and touching her. She would wear a skirt or some silky diaphanous dress to tease and titillate him. She always did when she flew to Texas. And he would playfully run his fingers across her knee and along the inside of her thigh.

Nazy called his cell phone when she landed and he timed it perfectly to pick her up curbside at the airport. He anticipated that she would not call attention to herself and act as nonchalant and inconspicuous as possible—but anyone with a functioning eyeball wouldn't be able to allow the dazzling beauty to go far without craning their neck to get a glimpse of her. Like a movie star escaping the paparazzi and trying to hide among the hoi polloi, all it took was just a glimpse that the woman was something special and any attempt at hiding in plain sight became an impossibility. As he stopped the sport utility vehicle, he saw Nazy emerge from the double doors dragging a small luggage bag. Men and women stopped and turned as she exited the double doors of the airport terminal. Hunter raced around the truck to open the heavy passenger door for her, deferentially and professionally like a chauffeur. From fifty feet away their eyes locked as they shared a smile. He watched her lower her head and maintain her pace as she played the part of an unhurried and privileged lady.

Unexpectedly, she broke into a run toward him. Her heels clicked on the concrete. Her long black hair, no longer bound by a clip, covered her shoulders and swayed with every footfall. A Presidential gold Rolex on her wrist sparkled in the sun as she urged her roll-aboard to keep up. Nearly every man and woman at the terminal entrance pivoted to watch the smoldering long-haired beauty rush to meet the American gringo. Nazy and Duncan nearly collided as they embraced and kissed. For the briefest of moments they were one, exquisitely fitted together like German engineering. She felt relief in the strength of his arms around her waist. A brush of his tongue across hers made her want more. She felt a fervent need to kiss him and press into him harder and deeper. She smothered his mouth in a blistering kiss, the kind of kiss men dream about. She wanted to jump and wrap her legs around him, but he started to pull away which brought her back to the present. She suddenly realized they were in a public place. It was so unlike her to lose her composure; it was so like him to be reasonable and rational after getting her all spun up. He would pay for teasing her with his tongue.

"I so missed you," said Hunter huskily after he pried her lips from his. He was surprised at her response. She really made him feel missed and loved and wanted. He felt a sense of urgency that they hadn't shared for several months. Crushed against his chest, she purred like an alley cat after a full meal, and he responded with a cruise missile of an erection. She could tell he was as excited to see her as she was to see him.

"I see that. I missed you too, Baby. Let's get out of here." As he helped her slide into her seat he capitulated to her sense of pace and timing. Knowing she wasn't to be hurried, he stood by the door and allowed a long exposed leg to linger outside the vehicle for an indelicately lengthy time. His eyes fell to the space between the tip of her high heel to the hem of her skirt which had been innocently raised to her hip. It took forever for that leg to get into the truck.

"You did that on purpose," he said, accusingly.

"I don't know what you're talking about," she said without a hint of a smile.

Being kissed like that and treated to the best show in town, that incredibly slow moving and stunning leg, convinced him he had made the right call to invite her. Now she was acting too coy for her own good. She would pay. He closed the door and put her bag in the back seat. After he got in and closed his door, he raked his fingernails across her naked knee making her laugh, flinch, and squeal. She knew what he would do so she grabbed his offending hand and held it away from her knee as they left the airport. She looked at him with loving, yearning eyes.

"You're incorrigible. I can't believe you're here. I've wanted to show you Colombia for a long time. I'm breaking rules by the truckload. But I see you brought *those* legs, so screw the rules!" Her conspiratorial smile urged him to hurry. He could see the effect of the vehicle's air conditioning on her nipples as they strained against her blouse. He was both shocked and pleased she wasn't wearing a bra. He realized it'd be difficult to drive with those things continuously in his periphery. Nazy just smiled.

Hunter followed the signage out of the airport and aimed the truck toward downtown. Departing the airport was a slow affair; at times the traffic crept along at kiddie car pace. The overcrowded highway didn't matter. They held hands tight. She leaned as close to him as possible over the center console and couldn't take her eyes off of him.

Nazy was excited to be in Bogotá and responded like a child seeing a natural wonder for the first time. "From what I could see coming in Colombia is beautiful. I didn't expect it to be this crowded. This traffic is very heavy."

"Sometimes it's as bad as DC beltway traffic. Just as crazy too!" Hunter accelerated with other cars down the two-lane expressway and jockeyed for position. He squeezed her hand to reassure her that he had missed her. He wanted the traffic to move along; he didn't want to get stuck behind any of the large diesel tractors pulling trailers as they belched thick black oily exhaust. It always found ways to seep into the truck's cabin.

Whether it was the excitement of having Nazy with him or the congestion of the roads that distracted him, Hunter didn't notice the closure of the motorcycle in the rearview mirror until it approached the rear of his truck. The movement of a motorcycle caught his attention as it suddenly filled up his outside mirrors. Something was odd about the two men on the bike—he didn't pick up immediately what was wrong with the emerging sight picture in his mirrors, but he knew something wasn't right. He continued to question what he was seeing in the rearview mirror as Nazy cooed in the seat next to him.

She was such a distraction, but the thought of being involved in a collision brought him back to his senses for the briefest of moments. He smiled at Nazy, released her hand, and turned his head back to his mirrors. She found his behavior confusing.

It wasn't that unusual to see a motorcycle speeding or weaving between cars and trucks. What wasn't immediately obvious in the rearview was the motorcyclist shunning a clear path around a large truck paralleling Hunter's vehicle. Any other biker in Colombia would've dipped the handlebars and accelerated around the lorry to get free of the congestion, but this one chose the least likely option and remained firmly in place behind Hunter.

Then the realization hit him. "He's not wearing the vest," he whispered.

"What?" asked Nazy. She stopped wondering why Duncan wasn't paying attention to her. Her voice registered her confusion and she saw a hint of concern in his face. She looked out her windows but nothing seemed amiss, just another motorcycle following in traffic. Motorcycles had been everywhere. As she turned to look over Hunter's shoulder her knee bumped into his hand on the gearshift. The incidental touching of her naked knee on his bare hand didn't get a response from him. She searched Duncan's face for answers, but he was fully focused on events behind them. His eyes rarely left the inside and outside mirrors. Growing fear had replaced the passion in the truck

"He should have numbers on his vest...and helmet. He doesn't have them. That's not good." He looked for an escape route, but in the snarled traffic, a way out was impossible. Nazy again spun in her seat to look over her shoulder. Hunter's gaze was transfixed on what he was seeing in the large external mirror on his door. The unmarked motorcyclists continued to ride the centerline or swerve behind their vehicle.

Hunter was forced to brake as a heavily laden lorry slowly passed on the left. For several seconds the motorcycle trailed behind him before making a disturbing dip to the left and then suddenly accelerating between the two vehicles. To Hunter, no vest markings and the aggressive move suggested they were likely the FARC. Only the FARC had the resources, informants, and spies to surmise who he was or why he was in Colombia. Only the FARC would be arrogant enough not wear the numbered vests. With five feet to go before the motorcycle was abeam the Toyota 4Runner's driver window, Hunter saw the Uzi come out from under the second man's windbreaker. Then he knew.

He yelled at Nazy to get down.

Just as the accelerating motorcycle came abeam of his window the man on the back of the motorcycle sprayed the truck's side with bullets. Hot lead pounded the vehicle's metalwork and side glass panels. Inside the Toyota the sound of hard supersonic bullets slamming into the vehicle's sheet metal was deafening.

The realization by the shooter that none of his bullets had penetrated the truck body or its windows briefly confounded him. It took him another half-second to realize the vehicle was armored against small caliber rounds. In the same half-second the men on the motorcycle realized they had blundered into a trap. At that synchronized instant Hunter swerved hard left into the motorcycle riders. Before the men on the bike could react and brake, the Toyota collided with them and squished them against the diesel's trailer sturdy metal structure. With the motorcycle and screaming men pinned between the two trucks, Hunter mashed the Toyota's brakes and continued heavy left pressure on the steering wheel, consciously grinding and pulverizing the men on the bike.

Being caught between the two moving vehicles immediately crushed the men's bodies and quickly disintegrated the motorcycle. The friction of the sudden stoppage of the Toyota grotesquely dismembered the men's legs and arms. Blood gushed onto Hunter's truck and the trailer of the lorry. When Hunter released the pressure of the steering wheel and turned away from the truck the remains of the men were lifeless bloody clumps of meat, bone, and shredded cloth. They fell from the smashed motorcycle and the rear tires of the lorry bounced over the two dead men and their smashed machine as if they were speed bumps. Fragments of arms and legs littered the roadbed like sausages and meat spilled from a grocery cart.

All the vehicles in both lanes of traffic behind Hunter had stopped as the drivers watched the horrific encounter. No one had expected the surprise attack on the Toyota to result in mangled bodies and a crumpled motorcycle emerging from under the tractor-trailer. Hunter watched in amazement as the lorry passed him; its driver blissfully unaware of the five seconds of mayhem behind him. Hunter moved to the left lane, sped to the next intersection, and hard-turned the Toyota. He pulverized the accelerator and headed back to the airport. He half-turned to Nazy, hunkered and shaking in the foot well of the sport utility vehicle and said, "Change of plans. We have to leave."

As the Toyota picked up speed Nazy and Hunter exchanged glances. With no further gunfire slamming into the truck, Hunter's calm demeanor suggested whatever danger they had encountered was over. Nazy slowly climbed back into her seat. She looked around to view the windows on his side of the Toyota. They were spider-cracked with small round clusters of crushed glass where bullets had struck the thick polycarbonate-reinforced glass. She still trembled from the attack. His hands gripped the steering wheel with white knuckles.

"I learned long ago you must have an armored vehicle in Colombia. There's a reason I rarely leave home without one. Never know when you'll need it." Hunter glanced over at Nazy to reassure her the threat was over. "I think we're ok for now, but we have to get out of town. We don't want to be questioned by the police."

"What happened?"

"Pretty sure it was the FARC—when the dude on the back of the cycle pulled an Uzi, I knew. He didn't expect we would be in an armored vehicle. It doesn't look like a typical American up-armored vehicle. It saved our lives."

Nazy shook and stuttered, "Why?"

"I don't know, Baby. I have to believe that I was made somehow—somehow my cover was blown. It's been a couple of years since the FARC actually came down from the hills and ambushed American contractors. It does not make sense. No one should know I'm here." He glanced at Nazy for a moment then looked straight ahead, both hands on the wheel. "It was stupid to break the protocol. I wanted to show you Bogotá, to get away and have a good time with you. I totally screwed that up. I'm so sorry, Baby."

Nazy repositioned in her seat, leaned toward him, and reached for his hand. It took a moment for Hunter to peel his fingers off the steering wheel. She brought his hand to her mouth and kissed it gently. Her hands were still shaking. So were his. He looked at her again. Hunter's eyes apologized profusely for putting her in grave danger. He knew better and was internally kicking himself in the ass. She took stock of the situation as the adrenaline spike subsided, even though her skin continued to tingle. She hadn't thought about Algeria in hours; spending time thinking about and being with your lover would do that. Even when getting shot at.

"I've always thought you knew how to show a girl a good time, Mister Hunter."

"Thank you, Miss Cunningham. Next time, no Uzis—I promise." He raised his left leg to provide steerage to the wheel as he unclipped his BlackBerry from his hip and punched buttons. The phone connection made, he spoke into the little back device. Nazy could only hear Hunter's side of the conversation with the Embassy's Chief of Station.

"Simon, I think a couple of FARC tried to take me out on the road between the airport and town. I'm heading back to the airport now and will be leaving immediately. The plan is to leave my rental at the curb…yes, yes, all my stuff is at the hotel, but there's nothing important there, they can have it. Yes, sir, that was the plan but I delayed—absolutely my fault; I should have left this morning. You need to tell the boss. He can either fire me or shoot me. That would be helpful—thank you, Simon. I owe you one—next time—if there's a next time, dinner is on me. Okay, goodbye."

As Hunter pulled up to the departure curb of the airport, Nazy asked, "Now what are we doing?" Nazy's hands had mostly stopped trembling.

"Well, I either take you back to DC, or we can go to Texas."

"I gave a lecture at the Marine War College this morning and I'm off for the next three days. You owe me dinner and you promised we'd go dancing."

"My place?"

"Maybe we can go to Gruene Hall for some dancing. If we stay home will you put on a little Moody Blues? Maybe play *The Other Side of Life*?" He guided the crushed, bullet-riddled and bloodied Toyota toward the curb. He nodded vigorously. He'd agree to nearly anything; he just wanted to get them out of Colombia as fast as possible. As fast as things were moving, he didn't know if the CIA Station Chief would be able to keep the airport police or the Colombian army from stopping them before they could get to his jet.

"Anything for you, Baby." Hunter kissed her hand. He slammed the truck's gearshift lever into park, shut off the engine, and tossed the keys under the floor mat. Reaching between the seats he dragged Nazy's bag from the back cushion. She kicked off her shoes.

"*You better!*" Nazy became aware of the growing crowd as people pointed at or gathered around the Toyota. Most Colombians had seen enough violence from the FARC to know that the truck displayed all the classic signs of having a run in with them or the Colombian National Police. Hunter and Nazy emerged from the blood-smeared vehicle and ran into the terminal as fast as her bare feet allowed. They didn't see a single policeman until they reached the Customs desk where the officer ignored Hunter and thoroughly ogled Nazy. They presented their passports. Once their visas were stamped and they were cleared to proceed, they passed through the security checkpoint and into the sterile side of the concourse.

After a short delay to settle the bill for fuel and parking fees, a white and red Gulfstream G-IVSP lifted off from Bogotá's El Dorado International Airport and turned on a northerly heading to San Antonio, Texas.

71

CHAPTER SIX

It had been a typical day in South Texas. Warm with an overabundance of sunshine, scant humidity, and not a breeze anywhere. It was one of those days where the natives were glad they lived in the Lone Star State, and the visitors wished they did. After taking a lazy tree-lined turnoff, they traded the view of metal buildings and mom and pop businesses lining the frontage roads of Interstate 10 for gently rolling hills and banked turns. Civilization was somewhere behind them. Ahead, the low mountain ridges of the "hill country" filled the windscreen. After several miles of deserted ranch gates and busy roadside fruit stands, the road discontinued its gentle peaks and valleys for a laser-straight two-lane blacktop paralleled by miles of fence posts, barbed wire, cactus and tumbleweeds, and creosote-soaked telephone poles. Few vehicles approached on the long stretch of road.

Carlos Yazzie lifted his eyes to the rearview mirror as a dark green Kawasaki Ninja approached at a torrid speed. On the long two-lane straightaway, the motorcyclist was a blur when he changed lanes and screamed past the Hummer2 at over a hundred and eighty mph.

As the green blur and hunched over man in black leathers and black helmet disappeared over the horizon the passenger of the Hummer said with a modicum of disgust, "That's crazy."

Yazzie said, "Yes, sir," as he turned off the road and onto the single-track smooth blacktop lane. He brought the big tank-like truck to a stop at the front porch of the ranch house. His plump little wife, Theresa, and Hunter emerged from the house and met the two men as they stepped from the truck. Introductions were made and Carlos offered to take Eastwood's bag inside, but the old Colonel demurred.

Theresa shuffled off to fix teas.

"Now this is a house!" said Eastwood. Arms spread wide, he surveyed the area and the breathtaking view. He hadn't expected an expansive log ranch home with a wrap-around covered porch capped with a tin roof.

"I stumbled on this property years ago and tore down the old building that was here to build this. It'd be very hard to drag me away from here."

"I can see why. It's beautiful. It's very well done, Duncan."

"Thanks, Colonel. I think Theresa has drinks inside."

Hunter steered Eastwood toward the living room. He offered one of the leather sofas as he headed toward the kitchen; Eastwood remained standing and took in the furnishings. A massive stone fireplace dominated the room, and the fire pit could have braised a buffalo. He noticed what appeared to be a LeRoy Neiman over the mantel. The flashy, brilliantly colored, stunningly energetic painting featured Duncan and his Corvette racecar—flying through the air—at a Monterey, California racetrack. Navajo rugs were scattered over flagstones while shelves featured American Indian pottery and *kachina* dolls. The walls were accented with watercolor paintings from local artists. Since Hunter was an old Marine pilot, Eastwood had expected an aviation theme not rustic southwest.

Then he saw something that made him stare in awe. He didn't know how he had missed it. Maybe it was the size of the room or the fireplace, but opposite the Neiman and suspended in the corner was an Apache war bonnet. Foot-long, white–tipped eagle feathers were arrayed across the brow with fancy beadwork and ermine trim. The six-foot long tails of feathers and leather barely grazed the floor. He hadn't seen one so closely before. Few things could make the old Marine stop and stare with mouth agape. The war bonnet was one of them.

"That's on loan from Carlos," said Hunter as he entered the room carrying a couple of ice teas. He could see the questions forming in Eastwood's head. "It's a long story. Have a seat." Eastwood hid his embarrassment with a smile.

The two men sat quietly, sipped drinks, and looked at each other. Theresa brought sandwiches. Eastwood broke the silence. "I usually know where to start and what to ask, but I have to say Duncan, I've completely forgotten what I wanted to ask you. I still have this vision of you landing that biplane on the Eisenhower—at night—no less. Being decontaminated and then flying off into the night. I know everyone on the boat asked, 'What the hell was that?' So how about I start with, how is your fiancée? That's off the record, of course."

Hunter nodded in repose. "Nazy's doing well considering the circumstances. She's back at work. I think she's getting better every day. You know how it is when a Marine or a trooper gets hurt—the rehab can be long and painful. She's signed up for karate and is in another grad school. To keep her mind busy."

"I'm glad she's doing well. When we were aboard the ship, I know Bill McGee was worried shitless about her."

"Sounds like him. He's here, you know."

"McGee?"

Hunter nodded.

"I thought he was still at the Naval War College."

"I made him an offer he couldn't refuse. He and his family moved here a month ago. We'll see him when we go into town."

"Any more adventures like Algeria?"

Duncan said coyly—official speak for no comment—"I don't know what adventures you're talking about, Colonel."

"Got it. Can't blame me for trying."

"No harm; no factor. If the roles were reversed, I'd be dying to know. But you know I can't talk about it."

"No need to know. Okay, I'll change the subject." Pointing to the painting over the fireplace Eastwood said, "That's quite a painting. I've a small ranch home near Lime Rock; inherited it from my grandfather. Never been to a race there; never really had the time."

"I raced there a few times when I was at Newport—great fun racetrack. I try hard but in reality, I *suck* as a driver. Like flying, driving a racecar is a very perishable skill. There's just never enough time to get good." Hunter smiled as he remembered the thrills of racing against the old Jaguars, Porsches, and Ferraris.

"From what I know and have seen it's highly unlikely you suck at anything. And that's quite a truck—the Hummer. You expecting a war or something?"

"That's a new line of business for us. Armored vehicles. Mostly Hummers. That's what Bill McGee is doing...primarily. We have a two-year waiting list for our conversions. Folks are waking up that there are a lot of bad people out there just waiting to do them harm. I call them 'friends of the former President.'"

"Your recovering warriors building them?"

"Yes, sir, they are. They're not as fast as most mechanics, but the quality is top block. What they lack in speed they make up in precision, excellence, and quality. The H2 was the prototype, our proof of concept vehicle. It has a thousand pounds of armor-piercing protection, and all the glass is bullet-resistant multilayer polycarbonate glass. Under the hood is a supercharged 700-horsepower Corvette engine; even the engine compartment is armored. The fuel tank was reinforced with quarter-inch ballistic steel; it's also bullet-resistant and blast-proof. Every vehicle my guys produce is a work of art that's also functional. They'll save lives." He reflected for a second about escaping the FARC in Bogotá and said, "Armored vehicles save lives every day."

"You can't tell it's armored from the outside—and I've been in a lot of hard-skinned vehicles over the last ten years. Your spiel sounds like a sales pitch."

"Kinda is. When a customer sees the Hummer and how well we've hidden the ballistics materials, the protection sells itself. There's a growing demand for armored vehicles. It's a sign of the times—crazy liberals and criminals are getting out of hand and people feel they need to protect themselves and their families. There's a reason police departments line up for the military surplus armored vehicles."

"For a demonstrator, that vehicle is a beauty."

"And a brute. I can't get enough of the Hummer 2s. And I love driving it just to irritate liberals in their squishy Prius' and Smart cars.

That truck terrifies tree huggers."

"That's not politically correct," said Eastwood, smirking.

"No, it's not," laughed Hunter. "If they're dumb enough to buy one of those things, I'm ornery enough to screw with them a little, especially if I see they have one of those idiotic hypocritical 'coexist' bumper stickers." After a few seconds of shared laughter, Hunter changed the subject. "Colonel, this is what I had in mind—we'll go into town and tour the garage; you and Bill can have a little time together, wander around and see what great work these guys are doing. I have a few small things I have to do in my office—I've a shipment of airplanes going to the Nigerian Air Force, and I have to see that the shipping paperwork is complete—you can imagine government regs are a killer. They're crated up and ready to go."

"Airplanes?"

"Powered gliders to patrol their oil pipelines. When I'm done I'll wander back over. Then we'll head out to the airport and see the rest of our air operations—like the garage. In addition to rebuilding old racecars or installing armor in SUVs, I've another group of guys manufacturing quiet airplanes. We also have a group of wounded warriors rebuilding old airplanes. We'll see how much time we have before I take you back to the airport."

The term "quiet airplane" intrigued Eastwood and bounced around his head like a BB in a boxcar. "Sounds like a plan." He paused for a moment and said, "I thought I'd see more aviation. Racecars and war bonnets were the last thing I expected."

"Let me show you the rest of the house and my office. That's where I hide when I'm home."

Hunter allowed Eastwood to stick his head into the bedrooms—he commented on Nazy's glamour photograph on the nightstand—as they headed to his office. Racquetball trophies and dozens of large airplane models filled a wall full of shelves. Another wall was covered with racquetball plaques, photographs and lithographs of airplanes Hunter had flown. Over the door hung an ancient propeller from a Fokker Dr1 of Bloody Red Baron fame. In one corner sat the remains of an F-4 ejection seat; a flying helmet and oxygen mask rested on the seat cushion. For a desk, a huge triangle slab of yellow and brown polished onyx was wedged into the corner near the window. On the corner of the desk was a small framed photograph of a vivacious red-haired woman draped over the side of a very old yellow Corvette convertible, the Disneyland castle was in the background. Hunter's dark brown Marine Corps leather flight jacket hung across the back of his desk chair. Below the embossed gold wings of a Naval aviator a black nametag read MAVERICK.

"That's more like it," said Eastwood, pointing. "You normally don't see spent ejection seats in houses. Like everything else in the house, Duncan, your office is most impressive."

Hunter grinned and said, "Thanks."

As Eastwood turned to leave the office he noticed an odd, long, thin-winged black airplane model on a simple, unmarked carved mahogany base sitting at the end of the stone tableau desk. Before Eastwood could ask about the little model, Hunter offered, "It's probably time to go into town." He didn't want to answer any questions about that one.

After retrieving his bag and thanking Theresa for the hospitality, the two men walked out of the house into bright sunshine. Hunter debated whether to take the Aston Martin but the H2 was at the ready by the porch. The heavy doors, laden with dozens of layers of Kevlar and ceramic plates, were perfectly balanced on their hinges. But like all massive weights, once you got them moving it was hard to stop them from the inertia. Hunter slowly closed his door and Eastwood followed his lead.

They talked of old Marines doing well as Hunter turned toward town. The only traffic was a motorcycle off in the distance and closing fast. With no other vehicles on the long stretch of road, Hunter knew it would be only seconds before the cycle, built for amazing speed and performance, would blow by them.

Eastwood said, "Just as Carlos slowed to enter the driveway, one of those guys shot past us like a bullet. They're insane."

Hunter nodded before transitioning to register his disgust. As expected, the motorcycle came up on the Hummer very quickly and then slowed significantly to pass them. With the Bogotá episode still fresh in his mind, Hunter stiffened slightly; Eastwood picked up on the man's reactions and was confused by his reaction. The rider pulled up beside them, waved innocuously, and then raced off in a cloud of dust and exhaust. In a few moments the bike was over a hill and out of sight. Hunter frowned but relaxed and maintained his momentum at the posted speed limit.

"I guess it was last week that I had someone try to kill me from...a bike." Hunter stared straight ahead and checked his mirrors. He was beginning to detest motorcycles. *No threat but that was weird.*

His comment stunned Eastwood, who struggled for words to ask a coherent question. He finally blurted out, "What do you mean someone tried to kill you?"

"He's coming back," said Hunter nodding toward the windshield. Eastwood's head snapped to the front. Hunter wasn't sure if it was the same motorcycle or another one. The rider was hunched behind the windscreen and closing fast. What had been a dark fuzzy point at a distance quickly turned to brighter shades of green when a machine pistol emerged from behind the windscreen and began to spit rounds. Hunter immediately swerved into the motorcyclist's lane in a spontaneous and undeclared game of "chicken." The motorcycle swerved onto the road's shoulder and sped past them. The biker wasn't able to discern if the bullets found the windshield and didn't know thick armor plating protected the radiator.

Eastwood saw the familiar flashes spit from the weapon and fell to the floor to get out of the line of fire. Every bullet slamming into the H2 was deafening. Hunter stayed steady at the wheel; he flinched as each bullet hit the glass directly in front of him. With each hit his confidence grew that the surrounding armor was protecting them. His eyes darted from mirror to glass, assessing and planning as the motorcycle shot passed them and braked heavily. Hunter mashed the gas pedal and sped toward town, trying to put as much distance as possible between him and the motorcycle.

The cyclist skidded to a power slide turning stop and, pulling the bike up on one smoking spinning wheel as it accelerated, raced back to the big black truck with extraordinary speed. The man on the motorbike released the long magazine and reloaded the MAC-10, and with 50 mph of closure speed ate up the distance between the two vehicles in seconds. The motorcyclist surprised Hunter as he steered the bike onto the road's shoulder to approach the passenger side of the truck. As the two vehicles hurtled side by side at 100 mph, the cyclist struggled with the recoil as he again raked the Hummer with automatic fire. Bullets slammed against the truck's armored metalwork and each round reverberated loudly inside the truck. The high-powered spent energy of each bullet created an echo chamber inside the Hummer. The cyclist emptied his pistol but couldn't comprehend why the driver and passenger weren't dead. Then he realized he was in trouble.

Hunter had monitored the situation with the cyclist on the passenger side of the vehicle and had gently eased the big truck to the right and onto the road's shoulder. The maneuver forced the cyclist to steer out of the way and brake to avoid hitting the truck. Hunter eased the trajectory of the H2 even further onto shoulder of the roadbed. As the cyclist tried to steer away from the encroaching truck he looked ahead and froze as a dark telephone pole filled his helmet visor.

Hunter and Eastwood heard the motorcycle hit the thick pole dead center. At 100 mph the impact of the Ninja broke the pole in two; the cyclist's died instantly as his face splattered against the dark brown timber. Hunter braced himself and crushed the brake pedal; the four tires stopped turning and the truck skidded to a smoky stop. Eastwood held on tightly to grip handles as he watched the scene unfold; Hunter's intensity and focus didn't waver. Almost before the speedometer needle fell to zero mph Hunter slapped the automatic gearshift handle into reverse and mashed the gas pedal. The power of all 700 horses under the hood was transferred to the drivetrain as all four tires spun in the opposite direction, digging into the rough rock-covered asphalt. He backed up to the scene of the impact. He flipped the gearshift lever into park, pulled a Kimber .45 pistol from under the dash, and jumped out of the truck. Eastwood turned to see what Hunter was doing, but the window glass around the H2 was like frosted glass—too pocked from bullets and spider cracks to see through. After a few seconds Hunter jumped back into the Hummer and handed Eastwood a MAC-10 machine pistol. "I think that's all of it except the spent brass."

The colonel pointed the weapon toward the floorboard and removed the magazine. He kept his fingers away from the unfamiliar weapon and struggled to ensure the MAC-10 was unloaded. As they reached the edge of the town of Fredericksburg, Hunter slowed the H2 to the posted speed limit. The men didn't talk as they drove down the town's main drag. The adrenaline spike of being shot at had flooded their systems, and they worked to calm their breathing and heart rates.

In one of the biggest tourist traps in Texas, all heads turned as Hunter drove the bullet-riddled Hummer down Main Street to his office and pulled into the former Chevrolet dealership's service lot. The men and women working in the repair shop heard the familiar rumble of the Hummer's Corvette engine as it pulled up and stopped in front of the eight-bay facility. They turned to look at the boss's truck only to find it riddled with bullet impacts. The side glass panels were crushed with coaster-sized impact points; the side windows were completely opaque from dozens of bullets fired at close range. Shock showed on the faces of the automotive artisans, craftsmen, and mechanics until Hunter and Eastwood stepped from the vehicle. The men and women, some ambulatory, others in wheelchairs or on prosthetics, surrounded the truck to take a closer look.

Bill McGee, former Navy SEAL, ran outside from his office just as Hunter tossed McGee the keys in a high arc. McGee, his thoughts mangled, fumbled the catch. The shock of his initial view of the Hummer was too distracting. He wanted to ask what happened, which appeared to be obvious, but he needed to retrieve the keys from the ground. As McGee fought for words, Hunter said, "Bullfrog, we might want to take some marketing pictures; we can say our vehicles have been operationally tested out. And please tell the whole team thanks for their great work—they saved two lives today." Hunter waved to the painters and mechanics and turned away, leaving several dozen battle-hardened men and women with their mouths still open. McGee quietly shook Eastwood's hand as the men looked at each other then at Hunter as he said, "Colonel Eastwood, we're going to have to do this some other time. Bill, can you or someone take the good colonel back to the airport after you guys finish catching up? I expect to be busy the next few hours. Take one of the other H2s."

Bill McGee nodded as Hunter and Eastwood said their goodbyes. The two men watched Hunter as he crossed Main Street to his office.

Duncan balled his fists repeatedly to try and stop his hands from trembling before he entered the old bank building that housed the offices of Quiet Aero Systems. Once ensconced in his office, he reflected on the similar attacks. *Twice in less than a week something's up and it's not good.*

CHAPTER SEVEN

Kelly Horne turned base leg of the Manassas Regional Airport, the runway over her left shoulder, landing checklist complete. The Piper Super Cub was becoming more difficult to handle in the prefrontal weather. Increasing winds weathervaned the little yellowtail dragger from side to side and bounced her all over the sky. She checked her watch. There wasn't enough time for another touch and go, so she radioed the control tower of her intentions: full stop. Enough was enough.

After an expert crosswind landing that would've made her father proud, she taxied clear of the runway, and still fighting the gusty winds, she headed to the row of T-hangars. Kelly shut down the engine and installed the protective covers in the intakes and over the pitot tube. She clipped a tow bar to the tailwheel and dragged the airplane into its parking space. A block of wood in front of one main tire was enough to ensure the airplane wouldn't roll into the door once it was closed. She locked the hangar and again checked her gold Rolex chronograph. It was time to get to the other side of the airport; she would be cutting it close.

Graduation from the CIA's Advanced Intelligence Officer's Course at "The Farm" was still weeks away. The rigorous schedule and months of training were rapidly ending. Instructors cautioned the class that during the final weeks of school students wouldn't be granted any time off unless there was a personal emergency. From the very beginning of the course the rules for budding intelligence officers were "never ask for time off." The senior instructor nearly fell out of his chair when Kelly requested a few hours of "personal time." She articulated she needed to get away from the intense "ground" school—the coursework to become an intelligence officer in the National Clandestine Service. She needed to get away from pistol ranges and spycraft. She needed to get away from the grunt work of following spies without being "made." She had enough of "shaking tails"—those skills used to readily identify you're being followed and the strategies to break any surveillance. She couldn't say she was sick of all the paperwork necessary to start a case file or generate an embassy dispatch.

Her senior instructor wasn't buying any of her excuses. He knew she relished and excelled in all of her regular courses—disguises, communications, weapons proficiency—even the tedious administrative coursework. Kelly never asked for time off while at the farm. She didn't need to. Kelly Horne was a SPINTAC student—SPecial INTerest Advanced Coursework. She was one of a handful of students slated for training to conduct a variety of "special activities." She was "DCI assignable," which meant special projects, special training, and special assignments. It also meant she passed the extensive polygraph with ease. On the first try. More an intern than a candidate, she would be "on call," 24/7/365. Being DCI assignable meant she could get a little time off when she asked. No questions asked.

Lieutenant Kelly Horne came to the CIA from the U.S. Air Force with qualifications as a jet pilot and little else. She had been one of a very few intelligence officer candidates that had been personally assigned to the program by the Director of Central Intelligence. One aspect of her special training included flying the types of aircraft one could reasonably expect to find in Africa and South America. Over the eight months of her time at The Farm she had amassed about fifty hours in different helicopters and acquired some twenty hours in a vintage DC-3. The Agency contracted for some flight time with the owner of one of the finest restored DC-3 Dakotas in America, named *Miss Virginia*. Taking off from a private airstrip near Bridgewater, Kelly and the owner of the polished aluminum airplane would fly around the Appalachians, do touch and goes, and navigate using the

1940s-era instruments. While she loved and missed flying the supersonic T-38s from her Air Force days, the time spent with the old man in his airplane was a near religious experience. She wondered if her father had been so fortunate to fly so many different types of aircraft.

Her mother had been a pilot too. Flying was in her DNA. Kelly needed to get into the air as much and as often as possible. She needed to feel the wind in her hair, to maintain her flying proficiency as well as master the fine art of landing tail draggers without ground looping the aircraft, or in the case of the Cub, dinging the propeller on landing.

Her instructor was unimpressed with her bullshit and crossed his arms. With a stern face and with a few flicks of his fingers he encouraged Kelly to tell him the real reason she wanted a pass off The Farm.

"I have a date. My father's coming to town and I'd like to have dinner with him."

His expression changed from stern and stoic to surprise, as if she had handed him free baseball tickets for the local team. He nodded and waved her away with a grin. She was special and SPINTAC students had some privileges.

Kelly opened the tiny door of the black Jaguar XKE and slipped into the dark red seat. A bump on the roadster's hood telegraphed the hidden V12 underneath the long sloping and louvered hood. She always marveled at the car, a surprise birthday present from her father.

She raced to the other side of the airfield and the airport executive terminal building. It had been months since she had last seen him although they spoke regularly through phone dates. Once in the lounge, Kelly expected to see her father but he wasn't in the lounge or in flight planning or the restaurant. She checked every available room, save the men's room. As she looked around the facility, movement from an aircraft on the ramp caught her eye. She recognized the familiar athletic shape of the greying man as he descended the airstairs of a white and red Gulfstream. She knew her father was probably doing well financially but arriving in a jet completely caught her off guard.

Wind blew his thinning hair all around his scalp as he stepped onto the tarmac and headed into the terminal.

He spied his little girl through the double doors as he pushed his way through. Both Kelly and her father broke out into giant smiles; he half-jogged to her and extended his arms as she virtually jumped into the arms of Duncan Hunter. After a hug and a kiss to his cheek she looked up into his eyes and asked, "Dad, a jet?" She demanded an explanation. Hunter changed the subject and waved his hand to dismiss the inquiry as gently as he could.

"Ah, it's old. I'm old. I like old fast things. Hey, I brought dinner. Theresa made us some fajitas; I thought we could eat aboard."

"Seriously?" She looked out at the Gulfstream and the airstairs beckoned. "Show me the cockpit?"

"What kind of aviator could deny that request? Eat first then I'll give you the nickel tour?"

"Of course!" She laced her arm in his as father and daughter walked out to the business jet.

After feasting on warm Mexican food and chilled salsa and chips, the two pilots climbed into the cockpit. Hunter pointed to switches, control panels, and instruments. Kelly took it all in. "It's a far cry from a DC-3," she said.

"This G-IV is the DC-3 of its day. I love the old Hummers—that's what we called them; we had Super DC-3s, in the Marines—and they were great airplanes. You're lucky to get some time in one."

"I know. It was absolutely magical flying it. So Dad, what brings you to Washington or can't you tell me?"

They sat comfortably in the cockpit seats as if they were recliners in a living room, but it was time for Hunter to leave. "Well, I have a polygraph scheduled for the morning and then a meeting with your boss. Hope to see Nazy tonight. She's been crazy busy."

"You still haven't...."

"Nope."

"Are you going...?"

"Soon. She's probably ready; she's not going to like it."

"Maybe you shouldn't say anything."

"I need to. It's time. I can't have the two women in my life not knowing each other. I thought after she lost the baby it was the right decision at the time not to say, 'Surprise, I've a daughter.' Poor timing. It's something I have to tell her face to face. The sooner the better; it's gone on too long."

"I'm sorry, Dad."

Before he let Kelly run off he had some unfinished business to attend to. He allowed her to climb out of the cockpit first and step into the cabin to wait for him. He reached for his flight bag and extracted a small box before backing out of the cockpit. He held the box to his side and said, "You probably need to get back."

"I do. Dinner was great. Give Theresa my thanks and my love. She was sweet to do that."

"I will. Kelly, I've something for you. It's a BlackBerry with all the bells and whistles, apps and unlimited texting and even international service. It's on my corporate plan so don't worry about overusing it."

"Thanks, Dad!" She was as excited as if she won the lottery.

Hunter grinned and asked, "Jag running ok?"

"Like a Rolex." She twisted her wrist for him to see.

For an instant, Hunter reminisced about buying the woman's watch while he was deployed aboard an aircraft carrier in the 1980s. He was going to ask Kelly's mother to marry him when he returned from his cruise through the Pacific and Indian Oceans. He had also bought a ring when the big ship stopped in Hong Kong but inexplicably, Kelly's mother had stopped writing. He had wondered what happened to her; he always wondered. He kept a photograph of the woman who had first won his heart sitting in one of his old Corvettes. A year passed before he found Kelly's grandmother's phone number; she told him Kimberly had passed away from cancer. The watch had never been removed from the box. Kelly had found it after her grandparents died. He remembered telling Kelly last year, "It's yours now," as he held up his left hand with his two-tone Rolex Submariner around his wrist. "I bought that one and this one at the same time. Kim got the

Presidential; I liked the two-tone. Pieces of art. Hasn't been off my wrist many times over the last twenty-plus years. I used to think of your mother every time I put it on. Now I'll think of you."

He walked her down the stairs of the jet. They hugged and he kissed her on the cheek. Hunter held Kelly's hands. Tears welled in their eyes; her hands trembled. She had cried many times over many things over the years. She had cried because her mother had abandoned her. She had cried because she didn't have a father. And she had cried when she had found her father eight months ago. Now the same insecurities that drove her emotions as a child flooded her mind—she didn't want him to abandon her again. When it came time for them to part, it was always very difficult to say goodbye.

By the time she slipped into the plush red leather seat of the Jaguar, she heard the distinctive sound of a jet's APU near the terminal building. Her head snapped toward the sound as she tried to find the jet through the fencing. She was confused and said aloud, "Is he flying that jet by himself?"

. . .

Nazy Cunningham sat up and moved until her back was against the headboard. She pulled the bed sheet over her long dark legs and tucked the top ribbon under her arms. In the subdued light, she watched and admired Hunter's naked ass as he padded across the oversized suite of the JW Marriott to the tiny refrigerator. Over-developed quadriceps and chiseled calves rippled with every step. She tried to find the faint remnants of racquetball bruises on his full and hard backside, but it was too dark for that. She could make out the long, raised, uneven scar on his Achilles and recalled his wholly unbelievable story of that injury. When he told her about it he made the funniest faces and gestures, and it always made her laugh. He had been in Amman, Jordan and was rushed to the Arab Medical Center's Hand Surgical Clinic after severing the tendon playing squash with a member of the royal family. He had exclaimed that his problem wasn't with his hand. And he admitted he felt like a fool when the head surgeon explained the "Hand Clinic" had been especially equipped to care for the severely wounded from Iraq and Afghanistan, and that the hospital had the finest micro-surgeons in the Middle East, specializing in hand and tendon reconstruction, and vascular and capillary repairs. When the doctor offered to send him to the orthopedic surgeon, Hunter reportedly told him, "Sorry Doc, I'm in the right place."

She loved looking at his body and his collection of "war injuries," as he called them. Nazy acknowledged that hers were healing up nicely too.

"I think you were checking me out, Miss Cunningham," Hunter said from across the room, returning with bottled water. He twisted off a cap and offered one to Nazy.

She demurred at Hunter's accusation and then smiled and took a drink. Her eyes never left his. "What's the word for...exquisitely shaped buttocks? You told me once."

"I do believe that's 'callipygian.' As in, the amazingly callipygian Miss Cunningham."

"How about the amazingly callipygian Mister Hunter?"

"Doesn't work like that, Baby. Pretty sure it's a feminine term. Male asses aren't beautiful. Guys, in general, *are* asses." She smiled at his retort as he slid into bed and tried to get under the sheet, but Nazy wouldn't yield a scrap of the material in what became an impromptu tug of war. He gave up. "If you look in the dictionary, you'll see a picture of your tight little hiney listed under *callipygian*." Hunter tried to stifle a ridiculous grin as he emptied the bottle of water. "I'm sure of it!"

Her looks gently scolded him. She was unconvinced but amused with his cleverness. He drew a finger across her leg, exposed during the battle over the sheet and said, "There may be a word for these legs too, but the only thing that comes to mind is...'*sezy*.'"

"That's not even a word! That might be a name somewhere in the world but I know that's not a word."

"It is now. When legs are so far past awesome, beautiful, and sexy, they must be something else. *Sezy*."

"You're crazy," she cooed. Their eyes locked again.

Hunter leaned into Nazy's forehead and in *sotto voce*, "Guilty as charged. I've said it before, I get around you, and my brain goes to mush. Just like when I first laid eyes on you. About killed myself." He initiated a gentle sweep of his nose across hers, soft and tender yet positively incendiary.

Nazy flashed a smile and took a sip of water. She recalled the day, the place, and the time that changed her life. She remembered he had glanced up at her sitting in the observation deck of the racquetball court as he ran down a ball headed for the back wall. Their eyes locked for an impossibly long second, and Hunter had temporarily forgotten what he was doing on the court. He tried to find and recover his focus on the little blue sphere's downward trajectory as it dropped toward the floor. He swung his racquet wildly but completely missed the ball. He was so off-balance that he flipped in the air, cartwheeled, and crashed heavily onto the floor as a trio of superannuated racquetball champions in the court with him looked on incredulously.

Nazy recalled that three old men had gathered around the much younger man on the court floor. She had not gone to the Newport Racquet Club to watch Hunter play racquetball but to spy on him and befriend him. She was tasked to find out information on him and one of his friends. She was a Muslim then, with another name and another past. *All that was long ago....*

As she lowered her head an avalanche of long black hair cascaded in front of Hunter's eyes. Her British accent low and thick she said, "That was a long time ago, but it seems like it was just yesterday I watched you in those silky black shorts and was mesmerized by your callipygian...."

Hunter quickly leaned over, closed his eyes and kissed her before she could finish her sentence. She moved into him and released the sheet from under her arm, brought her fingers up to his hair and closed her eyes. He slid under the sheet. Their warm bodies touched, tongues tickled. While barely touching his lips, Nazy guided her easily malleable lover onto his back; she crushed her breasts onto his chest. She moved to kiss him fully but then pulled away slowly; she brought a finger to his lips and said, suddenly serious, "I don't want to go home."

The words and Nazy's actions were incongruous; Hunter was completely confused. His eyes shot open in the dimly lit room. He probed her eyes for answers. Finding none he asked, "Why would you go home? I thought you're staying tonight. We'll go to the office in the morning from here. Is something wrong?"

"I'm a little...afraid."

Hunter tried to wiggle out from under her to sit up, but Nazy wouldn't let him. She straddled his torso and crossed her arms over his chest. It was a marvelous position to be in, and he wasn't going to argue. But he was still confused and growing more concerned. This wasn't like her. Nazy looked down onto a bewildered Duncan as he shook his head. He looked up at her and said, "What's going on, Baby?"

"I think I'm being watched."

Hunter thought she picked a fine time to tell him she may be in danger. Any beginnings of an erection became a memory. After the event in Colombia, Nazy would sometimes act as if she were still a little rattled, as if the assault might still be lingering in the back of her mind. It could have been a freshening of the horrors of Algeria, but he thought they had put that episode behind them and were focused on the future. They didn't speak of Bogotá or their quick retreat out of the country. Now it was too dark to see the green of her eyes, and that was just fine with him for the moment. He didn't want to alarm her any further and hadn't told her of his latest encounter with a motorcyclist with an automatic weapon. "Why do you think that; what's happened?"

She told him. He was now afraid for her. After being shot at twice in a matter of days, and with Nazy's finely honed senses and intuition sounding alarms bells, he took a mental inventory of every odd encounter or situation over the last month. His mind raced over the options and possibilities. She slid off his body and settled her head onto his shoulder. They held each other tightly while he looked up at the blackness of the ceiling, thinking and wondering if there was any connection. After a half hour of twitching, she settled down and dozed in his arms. Her arm and leg were draped over his naked body as if he were a body pillow.

Nazy breathed deeply on his shoulder as he lay still with his eyes transfixed on an imaginary spot above him. A string of disconnected thoughts from the past six months flipped through his mind, frame by frame, like photographs clattering into view through a mutoscope as he slowly turned the crank. Being shot out of the sky. Jumping from a burning YO-3A. Discovering Nazy's horrific injuries to her body and mind. Her therapy sessions and the aftermath of the flare-ups of her PTSD. She insisted on returning to work. She thought it'd help speed her recovery—confront the demons. However, she found she couldn't stand to be in an interrogation room with some of the older malevolent terrorists. She had lost her confidence. Her feelings of being abandoned and out of touch with Duncan were mollified with a new BlackBerry; it had applications—*apps!* She was so excited with all of the features. Not only could she talk to him and text him, *she could find him* wherever he was. Nazy would sometimes clutch it tightly, like a talisman. Now it was okay just to have it nearby on the nightstand, in her purse, in view. Little things helped, like attention to details, phone calls, and text messages; sweet obsessive love notes. They even used silly codes any teenager could break.

Her hair tickled his nose with every breath, but he wasn't about to move away or fall asleep.

CHAPTER EIGHT

"Have you been or are you now a Communist?"

The needle on the polygraph didn't quiver. Duncan Hunter was surprised at the new question and chuckled to himself. He said, "How about, hell no." The polygrapher recorded the reading from the monitor and transcribed the finding onto paper. The only accoutrement in the sterile room was a small picture frame above the man's head with a heavily shaded calligraphic saying: "In God we Trust. All others we polygraph."

"Have you been or are you now an Islamist or an Islamist sympathizer?"

Again, the polygraph needle didn't jump. The questions didn't bother him and the polygrapher wasn't surprised. Subjects that told the truth and had nothing to hide always acted a certain way when hooked up to the polygraph machine. As a contractor on a special access program, Hunter was polygraphed or "scoped" annually, and for 15 years the same polygrapher had always "interviewed" him. They had history.

This new series of lifestyle questions, as directed by the Director of Central Intelligence, designed to ferret out the closet communist or Islamic sympathizer and expose a person's innermost personal, political thoughts, and beliefs was having a profound effect on the blue badges, the civil servants in the CIA. For those with green badges, the contractors, it was just part of the harassment package. The new questions, strenuously objected to by a bar of Agency lawyers, had precipitated several unexpected outcomes. Nearly every State Department civil service employee that took the test was shocked at the first set of questions and failed the polygraph. During the subsequent redo, nearly every State Department employee again failed the polygraphs and follow-on polys. A failed poly meant the loss of one's clearance; a loss of one's clearance meant a loss of position and possibly one's job. The Secretary of State screamed at the Director of Central Intelligence for the undue scrutiny and called the enhanced polygraphs intimidation and harassment of senior State Department personnel. Accusations of witch-hunts and McCarthyism flew, along with the Secretary of State's spittle. Director Lynche wasn't making friends among the cabinet members, but the President backed his DCI. Termination notices at "State" were handed out like dollar bills at a strip club.

The first polygraph was the creation of a University of California at Berkeley medical student and a Berkeley Police Department detective. While a subject was asked a series of questions, the first device attempted to measure differentials in blood pressure, pulse, respiration, and skin conductivity in the belief that deceptive answers would produce distinct physiological responses which could be measured and differentiated from non-deceptive answers. The intelligence community found the device a marvelous tool to identify spies and those that had switched allegiances. Spies were trained to employ a variety of countermeasures to defeat a polygraph, but a good polygrapher, with thousands of interviews under their belt, could easily ferret out an undercover spy or someone with a questionable character.

With the recent unauthorized release of a CIA file on the former President, the Agency and the FBI were on an aggressive manhunt to find the bellybutton, the perpetrator or perpetrators who had removed the sensitive personal information and released it to Congress and the press. The newly installed DCI brought out a new set of interview questions reminiscent of the halcyon days of the House Committee on Un-American Activities. If the State Department wasn't screaming, then the incensed political left in Congress was howling. Those on the political right were stunned and speechless as, across the political spectrum, members of both parties lost large numbers of staffers to the

CIA polygraphers. Those that couldn't pass the "are you a communist" question could no longer receive or handle classified information in the performance of their duties.

After the polygrapher disconnected all the wires and hoses from Hunter's body, the short man told him he could put on his shirt. Show's over. There were others to bring into the small interview room to run through—what some called—a lie detector machine. "You had a couple of small anomalies—one when I asked about sharing classified information to those not authorized to receive it. What's up with that?" asked the balding little man as he held his pen over the form, hesitating to mark the blocks to indicate a "pass" and a clean polygraph.

Hunter broke out in a broad grin, confidence oozed with his response. "The short answer is—as you know—you're not cleared for that info, but among us girls, I was on a SAP and needed to get the help of the captain of the U.S.S. Eisenhower. I had to tell him something classified to get him to send a message to the President. It was a very unusual situation and the DCI is fully aware."

"Killed some bad guys, I hope," as the man placed a large X in the PASS block.

"I'll never tell," said a coy Duncan Hunter.

"You already did," replied the polygrapher. "Good work, Mr. Hunter."

"Artie, what the hell is going on? I've never seen this much hysteria at this place."

"Witch hunt. Leakers have taken intel and posted it on line. The President resigned, or don't you read papers?" The interviewer sighed and looked down at his shoes. "Normally what we see is intel released by a bona fide traitor to hurt the Agency, or the country, or for money. Happens more often that you'd believe. But the release of the President's file, well...." The man raised his head and paused before continuing. "...the President's file was *different*—you know what I mean? Every rational human knew there was something wrong with that man. He was bad from the get-go, and he was bad for the country.

It used to be that political appointees didn't get polygraphed, a real travesty of the system, but now they do. And, I tell you what. I'd love to shake the hand of the guy who released that file. Whoever he—or she—is, that...*person* was a true patriot."

Duncan Hunter held out his hand for a long second and said, "Artie, good luck with that. Thanks again for the good work. I know you've got more to do than bullshit with me."

The man called Artie was a career polygrapher and agency interviewer of over 10,000 polys, the unmasker of dozens of men and women who had inexplicably switched sides; he extirpated government spies with vigor and silent glee. He saw in his periphery Hunter's offered hand. The quiet little man with the advanced training reading micro-expressions hesitated for a moment and allowed his thoughts to catch up with his mouth. After he shook the man's hand, a stray thought slipped into his mind as Hunter turned away and walked down the hall. He furrowed his brow and squished his eyes together—something, some little thing that time, was just a little *too* different in Hunter's actions. Artie said under his breath, "He's just a pilot; a contract pilot. He wouldn't—couldn't have access to that kind of information." He harrumphed and shook away the thought Hunter left in his consciousness. He turned toward the interview room, then stopped and once more looked down the hall as Hunter rounded a corner and disappeared.

Artie shook his head and glanced up at the pithy saying in the cheap frame over his head. "Nah, couldn't have been. Impossible. But I will ask his ass next time."

· · ·

Abby Kesselring settled into her position to monitor the flow of arriving passengers at Terminal Four of the John F. Kennedy International Airport. She sat with her back to the recent arrivals and ignored them. Her job was to prevent anyone from entering the concourse without going through the security checkpoint. It was a very important job.

From 1968 to 1972, after more than 130 successful and attempted hijackings in the USA, the Federal Aviation Administration moved to tighten security. Commercial airlines were required to screen their passengers and carry-on baggage for weapons or explosives using X-ray machines, metal detectors, and personal searches. After 9/11, the U.S. Government federalized airport screening and removed the responsibility of air carriers to screen their passengers. The Department of Homeland Security and the Transportation Security Administration were charged with comprehensive airport security to prevent harm to aircraft, passengers, and crew, as well as to support the national security and counter-terrorism policies.

The airport security checkpoint was designed to ensure departing travelers couldn't carry either weapons or items that could be used as weapons on board aircraft, primarily so that they couldn't hijack the airplane. Passengers were still screened by walk-through metal detectors. Their baggage was subjected to enhanced screening via X-ray machines and explosives trace-detection portal machines. Arriving passengers would be ushered out of the concourse and out of the airport through outflow conduits adjacent to the security checkpoint.

Several directional signs warned arriving passengers that once they entered the one-way avenue and passed a clearly demarked threshold, they couldn't return. Other signage designed to alleviate passenger confusion and enhance throughput funneled arriving passengers into a secure corridor lined with marketing and informational signage. Ground transportation was directly ahead. Baggage claim downstairs. Additional directions pointed the way to other concourses. A large banner overhead announced inaugural nonstop service of the Nigerian Airways Airbus A380, the largest jumbo jet ever produced with the capacity to carry seven hundred passengers, would begin at the end of the month.

She sat quietly at the small desk in her Transportation Security Administration uniform. Hundreds of passengers arrived and passed her without giving her a thought. No one entered the concourse without first going through the security checkpoint. The TSA woman allowed herself a moment to look up at the Nigerian Airways banner. The twenty-foot sign was new, and she remarked to herself that she would be very busy on the day the big jet arrived.

It was her first time to manage the outflow position. She had mastered the operation of the X-ray screening machine and had monitored departing passengers as they passed through the magnetometer. She had learned to be polite when someone didn't fully remove all metal objects from their person and to always screen them again. She also learned what items were proscribed and prohibited from entering the concourse, mostly knives, bombs, and guns or anything else that was sharp or pointed or had an edge, which could be used as a weapon. TSA officers confiscated countless nail clippers and nail files because they had an edge. Even idiotic rules were rules.

After a couple of hours at one station, she rotated to another position. The easiest position of all was "arrivals" where she would sit on a stool and monitor passenger outflow to prevent anyone from unauthorized entry into the "sterile area" of the concourse.

The TSA concourse supervisor walked over to Kesselring at the outflow position and waited until a flood of arriving passengers had cleared the area. The man leaned over to whisper into her ear; he was cognizant of her headscarf and understood he needed to provide her plenty of space. He said, "In a few minutes there'll be a couple of airport policemen escorting three gentlemen through the outflow. You just wave them through. Got it?"

"Yes, sir," she said, nodding. Compliant. The young woman had seen airport police officers tour the concourses or meet special people coming off an airplane during her breaks or lunch periods, but she had never seen armed policemen pass through the magnetometers, only through the outflow portal. During the orientation training, she learned police officers were exempt from most airport rules and never passed through the magnetometers since they openly carried their service weapons. What was the sense of an armed police officer passing through a metal detector?

She had told her imam that the airport police never went through the magnetometers. The thin bearded imam was appreciative of the information and wanted to know about the air marshals. "Those sound like they're very interesting jobs," he told her.

Minutes after her supervisor walked away, two uniformed airport police officers and three men of varying heights and weights approached the outflow station. All were wearing casual clothes—khakis, polo shirts, sports coats, running shoes—one pulled a small rolling bag and the others carried backpacks. The two police officers half-waved at Kesselring; the three men in jackets lowered their heads. She smiled at the airport policemen as the five men walked through the exit, counterflow to the passengers who had recently deplaned.

After her shift was complete but before she went to her apartment, she attended mosque. She reported that airport police often escorted men through the outflow portal.

"I believe these men are armed; I think they're federal air marshals," she said. "Because they're armed, they're exempt from the magnetometer."

"You're doing well, my dear," said the imam with the long, grey bird-nest beard. "Allah is pleased with you." He gently patted the woman on the shoulder. She was unmarried. It was permitted. She didn't flinch or think anything of the gesture.

"I just want to serve Allah, my sheikh." Kesselring bowed obsequiously and departed the small office. She pulled a smart phone from her bag and began to touch the screen.

The wiry imam watched the young woman walk away. His lips pulled into a smile deep within his beard as a thin dark man approached while glancing back and leering at the departing woman. Once she disappeared from view the two men cheek kissed and held hands in greetings. The imam led the man into his office.

"Will she work?" asked the man with a broad nose and a single thick brow that stretched across both eyes. He toyed with a length of cord as he spoke looping it and tying it into knots. He smiled lazily.

The imam watched the man's delicate hands at work on the little rope and nodded. "*Insha'allah*, my son. Very promising. I think, yes. She will 'work,' as you say." He also extracted a loop of a similar cord and rolled it between his fingers.

"The *Ameriki* made it very difficult to get jobs with the TSA. I hope she'll be ready when we need her."

The imam brought his hands together as in prayer. He slowly and gently bowed. "*Insha'allah...Insha'allah.*" He paused for several seconds before asking, "What news have you of the infidel filmmaker?"

"We have found his house. In Connecticut." The man dropped the wad of cord into his lap, reached into the sleeve of the dishdasha and he extracted a folded piece of paper which he handed the imam.

The imam nodded. "Are you sure?"

"Pictures as well, *sahib*. He had a security company at his house. Many trucks for two days. I believe he added security cameras and alarms."

"Very well done, my son. Well done. Are you...."

"Yes, yes. I'm very interested in killing the blasphemer. Yes, yes." He reached inside his pocket again and withdrew a long, black, knife-shaped piece of dull plastic. The imam showed surprising interest in the weapon.

"What have you?"

"Very new, my sheikh. Carbon fiber dagger."

"Not metal; not knife?"

"Not metal; not for cutting. For stabbing. The infidels call it 'aerospace-grade carbon fiber.' Very clever these *aerospace* infidels; carbon fiber weighs less than aluminum and is stronger than steel. My sheikh, the salesman said one...*interesting* feature." He waved the dagger in the air. "Carbon fiber almost invisible to X-rays." He handled the weapon to the imam and said, "This can be hidden in luggage for airports; not metal—can go through metal detector."

"Very interesting. But no cut?" He wasn't entirely convinced of the weapon's utility as he fingered its edge and was surprised that while it was extraordinarily rigid and had a severe tapered edge, the long black shiv could barely cut paper or open an envelope.

"No cut—stab." He demonstrated a stabbing motion which seemed to please the imam.

"Have you plans for the infidel filmmaker? Bring me plans. Quickly, quickly." The imam returned the matte black dagger to the now wide-eyed, smiling younger man.

"Yes, my sheikh."

"Go. I must report." The imam turned toward the computer monitor as the younger man left the office, twirling the knotted cord around a finger. The imam's monochromatic computer screen took a very long time to warm up. Once he was able to see an image, he accessed an internet account and found the on-line auction he was looking for.

. . .

Bill McGee watched three men and one woman apply masking tape to the repaired and patched Hummer2. Nearly every mechanic was missing a limb or had severe burn scars. Scarred hands and fingers precisely applied strips of blue tape to areas that shouldn't be painted. Others masked off large areas and tires with barrier paper or plastic sheeting. McGee admired the way they worked together, the way they helped one another with playful banter and camaraderie. He'd been surprised that Hunter had hired such a diverse group of severely injured men and women. Now he knew why. He felt blessed to be given the opportunity to be part of such an operation.

McGee was intrigued that the men and women worked so well together; there was never a cross word. Each person was a special case. For any single individual the work was challenging, difficult, and for some, bordered on the impossible. Nearly every person in the garage suffered from some level of shell shock or battle fatigue syndrome, or the latest moniker Post-Traumatic Stress Disorder. Multiple combat deployments to Iraq and Afghanistan set the stage for extremely young men and women to experience or witness terrifying or traumatic events. Events that caused serious physical harm to their minds and bodies. Usually the damage came from an IED, an improvised explosive device, or a Taliban sniper. Some experienced the trauma of dismemberment or the death of their fellow soldiers.

The scenes of war overloaded the senses of the young men and women and caused feelings of intense fear, helplessness, or horror. It was as if an unseen hand suddenly turned on a motion picture camera as they relived the unexpected death or maiming of a fellow warrior. Their PTSD was a lasting consequence of these traumatic ordeals; a consequence that medication couldn't fix. Hunter had been encouraged that some studies suggested that early intervention with people who had suffered a major war-related trauma might reduce some of the symptoms of PTSD or prevent it all together. He also knew that group therapy could be very helpful by allowing disabled warriors to share their thoughts, fears, and feelings with other people who had experienced similar traumatic events.

When two disabled veterans worked together in the garage, there was little the fire team couldn't do. Sometimes two men, each with one arm, functioned as a unit. For any task that required work above shoulder height the vehicle was moved to a special booth where a series of sturdy ramps and scaffolding allowed the technicians to access the roof. Now that the Hummer was completely masked for the paint booth, a half-dozen smiling faces looked to McGee for approval. He patted the hood and returned to his office door leaning against it with his arms crossed. He cocked his head to scrutinize the work, waiting for the brief moment when everyone turned to look at him.

A week earlier when Hunter had brought the H2 into the garage one salty former Marine had said, "All shot to hell, and back again." Bullets had punctured the metal but not the ceramics or Kevlar. Scores of bullets had been absorbed in the polymer matrix windows. The metalwork had been repaired with welded patches and all the windows had been replaced.

He strode back to the Hummer. He was half-smiling as though he was thinking of something serious when he burst out with the announcement the group had been waiting for. McGee shouted over the din of other work being done in the garage, "Looks ready for paint!"

"It'll be beautiful again," said one man who stood on a prosthetic foot. McGee nodded his approval.

"Duncan likes his Hummers black," said a man who was missing a leg and a hand.

"...and, his Corvettes yellow," snapped a dark-haired woman impishly. She repositioned a mat of hair away from her eyes; her long sleeved coveralls hid the burns on her arms. Neon orange fingernail polish innocuously drew the eye toward her nails and away from her scarred hands. Once upon a time her hands had been beautiful and delicate, then a terrorist had blown himself up at the table next to her in a café in an Iraqi "Green Zone." After dozens of operations and skin grafts, the woman's hands were again...beautiful and delicate and strong.

"Well, he'll love this," said McGee aloud as he patted the hood. "This time, high-gloss polyurethane paint—I dare him to scratch this stuff. Night vision goggle cockpit lighting. You outdid yourselves. That's very nice work, guys." Confident the paint-prep work was done to the boss' satisfaction, the men and woman rolled the Hummer into the spray booth. As the paint booth doors closed the crew dispersed and went to work on other vehicles.

McGee walked out of the garage and got into another black armored Hummer2, a customer vehicle. It didn't have the extra features of Hunter's H2, just a basic up-armored truck. He set off for the town of Hondo, 80 miles south. He hadn't been on the road long before it struck him how well he had transitioned to this new normal. Instead of teaching war college students or leading squads of SEALs, with their incredible capabilities and training into the most hostile or austere of environments, he now led men and women of incredible fortitude and bravery whose shattered bodies and minds struggled to find purchase in the most hostile of civilian environments. As disabled veterans of America's wars, they endeavored to find housing, good work, and a safe place to raise a family. As an officer of SEALs he had worked to take care of and protect the hardy men of his elite SEAL Teams; now he worked to take care of and protect the somewhat fragile and damaged men and women of his and Hunter's businesses. The payoff and benefits were incredible, both personally and professionally.

Hunter had offered McGee a business opportunity, to team with him to build armored vehicles for clients across the United States. McGee spent a good portion of his day scanning the internet and trade magazines for Hummer2s, the boxy four-door off-road vehicle no longer built by General Motors. Once a week, a load of four to six Hummer2s, in various conditions and colors, would arrive by transporter. Every week a custom and fully "up-armored" Hummer2 would depart for a new home somewhere in America or Canada. Hunter's strategy of specializing in armoring Hummer2s, and other SUVs on a case by case basis, was a growing and tremendously profitable business. McGee spent a good part of his day managing the operation and interviewing and hiring disabled veterans to work on the trucks and on the racecars in the former Chevrolet dealership.

McGee also spent many hours interviewing former SEALs for Hunter's other business project, reconstituting the Full Spectrum Training Center outside of Hondo, Texas. Largely shuttered after the passing of Art Yoder, the retired Green Beret colonel and former business partner of Greg Lynche, the team of Hunter and Lynche had bought the property. When Lynche had had enough of flying the YO-3A in its new role, he walked away from the more kinetic counterterrorism work and passed the training center torch to Duncan to do with it as he saw fit. Hunter had continued some of the activities on the training center, mostly the firing and combat pistol ranges for occasional law enforcement units and the twice-a-year defensive driving courses for business executives.

The facility was significantly underutilized but Hunter didn't have the time or the skillset to return the special operations training center to its former glory. He believed the most highly decorated SEAL ever to wear the gold Trident could take the superbly equipped and specialized facility to a completely new level of capabilities. After McGee had rescued Nazy Cunningham from the troglodytes in Algeria, Hunter had offered the training facility as a token of his appreciation, a reward. It was an opportunity and gesture the old

SEAL couldn't refuse.

When McGee and his family arrived in Texas, Hunter completely opened his kimono and showed his new business partner all of the small businesses flying under the Hunter flag—quiet aircraft manufacturing, quiet technologies laboratory, antique racecar restoration, armoring garages, and the training facility. In a few short weeks McGee had become absorbed into the culture, leading recovering wounded soldiers and old SEALs in the pursuit of "special purpose activities," which allowed Hunter to focus on supporting CIA operations under a "black" or more formally, a "special access" program.

Law enforcement organizations and private gun clubs from across the country were ecstatic that the famous SEAL commander was back on the grid directing an operation he was eminently qualified for—leading the Full Spectrum Training Center. There was a yearlong waiting list to secure a seat.

Some former and retired special operations forces warriors migrated to the unique facility to update and maintain their perishable weapons skills for proposed or scheduled work. SEALs and former Green Berets spent hours on the firing ranges, indoor/outdoor tactical courses, and replica urban simulators before serving on personal security details or going aboard maritime vessels in pirate-infested waters. Their specialty, midnight parachute drops—both high altitude and low altitude jumps and openings—under night vision goggles, separated the men from the boys, the professionals from the amateurs. Inserting into unfriendly territories, killing the enemies of freedom, in several undetectable ways, under the cover of darkness, remained a highly marketable and lucrative skill.

As McGee drove the black Hummer2 through the gated compound he reminded himself that as gracious and as giving as Hunter could be, Duncan was also a very selfish man. Like the late Art Yoder before him, Hunter knew with McGee "in charge" of these lines of business, he would be able to spend more time with priorities. Hunter's main priority was to spend as much time with the woman he loved and cherished. *For all he's done for me, giving Hunter a little more time with Nazy is the least I could do.*

CHAPTER NINE

The Director of Central Intelligence, Greg Lynche, closed the meeting. Deputy Directors and other senior intelligence service officers around the conference table stood and gathered their notepads and coffee cups then made their way out of the conference room. Before Nazy Cunningham could get close to the door, the DCI said, "Nazy…stay, please." The request caught the attention of several of the more senior intelligence service executives; it was highly unusual and bordered on criminal activity for a male senior executive to be in a room alone with a woman. Human Resources wouldn't like the news, but no one would ever confront the director on his poor judgment.

Nazy improved her position from the far end of the table moving to sit beside the Director. When the last person departed and closed the door, Lynche asked, "What's the latest?"

"Sir, two dozen IOs are missing. Every intelligence officer who has gained access into al-Qaeda or the Muslim Brotherhood has vanished."

"Anything released on the web? Anyone claiming credit?"

"No, sir. No, that's why I think it's something far worse." Her worry accentuated by the tone in her accent and her demeanor displayed a crushing level of concern. "Director Lynche, there are only a handful of people who know who these men are and know their location, their posting and missions. Most of the ones who know just left the meeting."

"What are you trying to say, Nazy?"

"It's not any one of them."

"Agreed. So who is it? Do you know or think you know?"

"Yes, sir." Nazy closed her notebook and looked at Lynche directly, unblinking. "I think Rothwell is alive, or he provided our officers' identities and information to al-Qaeda before he died."

Lynche immediately shook his head and dismissed outright the bizarre comment. "He's dead. DNA match. From an arm and other collected, um, material. 14th floor. Explosion. Body parts. I need more to convince me he's alive." He refrained from being more graphic. "He's dead, Nazy."

"Director Lynche, before Dr. Rothwell left the Agency he accessed certain SAPs. And some other files."

"Like what?"

Nazy flipped open her notebook and read from a list of Special Access Programs. "JUGGERNAUT—the Soviet Union's clandestine war with the U.S. and the communist infiltration of the U.S. government. MATADOR—the Soviet Union's primary disinformation campaign. STARBURST—the infiltration of al-Qaeda. STEEPLEJACK—the infiltration of the Muslim Brotherhood. BLUE SHOES—the acquisition of man-portable tactical nuclear weapons from the former Soviet Union. PIPER ONE was ransom paid to stop commercial airliners from being shot down. PIPER TWO was ransom paid to stop anthrax from being introduced into the postal system. The Ortiz file—a mixed bag of old OSS items including a comprehensive listing of Nazi artwork stolen, I'm assuming, from European museums. Then there were WRAITH and NOBLE SAVAGE and Duncan's and my personal files."

"No Nazi gold?" Lynche asked flippantly, an attempt to lighten the mood. He didn't like where his Deputy Director of Counterintelligence was going or what she was intimating.

"There's a possibility, Sir. Our analysts believe there are documents in the Ortiz file that may provide the locations of the missing artwork, the missing gold, or both. We've made an extraordinary effort to authenticate the documents several times over the years as new intel was developed but have had no success in finding the art or the presumed gold. It's noteworthy that Rothwell personally took another look at the file; he had the encoded docs copied and sent to NSA. I'm waiting for an answer from my NSA counterpart to ascertain the whereabouts of those copies as well as the results of their analyses."

"There's more. I can see it in your eyes, Nazy. Those files are a mixed bag. I'm not sure what to make of them. I know enough of STARBURST, STEEPLEJACK, and BLUE SHOES to know those are Presidential…er, executive special access programs. E-SAPs. Eyes only level."

"Yes, sir, with the exception of MATADOR, they contain the identities of all but two of our missing intelligence officers. Our asset in Iran is new and is running in the black; you signed his assignment orders. The other one was in Liberia. The initial dispatch indicated he was almost assassinated and was able to escape the country. He's inbound to Langley, and we'll be able to debrief him in a few hours."

"Good. Remind me—JUGGERNAUT?" Lynche's furrowed brows needed filling in.

Nazy closed her notebook and recited from memory. "Communist-led intelligence services are aggressively recruiting leftist media leaders, academics, and university professors as spies and influence agents. Russia, China, Cuba, and even Angola have devoted significant resources to targeting and exploiting U.S. media and academia. While their intelligence services have been able to completely infiltrate the press—with one exception—mostly they've perfected placing agents in American universities, both instructors and students, under the assumption that a good percentage of leftist students will eventually move on to positions within our government, like Alger Hiss and others. Once in, they'll provide or help shape government decisions and policy." Nazy consulted her notes and said, "Academia and the media have been and remain key targets of foreign intelligence services. Each intelligence service has special departments to identify targets, collect information, and conduct 'influence operations.' Their greatest successes have been their ability to sway policymakers into particular courses of action or plant disinformation or propaganda through these influence agents. Once recruited at university, these agents are directed to enter fields that'll provide greater access to key elements of the U.S. government and intelligence community."

"And MATADOR? Disinformation?"

"MATADOR: comprehensive disinformation campaign from environmentalism to smearing the Pope to funding, ah, the global warming movement. Hundreds of concurrent programs."

Lynche's expressed surprise and urged Nazy to continue.

"As one example, the Soviet Union knew the Nazi leadership—including Hitler—was very attracted to what was an early form of environmentalism. The National Socialists was the original 'green movement.' The KGB pushed U.S. democrats and communists to be more aggressive and environmentally sensitive with respect to manufacturing war materials. In addition, because of their politics, the analysts couldn't believe the KGB had a hand in manipulating weather data and had funded dozens of British and American climate scientists; they were essentially on the KGB payroll. All the evidence pointed to first the Soviets then the Russians funding...." Nazy opened her notebook and quickly referred to her notes to ensure she got the terminology correct, "...*funding reputable-sounding phenomena.*"

"But it was just weather."

"Just weather. Another disinformation effort. There's hundreds of examples, actually. KGB. Behind all of them."

"I hate it when Duncan's right—you can't tell him I said that!"

Nazy beamed a Broadway smile. "Our secret, Director Lynche."

Lynche exhaled loudly. "Okay, the Soviets were the culprits behind all the chaos in the Middle East, and they funded liberal 'reputable-sounding phenomena' and terrorist projects. I'm not surprised. They've done that for years, all under the radar." He waved his hand to encourage himself to change the conversation. "Okay, WRAITH and NOBLE SAVAGE I know about. Yours and Duncan's files? I got the impression from Duncan that he was sure Rothwell didn't know you two were...*an item.*"

"Rothwell was obsessed with me, that I know. I think he may have been afraid of Duncan or was just curious since Duncan was an unknown contractor. He didn't trust and had little use for outside vendors. Duncan never said what he and Rothwell discussed when he visited the seventh floor; I know now that it was for NOBLE SAVAGE missions, targeting high value targets in the Middle East and Africa."

"The President wishes to continue that operation. The Deputy Director of Operations briefed me that they had some problems with, ah, having a contractor doing the work. So Rothwell did discuss it with at least the DDO and probably the General Counsel. Now that Duncan has an airplane up and running, the President is excited to restart the program. So you're aware of NOBLE SAVAGE? But you're not cleared for that."

"Director Lynche, I assembled the initial listing. Rothwell had me consolidate targets from different programs and files. It may have been 'Eyes Only' but I did all the racking and stacking. I didn't know how they prioritized the targets, and Duncan didn't tell me. That was the protocol. But it was obvious when a Mali warlord rose to the top of the matrix, Duncan meets the DCI, and a week later he's off on an adventure. When the warlord comes up missing, according to the papers, that's when I knew."

Lynche tapped his custom *banksia* pen on his pad. He bit his lower lip and looked at Nazy before breaking eye contact. She was drop dead gorgeous and was the fantasy of half of the men at the CIA, but she was family or as close to being the daughter he and Connie never had along with Hunter being the poster-boy Marine son they never had. Lynche thoughtfully nodded in repose. "Any issues with Duncan? I worry about him. Wet ops were never my forte but then, enhanced interrogation techniques wasn't either. He seems to be handling it well. How are you doing, Nazy?"

At the reference to government-sanctioned assassinations, she lowered her eyes for a second and then reconnected with Lynche's. "He can take care of himself. And I think I'm getting better every day, although I'm concerned I'm getting a little paranoid. I haven't been able to make any tail but I think I'm being watched. Telescopes or something. Or it may just be nerves; I don't want to believe it's this PTSD stuff or anyone from Algeria or Saudi Arabia. I just know someone is watching me." Nazy took a very deep breath. "I couldn't believe what I saw in Colombia—a man at point blank range tried to kill Duncan. Us."

With her final words, Lynche frowned at Nazy; he knew what he must do and what he was about to say wasn't going to make either of his adult adopted children very happy. He rubbed his eyes and said, "You're going to a safe house."

"Director Lynche…."

"There's no discussion, Nazy. I'd take you home so you and Connie could hide out in the basement and play cards or something. But if your assessment is on target—you're not prone to histrionics or ideations—then you're probably right, and you're on Rothwell's shit list. There's already been one attempt on your life—even if we want to isolate it and think that an assassination attempt by the FARC that was directed at Duncan. The further we unwind this ball of yarn, I don't like where it's going. I don't want to believe you're correct, that Rothwell is somehow alive."

"I don't think he'd hurt me."

Lynche chortled and reached for her hand for emphasis, "Nazy! Duncan told me about finding Rothwell in your hospital room. When Duncan told him that you were engaged, Rothwell was completely shocked and afraid. He couldn't get out of the hospital fast enough. His response was odd. If Rothwell's really running with al-Qaeda or some other terrorist organization, then he's fully vested in the dark side. And he's been chasing you…."

"Just about from the moment I set foot in the Agency."

"Nazy, it's apparent you hurt him badly when Duncan announced he's your fiancé. He'll find a way to get to Duncan to get to you—if he can't have you, he'll take great pleasure in destroying Duncan. Or worse, he'd go after both of you. If he *is* alive and is as wounded as I'm imagining him to be, he'll blame Duncan for all the problems of his world. He'll blame Duncan for everything that's happened to him, and, by extension, he'll blame Duncan for taking you away from him too. I'm not taking any chances with you—either of you. Where's Duncan now?"

"Updating his poly." Nazy squeezed Lynche's hand.

"I knew that. Plus, I'm seeing him this afternoon before my meeting with the President. I'll tell him. Okay?"

"Okay." Nazy sensed the shift from personal business to work. She again opened her notebook and was ready to provide answers to the Director's questions.

"Now, what do we know about our missing IOs?"

"Sir, the deputies will work each case. We went through the basic list at out meeting. I have a couple of updates. IOs have disappeared in Kabul, Abu Dhabi, Kuwait City, Cairo, Doha. We're waiting for some word from the Station Chiefs on their activities and whereabouts. I'm sorry to say some at the CTC expect crucifixion and beheading videos to show up on Al-Jazeera soon. For whatever reason, IRONMAN in Iran has been left alone and unmolested. I don't know how Rothwell could know of him as he was assigned and dispatched only after you signed his orders."

"That's unprecedented bad with one good."

Nazy nodded. "Two actually. There's IRONMAN and the one that escaped—MOOSE—out of Monrovia, Liberia. The report highlighted some quick-thinking airport manager intervened and rescued him. Embassy dispatch indicated the airport guy used an obscure Agency code to reprioritize a transient Navy aircraft to land in Liberia and take MOOSE to another airport. I suppose he told the pilot that he was a code one priority and flew him to the Azores. MOOSE is inbound for a debrief."

"That airport manager has to be LeMarcus, LeMarcus Leonard."

"That's what I thought but I haven't heard anything about him since we…last visited Monrovia." Nazy recalled the dizzying effort to interrogate Osama bin Laden at the Roberts International Airport. For twelve hours straight she asked questions of the world's most wanted "dead" terrorist before Hunter, as promised had put the terrorist "on a jet." Lynche shifted in his seat and checked his watch. He was in a hurry, and his tone and timbre demanded they focus on the mission at hand.

"MOOSE is inbound?"

"Yes, sir. You can count on one hand the number of people that knew who he was and where he was operating. If you exclude the outlier IRONMAN, every one of our IOs intersect with Bruce Rothwell. The DOs of CTC and NCS, and Rothwell. And with the IO untouched in Iran, an alive Rothwell seems to be the only solution that makes any sense...."

"Unless we have a mole."

"Not possible in this case. The old KGB—new FSB would need a half dozen in-place at *your* level, and after all the polys we've been through, someone would've popped up. You said yourself, these are E-SAPs; only the DCI and the President have access. No one goes through the DCI's burn bag. No, I'm afraid Rothwell's alive. Plus, there's more."

"Come on, Nazy, this can't get much worse."

"I'm afraid so."

"Okay. What do you have?"

"First, before I get to that, we just received another piece of intel; could be minor. I think it's huge. MI6 indicated the KGB investigated the missing Nazi artwork about twenty years ago—in Germany. You'll never guess who was in charge of that operation."

"*Vladimir?*" He opened his hands as if to say, "Surprise me."

"Not Vladimir—*Boris!* Nastakovich. Former KGB colonel."

Lynche asked in disbelief. "*Nasty* Boris? Russia's newest oil billionaire?"

"Yes, sir; you know him?"

"I do. Came up through the ranks of the KGB as a Lubyanka interrogator. Master of torture. Very nasty fella."

Nazy's eyebrows jumped. She continued, "Lastly, I believe several targets on the disposition matrix have also disappeared."

"I know what that means to me—what does it mean to you?"

"They've been warned, but only the high value targets with a strong AQ or Brotherhood connection, all of them in North Africa and the Middle East. My assessment is Rothwell was able to warn them that they were on a hit list, and they went to ground. Only the DCI and the POTUS, and informally me, know the names on the matrix. I don't know how anyone could have survived the bomb blast that reportedly killed him, but Rothwell is alive."

"You're brilliant, Nazy. Absolutely makes sense, and I'll defer to you—your sense in all this has been perfect. I'd like to know more when you're able to get more facts. Can you do that?"

"Do you mean can I provide answers from the safe house?"

"Yes. It's wired, a SCIF in a bomb shelter basically. After you debrief MOOSE send me an email on what he said and how he is. I also need the names of all the officers we've lost, then I expect you to head to *Spindletop*. You know the drill. We'll send Security to your house to get some of your things. Then again, that may not be possible. I'll work it. Expect the Security Chief to visit; she'll take special care of you." Lynche smiled sternly as he closed his leather notebook. He was finished and needed to complete his morning meetings. This evening he'd write condolence letters for the families of his fallen intelligence officers.

"Okay, Director Lynche."

"Nazy, you're doing it for me. I know it will be a pain." He broke out in a big disarming smile and said, "Besides, Duncan will beat my ass if anything happens to you and I didn't do everything to keep you safe. You have to trust me on this."

Nazy swore softly to herself. Her silver-green eyes flashed exactly like the wide-eyed Afghani girl immortalized on a National Geographic magazine cover. She didn't want to go to any safe house and be away from Duncan. She saw the dynamics of the operation turning into just that, another way that the disgraced Rothwell would keep Duncan from her. She cherished the few moments they could share. They didn't have many opportunities to be with one another, and getting stuck in a safe house with a security detail walking all over the place would never make for a romantic setting even if Hunter would even be allowed to visit. She nodded with resignation. "Thank you, Director...."

"Nazy, you're welcome. Listen, I love you guys, and I would never forgive myself if something happened to you." Lynche deftly avoided saying something he would've regretted. Nazy was still recovering from horrific injuries, and despite her outward strong demeanor, he was convinced she was still very fragile. He stood to signal the meeting was over. Nazy rose with him as a moment passed between them. He opened his arms as he would for his adopted daughter, and she stepped into his embrace. He said into her ear, "No lipstick; *ack!* I have more meetings!"

Nazy laughed as they patted each other's back and separated. Her killer smile buoyed him; she almost reached up and touched his cheek. Then a flash of inspiration struck her as they stood toe to toe. "Greg, check this out!" Nazy took his hands and led him in a few dance steps. Lynche was completely taken aback.

"You can dance? When did that happen?"

She released her grip and beamed, "I need to dance at my wedding. I've been taking ballroom dancing! Can you tell?"

"I can tell just by that little bit. Can Duncan dance? I think he'd be a clod."

"Oh no, he's very good." A flash of a smile tied to the memory of her and Duncan slow dancing to The Moody Blues, both of them naked, toe to toe. She had to stop thinking of Duncan.

"Is there anything he can't do well?" Lynche winked at her and waved his arms and said, "How'd this happen?" He was under the notion the former Muslima didn't know how to dance because dancing was, as far as he knew, prohibited in the Muslim world.

"I tried to take karate lessons, but all the instructors were more interested in me than teaching me. I found this ballroom dancing business and...*I enrolled.* My dancing partner is, uh, he's more interested in teaching me, and he gives great lessons."

Comic skepticism ran amok across Lynche's face. He had become more protective of Nazy since he returned to the CIA. He had brought her closer into the inner sanctum of the Agency leadership, and the President was supportive of her selection as deputy director of counterintelligence and her additional duty as special investigator into the death of the former DCI. Lynche didn't like the idea some other man was "handling" the breathtaking Nazy Cunningham especially when Duncan wasn't around.

She was amused with Lynche's expression. "Greg, he's gay."

"How do you know?" Skepticism replaced amusement.

Nazy frowned playfully. "I'm *not* dead. Thank you for worrying about me. That's so sweet. I'm okay and it'll be a great surprise for Duncan, if you can keep a secret."

"I can keep a secret—want to know one I've been holding for thirty years that involves Duncan? And the Ortiz file?"

"That makes no sense. The Ortiz file is World War 2. Duncan wasn't even born yet."

"Nazy, that's all true, but one of the things found in the Ortiz file was a bag of nails with another one stuck in a block of wood. Allen Dulles first looked at the nails in the bag that Ortiz brought and dismissed it; this Ortiz character looked at all the nails, concluded it was an aptitude test, and solved it in front of Dulles. The secret is we took that simple test and developed our own aptitude-screening program in the late forties and used it through the mid-seventies. Nearly every child and government worker and contracted executive in America took some form of 17 Nails. The findings from that exam were astonishing."

"Seriously?" Nazy was intrigued with the story but wasn't convinced any outcomes could have been considered "astonishing."

"Well, yes. When the leadership found out we had a simple method of testing high-level aptitude and problem solving, we developed a program to recruit the brightest of the problem solvers. Duncan clearly stood out from the rest after he took the test."

"I had no idea. But he wasn't recruited. He never left the Marine Corps." She was confused and she crossed her arms over her breasts to show she was finding it difficult to believe any of it.

"I was the 17 Nails program manager, and I tried, but he was too involved with the Marines so I put his file in abeyance. After we both retired, I finally got him to come work for me."

"Wow. I had no idea."

Lynche debated whether to tell he the rest of the story. He checked his watch and noted he had some time. It was a good story. "There's one more thing that came out of that program that has never been discussed, acknowledged, or divulged."

Nazy smiled and cocked her head. *Is he going to tell me?*

"You can never tell Duncan I told you this. There was an unintended consequence to all that testing with the nails."

"Uh huh?"

"Some of our researchers found out quickly that there's a *political* correlation to those who did well on the test and those that..., um, didn't."

"Umm, I'm not sure I follow you."

"Well, the test results showed that those that leaned left *politically* had a great deal of trouble solving the puzzle. Those that leaned right *politically*, solved the puzzle easily. Duncan set a record for how fast it was solved. I really do hate him!" He smiled and frowned at the same time.

She threw her hands to cover her mouth. "I suppose that's info no one would want divulged. Thank you for telling me."

"What was amazing was how fast the program was terminated once that bit of trivia leaked to the seventh floor; let's say some...powerful *liberals* in the Agency killed it. I guess I leaned left. I couldn't solve 17 Nails. I was very embarrassed until I saw the solution, which opened up another can of worms." He looked up at his wall clock and said, "But we have to go. See you later...*Miss* Cunningham." Lynche stepped for the door and began to open it for his Deputy Director of Counterterrorism.

"Nazy, a couple more things. Why do you think Rothwell accessed JUGGERNAUT; the infiltration of...."

She recited from memory, "The *Communist* infiltration of the U.S. government."

"We've had a lot of conversations about Russians. That can't be a coincidence."

"No, Sir. I'm not sure—what little I know is that the infiltration is widespread and their disinformation campaigns comprehensive. I've learned the USSR had hundreds of thousands in their disinformation army—maybe even a million people. We've analyzed only a fraction of the data. Interesting that our analysts were called off the program when they started to see or hear of communist infiltration at the highest levels of government even in the White House during World War Two and the Korea War."

"You think there's more here than meets the eye?"

"Greg, no disrespect, but you see history through the lens of what you've been taught. I've no such...*preconceived* notions. There might be something in there, but it's a huge file. If you release that file to me I'll look at it more comprehensively."

Lynche nodded at the woman's logic and said, "That would be great—I'll do that."

"My pleasure. Moreover, I'll have those names on your desk before I leave. Oh, Greg, you said you had a couple more things but only mentioned JUGGERNAUT. Was there something more?"

"Oh yes, refresh my memory what IRONMAN is doing."

"He's monitoring the nuclear facilities in, I believe, Natanz. Iran. It's their major nuclear reactor and processing plant."

Lynche recalled the rationale for the intelligence officer's assignment. "Their ayatollahs are directly responsible for toppling four Arab capitals. Their IEDs kill American soldiers. They would destroy Israel tomorrow if they could. This is what they're doing *without* a nuclear weapon." He shook his head to eliminate the image of a mushroom cloud over Jerusalem. There was nothing more left to say. The conversation was over. Lynche's body language said he needed to go. "Got it. Thank you, Nazy."

"Good day, Director Lynche." She turned her back to him and

headed out his office.

For two long seconds, he couldn't help but watch her perfectly shaped hips and exquisite bare legs as she walked across the carpet. Her legs had a way of erasing horrific images of mushroom clouds lingering in the back of his mind. He closed his eyes until he heard the door of his office close behind her.

CHAPTER TEN

"Mister Lynche! What a pleasant surprise!" Waggish sarcasm dripped with every syllable of Hunter's greeting as he closed the distance and found a spot to sit on the Scottish blanket. The two men shared a conspiratorial grin; Hunter shook his head in mild disbelief. Meeting the Director of Central Intelligence in the middle of Dewey Field, the U.S. Naval Academy's athletic grounds, would've been curious under any other circumstances. But Commissioning Week at the United States Naval Academy, the one time of the year when the Navy's Flight Demonstration Team—*The Blue Angels*—performed its routine in tribute to the new crop of Annapolis graduates, was a unique opportunity to get away from Headquarters and have a little fun. The former Chief Air Branch didn't have many opportunities to combine his passion for aviation with an official function.

The DCI's security detail, armed intelligence officers in white polo shirts, dark trousers, and warp-around sunglasses, hovered nearby but barely gave Hunter any notice. Hunter and Lynche had a long, warm, and personal relationship going back some 17 years.

Hunter noticed the tie and jacket were gone but Lynche would never give up his grey Joseph A. Bank's slacks and black Johnston Murphy oxfords. Lynche moved a light-neon green rubberized device out of the way so Hunter wouldn't sit on it. "Growler," said Lynche. Hunter acknowledged with a nod. The device generated a bubble of electronic noise and prevented anyone from eavesdropping on their conversation. He nodded when the lamp illuminated to indicate the device was energized.

"Well, *Director* Lynche, I'm sure you got that up-close VIP parking.

We peons have to park in the south forty and hoof it in."

The seventy-three year old, silver-haired Lynche leaned back and adjusted mirrored aviator sunglasses with a heavily lined and tanned hand. He looked out over the Severn River as he spoke. "Gave a lecture—I addressed the Midshipmen—and had lunch with the Superintendent. Rank has its privileges. Nasty business at the office when I return. Going to enjoy this while I can."

"You picked a great day for an airshow. Great seats." Hunter moved his arm next to Lynche's to compare tans; his eburnean limbs were an embarrassment. "I definitely need to get out and get some more sun. Thanks for the invite."

The DCI nodded. He anticipated the arrival of the dark blue and yellow jets. He'd seen the show many times over the years while sitting on the deck of the Annapolis Yacht Club with a glass of wine and a plate of calamari. He leaned into Hunter and said, "Nice work in Somalia—the al-Shabaab leadership has been nearly decimated—some say it was the work of rival gangs. They will no longer poach elephant tusks and rhino horn or kidnap sailors and tourists to fund their activities."

Hunter was serious. "That's what I like—a happy ending."

Lynche grinned an acknowledgement. "And then there's Colombia and Afghanistan. You've been busy."

"Thank you, Sir. Just doing my part to protect the environment. I did get pinged by a Coast Guard cutter; they must have a great radar to pick me up."

"They reported a 'radar anomaly' because one second you were there and the next you were gone. Like smoke."

Hunter nodded. "Radar absorption paint works."

Lynche said, "I take it the new airplane works well?"

"Yes, sir. 002 isn't as tight as 007, but it's very solid, and the Bobs are making it better every day. Per your directions the autonomous takeoff and landing software is installed and checked out. For the record, hands-off landings scare the crap out of me."

"This from a carrier pilot? I thought you guys got into that living on-the-edge stuff. I don't think I could do it."

"No, you'd probably piss yourself."

"That's not very charitable. But, you're probably right. You have the 'right stuff,' I know I couldn't defeat a missile or conceive of doing a 'dirty penetration' or land at night with my hands off the stick. I still don't know how you do it. I'd lose all my hair." Lynche allowed the complement to soak into Hunter's hard head.

"The war on terrorism is hell."

"Anyway, both Yo-Yos have the ATLS installed; the backup was just flight checked. One airplane has fresh radar absorption paint with some wild newfangled nanotechnology coating that absorbs something like 99.96% of light. While I've been busy, I want you to know your C-130 aircrews were, as usual, terrific and professional—an absolute pleasure to work with."

Lynche had authorized a CIA airplane to haul Hunter, the *Wraith*, and the support crew to Africa to track down pirate camps and locate hostages kidnapped from oil tankers and private sailing vessels. He had reviewed the FLIR video showing Hunter killing the pirates and sinking their boat. He said, "It took too long to find those people. Some of them have been missing for years. You might have been considered a hero, maybe even received another medal, if the NRO hadn't picked you up on one of their cameras. Pretty sure they caught you jerking off."

Hunter wasn't amused. "Nice try."

"I don't know—with you anything is possible." Lynche was enjoying the revelry; since becoming the DCI, he rarely had opportunities to let his hair down and poke fun at his best friend.

"Really—they saw me? How's that even possible?"

Lynche frowned at Hunter who nodded a signal that he already knew the answer. He said, "No need to know. Any more medals and you'll be the most decorated person in the Agency."

"I could never exceed the medal count of Pete Ortiz."

Lynche turned toward Hunter. He wasn't confused but sought validation. It was the second time he'd heard Pete Ortiz in the span of a few hours. He asked, "Who?"

"You don't know your Agency history? That's embarrassing. I expected better." Hunter shook his head in mock disgust, as if the quotidian CIA Headquarters with its teeming masses of intelligence officers looked upon the Wall of Honor and had no idea the Agency had heroes and patriots.

"Never heard of him."

"Bullshit." Hunter scowled at his best friend and knew he was lying. He could also play at that game. "Captain Peter Ortiz? OSS? *Two* Navy Crosses for leading French resistance efforts?"

"Oh, that guy. Another crazy Marine."

"The last of the manly men. He'd make today's liberals and girly men piss all over themselves just by walking into a room."

"Now, now...."

"I did fly with his son—Big Bird."

Hunter winked at Lynch just as the DCI suddenly erupted in laughter, culminating in an unnatural and lengthy coughing fit, exacerbated by some chronic minor lung condition from surviving multiple bouts of malaria. His security detail looked on ominously as Lynche struggled to recover his composure. Through very hard and very loud coughs, Lynche waved them away and fought for clear air.

Sometimes things Hunter would say or the way he would say them would send Lynche into red-faced, bellyaching laughter, resulting in a steady, hard coughing fit. It always happened when Hunter casually referred to one of his old military flying cohorts. What he said struck the old spook as belly slapping, Robin Williams funny.

Navy and Marine pilots demonstrated their sense of humor with the names they would call themselves, their "call signs." Geek, Goof, E.T., Mutant, Mongrel, and Rooster all highlighted some dubious personal characteristic. Like Big Bird. The names stuck forever even when the pilots retired, became old, or became general officers. Air Force pilots mostly went for the more dauntless call signs, like Killer, Mako, Magoo, Warpath, and Bullet, but they too were great people and unequivocal patriots.

Hunter loved and revered the Air Force instructor pilots that attended his courses, and he would address his graduate students by their call signs. Hunter was *Maverick* and Lynche typically called him *Mav*. Lynche was *Grinch*—Hunter mashed together "Greg" and "Lynche" to get the most obvious personal characteristic of the man— Lynche's sharp-witted and oftentimes caustic liberal tongue could quickly ruin Hunter's good time trashing liberals when Lynche got cranky. The DCI could be a Grinch under the right circumstances.

Call signs had introduced the formerly apolitical enlisted Marine Corps Sergeant Duncan Hunter into the world of politics. When a crusty new Marine colonel reported aboard his air station with the call sign "Assassin," Hunter was intrigued with the unique name. He was convinced it violated several Marine Corps policies—you could call yourself anything you wanted just as long as it wasn't vulgar or pornographic. He learned the man's basic story from several third-hand sources. The story made international news. An AP reporter had been on a Marine Corps CH-46 helicopter in Vietnam when the pilot rushed into a landing zone to evacuate wounded Marines. A Viet Cong soldier armed with an AK-47 jumped out of the bamboo in front of the helicopter. The dark little man with the straw coolie hat pulled the trigger to try to kill everyone in the helicopter's cockpit, but his machine gun jammed. The reporter watched the CH-46 pilot pull a .38 revolver from his holster, reach out the side window of the helicopter, and shoot the man struggling to unjam the Kalashnikov. An article followed, and the reporter accused the pilot of being an "assassin" for shooting the "defenseless man." This had taught Hunter the difference between liberals and conservatives, democrats and republicans, and he soon felt little but antipathy for anything liberal, until he met Lynche. He wasn't all bad; Lynche wasn't like any of the typical dumbass liberals he had met. He was smart, accomplished, professional, and a patriot, and Hunter loved him like the father he wished he had.

After recovering from his coughing, Lynche wiped tears from his eyes. He struggled to ask, "Big Bird?"

"Pete Ortiz, Junior. Flew in my back seat. Great RIO."

Lynche nodded, afraid to cough again.

"Marines are humble." Hunter deadpanned while stifling a shit-eating grin, hoping Lynche wouldn't break out into another bout of the hard, dry coughing.

"Well, *Mister Humble*, I've news for you. There's an investigation going on. Seems like someone released an Agency file on our former President." Hunter cocked his head to find Lynche had become more serious, introspective. He double-checked the Growler's flashing light to verify it was working.

"What do you mean?" Hunter asked but knew the answer.

"You know what I mean. It was totally expected; I'm just surprised it's taken this long."

"I'm a little confused," said the man who released the former President's file to the media and Congress.

"You know what MI5 is?"

"Military Intelligence, Section 5; U.K. counter-intelligence? Never heard of them." Hunter was unremorsefully sarcastic.

"They had their own file on the president as well. Now there's new information. KGB destroyed the official records of his birth and replaced them with fictitious documents. I still don't know how you knew he was bad, Mav."

"You mean that nasty indoctrinated child of the Left who told the world, 'We're the ones we've been waiting for?' Maybe it was his strong Islamic sympathies, or maybe it was the hint that he didn't know the Pledge of Allegiance or how many states there are in the *United States*? Commie bastard. I don't believe a damn thing a liberal or a democrat says. If their lips are moving, they're lying. The press helped maintain the fiction, and you know I don't have much use for corrupt media."

Lynche kept his voice low. "Ahem, well, yeah. On one hand, you're a treasonous bastard, but on the other, you're a hero."

"I know you liked the cut of his jib. You're awake now?" Hunter alluded to Lynche's voting for the democratic nominee.

"I am. The great and powerful Oz illusion is over. The awakening is spreading across the country. Some dumb national network biddy just came out and said words to the effect, 'We thought he was the next messiah.' They're crushed."

"They're *crushed?* I would think they'd be pissed because he was a Muslim masquerading as a Christian."

Lynche, ever the proper gentleman, said, "That's not politically correct. Be nice. No kicking when they're down."

"Bullshit—I say draw swords and run these idiots into the river— right over there! I'm really working hard to be nice."

"Anyway, you released the file and stopped it. I don't think you know how lucky we were. We are."

"What did Churchill *say…*'never give in, never give in, never, never, never—in nothing, great or small, large or petty—never give in except to convictions of honor and good sense. Never yield to force; never yield to the apparently overwhelming might of the enemy.' Good frickin' riddance."

Lynche stopped picking at the grass and looked at Hunter with exasperation. "That's impressive. You've been practicing?"

"*Never!*"

The field was full and noisy with hundreds of people waiting for the *Blue Angels*. Both men chuckled. *Hunter could get that way*, Lynche said to himself. Hunter patted Lynche's knee in love, respect, and admiration and asked, "You see Eastwood's show?"

"Heard about it. Near East Division's afraid of a backlash."

"I'm surprised we haven't heard anything."

"We have, but the press is suppressing it."

"That's surprising. The greatest power of the media is the power to ignore. Suppression for national security is antithetical to them. This is right up their alley. That would be a great story. This makes no sense."

"Some bin Laden wanna-be jumped in front of a camera and demanded that Eastwood be killed."

"Really? There's a lot of that going around. I haven't told you another fruit loop tried to kill me. But with that news, maybe they weren't after me."

"I can't believe you…. Hold it, another? I…."

"Mea culpa. I definitely screwed up in Colombia. I thought Nazy and I could spend a little time together."

"You're getting careless, Mav. So, there's *another* one?"

"Yes, sir. Last week I was with Colonel Eastwood. Just like the sucker in Bogotá, another dude on a motorcycle first tried to shoot us in the face. He came back around, pulled up to the passenger side of the Hummer and emptied a MAC-10 at us, but more at *him*. I thought it was for me but now…."

The concern and disappointment on Lynche's face was masked by other thoughts. *This is why you don't hire brilliant people for jobs like this. You hire smart people. Brilliant people get you into trouble. Maverick, you may be brilliant but you're going to get all of us in a mess!* Lynche exhaled in exasperation and let his thoughts dissolve in his mind. "Last week?"

"Yes, sir. You say some imbecilic, spittle-flying, wild-eyed, Islamic rage boy demanded that Eastwood be killed?"

"That's also *not* politically correct, but yes. It's the typical appeal to wealthy Muslims to bankroll rewards for the attackers willing to kill journalists serving in the Middle East, or maybe go after him in the States. He's previously called for attacks on U.S. diplomats when he asserted al-Qaeda would attack U.S. Embassies in retaliation for military activities in Iraq and Afghanistan."

"What a turd. I thought they were after me until the dude changed lanes. Eastwood might have been the target."

"Seriously?" Sarcasm and scorn flashed in Lynche's eyes. "Two cyclists with automatics in two countries; you're in both vehicles. And you think they were after him? What're the odds? Were they after Nazy, too? Please! You're a marked man, Mav. I think I need to lock you up, too. You're not that dumb...but damn. Suffer and learn; *pathei mathos.*"

Embarrassed, Hunter frowned at the curious reference to being locked up and appreciated Lynche's mastery of Latin, but he wanted to change the subject as soon as possible. He had broken dozens of personal security regulations and protocols just so he and Nazy could have a good time in an exotic place, but it could have exposed the mission as well as killed them both. Lynche had forgiven Duncan for his transgressions, but he would first let Hunter twist in the wind for his selfishness and stupidity. Lynch would get around to saying what was on his mind; he always did. Hunter had already learned his lesson and the admonishment; he tried to leverage his way out of the situation with a shift of topic. "Notice anything about today's group?"

"What are you talking about?" Lynche didn't appreciate the sudden change in the conversation, and his tone conveyed his displeasure. Maybe Hunter wasn't contrite as he was off playing one of his games. Lynche had seen this show before.

"Do you notice anything odd or strange about the other people out here? Enjoying the day; the airshow, maybe even demonstrating a little bit of patriotism?"

Lynche scanned from side to side, looked over one shoulder then the other. "Can't say I see anything out of the ordinary."

"No nose rings; no tattoos. No longhaired hippy types tatted up like a crop circle, no one flinging feces at cops or pissing on cop cars. No one here lives with their parents in the basement. They have jobs or they're in school. They're clean and smart; they have manners and they love their parents and little dogs and cats. And when we all leave here, this field won't look like a New Jersey landfill. In other words, not a lot of liberals. What do they call themselves these days—can't call them communists because that would be politically incorrect, but I understand the neutered and approved term for these eunuchs is progressives. That's right; not a lot of *progressives* here today. I suspect it's going to be a glorious day out here without any cowardly closet communists."

Lynche stuck his tongue deep into his cheek, frowned, and scratched a middle finger against his temple for Hunter to see. The men grinned at each other. Lynche said, "I was serious."

Hunter looked at his best friend and mentor. "I know. I think about it often. I thought it was just Soviet penetration, that the government is riddled with Red agents. In groups, cells, press rooms—

a nest of vipers actively pushing, enabling, and implementing the Soviet program. Now with this den of Islamic wolves...I don't know, Greg. Something's up with this red diaper baby band."

"You think?" Lynche shook his head in amazement. Two hit teams on two continents tried to kill his best friend and Hunter's dismissal of the severity of the situation struck Lynche as odd. He looked at his friend for a few seconds until the sound of a dozen turbojets rumbled in the distance, interrupting the banter and announcing the start of the air show. Hunter and Lynche stood and cheered along with the rest of the crowd on the field.

Hunter shouted, "The glorious sound of freedom!"

Six U.S. Navy F/A-18 *Blue Angels* set up for their first diamond formation pass. They came in low from the east, up the Chesapeake Bay and over the Severn River. Hundreds of spectators, midshipmen, their families and friends clapped and yelled their approval for the most spectacular air show on the planet. Individual opposing high-speed passes, six-jet triangle-formation wingovers, slow-flight where the nose of one of the big jets was held impossibly high, and gear-down loops were executed with precision and perfection. The jets dipped very low over the river at every pass. A few smart observers wore sound suppressors to diminish the constant roaring of jet engines just a few hundred feet away.

Hunter had seen it all before from inside the cockpit of a Marine F-4, but he loved the demonstration of skill and fearlessness of the team's pilots. Lynche, a pilot of Cessnas, dreamed of flying the supersonic fighters, but the closest he would get to the thrill of high-G flight was on the little patch of blanket at the Naval Academy's playing field. His eyes—always squinting—locked on the jets—left, right, and straight up. Wherever the *Angels* went, his eyes followed. Lynche unconsciously swayed with each turn and pass as if he were in one of the aircraft.

Hunter wasn't bored with the show but enjoyed watching the little kid come out of the old man he called his best friend and mentor. He felt a little sad that his friend had been unable to experience the thrill of high-speed, maneuvering flight.

They watched in rapt attention as the demonstration team approached their closing routine with the ultra-close, four-jet diamond formation low and slow over the river. The spectators couldn't begin to appreciate the extreme difficulty of the maneuver. Lynche was amazed but unsure of what he was seeing. Hunter was struck with awe, "Oh…my…God…." as the jets arced up the river and slowly spread out and away from each other.

"What?" Lynche demanded as the high-velocity noise level diminished. His head ratcheted between the disappearing jets and Hunter. He'd missed something Hunter had seen.

"Well, that was most likely the most difficult maneuver ever attempted by a demonstration team, and they did it just for you and the Navy's newest officers."

"What are you talking about?"

"Did you see how close they were to each other?"

"Yes, but…"

As Duncan spoke he motioned with his hands like airplanes flying in and out of formation. "Greg, for those few seconds, they were impossibly close, and I guarantee you'll never see flying like that again. Instead of half-dozen feet of step down, it looked like there was no more than eighteen inches separating the Sidewinder rails of the two outboard jets. That's insanely close—you can't do it without smooth calm air. You can't get four jets that close together without bumping wingtips or canopies. *Hell, you can't even park them that close!* But they did it for about five seconds. They're the greatest…and I didn't have a camera."

"It didn't look…*real.*"

"I know; a magician couldn't have done a better job than that. Show's over, Sir. The crowd is leaving. So Greg, what did you *really* want to talk about?" The men casually glanced around as people retrieved their blankets, lawn chairs, and coolers and headed off the field grass.

"A couple of things. My predecessor's death, for one."

CHAPTER ELEVEN

Six middle-aged men in dark suits filed into one of the conference rooms on the sixth floor of the Old Headquarters Building and took a seat. A lone framed picture—the Marine Corps War Memorial at night—hung in the middle of one wall, otherwise, the room was stark and dreary and devoid of character. A lone woman followed by a tall, young African-American man entered and took seats at opposite ends of the twenty-foot long, oak conference table. Nazy got right to the point. "What happened?"

Her voice came across as ungentle and grim. The intelligence officer assigned to the Special Access Program MOOSE, "Buck" to the other senior intelligence service executives around the oak table, took his time before answering. Notepads, pens, and a tape recorder recorded the undercover agent's every word. Buck glanced around the room and sucked in the cool, refrigerated air.

"I think I stumbled onto something...*in process*.... That's the best way to describe it. I had attended mosque a few hours earlier—like I had been doing for the last couple of weeks. I was approached—several times—to help with a project. The imam kept his eye on me as did others at the airport. I didn't want to appear overeager. At first, they kept me at arm's length. I don't know, it may have been the hotel I stayed at; it was the only place that didn't smell like a Mumbai slum, and it had a little beachfront that opened up to the ocean. Two days ago I was off work from the airport, getting some sun, reading a book on the beach when a dude I recognized from the mosque walked from an adjacent hotel. The beach was open. He tried to act casually but he had his hand behind his back. As he got close he said, 'We've been expecting you,' right before he pulled out a small automatic."

"You're not injured." suggested one of the SIS men. Nazy frowned at the comment and urged Buck to continue.

"I had sensed there had been a change in the demeanor of some of the men at the mosque; it was a subtle change. They didn't act...*normal*...normal, for Africans. I went over everything I had been taught and was sure my cover was unraveling. I almost convinced myself that it was nothing I had done, but after a while I suspected something was happening in the back of the mosque."

The men at the table scribbled on notepads. Nazy asked, "So you thought your cover had been blown?"

Buck nodded and looked the woman in the eyes. "At that point it was more a case of thinking that someone was coming for me. The guy was nonchalant, but when he said, 'We've been expecting you,' in reality, I was the one who was expecting him. As he approached, I put my book down and grabbed a handful of sand. When his eyes widened and his nostrils flared I knew I was about to die. As he brought his hand around I threw the sand into his face. He didn't expect it but tried to protect himself and brush it away. I pushed him, kicked him, and snatched a Makarov from his hand—just as we were taught at the Farm. He ran off. The gun never fired. I knew it was over at that point and raced to the embassy to tell the Chief of Station. The airport manager drove me to the airport and arranged to get me out of the country."

"What happened to the gun?" asked Nazy.

"I left it at the security office at the embassy with one of the Marines there. That was before I saw the COS."

Nazy asked, "What do you think they were up to?"

"Not sure. I don't know."

She continued, "Buck, you have to have some idea. You knew to go to the embassy for evacuation?"

"That's the protocol. The COS wouldn't say if the airport manager was a NOC, non-official cover. Probably couldn't say, but I ran into him, LeMarcus Leonard, at the embassy. I think the COS assumed we knew each other since both of us were working at the airport."

"He's not one of us," interjected one of the portly men.

"I didn't know that then, but somehow he knew I was Agency. I was a little confused when he said he was glad to know there's someone else he could trust at the airport."

"Is that a fact? Do we know that? We have a NOC airport manager?" barked one of the SIS men; his bushy brows nearly obscured his eyes when he frowned.

"We did," offered Nazy. "Buck, can we get back to the 'dude' as you called him, and the mosque. Something they said must have given you some hint?"

"Yes, ma'am. When you put together all of the—let me call them 'little things'—I think they were expecting an aircraft, maybe a special aircraft. I understand from Mr. Leonard that on his very first day on the job, I assumed it was several years earlier, an airplane landed and someone tried to smuggle a couple of dozen Philippine workers into the country. Mr. Leonard shared some of what he was doing in order to gain my trust and confidence. What were they up to? Both the airport guys and those at the mosque? That's what I've been trying to reconcile. They were or are expecting an aircraft. What it was or who was on it, I never got that far into the airport clique or the mosque. Something was definitely going on, going to happen. They get airplanes all the time, but this was something different. You could just sense it. A group at the airport knew something and could barely contain themselves. Like they were sharing a secret. I was part of the ground handling crew as were a couple of men from the mosque. I thought several times that they wanted to tell me, to bring me over to their side of thinking. I felt I had to be very cautious. I didn't want to move too fast."

"But you said the guy that tried to shoot you wasn't from the airport." Buck nodded.

One of the SIS men interrupted, "The Monrovia airport used to be a hotbed for Victor Bout's gun running. Do you think it was something like that—running guns? Smuggling Filipinos?"

Buck was unconvinced. "No. I don't think it was anything like that. But I just don't know. Again, I wasn't there long enough to penetrate the mosque or the inner circle at the airport. That was my mission. They were very suspicious of me showing up at the airport looking for work. I had papers; I found out later the majority of the guys around me didn't. 'How do you get papers after fifteen years of civil war?' one dude asked me. I told them I came from Ghana. Accra. I thought I was on the right track; I wasn't pushy or greedy; I let them come to me. I made friends and integrated with the airport workers. Then something changed, as if someone suspected I was CIA. It could have been someone found out I hadn't previously worked at an airport. Before I recognized the change in their demeanor, there was a casual mention of 'Catholics in Africa.'"

"How did you get into country?" asked bushy brows.

"A bus from Accra; my papers said I had worked at the airport. Specifically, I was a baggage handler."

"Any other questions?" Nazy asked. When there were no takers, she thanked and dismissed Buck. She and the men discussed the man's story, agreed on an action plan, and summarized the information to forward to the DCI. A discussion of the missing and reportedly dead intelligence officers took up the remainder of the meeting. Nazy concluded the briefing and accompanied the somber SIS executives off the floor. After Nazy emailed the DCI her debrief of MOOSE, she turned to leave her office only to find a very tall, very large, very buxom woman in a black pantsuit waiting for her.

Before Nazy could ask a question, the woman said, "Miss Cunningham, I'm here to take you away from all of this."

· · ·

Hunter shifted slightly on the blanket and looked away, out across the river. "Couldn't have happened to a nicer turd. Did the shithead traitor take up bomb making; did he cross some wires and blow himself up?

133

Curious minds want to know. I know he had a thing for good-looking women. Maybe he wanted to expedite and get to his forty virgins or something." While he played coy, Hunter knew exactly what had happened to the former DCI. It was one of the few secrets he kept from Lynche.

"It's more interesting than that. Jordan hasn't allowed the FBI into the country to investigate the bomb blast in Rothwell's hotel room. The FBI has been completely missing in action in nearly every other major terrorist investigation too. They didn't investigate the death of our ambassador in Libya. The Libyans wouldn't let them in and now the King of Jordan doesn't want the FBI to take a look. We had some special activities types in the area who were able to collect some human remains—so we got a positive ID through DNA. But the long and the short of it, we have no complete picture of what happened to him." Lynche scanned Hunter's profile for a clue; finding none he pressed his lips together and shrugged.

"Doesn't sound like you have a problem? What am I missing?"

"I even called my Jordanian cohort for some help."

"The Mukhabarat?"

"Yeah, I asked him what he knew. There was very little he would tell me, and what he did say wasn't helpful. Their forensics said C-4 was used and there were tiny helicopter parts in the debris. He blamed us." Hunter nearly winced when Lynche said there were tiny helicopter parts in the debris.

"May explain why they don't want to talk with the FBI."

Lynche continued, "Least of my problems, and I have several, actually. They're...the FBI is now crawling all over Langley."

"Why's the FBI at your place? Someone think inside job?"

Lynche's expression changed from apathetic to serious. "Not only does the FBI thinks the CIA outed the President, but that we also executed Rothwell."

"That's insane." Hunter wouldn't look at Lynche. He knew the career spook had been trained to read micro-expressions and would've read something curious in Hunter's response.

"Tell me about it. Lots of insanity going around. And it's not just Rothwell's death. There's the little matter of a certain file being released to Congress *and the media*. The radicals on the left and a majority of the Democrats on the Hill will crawl over broken glass to find—and probably kill—the guy who released the file on their President. Everything points to an Agency connection and they're turning over every rock to find him." Lynche patted Hunter on the back and playfully pushed him. "Congratulations, *Maverick*, in addition to all your other accomplishments, you're the most wanted and probably the most hated man in America."

"Seriously? The FBI is looking? Since when did unmasking the country's secret enemies become a greater crime than the commies' little secret war on America?" He acknowledged Lynche had congratulated him over the release of the President's file and not the attempted killing of Rothwell. Unless he told him, Lynche could never draw a bright red line between Hunter and the attempt on the former DCI in Amman, Jordan. Hunter was certain Lynche didn't know that Bill McGee had been in the Amman Sheraton Hotel when an explosion blew the former DCI out of his suite.

"Of course they are. What did you expect? The Attorney General's a holdover; he didn't resign when the President left."

"Another flaming communist working incognito to subvert the Constitution and advance totalitarianism far and wide."

Lynche ignored him. "The AG wants to know who got their hands on that file. So far, they have turned up nothing."

"Nazy's okay?"

"That's a two part question. Like everyone else who had a tangential relationship with the former-former DCI, she was given another poly. Three actually. I'm sure the Attorney General and the FBI Director suspect Nazy." Lynche turned to look out over the river. "After three different polygraphers, all she knew was that Director Carey had asked her about the file. She didn't flinch. She didn't take the Fifth. She told the polygrapher the DCI asked her to see if the archival record reflected if there's a file on the President and, if there was, where it was. Nazy confirmed what she told the polygraphers and the FBI. There was a file; the record reflected it was no longer in the archives, it had been removed, and the chain of custody record was clear. It was in the custody of the DCI. That was two DCI's ago. When she reported the information to the DCI he dismissed her, and she never saw or heard from him again. Then the FBI searched her office and safe. While they were doing that the agent asked her what she thought had happened and she said she had no idea but she was as surprised as everyone that the file popped up in the media and online."

"That's quite a woman." Hunter acknowledged and applauded Nazy's performance under the withering pressure of the FBI. If she had cracked, they'd all be heading to Leavenworth.

"I agree. Seems like you're a lucky man Maverick."

"What it seems like is that you guys can't hold down the job for more than a year." While Hunter grinned at his comment, Lynche wasn't amused. The two previous DCIs had died under mysterious circumstances. It was the beginning of a trend he didn't like. He blinked wildly until Hunter asked, "Part two?"

"I'll get there. I also had to open my safe. Of course it wasn't there. The chain of custody record card was there, but no receipt or indications of the transfer of the President's file."

Hunter tacitly acknowledged their conspiracy. He thought, erroneously, it was behind them. After all, there was a new President, and Hunter had even received a presidential pardon.

Several U.S. Navy SEALs had been murdered across America, beginning immediately after the reported death of Osama bin Laden. Another SEAL was convinced he was the next target. Captain Bill McGee, the most highly decorated member of Special Operations Command and the former commander of the vaunted SEAL Team Six, had reached out to Hunter for help. After flying to a safe location, the three retirees—Lynche, McGee and Hunter—forensically determined that the newly appointed and rabidly homosexual DCI was tangentially involved in the death of the SEALs.

During their discussions, McGee had indicated the President was a fraud, that there was a file on the man at CIA, and that the man who ultimately led the SEAL Team into Pakistan to snatch bin Laden had seen it. Hunter asked Nazy to try to locate the mythical file on the President. She had nearly given up on the impossible task when she stumbled upon a pair of books; the dust jackets indicated they were the autobiographies of the President. She opened the books only to find they contained pages of text and photographs of the man's secret life. Suddenly, Nazy found herself reading hundreds of classified documents—every scrap of the President's file—that demonstrated the man in the White House was someone other than whom he claimed to be. Everything the right wing and political pundits suspected the President of being was laid bare as factual.

Hunter had surreptitiously released the trove of documents onto the internet and provided hard copies to members of Congress and the major news media. It was unmitigated treason for someone with one of the highest security clearances in the intelligence community to release classified documents. However, some took a different view on the patriotism of the unknown releaser when the documents proved the President was a fully documented, and in the legal parlance, an "illegal alien." The President's fellow travelers, the media, every Democrat in Congress and his political supporters had committed a Chinese menu of felonies to maintain the charade of his Presidency.

Lynche continued, "Nazy's investigating Rothwell's death. What she's found is explosive."

"I've a fairly good imagination, if you recall; try me."

"We thought the Russians were only minor players...."

"And, now you know?"

"*Now*—they're clearly working with al-Qaeda *and* the Brotherhood."

Hunter chortled, "You mean just like the Democrats? I've always said they're a criminal organization masquerading as a political party."

"You're incorrigible. While you were out hunting bad guys I ordered everyone at CIA to be re-scoped. I also told the State Department if any of their people are holding an Agency clearance, they need to be scoped as well, otherwise no more access."

"That's huge. But everyone already receives a polygraph—what's one more?"

"I'm asking them if they're a communist. Or an Islamist."

"Oh, I know! I had mine this morning. I thought the questions were a dramatic shift from the norm. Whiskey Tango Foxtrot over?"

"I'm asking them if they're communist or are they an Islamist sympathizer. And now, with the President's approval, even political appointees get a poly. That should make you happy."

Hunter was confused and his furrowed brows and scowl only telegraphed his concern. "About friggin' time. What changed from the last time we had this discussion?"

"I know it's an old joke. State, Justice and much of the FBI is infiltrated…." Lynche gestured with his hands in the ether.

"I could have told you that; hell, that's not news."

"Well, now we're going to find out whose side they're really playing for. The infiltration is unprecedented, and I told the President it has to stop or we'll lose our country."

Hunter blurted, "Greg! The White House *was a sleeper cell*!"

"Why do you think I'm having everyone poly'ed?"

"You're starting to sound like me. That's spooky, Greg. Whittaker Chambers effectively said the same thing, and the House Un-American Activities Committee essentially proved the closet communists overran the government. Venona decrypts, Vassiliev Papers, Mitrokhin archives. Open source proof." Hunter's interest was piqued. "And I didn't need a polygrapher to prove it. I've even said so—how many times have I said Foggy Bottom is nothing but a snake's den of closet commies and liberals. They've hired their fellow traveler buddies for decades. You couldn't get a Republican in there even if he parachuted onto the building."

"You're right on that account." Lynche smirked at Hunter, who broke out in a broad smile. "We've had over thirty retirements just this morning; they dropped their papers and turned in their badges before they went to their polygraph. Everyone scheduled from State or

Congressional staffers has either retired, asked for an extension, or resigned. They're busy over there."

"Well, I'm shocked, shocked I tell you." Hunter grinned.

"There's more. People think the infiltration of Communists is a thing of the past, but this is going on right now. This isn't historical; this isn't the Fifties. Their secret warfare has succeeded in planting agents in agencies that deal with military, intelligence, and foreign policy issues. They're working hard to transform this country. I can't touch them; and no one can hold them accountable. The media won't touch it. There's treason going on in the Congress and the State Department."

"I knew it," said a smug Hunter. "The commies don't just want to influence the Democratic Party; they want to control it. People think the infiltration of the communist party is a myth."

"I don't mind being the head of the CIA—I parachute into the seventh floor—to use your analogy—and one of the first briefs I receive is that one of the unintentional consequences of the release of the Agency file is that it virtually stopped a coup. The old DCI had rooted out a number of good intel professionals and replaced them with lackeys. Same thing happened over at the DOD. Rothwell hadn't been in the office long enough to make an imprint."

"The moral to the story is the new President is a good start. Mav, the country and the Agency are in real trouble and we have to change direction. The CIA is my problem. The Justice Department leadership is totally corrupt. Can't do anything about them or the FBI, but as long as that AG is in place we have to be very careful. There's a lot of bad news, but one of the more interesting bits is that Nazy may have found a KGB link with Rothwell. KGB, AQ _and_ the Brotherhood."

Lynche's seriousness bothered Hunter, so he tried to interject some levity. "Aren't they called something else now? ABC, DEF, XYZ..."

"FSB."

"Ah, yes, the FSB. Whatever that stands for now—KGB was much cooler as the evil watchmaker of international terrorism. FSB sounds like a pansy liberal alternative rock band."

"Don't say it too loud or you too might get hit with a polonium-210 pellet. But you get my point," scolded Greg Lynche.

"I do. Any way I can help? Are we ever going to talk about part two?"

"Later. I need you for something else. What I'm dealing with is bad. Real bad."

"Greg, Algeria was bad." Hunter shrugged his shoulders and lowered his eyes. "Iran is bad; can it get any worse than Iran?"

Lynche glanced at the Growler again—green light—then out over the Severn River. He exhaled, "There's always Iran. We've no solution for Teheran; one of these days we will. I'm talking about suitcase nukes." Lynche's voice was almost a whisper.

Hunter realized they had been talking an awful lot about Russians; they usually dealt with narco and Islamic terrorists from Peru or Colombia or the Middle East; never Russians. Hunter inhaled a lungful of air and thought about the ultimate weapon of mass destruction. He exhaled and looked at his feet. "Sir, that's a whole other level of bad. I don't like where this is going. More *Russians?*" The two men had significantly reduced the volume of their voices. The DCI's security detail noticed the change as the two men leaned closer together, their heads almost touching. The Growler's light flashed every few seconds.

Lynche again glanced out over the Severn River. Hunter could barely hear him. "We've been in negotiations with a Russian billionaire—Boris Nastakovich. We call him *Nasty*. He claims he has one, maybe two suitcase bombs, and they're available to the first bidder—CIA or al-Qaeda. Only one problem."

"What's that?"

"He has all the oil and gas money he needs and he wants a trade, the suitcases for the lost Masters from World War Two. I suppose he wants to fill all the mansions he has with art or some such crap. Anyway, Nazis stole countless artwork from all over Europe; I think you know the story. It's all bullshit and Hollywood but Boris thinks the CIA has them in a warehouse."

"Do you have them?" Hunter asked.

"Please! I'd flip him the Mona Lisa in a nanosecond to get those *suitcases* off the street. I think with Algeria we've seen that you *can* blackmail the U.S. for profit and get away with it. Friggin' KGB billionaire colonel is the latest megalomaniac. You just have to have the proper leverage. We can't allow those...*things* to get into the hands of the bad guys. It's an easy jump for them to drop one or two in DC or Manhattan. Kill the country. It's no surprise al-Qaeda is also interested in finding the artwork. There's chatter that they're looking."

"Nasty has seen too many Nicholas Cage movies." Hunter smirked but listened closely.

"We think we know what's missing—an inventory—but we don't know where the artwork is—*none of it!* You'd think something would pop up on the black market after seventy years, and believe me we've been looking. Nope—they're really lost."

"Have any ideas where they may be or where they're not?" As soon as the words left his mouth, Hunter was hit with an old creeping memory screaming into his consciousness. He tried to listen to Lynche, but the little voice in his head was making more noise. He could hear the vertebrae in his neck squeak as he moved his head to look at Lynche. He tried to listen to both the internal and external voices. He could see Lynche's lips move, but he didn't hear a thing for a few seconds.

When Hunter recovered his composure he heard, "Nasty said he'd throw the other one in if we turned over the Nazi gold as well."

Hunter chortled and shook his head in disbelief when Lynche said, "Nazi gold."

CHAPTER TWELVE

The bulky, muscular man in the red and white checkered *keffiyeh* hurried across the room to whisper into the ear of the man at the head of the table. He ignored the ten men in cream-colored and white, high-collared *dishdashas*. Their *keffiyehs* draped across their backs and shoulders. With a mixture of black and grey beards, men from al-Qaeda—in black *keffiyehs*—and the Muslim Brotherhood—in white *keffiyehs*—lined the conference table, five to a side. At the head of the table, the man in the black *dishdasha* looked to be extremely uncomfortable. He was in great pain but strained mightily not to show it.

The man in black nodded gently as the messenger spoke and gestured. There was good reason for the man in the wheelchair to be conservative with his movements. A bomb had shredded his body when he was blown out of a hotel room. A black sleeve pinned at the shoulder indicated a missing arm and a black eye patch covered the collapsed socket that had once held a healthy blue eye. He was continually in pain, on the edge of agony. He carefully raised a heavily scarred hand to dismiss the messenger.

Once the huge Jordanian left the room, Dr. Bruce Rothwell said in perfect Arabic, "Peace be upon you and the Mercy of Allah and His blessings. Our brothers located the site where the artwork was hidden in Munich, but it wasn't there. The police detained a brother as he entered the hiding place. He was questioned and released. It was very telling, my brothers, that immediately after this the authorities issued a press release stating 1,400 pieces of artwork had been recovered from an 80-year old man's apartment. Apparently the old man had stumbled upon the cache and brought pieces to his building over a twenty-year period. They discovered the man two years ago—*two years!* The trove was valued at over two point five billion U.S. dollars."

The ten terrorist leaders around the conference table grunted at the news.

"There's one location remaining to investigate. Our brothers nearly bumbled their mission. They must be more circumspect."

This additional information pleased the men who nodded and softly spoke, "*Insha'allah.*"

The former Director of Central Intelligence also nodded and said, "Hopefully they will find what we seek. By my...*records*, there remain 5,000 pieces of decadent art and tons of gold yet to be discovered. Tens of billions of dollars. With our funding sources all but dried up, we must develop new funding streams. Contributions are down almost 90 percent. But with this undiscovered trove...." Rothwell nodded toward the men on his left, "We'll be able to fund more al-Qaeda priorities...to include those special weapons you desire."

The five men along the one side of the table randomly uttered, "*Insha'allah.*"

"And we'll be funding Brotherhood activities. For many, many years."

Five men on the other side of the table were more uniform and vocal, "*Insha'allah.*"

"Yes, *Insha'allah.*"

"You've done...well, Brother...Raqqa," said the oldest, greyest, and fattest of the Muslim Brotherhood greybeards. The doyen of the Egyptian Islamic Jihad, the most aged member of the group, struggled to speak as he had suffered a stroke recently.

Rothwell closed his eyes and motioned a bow, as much as he dared lest he shriek in pain.

The old man struggled with his speech. "All CIA spies have been...found and...disposed," teased the greybeard. He stroked the thin grey hair on his chin. "Your...assistance...has come at the most...opportune time. You're correct, donations have been...very poor for a very long time. This is...good news."

"There's the issue of the infidel, Hunter," reminded Rothwell. "And, the woman." He raised his one arm to emphasize the statements were questions. "Your part of the bargain was to *dispose* of him. You suggested it'd be a simple matter. I haven't heard any news. Do we have news of the infidel's demise, Brother Arkho?"

The man across the table from the al-Qaeda representative sighed and reported, "After weeks of surveillance, our brother *muj* in the infidel state of Texas seems to have had an accident...."

"What kind of accident?" demanded Rothwell. He shuddered as he spoke.

"He was riding a motorcycle and reportedly collided with a...telephone pole." Every man glared at the spokesman from the Muhammad Jamal branch of the Muslim Brotherhood. "His body was recovered and given a proper burial."

"Was the infidel Hunter involved? Was this truly an accident, as you say?" Rothwell waited patiently for an answer and let his mind wander. *Whether the accident was indeed God's will or merely part of some byzantine circumstance, accidents don't just occur when Duncan Hunter is involved.*

"*Sahib*, our sources believe it was an accident, but...."

Rothwell raised a damaged, burned hand; a bony finger gestured for the man to stop. "An accident may be possible if the scene of the accident was many miles away from where the infidel Hunter lived or worked. Pray tell, where was our brother found? Was he close to Hunter's ranch or was he far away?"

"Within five miles of the man's house. Just off the road." The man lowered his head in disappointment as he spoke.

"That was no accident. He killed our brother mujahedeen and made it look like an accident. Do we know where he is now?"

"He is... it's been very difficult to find him and keep him under surveillance. Our sources don't believe he's in Texas."

Rothwell murmured, "He moves around much. He is everywhere, yet he is nowhere."

"On the upside, *sahib*, the woman is under surveillance."

"But you don't know where *he* is." Rothwell glared at the man making excuses.

"He'll return to Texas. He will eventually return to his home. We'll get him."

Rothwell frowned and turned his head to eye the line of men from al-Qaeda. "My brothers from Kabul and Kandahar?"

Four men under black *keffiyehs* looked to their left at the angry petulant man at the far end of the table. The men didn't like to be put on the spot by the one with the evil, blood-filled eye. "It's difficult to get information from Colombia."

"What do we know? Do we know anything from Bogotá?" Rothwell strained to move his head from side to side, his questioning eye begged for an answer. He gestured with the scarred hand to emphasize more information was necessary.

The man from al-Qaeda spat through gritted teeth, "Our brothers also...had an accident."

"Another accident?" Rothwell closed his eye and exhaled loudly in exasperation.

"Our friends from the mountains found him and fired at his truck. The truck pushed them into a lorry. They're now martyrs."

Rothwell struggled to take a drink of water from a straw. His hand trembled; any significant movement shot pain throughout his body. He sucked air and exhaled, "That doesn't sound like an accident. That's a CIA defensive driving maneuver—pinch the attacker. He made the collision look like an accident." A sudden flash of inspiration struck him. *How would a contract pilot learn of the CIA defensive driving techniques? Would he have had some other access to classified materials...such as programs and files?*

The man from al-Qaeda scowled and responded with stinging vituperation, "It's difficult to kill this man. Why do you want this infidel killed? Three *mujahedeen* dead! Is this man a SEAL? Very hard to kill a SEAL."

"No. No, Navy SEAL. He's a pilot. Marine pilot."

The man from the Muslim Brotherhood became visibly frustrated with the man at the head of the table. "Brother Raqqa, Marine officers also very hard to kill. Very arrogant. We need more time. We'll get him. He's not been to see the woman."

"You sure he hasn't seen the woman?"

"Yes *sahib*."

"She's well trained. You watch the woman...he'll come to her like a dog in heat. Then you'll find the infidel. You wait and see." He had more salacious thoughts of Hunter and Nazy together. Not him. The old dream. She gave him a briefcase. *Could she have...?*

The antiquated terrorist from al-Qaeda in the Arabian Peninsula interrupted Rothwell's train of thought when he barked, "You find the decadent art. And, gold. We've much to do." The men from the al-Qaeda affiliates—Ansar al-Sharia, al-Qaeda in the Islamic Maghreb, al-Qaeda in Iraq, and the al-Nusrah Front, as well as the men from the branches of the Muslim Brotherhood—nodded at the assertion and looked at Rothwell for concurrence.

The pain was quickly becoming unbearable. He needed another injection of morphine; he needed to get out of here and return to his room for rest. Rothwell was resolute. He slammed his fist on the table and nearly blacked out from the pain. The IV port taped to the back of his hand remained firmly in place. "Hunter must die! That's the deal. Find and kill the infidel, and we'll fund your programs, our programs." Rothwell paused as he recovered from the exertion of the outburst. "Status of our new project?"

"Coming together. We're drawing recruits from across America. We will be ready soon."

"That's good news, my brothers. It's a good plan. I know of these things. It will work." He closed the meeting with, "May Allah give you success in serving the Sacred Knowledge and the religion."

Tensions around the table seemed to ease as Rothwell, now known as Raqqa, slumped back into his seat, exhausted from the closing prayer. One by one, the men from al-Qaeda and the Muslim Brotherhood rose and paid their respects as they left, cheek-kissing

Rothwell and lightly shaking his scarred and enfeebled hand. When the last man departed the conference room, Rothwell's Jordanian nurse, his red and white *keffiyeh* rustling behind him, hurried to Rothwell. As the nurse wheeled him from the room, he became more convinced he would have to take matters into his own...hand, if he wanted to see the infidel Hunter dead. Then, amid the morphine, a hint of an idea came to him. For a moment he was at peace; oblivious of the pain, aches, and stiffness of his slowly healing body as the idea slowly formed.

Although the Jordanian had transferred him to the hotel bed and had provided Rothwell with an injection through the intravenous port in his hand, a fresh wave of discomfort rolled upon him, saturating his nervous system until he could no longer move without yelping. But he could still think. Thinking was still painless. He thought of the woman. A very special woman that he had desired from the moment he first met her. However, the woman wasn't interested in him. She always rebuffed him. She even threatened to report him for his unwanted sexual advances. He wouldn't give up. He would never give her up.

The top floor of the Amman Marriott was virtually silent. Rothwell lay thinking, allowing the morphine to kill the pain. He hoped the ruffle of the drums throbbing in his head didn't presage his death. The sweet relief of the painkillers came in a slowly cresting wave, his senses obtunded, his rigid muscles became elastic; his sight grew dim, his ears heard only the never-ending tintinnabulation that could not be dulled or silenced through sleep or medicine.

He awoke with a start—not sure if he'd been dreaming or if his subconscious had been working on the problem. While at the CIA he had learned that once free of external distractions and stimuli, his brain continued to process data. The problem was how to kill Hunter, the man who took everything away from him—the woman he loved, the position he aspired to, and the gold he planned to steal from a terrorist. Hunter would pay, in some way. He closed his eye to conjure another ideation...with him and Nazy Cunningham together... entwined in front of a shackled Hunter, but that vision would not jell no matter how hard he tried or desired. His hatred for the pilot was too great.

Rothwell's labored breathing quieted. He lay motionless, cataleptic, fully awake and thinking. The ringing in his ears became a dull hiss. An unfocused eye stared at the room's overhead fan as thoughts and plans congealed. As the cocktail of analgesics wore off he again conjured up another image of the woman, naked, subservient. A smile crept across his scarred face as she writhed in joy at seeing him. The smile turned to anguish as she ignored him and welcomed the infidel Hunter with open arms. She handed him a briefcase and they ran away together. At first, Rothwell tried to stop her, and when he failed, he couldn't make sense of his ideations. He hated the man more than before. He whispered over the hum of the ceiling fan and the static in his ears, "If he can't be killed then can he at least be...*cornered... captured?*" The fan pushed cool air over his face as he raged against Hunter. "He's a thief! A thief that stole my life! And my...*my woman!*"

After several minutes Rothwell was again on the verge of sleep, his one eye shut. His mind was working to transition from daytime activities to nighttime rest when a flash of inspiration came to him, from the Holy Book...from Allah. He sighed and whispered, "Qur'an, five thirty-eight...." He was pleased with himself; a devious smile presaged the thought, "*That's what I must do. When we find him, I will ask him. Before I kill him.*" He nodded at his genius and settled down, and his anesthetized brain slowly allowed him to fall asleep.

• • •

Hunter mewled as if he'd been wakened, "Nazi...*gold?*"

"That's what I said. *Are* you listening? This is serious shit." Irritation and frustration now dominated Lynche's face. The men were almost nose-to-nose. The Growler kept flashing.

"What's...*Nazi gold*...look like?" Hunter stumbled through the question as he recalled happy days in post-war Germany on the best kid's bicycle ever produced, racing through the woods and splashing through the leaves. He reached for his billfold.

Lynche's security detail noticed the man on the blanket with their DCI make a deliberate move to withdraw something from a hip pocket. They were conflicted. The rules of engagement were no sudden or stealthy moves that could be construed as a threat to the DCI but Hunter was "a friendly." No threat.

"I don't know. What does any gold look like? But it's lost. Reportedly, rumored, over 300 *tons*. I don't know everything, Mav. Jeez. Well, we kinda know something. It's not the nice big shiny anodized gold bars with intricate swastikas from *Goldfinger* or some such crap. Some…very few samples have emerged over the last 65 years."

The security detail relaxed as Hunter withdrew his wallet and began fishing for something in one of the billfold's hidden pouches. Hunter removed an opaque plastic sleeve from behind a rack of credit cards and then withdrew something round and shiny. He flipped the item toward Lynche, who also had begun to monitor Duncan's strange action.

"Like that?" asked Hunter.

Lynche's first surprise was something being thrown his way. The high arc gave him enough time to react and catch the spinning item. His second surprise was the weight of the coin as he caught it. The shock came when he opened his hand to reveal what he had snatched in midair. An eagle and swastika were crudely stamped into the top of the thick round coin. Below the Nazi emblem, 1943 had been stamped into the metal. Lynche raised his head and said softly. "Where'd you get this?"

Hunter told him the story, and then told him he had fifty of the coins. "You're the first person to see that in forty years. I think it's the gold taken from the mouths and fingers of Holocaust victims. Stamped into coins; doesn't look like it was totally melted or stamped very well. Very crude. I was just a kid who collected coins. I've never seen any others like them."

Lynche closed his eyes and shook his head, then he looked at Hunter seriously. *You're always doing shit like this to me!*

Hunter said, "Maybe where I got this is where the Masters are stashed as well. It was big and dark; I thought it was a deep cave. I couldn't see very well. I got far enough in, just enough to find that, snag a bag, and beat feet. I just knew there was more *stuff* in there, but I wasn't going back. The entrance was very well hidden. It's been a long time; I would think someone had to have found that entrance by now. *It's on an air force base!*"

Lynche recovered enough to slowly finger the coin and reply, "That these were on an air force base is precisely why they may not have been found. If someone did find it, they'd probably do what you did—get something small and get out. Anyone lucky enough to stumble on...your little hiding place would have had to have known that if they tried to advertise it, someone would've squawked and the government would come down upon them like a ton of bricks. And if they tried to smuggle anything out and sell it, the authorities would eventually find out and toss them in jail." Lynche tapped his knee with his free hand. "But if it was on an air base, behind a fence...you've *fifty* of these? This is about two ounces. You remember where you got this?"

"Like it was yesterday. It's on the other side of the runway at Ramstein Air Base. I bet I could find it in ten minutes."

"Not if it's on an American air base." Holding up the Nazi gold coin, Lynche said, "I'm sure al-Qaeda is looking for these as well as the location of the suitcases. They're hurting for money."

"Al-Qaeda? Where did that come from?"

"And Nazy thinks Rothwell is alive."

"*What?!*"

"There's no good news in any of this." Lynche looked toward the river before turning back to look at Hunter and whispered, "Ready for part two? Overnight, we've lost a number of intel officers throughout the Middle East, Europe, and Africa but not the one in Iran. Nazy says it indicates Rothwell is behind it somehow. She made a compelling case, and I'm convinced." Lynche continued to examine the heavy Nazi coin.

"She didn't say anything to me."

"She came to the conclusion this morning with the news we lost a dozen officers overnight. One more piece to the puzzle. She thinks there's surveillance on her—I'm not taking a chance if there is or isn't. I'm moving Nazy to a safe house."

"She said she was afraid someone was watching her. She didn't go home but went straight to Langley. That's smart. Thank you, Greg."

"Who's your buddy, who's your pal? Anyway, before he disappeared, Rothwell accessed several Special Access Programs and files. One was your buddy's—the Ortiz file. Nazy found the lists of the missing Masters; she thinks the file may also hold the key to finding the locations of the lost artwork as well as the missing Nazi gold. The list of artwork was extensive, but there were no locations; there were some documents in the file which were encrypted. It appears Rothwell, in one of his final acts, got the NSA to decrypt them."

"Crap. If it's Rothwell, what's he doing now?" Hunter labored to pretend he was just interested and wasn't crushed that his nemesis wasn't dead.

"Well, that's the billion dollar question. We think he's gone over to the dark side, likely selling intel. It's a classic response to identify all the undercover officers in the field and their locations to establish your bona fides. The killing of Americans and her spies would put him in good standing, and if he brought money or the ability to generate money, he could be in a leadership position. Protected. With those SAPs, Rothwell knows absolutely everything, and as the DCI, he had to approve everyone working covertly, by name. So he knows them all. Except the one I deployed."

"That's bad." Hunter shook his head in disbelief. He thought Bill McGee had been able to kill Rothwell. Now there were so many questions, unanswered questions and new threats. All of a sudden being targeted twice took on new meaning—*Rothwell!*

Lynche nodded. "It gets worse. Nazy thinks Rothwell may have been run by the KGB...FSB...*KGB!*"

Hunter's head snapped toward Lynche in disbelief.

"I had Nazy look into an old Soviet infiltration file as well as Rothwell's history and career, and she spotted a curious entry in his file. After our former President got into the U.S. with bogus documents, Rothwell did too. Their birth certificates have KGB fingerprints all over them. Complete forgeries."

"*The KGB was running our DCI?*"

"Quiet please. Well, he wasn't always the DCI—he was an agent and came up through the ranks; just like me. It's the ultimate intelligence horror."

"Are you saying you're the ultimate intelligence horror?" Hunter's wry grin wasn't appreciated.

"I mean he knows everything. And I mean everything. We're doing what we can to mitigate the impact, but it may be too late. We'll get through it, but a couple of dozen families have been destroyed, and all of our efforts to infiltrate AQ and the Brotherhood have been set back years. Worse case, if he *is* alive, he may be running their financial elements. It'd be a perfect fit for him. Funds have dried up from Europe, the price of oil is dropping, and they're in dire straits. But Rothwell is a master of the game and knows how to get money. Selling intelligence commands high dollars."

"Are there any shiny dimes in this pile of pony shit?"

Lynche said, "Time isn't on our side. Oh. Break—Break. The President wants *Wraith* to take a crack at some nuts in Nigeria. There's been several more kidnappings, an upsurge in pirating private sailing boats, and some other nasty things."

"Nasty things?" Hunter had seen that look before. Lynche nodded without looking at him.

"I know you can handle it." Lynche's voice was hushed.

Hunter replied, "If you're talking nasty then you're talking Boko Haram. Where murder and raping are *au courant*. Are you kidding, *Director* Lynche? What you're asking for is impossible."

"Which you've developed to be your specialty...."

The airshow crowd had virtually disappeared leaving the five CIA men alone and exposed in the middle of the field. The security team was getting more nervous by the second; having their boss out in the open for an extended period wasn't part of the brief.

"You want me to go to Nigeria? Northern Nigeria. Do you even have a single intel officer in that part of the country?"

"Yes, yes, and...um, unfortunately not yet—but I'm working on it. We had someone inside but he too, was killed last night. I've dispatched more help, pilots and additional intelligence officers." Hunter missed the unnatural twinkle in Lynche's eyes.

"You *are* trying to get me killed. What did I ever do to you?"

"Well, you *do* keep poking at my *liberal*...leanings." Lynche chuckled and fingered the gold coin. "Seriously, the intel suggests they're making a huge push into the northwestern part of the country and have specifically targeted young girls, Christian girls, to sow terror. The Nigerians are too afraid to do anything and the President wants an effort. You impressed him in Somalia, Colombia, and Algeria; he thinks you can do anything. And I have to agree with him." Lynche offered to return the Nazi coin as a screw turned in his head. *What are the chances?*

Hunter refused. "Keep it." He turned to look at the river. He was suddenly distant and alone in thought. "I almost got killed last time. Fruit loops are shooting at me." He took a deep breath and exhaled. "At least Nazy is safe." He wasn't sure Rothwell was somehow behind the recent motorcycle assassination attempts and any surveillance on his fiancée. But the former DCI instantly became the prime suspect.

Lynch noticed the change of mood in his friend. He sensed the mission in Algeria was much more dangerous and challenging than Hunter had let on. There was the official version of events. When it came to a full debrief, Hunter was just as bad as the media he despised. He'd leave out crucial details for whatever purposes suited him. It was time to get some answers. "We need to talk about Algeria."

"What about Algeria?"

"Your Algeria after action report. All you said was, 'At low altitude, with the aircraft on fire, I parachuted to safety.' I know there's more to it. Has to be—I've flown with you. I know."

"You, more than anyone else, know what to say and what not to say. How many times have you started to tell a story but had to pull back because I didn't have a need to know?"

"You completed the mission. But there are some questions."

"There are some things that don't need to be discussed or become part of the official record."

He knew some secrets were not and would never become part of the official record. For neutralizing the surface-to-air missile threat to commercial aviation and for the recovery of billions of dollars in gold coins, the President rewarded Hunter ownership of a corporate jet which was used to transport the ransom from the U.S. to Algeria and that he used to escape from Algeria.

Lynche knew some details. Hunter had taken possession the Gulfstream 550 under the official pretext the aircraft had been abandoned and recovered in North Africa. They hadn't talked about the new airplane, primarily because the two men had other issues to talk about. However, not discussing the new jet was in itself curious, and in retrospect, Hunter not sharing the details of it's unusual acquisition bordered on being a secret.

"We've never had secrets," Lynche implored. Since walking off the YO-3A program and becoming the DCI, he had remained interested in Hunter's activities, both his CIA-related and some of his commercial enterprises.

"Yes we have, but this is different."

Lynche stared at Hunter. Lynche's eyes demanded the whole story. With his free hand, he gestured for Hunter to talk.

"Greg, I'm guilty of not saying I was scared shitless after I was shot down, that I was fighting for my life. I didn't want to be caught. I knew if I were captured, I'd kill myself before I gave those bastards the privilege of slicing my fat little body to ribbons or the pleasure of chopping off my head. But more than that, I'm guilty for not saying, for the record, *your predecessor* was in on it, somehow." The two friends locked eyes.

The goal of the special access program was to neutralize budding terrorists before they could become a problem. If the CIA had eliminated the young Osama bin Laden when he was thirty, he wouldn't have been in any position to facilitate the deaths of 3,000 Americans on September 11, 2001. Hunter had removed a few major targets in Africa and the Middle East before receiving the mission to Algeria. That target was suspected of shooting down commercial airliners with shoulder-launched anti-aircraft missiles and collecting hundreds of millions of dollars in gold as insurance. Pay the ransom and American airliners wouldn't be shot down.

The intelligence was outstanding. The aircraft arrived at the expected time and at the expected remote location. Hunter had crossed the Mediterranean Sea from a private airstrip in Spain to be in position off the coast of Algeria. Then the target spotted the black aircraft in the midnight sky over a mile away. Hunter would never forget how the man looked straight up at him in the forward looking infrared sensor and then fired missiles at him—the second missile blew off the wing of Hunter's quiet spy plane.

In over a hundred nighttime missions, not a single person had looked up; not one, not ever. The YO-3A was small, silent, matte black and should have been impossible to discern in a night sky. Hunter was convinced that somehow, the *Noble Savage* target expected him. Not simply *expected* but knew exactly where and when to look for him—the target had to be given a clue and a window of expectation.

But in the tightly controlled sphere of special access programs, where only a few people with a "need to know" would ever even have tangential knowledge of the program and its players, one person stood out as a possible informer—the former DCI. Not only was he capable of informing the target, but under some improbable hint of circumstances, he may have had a motive. However, proving motive and opportunity remained a problem.

Hunter was just a contracted employee of the CIA and had no direct access to CIA files. He was on a special access program and had no need to know anything else. It had been true that DCI Rothwell was in significant trouble, politically and personally. Congress called for his resignation, and he was under investigation for sexually harassing or having an inappropriate relationship with a number of women. Rothwell's storied career was about to crash about the time Hunter bailed out of his crippled airplane.

When he learned the DCI had been in the immediate area when he was shot down over Algeria, it may have been a tiny thread but it was a huge bit of tangential information. In any other context, having Rothwell in the area made absolutely no sense, but it was all too coincidental for Hunter, especially when the ransom aircraft contained $100 million in U.S. gold coins.

"The guy was a creep. If he were a Republican, he would've been nailed to a cross. He sent Nazy over there to execute the bag drop. He nearly got her killed. I know he was in on it. And, if he's still alive…."

Lynche asked, "I might understand why you left that info out of the after action report. But why do you think he was in on it?"

"Seriously, Greg? Look at what these KGB colonels do when they get a bit of information and have a little power—they knock off the competition, consolidate their power, steal whatever is worth stealing, and sell it to the highest bidder. Next thing you know, Vlad's a billionaire. As a corrupt civil service employee about to be shit-canned, he knew my target was to receive a shipment of gold—and he looked at it as his retirement fund or something. That's my major problem—why? Here's how I know that he was in on it."

"There had to be friendlies with him in the area; NCS guys loyal to him would rush to the hangar and clean up the site and run off with the gold. That's what I think is the 'how.' The 'why' continues to bother me. Being a KGB plant only befuddles part of the answer. I didn't report that aspect of the mission. I suspected the DCI was behind it. I *think* I know—but I just don't know how he did it; I didn't ask the asshole who shot me down—I just killed his ass and took his airplane and got the hell off the continent. There has to be more to it than Rothwell was just a greedy bastard."

Disparate thoughts clanged around his head. *American gold. Nazi gold. I thought I understood why he wanted the American gold. But why… would…Rothwell want the Nazi gold? Did he also know of the suitcase deal? Even former DCIs know everything. Shit! He had to know.*

Lynche listened intently and was confused by Hunter's diatribe and far away stare. It was rare for Hunter to open up and be overly serious. His outbursts were typically spontaneous asymmetric assaults on liberal politicians. He hung his head for a moment. Hunter lowered and shook his. Lynche whispered, "I need your help."

"You know I'll do anything to help you." One would die for the other. If Lynche needed help, Hunter was in with both feet.

Lynche quickly stood, reached for a corner of his blanket, and pulled hard. Hunter, lost in some far-off thought about Nazy, Bruce Rothwell and Nazi gold rolled off the blanket and onto the field grass. Hunter lay spread-eagle and looked up at Lynche with incredulous eyes and feigned ire. Lynch's security detail flinched but saw the levity and, stifling wry smiles, returned to their watch.

"Seriously?" laughed Hunter as he rolled over onto his belly.

"I'm glad you feel that way, Maverick. I'll take you up on your offer."

Hunter shot up to a sitting position, mashed his brows together, and said, "What offer?"

"You said, 'I'll do anything to help you.' I accept." Lynche smiled and folded the blanket. "I knew I could count on you."

Hunter started to stand, but he was stunned, strabismic with confusion. Lynche offered a hand to Hunter and helped him to his feet. "So, I'll see you tomorrow evening; don't be late. Bring a toothbrush; we're going to Germany. Oh, by the way, if we find more of these I'll let you see Nazy. But we've work to do."

Hunter handed the DCI the little green box that was the Growler. "We're going to Germany?"

Lynche held up the vulgar gold coin. "You haven't ever let me down and, as you've said countless times, I'm beginning to believe you're the luckiest shit I know. We're going to see if there's any luck left in that Midas finger of yours and if there are any more of these. Regarding Miss Cunningham, it seems that when anyone gets next to you, someone tries to shoot you. I can't afford to have one of my most trusted intel officers be seen with you, so I'm quarantining her until we get this mess resolved. She thinks she's being watched and with all of the intrigue surrounding you two, I doubt she's wrong."

"On these things, she's never wrong. But…."

"No buts, Mav. Nazy's and your pictures may be out on the web after your little stunt in Bogotá. Where she's at, she's safe."

He shook his head as Lynche offered his hand. The men shook hands as Hunter considered the impossible. *If someone's watching her, Rothwell must be behind it.* His reverie was snapped as Lynche's words refocused his attention.

"I'll meet you at Reagan, executive terminal; seven *P.*" As an afterthought, Lynche asked, "What are you doing tonight?"

"Well, Nazy and I were supposed to have some time together—I promised her we'd go to dinner after I meet with Colonel Eastwood to finish our interview. I suppose there's no hurry if you have Nazy quarantined."

Lynche patted his pocket and said, "Spies allergically avoid contact with reporters. Be careful."

Hunter protested, "I'm always careful! Besides, I'm not a spy. I'm a pilot."

"Right. I'm sure that was Gary Power's defense. Keep believing that. Anyway, such a deal I have for you. If you prove to be right, I'll let you see her. Have fun being Marines. Please try not to get your ass shot at between now and then." Lynche switched off the Growler, winked at Hunter, and walked off. The security detail gravitated to their director like a movie star with trailing paparazzi.

Hunter wasn't done; he called out. "Director Lynche!"

Greg turned, exasperated. "Yes?"

"If he blew the whistle on our guys in the ME why wouldn't he blow the whistle on our guys in Europe and Russia?"

A long few seconds passed between the friends when Lynche acknowledged, "Good point."

"Hey, if you weren't in such a hurry we could go to Pax River, I'd introduce you to the *Blue Angels* before they left."

A skeptical Lynche shouted, "How do you know anyone in the

Blue Angels? And don't say he was at the war college."

"Ok, the skipper was a classmate of mine in Newport."

"Is there anyone you don't know from the war college?"

"He told me I've an open invitation for a back seat ride, but you always have me on the road."

"I knew it going to be my fault. I'd give my left hand to ride in an F-18."

"I know. I'll see what I can do."

Lynche frowned at Hunter.

"It's all in whom you ask."

The DCI nodded and dismissed Hunter's impossible comment with a flick of his hand, turned and walked away.

As Lynche and his detail strode to their black Suburban, Hunter returned to the concept that Rothwell could somehow be alive and behind the assassination attempts. He threw his hands to the sky to beseech the intel gods and asked aloud, "Whiskey Tango Foxtrot, over?" When he didn't receive a reply to his interrogative, Hunter walked off the field and headed directly to the Midshipmen Store near the main gate. As he walked he sent Bill McGee an email asking, "You interested in riding in my back seat when I go to Africa?" Mindful of the numerous monuments and lawns which were not to be walked upon, Hunter sent Kelly an email apologizing that he'd be unable to attend her graduation—but he'd think of something to make it up to her.

The walk to the main gate allowed much of the information that Lynche shared with Hunter to percolate a few latent synapses and generate some questions that Hunter wished he had been quick enough to ask. He'd ask them on the jet to Germany. As Hunter approached the Leftwich Visitor Center he finished an email to Nazy. "Hope you're ok—I think Greg is trying to keep me away from U because of Bogota—my punishment. I'll be gone for a while; hope to CU and talk with U soon. Know ILY, Baby. Be safe."

CHAPTER THIRTEEN

Within an hour of the DCI giving the order to evacuate the deputy director of counterintelligence and deploy her to the safe site, an extraction team had assembled and flown her out of the Langley headquarters complex on a Marine Corps "white-top" helicopter. The team deposited her and two armed intelligence officers at the Sky Bryce Airport, a few miles south of the mountainside safe house. An armored SUV met her and the security detail and whisked them to the fortified hilltop retreat. The security chief assembled a counter-surveillance team and a security detail before embarking on a shopping trip for provisions.

Two black Suburbans rolled past the gas station and the convenience store that was the town of Columbia Furnace. They headed west up through winding roads toward the top of the Blue Ridge Mountains. After a half-hour of climbing tortuous roads and hairpin switchbacks, the vehicles turned onto a single-track dirt path. At the end of the well-worn driveway an invisible signal caused a tall wrought-iron gate to jerk to life. The barrier silently trundled across the path and latched into a matching brick and mortar fixture on the other side. Once the convoy had passed, the gate rolled to a close and sealed the compound. Two shadowy figures emerged and pushed huge wooden barn doors apart allowing the vehicles to enter the old red outbuilding. As four more silhouettes joined the other two, one improbably large dark mass emerged and led the group through the pines, like a fullback running through linemen. The collection of shapes hurried toward a sprawling ranch-style house hidden among the trees.

Spindletop sat atop a Virginia mountain ridge in the Shenandoah Valley. The view of the fog-shrouded basin on a moonlit night had drawn Paul Spindle, an early member of the Office of Strategic Services, to purchase the property. In the 1980s when he could no longer care for himself, he donated the land and the house to the CIA. The house had been refurbished several times over the years and upgraded with the latest electronics and security systems. It had become a place to debrief and interview high value political figures and defectors from foreign intelligence organizations. Some defectors who passed through 'the house on the hill' became Agency assets. Interview teams and polygraphers would sometimes take the communists into one of the surrounding towns for dinner and a beer.

More recently, Agency leaders used the house to evacuate CIA executives and other high-ranking but otherwise "covert" intelligence officers from possible terrorist group retaliation. Other Agency employees were brought in when a surveillance team was detected targeting them. Being sent to the "Bunker," as it was affectionately called, was an *in extremis* situation used to remove the executive or covert officer, and sometimes their family, to a comfortable place that was safe and far from the Washington, DC area. A heady group from the headquarters security office escorted those that came for "a visit," a euphemism for an evacuation. The head of the security team never missed a chance to visit the Bunker and take care of her clients.

"You were right; there's surveillance on your street and they didn't look like friendlies," the redheaded hypermammiferous woman said as she barged into the well-furnished and heavily curtained living room. She and the five slender women trailing behind her were laden with shopping and grocery bags and pizza boxes. The smaller women carried loaded sidearms that hung from their waists and were strapped to their legs.

The six women, from round and towering to tiny and muscular, lined up in an arc. All eyes fell to the graceful and willowy woman in the business suit and tennis shoes who was sitting at a long worktable. The table was covered with a bank of computer monitors, CPUs, keyboards, and mice. The firecracker of a woman, Anna Comstock, the *über*-zaftig chief of security, continued her assessment of the situation. "Pretty sure they're Muslims, my dear. Unsavory looking creeps. But we're here, and we're not going to let anything happen to you. Dinner is served. Hope you like pizza." The women with guns and bags smiled at the CIA executive as they moved to the kitchen.

The shapely, but not nearly as buxom woman arose from her chair. The Deputy Director of Counterintelligence was overwhelmed and unconsciously brought her hands up to her cover her mouth. The severity of the situation finally hit her. She was close to tears and the chief of security could see it.

Anna Comstock, the former Marine Corps drill sergeant and military policewoman had seen it all before. Agency executives or undercover agents performed their duties as overseas intelligence officers while living on the edge. Then a sliver of intel would come across the wire showing that the cover they had worked so hard to maintain over a career or a lifetime had somehow been blown. The revelation that they and their families were now exposed to the vicissitudes of retribution or terrorist attack was devastating and oftentimes crushed the strongest of psyches. Naturally maternalistic, Anna sidled up to Nazy and said, "We'll take care of you; we're not going to let anything happen to you."

"I'm not worried about that, Anna. I appreciate your help and compassion. Seeing all these girls excited to take care of me, to protect me, it's just...I...don't know how to say an appropriate thank you."

"Well, you're welcome, Nazy. All part of the job. I haven't lost a soul in a hundred years, and I'm not going to start now. So you just leave the worrying to me. You do what you have to do, and we'll get this threat behind us. We do this more often than you think, although this time it's an all-girl crew, right out of school."

"Okay, thank you, Anna." Nazy scanned the bags the massive woman was still holding. She didn't see her backpack, her "go bag" that she kept at her home for emergencies. "So, I take it you weren't able to go to my house?" Nazy had hoped the counter-surveillance team would've been able to shake the coverage near her house and pick up a few of her things to wear while she was "deployed."

The energetic woman started unloading the bags and gesturing to Nazy to come look. She was excited to show Nazy what was in the disparate shopping bags. "Wasn't prudent, Nazy. Wasn't prudent. Stopped by Wal-Mart and picked up a few things. You know the contracting officer would kill me if I had gone to Victoria's Secret for your underwear. That's one cheap bastard." The woman's expression flipped from scowl to smile as she raised one bag, seemingly to indicate the flimsy plastic bag contained panties and bras of dubious quality and unknown quantity. For a woman who appreciated her sexy lacy dainties, more for Duncan's eyes than comfort, Nazy resigned herself to wear whatever was in the bag. She appreciated the effort and wouldn't complain. If wearing Wal-Mart undies was the worst thing she encountered while at the safe house then it'd be more than okay.

"Whatever you have will be fine. Thank you, Anna. I apologize for the trouble."

The huge security officer grinned. "Oh, no girl...no trouble at all. You should have seen the clerk look at me when I asked for something in a size five or six. Wait, there's more." With a flourish worthy of a Las Vegas magician pulling a rabbit out of a hat, the Agency's top security executive extracted a fluffy yellow sweatshirt from a black paperboard bag. "The Director asked me to see if I could find one of these. I stopped at the Chevy dealer in Manassas and, well, I hope this will work. It's a large—it'll probably swallow you, but it was the only one on the rack...that might fit *that* rack." She nodded at Nazy's bosom and then winked at her. The former Marine was crude and incorrigible, and everyone loved the no-nonsense Anna Comstock. Nazy was temporarily left speechless.

At the sight of the bright yellow jersey with black lettering, Nazy pinched her lips and squelched tears. Every night for over ten years she had always slept in one of Duncan's yellow Corvette Racing jerseys or sweatshirts. It was her one real vice. The only time Nazy didn't wear one of the ultra-soft and billowy yellow shirts was when she was in the hospital recovering after surgery or when she slept alongside Duncan. How the DCI knew that tiny bit of information was anyone's guess, but it obviously had Duncan's fingerprints all over it. Nazy dabbed her eyes, bundled and hugged the shirt, and then dropped it in the middle of her lap.

A flurry of activity broke into Nazy's thought as short-haired women filed out of the kitchen with pizza slices on paper plates and plastic cups filled with tea or water. Anna Comstock moved the bags off of the sofa and carried them down the hall to the bedroom. Her voice caromed off the wood paneled walls as she returned. "We got jeans and sweat pants and shirts that will more than accommodate your girls." The comment elicited grins and embarrassed looks from the younger intelligence officers who were all lithe, thin, and curvy; just not busty.

A red-haired woman brought Nazy a plate, a drink, and a smile. She struggled to keep her eyes off the striking, olive-skinned, brunette with the dark green eyes.

Nazy's eyes were instantly drawn to the gold Rolex watch on the young woman's wrist. She caught herself staring at the watch, then returned her smile and thanked her for her thoughtfulness.

After emptying a cup of water and taking a plate of food, Anna Comstock continued to dominate the conversation as she spoke to the women in the living room. "Alright ladies, listen up. Since we now have all of the team together there are some things you need to know. Our Miss Cunningham is the deputy director of counterintelligence. She's being surveilled by an unknown group, and the FBI is on the case. Our job is to provide personal security until such time as the threat has been eliminated or neutralized. I expect Miss Cunningham to continue her work—*inside*. Nazy, we can't have you go outside at any time unless it's an emergency. The property's wired so you can access all Agency networks just as if you were in your office. The property's also protected with seismic and thermal sensors and cameras."

"For everyone here, there's no need for anyone to be outside unless we make a food run. The ladies here will take shifts in the control room to monitor our surroundings. There are backup generators for uninterrupted power; the basement is a safe room if, somehow, someone gets through the layers of security and the shit hits the fan. If that happens, we're not here to be Jane Waynes at the OK Corral. Everyone will head below to the safe room and wait for help or the all clear signal. Understand?"

Anna Comstock scanned the armed women for concurrence. Nazy nodded as well. "Good. The Bunker has an armory and is an alternate control room. Reinforcements will be on the way and will be on site within minutes. I don't expect anything crazy to happen but we have to be prepared, be alert, and be ready to respond to any threat. Got it? Any questions? None? Okay that's good."

Nazy thought the security chief was being a bit melodramatic but allowed the thought to dissolve as Comstock introduced the security team. After the first four women introduced themselves and outlined their responsibilities, the last of the security team said, "Miss Cunningham, I'm Kelly Horne, your full-time personal security assistant. Anywhere you go, I'm to be by your side. I'm not to let you out of my sight."

The comment sparked a smile from Nazy, suddenly mischievous. "Even the bathroom?" She didn't expect a lack of privacy for the most basic of body functions.

"You can leave the door open ma'am."

"Shower?" Nazy was intrigued.

"I'll just be in the room. I promise I won't peek."

"What about when I'm in bed?" *Seriously?* Nazy's eyes panned to Anna Comstock and beseeched validation. The security chief crossed her arms atop her massive breasts and nodded.

"I'll just be in the room. I'll be quiet."

"What about you—when will you sleep?"

"During the day, when you're at work, ma'am."

Nazy took a bite of pizza and reflected on everything the woman had just said, and how it was said. While it was...*polite* and *professional*, it was rare for an Agency officer to be *that* polite and *that* professional.

Only Duncan was naturally *that* polite and *that* professional. While that thought was running loose in her head, she sensed there was something vaguely familiar about the red-headed woman who would be, figuratively, attached to her hip. Nazy looked into the eyes of the young lady and searched her face.

With a disarming smile, Horne tried to convey her duty wasn't personal but purely professional. It wasn't working.

"Okay, Miss Horne, I sense you and I will become very close before this is over."

Kelly replied enthusiastically, "That's my hope too, Miss Cunningham." She quickly realized her gush of enthusiasm might have been too strong; she was embarrassed and blushed. All of the women noticed Horne's enthusiasm and over-eagerness and collectively grinned.

The room was quiet before the awkward tension in the room was broken as Nazy and Kelly Horne spontaneously broke out in laughter; then every woman in the room erupted and giggled like teenagers at a slumber party. Nazy said, playfully, "Just not *too* close, Miss Horne."

Nazy and Kelly smiled at each other as the other women finished their food. Nazy returned to the thought that there was something about Kelly that was different from the other intelligence officers in the room. As Horne got up and headed toward the kitchen, her movements stirred odd thoughts in Nazy. She sensed they weren't exactly *sexual* but couldn't pinpoint the source of her concerns. She soon dismissed them. Comstock began to direct the other women in the room on the features of the house and Nazy lost interest. She moved to the table and checked messages on her BlackBerry. Duncan had sent her a short *billet doux* eliciting a quick smile and a salacious reply. She returned to her computer and blocked out the noise in the room.

Kelly Horne was shocked that she had been assigned to guard her father's fiancée and embarrassed that she couldn't control her emotions when she came face to face with Nazy. Anna Comstock had told her that the DCI had personally made the assignment—"You're DCI assignable, cupcake, so he has his reasons." She struggled to make sense why the DCI would be so interested in a newly graduated intelligence officer. She would protect Nazy; her father would probably never know of her assignment. Kelly turned to see Nazy studiously at work; she was much more beautiful than her picture. It saddened her that Nazy would probably never know Duncan had a daughter. It saddened her that her father had squandered his opportunities to tell Nazy.

A string of classified emails from the National Security Agency and Special Operations Command filled Nazy's classified email inbox. One by one, she sifted through the high priority "red flag" correspondence looking specifically for the "decrypts" from the NSA Crypto-Analysis Section. Although CIA had their own section of code-breakers, the former DCI bypassed the in-house analysts for the NSA to get an executive "eyes-only" assessment of some WWII encrypted documents. Once Nazy determined Rothwell had made the request to NSA, DCI Lynche overrode the previous Director's request for decryptions and asked the NSA Director to forward the findings of the crypto-analyses directly to Miss Cunningham.

Before shutting down her workstation and heading to bed a "red flag" email from the NSA Deputy Director got Nazy's attention. She read the subject line: GRID COORDINATES. An executive summary defined the mission, how the line-by-line analysis was accomplished, and challenges encountered with decrypting the Nazi document. Attached to the email were multipage documents, which pinpointed each decrypted grid coordinate, outlined the location, and provided the name of the closest landmark to the precise point on Earth. Each decrypted grid coordinate location also came with several layers of satellite imagery.

She sat up in her chair when another high-priority email from the NSA Deputy Director came through. The subject line: CHATTER RE: GRID COORDINATES. She read the NSA email three times before she understood the unofficial NSA-generated acronyms and forwarded the NSA findings to DCI Lynche. She provided a short narrative of immediate and actionable intelligence relayed by the

German intelligence service: BND reports AQ + MB chatter suggesting teams have rough 'grid coordinates' and looking for lost artworks. Of the 20 decrypted 'grid coordinates' 18 locations confirmed 'once held' materials. One location 'in excavation since 2011.' One location on USAF base near Ramstein-Miesenbach. Contents unknown.

Nazy gathered her papers for a burn bag and was about to shut down her computer when DCI Lynche surprisingly responded to her email: Maybe we'll beat them to it?

She wasn't sure what he meant. After a moment's confusion, Nazy figured out the meaning of the cryptic question. She typed, "They shouldn't be able get on the base."

Seconds later, Lynche replied, "Let's hope not."

CHAPTER FOURTEEN

The Capital Grill steak house was full of businessmen and women in their Brooks Brothers and Burberry suits, flashing gold Tag Heuers and stainless Breitlings and enjoying the fruits of their labors as the engines of commerce. Wine bottles flew out of diamond-cubed racks; the wine splashed into a smattering of goblets on heavy linen-covered tables. A train of obsequious waiters poured water into bulbous glasses from carafes held three feet above the tables. A hostess walked by with a tray of desserts, each as big as a brick, enticing the thick men to indulge and splurge while the curvy women recoiled in mock horror and forced themselves to abstain.

Eastwood and Hunter were largely indifferent to the background noise of corporate executives' gruntings, intrigues, the under the table footsies and other bawdy shenanigans. They carved steaks as thick as a bodybuilder's forearm and talked about their life in and out of the Marine Corps.

As he chewed a piece of beef, Eastwood waved his knife in dismissal. He didn't want to reflect on the old past but was willing to discuss the new past. He said, "I thought I was dead, point blank range. Your fancy truck and fancy driving saved my life."

Hunter popped a bit of steak into his mouth. His BlackBerry buzzed on his hip; he'd look at it later.

"You didn't flinch. I've been in a lot of combat but nothing that close. I about pissed on myself. I never said 'thank you.'"

"My pleasure, Sir," Hunter said with a smile.

"I'm going to need one of those Hummers, I'm afraid."

"I'll give you the *fatwa* special. After your TV special, you may

NO NEED TO KNOW

need one sooner rather than later."

"I'm serious. And, you're right. However, that show needed to be done. There's something going on, and it's happening right under the FBI's noses and in front of America's eyes."

"You're not going to get any pushback from me. I've been saying—privately—the liberals and commies have been running roughshod over the government for years, and now it's the Islamists who want a piece of the action." A quiet moment passed between the two men, as if one had uttered some secret challenge code word and the other had responded with the correct answer. Now they could talk freely; they were friends that shared special secrets.

"Well, I have to tell you, Duncan, they were well on their way—and there's nothing that could stop them. But whoever released the President's file....that put a stop to it. Overnight. And probably set their operation back for years."

"Some would call him a traitor for divulging classified material." Hunter wiped the smirk off his face with his napkin.

"Damn hero in my book. Of course, the left and the Islamists will cut his head off if they ever find him."

Hunter broke into a huge smile as he chewed a slug of beef. Eastwood noticed. He leaned back and again pointed his knife across the table. Hunter swallowed and took a drink and asked, "Ever see the old movie *The Conspirator*? Liz Taylor, Robert Taylor?" Eastwood shook his head and narrowed his brows. "If I recall my movie history correctly, there's a line in there where the Robert Taylor character is asked by his communist handler, 'Are you a thinker or a doer? The Communist Party needs doers, not thinkers.' Something like that."

Eastwood shook his head and wondered where the conversation was heading.

"It took me a while to understand that the liberals, communists, and Islamists have plenty of thinkers but it's the workers, the true believers—*the doers*—that are the problem."

"It's why they call them workers."

"Right, working to destroy America."

Eastwood smiled, gestured the knife toward Hunter and said, "You have to be careful with talk like that. Might find yourself getting shot at or something."

Hunter grinned right back, "That might explain our buddy trying to kill us. They're everywhere and they're trying real hard."

"They *are* everywhere, that's the problem."

"Those workers are working to collapse the government. I'm trying to do my little piece to put Achmed Carbomb Mohammad out of work. How's that?"

At the quip, Eastwood struggled not to choke on a chewed wad of fillet. Once he had wiped tears from his eyes and recovered sufficiently, he asked, "What's the greatest thing you've ever done in an airplane?"

"Besides landing a Staggerwing on a carrier? In the Marines I was a team player; never really had the opportunity to do anything that you'd classify as 'great.' There's not a lot you can do that could be considered crazy either when you have a guy in your back seat who's usually senior to you. To me 'great' is what William Overstreet did when he flew his P-51 Mustang through the Eiffel Tower arches while pursuing a German Messerschmitt."

"Just being in the Marines was the most amazing time in my life. Saw so much—good and bad, especially when I crewed search and rescue helicopters. The saddest day of my life was when I put a baby in a body bag. Parents were shitfaced drunk and their toddler walked away from a campsite and into a lake. I've rescued downed pilots and transported half-dead people to hospitals. It was the greatest thing ever when the guys that were at death's door—on a stretcher on the floor of your helicopter, blood leaking out of them faster than the flight nurse could pump it into them—walked into the office to tell you 'thank you' for saving their life. Things like that will change you. All of us have a story. But I have to say every day I got to fly the F-4 was an adventure—the most fun you can have with your clothes on."

"You're not the typical Marine. I thought I'd seen it all, working in the White House, working with spooks at Langley, the movers and shakers at State and DOD. But you're different. I still find it unbelievable that you flew a biplane onto the *Ike* and got the President to authorize a strike in Libya. Now that's a...what's the term; a *rara avis* among us mere mortals."

"I don't know what...*strike* you're talking about, Colonel." The huge steak knife waved in a circle and Hunter stifled a grin.

"I'm just glad you're on our side and that I got to see you in action. I've seen Delta and SEALs and Marines at work—*as a team*, but you're on a different planet." Eastwood sensed he may have pushed too far and beat a retreat. "I hope Nazy is doing well. It was apparent to me she was another rare bird operating on a different plane. She was out of place in Algiers. I could see it—and I think the bad guys saw it too. I think that's why they snatched her."

Hunter debated whether to say anything at all. He realized Eastwood could be *useful*. "You and McGee saved her life; for that I'm eternally grateful. I wouldn't be talking to you, probably, if you hadn't been part of that."

"I know that's a delicate subject. My CEO wanted to know what happened to the Chief of Station in Algeria. I didn't tell."

"Thank you, good sir."

"That whole episode was simply incredible. McGee and I were finishing our beers and telling war stories. I remember she waved at the SEALs at another table and acknowledged the other embassy people in the cafeteria with a wave and a smile as she left. She was in jeans and a white long sleeve shirt. The next time I saw her McGee had her in a bloody sheet as he worked furiously to put her back together. I swear the big guy was crying; I nearly lost it. It was like being back in Nam. Heartbreaking."

Eastwood was suddenly lugubrious. As a lieutenant he had seen war up front and personal in the rice paddies of Viet Nam. He had carried severely wounded Marines to safety and was wounded several times during his time "in-country." Reliving the horrors of combat or the results of terrorism was always traumatic and painful. Some handled the stress better than others did. Eastwood considered himself one of lucky ones.

The men sat quietly; Hunter lowered his eyes to let the moment vaporize. He remained emotionless and slowly waved off Eastwood's comments. It was time for the colonel to be useful. "What do you know about Bruce Rothwell?"

"The DCI, I'm sorry, former DCI?" When Hunter nodded, Eastwood continued. "Not much—never met him. Only know what was in the papers. Trouble with a woman, maybe it was women. Disgraced. Resigned." His eyes begged for verification.

"He converted to Islam years ago." Eastwood dropped his knife on his plate.

Eastwood asked, "Are you shitting me? Are you saying the former President *and* the DCI were closet *Muslims?*"

"That file proved the President was—yes. Different times, not together that I know, but yeah. Seems so. Could be a trend."

"Wow." Eastwood considered the ramifications of the intel. He'd had intel leaked to him before but nothing on the scale of the former DCI's religious philosophy. "How do you know that?"

Hunter replied, "Come on, Colonel, it was open-source at one time." He slowly shredded a piece of the red meat while Eastwood tried to comprehend the consequences of Hunter's astounding revelation. Thoughts and apologies of bringing up Nazy were gone.

In his telecasts, Eastwood purposely steered away from and avoided commenting on the former President's publically declared faith as a Christian. The release of the CIA file exposed him to be a British national as well as a Muslim with highly probable ties to al-Qaeda. The revelation forced him to resign. The knowledge that the former DCI was also a Muslim, with access to the nation's greatest secrets, was explosive. Did Hunter intimate or mean that al-Qaeda also had a man running the CIA, however briefly? Moreover, as the ultimate horror, if those two were somehow able to get "into the system," how many more were in government?

Suddenly, Eastwood's steak lost all taste. Hunter looked as if he were a tiger grazing on a gazelle, a steady stare in some faraway place.

"So, what does it mean?" The old warrior looked tired, beat, as if he'd been in an all-night firefight, and still needed to clean his weapon before turning in.

"To me it means, like the Communists of the 50s, 60s and 70s, al-Qaeda has fully infiltrated the highest levels of the media and the government, and few people in America know or care. Moreover, you just had a special on how well the Islamists have infiltrated America under the cover of mosques, and now millions of Americans know you've shined a light on these roaches. Like the left and their fellow travelers and commies, whenever you expose them it's like stepping in a fire ant mound. They instantly attack and try to kill you with ten thousand bites. The commies were bad, but I think having to deal with these radical Islamists is going to be an order of magnitude worse. They want to kill you."

"How do you think they did it?"

"How'd they get in? The President's file clearly showed he used bogus documents, thuggish tactics to get elected, and a phalanx of lawyers to crush anyone who dared challenge him and his bona fides. That's organized crime in any other person's book, only in this case it was facilitated by democrats and commies, in my humble opinion. Then there's a fawning press and red media—fellow travelers all—they were able to hold off any scrutiny of the man. Fooled the voters. But, when it comes to Rothwell, well, I just don't know. I was under the impression he came up through the ranks. The rumor was he converted to infiltrate a terrorist group."

"I think what we learned from Whittaker Chambers is that these things are deliberately planned and coordinated with some goal in mind. Like the American Communist Party did on so many levels, the true believers worked their way into media and jobs with the government, to steal secrets and to collect intel. And, at the very least, I think their ultimate challenge to overthrow the government was to affect policy. Once they become the ultimate decision maker, like the President or the DCI, it's hard not to follow the directions of those leaders, however screwy their policies are. People just won't believe their leaders are communists or radicals or are deceptively evil."

Eastwood was troubled by the communist connections in the conversation. He had often thought there's a link between the communists and the radical Islamists, but he could never find anything that linked the two together. As he listened to Hunter he sensed he was about to discover the faultiness of his logic.

"I think you have to look at what the left did during the Cold War. The democrats didn't come out and vocally articulate their support for communism—what they did was personally attack the anti-Communists. McCarthy wasn't the best spokesperson as an anti-communist, but he was right. All the guys with security clearances at CIA and State knew he was right when he said there were commies in the State Department. The Venona Papers and the Mitrokhin Archives peeled back the innocent veneer of the commies hiding in government and named names. Reality was hidden behind the curtains of top secret security clearances and special access programs. What did the democrats and the press do? They targeted the people that were anti-Communists. If you were seen as an anti-commie then you were ridiculed as a zealot."

"Now the left is doing the same thing with Islam. They've taken up the mantle of radical Islam. Just as they did during the Cold War, they don't overtly support radical Islam, but they attack people who are anti-radical Islam. They deflect any discussion that might be had while they demonize people as Islamophobes and smear them—which is the same strategy they used to suppress the voices opposed to communism. Only difference is, while the democrats try to smear you the Islamists just want to kill you."

Eastwood asked, "For all of his lofty speeches, are you saying he was Damien Thorn? Stalin reincarnated?"

"Regarding the former President, he always spoke for the hard left. The left believes we're the greatest source of evil on the planet. Because when we, Western civilization, are in power, they can't get their way. When the left—the socialist left and especially today's democrats—is in power, they kill or try to kill those that oppose them. Lenin and Mao are their heroes. The 'doers' on the left would kill us or imprison us by the trainloads if there wasn't a Second Amendment." Hunter sliced another piece of beef, stabbed it with his knife, and slowly popped in his mouth.

Eastwood was very near speechless. With approving head nods, he worked up the courage to say, "Wow. Duncan, that's it. It all makes sense to me now."

"Look at what he did with Iran. The Iranians aren't looking for anything but to develop a bomb to annihilate Israel."

Eastwood approved the change in topic. Iran *was* in the background of every conversation regarding terrorism. They were a wildcard—their influence was everywhere, as widely viewed by the intelligence community, the DOD, and strategic think tanks. If and when Iran achieved the technology to build a nuclear weapon, the Iranian clergy would give their terrorist proxies those weapons to achieve their goals.

"I used to think al-Qaeda, the Brotherhood, and the radical clergy took a page from the Iranian embassy playbook to try and do in Iraq and Syria what Khomeini did in Iran. Foment unrest, step into the breach, and you're in power. Those corrupt ayatollahs only want more power. The people of Iran don't want a nuke but building the bomb is protection for the clergies to rule Iran forever. You can never trust them."

"I agree," said Hunter. "That's just one of many examples to prove *he wasn't on our side.* I always wondered why the President would support our enemies. Never made any sense." Eastwood's eyes begged for an answer.

Hunter leaned over his plate to keep his voice down. "He wasn't on our side. Those documents showed he was born a Muslim and was raised to be a communist." He cut his remaining steak while his eyes were transfixed on Eastwood's. "Those items were never reported by the Post or the Times."

Eastwood frowned, "Liberals and democrats did everything in their wheelhouse to kill the contents of that release. They tried to discredit the storyteller, but no one knows who released that file. Liberals do everything they can to kill horrific stories. I think these stories need to be told."

"Sort of like Paul Revere. Another great American patriot."

"I'll take that as a compliment."

"They don't like to have a light shone them—that's always an interesting reaction. When you highlight what they're doing they get ugly or even deadly." Hunter smiled broadly at the thought he and Eastwood were simpatico in their understanding of the destructive and stealthy nature of America's radical liberals.

"That's true; enough about me. Why do you do it?" Eastwood was momentarily distracted and was forced to wave at another well-wisher across the room who had recognized him.

"How about another story?" Eastwood broad smile encouraged Hunter to continue. "I was in flight school with another former enlisted Marine. He'd been a Marine Security Guard in Athens. He married the British ambassador's daughter, went to OCS, and was my neighbor going through the program. Both of us were tearing up the syllabus with great grades, having a grand time when he blurts out he's not going to ask to fly jets. If you fly fighters there's a real chance you'd be ordered to drop a nuclear device on an enemy, and he said he couldn't do that. Doing something like that would be against his conscience. I said if my country needed me to drop a bomb on our enemy, then that's what I would do. I learned then and there the real difference between thinkers and doers, and when you get the opportunity to do something for your country; you have to step up and be a man and do it. I've been given the opportunity to do great things for my country, I like to think I didn't hesitate to step up to the plate. Speaking of plates...." Hunter waved down the dessert hostess and took a Brobdingnagian wedge of key lime pie.

When Eastwood shook his head to defer dessert the server asked for his autograph. Hunter watched the transaction with fascination. *It must be like that wherever he goes.*

As the pretty waitress walked away Eastwood's eyes followed her until she turned and disappeared. He turned back to look at Hunter and said, "Where were we? Oh, yeah, great story. I understand. Some of us come around to the obvious and others remain on the sidelines. Think of all that's going on in the world. Africa is being set on fire by radical Islam, Iran is working overtime to develop nukes—they're not developing intercontinental ballistic missiles to deliver Chinese food. The Russians are trying to reconstitute the old Soviet Union and threatening their neighbors. And Islamists everywhere—to include here at home—are stepping up their game to finish what Hitler started and what Stalin envisioned. Eradicate Jews and Christians, attack the U.S., and turn America communist. They were able to get one of theirs into the White House and now, you say, the CIA. They've been very lucky. They're making headway. We're in real trouble."

"I agree. The Islamists have changed tactics. They're now using converts. You know McVeigh was helped—aided and abetted—by several...*Islamists*."

"I know," said Eastwood.

"You can always tell the media are hiding something when they obsessively focus on atrocities someplace else in the world. Like your unreported war stories, they're something that was well documented by a local reporter but totally ignored by the liberal media. McVeigh had help from a trio of Middle Eastern men the day before and the day of the Oklahoma bombing. The media would never look at the facts, never report it. News like that has to come out in a well-researched book. I think there has been more *unreported* mayhem caused by homegrown wannabe terrorists via converts than your average American could possibly believe. For example, our media will never report that the Czech Republic President not only warned about the rise of Islamic terrorism around the globe, but also described how the Muslim Brotherhood had a hand in developing and training the leaders of almost every Islamic terror group worldwide. One of the greatest powers the media has is their power to ignore. You know that's true."

Eastwood nodded. "I do. And it's true there's been a shift to rely on local talent; men they recruited, trained, and trust. They want them to look like they came out of the heartland of America."

"Yes, sir. Colonel, your special was important; you're adding to the body of work to unmask these wannabe terrorists who want to get into the big leagues. We're in real trouble."

Eastwood indicated for Hunter to continue.

Hunter chose his words carefully. What to say and what not to say? Eastwood wasn't just a reporter; he was now a friend. He marshaled his thoughts and finally unleashed a jumbled potpourri of what concerned him. Nothing was classified, just sensitive. He lowered his voice and said, "We need to be careful. I've been shot at twice. I don't know who's behind it. Is someone pissed off at me or you? Maybe it was someone trying to get at you for your video—the biker seemed to recognize you. When they die trying to kill me—*us*—it's hard to ask them questions. I'm not interested in interrogating them when they're shooting at me. Know what I mean?"

"I do."

"If you're attacked when I'm not around, then I'll start to believe you've a bigger problem than I do. Everyone in this building knows who you are. You have a *fatwa* on your ass. I'm a nobody. I think when they come after me it's probably not the FARC but just the *Islamists* from one of your mosques. Maybe I'm right; maybe I'm wrong. But we're in someone's crosshairs. We must be smart, and we must be very careful."

"Crapola."

Hunter relished his pie and wiped the smile off his face with his napkin. He asked, "You conceal carry?"

Eastwood shook his head slowly. "It's illegal in Maryland."

"So is smoking dope and crossing the Rio Grande without a green card, but everyone does it. You should carry a weapon and you need to wear body armor." Hunter signaled for the check. "I'll give you my local truck until we can get you one of your own."

"Your truck?"

"Yes, sir. It's not a Hummer but it will do."

"What about you?"

"I'll be fine. Again, everyone knows you."

"How will you be fine? I don't know what to say, Duncan."

"There's a pair of competition Kimber 1911s...."

"Forty-five cal? ACP?"

"Yes, sir. Automatic Colt Pistol with competition fixed and laser sights. Under the dash. Just push up on the doors—you can't miss them, both sides of the steering column have spring-loaded panels—the doors drop down. Mags in the console—230 grain jacketed hollow points. Squeeze the handgrip and the Crimson Trace laser will light up your target. Take the truck home and check the underside thoroughly before driving it if you park it in an unsecured space for any length of time. It'll protect you from anything but a big bomb." Hunter dragged his BlackBerry off his hip and checked his messages.

"Duncan, that's most gracious, but what are you going to do? How are you...?"

"I'll take a cab; no factor. I'm in a hotel not far from here. Only a few people know I'm here. But you can't go anywhere without someone wanting to tell you 'howdy' and send you a bottle of wine, buy you a beer, or get your John Hancock. I'm invisible."

Eastwood acknowledged his celebrity without a smile. "That's probably true. Then what?"

"I'm heading to Europe tomorrow."

"What are you doing...*in Europe*? Oh, that's right...."

The two men raised and touched their water goblets together in toast, and said, "No need to know!" Eastwood apologized for being nosey. "Reporter habits are hard to break," he said.

The valet brought a black Chevy Tahoe up to the curb and eyed Eastwood and Hunter suspiciously. He had never before seen or driven an armored vehicle with two-inch-thick windshields, and the experience unsettled him until Hunter slipped him a $20, then he scurried off to park a Maserati. As the old Marines exchanged handshakes, Eastwood said, "I don't know how to thank you."

As Eastwood crawled into the SUV Hunter said, "Try not to get it shot up. Stay safe, good sir. I'll see you soon. Any questions—that is, any that I can answer—send me a text message or just give me a call. We'll stay in touch. Semper Fi, Colonel."

"Semper Fi...*Maverick*."

Hunter touched his fingers to his brow in an informal salute; he turned his attention to his BlackBerry as Eastwood steered the Tahoe away from the curb. He waved down a taxi, got into the back, and gave the driver directions. Duncan pressed the keys of the handheld device with a finger and told Nazy he missed her and he loved her and he hoped he'd be able to see her soon. He sent a short text message to Kelly Horne informing her he was thinking of her, and he pushed an email to Bill McGee: "Just gave my Tahoe to Eastwood; need 2 more; 1 for me and 1 for Nazy, maybe ASAP. Off on another adventure. Still plan to jump on schedule. OUT."

The taxi ride to the JW Marriott was uneventful. Hunter didn't spot any surveillance on the way to the hotel or in the hotel. He brushed his teeth, dropped to the floor and did a hundred sit-ups, then flipped over onto his belly and counted out sixty push-ups. When he got to his feet he removed a six-inch .357 Colt Python from his overnight bag and slipped it under what would've been Nazy's pillow. He set the alarm on his BlackBerry, killed the lights, and was asleep in minutes.

CHAPTER FIFTEEN

"So we're going to just waltz onto an Air Force Base and they'll roll out the welcome wagon?" Hunter flashed an insincere and smug smile at the Director of Central Intelligence. The soundproofing in the Gulfstream allowed intimate conversation between the fore and aft seats. The DCI's security detail continued to sleep out of earshot at the rear of the jet.

"Last night while you were playing Marine with that 'reporter' I was busy with the President, the SECDEF and the Air Force Chief of Staff. And 'no' I didn't tell the latter exactly what we'd be doing, but I told them that to be successful, we're going to need a lot of help, a full seven-level security team. The President is fully briefed; he indicated this could be world changing. Whatever we need will be at our disposal."

Lynche never looked up from his laptop. He pounded the keys like Hunter, primarily with index fingers flying across the keyboard, like a college professor who was too busy with his work to learn how to type. When he stopped pecking, he looked up to check his work on the screen. The DCI was distracted with the haste and direction of their mission as he pondered yesterday's meetings: first with the President and then the Secretary of Defense.

The President was skeptical of Lynche's hunch that a trove of Nazi gold and art sat unmolested under a U.S. air base in Germany for nearly seven decades, but Lynche had convinced the President completely when he said, "Duncan Hunter gave me this." He tossed the chief executive the swastika-embossed gold coin, just as Hunter had done to him. President Hernandez stared at the coin, his eyes wide and mouth agape. Examining both sides—overwhelmed by the revelation and the cascade of effects this discovery would precipitate—Hernandez was speechless. He had finally raised his eyes to Lynche and said he'd fully support this mission as he lifted the phone and hot-lined the Secretary of Defense. Within 20 seconds the SECDEF was on the line and was told DCI Lynche would be at the Pentagon in 30 minutes to brief him on a POTUS-directed mission requiring full DoD support.

The Secretary of Defense's simple "Yes, sir," earned a genuine "Thank you, Tommy," from the President who immediately hung up, smiled broadly at Lynche, and extended his hand for a meaningful shake of thanks, safe travels, and good hunting. With the clasp of hands, the President also returned Duncan's gold token quipping, "I don't need swastikas in the White House."

On the road to the Pentagon Lynche realized he hadn't shared with the President the increasing probability that Rothwell was still alive and becoming an increasing threat.

Less than 27 minutes later and, as promised by the President, Lynche was in the SECDEF's office relating the essence of the real mission, the details of a deceptive cover story, and outlining what he needed for his operation.

Secretary Wilson called in two of his staff members—full colonels. He directed the first to prepare the U.S. Army's CB/RRT, the Chemical-Biological Rapid Response Team, for overseas deployment. They needed to be ready to depart in three hours and they all needed Top Secret security clearances. "For now we're saying it's real-world." He directed the second to fetch the Air Force Chief of Staff.

Plucked from the racquetball court, Air Force General Harbaugh arrived panting and sweaty in his PT gear within three minutes. Secretary Tommy Wilson stepped into his private bathroom and emerged with a plush white towel that he tossed to Harbaugh.

Secretary Wilson picked up a hotline to the Commander of United States Air Forces in Europe: "I'm initiating a no-notice exercise of the CB/RRT to Ramstein Air Base where they will be exercising their capabilities in your AOR. The only USAFE resources required will be one of Ramstein's training areas, your normal airfield operations folks to receive and service three or four aircraft, transportation assets—vans, deuce-and-a-halfs, and whatever else they need, and Security Forces for perimeter control—they'll need their chem gear. The exercise director is with me now and will arrive at 0800 to set up the training area. The RRT will need to be in place ready to execute the deployment order two hours before his arrival. Take no action until he arrives and initiates the exercise. This is a Top Secret exercise with POTUS interest."

Lynche stopped for a moment and scanned the screen with a finger, reading what he had typed. He said, "The Smithsonian Administrator wasn't very happy when I told him I might need some help. In case we find something, we have a couple of guys on standby over there, kind of on retainer with all the tickets."

"Seriously? Why would anyone at the Smithsonian Institution need TS with SCI?" Hunter screwed up his face while crossing his legs. The confusion in his head spread across his face as his eyes pleaded for a reasonable answer, but the DCI never looked away from his computer and simply ignored him. Hunter couldn't understand why anyone so far outside of the intelligence community would need a clearance and access to secret materials. With a touch of sarcasm, he asked, "Many commies over there?"

Lynche glared at Hunter over glasses perched on the end of his nose. The look was enough for the younger man to get the message. Hunter countered the rebuke by consulting his BlackBerry for new email but returned it to his pocket when it was obvious the aircraft hadn't descended to an altitude where the device could receive a signal from a cell tower. He thought of Nazy and wondered what she was doing ensconced in a safe house.

The DCI continued to work on the computer through the descent and landing at the air base. Hunter knew the DCI better than anyone at the Agency. He had flown with him for fifteen years, and they had been business partners. Hunter had never seen him so focused on a computer monitor and wondered what he was doing. *Probably some secret squirrel shit—he is the DCI after all.* Hunter finally asked, "What are you doing, good sir?"

The aircraft touched down as Lynche looked up from the monitor, then said in a hushed tone, "I told you some of our IOs were killed. I'm writing letters of condolences to their families." The two men locked eyes. Hunter mashed his lips together and nodded. Lynche continued pounding on the laptop keyboard.

The Director of Central Intelligence cautiously stepped down the aircraft stairs to a welcoming crowd of one. Behind him a pair of F-15E *Strike Eagles* roared down the runway in afterburner. He smiled broadly at "The Sound of Freedom" as Hunter called the deafening triple digit decibel and ground shaking operation. His smile could have been interpreted as a greeting to the general officer approaching the business jet.

A major general wore a trim blue uniform with the silver wings, wreath, and star of a command pilot. She walked toward the aircraft as the airstairs were lowered. She saluted informally and greeted Director Lynche as he stepped from the white and blue Gulfstream G-550. Hunter and the intelligence officers followed.

She shouted over the departing aircraft noise. "Welcome to Ramstein Air Base, Director Lynche; it's an honor to have you visit our facility." Her gravelly voice sounded like Janis Joplin; her handshake was as firm as a gymnast's.

Lynche maintained his grip on the woman's hand and placed his other atop theirs to show his appreciation for the general's warm welcome; he leaned in closer to be heard over the jet noise in the background. He read her nametag. "Thank you, General Volner. I hope our visit doesn't disrupt your daily routine too much. I do a little flying myself and appreciate the sound effects!" He shook her hand and then released it.

The Air Force general officer smiled back warmly as the F-15s rocketed out of sight and hearing. She recalled the directions and expectations from the Air Force Chief of Staff. The four-star general indicated the DCI's visit was to be very low key with no public affairs photographers or extraneous personnel on the ramp while the CIA's top spy and his security detail were exposed. Ensure the jet is parked in a secure area. "The DCI may or may not introduce his entourage. He'll need a van, some flashlights, and a driver with a clearance. He wanted to land under the cover of darkness but his schedule is too compressed. He and his team should be, if you're lucky, back airborne within thirty minutes."

She said, "Sir, I've talked to the Chief of Staff. We have what you need and are ready to take you wherever you want to go. The CB/RR Team is aboard the base awaiting your direction."

Lynche offered, "Thank you, General Volner."

The major general snap-tuned away from Lynche, unclipped a Motorola hand-held radio from her waist, and barked a few words. Well away from the aircraft's wingtip, a blue Air Force van waited. An R-11 fuel truck drove to the front of the Gulfstream and the uniformed driver bounded out of the vehicle to refuel the executive jet. Lynche was personable and continued an intimate conversation with Bonnie Volner as they walked across the parking ramp to the van. Hunter and the security IOs were ignored. They trailed the man and woman at a short distance.

The pilot and copilot had followed Hunter and the two intelligence officers down the jet's stairs. The pilot proceeded to vector off to the most obvious landmark on the base, the control tower. He hiked some 500 yards to the base operations building to file a flight plan for the return trip, while the copilot assisted the fuel truck driver with refueling the Gulfstream. He made sure the driver wouldn't take an unauthorized tour of the inside of the jet. The woman returned her radio, a "brick" in Air Force parlance, to her belt.

Hunter raced to the vehicle and opened the door for the general and the CIA director. At this demonstration of manners, Volner smiled a thin thank you and Lynche frowned under furrowed eyebrows. The security detail climbed to the back of the van as Hunter took the time to check his surroundings. He scrutinized the hangars, flight line, the control tower, and the woods across the runways. Nothing looked familiar and thoughts of failure crept into his mind.

. . .

Three men in German Army camouflage uniforms moved cautiously and quietly through a patch of dense, deciduous forest and matted patches of thick leaves. Each step was thoughtful and deliberate. One man followed the other, stepping in the same place as the man before him. The man who led the trio wore headphones under a helmet and waved an all-terrain metal detector from side to side, searching for buried targets. After ten minutes of searching he had located and marked several buried seismic sensors. He signaled the path they would take to the perimeter chain-link fence. Another soldier removed a short pair of bolt cutters from a backpack and severed a single wire about five feet from the ground and another near the base of the fence. The man returned the cutters to his bag and threaded the cut wire through the links of chain. The three men stepped through the opening. The man with the metal detector continued to lead the way through the trees and thick bushes.

. . .

"I'm looking to be out of your hair in very short order," said an optimistic Greg Lynche to the bewildered general officer. She was still unsure why the CIA Director had come to Germany and commandeered her air base. It would've been nice to know what she was getting into. She had a career to protect.

"The Chief said I was to provide you with anything you need or want. I'm still a little unsure what you're looking for." General Volner sat next to Lynche in the seat behind the driver who had been introduced as Colonel George.

"General Volner, we've some intel that there may be, well, a hidden

NO NEED TO KNOW

underground entrance to a cave or a facility on the airfield that goes back to the war." The comment piqued the general's interest.

"Director Lynche, I'm not sure where that would be. All our facilities were built in the fifties and added on through the decades. The only trace of anything that goes back to the war era is an old runway which was part of the original autobahn and was used for Luftwaffe aircraft operations."

"That may be it—my source claims to have been there and can take us to the spot."

"Well, that's interesting." General Volner waved her hand in the general direction of the other side of the airfield. "The history of this base has always been steeped in a little mystery. Unlike every other aerodrome no airplanes were found when the allies overran the area. There may be something to your intel, but I would think that if there were a hidden entrance it would've been found long ago since U.S. forces have been on this base since the late 40s."

Lynche offered, "That's my view as well. I'm under no illusions that this is anything more than a wild goose chase, but my source has been unnaturally...ah, *right* on these issues. That's the reason for the RRT. If he's right we'll need the security. If he's wrong, well, we'll pull chocks very quickly. Everyone can return to their daily routine and forget any of this ever happened."

The general gestured a guiding hand toward the base operations building and hangars as the van passed through some of the flight line security checkpoints. Lynche exchanged smiles with the slender woman as she served as something of a tour guide on the part of the air base infrastructure supporting military aviation. They chatted like long lost friends. In the back of the DCI's mind as he saw the air force base buildings and cargo airplanes and fighter jets, was his suppressed desire to watch the "fast movers," the big-engine fighters takeoff.

General Volner spoke into her "brick" that "Ramrod was off the net," and maintained a friendly two-way conversation with Lynche. The colonel driving the van struggled not to look at the CIA men. The security detail, two unsmiling intelligence officers in dark sunglasses who had given only their first names and last initial when introduced, sat quietly behind Lynche and the general.

Hunter was in the rearmost seat of the van. He looked left and right trying to reignite the embers of a forty-year old memory. It was impossible to remember the layout of the airport and the runways. As a child he wasn't allowed to be on the active part of the airfield. Buildings come and go; runways are nearly forever. The old runway was a strip of the old autobahn and had been decommissioned. A fragment of it now served as an access road which intersected the base's perimeter road. As Hunter entered the van, he had asked the colonel to "drive the long way," to the perimeter and access roads.

"We can do that," said the incurious and compliant colonel.

"Director Lynche," began General Volner, "There may be something to your intel. You know there used to be an Air Defense Operations Center that was very close to this facility."

"The old Kindsbach Cave. Yes, I'm familiar with the ADOC. I served a couple of tours as the Agency liaison in the 70s and 80s. I used to fly into and out of Ramstein in those days; let's say an Air Force Constellation was a bit more primitive and Spartan than a Gulfstream."

After Lynche finished chuckling to himself it was his turn to recall old war stories. He explained that the ADOC had been a huge underground bunker complex, a mixture of natural caves and concrete, and was a former Nazi western front command headquarters. He recalled the history as he had been told. The French took control of the facility after World War II and after extensive renovations, the "Cave," as those with a need to know called it, had been converted into Europe's best equipped underground combat operations center for NATO forces.

"Because of the history of the Kindsbach Cave complex and the other bunkers in the area, I didn't think it was too far 'out there' to believe there may have been another bunker or a section of a cave that hadn't been discovered or was used for other purposes. As I recall, after the war the French had to be told of the Cave's location and purpose even though hundreds of soldiers had crawled all over the area as they looked for Germans."

He turned over his shoulder to look at Hunter and said, "We'll see if Mister H. can lead us to the Promised Land." All eyes turned to look at Hunter in the back of the van. The driver checked the interior mirror to find the spook scanning their surroundings.

"Nothing like a little pressure; thank you, Director Lynche." Hunter sat quietly in the back seat while the bird colonel drove his boss and her guests around.

The driver pulled off the decrepit and overgrown access road and slowed down to negotiate some deep ruts. Then Hunter said, "Colonel George, at that dogleg ahead, we need to stop." Everyone in the van became alert with anticipation.

The driver said, "Roger."

The general turned to Lynche, "Could be exciting...."

Lynche replied with a frown, trying to manage expectations, "...or it could be a bust."

One of the security men asked, "What are we looking for?"

Hunter replied, "An opening to a cave."

The general turned to look ahead as the van decelerated. "There's no cave, only a hill with thick trees."

After three minutes of cautious driving over an obviously unused road, a voice from the rear of the van shattered the suspenseful ambiance. Hunter barked, "We're here. Let me out."

. . .

Three men cautiously approached the target which, according to the hand-held GPS, lay a hundred meters directly ahead. They had made it through the thickest part of heavy woods and walked carefully down a slight but slick incline when they heard a vehicle approach. The leader froze in place assuming their entry onto the air base had been discovered. Their efforts to find and avoid the seismic sensors buried inside and outside the perimeter fence must have triggered an alarm somewhere in a radio control room. The men were well-trained, and without a hand signal, they stopped walking. Questioning eyes asked the leader the imponderable—*were we detected?* The leader hushed his teammates. The interlopers retreated to a hiding spot where they would be able to observe the vehicle. Hiding behind trunks of evergreens and oaks was the least of their worries. The leader hoped that whatever vehicle was approaching was on a routine patrol and would pass quickly. Their hearts slammed in their chests in trepidation as they hoped they hadn't tripped a hidden seismic or an infrared sensor.

. . .

That's it! The memory of being on a yellow Sting-Ray on the dirt road among the trees, looking back toward the hill with a handful of gold coins in his pocket flashed in his mind. Hunter realized that his old memories had been made through the eyes of a young boy. Everything he could see was much closer and smaller than he remembered. As they left the flight line he had noticed that the old gymnasium was much smaller than he remembered; the old hangars, which used to tower over him as he rode his bicycle seemed much smaller too. The hill in front of him painted a picture that was smaller and more heavily wooded than in his faded memories, *but this was it!* It had been a little scary then, now it was just foreboding.

. . .

As a large blue van stopped near their target, the three men looked nervously at each other. They expected security forces to emerge from the vehicle. The leader lowered binoculars and imperceptibly shook his head. He extracted a Markov semiautomatic pistol from his shoulder holster. The other men understood the unspoken change in mission as they drew their weapons and waited for a signal.

. . .

General Volner stepped down from the van as everyone else extricated themselves from the vehicle. Arms akimbo, they looked about trying to discern what was so special about the area. Hunter was last to disembark. As soon as he was free of the van he jogged to the top of the hillock, and mindful of what happened to him the last time he was up on the hill, carefully scanned the ground for a sign, a hint of an opening. He was certain he was correct and looked over his shoulder, back toward the air base to align the diaphanous memory with the current sight picture. Hunter tested the ground in front of him with a cautious toe. He had the distinct recollection of riding to the top of the hill then gaining the courage to ride down the most vertical portion of the hill, the part of the hill which was free of trees and obstacles and would scare a kid on a new bike.

Lynche and Volner exchanged glances; the intelligence officers spread out and cursorily scanned the area for threats and found none. The driver watched the men in sunglasses amble about and then turned his eyes onto the man on the hill. The CIA Director and the Air Force General focused on the shrinking image of Hunter as he slowly and methodically took a few steps to the right and then to the left.

Hunter scrutinized the ground as he looked for a sign. He lifted his head as if he recognized a landmark ahead and walked toward the apex of the forested hill, and then...*disappeared.*

Lynche and Volner saw Hunter go down but the image of him falling below the crest of the hill didn't immediately register. The driver didn't believe his eyes when the man vanished between eye blinks. No one moved as their brains tried to process what was essentially a magic trick. Now you see him; now you don't!

After a few seconds Hunter's distinct but muffled voice emanated from the hill as if he were in a culvert. "*Found it!*"

The words galvanized the four men and woman as they scrambled to the top of the hillock where Hunter was last seen. General Volner ripped the radio off her belt; she activated the Rapid Response Team and directed the Command Post to send an ambulance to their location.

. . .

Across the road, the three men in the wood saw and heard enough of the activities below to know they hadn't been detected, but they were too late. The race to find the opening, the prize, apparently had been won by the enemy. Dejected and furious, the leader put the GPS into his pocket and indicated to his men that they would stay and observe. They might still have a chance to investigate the area and locate the entrance suggested by the rare WWII sixteen-digit grid coordinate. An eight-digit grid coordinate would define a given location within ten meters, but a sixteen-digit grid coordinate would bring you within one meter. Global Positioning Systems now did the work of computing and transforming grid coordinates into navigation directions.

The men's collective mood changed perceptibly. Failure to complete their mission meant they would probably die for their failure. They raged within, but they would wait and see what transpired, putting death on hold for as long as they could.

CHAPTER SIXTEEN

Blood streaked down Hunter's forehead as he waited for reinforcements. Lynche and General Volner rushed up the hill side by side and quickly found a manhole-sized sinkhole in the thick leaf litter. Lynche called out, "Maverick, you okay?"

"I cracked my forehead on the rock. Bleeding like a stuck pig. I'll live."

The security detail spread out and tested the ground for stability. The driver raced down the hill to meet the ambulance and the Rapid Response Team. The slightly overweight man was getting a workout. Lynche and Volner were comically cautious as they lay flat, crept up, and peered over the edge of the leaf-compacted void. Directly below them they saw the chisel work and drill cuttings of a stylized and elongated eagle atop a simple yet artistic wreath. It was spread across a huge flat-faced granite boulder. Hundreds of shallow drill holes formed arms at right angles creating a swastika inside the wreath. They saw Duncan standing with one hand on a hip and the other resting against the rock face under the emblem of the Nazi party. Bloody brown leaves were everywhere, a sign Hunter had tried to stem the bleeding of his forehead. He leaned against old grey pebbly concrete as he turned and looked up at his rescuers. With the Nazi insignia hovering over Hunter's head, the sudden assault on their senses, Lynche and Volner thought they smelled the stench of evil in the odor of decaying leaves.

"Leaf litter is thick. The entrance is at least ten feet below me," Hunter offered. "We're going to need help to get in. A lot of help. There's forty years of composted leaves under me and out to the sides.

You guys maintain your position and don't move around—I'm not sure how stable the sides are—they were open the last time I was here. Don't need you falling in and cracking your ass." Hunter wiped blood from his face with the sleeve of his shirt.

General Volner looked at Lynche as she spoke into her radio brick, "Command Post, Ramrod. I need a ten-man working party with shovels and rakes at my location, copy?"

"Roger, copy, Ramrod; ten-man working party; shovels and rakes. Will call when they're on the way. RRT activated and en route to your position. Command Post out!"

Lynche recovered from the shock of finding the entrance and finding Hunter injured. "You sure you're okay?"

"I am—not sure if I'm going to need a stitch or what."

"What do you think this is," General Volner asked the two men from the CIA. She hadn't been told Hunter had extracted pieces of gold from the cave and had no idea what lay beneath them. As Hunter kicked clods of composted leaves from one side of the hole he was in, Lynche put the discovery into perspective.

"General Volner, *Bonnie*, this just became a national security issue. Once we get Duncan out of there and see what's inside, the game could completely change in a microsecond."

Curiosity stoked her imagination. "You've an idea of what's in there?" she asked, ignoring Hunter at work kicking clods of compacted leaves.

"Call it more hope than an idea," offered Lynche, trying to be vague and noncommittal.

"Don't tell her she has no need to know. This is her place and we need her help." Hunter looked up at General Volner mischievously; she smiled as Lynche frowned. Lynche sometimes wished that he could just throttle the insolent Hunter when he spoke out of turn.

•　•　•

As several trucks arrived filled with heavily armed women and men in camouflaged battle dress uniforms, some with shovels and garden rakes, three Middle Eastern men retreated from their hiding place to a better-protected position. The leader used a powerful Nikon digital camera to take some pictures of the evolving scene below. He took several photographs of a road and a hill overrun with men and women in uniforms, some with external body armor and some carrying black M-4s, at the ready. Some of those in black formed a blocking guard. He took pictures of a squad of workers who toiled with shovels on either side of the hill removing what looked to be dirt and detritus.

The leader observed the ever-increasing activities and arriving equipment. He took little solace that, while they might have been able to find the opening, they hadn't prepared well enough to enter the concealed location. It'd be another thing the master would criticize them for as he condemned them.

He took more pictures of the man who had raced to the top of the hill only to disappear and then re-emerge with an injury. Medical people tended to him in the ambulance. The leader continued to take photos of the growing operation until the man with a head bandage emerged from the white truck with the large red cross. He watched intently as the injured man raised his head to look up the small hill at the progress being made.

Through the zoom lens, the incursion team leader could easily read the man's body language even at a distance of a hundred meters. The man with the bandage on his head was on guard even when all the effort and interest was focused on the hill. He glanced in the general direction of the leader and his men. Then, before he stepped off to return to the action, the man with the bandage slowly turned his head as if he had forgotten something or heard something. The leader snapped a photograph just as the man looked up in the exact direction of the leader. The three men stared at the lone man looking up at them as if he knew the team was there. They were wide-eyed and gasped for fear of being discovered until the man with the plaster dispassionately turned away and returned to the hillock to monitor the excavations.

With the man's back toward them, the leader gave a nod to order retreat. The three men stealthily backtracked and departed the area.

．　．　．

By the time Hunter was patched up with three stitches, a washed face, and a massive white bandage that nearly covered his forehead, the working party had cleared out the channels between the rock face and the grass-covered concrete backstop. With the opening to the cave cleared a team of demolition experts with metal detectors and a small tracked robot checked the entrance for bombs and booby traps. Hunter walked up to the DCI, who was pushing buttons on a BlackBerry with both thumbs, and said, "What are we waiting for?"

Lynche turned to him, inspected the emergency medical technicians' work, grinned, and harrumphed. "What did you get— thirty stitches? I can't take you anywhere! Okay. Once it's clear we can go in. Any minute now. Anyone tell you that you look like you've been in a fight with Mike Tyson?"

"Concrete hands, concrete walls; same difference. So what do you think?"

Lynche crossed his arms and raised an eyebrow before he said, "Depending on what we find, this may go full black. Only you and I can go in for the initial assessment—don't bring anything out unless it's essential. Looks like they're ready for us."

"We have to take the general with us," said Hunter.

Lynche shook his head.

Hunter nodded and raised his eyebrows for emphasis.

Lynche remained stoic for a moment until his defenses collapsed. "I'm going to regret ever hiring you," he snarled.

"Invite her! Let's get this show on the road!"

Once a pair of small tracked vehicles with cameras and mechanical claws whirred out of the cavern, two men positioned a pair of floodlights at the entrance. A portable generator fired up and the lamps illuminated much the area between the cavern face and the inside of the vast room. Lynche indicated for Hunter to go first; he led off—bounding off to the right with a big metal flashlight in hand.

Adrenaline made Hunter's skin tingle as mustiness assaulted his nose. The more steps he took into the heart of the cave the faster his heart pounded in his chest. A mere dozen steps inside he spied an incalculable number of rotten cloth bags and a pyramid of gold coins. A foot imprint from an old Converse tennis shoe marked the spot where a young Duncan Hunter had snatched a bag of coins forty years earlier. He was so engaged with the memory that he didn't hear Lynche talking until the DCI raised his voice. "Mav, check this out." Lynche and Volner had taken a divergent path—to the left—and found countless crates of various lengths and widths and heights resting atop a floor of wood pallets. As far as the light from the floodlights could reach the left side of the cave was awash in tall thin crates. Hundreds of crates. General Volner intuitively knew what was in the crates but she was speechless.

"Must be artwork. There are even boxes...all kinds of shapes—maybe Ming vases are in those." Hunter was in awe; Lynche was grappling with the meaning of the number of crates and boxes when he looked across the room where Hunter had been. General Volner saw what Lynche saw and struggled with the weight of her slacked jaw.

Looking like a cross between a room-seized Carlsbad stalagmite and a Hershey's chocolate Kiss was an avalanche of bright coins piled nearly to the top of the room's ten-foot ceiling. Gold coins spilled at critical angles from rotten moneybags and cascaded over what had been stacked crates. The pine from the gold-carrying crates had decayed and collapsed. It lay in scraps at the base of the mound of coins.

The treasure finders crisscrossed the room. They had not anticipated such bounty. Hunter checked the weight and sturdiness of the mahogany scaffolding protecting the enclosed artwork. The wood was dirty, dusty and greyed, but unlike the pine pallets, still very solid.

From wall to wall, floor to ceiling, the natural subterranean storeroom contained crates, boxes, containers, chests and cartons of every size and shape. In the light and hum of flood lamps, Lynche, Volner, and Hunter quietly exchanged appreciative glances. Then the spry 73-year old DCI snapped his fingers and pointed at his old flying partner; "You're a friggin' genius and better than Howard Carter." Volner labored to comprehend the possibilities, the range, and scope of the contents of the cavern. Each wondered what wonders could be hiding inside each enclosure.

Not many photons from the floodlights penetrated the far reaches of the cave, but the outline of a garage-sized door beckoned. Hunter flipped his flashlight beam into the darkness. There was a sense of urgency in his voice. "Greg...."

Lynche and Volner converged to join Hunter. They walked into the greyness; their flashlights combined to illuminate the large vertical metal structure. Not only was it a door, it was open.

Three bright rays punctured the blackness as columns of ancient dust, disturbed from a long sleep, sparkled in the torches' light. The three individual flashlight beams consolidated and focused into one intense beacon illuminating the machinery, workbenches, jigs, and tooling of an ancient aircraft manufacturing facility. Silently they panned their lights along the walls, the ceiling, and the floor. Hunter ignored a smattering of packing crates and wooden boxes, and concentrated on several dozen different aircraft structures—fuselages, wings, elevators, tails, empennages—in various stages of assembly. Some airplane parts rested in jigs or fixtures, or rested on the floor or upon huge workbenches. Other structures were stacked along a wall or suspended from gantries. Lynche and Volner moved toward the aircraft structures and ignored the stacked crates and other shipping containers, too.

Hunter had read about some of the Nazi's secret aircraft projects and had seen many archival photographs taken by American soldiers. He didn't give a crap about the artwork strewn around in boxes or crates; he was overcome with curiosity at what looked to be newly discovered aircraft. He broke the silence with a loud, "*Wow!*" His voice reverberated in the cavern.

Lynche said, "Whoever worked in this facility apparently evacuated. It looks like their work was interrupted."

Hunter looked at Lynche to see if he was supposed to reply. Lynche waited for an answer. Hunter disagreed. "I don't think so, sir. I'll bet the aircraft work was ordered abandoned to accommodate the art and gold. If some Nazi general thought the war was lost and was dispatched to find suitable hiding places, this would've made a perfect location. There are likely some undiscovered graves close to here; they couldn't afford for any of the workers to return to the location and find....this." Hunter spread his arms wide for emphasis. General Volner nodded and Lynche frowned; he hated it when Hunter was right.

The aviation historian among them gravitated to a smallish sleek airframe with an unusual 120° V-tail. A dusty set of forward-swept wings rested against the bullet-like fuselage on the floor. Lynche saw what Hunter's flashlight was focused on and quickly and gingerly stepped around Hunter to look at the strange bullet-shaped cockpit. When Hunter arrived at the structure he ran his hands over the fragile and rotten doped fabric covering. He scanned the canopy rails for the data plate, but Lynche found it first on his side of the fuselage. The DCI screwed his face in stupefaction and clamored, "*Bugatti* made airplanes?"

Hunter was astonished and walked around the structure to see what Lynche had found. "*Bugatti*? Are you sure? Let me see that. Wow—this must be...."

"It says Model 110. Did he really build a hundred of these?"

"Greg, come on. I vaguely recall old man...*Ettore Bugatti* thought he could design a racer for some cross country competition...." Hunter's Italian was pathetic.

"The *Deutsch de la Merthe* Cup Race," announced General Volner as she walked up to the airframe. "Engineering and art." She unwittingly poked a hole through the fragile covering with her finger. "This...*design* is so amazing, so far ahead of its time, but you'd never catch me in that thing." She wiped the ancient detritus off her hand onto her pants leg.

Hunter grinned and said, "I think you're right. If I recall, the original concept never flew for technical reasons, but the design was so advanced that Bugatti thought he could sell a militarized version. This must be it." Turning his head away from the tattered racer Hunter shone his light in another direction. When his flashlight illuminated an acre of aluminum and rivets he was nearly too dumbfounded to speak. He moved the torch to different parts of a goliath airplane. "Oh, Greg...*look at this*! From here it looks like...a jet-powered...*glider! Look at those wings!* It's like a U-2 on steroids...*and I think that's a bomb bay.* I've never seen anything like this from this era. This is completely new. Lockheed's Kelly Johnson would be astounded." Hunter's voice reverberated in the structure; the echo dissipated into the distance as he stepped gingerly around scattered aircraft structures and work benches to get to the long slender airframe. "I think it's supposed to be a super-high altitude bomber."

Hunter thought that the monstrous German aircraft looked like it could be assembled and disassembled quickly, much like his YO-3A which was re-engineered to be quickly assembled for operations and disassembled for transportation. This was just on a larger scale. He recalled the Nazis had built some of the largest weapons of that era, like the 155-foot long Schwerer *Gustav* railway gun and the six-engine Messerschmitt Me 323 *Gigant* transport aircraft. He realized there was only one reason to develop an aircraft that could fly high enough to escape the fighters of the day, and it wasn't to take pictures like Lockheed's jet-powered U-2 glider which had flown high over the Soviet Union during the Cold War.

He stood still and stared somberly at the unique aircraft for several seconds before he said, "The Nazis conducted a lot of high altitude research and human experiments on the prisoners at Dachau. They subjected victims to high altitudes and froze them in order to understand the dynamics of long-term high-altitude flight. There must have been another opening over there to take this out to fly." He pointed his flashlight to a wall of dirt. He didn't say that the only reason to develop such an aircraft was to deliver a single bomb, a nuclear bomb. Hunter knew two well-placed thermonuclear devices had stopped the war in the Pacific. He reminded himself that 19 hijackers started another war on 9/11.

General Volner shined her light to the roof and said, "I think the old runway, the old autobahn is...is the ceiling. This is just astounding. I don't know what to say other than thank you for allowing me to be a part of this. This is amazing."

Lynche said, "More crates, more artwork back in there. Has to be in the hundreds. I've never seen anything like this. It's unbelievable." He walked over to the huge aluminum aircraft and slammed Hunter on the back, nearly knocking him over. "Damn, Mav, you did it to me again."

· · ·

At the base of the airstairs of the Gulfstream the DCI shook hands with General Volner one last time. It was unusually quiet on the tarmac, no jets taking off or landing. Bright sunshine pummeled their faces. He smiled broadly; the heavy lines around his eyes were getting a workout. Still stunned from the enormity of the past two hours, she nodded in the direction of the cave of artwork, gold, and Nazi aircraft and said, "Director Lynche, thank you again for allowing me to be a part of this. I suppose you have much to do; is there anything else you need from me?"

He cautioned her to avoid accidental disclosure. "We'll need a good cover story to account for all the activity that'll come to your facility. I'll work on that. The Rapid Response Team will provide the treasure trove the appropriate level of security. I must brief the President on this as well as the SECDEF and your boss." He gripped her hand a little more firmly and placed his other over hers and said, "I'll tell them you were instrumental in the success of our mission; I don't think that'll hurt you too much. I suspect in a matter of hours there will be a cast of hundreds converging onto the base. I don't know who all will be involved in the security and recovery effort. I'll work all the particulars once I'm airborne. You've been very helpful, and I thank you."

The general saluted the DCI before he started up the airstairs.

After takeoff the pilot of the Agency's Gulfstream raised the landing gear in the calm afternoon air and headed west. The copilot energized the autopilot, the software programmed to take the Great Circle route to Washington DC, flying just south of the tip of Greenland and jetting down the coast of Canada and New England to Washington DC. Three wooden crates, ostensibly containing paintings and an urn, rested in the aircraft's cargo hold along with a shoebox full of gold coins.

Once aboard Hunter rested in a recliner and yawned. He didn't interrupt Lynche while he worked at his computer. The Director sent FLASH Precedence messages to the White House, DOD, and CIA headquarters command post. He directed his deputy director of operations to assemble a team to develop a cover story and begin to deploy the Smithsonian recovery team to the German air base. He then finished with the last of the condolence letters, snapped the electronic notebook closed, patted Hunter on the shoulder, and was about to repair to the private bedroom at the rear of the jet when Hunter held up his hand. Lynche anticipated good-natured ribbing and moved to take the upper hand. "Rank has its privileges and you need to continue to respect your elders."

Hunter grinned at his best friend and then became quietly serious, "Director Lynche, you said, Rothwell...*knows... everything.*"

Lynche returned to his seat; his furrowed brows indicated he was obviously confused. "That's right."

"Would he know all the safe house locations?"

The question caught Lynche unaware and he searched for an adequate response. "Nazy's in the most secure location we have."

"If you know...he knows; doesn't he?"

The DCI pouted and acquiesced. "It's possible. Before I retired we didn't use that location for something like hiding one of our senior executives."

"I've a bad feeling…."

"Not to worry. She's safe and you'll see her soon; that was the deal."

"Thanks, Director Lynche," said Hunter as he looked over to the DCI's already asleep security detail. "I'm not sure when I'll be able to see her—I've a bunch of things I have to do. You know you're ruining my love life."

"You ruined my retirement by volunteering me for this job, so we'll just consider it even. What are you missing that's so important?"

"Primarily a night jump at the training center. UAV conference in DC. Corporate Council on Africa meeting. Teach a class—I'll reschedule. Board meeting. Same old stuff. Not much."

"Tell Nazy you have a daughter? Plan for *Noble Savage?*"

Hunter glanced at the two snoring security officers. He was suddenly tired. "Yes, I have to tell Nazy. And Boko Haram; how could I forget *that?* Can I at least know how Nazy's doing"

Lynche patted Hunter's shoulder. "I'll get an update before we turn in. Maybe the threat climate has passed and we can all return to normal ops."

"You're a gentleman and a scholar, Grinch."

"Don't you ever forget it, Mav." Lynche turned and repaired to the sleeping berth at the rear of the jet leaving Hunter to plan for an incursion into Nigeria.

· · ·

The man discarded the photograph of American uniformed men and women carrying black assault rifles. Photographs of men with shovels digging into a hill were tossed to the center of the table. Other photographs of portable light units, small tracked robotic vehicles, and soldiers with metal detectors working near an opening in the side of a hill were perused and discarded. A photograph of a man standing at the crest of a hill flew across the conference table. Scarred fingers held the photograph of a man with a head bandage emerging from an ambulance. The man's head was low; his face obscured.

Rothwell was livid with the news that a group of uniformed soldiers and civilians had interrupted his reconnaissance team in Germany. All they had to show for their efforts was a few photographs and, by extension, their failure to locate and acquire the spoils and booty of Hitler. Another picture was offered to the man at the head of the conference table who was on the verge of hyperventilation. He knew the man who looked up into the trees and into the camera. Rothwell knew who he was before he saw the man's face; he recognized the man's shape and build.

He took one short look, mashed his one eye closed, and dropped his chin to his chest as he softly said, "Hunter. My brother. You were looking for the infidel—he's in Germany." Rothwell tossed the photograph to the vile man from al-Qaeda; the print effortlessly glided above the table top and was stopped by the man in the black *keffiyeh*.

Rothwell was just one color—angry—and crushingly disappointed. He strained to check his fury and his breathing. "We must kill this man, this Hunter. He is everywhere; he is nowhere. Now that he's found the treasure, he'll go to the woman. Find her and you'll find him."

He suddenly brightened as he mulled this last directive. A long suppressed memory became clear; a hint of cruelty lined his lips. He hissed, "I know where the woman is. I know where to find the *takfir*." Rothwell scribbled notes onto a tablet and handed it to the al-Qaeda man closest to him who passed it to his leader.

The men from the Muslim Brotherhood and al-Qaeda sneered at the man in the photograph as it was passed around. They nodded indifferently at Rothwell's latest utterance. The old CIA spy was becoming a burden.

Rothwell furiously slammed his fist onto the table. "My brothers, this setback makes no difference at this point. Whether we found the artwork or not, we still have other funding strategies in the queue. It's time to activate *Anjam*. We've much to do. Go! At all haste. Go! *Allahu Akbar!*"

. . .

Before terrorism came to commercial aviation, flying was an esteemed event, a unique opportunity where men and women of wealth dressed in their finest habiliments to ride in relative luxury to virtually any spot on the globe. What used to take days or weeks in ocean or continental crossings could be accomplished in hours. However, when the targeting of tourists confined in large jet aircraft became the business of the terrorist for politics and profit, airlines and governments reacted to the mushrooming threat. They set into motion the protracted and tortuous death of the once wonderful experience of airline flying.

International terminals became large bus stations of controlled chaos as jumbo jets from around the planet offloaded and boarded hundreds of passengers under the watchful eyes of surveillance cameras, airport security, and law enforcement personnel. After passing through the inconvenience and unpleasantness of airport security, after being unshod, unburdened, unfrocked and undressed, queued for mandatory irradiation—and for a very special few—fondled, molested, poked, prodded, and otherwise embarrassed and humiliated, thousands of travelers raced to get away from the uniformed minimum-wage men and women with their rubber gloves.

Passengers would hide in retail stores, restaurants, restrooms, airline lounges, and departure gate waiting areas to regain their dignity and composure before confronting the final phase of discomfiture of long-distance commercial airline travel. For some voyagers, escaping the vicissitudes of the security checkpoint only to be seated in the coach and economy classes was akin to tumbling from one level of Dante's *Inferno* into another, especially when trapped in the middle seat between Jabba the Hut and the perpetually unshowered Tiny Tim.

Harried passengers and patrolling airport police officers ignored the three female TSA officers sitting at the Boar's Head tavern on the concourse. Law enforcement officials strolled along the walkways quietly demonstrating by their presence that the traveling public was safe and secure. Travelers were too focused on getting to their airplane or retrieving their luggage to pay much attention to three uniformed women wearing *hijabs* in the international terminal of the JFK International Airport. The only thing noteworthy about the three women was the color of their *hijabs* which matched the color of their dark-blue uniforms.

Transportation Security Officer Abby Kesselring offered to her tablemates, "I realized the best way to understand Islam was to take a walk in their shoes. I climbed out of my comfort zone, attended mosque, and began to wear the headscarf. At first it was more of a science project—an experiment—than a commitment of faith." The recent convert to Islam looked forward to talking with her fellow Muslim women during breaks and lunch periods.

"The *hijab* isn't a symbol of oppression," the tall African American woman insisted. Eboni Whittle, the TSA's Behavior Detection Officer, said, "I really feel liberated wearing the *hijab* and always have. It's a sign of modesty and respect, and I feel beautiful and empowered. How's that a bad thing?" The women looked at the other girl who raced to finish what she was eating.

"I've never been ashamed of being Muslim," said the pudgy Arabic woman. A trained bomb appraisal officer, Amira Mohaned swallowed the last of her humus and chips and told her narrative of when she started religiously wearing the *hijab*. "I didn't wear it when I was a little girl or throughout high school. I used to wear capris and shorts like the other girls, but one day I met a girl like Abby, someone who had converted, wearing the *hijab*. I felt guilty, stopped dressing so provocatively, and started wearing it again. Her commitment made a lasting impression on me. We should only wear the *hijab* when we're most comfortable doing so."

Kesselring offered, "It was never forced on me; I don't think I would've worn it had it been forced on me." She noticed her friends wore neither fingernail polish nor lipstick, but their eyes were detailed with eyeliner and dark eyeshade. She thought it'd be hard to give up her dark fingernail polish, but as she looked at the other women's bare nails, she decided it wouldn't be so difficult to remove the polish and have fingers *au naturel.*

Whittle gestured with her hands. "Of course, if it's forced upon you, you won't understand its significance and importance. Coercion doesn't work; it's counterproductive. Some parents demand the *hijab* for their daughters and you see that when they do that, most girls rebel. I certainly did."

Passengers and airport workers came and went through the restaurant. The TSA women ignored them. Mohaned interrupted Kesselring, "I agree; you have to be drawn to it; want it; accept it. It's not worth it to just go through the motions. You have to be confident and committed. Islam doesn't consider just your actions but also your intentions. Wearing the *hijab* reminds me to be sincere and be myself."

The Arab woman gathered her trash and stood. "This was fun, but I have to run."

Kesselring asked quickly, "Did either of you see that vile TV special on mosques? All lies. My imam is livid."

The other women nodded. "We'll talk about it tomorrow."

The blue-eyed Kesselring also nodded, checked her watch, and cleaned her area. She didn't want to be late and be subject to the vituperation of the lead transportation security officer.

Kesselring wanted to tell more of her story and looked at Whittle. "I don't know everything about who I am or who I want to be. I wasn't a good girl to my father and fought him at every turn. He called me anti-establishment, an anarchist, and even a radical. I wanted to do crazy things to antagonize him and piss him off, but I really never had the guts to do anything. Converting to Islam about gave the old man a stroke, so I was feeling vindicated, in a way. Now I feel I'm taking the steps to being a better person. This old hippy girl is trying to be a good Muslim."

"It looks like you're doing good, girl. Keep it up. We gots to go!" Whittle and Kesselring walked together and chatted about the different ways to wrap a *hijab* until they reached the concourse security checkpoint. Whittle waved goodbye as Kesselring reported to the lead

TSO for her assignment. Before directing her to the X-ray machine the lead TSO asked if she would be available to work some extra hours as they would need extra screeners for the upcoming new Nigerian Airways service.

She felt tension build-up with the thought of hundreds of depressed and cheerless passengers pouring through the checkpoint, but the anxiety melted away when she reminded herself that she could use the extra money. She put on a happy smile. "I can do that. Thank you for thinking of me," she said.

"It's a once a week flight for now. We'll be slammed as it's 700 pax. All our X-rays and magnetometers will be manned, up and running. I appreciate it, Kesselring."

She acknowledged the gratitude of the lead TSO and took her position behind an X-ray machine. She reminded herself she'd have to tell her imam of the change in her work schedule and that she would likely miss prayers.

CHAPTER SEVENTEEN

"Gentlemen, this course of instruction is 'sniper fire from a ship.' At the end of this training element you'll be able to engage targets out to 600 meters, in pitch and roll, in most sea states. You've a standard human silhouette on the left, an outboard motor silhouette on the right. Shooters and spotters take your positions."

The man's deep radio-announcer voice reverberated in the metal enclosure surrounding the six-axis, full-motion simulator at the Full Spectrum Training Center outside of Hondo, Texas. He directed the two teams of two to climb the ladder and take their positions on the deck of the simulator. The shooters, wearing yellow polarized shooting glasses, took their place. As they settled in the prone firing position they readied their weapons. Each shooter was armed with a highly modified sniper rifle with a complex optical system mounted atop the receiver in place of a riflescope. The tracking system incorporated the same tracking and fire-control capabilities found in fighter jets. The spotters carried sniper spotting scopes on nine-inch tripods.

Sporting a white-haired flattop, Captain Bill "Bullfrog" McGee, U.S. Navy retired, and another former SEAL, Master Chief Steve Malagorski, climbed the ladder. The men waited for the teams to settle in on the left and right sides of the platform that replicated the steel non-skid decking and edging and guardrails found on most container ships. McGee stood in the center of the platform while the other SEAL moved to the instructor's station at the rear of the training device.

"Killing pirates or disabling their boats from a moving vessel is an art form, and this is the only training aid in America designed and constructed to simulate shooting a sniper rifle from a ship at sea." He gave a "thumbs up" to the SEAL behind him to energize the platform and begin to "rock the boat." Hydraulic pumps buzzed to life, and the simulated ship's deck began to sway to the right then to the left. McGee allowed the men a few moments to acclimate themselves to the rolling deck. "You have to feel it and anticipate the apex of the ship's roll—as Master Yoda might have said, 'you have to become one with the deck.' Take aim and see how your sight picture is constantly changing with every swell of the ocean. Notice what happens when you reach the apex of the wave; for a brief moment all motion stops and you've an opportunity to put crosshairs on the target and hold it through trigger pull. Can you see that?"

One shooter said aloud, "Well, I'll be—*them* are ducks!"

McGee continued. There was a definite growing rhythm and flow to his sentences. As the "ship" rocked with the waves so did his words. "You can see it and you have to be conscious of it. Right-handed shooters have better accuracy as our boat rolls to the left; left-handed shooters have better accuracy as our boat rolls to the right. You control your breathing and your pulse as the boat rocks to the right—now I want you to dry fire at the apex. Time it so the round goes downrange at the exact moment when the ship stops shortly and reverses directions. Spotters, you can be very helpful talking to your shooter as the pendulum swings to the killing point. Shooters, you know your trigger release point and your pulse, and you can control them and synchronize them to take the shot at the apex when you and the boat are stopped for that fraction of a second. Can you see the perfect sight picture at the apex? Tell me now if you're having an issue."

"Your silence tells me you're comfortable with the process and the timing. Breathe...squeeze. At the top of the apex...fire... reload. This is the ultimate confidence maneuver; once you master this in roll then we'll work your sight picture in pitch. Pitch is the motion where you can most easily kill their boat."

"Okay. I think you're ready to go. Sound suppressors please! Shooters, lock and load! Ready on the right? Ready on the left? All ready on the firing line? Shooters, when your targets appear you may commence firing!"

Shooters and spotters worked together as the simulated ship's deck rocked left and right. After several misses both snipers began to synchronize their sight picture and trigger pull to better stabilize their positions and hit the targets consistently. After several simulated "waves" the shooters gained confidence in their ability and their groupings tightened. With the guidance of their spotter, the snipers gradually moved impact points to the center mass of the human silhouettes. One round after another was expertly sent 600 meters down range. Once the shooters were synchronized with the swaying training device and got "dialed in" to the target they began to target the heads of the silhouettes. McGee lowered his binoculars pleased with the results. He barked, "Cease fire! Cease fire! Clear all weapons; open your bolt. Do we have any saved rounds? Any saved rounds? No saved rounds. Shooters, safety your weapons!"

McGee stepped forward to check the open bolts of both weapons and said, "That was excellent. Outstanding. Please notice your surroundings. What do you see?"

"Bullfrog, I think you increased the roll a little," said one of the shooters.

"Very good, that's exactly what we did. You'll rarely encounter sea states as high as what we're experiencing now on a huge container ship. We started with sea state two—very smooth seas—and now we're at sea state six. Pirates and containerships will avoid rough seas. But you naturally adjusted as Malagorski increased the sea state, and you still killed pirates at 600 meters. That's well done. Are you ready for pitching seas?"

After fifty rounds were expended as the "ship" pitched with the simulated bow rising and falling, proud and confident shooters exchanged their positions with the spotters on the simulated deck and the process began anew.

The training device had once been a full-motion simulator for a small helicopter until Art Yoder, the original owner and operator of the training facility, and Duncan Hunter acquired the simulator from military surplus. They removed the Huey helicopter cockpit from the deck and converted it to a shipboard sniper platform. The commander of the United States Naval Special Warfare Development Group was very interested in the unique training device that replicated the wave action of a ship at sea at various sea states and soon contracted ten weeks a year for all SEAL snipers to go through the Hondo facility. The word got out to the special operations community of the special purpose firing range. Soon retired and former SEALs and other special operations forces—U.S. Army DELTA, Green Berets, Rangers and Marine Corps Raiders—filled up the training schedule for fifty weeks a year.

After completing the training the men were sent to security details around the globe to protect shipping containerships and large commercial fishing vessels. Small two-man sniper teams used armor piercing rounds to disable the pirate's boats in any sea state during the day. At night the teams used night vision scopes atop the sniper rifles to spot attacking pirates and terrorists. Silencers were rarely used aboard ship as the report of the big bore rifles was often a deterrent. Only the most determined pirates would assault a ship with former special operations forces men aboard.

Success was measured by a stunning drop in the number of hijacked ships in the heavily pirate-infested waters of the Malacca Strait and off the many national coasts of Africa. More snipers aboard ships resulted in fewer and fewer attacks on the high seas. In some areas along the African coast FSTC-trained snipers put hundreds of pirates and terrorists out of business as armor-piercing rounds destroyed inboard and outboard motor engines. This forced the pirates to find other ways to raise monies. The cost of acquisition and conversion of the simulator had been recouped within a few months of operation.

McGee refined the hands-on training as well as other aspects and capabilities of the FSTC. He and a handful of instructors taught primary and refresher courses in defensive driving. They taught anticarjacking techniques and the delicate art of driving backward at seventy miles per hour before spinning the car 180° to continue in the same direction in a high-speed escape. Weapons familiarization taught students to identify, disassemble, and fire weapons from around the world. The firearms training was a holdover from the late Art Yoder's Delta Force days. If there was a smidgeon of a chance that someone might come into contact with a foreign weapon in a prisoner or hostage situation, that person needed to know how to use that weapon. McGee absolutely agreed with the strategy and greatly expanded the arsenal of weapons for the FSTC. They began providing weapons familiarization and other self-protection services to corporate executives and their international business development and program managers.

Some capabilities remained strictly the purview of active and retired Special Forces personnel. Every few months McGee led nighttime, high-altitude, low-opening as well as low-altitude, low-opening recertification parachute jumps for these august professionals. Every man wore lightweight, helmet-mounted, AN/PVS-23s night vision binoculars used exclusively by U.S. Special Forces.

After years of operating the FSTC at a significantly reduced capacity following the death of Colonel Art Yoder, Hunter knew what it'd take to return the facility to its former glory—another charismatic and world-class leader of Special Forces operators. He never thought his friend from the war college would be interested in a move from the clean classrooms of academia and beautiful New England to the grit and grime and the heat of special operations. He couldn't conceive of a situation where anyone would purposely move from the cool of New England to the dusty hotbox of San Antonio. Hunter was wrong.

McGee was one of a handful of African-Americans serving with the vaunted U.S. Navy SEALs—Sea, Air, and Land—and the only African-American officer ever to command the Naval Special Warfare Development Group or DEVGRU, the maritime branch of the United States' four secretive counterterrorism and Special Mission Units. Captain McGee rose through the ranks to become the commanding officer of SEAL Team Six due to his unique and meritorious ability to execute the most challenging, difficult, and dangerous missions. He was the best of America's best warriors; the most accomplished, the most decorated, and the most successful SEAL in the history of the Naval Special Warfare Command. When 19 terrorists commandeered four jets on September 11, 2001, the Joint Special Operations Commander called Captain McGee and directed the nation's 911 counterterrorism reaction force into the mountains of Afghanistan to find and capture bin Laden. SEAL Team Six chased the master terrorist into the mountains of Afghanistan but came home empty handed.

Captain "Bullfrog" McGee, the former commander and the "head frog" of the Leap Frogs, the Navy's Parachute Demonstration Team, met a civilian, Duncan Hunter, at the Naval War College. The two became fast friends. The massive body builder in his sparkling white uniform and the athletic racquetball player in a black business suit made an inseparable odd couple as war college students. McGee credited Hunter for saving his professional life after the humiliating failure of not finding Osama bin Laden, Duncan Hunter owed Bill McGee a hundred lives for saving the love of his life, Nazy Cunningham, from being butchered by Islamic extremists. An offer to return to the "Spec Ops" world and train former members of Special Operations Command and SWAT law enforcement officers as the director—and owner—of the Full Spectrum Training Center was too good for McGee to turn down.

After other FSTC instructors processed six more sniper teams through the wave simulator, McGee met with a group of four special operations warriors and loaded men, parachutes, helmets, altimeters, gear bags, gloves, and night vision goggles into a four-door, four-wheel drive pickup truck. The drive over the unimproved and dusty road to the Hondo Airport was made in relative quiet.

Thirty minutes after leaving the training facility, McGee stopped the pickup at a security gate, waved a security card against a card-reader, and entered the airport, and headed for the tiny terminal. Two aircraft were parked adjacent to the old terminal building, an unremarkable white single-engine turboprop Cessna Caravan and a Gulfstream G-IVSP with faded red and gold stripes running down the length of the fuselage.

As the pickup stopped at the airport terminal building a man descended the stairs of the corporate jet. McGee checked his Seiko dive watch in feigned disappointment. As heavy muscular men in black free fly suits stepped from the truck, McGee said to the man from the jet, "Cutting it a little close? What's that? Looks like you got beat up by a Girl Scout troop. Are you sure you didn't grow up on a padded playground?" McGee tossed a wadded, black, poly-cotton parachute jumpsuit to the smirking man with a cell-phone-sized bandage on his forehead. The man saluted informally with a touch of his fingers to his brow.

"And miss a night jump with you, Good sir? Not bloody likely!" said Duncan Hunter.

. . .

"Where're you from?" Nazy Cunningham crossed her legs, shrugged her shoulders, and silently begged for more information. She took a bite of lasagna and listened. Dinner was served late as the old electric oven took its sweet time in heating the pan of pasta and rolls. No one seemed to mind; the security detail went about their duties while the deputy director of counterterrorism worked on the computer in the makeshift SCIF. Once dinner was officially declared "served," the three women on duty gathered around the dining table. The other two women assigned to the security detail were either patrolling the grounds or were downstairs in the basement control room monitoring sensors and cameras.

Mealtimes were usually catch-as-catch-can affairs; sometimes an intelligence officer would assemble a meal of cold cuts and chips and put out a plate for lunch. But the dinner meal was prepared by the "mom and pop" general store at the bottom of the hill. When someone got hungry the security women and Nazy usually served themselves.

Tonight was different; the tension at the safe house had been greatly reduced with the news Anna Comstock brought. The FBI arrested several men conducting surveillance on Nazy's residence. The women in the house were more relaxed and half of them ate together at the table for only the second time since the security detail began. With the news that the security detail could soon be coming to a close there was a sense of urgency to know a little more about each other and especially about the Agency's senior executive they were protecting.

The short-haired blonde with a .38 Beretta strapped to her thigh thought the senior intelligence executive was talking to her and went first. "San Fran. I was a cop in grad school and my professor suggested I see her after class. I figured she wanted to ask me out or something creepy—it was Frisco after all—but I was blown away when she said I had those special qualities the CIA was looking for. I applied and the next thing you know I'm in a room with a polygrapher. About a year later I'm at the Farm in the National Clandestine Service."

Nazy pecked at her plate and asked the next girl, "And you?"

"Originally Golden, Colorado. I was an Army intel officer at Fort Meade—NSA, SIGINT and a Russian linguist. Got caught in the drawdown after we pulled out of Iraq and needed a job. I didn't want to serve beer at a bar at home; saw the Agency recruiting poster at the BWI airport and applied. And, here I am."

"Everyone an only child?"

The three armed intelligence officers looked at each other and eventually nodded in unison. Nazy said, "Me too. Is that odd?"

"We're so new, most of us are right out of school, I'm not sure what normal is really," said the redhead right before she stuffed her mouth with salad. Nazy again noticed the glint off the woman's gold Rolex and glanced at her wrist—the watch was just like hers. *Isn't that odd?*

"I've wondered how all of us came to this place. It seems everyone has an unusual story, and what separated us from others is what binds us together today. We're all very different from the norm. I could be wrong." She panned her eyes at the three women sitting around the kitchen table. "You were a police officer; you were in the Army; what's your story, Kelly?"

Kelly Horne wasn't prepared to talk—she had just started chewing on a mouth full of food and gestured "one moment" to the group. Nazy was embarrassed for putting her on the spot when she could be least expected to respond. "I should tell my story, if you're interested."

Heads nodded around the table. Kelly was relieved she could eat as well as listen to Nazy's life story. She hadn't learned much from her father about the woman he was going to marry.

"Nazy Cunningham, born and raised in Amman, Jordan until I was ten years old; I was then educated in Switzerland and England. I understand I've an accent; I thought it was you who talked different." Nazy flashed a disarming smile and tossed back her voluminous hair; the other women returned the smile and waited for her next words.

There was no doubt in Nazy's mind what she would say next. She wouldn't tell them she was born Marwa Kamal, that her father was the head of the Royal Jordanian Court in the service of His Royal Highness, the King. She wouldn't tell them that after attending Yale Law School she had run away from her abusive husband in Amman, returned to America, and had been blackmailed to spy on a man named Duncan Hunter. She would provide the official cover story the CIA had developed for her after she had been vetted for a week. It had been a week of a brutal battery of interviews and polygraphs after which she was given a new name, a new history, and a new job at the Central Intelligence Agency.

She continued with the fiction of her life. "I studied law at Oxford. I met a military man...."

Kelly's attention was piqued. The other women in the room also sat in rapt attention.

"... who was on an exchange program with the Royal Navy. He was an American Navy jet pilot. I fell madly in love with Lieutenant Commander Jeff Cunningham. We married and a month later he disappeared on a training mission over the Indian Ocean. That was twelve years ago. Then I was recommended by someone—probably like you, a recruiter if you will—and with the new war in Iraq just starting there was an urgent need for native Arabic speakers, and I fit the bill. I'm here; I'm glad to be here and proud to serve. I believe I'm one of the luckiest women in the world." Nazy returned to her plate of food and waited for the other woman to tell her story.

The blonde asked, "That's a beautiful ring."

"I'm engaged," Nazy said softly and then brightened and said, "Another...pilot!" She thought she'd been clever then added, "A wonderful man."

The brunette offered, "And you found Osama bin Laden?" She had heard the rumor and wondered if it was true.

Nazy mulled over her response; the room was quiet in anticipation of the release of a national secret. "Well, *someone* had to! Don't believe everything you hear and don't ever believe what you see in the movies!"

The four women laughed heartily. Nazy winked at the group. They picked at their plates. For the ten minutes of down-time, the atmosphere in the room was joyful, almost festive. All eyes turned to the lithe woman with the flaming red hair.

Kelly, the only intelligence officer who quietly said grace before every meal, asked, "Are you still a Muslim?"

All the levity in the room was crushed by the bombshell question. The question wasn't tinged with any malice and Nazy wasn't taken aback; she smiled in amazed admiration.

"Oh, no. I renounced Islam long ago, and I'm now a Christian. I missed going to church this morning, but you girls weren't going to let me out of the house no matter what I said." The women exchanged smiles and nodded at each other. With a potentially awkward situation diffused and behind them. Nazy nodded to the only girl that hadn't told her story; the girl with the gold watch. "It's your turn, Miss Horne."

Kelly started off slowly, embarrassed yet cautious; fearful she would say something else that was inappropriate. She apologized as she started; her view of her life story was one of longing for parents she never knew because her mother died in childbirth. Kelly reluctantly told the story of how she was raised by her grandparents, and how she worshiped the photographs of her mother who had been an Air Force officer, a pilot of jets. She had worked hard in school and won an appointment to the Air Force Academy. After graduation, she went to flight school and also became a pilot—like her mother—and surprised herself by doing very well. She ultimately became a flight instructor. The work was thrilling, the flying exhilarating, but her life was empty. She often wondered if her father was alive. Could she ever find him? If he was alive, did he know he had a daughter and would he even want to know her?

All of the women around the table were saddened by her story; the joyfulness and levity of the evening had vaporized like smoke, replaced by a heavy fog of unrequited pain and sorrow. Nazy placed her hand atop Kelly's; her green eyes suggested to Kelly she didn't need to say anything else.

The younger women were now emotionally involved and demanded to know if her quest to find her father was ongoing. Had she ever succeeded in finding him? Kelly couldn't look at her father's fiancée but nodded at the other women and smiled as tears welled in her eyes. Nazy squeezed Kelly's hand as all the women moved closer together to show empathy and support as well as solicit the answer to the question: So, what happened when you found him? "He embraced me and we cried. He never knew he had a daughter. He's a wonderful handsome man, and like me he was a jet pilot!" Nazy and the two security women squealed their delight as they moved around the table to give Kelly a hug. They bombarded Kelly with questions. Someone handed her a napkin to stem her tears.

"He didn't doubt you?" asked the blonde.

"No, I received my mother's diary after my grandparents passed away; that's how I found his name. He read it. It answered the questions he had, why my mother pushed him away, and never told him about being pregnant with me. He never knew."

Nazy asked, "Any troubles becoming his daughter? How did his wife take the news?"

Kelly thought about the question; she debated how to answer it. After a long uncomfortable pause, she slowly turned toward Nazy and looked her in the eyes and said, "He's trying to find a way to tell the woman he loves that he has a daughter. I know he loves her very much, but she's been through a hellish period in her life, and so he feels it may not be the right time. And I agree with him; it's probably not the right time to tell her. What I know of her is that she's an amazing woman; unbelievably beautiful, smart, accomplished. I think she would be a great friend, and if she wanted to be a mother, she'd be the best mother I never had. I would try to be the daughter she never had. I know he wants to tell her. Hopefully he'll be able to tell her soon. Not knowing what she thinks is killing me."

Electricity sizzled between the women. Nazy blinked wildly as Kelly broke eye contact and turned toward the other women at the table; her eyes again glimpsed Horne's gold Rolex. She glanced at her own watch, identical in every way to Kelly's. Nazy didn't hear the other members of her security detail emerge from the basement of the safe house to get some dinner and assume their watch. Kelly and her tablemates cleared the table of dishes and silverware and smart phones, leaving the Nazy alone with her thoughts.

Later Nazy emerged from the bathroom in black sweat pants and her yellow sweatshirt; Kelly was pushing buttons on her BlackBerry while sitting in her chair in the corner of the room. Nazy smiled at her security guard, turned off the light on the nightstand, and said, "Good night, Miss Horne."

"Good night, Miss Cunningham."

Nazy lay still thinking...the picture...the long red hair. *The old flame.* He bought her a ring...and a gold Rolex.

Kelly stared impassionedly at the foot of the bed.

After thirty minutes, Nazy whispered, "Kelly?"

"Yes...ma'am?"

Nazy reached up to turn on the nightstand light. She sat up in bed. She could see hints of Duncan in the woman.

The two women looked at each other for a very long time.

Kelly trembled inside. *She knows!*

Nazy struggled to find the words to speak. Her thoughts were a jumbled mess of incongruous notions. *It's her! How is it possible?* Nazy shook her head in disbelief. *I must talk with her....*

Nazy slid out from under the bed covers and stood; Kelly struggled to stand, afraid to move. When Nazy held out her arms Kelly's anxiety and fear melted away.

Inertia drove the women together; they embraced and held each other tight. After a long hug they sat on the bed, held hands and cried and talked until dawn.

CHAPTER EIGHTEEN

As the DCI walked across the 16-foot inlaid granite seal of the Central Intelligence Agency, he acknowledged the greetings and salutations of intelligence officers and the heavily armed guards in black battle fatigues with slung M-4s. He continued toward the bank of access control terminals and swiped his blue badge across the turnstile reader; green lights flashed approval, small doors opened, and he proceeded through. High overhead in the atrium, large scale models of the CIA's greatest aircraft—the A-12, the U-2, and the D-21—were suspended from the ceiling.

The lift to the top floor executive suite was swift. Lynche stepped out of the elevator. He stopped in front of his secretary's overflowing L-shaped desk and said, "Good morning, Penny."

For twenty-plus years, Penny Mayo had been the personal secretary for the last ten Directors. She was a fixture at the Agency and the gatekeeper for the DCI. Intelligence officers, newbies to executive, knew not to get on her wrong side, or they would never get their case files in front of the DCI. Her only gap in employment on the seventh floor was when a former DCI ignominiously replaced her with his own longtime male secretary.

Penny Mayo was a mature beauty, like Miss Moneypenny of James Bond fame. She was thoroughly competent and discrete and completely infatuated with an infrequent visitor to the executive office spaces, a contractor named Duncan Hunter.

"Good morning, Director Lynche. You've a full schedule today, and your anniversary is tomorrow; you have reservations at Bertucci's for eight o'clock. Coffee is on; you have Mr. Hunter at seven followed by the FBI at eight-thirty. The conference room is booked for the nine-o'clock, and you have a Congressional hearing at two pm." Mayo placed the Agency's message board atop the dark granite counter top. Lynche ignored the woman's unusually revealing dress and the items trying to ooze out of it.

Lynche lifted the heavy, thick, aluminum "container" and placed it under his arm. "Thank you, Penny." He entered the inner sanctum of his office. The coffee was indeed brewing as the aroma of Colombian Black, a gift from Duncan, filled his lungs.

Bare walls and empty custom bookcases painted a stark contrast to the mess on his desk. A foot of files rested in his inbox; every file save one displayed bright red borders and red SECRET or TOP SECRET headers. Each had a signature routing slip clipped with like–colored paperclips. Lynche withdrew the blue bordered PRESIDENT's EYES ONLY file; he cut the metal sealing tape and reviewed the approved Presidential cross-country authorization orders for the upcoming *Noble Savage* mission. Lynche initialed the routing sheet and flipped the file into one of his outboxes labeled SAFE.

Two red-bordered SECRET files read FBI in large red letters. Lynche reviewed the FBI status report; their agents were still looking for the traitor who had released the President's history file. The FBI's investigation discovered a deceased and long buried senior CIA analyst had acquired over two hundred documents from different intelligence agencies and commercial institutions. The former Near East Division Director had started a file on an unexceptional and undistinguished young man, reportedly from one of the former British colonies in Africa, who had tried to be discrete in visiting some of the leaders of major terrorist groups. His curious and noteworthy activities had moved from a "minimal" level of interest to "keep informed," and the tall thin man was monitored and mentioned several times "in dispatch" by U.S. and other intelligence agencies. Over the years, other dispatches from various Middle East embassies had filled the file on the mediocre terrorist-tourist. The interest in the man changed when the Near East Division Director learned the British subject suddenly appeared to have acquired a U.S. passport. Israeli and British intelligence documents proved the man who became President used counterfeit documents to secure college admissions, a social security card, a driver's license, and a sheaf of other papers necessary to establish his American bona fides. Lynche tossed the file into the outbox. "Blah, blah, blah." *Old news.*

The second file was a comprehensive essay of the threat assessment on Nazy Cunningham. The FBI detained several Middle Eastern-looking men who had been identified as members of a surveillance team. Four men were arrested and interviewed for failure to produce passports, driver's licenses, or immigration documents—they had little to say. Lynche scribbled a note on the cover sheet to terminate the *Spindletop* operation but to maintain a security detail for the deputy director of counterterrorism's residence and her person when she wasn't at headquarters.

Lynche signed graduation certificates for the Advanced Intelligence Officer's Course and scanned the follow-on change of duty stations for the graduates. He verified that Kelly Horne received a follow-on assignment as a pilot. He confirmed that her first duty station was Abuja, Nigeria where she would conduct airborne ISR—intelligence, surveillance, and reconnaissance—missions in the West Africa region. *Not a great place to start but that's where I need a good pilot.* He initialed the cover sheet and placed the file in his OUT box. The Colombian roast was ready.

Lynche signed the signature sheet on the front of the message board. A collection of Embassy dispatches, classified Secret, filled the center section of the board; a paper file fastener held the flimsies tightly in place. He speed-read each dispatch summary from the Chiefs of Station and made comments in the margins. He looked for a special dispatch from the embassy in Ashgabat, Turkmenistan and found it near the bottom of the stack. He read the COS' narrative carefully.

The DCI spun 90° and logged on to his computer. As the machine processed through all of its security algorithms, Lynche jumped up, fixed a large mug of coffee, then returned to his huge ornate judge's chair. He referenced the special access program BLUE SHOES—the program to acquire the missing man-portable tactical nuclear weapons stolen from the former Soviet Union—to verify the codename of the prime suspected seller. Named after one of the three goddesses of Mecca, pre-Islamic Arabs believed *Manāt* to be the goddess of fate who snatched men away from their families and homes and robbed them of their existence. It was a suitable codename for the merchant of death and auctioneer of weapons of mass destruction.

Lynche pounded out an email to the COS in Turkmenistan: "Contact MANAT. Set up mtg to inspect our offer."

. . .

New York Times
Editorial by Demetrius Eastwood

The investigation into the recent hotel bombing in Amman, Jordan has taken on a new twist: Did the blast target a US Agent who defected to al-Qaeda?

A former American intelligence officer is believed to have been in the immediate area of the early morning bombing at the Sheraton Amman Al Nabil Hotel on October 24, 2012. According to people familiar with the investigation, DNA analysis of human remains found at the hotel confirmed the defector's identity. Intelligence officials described the former American officer as the highest ranking defector ever to cross over to the terrorist network and called his defection one of the most damaging to America's national interests. The identity of the intelligence officer is a closely guarded secret, and sources would neither confirm nor deny the remains belonged to the former Director of Central Intelligence, Dr. Bruce Rothwell, citing national security considerations.

Dr. Rothwell was last seen boarding a government-chartered jet in Washington, DC a month before the hotel blast. The Federal Bureau of Investigation has tried to send forensics teams to Amman, but the

Jordan Intelligence Service has reportedly not allowed investigators into the country. Three attempts to discuss the matter with Jordanian intelligence services were rebuffed.

Before being appointed Director of Central Intelligence, Rothwell was a deputy director at the National Counter Terrorism Center. Unsubstantiated reports say Rothwell infiltrated Islamic extremist organizations overseas and converted to Islam. His understanding of Islam and his fight against radical Islamists helped propel him through the CIA's ranks. It is unknown whether the former officer's al-Qaeda sympathies were missed during the Agency's polygraph process or manifested themselves later.

The intelligence official said the combination of Western intelligence training and devout jihadist beliefs would've made him among the most dangerous of al-Qaeda operatives. Dr. Rothwell didn't have a military background. He received a PhD in political science from the Josef Korbel School of International Studies at the University of Denver. His dissertation centered on counterterrorism policy and politics of Islamic countries. Because of his appearance, Arabic language skills, and a very high degree of competency he rose to the highest levels in the intelligence community.

.   .   .

Duncan Hunter, sporting a new small bandage on his forehead, spent an inordinate amount of time leaning over the counter to talk with the secretary. After a few moments, he and Bill McGee were guided into the DCI's office. Penny Mayo had made the hour-long appointment for Hunter and McGee, and she had dressed to the nines for the occasion. The form-fitting dress with a plunging neckline was out of character for her any other time except when Hunter was on the DCI's calendar.

As Hunter closed the DCI's door behind him, McGee admonished him. "You're going to break that woman's heart." Hunter didn't have time to respond as McGee and Lynche met in the middle of the room, shook hands and gave each other a little man-hug amid raucous salutations and greetings. McGee offered his heartfelt congratulations for Lynche becoming Director.

Lynche pointed at Hunter and said, "I know! You can't take him anywhere, I swear."

"I don't think I told you but he was viewed as some kind of ladies' man when we were at the Naval War College. The way your secretary looked at him would've given even an ugly man hope."

"Ladies' man? That's so hard to believe. I don't know what women see in him. Penny and Nazy must be half blind."

Hunter folded his hands and scowled at his friends. "*Director* Lynche, are we going to get a brief or did we stumble into the wrong office—I thought slam grams were next door."

Lynche said, "Don't get your panties in a wad, Maverick." As the men took a seat the DCI continued, "Bill, how was the night jump? I'm surprised he didn't come through the door on crutches. Look at him. He has a history of...ah, getting hurt."

Hunter gave up any pretense of being there for a meeting and allowed the men a free fire zone. It was all in good humor, and if he hadn't been the subject of the good-natured ribbing, he would've gleefully poked at the other men. He convinced himself that if they didn't love and respect him they wouldn't feel comfortable poking at him; it was the ultimate compliment among friends. It was just a little unnerving when he was being attacked from both quarters. It'd be over soon. He grinned and took it in stride.

"I've a couple of thousand jumps over a thirty year period and Duncan has what...."

"Less than a hundred in the same timeframe."

"So I expected the worst." McGee winked at Lynche.

"What he's trying to say is I didn't kill myself but it was...."

"Definitely colorful," said McGee. "He can't land for crap."

The three men broke out in laughter; Lynche was the worst. For years Hunter had done everything better than Greg—on the pistol range, in the airplane, on the racetrack. For Lynche, it was a great feeling that Hunter could be human and screw up now and then. McGee made gestures of a rolling ball to suggest that when Hunter landed he just kept rolling and rolling until he came to an ignominious splat. "He could control the competition rig but with NVGs—well, you know there's virtually no depth perception—he didn't time his flare right and crumpled up in a little ball. I expected compound fractures, but when it was obvious he was ok, I nearly gave myself a hernia I laughed so hard."

"It's a good thing I took gymnastics and learned how to tumble. I could've broken my legs."

"Or your neck. Bill, he's the luckiest shit I know. I hope it holds during this op." Lynche retrieved a thick file folder and passed it to the men. "Oh, before we get started, I got a call from the President. He wanted me to tell Duncan, 'thank you' for your last mission. The FARC's moving their operations further into the mountains. Duncan poked a few holes into a number of fast boats that I understand were hidden along the waterways in the jungle. He also sank a sub and a thousand pounds of cocaine."

McGee said, "Who said the war on drugs doesn't work?"

Hunter smiled and gave Lynche and McGee a gentle nod. Then he said, "Dope smoking, coke-snorting liberals for one."

Lynche scowled and McGee smiled at the comment. With no other segue, the three men dove into the mission brief. "Bill, a little history. The President and my predecessor initiated a program to find and kill terrorists before they could bud into something more lethal, sort of culling the herd of Islamofascists before they get out of control. The primary concept is if we had killed bin Laden when he was a younger man we wouldn't have lost 3,000 lives on 9/11. So under an Executive Special Access Program, the POTUS and the DCI developed a list of....*candidates,* a list of potential targets and prioritized the individual terrorists and financiers for targeting."

Hunter added, "We get a warning order, based on the movements of a given person or a group, such as: 'General Omar is expected to be feted at a tent in the middle of the Timbuktu desert, mostly likely between the hours of dusk and dawn.'"

McGee listened intently and Hunter waited for Lynche to continue. "This list is fully in the 'need to know' category only to be discussed inside this office. Internally, it's called a 'disposition matrix' and not the 'President's kill list.' We leverage the unique capabilities of the modified YO-3A to take direct action on those in the matrix. I provide the execution order. I'm responsible to identify which target is the priority and provide as much information as possible to ensure mission success. I start the process by informing the POTUS we've an opportunity to excise a candidate from the matrix and requesting presidential cross-border authorization. As a SEAL, you're aware that only the President may authorize clandestine assets to cross the borders of another country. Then Duncan provides the basic concept of operations; aircraft movement, mission execution, and then retrograde all assets out of country. Infiltrate and exfiltrate clandestinely."

"Like a normal SEAL op," offered McGee.

"Probably, just now with an airplane," said Hunter.

Lynche continued in hushed tones. "This is an Executive Special Access Program—not many like this one. All my time with the CIA, I never knew of such a thing—we had SAPs that required Presidential approval and were limited to those with a need to know. Unfortunately, sometimes the number of people that needed to know grew so big that we had to cancel an op because of risk mitigation. So when I took this job and found out Duncan was doing *Noble Savage*, I have to say, I was surprised. There were times I didn't think he was trainable, but he never told me about the program. You're on the program now—taking my place as the sensor operator."

McGee nodded and turned to Hunter for confirmation.

Lynche continued, "There's something special about Duncan and his relationship with the President. The former DCI knew it was very controversial for the President to personally take an interest in eliminating terrorists or bankrollers of terrorism. Duncan and the President have some history, and the opportunity to conduct these direct action operations is limited to the period when the President is in office."

"Then the complete file is destroyed?" asked McGee.

"Like it never existed."

"What about the aircrews?"

"Agency assets for quick launches. Air Force Special Ops MC-130s to carry the airplane's container when a more persistent presence is needed, such as for the non-kinetic Weedbusters operations. They're not aware of the nature of the *Noble Savage* mission. No need to know."

"I'm astounded that this mission hasn't been...what's the word I'm looking for?"

"Federalized?" said Hunter. McGee nodded.

"Duncan?"

"This work would never be done by a contractor and the President had to authorize it. I understand the previous DCI expressed his concern that government agents should be doing work that was 'inherently governmental.' The President asked him if he had anything that approached the *Wraith's* capabilities in-house. Although he had only been on the job for a short time, Rothwell had enough knowledge of the capabilities of Air Branch and the Clandestine Service to know the Agency did not, and neither did Special Operations Command. The President asked me directly if I would help him eliminate the worst of the terrorists."

Lynche asked, "Bill, your last job was Algeria?"

"Yes, sir. We were to help recover a cache of MANPADS."

"That expertise was well within your wheelhouse?"

"All SEALs are trained to be proficient in every rifle, assault weapon, and pistol manufactured from every country. We are trained in every man-portable shoulder-launched weapon ever made, to include the Soviet one, two, and five kiloton 'suitcase' tactical nuclear weapons. If we couldn't carry it, we ignored it."

Lynche nodded when McGee finished. "That could be helpful one of these days." He turned to Hunter and suggested, "I envision the

Boko Haram mission to be a composite op—possibly several 'quick launch' flights into northern Nigeria with recovery at another location, another country. I'm sorry to say we've lost a couple of unmanned systems in that area, but they provided the necessary intel we needed for this operation. Up until those flights, what we knew of the Boko Haram leadership was thin at best. Senior analysts had identified only a few of the primary leaders. It's been difficult tracking them. We had few assets on the ground, and they hadn't been particularly effective. We aren't sure why. Nigerian security forces uncovered Boko Haram camps in Cameroon. The northeast quadrant of Nigeria is virtually under total control of Boko Haram, and their leaders are expanding their influence, we believe, into western Nigeria."

Hunter and McGee had several questions milling about their craniums. Why wasn't the Nigerian Boko Haram leadership targeted earlier? They surmised it was because of a recent string of atrocities, not reported in U.S. media circles but explicitly covered on British and Canadian websites. They reported the killing of children by the Islamic terrorists to force large numbers of non-practicing Muslims to get with the program and become good Muslims or die. For Christians in the northern half of the country, it was a case of convert or die. Classified briefings highlighted the Nigerian military was ill-equipped to stop the carnage in the north. When they were deployed to offer protection, the soldiers were disbursed in small numbers, so they were easily overrun or ambushed. When the Nigerian's were caught, they were butchered. Mutilated soldiers sent a signal to the Nigerian Army not to enter the house of horrors that was northern Nigeria.

Lynche continued, "A couple of months ago, the Boko Haram leader, Ali Dakatumbo, scoffed at the million-dollar bounty put on his head by previous administrations. He vowed to decapitate and mutilate more people in his jihad, but only when he isn't capturing and raping young girls. He has kept his promise."

"A blood-soaked tick like that has got to go," said McGee.

Hunter concurred with the obvious. "Someone has to stop the madness—send a signal we're not going to take it anymore. That we

232

can reach out, anytime and place, and put them away."

"And their friends," suggested Lynche. "Here's where we're at. The intel is strong they're moving west, most likely in order to rob banks and of course, to capture more girls. So, whatever you can do in the short time you're there will be helpful."

Hunter opened the dark blue PRESIDENT's EYES ONLY binder and placed it between him and McGee to peruse the contents. Greg Lynche continued to speak. "Nigeria is a hot button and a priority. I've come up with a list; there are ten desirable targets. We expect there'll be more than their core ten-man leadership cadre."

Hunter said, "They probably need a new inventory of girls. They're heavy into slavery and the sex trade."

McGee considered Hunter's comment and asked, "Can't use a drone to take them out?"

Lynche shook his head. "For obvious political reasons, and the logistics require too heavy of a footprint. And, if they snatch a busload of girls, it wouldn't look good if the innocent got killed in the process. This operation requires stealth and precision. We believe there's a very narrow window for an intercept. This is predictive analysis; you may not find anything when you get there. You'll try to find them over three nights, you'll return to Liberia after the surveillance mission. We have good landing rights there. This one's very time-sensitive. If there's no one home, I want you out of there. I trust your judgment. So watch your top knot. That's an order."

Hunter and McGee absorbed the contents of the EYES ONLY dossier as Hunter formulated a basic assault plan. The list of men resembled the unclassified FBI's Most Wanted List with the exception of red TOP SECRET stamps at the top and bottom of each page. Hunter summarized what he knew. "A gang of psychotics have raided a number of villages with Christian girls. They kidnap and drag them off into the bush. They threaten to sell some of them as sex slaves while others are forcibly married to their captors or are forced to convert. There are several large girl's schools in the northwestern part of the country that haven't been targeted. The people that live there think they're safe."

Hunter articulated, "Look at what Boko Haram does in the name of Allah. The left wing press ignores them; if they were a Christian terrorist group they'd be in the paper or on TV every day. They've been slaughtering people all across Nigeria for at least five years with little interference from the army."

"I agree the press hasn't covered them," offered Lynche.

"Scum like that deserve to meet Allah," said McGee quietly.

After two minutes, Hunter returned the binder to the DCI. The tone in the office was somber. As a distinguished member of the Navy SEALs, Captain McGee had been sent on missions to kill the enemies of the United States. Now he and Hunter would be going to kill the killers of innocent children and the butchers of families.

McGee recalled he had never felt remorse when he killed the enemies of America and wondered what he would feel when he targeted the murderous Boko Haram. They were not, in the classic sense, the enemies of the U.S. However, the killing of children and the slaughter of hundreds of innocent men and women, fathers and mothers were the enemies of humanity.

Hunter and McGee left the DCI's office, and Hunter tried not to flirt during a short goodbye with Lynche's secretary before they entered the elevator. Duncan could tell something was bothering McGee and he asked, "What's bugging you?"

"Just thinking what I'm going to feel when we get there...."

"What do you think you'll feel?" Hunter was confused.

Just as the doors of the elevator closed, McGee turned to Hunter and said, "Recoil?"

CHAPTER NINETEEN

"Uh huh. The reaction to your special has been one of two extremes, Dory—those on the Right loved it while those on the Left despised it. That Islamic Council group is demonstrating again, demanding we pull the tape and issue a public apology. They want you fired as well. Because of your show describing Muslim radicalization and Islamic terrorism, they've initiated an online petition to boycott all of our shows and advertisers. And they sought to block the network's broadcasts into the 57 Organization of Islamic Conference countries and the Palestinian Territories."

The CEO of the conservative television network talked to the window of his 45th floor New York City office. Ten-foot high glass panels surrounded the tennis court-sized corner office. The view of the surrounding skyscrapers was breathtaking, distracting, and disorienting. Demetrius "Dory" Eastwood stood next to the old greying man, his hands clasped together in front of him, his head hung low. Eastwood didn't know if he was being commended or if the CEO's words were the prelude to getting fired.

"It was fine piece of work. They're one of the most extreme branches of the Left and continually attempt to reshape our broadcast content. It's a story that needed to be told...."

"I sense a but...." Eastwood furrowed his brows with concern and waited for the old man's verdict.

He shook his head thoughtfully before speaking. "Uh, no, no, no. You struck a nerve, uh, with the opposition, and when that happens they go into full wailing mode. They screech and scream—they're ridiculous. Please know the venomous ad hominem character attacks

NO NEED TO KNOW

thrown your way suggest that your assailants lack any argument or evidence to counter your fine work. You reported the facts; we don't have to embellish them. We'll let the audience decide." Eastwood was pleasantly surprised when he received a pat on the back and a sly grin from the boss.

"These propagandists push the media and the Hollywood elites to rewrite history to mask Islamist influence and to promote messages denigrating Christianity. They function exactly like the organized Left using infiltration, disinformation, and lawsuits. It's essential to discuss Islamic terrorism as a war of ideas, and media interference isn't allowing an honest dialog. Your show was terrific and on target. Good work."

"Thank you, Sir," said a semi-relieved Eastwood. "What we've uncovered is a network of true believers; it's an organization. There are 800,000 members on social media. Only 4,000 or so of them are 'active' in the politics. Of those, forty are what we can call 'true believers' and the worst part: virtually all of them are leaders of mosques in New England. The intelligence community knows it's a problem. But the FBI isn't doing a damn thing."

The bowling pin-shaped man was quick on his feet. He spun around from the vertiginous edge and wall of glass and headed for the opulent, mirrored, and well-stocked bar. As he sprinted across thick carpet, he said, "Uh huh. You know, Dory, the flak is greatest when you're over the target. And you dropped a bombshell on their asses. I love to see them flip and jerk; the only thing missing is blood shooting from their eyes. There might be a little of that before it's all over."

Eastwood missed the man's turn and hurried to join the CEO as he headed for the thick black-granite bar. "Yes, sir."

"Uh huh. Your team did a masterful job in Africa; the video from Libya and Algeria was timely, amazing impact. It woke up the good half of Congress. What do you want?" He used a finger to point at the vast collection of whiskeys, rums and ryes, scotches and vodkas, and wines and liqueurs.

Eastwood was a bit embarrassed, but said, "Something diet or water will be fine. We received confirmation from the Algerian Deputy Foreign Minister that intelligence reports showed both groups had been coordinating. We had doubts that coordination existed between al-Qaeda and the Brotherhood. The CIA refused to believe it. Or at least they said it was unbelievable."

The comment didn't affect the CEO as he placed a couple of chilled bottles of water on the counter. He took a quick drink and said, "Uh huh. Dory, you know I've wanted to do a story about the AQ affiliates in equatorial Africa; how they recruit and train...."

"You mean like al-Shabaab or Boko Haram or some other AQ or Brotherhood spin-off? After Algeria, we proved that coordination exists between al-Qaeda and the Brotherhood, it's not that far of a stretch to believe Boko Haram and even al-Shabaab in Somalia are also working with them or at least receive some funding. Al-Qaeda and the Muslim Brotherhood act like terrorist motherships."

"Uh huh. I wanted you to go and tell that story. But you've resisted. You had no problems with chasing down a story in North Africa. I think the hotbed of African terrorism is in Nigeria."

"Sir, I don't think that's a good characterization. I was up to my neck in something big, and every rock I turned over led to something worse; the department head wanted me to drop what I was doing and head to Nigeria. It was a judgment call. I didn't know where the direction to coordinate came from, but I couldn't imagine anything that was more important than reporting on an impending assault on our embassies."

"Uh-huh. I wondered what the issue was."

"It was *essential* that I stayed on the trail of the radicals as they moved from one embassy to another. I think if we hadn't broadcast our warning from Algeria, the embassy could have been completely overrun. When the embassy was assaulted with rocket propelled grenades, they were prepared to evacuate and only one person was injured."

"Uh-huh. That reminds me, did we ever get a follow-up with State on the one casualty? It seems she either disappeared into the ether or someone's not talking."

"Sir, we're not going to get anything out of State because, well, she wasn't State Department."

The CEO of the network immediately knew Eastwood was holding back information and a potentially explosive story. "CIA? Uh-huh. Well, that changes things, doesn't it Dory? That would make an interesting story."

Eastwood looked at the man in earnest. "We can't tell it, Sir. Even a hint of a story would expose their cover—I...cannot do it." Eastwood was at a loss for words as anxiety welled in him; he was afraid the boss would demand pursuing the untold story. And if the boss insisted, Eastwood had prepared himself to resign. The threat of resignation wasn't a simple bargaining chip. The CEO took his time and mulled over Eastwood's refusal. "Dory, what do you think would be the best use of your time and effort?"

"Well sir, I think the best use of my efforts is to seek out the important but uncovered stories. Stories like what has happened to the former CIA chief, are al-Qaeda and Iran working together, and *Is Your Neighborhood Mosque a Sleeper Cell*—areas where the reporting is non-existent and partisan claims and counterclaims make it impossible to get to the truth because the most publicized versions of an event are plainly dead wrong."

"Uh-huh. Well, you're talking about taking on media malpractice. We've seen the media heading down a dangerous path to censor or block stories that don't align with their preferred agenda. We're not going to do that."

"But sir, there's a tendency in the media—I have to say those on the other side of the street—to censor or block stories that don't fall in line with the message they want sent to their viewers."

"Agreed. That's really a very dangerous perspective to have."

Eastwood was surprised at the CEO's insight. He shouldn't have been; the man was a genius. "Sir, you're right. It seems that when the media weaves these richly documented tales of injustice it just sends up my bullshit flag. This work is, more or less, tailor made for me. I think

I'm pretty good at exposing their BS."

"Uh-huh. Well, I've always admired your honesty, Dory. I've always respected your view of the situation and assessment of the conditions when we send you into harm's way, as well as your ability to—as you say—expose their BS. Those are your areas of expertise and not mine. If you say we can't discuss the CIA link, then I'll place it 'on ignore' and hope one of these days you'll be able to tell me the rest of the story. I deserve that at least."

"One of these days, Sir, I shall. Thank you."

"Uh-huh. Okay, Dory. I'll hold you to it. A change of subject; have you received any feedback on your *Times*' editorial? Do we know anything on the disappearance of the CIA Director?"

"What I hear from my sources is that he defected and may be dead from a bomb blast in Amman. I hope to have a follow-up report."

"I look forward to reading that."

"It's an odd one. My Agency contacts insist their leadership has closed all discussion on the issue."

The CEO hadn't moved from behind the bar. He plopped his chin in the cusp of a hand and stroked his stubble. "Uh-huh. We may have some shortcomings at times, but unlike the leftist progressive lemmings that dominate the other networks, we're not ever going to expose military or intelligence operations or their people. We've thrived by a code of ethics—not the easiest thing to do in this business. When I started this network, I vowed we wouldn't become a propaganda tool—for any of the political parties—and we're not going to start as long as I'm in charge."

"Sir, it's taken some time to wake the folks up to the lies they've been fed, but I think they're becoming quite aware which networks have been carrying the water of one party and which one has tried to be fair and balanced. Nothing in today's world is so black and white. I think we strike a better balance than any of the other brand Xs."

"Uh-huh. Good show, Dory. Back to Africa. The independent newspaper in Lagos reported that al-Qaeda has taken control of the country's Boko Haram terrorist group. They're probably funding a major part of it when they're not poaching elephant ivory or selling little girls. I'd like to do an exposé; something hard hitting. Build on your special; show that the specter of al-Qaeda and the Brotherhood isn't limited to North Africa and the Middle East. Wake up 'the folks' as you called them, and show the world what's in store for them if they ignore the problem of Islamic extremism. Show them what happens to countries that don't or are unable to control their radicals. Can you do that?"

After affirming and exiting the office, Eastwood stepped from the elevator onto the 27th floor and into the warren of reporter's offices and supporting team member's cubicles. Since he didn't have a television show, he didn't have one of the choice corner offices reserved for those that went in front of the camera five days a week, but his 20'X20' space still had an outstanding view of Times Square. He barked at his secretary and the other members of his reporting team—Marty Marceau, Karl Mann, and his driver Khalid al-Alawaki—to come into the office. One by one, they entered and crowded around the small round table as they waited for Eastwood to join them. Khalid was completely mesmerized with the view below his feet.

"Give your passports to Beth for visas; we're going to Nigeria. They need to be overnighted."

"Flights?" asked the secretary.

"If possible, see if they have a direct flight to Lagos. I don't want to fly through Europe unless we have to. A four-star hotel and a four-wheel drive rental."

The frail woman with the dull silver pixie haircut nodded.

"I don't know how hard it'll be to find out where the airlines stay, where the aircrews stay, but that hotel should be our first choice and priority. Abuja for a couple of days. If you can book them that's fine; if not, we'll deal with it when we get there."

Camera operator Marceau asked, "Boko Haram?"

Eastwood said, "We knew this was coming."

Marceau asked, "Are we really going to jump on a Nigerian jet? Have you any idea what the accident record is for Nigerian air carriers?"

"But they have new airplanes—don't you read the press releases. Besides, it's a little less shaky than the Nigerian princes who keep sending me letters and emails trying to get me to send them money so they can get their gold out of a Nigerian bank." Eastwood sucked in a lungful of air. "No doubt this is going to be one of our more challenging, more dangerous assignments."

Karl Mann, photographer extraordinaire, suggested, "Well, we talked about this before, before we left Algeria. I'm surprised it took the old man this long to pull the trigger. *Machts nichts*, as we discussed before. For this we're going to need night vision and low-light camera equipment. I can get that if we've the budget."

Eastwood interrupted, "Karl, we have the funds, and you need to get enough NVGs for all of us. See if you can get the Gen Threes, panoramic night systems, head straps, extra batteries—the works. Top of the line. And body armor."

Former Libyan contract driver, Khalid al-Alawaki, turned his eyes from the window and watched the men plan for Nigeria. His English was passable and improving, and he was always asking questions. The back-and-forth ping-pong ball discussions didn't make much sense to him and he sought an opening to ask for clarification, "What is this *Broken Harem?*"

Eastwood grinned. He didn't see the value of correcting the man and said, "Terrorists. Sub-Saharan African terrorists."

The man from Libya looked dismayed and said, "Again?"

. . .

The black BMW 750 sparkled in the high sun as it pulled through the narrow sally port and out onto the street. Mechanical arms attached to hydraulic rams closed the heavy wrought iron gates as the vehicle drove away from the dark and foreboding headquarters building of the General Intelligence Department. Armed guards saluted the unmarked vehicle as it approached, while another guard raised the compound entry barrier. They knew who was in the powerful luxury car and rendered the appropriate respect. The long and wide BMW was the car of choice for safety and security. Not a single member of the Royal family or the intelligence community leadership had been killed while riding in one of the specially-armored BMWs.

Major General Faisal Ali Faisal checked his thin gold Armani watch as he headed off the Army post and into downtown Amman. The head of the GID, Jordan's equivalent of the KGB, reported directly to His Majesty and rarely ventured far from the protection of his office building or his home in a heavily guarded compound. Attempts on his life every few months kept him on his toes. He was arrogant and deadly, and he wielded his power with a heavy hand. This was expected of the head of the GID, who was also the head of the Mukhabarat, the dreaded and infamous Jordanian Secret Police.

The big black car pulled in front of the Amman Marriott Hotel and was left idling. Ali Faisal sneered at the doorman as he walked around the vehicle and into the building. He bypassed the X-ray machine and the magnetometer in the antechamber and strode to the elevators. Once inside he inserted a key into the panel of buttons, and the lift raced non-stop to the top floor.

A brawny Jordanian male nurse in a flowing red and white checkered *keffiyeh*, bowed as he opened the door and indicated for the husky gentleman in the business suit to enter. Bruce Rothwell was standing unsteadily as the GID director hurried across the room to greet his old friend from the CIA. "Peace be upon you and the Mercy of Allah and His blessings." Both men leaned forward and lightly cheek-kissed, alternating cheeks, three times and hugged gently—an expression of respect as well as their long and close friendship.

Rothwell, when he ran the CIA's counterintelligence division, routinely bypassed the well-established protocols required by the Jordanian government and dealt directly with the head of the Mukhabarat in order to expedite the process of sharing time-sensitive information or being directly furnished with top-rate intelligence coming from the battlefield. Rothwell was rarely received in the sterile and austere Mukhabarat offices. Ali Faisal usually met with his American counterpart in one of Jordan's luxurious American hotels, mostly for the free food and drink. As was the custom when greeting close friends, Nizar, Rothwell's nurse, offered the men strong Turkish tea. Rothwell recommended the pistachio pastries delivered fresh from the Babiche Patisserie, Amman's best bakery.

Ali Faisal sat quietly as Rothwell was assisted to his chair. Once the nurse had left the room, the two men talked of the old days, of families and friends.

"How can I help you, my friend?" asked Ali Faisal.

Rothwell's hand trembled but his voice was strong. "I would be forever grateful for a little assistance, my friend, my brother."

"All you have to do is ask. I owe you so much."

After an hour, an ashen Ali Faisal returned to the BMW's ice-cold interior and sat quietly for several seconds in stunned silence, incredulous. He glanced back toward the entrance of the hotel as if he were waiting for someone to join him. Before he drove out from under the hotel awning and into the sunlight he said to himself, "You should have died, my brother. What you ask is insanity. Why not just have me attack the Royal family?"

. . .

Transportation Security Officer Kesselring glanced at her smart phone for the latest messages on the online social networking service. She steadied herself as the Lead TSO tapped his watch and gestured for her to go. It was lunchtime and the three female TSA officers were becoming a fixture at the Boar's Head Tavern. The young uniformed women in tight blue *hijab*s, each with a smart phone in her hand, would arrive within seconds of each other. They came from different parts of the concourse—the security checkpoint, downstairs where baggage was screened, sorted and routed to their aircraft, and from upstairs in a small control room holding dozens of surveillance monitors to systematically keep track of and collect information on the behavior of passengers on the concourse. As if choreographed, the women converged on the tiny table in the corner of the semi-enclosed, walk-up-to-order diner. They giggled at the synchronicity of their actions as they met. As if they hadn't seen each other in weeks, the reunion was a joyous and intimate affair. Hugs and cheek kissing presaged the procurement of iced tea and halal sandwiches from the vendor.

When patrolling airport policemen approached with a smile, the three ladies waved and chatted vivaciously. The warm camaraderie was a way to acknowledge they were part of the larger airport security team; they were all there protecting the traveling public from the range of threats that could interfere with safe travel. The older police officers would stop and talk to the three women because they were easy on the eyes. The women waited impatiently for the policemen to leave. The TSA officers were on their lunch break, and they had much to talk about before returning to their posts.

Her work friends teased Kesselring gently when one policeman showed an unusual level of attention and interest. Eboni Whittle was clear, "Abby, he definitely likes you." Amira Mohaned nodded concurrence and unconsciously bit into her lip; she was a little jealous of the attention.

Kesselring wasn't interested in a man or a police officer. She was more interested in the string of messages she'd been following on her cell phone. "This week on Twitter, jihad supporters are discussing young men who quit their studies in America and England to join the jihad in Syria and Libya Islamic State. Have you heard of this?" she asked quietly, as if it were a secret.

"Where have you been, sister? At my mosque there have been many boys who join the jihad. There's much interest in Syria and Libya. They come and they go. I never see them after they leave. They're very brave," said Whittle.

"But no women," admonished Mohaned. She waved her finger to emphasize "no women."

"No women? Are you sure?" Abby was confused and hurt. The

work at the airport was boring, monotonous. The text messages indicated that many students enrolled in universities in the U.S., Britain, Australia, Germany, and elsewhere were leaving school to join the thousands of foreigners who were fighting in Syria. The men looked forward to being in a martyr's brigade.

"Please keep your voice down. And, please tell me you're not thinking of doing *that*?" Mohaned was concerned. The only women she had heard of joining the jihad against the West and the Great Satan became suicide bombers or wives of the jihadis. She was afraid for her friend.

"I want to serve Allah," Kesselring said quietly. She glanced around to ensure no one could hear her. "My imam said Islam isn't in America to be equal to any other faith but to become dominant. The Qur'an should be the highest authority in America, and Islam the only accepted religion on Earth."

The other women nodded fervently. "I've never seen a woman leave for jihad. You must be very brave to think of joining the fight," said Whittle. "Talk with your imam. A decision like that has to be discussed."

The three smart phones on the table began to ring alarms in unison; some GPS synchronization signal kept every cell phone on the correct time, to the second. The lunch break was over and it was time to return to work. The women tapped "an app" to kill their vibrating cell phones and the strident sounds.

"Please don't," begged Mohaned. Whittle seemed to second the entreaty by shaking her head gently.

"I'll talk with my imam. That can't hurt." Kesselring remained upbeat and shunted off the disappointment from her friends. *They should also want to serve Allah. If you aren't serving Allah, then what's the point of Islam?*

Abby Kesselring raced back to the concourse security checkpoint while Eboni Whittle and Amira Mohaned walked off together. Over her shoulder Whittle said, "White girl gonna regret that conversation."

. . .

The DCI stood and raised his hand, affirming he would tell the truth, the whole truth, and nothing but the truth. As the white-haired gentleman from Langley took his seat, admiration, curiosity, and concern adorned the faces of the fifteen senators in the closed door hearing of the Senate Select Committee on Intelligence. There were no sounds from the annoying clicking from digital SLR cameras or the rustling of photographers jockeying for position or onlookers elbowing each other in the visitor's seats. There were no staffers sitting behind their senators, and there were no CIA lawyers or intelligence officers sitting behind the DCI. Greg Lynche sat alone at the long table and read a statement into the record. It was the first time he had testified before Congress.

From their elevated seats, the Democrat members of the committee hectored, lectured, and used their opening remarks to complain about the sorry state of affairs at the CIA, specifically the new polygraph questioning. They acted like angry schoolchildren and sought to lay blame on the new President.

After an hour of vitriol and vituperation from the Democrat members of the committee, the Republican members were afforded a chance to speak. They praised the man at the table for his service to the country and expressed appreciation for his professionalism and leadership, especially at this time of unrest and distrust. After another hour of spirited back and forth dialog, the junior senator from Florida asked the DCI what threshold must be broken before an intelligence officer takes action to collect intelligence on a "person of interest."

"When a person of interest comes to our attention, basically, an intelligence officer working the case makes a decision 'to pursue' and will create a file on that person of interest. What we know is a file was generated on our former President in the eighties when both our embassy and our allies' embassies in Pakistan first photographed and tracked the movements of several foreign students who were attending American universities. They traveled to Afghanistan and Pakistan to partake in what we called 'terrorism tourism.' They travelled on their foreign passports and received visas for entry. Those actions were sufficient for a case officer, in this case, stationed in the U.K., to initiate a file on these persons of interest and start a timeline checklist."

Most members of the committee were riveted to their seat with interest in what Director Lynche had to say. However, half of the Democrat senators had their heads down, childishly playing video games on their smart phones.

"These were generally Muslim men who were supporters of jihad. Some left their universities in the United Kingdom and America to attend terrorist training centers, intending to join the jihad in Afghanistan and fight against the Soviet invasion and occupation. Many hundreds of Brits and AmCits—American Citizens—did this every year. It wasn't something new or odd. We've seen this activity before."

"But not all were interested in going to war against America," barked the short, weaselly, junior senator from New York.

"That's true. *Some* were not so motivated to join the jihad and attended mosque in Pakistan a single time, for example. Others that were interested in joining the jihad repeatedly attended certain mosques where the imams were vociferously anti-American. Analysis of the intelligence, from dispatches from the British embassy to MI5 and MI6 in the President's file, strongly suggested the President met with Osama bin Laden as well as attended a mosque in Pakistan which was noted for its role in screening applicants for jihad and forwarding candidates to the training camps."

Out of order, the senior senator from California interrupted flouting her role as Committee Chair, "When you say 'strongly suggested' are you saying you've no proof?"

"No, Senator, that part of the file was well-supported by photographs, transcripts, and dispatches. I can't reveal the means and the methods, but suffice it to say our allies have the originals. There are dozens of eight by ten glossies of our former President, as a student, bowing before Osama bin Laden, kissing Ayman al-Zawahiri on the cheek, attending the mosque which was the conduit to the al-Qaeda leaders, and so on. The photographic evidence from our allies is extensive. Noteworthy, only some of those photographs were released with the file."

The Republican vice chairman of the committee asked, "Director Lynche, was there any chance the KGB or some other counter-intelligence agency was able to insert fictitious documents or photographs into the MI6 archives?"

"I don't believe so, Senator. Those photographs were date-stamped, cataloged and archived well before the President appeared onto the political scene in the U.S. It's an issue of timing and the chain of custody documents indicate the physical records of our allies haven't been accessed or altered, with the possible exception of his birth certificate."

The junior Republican senator from Texas asked, "Director Lynche, do you have any idea who released the file and why?"

Director Lynche had practiced answering the question. "Senator, my Agency and the FBI are continuing to investigate. If we ever determine who, then we'll probably learn the why."

The Democrat committee chairwoman became nearly mercurial at Lynche's non-answer and spat, "In your view is the person who released that file a traitor or a patriot?"

The Director of Central Intelligence took several seconds before answering. "Senator, if we find him, I believe he'll be considered innocent until proven guilty."

The Senator from California was furious and screeched, "The witness is excused."

CHAPTER TWENTY

McGee sat with his feet and hands lightly on the copilot controls as Hunter taxied the Gulfstream into position on the runway at the Dulles International Airport. "Your jet," Hunter commanded as he ran up the throttles, checked the engine instruments, and held the straining jet with his toes on the brakes.

"My jet!" said a near hyperventilating McGee. He couldn't believe Hunter offered to let him fly the corporate jet from brake release through takeoff. Hunter wasn't concerned with McGee's pilot technique and "rode the flight controls" with a deft touch and pressure on rudder pedals and yoke, as he talked the old SEAL through the process. Once they were airborne and Hunter retracted the landing gear, McGee could no longer feel Hunter's light instructional influence on the controls. He was flying the jet.

Hunter made the appropriate radio calls to Departure Control and ATC, and allowed his friend the joy of controlling the big jet through the sky. Although the airplane had an automatic trim feature, occasionally Hunter would use the trim button on the yoke to fine tune the pressure McGee felt on the flight controls as they climbed to their assigned cruising altitude. As the Gulfstream approached their level-off altitude Hunter said, "My jet."

A life-long SEAL with no formal flight training, McGee had watched Hunter and Lynche coordinate the flying duties in the company's Gulfstream or Lynche's Cessna Skymaster. He knew how to accept command of the aircraft and to relinquish the flight controls. "Your jet," said McGee as he took his hands off the yoke and raised them in front of him to prove he was "free and clear" of the yoke and his feet were off of the rudder pedals.

Hunter engaged the autopilot, disconnected his radio headset with boom mic, and motioned for McGee to do the same. He ensured all cockpit microphones were disconnected. After turning up the cockpit radio speaker to monitor the FAA air traffic controllers, Hunter began a classified discussion. "What we're going to do tonight is get you snapped in on the *Wraith's* sensors: FLIR, laser designator, and the gun. Our mission is to "ops check" the gun. It's a laser-designated, .70 caliber rifle, the product of a pair of TS programs from the Science and Technology laboratories."

"S&T? Seriously?" McGee's raised eyebrows and grin suggested he was surprised and impressed that the CIA would allow a contractor to not only have access to top-secret weaponry but would authorize its employment.

Hunter understood McGee's confusion. "Yes, sir. They kinda had to give me the system if I was going to do the work."

The man of very few words nodded. "I'm not familiar with any recent systems—I've been out of the business for so long and when you're out of pocket you never have a need to know. When I was active duty I knew everything and I trained on everything." As Hunter nodded in acknowledgement, McGee said, "But I do know seventy caliber ammo is, uh, *illegal*."

"The goal was to develop a very long range sniper rifle using special purpose ammunition. The bullet has a seeker head, just like a missile on a jet, which, I'm told, would provide a probability of kill of 98% out to three miles. Even I can't miss."

McGee was suspect of the effectiveness claim. Hunter anticipated the skepticism of the professional marksman; he said, "It's closer to 100% effective as long as you're inside three miles and keep the pipper on the target. It's not 'fire and forget' ammo. It has a few quirks; it always hits a little up and right."

"That's stunning accuracy."

"I know—from an airplane! Amazing stuff." Hunter explained the gun was the product of the Intelligence Advanced Research Projects

Activity, a research entity under the Director of National Intelligence. IARPA challenged industry to come up with a long-range weapon to kill vehicles by splitting the engine block or breaking an axle, hence the super-large caliber. The main challenge was designing a seeker head into the nose of a bullet.

When a round was fired by a conventional powder cartridge the bullet's seeker head was subjected to over 1,000 Gs and the failure rate was nearly 100 percent. Agency researchers determined through experimentation that a hybrid propellant source, a two-stage cartridge of black powder and a tiny solid rocket booster, eliminated the severity of the G-load on the electronics in the bullet's seeker head. The two-stage strategy decreased the G-force to a level that didn't destroy the circuitry. A very small, slow-burning conventional black powder charge would push the bullet out of the barrel and light off the solid rocket motor that used the same chemical compound as the Space Shuttle's solid rocket boosters. A very gentle twist of the barrel's rifling provided the initial stability for the bullet's flight; then tiny triangular fins popped out of the four-inch long projectile when it was free of the barrel. At that point it was no longer a ballistic projectile but a guided missile which "flew" to a laser-designated aiming point.

McGee said, "I heard they tried to develop such a system. Never expected it to be given to anyone to put on an airplane."

"I'll give you three shots at varying distances to snap you in. I'll start at one and a half miles and then we'll work our way out."

"Sounds great." McGee wanted to fly the aircraft some more.

The two men settled in their seats as Hunter plugged his headphones in and exchanged a series of radio calls between Houston Center and the FBO in Fredericksburg.

"We'll take the Hummer."

"Which is *repaired*, I want you to know." The men grinned broadly.

"Thank you, sir; I forgot all about that. Anyway, we'll take the *repaired* Hummer to a remote field near Del Rio. We'll drive through Uvalde, the site of the National Gliding Championships. They get hundreds of sailplanes through there so our long narrow trailer, which obviously holds a sailplane, won't even raise an eyebrow as we pass through town. You haven't met Bob and Bob. They're the support crew for the YO-3A. It'll be just the four of us."

Hunter detailed the long relationship he and Lynche had with the former Vietnam veterans who had been the mechanics and crew chiefs for the small fleet of U.S. Army YO-3As in Vietnam. One Bob was taller than the other Bob and sported shoulder-length gray hair. The shorter Bob was heavier, bald, and had a long scraggly grey beard. "They're in their seventies and, really, for the past 15-16 years, they've maintained the *Wraith* in better than new condition. It's going to be a sad day when one or both of them tell me they've had enough. They roll the aircraft out of her container and put her together. They hook up everything—fuel lines and all the electricals are quick disconnects, and the flight controls are connected with bolts and pins in clevises. Then they tape the seams; it's a sight to behold. They're very fast but the last couple of times, I can tell they're beginning to slow down. It's obvious they're not getting any younger."

"Did you say taped? I don't remember seeing any tape."

"Yes, sir. Once it's all bolted together and all the connections hooked up, then they tape all the seams to ensure the airplane doesn't whistle when it's airborne. While they're doing that, I'll drop a few IR chem-lites on one side of the runway, put up a target at the end for you to shoot at, and drop a few more chem-lites on the way back. Then we'll get into the airplane and prepare to launch. You're familiar with the parachute harness; it's no different than the one we used for our night jump. I'll fire up the engine and we'll be airborne in under a minute."

"Seriously?"

"Or less. If the engine doesn't fire off, we abort. If the engine quits on takeoff, we abort—I'll put it back on the runway. If the engine quits after takeoff, I'll see about turning it around and landing on the downwind. If we have an emergency, I'll tell you to bail out. I'll jettison the canopy and you go first—dive over the trailing edge of the wing. You go left, I'll go right. The parachutes are black competition ram-air canopies, just like the chutes we used a few days ago. NGVs on our helmets; just like a couple of nights ago."

"We used to pack our own chutes. And reserves."

"I can see SEALs doing that. I don't have the time; I've an FAA-certified parachute rigger that inspects all of them."

"You were doing this when we were at the war college?"

"Not exactly. I really was just a student."

"Why were you there, really? You never told me."

For the next two hours, Hunter told McGee what he and Greg Lynche did for the Central Intelligence Agency. McGee reciprocated and told Hunter about some of his more entertaining "exploits," such as boarding vessels at sea, hostage-rescue situations, and killing the enemies of America, primarily communists and Islamists. As McGee was enjoying the view from the cockpit and the aircraft was on final approach into the small county airport, Hunter said, "Rothwell's not dead."

McGee's head snapped around. "That's not good."

"No. It's not."

"He'll be pissed off. I know I would be."

. . .

Two vehicles, one pulling a sailplane trailer, exited the town of Uvalde on Highway 90, heading west. Hunter contacted Bob and Bob in the trailing crew cab pickup truck on a handheld radio over a discrete encrypted frequency and briefed the mission. The two septuagenarians recalled they had done this run once before, a year ago; same mission, same sense of urgency, same ingress and egress procedures. Nothing new except this time there was someone new in the backseat. And he was a monster.

The moon was nearly full which did nothing to calm Hunter's emotions as he pulled up to a heavy gate; a sign mounted on the fence announced: U.S. Government Property, U.S. Air Force Auxiliary Field Spofford, No Trespassing. Hunter flicked a couple of switches which killed the tail and brake lights. McGee watched in amazement as Hunter jumped out of the Hummer2 and wrestled with the huge chain with multiple ancient locks securing the gate to a telephone pole-sized mounting post.

It's better to beg for forgiveness than to ask permission. A year had passed since Hunter had last accessed the combination locks used by the U.S. Border Patrol to gain access to ranches as they pursued illegal aliens across private property. The mission hinged on getting onto the auxiliary field and not being discovered breaking and entering. Two large Master locks linked the hefty chain together in a way the ranchers could unlock one to gain entrance or the Border Patrol could unlock the other to do the same. Hunter ignored the US Government lock and chose the burly antique lock with U.S.B.P. stamped on the side. As he rotated the thumbwheels he bet the Border Patrol had never changed the combinations of the thousands of locks which hung on thousands of ranch gates in the Del Rio sector. As an aviation historian, he could never forget—2-7-0-7—the designation of the old Boeing Super Sonic Transport design. He always thought it was a given not a single Border Patrol agent had ever heard of a Boeing SST.

He pulled at the shackle and the lock unlatched easily. He swung the gate wide allowing Bob and Bob to drive the pickup and trailer onto the property. McGee drove the Hummer past the gate as Hunter closed and locked it behind them. Bob and Bob had turned hard right and stopped. They jumped from their truck and began to extract the YO-3A from its container. They worked furiously to install the wings, put a little gas in the tanks, and perform a functional check of the flight controls.

Hunter directed McGee to drive along one edge of the runway as he dropped chem-lites every 200 feet until they reached the "1 board" signifying the first 1,000 feet of the runway. McGee raced the Hummer to the far end of the runway; he noticed the greatly muffled engine exhaust of the Corvette motor. It was virtually silent. He looked at Hunter who seemed to have read his mind; Duncan pointed at a bank of switches. McGee knew SEALs wore the new generation of a wearable sound-cancelling system for shooting silently in close quarters; he never expected to see a similar system on a vehicle the size of the Hummer.

At the end of the runway, Duncan slid out of the truck and set up a full scale silhouette target of a man; three large holes the size of a weightlifter's thumb were grouped near the left shoulder, the results of Hunter's initial gun trial of a year ago. On the return trip on the other side of the runway, Hunter dropped more chem-lites. They were nearly ready to go flying.

Working with the practiced choreography of a NASCAR pit crew, Bob and Bob had attached the aircraft's wings, hooked up the fuel lines and flight controls, and installed black speed tape over the joints that were known to make noise at slow speeds. Hunter bounded out of the Hummer and raced up and onto the wing. He leaned into the aft cockpit and loaded the gun with three rounds. McGee finished connecting his parachute before he crawled into the aft cockpit.

Just as Bob and Bob finished taping the last of the aircraft's exposed seams, McGee and Hunter climbed into their seats and pulled on their night vision goggle-equipped helmets. Hunter flipped the YO-3A's battery switch and started the engine. The Continental 360 was eerily quiet to McGee. He felt a strong vibration in his seat from the engine torque against its engine mounts but there wasn't the expected 150 decibel sound of engine exhaust. The YO-3A's exhaust gases were diffused through two large conformal mufflers—from 1960 Buick Electras—that ran along the fuselage. In the noise suppression headset, McGee could hear himself breathe but couldn't hear the engine exhaust.

For this mission, Bob and Bob had installed the stubby low-profile, three-bladed wooden propeller, another top secret design. Hunter told McGee to watch his hands as he lowered the canopy. The men flipped night vision goggles over their eyes, and Hunter checked the flight controls to ensure they were hooked up properly. In the NVGs, the runway was clearly outlined by the chem-lites. He jammed the throttle to take-off power. McGee noticed that what Duncan called the "1 board" came very quickly, then with a slight backpressure of the control stick, they were airborne. He was surprised the aircraft weathervaned into the wind as it tracked down the runway. He realized why Hunter had dropped the chem-lites. The nose of the tail-wheel airplane was cocked up and obstructed the view of the end of the runway; the chem-lites showed them where they were on the runway.

Hunter retracted the landing gear, energized the FLIR and lowered it into the airstream, and scouted the area for Border Patrol vehicles. A couple of vehicles on Highway 90 disappeared off in the distance. He and McGee spoke in spurts as they silently zoomed to 1,000 feet above ground level. Hunter turned toward the auxiliary field and announced he had selected GUN on the multi-function display panel. McGee could feel the gun assembly unlock and then rotate out from the lower confines of the fuselage; another faint shudder in the airframe indicated the gun was locked into place under the belly of the YO-3A. A position light on the MFD confirmed it was "down and locked." Targeting symbology overlaid on the FLIR image was displayed on the MFD. Initially, it was all a bit overwhelming for McGee, but at the same time, the displays were intuitive. His job was to acquire the appropriate targeting "sight picture" and shoot. Hunter's brief began to make sense.

"Gun coming hot," announced Hunter.

"Roger, gun hot." McGee focused so intently on the MFD he didn't blink.

McGee was mesmerized by the quality of the thermal imagery. Hunter selected Gun Master Switch and called "hot" in the microphone. The shorter Bob answered, "Roger" into the handheld radio as both men on the ground slid into the armored Hummer and closed the doors. Even a mile away from the silhouette, Hunter wanted the Bobs protected from any ricochets.

"Okay, Bullfrog. You can slew the barrel left or right with the controller. I found it's better if I steer the airplane and point it with the gun, so that the airframe and the gun point at the target as I close on it. With you as the shooter, all I have to do is fly the airplane. You can point and shoot. Shots ahead work well; shots abeam aren't very effective. You see the silhouette?"

"Tally ho."

"Your gun, sir. I'll give you range."

McGee moved the joystick control left and right to discern the feel of the electro-mechanical targeting system and watched as the barrel programmed left, then right. He placed the crosshairs of the targeting system center mass on the silhouette. Hunter called out the range to the target. "1,000 feet of altitude, coming up on 1.4 miles. 1.3. 1.2. 1.1. Your target!" Hunter illuminated the target with the laser designator, "tagging" the target as the computer software computed the firing solution onto the established laser "tag" on the silhouette and fed the information wirelessly into the electronics of the bullet head.

"Fire in the hole!" McGee depressed the trigger switch on the control stick as the rifle underneath his seat bucked and spat out a round. Two green circles appeared on the thermal image as the bullet's projected flight path made constantly computed and incrementally finer corrections. The circles decreased in size while increasing in intensity as the firing point solution intersected with the "tagged" laser spot and locked onto the target. When all the software algorithms were satisfied, less than a millisecond after McGee squeezed the trigger, the gun fired automatically. As the projectile left the muzzle of the barrel, the FLIR display of grey and whites "washed out" as a momentary white screen, but quickly recovered and displayed the real-time thermal images as the aircraft flew through the hot gases of the propellant charge.

Hunter urged, "Keep the pipper on the target." The integrated intelligent tracking scope mounted atop the rifle relayed sight-picture data into the multifunction display, overlaying the FLIR and the targeting images.

The delay after pulling the trigger, the lack of recoil, and muzzle flash surprised McGee. He was so accustomed to the instantaneous recoil of a full trigger squeeze of a rifle that a thought of a misfire flashed in his head. However, within a blink of his eyes, McGee was

257

startled by the firing and the flight of the bullet as the FLIR traced the white-hot round into the silhouette.

The round struck the silhouette up and to the right, just slightly off center of the tagged aiming point. McGee shook his head in disbelief at the incredibly fast and exhilarating display of technology just as Hunter announced, "We're setting up for a two-mile run. I'll give you a half-mile buffer."

"Roger. That was very cool!" McGee was dazzled that the system was much more accurate than he had envisioned or imagined. His mind wandered a bit with a quick thought. *What could a system like this could do for a sniper in the field; could a SEAL hit targets at three miles without missing?*

"I know. High coolness factor." Hunter turned the aircraft hard to the right, checked for the thermal signatures of vehicles in the FLIR, zoomed in for greater definition, and then turned right again to set up for the next gun run.

The runs at two and three miles were made with similar results. At two miles McGee aimed more left and a little lower. The bullet struck the silhouette between the shoulders where a human's heart would be. At three miles, McGee placed the tagged aiming point closer to the silhouette's left ear and the impact point was within two inches of the laser-tagged spot. The bullet blew a thumb-sized hole between the silhouette's imaginary ears and eyes. Hunter rolled a thumbwheel on his throttle quadrant to zoom in on the FLIR image. The gyroscopically stabilized picture was clear and steady.

"I call that a kill. Nice shot. Ready to head back?"

"I am. That's an incredible system, Duncan."

"Now the fun part."

"Fun part?"

"Getting down and getting off the field. We made a lot of noise. Even out here among exotic animal ranches, nobody's supposed to be shooting at night, so we have to hurry." Hunter turned off the autopilot and turned back toward the airfield. He selected the gun to STOW and began to search for signs of vehicles in the FLIR. Nothing hot popped up in the thermal sensor; no vehicles, no illegal aliens, no ibex, or kudu, or white tail deer. He stowed the FLIR as McGee enjoyed the clear nighttime view from the backseat.

"If I thought we had the time I'd program the airplane to land hands-off by activating the automatic takeoff and landing system, but I really want to get down ASAP and get out here," said Hunter.

"I'm along for the ride."

"I hope I don't scare you."

"I've seen you drive and you're not all that scary."

Hunter headed to the field and to expedite his decent pulled the throttle to idle and cross-controlled the flight controls—full right rudder deflection with full left control stick deflection. In this slip, the glider-like YO-3A uncharacteristically dropped from the sky like a stone. McGee was pushed to the side of the cockpit by the awkward flight mode; he thought they were going to crash. At twenty feet of altitude Hunter centered the flight controls, lowered the gear, and touched down well down the runway. The Bobs' support vehicles and trailer were dead ahead.

"Okay, I lied, *that* scared the crap out of me."

Hunter coughed as he laughed.

Five minutes after the engine was shut down, Bob, Bob, and Hunter pushed the airplane into its container. McGee drove up and down the runway to retrieve the chem-lites and the target silhouette before they departed the airfield. Hunter closed the gate, latched the shackle, and jumped into the Hummer. He pushed a bank of switches and brake lights came on and the mighty rumbling of the Corvette race motor mysteriously reappeared. A right turn onto the highway and he floored the pedal shattering the night with the sound of all four tires spinning on the Hummer2. The men laughed like kids at a carnival and bumped fists. McGee beamed, "Gotta love it when a plan comes together!"

. . .

The men were on their knees on dark prayer mats in twenty rows. The women were always at the rear of the mosque. They waited for the Call to Prayer to fade. The congregation was oriented in the direction of Mecca, specifically toward the Kaabah. When the imam stood, the congregation stood. When the imam ascended the *minbar* and raised his hands, the congregation raised their hands in supplication. The mosque reverberated when the congregation said, "*Allahu Akbar.*"

Men and women folded their hands over their chests while staring straight ahead, trancelike. The congregation recited the first chapter of the Qur'an. When they finished they uncrossed their hands and again said, "*Allahu Akbar.*"

After coming to a sitting position, after all the *rak'as* were completed, the congregation recited the second part of the Tashahhud. When they were done, each man and woman turned to his or her right and said, "*Assalamu'Alaykum Wa Rahmatullah Wa Barakatuh.*" *Peace be unto you and so may the mercy of Allah and His blessings.* Abby Kesselring, along with two hundred followers in the congregation, inhaled deeply and whispered, "*Allahu Akbar.*"

The imam stood in the *minbar* and preached for an hour. Abby Kesselring was energized when he said, "Anyone who works to raise awareness about our work or is willing to help with our work in Africa and Iraq and Syria is a jihadist for Allah. Every single one of you who gives any kind of support to help his brothers in Egypt or Sudan or Libya is a jihadist for Allah. Every single one of you who spreads the word to raise the awareness among the others about what's happening in the Muslim world is a jihadist for Allah. Those who subject themselves to martyrdom for the sake of God and who defend themselves and their families, not only those who are performing the jihad, but every single Muslim who has sympathy toward what happens in Islam is a jihadist for Allah. *Allahu Akbar!*"

Kesselring was transfixed with the imam, his presence, his words—the word of Allah. When the imam asked, "Now, these crusaders, that is the Christians, are they infidels?" She joined with the congregation's raucous, "*Infidels!*"

"Infidels are attacking all of Islam. I thank Allah the Iranian government was able to legitimize their nuclear program to the world." The grey bearded imam continued, "The agreement will ensure there will continue to be very big strides in their technical progress. The enrichment rights of the Iranian nation are now acknowledged by the world powers. The agreement is a rejection of those *arrogant* regimes, and we know who they are, those who had tried to deny them. We join together, brothers in arms, for the full elimination of the *arrogant* powers and the destruction of the *arrogant* regimes!"

"Islam uplifts the Muslims and debases the non-Muslims." The imam raised one hand, which was symbolic of Islam, and lowered his other, which was symbolic of non-Islam to drive home the point to the audience. The sheikh continued his harangue and affirmed that some non-Muslims have "rights" under Islam. He called on the men and women "never show any love for Christians, even if they're your neighbors."

"Always recall, when infidels encourage us to treat each other as 'brothers and sisters' and say 'we must live as one nation,' regardless of religion—always recall these are poisonous and treacherous words. These teachings contradict the Sharia."

When the sheikh finished he stepped gingerly down the steep stairs of the *minbar* he turned to the congregation and said, "*Assalamualaikum Wa Rahmatullah.* The two hundred-strong congregation intoned, "*Allahu Akbar.*"

Kesselring waited in the back of the mosque until it was permitted to approach and speak to the imam.

"Honorable Sheikh, I understand young men have quit their studies in Europe to join the jihad in Africa and Syria and Libya."

He nodded toward his office and stepped off, leaving Abby to follow. Once they entered the cigarette-smoke filled room, she closed the door as directed and waited for the man to speak.

"You've heard of this?" the imam asked with surprise.

"I have, my Sheikh. I would like to join the jihad."

The imam pulled at his beard and looked dispassionately at the young convert. There was fire was in her eyes, and she displayed the expected fervor of a budding martyr who would submit and subject herself for Allah. Her anxiety grew with every passing second as he studied her. The thought of controlling the woman, making her submit, made him grow hard. He stroked his beard and considered the possibilities.

The imam thought introspectively for what seemed like an interminable time for Kesselring. When he finally spoke he said, "There are roles for young women *here* to perform the jihad."

She was confused. "Jihad, here in America? Honorable Sheikh, I do not understand."

He continued to stroke his beard. He was so pleased with himself. After several seconds he answered. "My dear, do you know how to hide a weapon in baggage? That which must pass through your machine?" The imam smiled broadly showing foul teeth through a mess of his beard.

The confines of the imam's office suddenly closed in on her. She felt her heart slam in her chest and could hear her blood race through her ears. Abby was no longer confused. She understood how one could perform jihad in America. She was excited as she nodded with a thin smile. "*Allah is very Akbar,*" she cooed.

. . .

The telephone call came through at the designated time; a frail hand lifted the receiver and brought it to his remaining ear. Bruce Rothwell didn't speak and didn't move. He hated to acknowledge the surveillance placed on Nazy Cunningham had failed and the watchers were in custody. Their mosque was now under investigation and surveillance. The voice in the receiver said the woman hadn't returned to her house, and the other possible locations all appeared to be deserted, all except the one on the hill. After a minute Rothwell said, "That's the one," and replaced the handset. He sat contemplating what he had heard and what he had encouraged. He spoke just above a whisper, "Nizar."

The adipose nurse expected to be summoned at a moment's notice and hovered nearby in the adjacent room. He responded in a trice, bowed, and waited for the command.

"My book. And more juice and sweets."

The Jordanian spun and left the sunroom. He returned with an electronic notebook. He held it front of the man with one eye and released it when Rothwell could demonstrate he had a firm grip. As Rothwell touched and swept his fingers over the sensitive pad, touching a sequence of numbers to unlock the computer, Nizar brought a tray of pistachio-covered pastries and a carafe of orange juice. The Amman Marriott featured navel oranges for their many western visitors and *jaffas* for the locals. Rothwell had made it clear he preferred the sweet and fine *jaffas,* freshly squeezed at room temperature, over the bitter navel oranges. Nizar maintained a large bag of *jaffas* in the suite's kitchen. He was forever squeezing dozens of the small oranges to fill the carafe.

Rothwell nibbled on the nut-covered snack and drained his juice as he logged in to the world's largest on-line auction website. He located the individual auction he was looking for and selected the option to "Ask Seller a Question." When he reached the appropriate page, he awkwardly typed, "can you ship immediately anjam." He repeated the process with other auctions in the U.S.

Al-Qaeda and the Muslim Brotherhood were continually seeking ways to communicate with members of their networks while avoiding the scrutiny of the CIA and the NSA. The use of on-line chat rooms kept intelligence community analysts on their toes, but it soon became apparent to the CIA and NSA analysts that all the chatter in the chat rooms was an orchestrated disinformation campaign. The use of public on-line auctions to pass coded information was the brainchild of the former DCI. He started using the on-line auctions after an NSA cryptoanalyst had complained bitterly about their inability to close the unmonitored on-line auction's communication system between buyers and sellers.

Nizar took the electronic notebook and slipped it under his arm while he helped his master to his feet. Rothwell lifted the white *dishdasha* and adjusted the belt on his trousers. He realized he had lost so much weight that his clothes had been falling off him, although his strength was quickly returning.

Rothwell leaned on Nizar with his only arm and shuffled painfully as the two men made their way to the bedroom. The nurse detached Rothwell's *keffiyeh* and *dishdasha*. He helped his employer onto the bed, hooked up the IV port in Rothwell's hand, and started the flow of fluids and drugs into the man. Once he closed the bedroom door, Nizar raced out of the hotel and into the marketplace for more tins of pistachio pastries and more *jaffas*.

CHAPTER TWENTY-ONE

A line of black Suburbans passed single file through the heavy wrought-iron gate and drove into the barn. A minute later three women emerged from the side of the old wooden building carrying long aluminum pans, boxes, and grocery bags. The chief of security led the women into the safe house and barked orders as she sat down the large food pan she had been carrying. "All hands on deck! Muster! Kitchen table! Move it, move it!" The old Marine drill instructor in Anna Comstock was on full display when she was on a time sensitive schedule. Instead of herding Marine recruits to chow she "mustered" her lollygagging civilians for the evening brief and assignments. She had a long drive ahead and wanted to be home in her bed before midnight.

Nazy and Kelly turned and looked at each other rolling their eyes at the directive, but they complied. Nazy jumped from her workstation as soon as the computer screens closed down. She logged off her computer while Horne checked the bank of monitors for any movement outside the safe house. They hurried up the stairs and gathered around the kitchen table to wait for "the word."

By the time the women reached the kitchen, Comstock had ripped the cover off the pan of hot food. The rich and spicy aroma of pulled-pork barbeque filled the room. Plastic containers of potato salad and coleslaw were opened, and paper plates were passed around. The women helped themselves to the night's offerings.

Anna Comstock said, "Listen up. I thought we might be getting out of here, but that's not going to happen for a few more days, I'm afraid. I've good news for some of you; we've some ladies that need to get on the road for their follow-on assignments. More on that in a minute." Comstock nodded at Nazy and said, "The FBI hasn't fully closed your case—they report that there's still some unusual activity on the streets of Miss Cunningham's neighborhood. They won't recommend termination until they're certain all surveillance activities have been eliminated."

The six women around the table nodded; Nazy and Kelly exchanged glances and faint smiles. Since Horne's revelation about her father, they had become somewhat inseparable. Some of the women in the detail cattily suggested Horne had crawled into the bed of the CIA executive, and they were now bosom buddies. They strained to find hints of impropriety or fraternization between Nazy and Kelly Horne, but had given up their quest as nothing the women did could be construed as improper or overly familiar.

"Horne and Gabriel," barked Anna Comstock, "pack your trash and be ready to move out. Your follow-on assignments were signed off by the DCI, and you have jets to catch in the next couple of days. You've visas and shots and briefings and, well, you'll be busy until you hit the airport. Thirty minutes and we're out of here. Questions?"

"Do you know where we're going, Anna?" asked the intelligence officer Gabriel.

"Africa. You're going to Luanda—I think that's how you say it. Communist Angola. Horne, you're going to Nigeria. Not communist but I hear they have a Muslim problem. Haven't been to either of those places; you remember you signed up for a life of adventure. It'll be exciting. Horne, I understand you'll be doing a lot of that flying stuff that scares the crap out of me."

Kelly had expected orders, but not so soon, and she hadn't expected Comstock to know where she was going or what she'd be doing. She chided herself for being naïve; of course the tentacles of the Agency's security department were everywhere, and there was little the big busty woman from Little River, South Carolina didn't know. Kelly wasn't ready to leave the safe house or Nazy's side. Those that came to *Spindletop* never wanted to leave.

Nazy walked across the room and placed her hand on Kelly's; she sensed Kelly's shock and didn't want Kelly to dwell on bad news. She knew from experience it was unhealthy to fixate on the negative. It was better to be distracted with something positive rather than allow oneself to tumble down a rabbit's hole of misery. Nazy interrupted Anna's monologue and gestured to the other women to be quiet then asked, "Kelly, could you bless this meal?"

The women around the table were initially startled but recovered quickly and tacitly agreed. They held hands with one another and lowered their heads as Kelly Horne reluctantly offered, "Bless us, Oh Lord, and these gifts which we're about to receive. We look at the food that has been prepared by loving hands, we look into the faces of those that love us and whom we love. We thank you as you bless this food and bless this time we've had together. Amen." Kelly raised her head and thanked Nazy with a nod.

"That was beautifully done. Thank you, Kelly," said Nazy. Others around the table agreed.

After a quiet start to dinner, the irascible Comstock jumped back into her spiel. "Okay, we'll be down two sets of eyeballs for the night; that means a reshuffling of the watch schedule until reinforcements arrive tomorrow. We still have the quick reaction security force at the bottom of the hill if we need augmentation. They're all young, good-looking studs, and since y'all are young, good-looking babes, well, it just wouldn't be prudent for me to mix such a combustible combination. Too many distractions, if you know what I mean; and I know you do. So, Miss Cunningham, I don't think you need anyone in your room anymore; it's a luxury we can't afford. Horne and Gabriel, you ready to go?"

The four remaining women of the security detail took up their posts; two in the basement bunker to monitor cameras and alarms and two upstairs to provide physical security as needed. Nazy thoughtfully hugged Anna Comstock before the security chief chugged out the door like a steam locomotive leaving the roundhouse. Nazy hugged the intelligence officer, Gabriel, and told her, "Thank you" as the young officer departed *Spindletop*, a pack on her back and a weapon at her side. Then Nazy hugged the intelligence officer, Kelly Horne, long and hard. They had already promised to stay in touch and would notify each other if Duncan ever said anything about having a daughter. The fact that they already knew would be their little secret.

The ride down the mountain was made in abject fear. Anna Comstock drove the big black Suburban well past the edge of comfort for the young intelligence officers; both women exhaled sighs of relief when the road leveled out. Comstock accelerated down the Interstate 81 on-ramp heading east. After ninety minutes of listening half-heartedly to Comstock's words of wisdom on the secret of how young women can succeed in the Agency, Kelly felt her BlackBerry vibrate. She opened the screen to see she had received a text message: "If Duncan is going to have another woman in his life, I thank God it is you. Love, Nazy."

As a black Suburban was waved through the CIA security checkpoint and approached the New Headquarters Building, seismic sensors at the base of the mountain of *Spindletop* triggered alarms in the basement of the Bunker.

· · ·

The two-hour drive out of the concrete forests of Manhattan skyscrapers to the rolling hills of Connecticut's farmland was easier than the two men could believe. Traffic was abnormally light even for the late hour, and try as they might, they couldn't discern if another vehicle was following them. When he wasn't checking the traffic in the outside mirror, Dory Eastwood continually looked over his shoulder. He let his guard down incrementally and relaxed as he surmised that no one had followed them out of New York City; he turned to his driver and said, "Khalid, I don't think we're being followed."

"Yes. No cars follow."

Khalid al-Alawaki pulled off the interstate highway and headed north to Eastwood's home so his boss could pick up fresh clothes, check on his house, and stop the mail. He checked his mirrors before taking the exit; he was confident there had been no surveillance trailing the big black truck. As a long time professional taxi driver in Libya, he had been tailed several times by government agents during Qaddafi's reign and learned quickly how to shake off surveillance and hide if necessary.

Eastwood found Khalid to be a man of many talents; he had proved to be an excellent driver in the most hostile conditions when they journeyed across Libya, Tunisia, and into Algeria. He had an uncanny ability to foresee trouble and steer around it. After terrorists killed the American ambassador Eastwood had hired the thin dark man to drive his video crew from Tripoli to Benghazi.

Shortly after arriving at the burned-out consulate building, Eastwood and his crew found something that they never expected to find, a large flag draped over a compound wall. The flag was bright green, the color of Islam. Neatly centered in the flag were two crossed swords bracketing a Qur'an. At the bottom of the flag were white Arabic letters. Eastwood couldn't read Arabic, but he knew what they spelled out. *Strike terror into the enemies of Allah!* The flag wasn't the flag of al-Qaeda but of the Muslim Brotherhood.

As Khalid drove Eastwood and the video crew across North Africa, the war correspondent observed and reported on the strange movement of men on a decrepit bus as they followed it from Tripoli to Tunis and Algiers. Each time the bus stopped, it was at a mosque adjacent to or near the semi-restricted areas dedicated to foreign embassies, known the world over as "Embassy Row." The men would spend the night in the mosque, and then a few hours before daybreak they would pour out of the mosque and organize into groups of protesters. Others with AK-47s and rocket-propelled grenades would assault the American Embassy. When Khalid volunteered to go into the mosques to determine what the "bus men" were doing and planning, Eastwood was convinced the man from Libya wasn't a typical Arab.

Khalid proved his worth gathering intelligence, which helped

Eastwood broadcast a warning to his New York network, transmitting video of the impending assault force on the embassy in Algiers. In addition, when it came time to evacuate embassy personnel, Eastwood facilitated the passage of a new crew member, Khalid al-Alawaki, onto a U.S. Navy helicopter. For his services to protect Americans, Khalid was given U.S. citizenship and work as a taxi driver in New York City. Eastwood and the network leaders knew a man of Khalid's talents could be useful whenever Eastwood and the crew travelled to Arabic speaking countries.

Now he followed the directions of the GPS and asked Eastwood "if the machine was correct." Hunter's Tahoe was fully equipped with all of the options expected of a corporate executive's personal armored vehicle, including satellite radio, and Eastwood kept them entertained listening to Oldies on the 50s, 60s, and 70s channels. Khalid reveled in hearing the old songs he remembered singing when he was a young man in Tripoli. His father worked at the old Wheelus Air Force Base before Qaddafi shut down the American air facility and the Islamists shut down the radio stations that played the decadent American rock and roll music.

Khalid loved the sturdiness and firmness of the heavy truck while Eastwood loved the feel of security of the big Chevy. On the drive from Washington, DC to New York City, Khalid complained the truck got 'velly' bad gas mileage due to the supercharged motor and the additional ton of armor plating encapsulating the driver and passenger compartments. Thick bulletproof glass and ballistics-grade ceramics surrounded the vehicle. A savvy terrorist might recognize the subtle differences between a factory Tahoe and one which had been through Hunter's shop in Texas. Eastwood recalled Bill McGee's words of wisdom, "Fortunately there are very few truly savvy terrorists anymore; and we need to kill those that are trying to become a little savvier."

Never before had the trip from the network headquarters in New York City to his house near Lime Rock seemed so quick. Eastwood credited their record time to being distracted by looking for surveillance as well as listening to the old music. As Khalid pulled into the town's main intersection—left to Eastwood's house, right to the world-famous race track—Eastwood said, "One of these days I'm going to go to a race there."

"Racing? NASCAR?" inquired the always inquisitive Khalid, as he followed the GPS and turned onto Well Hills Road.

"I don't think so—more like a Formula 1 and Grand Touring course, if that makes any sense. I've a friend that raced an old Corvette out there. He told me, 'Behind every great Corvette is a Jaguar, a Porsche, and a Ferrari.' Or some such bullshit." Eastwood laughed at the skilled witticism but Khalid didn't understand the *double entendre*. Eastwood tried to explain the meaning but had to stop and give directions as they approached the driveway to his house. The mailbox at the end of the driveway marked the way. The woman's voice from the GPS claimed, "You are at your destination."

A mailbox and the face of a dirty white car appeared in the headlights on the left side of the roadway. As Eastwood looked at the dull vehicle with curiosity, Khalid braked the Tahoe and asked, "Is that your car?"

As the truck closed the distance to the driveway, Eastwood noticed an orange card attached to the driver's door handle. He had seen similar bright orange tickets on abandoned or disabled vehicles. Police or sheriff departments identified broken down automobiles with the tags and gave the owners a date by which they would have to move their car; otherwise, that vehicle would soon be taking a ride hooked to the back of a tow truck to an unlovely auto pound. "No—it's broke down. Orange ticket means the car is disabled, and the owner has to move it soon."

Eastwood's eyes were riveted on the vehicle as Khalid slowly pulled off the asphalt, sweeping the bright lights across the face of the car as they turned left onto the drive. Eastwood turned in his seat to get another view of the disabled vehicle, but it was lost in the moon-free darkness. He didn't find it odd to see a vehicle broken down along the road; it wasn't an unusual occurrence when one lived around a race track. But it was curious that the vehicle had been left so close to his property, and that it hadn't been recovered. The faint klaxon of alarm bells in his cranium were extinguished when Khalid began to speak.

"In Libya an abandoned car would be...how do you say?"

Eastwood turned back in seat and looked ahead. He was still thinking of the car when he said, "Stripped. Someone would take all the parts off of it."

"Yes. *Stripped.* I'm surprised abandoned cars not *stripped* in America." Khalid drove slowly, intently focused on the dual ruts in the grass Eastwood called a driveway.

Eastwood added, "Downtown New York—any large city—that car would also be stripped. Different set of rules out here in the country. There's more respect for property that isn't yours." Khalid nodded while focusing intently on the tire paths ahead.

The bright high-beam lights of the Tahoe illuminated the dark one-story ranch-style house as they crept down the slight declivity. Before Khalid brought the three-ton vehicle to a stop, Eastwood touched a panel under the dash and above Khalid's foot. Khalid jumped as a huge black semi-automatic pistol dropped down near his knee. Eastwood ignored Khalid's surprise, snatched the .45 caliber gun, racked the slide to check a round was chambered, jumped out of the truck and entered the house.

Lights blazing through the windows showed Eastwood's progress through the house: Khalid thought his boss had probably turned on every lamp. After a few minutes, the lights started to go dark again before Eastwood exited with a pair of overstuffed camouflage-print backpacks. He had changed out of his business suit into his more traditional ensemble of tan cargo pants and a billowy white denim shirt.

After Eastwood stowed the backpacks, fastened his safety belt, and unloaded the Colt, he leaned over the center console and replaced the weapon in its holder, and reset the trapdoor. Once the truck doors were closed, Khalid drove away from the house and aimed the Tahoe back from whence they came.

Khalid drove up the dual-track road. Well before they got to the mailbox near the highway's roadbed, Eastwood said, "Khalid, I need to stop at my mailbox—I should have done that on the way in."

Before Khalid could respond, a whitetail deer sprang out of the trees on his left and turned to parallel the slow-moving Tahoe. Khalid was wide eyed—he had seen dead deer on the side of the roads in America, but he had never seen one alive, or so close. He could look right into the deer's big black eye and it frightened him. He gripped the steering wheel tightly as he struggled to keep the truck on the path. The deer—right outside his door window—gently bounded alongside the vehicle. His head flipped back and forth—from the deer to the road—as if he were watching a professional tennis match. He was shocked and speechless. The sight of the deer running beside him was fascinating and incredible; another indescribable new experience in America.

Eastwood was also startled by the whitetail bounding just a few feet away. He marveled in silence as the doe ran and jumped to keep pace with the black Chevy, always maintaining a safe interval from the truck. As the deer and Tahoe slowly approached the highway, the headlights illuminated the mailbox and the disabled car. Eastwood suddenly remembered the mayhem he had seen at other times as drivers instinctively tried to avoid hitting a deer but lost control of their vehicles. He knew the deer would die if it ran across the road and was hit by a passing vehicle, and he needed to be well out of the way if a vehicle were to unintentionally depart the highway to avoid the deer. He yelled, "*Stop! Khalid!*"

The Libyan heard the directive and snapped out of his trance. He mashed the brake pedal with both feet as the doe shot ahead of the truck and continued its bouncy path between the abandoned car and the old wooden mailbox. Eastwood checked to his right for approaching traffic. As the Tahoe came to a stop, both men watched the deer as it bounded in front of the disabled car.

A huge yellow flash of light blinded the two men; the blast wave rocked the Tahoe. It was followed by a debris field of deer and car parts. The men instinctively ducked to protect themselves, but the

Tahoe's sheet metal, armor plating, and bulletproof glass withstood the blast, although the vehicle rocked wildly. The concussion was deafening. A dingy grey mushroom cloud rose from the remains of the disabled and burning vehicle, barely illuminated by the Tahoe's single undamaged headlight.

Spider cracks appeared across the windshield. Khalid was dazed and confused; Eastwood's senses were on full high alert. "*Drive Khalid! Right turn! Go, go, go!*"

Khalid's hands shook as he turned onto the highway, but he was composed enough to ask, "What happened, Mr. Dory?"

"That was an IED, Khalid. Improvised Explosive Device—a car bomb. Proximity fuse—probably set for when someone, like me, went to check the mail. Definitely proximity fuse—otherwise, if it had been a remotely detonated bomb, they would've waited until I went to check the mail. We're lucky to be alive."

"Good to have this truck." Khalid patted the dashboard.

"That was our good luck deer; saved my life and yours."

Khalid could see his boss was very shaken by the bomb. He had nearly wet himself from the evil eye of the demon doe, and the devil that tried to kill his Mr. Dory was even worse. He kept the radio off for the remainder of the trip and quietly followed the GPS back to New York City. Eastwood stared out the window.

As his pulse rate returned to normal, Eastwood extracted his smart phone and keyed in a message to tell Hunter his truck had again saved his life. He ruminated over the message for several minutes before deciding it was too soon to inform Hunter of the details of the evening. He shut down the tiny device without sending the message.

CHAPTER TWENTY-TWO

The pilot of the dark grey U.S. Air Force Special Operations Command MC-130 expertly flared the big cargo plane over the runway threshold of Lajes Field, Azores. The main landing gear touched down within the first thousand feet of the runway. When the nose wheels contacted the concrete, the copilot reversed the propellers and the Hercules quickly slowed. The pilot coordinated the use of the tall rudder to ensure the aircraft tracked perfectly down the runway centerline. He applied the brakes, easing the airplane off onto the taxiway at midfield and trailed the FOLLOW ME truck to the parking apron. The aircrew performed their after landing checklists and started the auxiliary power unit. Once stopped in their assigned parking spot, the pilot secured the inboard engines as the crew chief lowered the crew door and stepped out of the aircraft. He walked to the front of the aircraft and signaled "Cut engines" with his hand. As the outboard propellers and engines wound down, the loudest noise on the ramp was the high-pitched scream of the small turbine of the auxiliary power unit. After a few minutes, the APU was shut off and all was quiet on Lajes Field.

At touchdown, Hunter's BlackBerry vibrated and rang, signaling a string of emails and missed calls. Because of the din of hydraulic pumps actuating during the lowering of flaps and landing gear, Duncan missed the incoming messages. Bob and Bob emerged from sleeping bags while McGee stepped down from the cockpit where he had been the guest of the aircraft commander. Sitting in the jump seat through the landing, he watched the crew and listened to their radio and interphone calls. With a commanding view of the islands and runway, he relished his time in the cockpit as the Hercules crossed from flying over the ocean—"feet wet"—to flying over land—"feet dry."

The Air Force FOLLOW ME truck driver drove the MC-130 aircrew and the YO-3A crew to the billeting office. The old guys, Bob and Bob, rode in the rear seats while Hunter and McGee crawled into the truck bed with the rest of the enlisted aircrew. Once the overloaded vehicle stopped in front of the Mid-Atlantic Lodge, the flight engineer jogged inside to check in the flight. Prior to dispatch from Andrews Air Force Base, the loadmaster had secured rooms for everyone on the airplane—standard procedure on these missions—to ensure there were limited records of who registered at the lodging facilities. After a few minutes, the flight engineer bounded out of the Lodge office and handed keys to everyone in the pickup. He also flashed the keys to a van.

With his Yankee White clearance and Code Two VIP designation, Hunter was the mission commander and was accorded distinguished visitor privileges although he wasn't identified by name. As he had done with previous *Noble Savage* missions transiting Lajes Field, he ensured everyone on the MC-130, officer, enlisted and civilian received a DV suite. The Mid-Atlantic Lodge didn't quite approach the four or five-star accommodations Hunter was used to but they were more than adequate for a 24- to 48-hour layover. Every DV suite overlooked the Atlantic and provided breathtaking views of the ocean and sunsets, something the Marriotts rarely featured. Rank has its privileges.

Lajes was one of the best-kept secrets in DOD. Located on the eastern-most part of the island of Terceira, Lajes Field had been regularly used by NATO and non-NATO aircraft. However, with more aircraft movements relying on aerial refueling, Lajes no longer received much traffic—a perfect place for a Special Operations MC-130 and her crew to spend some time resting for the long and challenging mission ahead. U.S. Air Force support had been downsized; the DOD ramp was typically deserted except for an occasional transient MC-130 or KC-135. Aircrews that spent the night were treated to great rooms overlooking the ocean. The local food was fantastic and the transportation to and from town was safe and pleasant. And the entertainment was discrete. What happened at Lajes, stayed at Lajes.

It had been a year since Duncan Hunter last walked along the covered porch and wooden deck. He quietly entered the same VIP suite he had used when he embarked on his last mission to Algeria. It was difficult for him not to think about that mission, how it unfolded and how it ended. He had brought the YO-3A to Lajes and less than 24 hours later he had been shot down.

Hunter deposited his backpack and helmet bag into a recliner chair and proceeded to the refrigerator. Unsurprised it was fully stocked, he removed a tall rectangular carton covered in Arabic script with a picture of an orange. He pulled the plastic plug and gulped the drink from the container as he walked toward the center of the room. He yawned in front of the large picture window as he admired the bioluminescence of the ocean surf a few hundred yards away. His BlackBerry chirped and buzzed and reminded him that he had much to do before the crew headed across the Sahara to drop him and McGee off in a tiny country no one had ever really heard of.

Unlike the Algerian mission, the mission from Benin into Nigeria would add a new dimension—the addition of Bill McGee as the YO-3A's sensor operator. McGee had no formal training as a pilot or sensor operator and brought few talents to reduce the cockpit workload during the intense phase of mission execution. But to Hunter, he brought more than enough skill to offset his lack of flying experience. Once Hunter slipped the quiet aircraft into the mission profile and began to monitor the activities of terrorists, his workload had only just begun.

As a solo pilot he always had to be mindful of flying the airplane and keeping the aircraft airborne in a turn as he scanned the target area for an opening and opportunity. Whether it was to kill opium poppies with a laser or target a terrorist hiding behind a hostage, the first priority was to keep the aircraft safely in the air. The ability to handle multiple and diverse tasks simultaneously, while keeping a very slow-flying aircraft airborne, was akin to a professional juggler who spun a dozen plates on sticks while juggling chainsaws. Something could always spin out of control in an instant and cause a crash. But, more insidious, there's always the possibility of experiencing nighttime visual illusions or misperceptions leading to mishandling the airplane at low altitudes and low airspeeds. If he was distracted and missed the warning signs that the aircraft was about to depart controlled flight, there was no safety margin for recovery. After being shot down and hunted down by professional special operations soldiers, Hunter realized that, if he were to continue flying the Agency's incredibly risky *Noble Savage* missions, he needed a little help.

He'd seen the business executives who took their pretty and leggy corporate vice presidents to iconic or romantic places like Monaco or Paris. But when the same business executives traveled to the really nasty places on the planet, they took along former special operations colonels they had hired as vice president for "special projects" or personal security. Having one airplane shot out from under him was enough, and the addition of McGee in the YO-3A cockpit was welcome. McGee had closed with and killed America's enemies on the ground in close combat—even hand-to-hand—for 35 years, and he was more than enthusiastic to do something different. Riding in the back seat of the quiet airplane was thrilling and exhilarating, and he was looking forward to the mission of hunting down and killing the murderers of children.

After the two crews returned from town after a night of food and drink, Hunter and McGee walked back to their rooms. They sat in Adirondack chairs on the deck in front of Hunter's suite, and watched the sparkling white surf crash onto the moonlit beach. McGee did most of the talking. He talked about how Angela and his girls were assimilating into the west Texas culture, how inexpensive homes were, how he didn't like the number of boys hanging out at his house, and how his life had changed by relocating to Texas and becoming Hunter's business partner. He didn't mention the substantial increase

278

in income. Later as McGee said good night and turned in, Hunter repaired to his room and focused on the upcoming mission.

Every deployment checklist item had been checked and double-checked. The YO-3A, the FLIR, the gun, and McGee had performed flawlessly during their test run. Bob and Bob had removed the special purpose three-bladed prop and installed the larger six-bladed propeller for greater speed and performance. The MC-130-capable container was loaded with tools, fuel and oil, and spares—spare tires, spare instruments, spare parachutes, and even a spare canopy—and several silenced weapons. It was stowed in the cargo hold of the Hercules.

There hadn't been time for McGee to be custom-fitted for a shoulder holster for a revolver or an automatic pistol for the mission. Somewhere over the Atlantic Ocean, Hunter showed McGee a pair of Kimber Model 1911 .45ACP pistols with hollow-point ammunition, fixed silencers and conformal-grips, and laser sights. The SEAL admired the workmanship of the 16-inch long firearms and the extra features. "Expecting trouble?" he yelled.

"I thought it was a SEAL axiom, you can never have too many weapons?" Hunter shouted over the constant din in the MC-130 cargo bay as he cleared the weapon showing McGee the empty chamber and then handed McGee the 1911 and several full magazines for the pistol.

"Something like that!" McGee nodded at the hollow-point bullets in the magazines and slipped the magazines into his lower flight suit pockets. The weapon looked odd with the silencer protruding out of the pocket of the survival vest.

Hunter rummaged through his helmet bag and extracted a plastic bag the size of a paperback novel. He held up the first aid kit to McGee, who smiled broadly. "This has a little bit of everything, anti-malarials, ciprofloxacin for anthrax, atropine for nerve gas. Iodine, Chap Stick, aspirin, bandages. One for you, one for me."

"Sutures?" interrupted McGee. A quiet thought passed between the men; their eyes locked for the briefest of moments. He recalled that after rescuing Nazy Cunningham from some Muslim butchers, he had used all of the bandages and sutures in his first aid kit to save Nazy's life. Hunter allowed the thought and image to pass and nodded to the big man.

"Yes, sir. Thirty field and thirty steri-strips." He rummaged through the first aid kit and extracted a foil-sealed card. "Also, twenty potassium iodide tabs for...."

"Radioactive poisoning. You've thought of just about everything."

"I'm always looking to improve my odds of staying alive. I added the potassium iodide when I restocked the cipro I used in Algeria. Your bag and mine are identical."

McGee and Hunter zip-locked their first-aid kits closed and slipped them inside the pockets of their survival vests.

Hunter continued through his mental checklist.

Prepositioning to the Azores after the short-notice "go order" went off without any problems, unlike the mission to Algeria where an older Agency Hercules had experienced some minor mechanical issues. The Algeria mission had been fraught with distractions and problems. For the mildly superstitious Hunter, trouble in the little things meant you could expect trouble in the big things. Consequently, he planned and table-topped his missions to the nth degree to reduce risks and surprises.

The Air Force MC-130J was a new model and the aircrew was professional and responsive. Like all good Special Operations Forces mission aircrew, they arrived when they said they were going to arrive. There were no issues, no problems, no surprises. Halfway across the Atlantic, the enlisted aircrew and the two Bobs rehearsed their mission tasks. Hunter and McGee prepared their black flight suits, survival vests, and flight helmets. They mounted and connected the night vision goggle systems to their flight helmets. The flight engineer acknowledged she would raise the upper cargo door and lower the cargo ramp after landing at the remote airfield. The aircrew learned that immediately after touchdown, the YO-3A would roll out of its container and down the ramp of the Hercules. Bob and Bob would need some assistance and instructed two able-bodied backs on their duties to help install the wings while the old guys attached the flight controls, fuel lines, and electrical connections. The YO-3A would be assembled and taped and the engine started within four minutes of the MC-130's full stop. A minute later the Hercules would be airborne again, trailing the YO-3A before heading to the designated rendezvous point, or in the case of an emergency, the alternate landing site.

McGee and Hunter discussed their roles and responsibilities after completion of the mission. Bob and Bob and the aircrew would expeditiously disassemble the wings and disconnect the flight controls and all of the "quick disconnect" couplings. Hunter would jump out of the cockpit and connect a cable to the YO-3A's tail wheel. When the wings "were dropped," he would winch the airplane back into her container. Disassembly would take three minutes and a minute later, they'd be airborne. That was the plan. It always worked. No issues, no problems, no surprises.

Hunter awoke his BlackBerry and sent Nazy an email that he was on an adventure. That was their way of communicating that he was "safe on deck" somewhere out of the country and would be incommunicado until he popped back up on the grid. The implication was he would be home in a few days, and he would see her when he returned to the Washington DC area to meet with the DCI for the mission debrief. He continued typing a love note and signed off that he missed her and looked forward to talking to her soon. Several business-related emails remained in his inbox and he answered them one by one. He sent emails to Kelly Horne and to Greg Lynche's home account. One went to the ranch foreman, Carlos Yazzie, and a short one to Demetrius Eastwood. He wondered if the Tahoe was still in one piece, but he rationalized that no news from Eastwood was good news.

After his nightly routine of push-ups and sit-ups, he set the alarm on his BlackBerry, crawled between the sheets, and fell asleep.

∙ ∙ ∙

Nazy Cunningham raced off the airplane. She ran through a labyrinth of narrow tunnels and switchbacks before she spilled out into a vast room of indeterminate shapes and people. She stopped and searched...for Duncan. When she didn't find him, she ran again. She turned and ran; she scanned the fuzzy faces of people as she ran...but there was no Duncan. He promised he would be waiting for her. Nazy heard her boots as they clicked on the floor as she ran...down the concourse, past the departure lounges, around faceless people toward the place called "baggage claim." She had to find her bag. She had to find Duncan. Her heart throbbed in her chest, her chest heaved; and she ran. She had to find Duncan...to surprise him...*yes*; she *would* surprise him when she saw him.... Yes! Yes! Nazy would run and jump into his arms when she saw him!

When she rounded a corner, through the shadows of people, she saw the familiar shape—*she found him*! He smiled. Bronze eyes shimmered and reflected his love for her. He opened wide his greatcoat as she jumped into his arms and wrapped her arms around his neck, then her legs slowly wound around him. He enveloped her, covered her with the long, warm, wool coat. *I found you! I missed you!* Nazy said breathlessly, as she leaned down and kissed him, and sucked the air from his lungs through his mouth. *I have a surprise for you!* Duncan would be very surprised! *I so missed you and I want you to know how much!*

A klaxon, loud and strident, startled her; she looked away as the luggage system over Duncan's shoulder began to rumble and move and then...something...tugged vigorously at Duncan's coat....

"Miss Cunningham!"

She shook her head and fought against the unseen hand pulling at her...pulling her away from Duncan.

"Miss Cunningham! We have to go!"

Nazy tried to scream *No! No! I found you! I don't want to go! Duncan don't let me go!* What came out of her mouth was guttural, primordial, disturbed.

"Miss Cunningham; we have to go, NOW!"

Nazy's eyes sprang open and she blinked wildly; she shuddered, fully disoriented as one of the security women dragged her from her bed. The sounds of alarms in the house were very loud and the flashing red lights were frightening. Some distant instinct told her she was in danger and she had to run.

"*Nazy; we have to move, NOW!*"

Nazy stumbled in confusion but found her legs as she was pushed out of the bedroom, through the SCIF doors and down the stairs to the safety of the bunker room. The hazy image of her reunion with Duncan popped like a soap bubble, replaced by the shrieks of alarms and of familiar people running and shouting.

For several hours the four security women had been stone cold silent. Some monitored the security cameras while the others rested or read until the intruder alert signal had sounded in the basement. Seismic sensors registered several heavy mammals moving through the woods near the compound. A second later, one of the security women raced into the darkened bedroom, struggling to awaken the fully incoherent Nazy Cunningham and to get her into the bright lights of the basement of the safe house. Once she staggered past the inner door threshold, the woman who had pushed her down the stairs turned to lock the inner and outer doors of the SCIF and slam heavy dead bolts into the steel frames. They were now as secure as a safety deposit box in a bank vault.

Nazy couldn't return to her dream as the seriousness of the situation forced her from slumber. The expected adrenaline rush of the emergency had yet to kick in. She was in a state of disbelief and was still "a sleepyhead," as Duncan called it. She wondered why she was holding her running shoes to her chest; someone must have put them there. After a full minute the adrenaline kicked in and Nazy came around to being fully awake. Once she was aware of her surroundings, she watched in amazement as two women hovered over the security workstations—two monitors on each desk displayed twelve camera feeds on each monitor. The other intelligence officer held a telephone receiver to her ear in one hand and a microphone in the other. Nazy heard the excited women relay information; the director of security was apparently on the other end of the hardwire telephone, and she surmised the woman was talking on the radio to the additional CIA security forces lodged at the bottom of the hill in Columbia Furnace.

The woman who pushed Nazy into the Bunker and locked the SCIF doors sprinted to an ugly grey wall locker and yanked body armor vests out of its recesses. When the final SCIF door was locked the alarm in the basement abruptly stopped, much to the relief of the young women. Nazy had ignored the siren. *This cannot be happening!*

The security team monitored the network of security cameras and prepared for an attack. No longer the priority, Nazy was completely ignored; the priority now was to monitor the situation and stay alive until reinforcements arrived. The woman on the telephone barked into the receiver, "Anna! We've five hits on the 1604 sensor and five more hits on the 1599 sensor. Bottom of the hill, west of the house. Contacted the augmentees at the Furnace; they're en route. Still no video of anyone or anything."

One of the women at the long work table shouted, "Becca! *Video contact!* Camera ten—five men with rifles! *Those aren't Boy Scouts with...AR-15s. No they're AK-47s!* Shit, camera two shows five more men with AKs. They're probing the outside concertina!"

Nazy slipped her feet into her trainers and moved in to get a better view of the monitors. Ten startled eyes focused on the single monitor. The video feeds from a dozen hidden low light and infrared cameras in the west quadrant of the safe house acreage clearly showed green night vision images and eerie black and white thermal images of armed men at work, ready to puncture the safe house line of defenses.

She unconsciously held a hand to her mouth in fear, the fear of being stalked and preyed upon again. She turned away from the monitors and picked up a black body armor vest. She pulled it over her head and tightened Velcro straps around her waist. Once it was secured over her yellow sweatshirt she walked to one of three sofas. Two women of the security detail watched Nazy as she staggered away from the camera monitors and found a place to sit. Once she settled in, Nazy planted her face into her lap, wrapped her arms around her head, and cried. The women of the security detail noticed that their charge had taken to the couch to await her fate. Glances ricocheted between the four intel officers as they telepathically resolved that they wouldn't allow any harm to come to the CIA executive; not on their watch, not ever. The women were well trained and well protected by an array of systems, both electronic and structural. So far, they had just monitored the evolving situation and hadn't been compelled to activate the protective systems.

Days earlier when they had been assembled as a security team, every member of the safe house security detail had walked the property's 100 acres during daylight hours. The chief of security expected the women to get a sense of their duties and the limits of the *Spindletop* property. Among the oak and evergreen trees, the women walked to the four corners of the government property inside the fence. They touched the signs spaced 50 yards apart which read:

WARNING

RESTRICTED AREA

It is unlawful to enter this area without the permission of the Installation Commander

While on this installation all personnel and the property under their control are subject to search.

USE OF DEADLY FORCE IS AUTHORIZED.

The sturdy chain link fence was topped with thick concertina wire, and large coils of razor wire were expanded like a concertina on both sides of the fence. Anyone who came upon the razor wire and the signs in what would be considered a forest would have no doubt they had found an official government facility and that facility's defenses were not meant to be breached.

The lanky deputy chief of security had briefed the lithe athletic women where cameras were located. He also told them the general location of a battery of seismic sensors. The sensors were installed on the outside as well as inside the fence, or what the deputy called, "inside the wire." In the confines of the Bunker, the deputy chief of security explained the most obvious lines of attack—a frontal attack— through the front gate. He noted the least expected line of attack—a

1,200-foot climb up the steep mountain that flanked the sides and the rear of the property. "But you've little to worry about; this house is well protected inside and out. As you see inside, it's a vault; and outside, you have an emergency 'High-Output User-autonomous Defensive System.' HOUNDS. It's a last ditch system; for those that may have been in the military, it provides what's called 'final protective fires.' Think little robots with artificial intelligence controlling extremely high output fires—or rounds of ammo. We call it the 'HOUNDS from Hell.'"

"Listen up—it's very intuitive. To protect this property in an emergency, you activate the system with one click of a mouse from the control station in the bunker. Then select the targets from the camera system with a double click. Six tracked robots with microwave and infrared sensors will leave their charging stations near the barn and will locate and close in on your selected target or targets. Once the HOUNDS sense the targets, they flip into autonomous mode and engage any moving object. Hounds can pick up the slightest variation of movement, meaning they can detect the rise and fall of the chest of a human breathing from 100 feet away. Once the targets are acquired, the HOUNDS lock onto and engage them, subjecting the targets to the withering fire of an electrically-driven Gatling gun. The control rate of fire is 2,000 rounds per minute with three-second bursts of about 100 rounds of twenty-two caliber long rifle ammunition. There's five thousand rounds in the bucket. The HOUNDS can launch smoke or fragmentation grenades for final defensive fires. There are no known defenses to this recently installed system. And ladies, you cannot be outside the safe house when the HOUNDS are released and are on the prowl. You'll see a 'recall' icon on the security panel which will interrupt the HOUNDS' work and send the pack of six critters back to their stations. The HOUNDS should eliminate or delay any threats until reinforcements arrive. That's the end of my brief. Questions? If not, good luck."

· · ·

On the telephone, "Becca" provided a continuous dialog of what she witnessed on the monitors. "Anna, we've ten men wearing night vision goggles and carrying AK-47s. Looks like two are beginning to cut through the first bundle of concertina wire...outside the wire." Anna Comstock listened intently from her office at CIA HQ.

"You sure?" asked an incredulous Comstock. *I should have never left! Damn!*

"There's no doubt what they're doing Anna—they have those large handle...wire cutter things."

"Bolt cutters."

"Right, two men have bolt cutters and they're snipping away at the concertina and have just started to pull the rolls away from the fence. They'll start cutting the chain link fence any moment."

"Becca, I'm on my way back to the house and the security men are on their way; ETA eight minutes." Anna Comstock's massive chest heaved as adrenaline was dumped into her system by the gallon. She hadn't ever lost a special interest person or a CIA executive. There had never been an attack on a CIA safe house before, but now there's a sizable, hostile force working its way up the mountain. The prize in the Bunker must be an incredible threat to someone. Anna Comstock would never have believed what she was about to do.

As she played mental gymnastics with the lives of her security detail and her career, the woman called "Becca" said, "Anna, we're all in body armor; we're locked and loaded. The SCIF is locked, and we're ready for them until the cavalry arrives."

. . .

One by one, the four security women extracted their service weapons and racked the slides of the .38 Berettas to chamber a round. Once locked and loaded the weapons were safetied and returned to their holsters on their hips. One security officer snatched a pair of ten gauge shotguns from the weapons vault and placed them against the workstations. Only Nazy didn't have a weapon on her person, but there were several M-4s in weapons safe locker just three steps away.

. . .

The security chief racked her brain as to why the attack on the safe house was happening. *Only a handful of people know of Spindletop! Only a handful of people know Cunningham is here! How is this possible?* Her next thought was more pessimistic. *I need to up-channel the news to Director Lynche.*

. . .

Two women sat transfixed in front of the bank of monitors. Nazy recovered her composure and wiped her eyes; she stood and walked over to stand between the two women controlling the security cameras. She placed a comforting hand on each woman's shoulder and dispassionately monitored the activities of the security force protecting her. Her mind wandered to another nightmarish place and time that she had struggled to put behind her. She was just now starting to dream again...of Duncan and her...in beautiful places. She didn't want to go back to the bad places of horrific dreams; she would rather die first. And if she were going to die, she wanted to die in Duncan's arms, not in the grips of savages. She stared unblinkingly at the monitor as she watched Muslim men come for her yet again.

Nazy was shocked back to the present as she heard the young woman called Becca shout, "Anna, they've cut the links of the chain link fence. Anna; they're inside the wire."

Anna Comstock checked her watch and realized the quick reaction force coming up from the tiny inn at Columbia Furnace wasn't going to be able to respond quickly enough; they wouldn't make it in time. She prayed she was making the right decision when she said, "Becca, I need you to release the HOUNDS. *Release the HOUNDS, dammit!*"

The two women sitting at the monitors were close enough to hear Anna Comstock's voice come though the telephone receiver. They shared a quick glance and acknowledged the order. The woman seated to Nazy's left said, "I've got it." Nazy's eyes grew wide.

Alice Prince shook the mouse to find the cursor and placed it on the HOUNDS icon near the bottom of the monitor. She clicked the left button once and activated the system. A Windows box opened and six stroboscopic lines, varying from low to high intensity appeared. She scrolled the mouse and double clicked to select the targets as each man stepped through the hole in the fence. She also targeted those already inside "the wire." Ten pulsating red circles, each the size of a nickel, tracked the men as they moved through the fence and the concertina wire. Green lights flashed in the Windows box in the middle of the control monitor indicating six tracked robots had been activated and were powered up. Another small Windows screen with two buttons appeared, RELEASE and RETURN. Intelligence Officer Prince exhaled as she panned the cursor over and clicked the RELEASE button. One after another the six flashing green lights turned solid green. Video shots from each HOUNDS appeared on the control monitor. The lawnmower-sized machines shot away from their charging stations at the side of the barn, turned, and zipped down the hill. The computer system continuously fed targeting data to each HOUNDS as the wide rubber-tracked, electrically-driven vehicles, split into two echelons of three. The five women watched the screen as the armed robots acquired their targets and attacked in enfilade. Nazy turned her head; the four intelligence officers looked on in stunned amazement.

All six HOUNDS fired simultaneously; the sound from the robots was a deafening mélange of zip and crack. The sounds from the infiltrators were truncated grunts as thousands of bullets found their marks.

The twelve small barrels of each Gatling gun spun rapidly as they spat five hundred rounds in twenty-second bursts. Three thousand rounds of .22 caliber long-rifle intermeshed from left and right and saturated the narrow killing field with the small-bore ammunition. Death was nearly instantaneous as a thousand tiny rounds cut into the men's unprotected flesh. Sensors on each HOUNDS monitored the killing field for movement. After two minutes, intelligence officer Prince moved the cursor on the monitor and selected RETURN. One after the other, each HOUNDS pivoted 180º and zipped back up the hill, spun 180º and slipped into its docking station, barrels pointing outboard.

When the last HOUNDS was safely secured in its charger and the system was de-energized and shut down, two glossy black Tahoes trundled up to the driveway gate. A dozen armed men, with IR reflective tape on their clothes to identify them as friend for the HOUNDS, poured from the vehicles. Some had drawn handguns and shotguns; some exited the trucks with assault rifles with night vision scopes jammed into their eye sockets as they scoured the area. Red dots from laser pointers danced and flickered across the ground, the safe house, and the barn as the men searched the grounds for hostile intruders. Several men spread out along the ground and the fence, their weapons pointed into the void behind the safe house. An intelligence officer was screaming into a radio microphone demanding a SITREP from the Bunker. Other intelligence officers touched their earpiece receivers, straining to hear a voice or a signal. Everyone was on high alert and their senses were overloaded, anticipating a sudden rush of armed men over the crown of the hill.

The smell of thousands of fired rounds hung in the air. The residual warmth of the IR signatures of the bodies shone bright white in helmet mounted FLIRs.

The five women in the bunker silently looked at each other and the monitors. The surreal scene and the sounds of silence was shattered when *"Well!?"* erupted from the telephone receiver. Outside the ranch house of *Spindletop*, the head of the quick reaction team screamed into a microphone, "Come in Bunker Control! Come in Bunker Control! What's your status?"

At CIA Headquarters, a horrified and agitated Anna Comstock

bellowed from her telephone, *"Someone talk to me!"*

Nazy Cunningham took the receiver from the shocked intelligence officer and said, "All clear, Anna. We're okay. The HOUNDS did their work and they're back in the barn. The augmentees have arrived and they're reconning the area." Then responding to the electronic speaker between the pair of monitors, she depressed a red button on a desk top microphone to inform the QRT leader that everyone in the house was safe and that someone would be coming to the door to let them in.

Nazy patted the girls at the workstations on the shoulder to break their trance. With no training or simulator to replicate the killing of men *en masse*, they had been shocked to the point of incapacitation. Wordlessly, the women at the workstation pushed away from the desk, turned to Nazy, and nodded. The intelligence officer, Alice Prince, picked up a shotgun, slung it over her shoulder, and then unbolted the heavy SCIF door.

Nazy was the last to leave the bunker. She looked around at the monitors, the weapons safe, and the furnishings of the room. The basement was a mess and she automatically picked up a shotgun and a pair of M-4s and returned them to the weapons vault.

Strange curious thoughts crept into her mind. She was surprised her PTSD hadn't flared anew with all the excitement, suspense, and fear of the last few minutes. She thought she would've been more emotionally shattered and was sanguine that she wasn't. Then she wondered if the women charged to protect her would be similarly affected after witnessing the killing of the invading force. What they watched intently hadn't been a drill or a video game. Only time would tell if the actions of the evening would affect their minds long-term. It certainly was going to be a night she wouldn't forget. She tried to make some sense of the men coming up the hill and cutting the fence to get into the compound. She wondered what Duncan was doing; she wondered what she would be able to tell him of the night. They had their little BlackBerry code, but then she then realized she had left her device in her bedroom. She started toward the SCIF door to retrieve it.

She wasn't prepared for the thought that made her stop in her tracks. She inhaled sharply and wondered if the men on the motorcycle in Colombia could have been after her and not Duncan. As she opened the bunker door and headed up the stairs, she ran through all the scenarios that would explain how her cover could be blown and how they had found her.

CHAPTER TWENTY-THREE

The wind roared along the front of the Ronald Reagan National Airport terminal as Kelly Horne stepped from the taxi in the pre-dawn twilight. One strong gust nearly knocked her off her feet while another caught her off-balanced rolling bag and flipped it over. Preoccupied counting his fare and tip, the Middle Eastern driver offered no help to the young woman as she fought her bag in the wind. Between gusts she tossed her pack onto her back and returned the upended bag to its correct orientation. She pulled the recalcitrant rocking roll-aboard through the automatic doors, bypassing a pair of lethargic skycaps. Kelly shook her head in mild disgust and thought: *East coast men have no manners.*

She negotiated her way through the crush of early morning travelers and queued in the International Departures line. Hundreds of travelers behind her shuffled their feet and luggage as they made their way to ticket counters or the security checkpoint. As she lugged her belongings and waited in line, she realized she was thoroughly exhausted. With no sleep and an unrealistic and expedited departure schedule, she wasn't a happy girl. She tried not to show it.

A ticketing agent waved at her to approach the counter. Kelly submitted her "traveling" passport. The blue cover U.S. tourist passport was relinquished, scanned, and returned. "Thank you, Miss Ledford. One bag to Lagos?"

"Yes, please." The ticket agent punched keyboard keys and slapdashed stickers and tags onto her bag. Processing through the security checkpoint was easier than Kelly had expected. She wondered if the CIA had somehow put a code on the ticket to alert the TSA

Security Officers to expedite her passage to the departure gate. That scenario wasn't likely Kelly reminded herself. She would play the role of a Christian missionary until she checked into the U.S. Embassy.

Boarding the aircraft was slow, but finding her seat was quick. She tossed her backpack into the overhead compartment, took her seat by the window and closed her eyes. Kelly awoke with a start when the flight attendant announced, "Welcome to JFK, please remain seated until the captain has turned off the fasten seat belt sign." She shook the sleep from her mind as she ran her fingers through her hair. She glanced out her window only to see the largest airplane she had ever seen make its landing approach.

.   .   .

The massive green and white Airbus A380 touched down gently on the centerline of the longest of JFK's runways. Thrust reversers deployed as the world's largest jumbo jet—a million pounds of aluminum atop twenty-two wheels—lumbered down the runway, continually braking until its speed was reduced to a crawl. Acres of fuselage and a six-story tail sported the livery of a giant Nigerian flag—sea-green bands flanked a white middle—as the aircraft rumbled down the runway. The safe landing of the monstrous, sparkling new Airbus marked the completion of its maiden voyage to America from the heart of Africa. The pride of Nigerian Airways and the Nigerian people were on full display.

The four-engine Airbus 380 was a relative newcomer to America. With 700 seats, the three hundred million dollar airplane was a tour de force of engineering and economics. Developed in secret as an ultra-high-capacity airliner, Airbus launched the fifteen-billion dollar program to break the dominance Boeing had enjoyed in the jumbo aircraft market since 1969. With hundreds of improvements and upgrades, *The Nigerian Queen* was the newest and latest of the A380s produced and delivered.

As *The Nigerian Queen* cleared the runway, two huge fire trucks drove to a predetermined position on opposite sides of the taxiway. The pumper trucks' water cannons rotated up at a 45° angle to welcome the inaugural flight.

As the ponderous Airbus slowly turned off one taxiway and onto another, a crewmember emerged from a small emergency hatch on the crown of the jet. He thrust a pole into the air and waved the national colors of Nigeria. The man struggled to hold the green and white flag against the wind rushing up and over the front of the tall airliner. When the aircraft approached the gauntlet of fire trucks, narrow columns of white and green water spurted from the opposing water cannons creating a spectacular rainbow effect as the Airbus continued to taxi under the ceremonial water arch. With the first splash of water in his face, the man with the flag ducked back inside and immediately closed the clamshell hatch with a wet splat. The aircraft was completely drenched as it passed through the water salute. Once clear of the welcoming fire trucks, *The Nigerian Queen* taxied to its arrival gate.

· · ·

Transportation Security Administration security officers had never seen anything like the chaos outside the security checkpoint. Hundreds of media, well-wishers, and curious passengers from across the airport had been herded into special event areas; photographers elbowed each other to video throngs of passengers as they exited the concourse. Inside the terminal, local and international media jockeyed for position to interview the passengers and aircrew. They were largely ignored or rebuffed.

The return flight of *The Nigerian Queen* had been a sellout with all 700 seats reserved a month in advance. No longer did American passengers have to fly through Heathrow or Paris or Frankfurt to get to Lagos. A few yards away, a crush of people scheduled for the outbound Nigerian Airways flight found impassible traffic jams for departing passengers and long waiting lines at ticketing and security.

Reporters blamed airport management for the poor design of the terminal infrastructure. It wasn't designed to process a 700-passenger flight.

The noise of the departing passengers inching their way through the extremely slow-moving lines of the security rat maze was deafening. TSA officers manned every available magnetometer and X-ray machine. Tickets and passports were checked. Passengers were given directions to process through a designated line to have their bags and belongings subjected to X-ray screening, and their person subjected to a walk-through metal detector.

Sitting behind her assigned X-ray machine, the woman in uniform and wearing the *hijab* was anxious and nervous. The crowds waiting to be screened were unbelievable; there were twice as many people in line as when the Boeing 747s departed. She glanced at the clock and then at the men and women in the queue waiting to have their baggage and belongings screened.

Abby Kesselring focused intently on the monitor screen, scanning the multicolored images of various shapes and sizes, looking for the telltale forms and features of weapons and instruments of harm and mayhem. She developed a rhythm and quickly processed the passenger's possessions—people in her line were moving faster than the other X-ray screening stations at the security checkpoint. Passengers in her line were grateful for the speedy processing as they raced away from the security checkpoint. The passengers in the other lines lamented that they had gotten into the wrong lane.

She processed passenger bags through her X-ray machine effortlessly. Then she saw in her monitor the image of three-sticks of dynamite, some wires, and a clock. She stopped the conveyor belt and stared at the image of a time bomb that was just inches from her face.

After several deep breaths, Kesselring called for a supervisor as she had been trained to do. He approached the stainless steel cabinet housing the X-ray machine and calmly verified that the image on the monitor was that of a classic time bomb. He could also make out the faint outline of the plastic material which encased the bomb components.

Exasperated, the Lead TSO officer approached the traveler whose bag was ensconced in the X-ray machine; he followed the protocol for identifying suspicious items highlighted by X-ray. He wouldn't remove the bag from the X-ray cabinet until he asked the woman, "What's in your bag?" The dark haired woman in a trim business suit flashed her Federal Aviation Administration badge and said, "OTP." The Lead TSO officer signaled Kesselring to release the conveyor belt to allow the bag with the dummy bomb to pass through the X-ray machine. The FAA woman unzipped her bag, presented the green-rubber, rectangular Operational Test Piece for the TSO Lead and TSO Kesselring to see. She returned it to her bag before she walked off.

The TSO Lead shook his head to indicate to TSO Kesselring that he wasn't thrilled the FAA was performing impromptu security checks during the departure window of the world's largest jet. But that was exactly when the FAA and airline executives would test and check the security system, during periods of high passenger throughput, or when they believed some of the X-ray machine operators might not be as thorough screening bags and their contents as they should be.

The TSO Lead patted Kesselring on the shoulder and said, "Nice job. Good catch." He glanced at the image of the training aid still on the screen as he walked to his office to file the report of an FAA test and the TSA's successful detection.

TSO Kesselring's heart continued to slam inside her chest as she realized she had been watched. She struggled to compose herself. After several deep breaths, she started the conveyor belt to begin processing more bags. Moments later the image of four automatic pistols stacked side-by-side—handles up—appeared on her monitor. She looked up at the man passing through the magnetometer and then quickly lowered her eyes.

She was stunned to see actual weapons in the X-ray machine, not those encased by plastic of operational test pieces. She blinked once and pressed the conveyor button to send the bag through to be picked up at the end of the machine. Kesselring wanted to make eye contact with the brave jihadi who retrieved the backpack, but she demurred knowing he wouldn't look at her. She trembled in her chair. Her temples pounded and she thought she could hear the blood racing through her veins. She really didn't see the images of bags and shoes and computers that followed through the X-ray machine like the pages in a book. She realized she was now part of the jihad against America. She unconsciously touched her *hijab*, then she calmly returned to screening the contents of an uninterrupted chain of grey tubs.

After waiting for many dozens of people before her, it was finally Kelly Horne's turn to take off her shoes and remove her computer from her bag. She placed them in a plastic container on the steadily moving conveyor and sent her possessions down the chute into the maw of the X-ray machine. Kelly glanced at the X-ray machine operator and thought it was irregular for the woman to be wearing the headscarf of a Muslim. She found it peculiar that TSA would allow nonstandard uniform items. Since she didn't know the TSA's grooming and uniform rules and regulations, she let the curiosity pass. With her next thought she hoped her backpack would pass without being subject to a secondary inspection. It'd be hard to explain being in possession of multiple passports with different names.

The TSA officer in the blue *hijab* looked bored and didn't look up from her monitor. Horne was grateful she was in a line that moved quickly as the operator expedited every bag through the screening machine. In stockinged feet, she shuffled to the standing metal detector device and was waved "to come through" by a TSO officer. No lights or alarms sounded as she passed through to the other side of the magnetometer where she was reunited with her backpack. She slipped on her running shoes and put her computer back in her bag. Kelly took another glance at the woman behind the X-ray machine then turned and stepped into the throng headed toward the Nigerian Airways departure gate.

Two men with strong Middle Eastern features, wearing jeans and sports shirts, innocently engaged in light banter and mild arm gestures as Kelly Horne passed. They casually eyed the good-looking women coming from the security checkpoint but were more focused on the movement of passengers leaving the international concourse. From under dark bushy brows, one of the men continually peeked at the single TSA officer positioned near the exit.

A nearly imperceptible nod alerted one of the men to shift his position. Their expressions changed marginally when three uniformed policemen approached the desk of the TSO officer stationed at the exit. The airport police escorted two noticeably muscular African American men who wore dreary sport coats with backpacks slung over their shoulders. The police and the TSA officer conversed quietly for a moment before the TSA official waved the five men through, bypassing the security checkpoint. As the policemen bantered with each other, the other men stoically walked counterflow to the steady stream of arriving passengers before joining the natural flow of passengers striding to their gates.

The Middle Eastern men suppressed any facial expressions, glanced at each other, and turned to follow the police escorts. They integrated into the mass of outbound passengers like lost fish rejoining their school.

Demetrius Eastwood's presence in the security passenger control maze created a major commotion as he was instantly recognized when he pulled off his soft camouflaged Tilly hat. His video and support crew were used to the man's celebrity wherever he went. While they ignored Eastwood's fans, they kept an eye open for any of the haters and political liberals that would pop up at the most inopportune times, usually at airports and hotels. But there were no antagonists in line for the direct flight to Nigeria as Eastwood signed countless autographs and posed for pictures with short-haired men and women who wanted to kiss or hug him. The TSA officer that checked Eastwood and his video and support crew's tickets and passports noticed the hundreds of visas, stamps and additional pages sewn into three of the men's well-worn passports, evidence of the men's sustained worldwide travel. The fourth member of the group, Khalid al-Alawaki, smiled broadly as he submitted his ticket and newly issued U.S. Tourist passport with one

Nigerian visa. He bounced on his toes until he was waved through.

After a quarter-hour of the steady and relentless crush of hot and displeased passengers, TSO Kesselring was flushed and exhausted. She stopped the conveyor belt, adjusted her damp *hijab,* and stood. She waved to the TSA supervisor to indicate she needed assistance. The supervisor frowned with concern and converged on the X-ray screener. "I'm sick and I need to be excused," she croaked. The TSO Lead snapped at another TSA officer to assume Kesselring's position and sent her away with a caveat not to give to him whatever "bug" she had. The TSA supervisor demanded she go home and get better.

She retrieved her bag from her locker and then stepped out onto the concourse. She stole a glance down at the crowd at the Nigerian Airways boarding gate then hurried out of the airport.

Abby Kesselring had no second thoughts about allowing weapons to be smuggled aboard an airliner. She smiled at the thought she was now a jihadi and had to escape. She had to flee the airport lest a TSO supervisor stumble onto security tapes which would show four semi-automatic pistols had passed through her X-ray machine and were on the "sterile" side of the airport concourse.

She didn't go home to get some rest; she picked up her bags and went to her mosque to communicate her success.

Four hours after landing, *The Nigerian Queen* boarded every one of its 700 passengers, and the aircraft pushed back from the gate without fanfare. The largest jet in the world taxied to the runway for takeoff.

CHAPTER TWENTY-FOUR

Network correspondents with no knowledge of aircraft or airlines operations rambled incoherently into microphones while photojournalists hunkered over the viewfinders of their cameras as *The Nigerian Queen* taxied into position on the distant runway. The festivities of the inaugural flight were but memories save for the few airline and airport employees remaining on the concourse silently waiting for the Airbus to takeoff and depart.

Inside the airplane passengers marveled at the roominess of the new jet: the ceilings were taller, the seats were wider, and the distance between the seats was longer than any other airliner they'd experienced. The expectation for the majority of travelers was sybaritic excess and wonder—wondering about all the buttons on the seat and video monitor control panels. Frequent travelers were in awe of the mighty airplane and were ecstatic to be one of the first travelers to fly directly to Nigeria, no longer having to change planes in Europe. Few passengers paid attention to the list of airline emergency instructions; fewer still heard, "This aircraft is equipped with aisle path lighting which is located on the floor in the left and right aisles."

Shortly after takeoff, waves of passengers' seats in the first and business class sections fully reclined into lie-flat beds; sleep masks shut out the light, airline blankets shut out the cold, and earplugs shut out the sounds of other passengers and flight attendants in the two premium class sections. In the last row of the business class section, Kelly Horne was asleep in the appropriate long-duration configuration—earplugs in, mask on, pillow and blanket employed— near one of the oversized windows in the super-sized jumbo jet.

Two African-American men with rumpled sports coats had settled in their aisle seats. One sat on the lower deck with the cockpit door in view, and one sat in one of the emergency exit rows in the upper deck. The man at the front of the airplane rarely took his eyes off the cockpit door as he casually monitored the comings and goings of the passengers who approached the toilets and the flight attendants who serviced the lower deck business class area. He sat across the aisle from an old retired Marine Corps officer, now a war correspondent for one of the networks. Eastwood and the man talked across the aisle sporadically during the flight.

In the rear of the business class section, a Middle Eastern man unbuckled his seat belt and retrieved his backpack from the overhead storage bin. He placed his bag on the floor near the footrest of his seat. He then sat glumly in his seat until after the first meal had been served.

After a couple of drinks cameramen Marty Marceau and Karl Mann stretched out and went to sleep in the center seats of the business class section. Eastwood and Khalid al-Alawaki remained awake. Eastwood reclined his seat with his feet up to ward off any chance of deep vein thrombosis; he pecked on the keyboard of a laptop computer while Khalid stared dreamily out of his window.

Khalid sat in disbelief of his good fortune. He had never experienced such wealth and opulence and service. The only other times he had been on a jet were in military transports, strapped in slung nylon troop seats flying off the U.S.S. Eisenhower or in the back of an Air Force C-17 Globemaster.

Khalid was the eyes and ears for Eastwood in all things Islamic. A Coptic Christian, he had learned the survival skills necessary to live in Muslim Libya. He lived and functioned as a Muslim. He learned Islamic prayers, Arabic, the Qur'an's interpretation, the *hadith*, and Islamic history. He attended mosque by day and reported what he heard and saw by night. Khalid had a knack of getting out of a jam, especially when an AK-47 was pointing at him. His undying devotion and fearlessness endeared him to Eastwood.

Eastwood glanced across the aisle at the sleeping man who hadn't removed his jacket, then over at Khalid before he returned to his computer. He worked furiously drafting emails to associates and informing his fellow former Marine that his armored Tahoe had been damaged and was in the network's underground parking garage. Eastwood was surprised the new jet didn't have a working inflight internet capability but figured that when they landed one of the local internet providers would pick up the queued messages and pass them on. Finished with his work, he shut down the laptop and pushed one of the many buttons on the seat control panel which unfolded his seat and turned it into a bed. After several yawns, he also shut down for the long flight.

· · ·

Nazy Cunningham stood in front of the desk of the Director of Central Intelligence. The Chief of Security, Anna Comstock, stood next to her, coughing into her hand to clear her throat. The air of the office was oppressive and stale with rancid nanoparticles of sweat intermittently wafting into the atmosphere as they burst from the drenched armpits of a highly caffeinated and apoplectic Greg Lynche. The women wrinkled their noses as Lynche waved his arms, unable to speak, trying to find the right words but failing. He retreated from his histrionics by placing his head in his hands to calm himself. "No one hurt?"

Comstock coughed, "Ten intruders are dead. Agency personnel all safe."

Lynche peeked through spread fingers. It was a subconscious gesture of leaving his hiding place to face the consequences. From the moment his telephone rang at his house with the duty officer informing him *Spindletop* had been attacked, he had feared the worst.

Of course, the safe house would be attacked. Rothwell knew everything—he knew the Agency leadership would send Nazy away to hide until a counter-surveillance force could ascertain and qualify the nature of the threat on the deputy director of counterterrorism. And Rothwell knew of the unique safe house, that *Spindletop* had been used for debriefing high value defectors. He would've logically assumed the Security Chief would suggest evacuating a senior intelligence service executive suspected of being under surveillance to the mountaintop house.

Hunter's question, once casually dismissed by Lynche, now resonated with alarm: *If you know, he knows; doesn't he?* Lynche's liberal *laissez faire* assessment of the selection of the safe house to hide Nazy could have been fatal, and he would've had only himself to blame. As he sat there looking up at the two women, excoriating himself for being a fool, he capitulated and acknowledged he should have just countermanded the initial order and redirected Nazy and her security team to a larger facility with better security.

"Were we just lucky this time Anna? Or what?"

"Director Lynche," interjected Nazy, her accent was more pronounced when she lowered her voice. "*Spindletop* was probably not a good location for this operation. The premise that I could continue to work with heightened security all around me wasn't completely logical. No one was injured; all of the fail-safe protection systems worked as advertised, and we evacuated to the conference center—which is where we probably should have been in the first place. I could have said something. I should've said something."

Anna Comstock put her hand on Nazy's back and said, "I think the real concerns are, who were those men and what were they doing on the hill?"

"And who sent them," interjected Nazy. No one mentioned the elephant in the room—who knew about *Spindletop* and why they would orchestrate an attack. Lynche hadn't briefed Comstock on Nazy's analysis that the former DCI, Dr. Bruce Rothwell, was likely behind the assault. At that stage of the investigation, Comstock didn't have a need to know the particulars and the specifics. Now her mission was complete and she needed to return to her normal duties.

Lynche extracted his face from his fingers and sat up straight. "The

FBI is on the case. Anna, I didn't think Miss Cunningham would be in danger at the house, and I thought she could continue to work. There's only a handful of people that even know about it—that's what's disturbing."

The air was again breathable, but Comstock wanted out of the office. For the first time she sensed the DCI wasn't being entirely honest with her, that he just wanted her to leave, and it pissed her off. But she had work to attend to, like determining the identities of ten men, why they were after one of her senior executives, and where they came from. She offered Lynche a face saving mea culpa, "Director Lynche, we need to know what you want to do with Miss Cunningham. I can take her back to the conference center or even the Farm—no one would dare go after her if she were in one of those facilities."

Nazy looked at Comstock and then at Lynche. She thought she should have some say in where she should go, but Lynche frowned and blurted out, "I'm leaving for Germany in a few hours; Miss Cunningham will accompany me. No one will think of looking for her in a jet or, for that matter, in Europe."

The two women looked at each other with incredulity, disbelieving what they had just heard. The Director of Central Intelligence began to move papers around his usual trash heap of a desk; he was back to being the Director of the CIA and was no longer lamenting on his deficiencies in the safe house operation. Director Lynche dismissed Comstock; "That'll be all, Anna. Again, thanks for all your help."

As Comstock turned and exited the DCI's office, Lynche asked, "Miss Cunningham?"

"Yes, Director Lynche."

"Do you have a bag packed for an overnighter?"

"I do, but...."

"Bring it. I'll pick you up from your office at eleven and we can walk down together. I'll brief you when we're airborne. You're not going to believe what your fiancée has done."

"I can hardly wait to hear it. See you shortly, Sir."

As Nazy turned and walked away, Lynche struggled not to watch her depart his office. But he was a man, and the shapely and leggy woman had a way of making men's eyes follow her. After she closed the door behind her, Lynche blinked, exhaled, and said to the computer monitor beside his desk, "Hunter, you're the luckiest shit on the planet."

. . .

As *The Nigerian Queen* reached its cruising altitude, Abby Kesselring entered her mosque on the south side of New York dragging a bag and wearing an arrogant smile. Ebullient to be part of the jihad, her enthusiasm was obvious, and her imam smiled at her through his wiry grey beard. He rubbed his ubiquitous knotted cord with one hand and gently directed the young woman to his office, then invited her to sit.

"Concerning the Islamic caliphate, this is our dream, and we hope to achieve it. Your help today brings us closer to our dream. Our first goal is the overthrow of America, then the renaissance of the Arab world, and then the dominance of the world. This will come gradually, one step at a time. You've done well, my sister." The imam gently touched her shoulder as an acknowledgement of doing well.

Pleased with herself, Abby gently nodded. She was ready to move to more exciting missions. Having packed and vacated her apartment as planned and directed, she looked forward to again serving Allah in a new assignment. She was so very happy with herself and so giddy with success that she was oblivious to her surroundings.

The imam continued to finger the braided cord and speak of her good work, but she heard little of what he said. When he casually stepped behind her—a movement that would've previously made her nervous and unsettled, however momentarily—she ignored the man's shuffling and words. She closed her eyes and focused on her successes, relishing how easy it had been to help smuggle weapons through the airport and identify air marshals for her fellow *jihadis*. She was also pleased with the way she rejected her parents, especially the way she stuck it to her gun-toting, Bible-thumping, know-it-all father. She knew her imam had to be very pleased with her for passing several of the most difficult tests of loyalty and faith. She never saw the loop of cord as it snapped over her head and jerked around her neck.

The imam had separated the ends of the loop of cord and he gripped the ends. His nostrils flared, and his knuckles turned white as the knotted rope chewed into his hands. He pulled Kesselring backwards out of her chair.

Her eyes bulged the instant he pulled the rope tight, and she immediately fought the garrote. She tried to scream, but nothing came out of her crushed larynx. She didn't understand what was happening to her. She kicked and clawed at the cord but with no blood or oxygen going to the brain, she quickly exhausted herself. As her life ebbed away she quit fighting and fell limp.

When the grey haired imam was sure the woman was dead, he viciously ripped off her *hijab*. He then removed her slacks and her underwear. After a short pause to admire his handiwork and her naked white ass, he unbuckled his trousers.

· · ·

Hunter and McGee lounged in oversized chairs in Hunter's suite watching the news on the large television monitor. Hunter vigorously pressed buttons on the remote control in an attempt to find something worth watching. As he scrolled through flashes of images from the different channels, he was surprised to see something he recognized. He mashed a few more buttons to return to the channel that caught his eye.

The image of a green and white Nigerian Airways Airbus A380 filled the monitor's margins; the header banner indicated the picture was televised by Al-Jazeera. The Africa channel. He thought the gold-colored emblem in the corner looked suspiciously like a stylized bug with legs, a tail, and eyes and ears. The crawler across the bottom of the screen stated in English that a new direct flight was now possible from

Lagos to New York City. McGee watched in rapt fascination as fire trucks sprayed water over the massive airplane. Hunter laughed when a crewmember who waved a flag from the top of the jet had to scurry like a rat back inside the airplane just as walls of water converged on him.

Duncan read confusion on the big man's face and said, "That's a water-cannon arch, kind of a salute by the airport fire department. They do those ceremonial things for pilot retirements, inaugural flights, and aircraft retirements. You're not supposed to have any doors or windows or emergency hatches open though. He was proud to wave that flag...." The two men laughed heartily as Hunter smashed a big red button on the remote control and shut down the television. It was time to go.

The start, taxi, and takeoff of the U.S. Air Force Special Operations MC-130 was made without any issue. The pilot, copilot, and flight engineer continually scanned the engine instruments and system indicators for signs of trouble from climb out to their assigned altitude. As the Hercules flew toward the African continent on a direct heading for the tiny country of Benin, the outside visibility quickly degraded, and the ride became significantly rougher. Dust and sand carried aloft from the Sahara obscured the ground and the coast, and the crew relied on the autopilot to navigate through the turbulent air. Level at 15,000 feet was a technical term, more an average, as the Hercules yo-yoed up and down hundreds of feet at a time while maintaining cruise airspeed of 300 knots. The pilot asked the flight engineer how their special passengers were doing.

"They're in sleeping bags. Asleep."

"Of course," said the pilot with a smirk.

"They sleep a lot," offered the copilot, matching the smirk.

"Be nice; one of these days you'll be old."

The flight engineer was bouncing around in her seat and she didn't like it. She offered her displeasure as only an aircrewman could, "Only seven more hours until we're out of this bullshit."

CHAPTER TWENTY-FIVE

An amalgamation of American engineering and artistic excellence, the G-550 proved that not all corporate jets were created equal. There's nothing else quite like the ultra-wide-cabin aircraft from Savannah, Georgia. With the exception of the pilot and copilot, those that approached the aircraft did so in hushed awe and settled in the cabin as if they had just discovered a how the rich and famous traveled. Most government employees usually rode in the center seat in the back of commercial airliners or in the troop seats of military airlifters. It was what the government travel regulations mandated as lowest cost, technically acceptable transportation. To fly on the DCI's aircraft was a treat.

Secure discrete air travel hadn't always been the case for the intelligence community. After the 2001 terrorist attack on America, as the war on terrorism mushroomed into a series of threat assessments on facilities and personal protective services for senior executives, highly protective and secure transportation became the new normal. Suddenly every GS-14 and above needed an armored car to get across town, and nearly every general officer or senior executive needed a corporate jet to fly across the country or the ocean.

Terrorist organizations such as al-Qaeda and Abu Nidal had longstanding fixations on targeting politicians and intelligence executives riding within aircraft. They had no compunction about bombing or shooting down an airliner full of civilians to get at a single government executive or intelligence officer they believed was working undercover. The targeting of intelligence officers and executives by hostile terrorist groups gave rise to the acquisition of several dozen corporate business jets in different sizes for different missions and effective ranges. Gulfstreams, Bombardiers, Learjets, Falcons, and other twin-engine jet aircraft with subdued markings were purchased or leased to quietly transport government executives and their bodyguards while reducing the targeting threat on commercial airliners.

Low-level and mid-grade intelligence officers, who were still able to travel clandestinely, flew undercover with multiple passports and disparate aliases, while the senior intelligence service executives, politicians, and other high-value, low-visibility persons took the corporate airlift. But for every action there's an equal and opposite reaction. When the U.S. government invested heavily in counterterrorism measures for transportation, other informal structures immediately sprang up to find and track government corporate aircraft movements and the movements of Senior Intelligence Service executives.

"Tail Watchers" monitored the comings and goings of government corporate aircraft—and their passengers—and were rewarded handsomely by the intelligence services of the former Soviet Union, al-Qaeda, and other nefarious terror support groups. Liberal and Islamic groups sprinted to be the first to identify the aircraft by photographing and tracking SIS executives and high value persons boarding and disembarking from the long-range jets. Less generous awards awaited those who merely confirmed an initial report that a senior intelligence officer was on the move.

Flyover America didn't have a need to know when or how their intelligence officers were traveling in the course of their duties. But armed with a computer and an internet connection, a network of tail watchers competed to find and track America's spies. And track them they did, easily and effortlessly. Tail watchers learned to discern between government and civilian travelers when they boarded the private jets. They noticed early on that there were two types of passengers: those that had their luggage handled and stowed by the aircrew while their meals were catered by the finest catering services, and those that managed their own luggage and carried their own food aboard the aircraft. The tail watchers ignored the former and reported on the latter, who were always government executives. So when six men and a woman carrying Subway sandwich bags and pizza boxes and dragging roll-aboards crossed the executive terminal ramp, their activities were enough for a pair of tail watchers to leap into action.

In a high-rise apartment building, overlooking the executive terminal at the Ronald Reagan National Airport, two men with high-powered binoculars and telescopes attached to digital cameras shot dozens of photographs and real-time videos. Once the passengers were aboard, the men immediately downloaded the images of the passengers and inputted the "tail number" of the aircraft into the tracking matrix database. Within minutes some nameless entity deposited many hundreds of dollars into the tail watcher's on-line bank account.

High over the Atlantic, hugging the Eastern Seaboard as the G-550 arced its way toward Europe, Nazy and Lynche sat opposite each other and finished their submarine sandwiches. He thought that it was incredible that such a thin woman could put away so much food. Lynche's security detail were satiated with pizza and were asleep at the front of the airplane, capitalizing on the old military axiom: when given an opportunity to eat, you eat; if given an opportunity to sleep, you sleep. It was going to be a long flight.

Nazy looked over her shoulder to verify the security men behind her were out of earshot. "Director Lynche, you said I wouldn't believe what Duncan did. Is that the reason we're going to Germany?"

He had forgotten he hadn't told Nazy why they were heading to Europe. He blurted out, "He found the lost Masters. And the Nazi gold." Lynche beamed like a lighthouse on a clear night.

Nazy couldn't speak. Lynche was familiar with the malady and laid out the plan to her. With the President's concurrence, Lynche would offer some of the paintings in exchange for the Russian suitcase nuclear devices. He didn't want to deal with the devil but reconciled and waxed philosophical, "that there are exceptions to every rule." The artwork could've easily rotted away for all eternity; now they were being put to good use as a bargaining chip to recover some of the failed Soviet Union's missing man-portable nuclear weapons. A thin smile punctuated other thoughts rummaging through his brain attic. "Boris knows we've recently found the artwork, and he's very interested in a swap. He'll meet us and inspect the art. He may bring an art expert to validate the collection, unless he's an art expert. With the KGB, you never know."

"Don't we have to verify he has the WMDs?" asked Nazy.

"We do, and I anticipate they'll be some offering on how we'll do that if we can make a deal. Obviously, he's not going to bring thermonuclear devices on a plane with him so I expect someone will make a trip for us to inspect the devices. There are still a number of questions we're dealing with. That's one of the reasons I wanted you to come along—you're a calming rational voice when there's so much testosterone in the room. KGB colonels are bullies, and when they have something you want, they can be insufferable especially after a half bottle of vodka. It may be a mistake to bring you along, or it may be one of the smartest things I've ever done. My track record lately hasn't been too good."

A polite smile preceded, "Thank you, Greg. We'll see what we can do dealing with this devil." After a few quiet moments of the two spooks keeping their thoughts to themselves, Nazy asked, "Where's Duncan now?"

"Africa—Nigeria."

"Boko Haram...*leaders?*" Lynche nodded. Nazy shook her head slightly; her hair wandered over her shoulders. "I worry about him. I wonder what this is doing to him...to his mind."

Lynche was immediately alert; he didn't expect the change of direction and suddenly realized he should have been wondering too. Lynche had his own problems that he was worried about but he pushed them into a corner for the time being. "Have you seen a change in him?"

Nazy shook her head vivaciously. "I haven't, but then again, I don't see him as often as I did, as I used to. I hardly see him at all now since he has another airplane. He's working at a furious pace with the business and for us. And he's still teaching school! His workload is overwhelming to me. He's gone much of the time."

"I've definitely kept him busy. Maybe too busy, if I read your level of concern right." Lynche looked into Nazy's eyes and realized he was reading something else; her body language shifted uncomfortably. She had something else she wanted to say and he'd be patient. It was going to be a long flight.

Nazy asked, "Do you know about his daughter?"

Lynche strained not to blink or say anything stupid. He nodded. He had no idea how she was going to react but her actions spoke of calm and introspection.

"I have this notion you personally assigned Kelly to be on my security detail. She obviously knew about me, and I figured it out; I mean how many new IOs have a gold Rolex identical to mine?" Nazy held up her hand and admired the timepiece. When she looked back at Lynche, she realized he was about to pop from nerves. His face was red; he couldn't speak and didn't know what to say. She continued, "I'm okay with it. I really am. She's a wonderful girl and I think she wants to be like Duncan. You know how he is; in a very short time he'll impress you beyond your wildest dreams. Kelly thinks he's the most amazing man she's ever met and cannot believe Duncan is her father."

Nazy's cool demeanor allowed Lynche to find his tongue and heave a sigh of relief. "Well, Duncan is the most amazing man I've ever met, and I've known a few—a few Presidents, a few DCIs, more than a few generals and admirals and members of Congress. But Duncan is in a category all by himself—definitely unique in many ways. He's a gifted athlete and a big brain. He thinks so far out of the box I've often thought his mother dropped him on his head and something went off in his cranium, turned him into some sort of prodigy. Probably could have been a brain surgeon."

"But he wanted to fly. He achieved his childhood dream. How many people can say that?" Nazy smiled, showing her perfect teeth, and shook her head in wonder. Lynche joined her in the smile as he synchronized their head movements.

"Duncan says he's the luckiest guy he knows. I have to agree. You two make a great couple." He thought Nazy might cry, but she didn't.

"Thank you." Nazy patted his hand and pinched her lips. *I…am the luckiest person I know!*

He allowed Nazy some time to consider what they had been discussing, then he stood and collected the refuse from the tiny table. Her train of thought was interrupted when he said, "Nazy, we ought to get some sleep. You take the bed in the back."

Confounded by the directive, she ushered, "I can't do that—that's…*the DCI's private…suite.*"

"You can and will; don't worry about the silly protocols—you're the one who got no sleep last night. These chairs recline—they're so good for my bad back you just can't appreciate it—trust me. If you weren't here I'd be sacked out in one of these chairs and would've sent one of the security detail to the back. Go." Lynche slipped off his shoes as if to say, *"Move it Cunningham; you're cutting into my sleep time."*

Nazy knew it was useless to argue so she capitulated. "Okay. Again, thank you. Good night, Director Lynche."

"Good night, Miss Cunningham."

As Nazy disappeared behind the small door at the rear of the jet, Lynche spread out in the recliner and tried to relax. Discussions of Hunter and Nazy frequently brought his thoughts back to a time in Liberia where he had witnessed a clash of civilizations when Nazy interviewed Osama bin Laden. He was strapped in a chair as Lynche looked on and Hunter threatened the master terrorist. He could still see OBL's fear as Duncan took battery jumper cables, opened wide the menacing toothy clamp, and temporarily attached it to the unprotected hand of bin Laden. The mastermind of 9/11 bucked against his restraints and screamed against the layers of duct tape across his mouth. When Hunter raked the positive and negative cables together in front of OBL's face, molten metal and sparks flew and filled the room with the biting smell of burnt metal. Lynche couldn't move or speak when Hunter threatened bin Laden with crushing the man's testicles with the battery cables and hooking him up to the battery. Evil was in Hunter's eyes that day as if hurting OBL would somehow ameliorate all the pain and suffering of the men, women, and children who died on September 11, 2001.

"We've all got a little bit of devil in us," said Hunter as he and a Navy SEAL carted the limp body of OBL out of the station master's house for places unknown. Only later, in the cockpit of another smaller Gulfstream, did he tell Lynche what he'd done. "I kept my promise—I put him on a jet."

"But we're the only jet on the field." Lynche was confused and when his partner didn't immediately respond, he then realized there *was* another jet on the field—an abandoned Russian "business jet." Lynche knew the three-engine airplane was the home of rats and mambas. No one would go anywhere near it.

Evil comes in many forms—sometimes it sits right next to you, if one were to believe it was evil to let rats gnaw on the flesh and bone of the world's top jihadist. Lynche could hardly believe that Hunter could conceive of such a way to die. It was better for the mind to believe the official narrative where OBL had been given a burial at sea after being snatched from his bed in Pakistan.

Yes, we've got a little bit of devil in us. As a liberal man, Lynche thought what Hunter did was heinous and abominable, but at the same time, OBL's body had to be disposed. He solved the dilemma like he had done so often with difficult problems. There's an evil elegance having rats turn bin Laden into tiny brown pellets. Lynche shuddered at the thought. One bad thing of making a deal with the devil is that he always comes to collect when your guard is down. The vision of OBL screaming while being eaten alive woke Lynche nearly every night for months. When Lynche stopped flying with Hunter, the nightmares stopped.

He looked over his toes to the door at the back of the jet, then closed his eyes. He would never tell Nazy or his wife that the nightmares had started again, this time with Nazy and Connie screaming while being burned alive from some terrorist who detonated a suitcase nuke in Washington DC.

. . .

The leader from the Muslim Brotherhood in Egypt sauntered onto the top floor of the Amman Marriott and into the executive suite. Those sitting around the conference table immediately ceased the badinage enjoyed by the majority as all eyes turned toward the man with the temper. His tenebrific expression conveyed he was furious about something, and he glared at Bruce Rothwell as he walked past him. Abdullah Muwaffaq noisily took his position at the foot of the table. The other members of the Muslim Brotherhood got out of his way as the Egyptian chuffed his irritation. He reeked of freshly smoked shisha; those sitting next to him barely noticed as he plopped into his seat and dropped his arms on the table with a thud. He waved a gnarled hand that was missing two fingers as he shouted and pointed toward Rothwell, "Raqqa, many Brothers were killed trying to capture the woman. *I am not* convinced it wasn't a trap!"

The jovial mood which had been present earlier immediately shifted to gloom and distrust as the accusation of treachery was tossed onto the table like a dead monkey. The first order of business was to determine what to do with the dead monkey on the table. The former head of the CIA had been in this situation many times before. When high-risk clandestine operations didn't go as planned, squeamish operations managers or protective intelligence officers often railed at political appointees or the one at the head of the table, venting their displeasure and frustration when good men were killed in an operation that went south for no apparent reason.

Rothwell calmly directed his good eye to the angry Egyptian and said, "Brother Arkho, compose yourself. We had agreed—unanimously—to the plan. I sense things didn't go well. What do you know; what have you learned?"

The man from the Muslim Brotherhood didn't appreciate the condescension in Rothwell's voice and became enraged. He tried to stand, but his fellow Brothers on either side of him pulled him down and patted his arms to calm him. His oversized Jordanian nurse, sitting against the wall behind him, banged his chair slightly as he raised his head to assess the situation. All eyes, save Rothwell's, turned toward the muscular man—even those of the al-Qaeda man sitting behind a laptop computer. There was malice in the Jordanian's eyes and malevolence in his posture as he moved to the edge of his chair, like a cougar pawing at the edge of a rock, ensuring his purchase and calculating his intercept point before leaping onto its prey. All eyes shifted back to Abdullah Muwaffaq for his next move. The man behind the laptop monitor returned to his computer work.

Rothwell's voice was suddenly silky, ominous, sinister. "Brother Arkho, so we may move forward, what do you know?"

"Ten mujahedeen found and approached the compound... they, uh, entered...and *dragons* killed them."

The raised eyebrows of every man in the room indicated their confusion. They looked at each other, extremely circumspect given that dragons were myths and therefore, not to be believed. Even Abdullah Muwaffaq found it difficult to utter the incomprehensible. After several moments to assimilate what the man from Egypt had said, Rothwell offered an olive branch. "Brother Arkho, I was aware of the CIA spies within your organizations, and I was aware of the leaders of your many groups targeted for assassination by the American President, but I'm unaware the CIA has employed legendary creatures, be they serpentine or reptilian. If you please, may we start anew—as Brothers in arms—to resolve and understand this latest obstacle?"

The huge Jordanian, reading the body language of the group, slipped to the back of his chair and lowered his head as if he were dozing. The men of al-Qaeda and the Muslim Brotherhood nodded a collective and encouraging assent; they traded racing hearts and anxiety for minor nervousness. They waited for the Egyptian to explain himself.

Muwaffaq was deeply embarrassed. The group of terrorists would hold on to his every word. He gathered his thoughts and nodded slightly before he said, "Please, forgive my impertinence and disrespect. The sole survivor...reported everyone was silent and progressed with caution. They found the fence as expected. He took up a position between the fence and the bottom of the mountain when he heard the roar of the dragon. He looked up at the top of the slope as the dragon roared and spit fire. The light of fire illuminated the area, just like a dragon. Then it was silent; the *muj* called out his Brother's names. Only silence. He raced back to the mosque, afraid the dragon would come after him. My Brothers, I know it sounds incredible, but that's all I have."

Rothwell was disturbed by the man's testimony. He searched his memory of the safe house and its capabilities; it was just a house to debrief defectors; it was just a house with a SCIF in the basement; it was just a house located high atop a mountain in the Shenandoah. *At my level...I might not know of all the specifics, all the capabilities of the house. At my level...I wouldn't know of all the inherent security capabilities of the safe house—ah, yes, Spindletop! I never visited Spindletop. Although it was an Operations facility, I had no need to know what defectors visited Spindletop. I had no need to know the outcomes when defectors were debriefed. I had no need to know, but I should have known. I obviously missed something. Dragons make no sense. Something from the S&T labs maybe? Probably.* "Brother Arkho, I can assure you I'm unaware of any *dragon* in the employ of the CIA. But it does sound like the mission was compromised—somewhere, somehow. I won't lay any blame at the feet of my Brothers in this room. Until we've more information on what happened to our *mujahedeen* Brothers, I suggest we try to determine...we need to find out where your Brothers are now. They couldn't just disappear like shisha smoke in a stiff breeze. Do you not agree?"

Ten heads nodded at the sagacity of the man at the head of the table. He had diffused the potentially explosive situation. Abdullah Muwaffaq had been embarrassed, now he was humble as he stated that he agreed.

The eyes of the terrorists bounced from chair to chair when the man behind the laptop computer announced, "Raqqa, is this the infidel Hunter?" He pointed to an image of Duncan Hunter in a black business suit, leg crossed, and relaxed that was displayed on a projection screen at the far end of the table. At the grainy visage of

Hunter, Bruce Rothwell's anxiety level spiked and his heart raced, his hand suddenly clammy. All eyes turned to the former CIA Director for an answer. *"This is the infidel that can't be killed?"*

Through labored breathing, Rothwell croaked, "That's the infidel Hunter! *What, what do you have here?* Where, where did you get that picture?'

"Brother Raqqa, this is a video from the infidel's school, Navy War College. Ten years past." Everyone in the conference room watched in rapt attention as the man identified as Hunter ignored the camera and gave his attention to the speaker on the dais.

The video showed a slim man sitting in the front row of an auditorium. Nizar, the Jordanian nurse was unimpressed and resumed his hunched over dozing. The other men scrutinized the short video until it abruptly transitioned to a different scene of the military school. "Go back! Go back!" hollered Rothwell. "Can you freeze the image when you bring it back?"

Seconds later, the image of Hunter filled the screen.

The top al-Qaeda man said, "The infidel is sitting next to the Black Ghost."

Rothwell's head rocketed to the old Osama bin Laden lieutenant. His one eye stared at the man and his wire brush of a beard. "Who?"

"The Black Ghost. The Navy SEAL. *McGee.* He killed many, many *mujahedeen*. Immediately after we struck the Great Satan, the Black Ghost was sent to find the Sheikh. Sheikh bin Laden learned the Black Ghost was sent to Afghanistan to find him, so he *repositioned* to Pakistan by the most expeditious means possible. We monitored the Black Ghost in America for many years. For some time, we believed the Black Ghost was responsible for finding and killing Sheikh bin Laden, Peace be upon Him; some Brothers watched the Black Ghost's house. Our Brothers *disappeared* and their mosque caught fire. Suspiciously. Many Brothers and sisters died. The Black Ghost is an evil spirit."

Some of the men watched the infidel Hunter bounce one leg over the other; others focused on the huge black man with tiny gold-rimmed glasses and a brilliant white uniform sitting on the other side of Hunter, partially obscured. Rothwell noticed the men from the Muslim Brotherhood seethed at the image of the infidel Hunter, indelibly imprinting the hateful and arrogant man in their minds, while the men from al-Qaeda curiously displayed reverence and fear when looking at the Navy SEAL, McGee.

A minute passed before Rothwell pounded his hand on the table to get the attention of the group. The discordant thumping achieved the desired effect. "My brothers, the purpose of our meeting is to acknowledge that *Operation Anjam* is in play. They will do anything to get their airplane back. We'll soon have sufficient funds to push our agenda, your agendas. Our Brothers are in position. Soon we'll submit our demands. *Insha'Allah.* Agreed? Good. Now, could someone tell me why the infidel Hunter is sitting with this Black Ghost, this murderer of Muslims?"

The murmur around the conference table was sibilant, like the wind rustling fallen leaves. From the al-Qaeda men with their black *keffiyehs*, their wordless response was confounding, perplexing. From the men from the Muslim Brotherhood, their response was discomfiting and full of chagrin. Seeing the mortal enemies of both organizations sitting peacefully, side by side, obviously meant something, but no one could offer an answer. Before the man from the al-Nusrah Front could offer a suggestion, the man with a black beard in the white *keffiyeh* sitting behind the keyboard of his laptop computer interrupted the buzz around the table. "Brother Raqqa, excuse me. I may have something new from the watcher's network. *See-ah-aaa* aircraft departed the Great Satan's capital...six men and...a woman." The conference room became morgue quiet; every head turned toward the man at the head of the table.

Rothwell allowed his eye to drift to the man behind the computer. "Do you have photographs?"

"Attached video. I'll retrieve and play." Heads and eyes turned toward the silver screen; the projector hummed and flashed a very good quality picture of a man and a woman walking together, side by side, with five other men following, carrying boxes and bags and dragging luggage with wheels. Rothwell recognized the jet. It was the same aircraft he had flown in during the last days of his tenure as the Director of Central Intelligence. The picture was disturbed; the image vibrated sporadically and vigorously as the camera zoomed in on the woman and the man.

Rothwell barked, "Freeze it!" when the woman turned to speak to the man on her right. Rothwell recognized the man to be Greg Lynche, the new DCI; and he recognized the woman with her hair pulled back into a tight knot and a long ponytail. He hadn't seen her in months, and again she took his breath away. Every man in the room, even the big Jordanian nurse, stared at the striking woman on the screen. A couple of men from the Muslim Brotherhood tapped their fingers, thinking. The leader from the Muslim Brotherhood in Egypt turned to Rothwell and asked, "This your woman? She is *takfir*?" While all eyes turned to the former CIA chief to await his answer, the man from Libya suspected the woman on the screen had willingly abandoned Islam. The sentence for apostasy, *irtidad*, under Sharia is execution, and he said so. "She is a traitor to the faith. She must die Raqqa."

"All in good time." Seeing her again, surrounded by men who would do anything for her, convinced him that she was treacherous enough to hide the President's file and give it to Hunter.

A chime from the laptop computer interrupted the group's focus on the woman. Rothwell ignored the hint of accusation that he lusted after a woman who left Islam. His eye was drawn to the pop up window in the lower corner of the screen. An email had been received. The sender's name was blocked. A pithy response to an unknown question was spelled out in the tiny box. "Done." Rothwell smiled at the message and returned his eye to the group. He nodded and said, "Is she not remarkable? It will be a thrill to punish her for her heresy and snuff the life from something as exquisite as that."

"*Insha'allah, Insha'allah,*" uttered the men around the table, their eyes returning to the image on the screen.

With a wave of his hand he dismissed them. "May Allah give you success. Go in peace, my brothers."

CHAPTER TWENTY-SIX

As soon as the Special Operations MC-130 entered Benin airspace, the pilot pushed the aircraft to a lower altitude and retarded the engine condition levers to not over-speed the quickly descending aircraft. The pilot and copilot donned helmets and night vision goggles for the ingress to the dirt landing strip. The sensor operator in the cockpit scanned ahead of the flight path with the FLIR to determine any hint of a thermal signature of man or beast near or on the runway. Finding "hot spots," the white-hot images of wildlife, was a common occurrence when flying into a remote African runway. Lions were virtually extinct in the area, but hitting a water buffalo that decided to run across the runway could ruin the mission and possibly kill the crew. The approach into the field under NVGs was the most dangerous part of the mission.

The cabin became awash in red lights that signaled the landing phase and marked fifteen minutes to touchdown. As the cockpit lighting was switched to the aircraft's internal NVG-capable systems, the instruments and controls became fully readable by the aircrew with their night vision devices. Instruments, knobs, switches, circuit breakers, and caution and warning lights were displayed in shades of green. In the cabin, young men in green flight suits sprang into action as the two old but spry YO-3A mechanics, Bob and Bob, prepared their special purpose aircraft for deployment. They opened the doors of the spy plane's shipping container and locked them in place.

Thirty minutes earlier the taller Bob had squeezed into the YO-3A's container to unlock a safe where the hybrid propellant bullets were safely kept while in flight. He reached over the Yo-Yo's empennage and handed Hunter two of the twenty-pound, ten-round, foot-long magazines of the state-of-the-art, laser-designated, .70 caliber ammunition. Hunter demonstrated to McGee how to load the airplane's gun. He opened the sensor access panel on the left side of the YO-3A, then he and McGee checked to ensure the rounds were fully seated into the gun's magazine port before closing the panel and taping its seams. McGee hoped they had brought enough ammo.

It was show time. Under a red light in the cargo area, Hunter and McGee slipped out of their traveling clothes before donning black Nomex flight suits, black flying gloves, and the black tactical boots favored by Special Operations warriors. Hunter extracted a black leather shoulder holster—with a hideous black revolver—from his helmet bag. He nestled the weapon close to his chest under his left arm. Bill McGee checked the silenced Kimber 1911 .45 ACP in the pocket of his survival vest. In a synchronous motion, the men donned their flying helmets with binocular night vision goggle systems mounted to the front. Both men snapped chinstraps and flipped the NVGs up and out of the way.

McGee had mirrored Hunter's preflight ritual up to the point when Hunter threaded his arms through the shoulder harness for the heavy, black six-shooter. Duncan pulled the six-inch .357 magnum Colt Python from the holster and opened the cylinder to verify that five hollow-point rounds were loaded in the revolver. He precisely closed the cylinder and ensured the empty chamber was at the twelve o'clock position. The old SEAL watched and understood the hammer wouldn't be able to strike a cartridge's primer in the case of a hard landing or other sudden impact. *Marines aren't as dumb as they look* McGee thought facetiously—real men don't ever fly with the hammer of a revolver positioned over a live cartridge.

The other trick Hunter learned was to always carry the biggest damn gun and the hottest ammunition you can handle. "I never carry anything in the Python that's not capable of taking down a grizzly," he said to McGee the first time the SEAL saw Hunter handle the big Colt. "I hate confessing I'm an ophiophobe, but I love this snake. It's a baddass gun—the most beautiful handgun ever made. Trigger breaks at three pounds. There's no take up or over-travel. It's like a cannon going off in your hand. Bang." Hunter felt the .44 magnum had plenty of stopping power but it was too large and too heavy, but the.357 magnum was just right for his hand and frame. If someone was hit with a .357 magnum bullet, they stayed down. Hunter was living testimony that the Colt Python had plenty of stopping power and was more than enough of a weapon. He had killed a pair of Algerian special operations soldiers that had been chasing him. He credited the big-bore Colt for saving his life, and he had become quite fond of it. McGee suspected Hunter liked the revolver because the combat rig looked great slung under his arm. It *was* very *manly*. For the SEAL, the revolver was for show; the silenced semi-automatic was for combat operations. When Hunter pulled another silenced, Kimber 1911 .45 pistol from his helmet bag—identical to McGee's—and slipped it into a pocket of his survival vest, McGee said, "Duncan, I think you're a threat to the existing social order."

Everyone in the cabin jumped at the sharp sound of the hydraulic system lowering the flaps. Three special operations mechanics moved toward the rear of the airplane; the loadmaster lowered the cargo ramp and raised the cargo door. The seven men in the back of the Hercules looked out of the opening into the inky blackness of African jungle. The men didn't need to check their watches; they knew it was two minutes to touchdown.

The next audible clue that landing was imminent was the sound of the hydraulic systems repositioning the flaps to full down. The aircraft slowed quickly and pitched nose downward, and the C-130 Hercules gently swayed in the calm night air. Seven men positioned themselves for the final phase of landing. The flight engineer moved to the cargo ramp controls while the two Air Force mechanics moved to the cargo ramp hinge. Bob and Bob crawled to the rear of the YO-3A container and released the locking pins which secured the airplane in place. The old men were jostled from the additional drag of full flaps and from the tires and wheels being lowered into the airstream. The cabin lights flashed three times. On glide slope, on course. Sixty seconds to touchdown. In less than five minutes, Hunter and McGee would be airborne.

The FLIR sensor operator called out through the interphone system "the landing environment is clear," meaning no humans or large mammals were anywhere close to the runway. A young mechanic blessed himself with the sign of the cross. Hunter and McGee slipped into their parachute harnesses and buckled the chest closures as they peered out of one of the cabin's porthole windows—nothing but pitch black.

No landing lights illuminated the runway. The special operations aircrew had trained extensively with their night-vision goggles to land the big cargo airplane in the most remote and austere environments. Rarely did the men and women of AFSOC get lucky and land on a prepared runway, even if it was dirt.

The night vision goggle systems were extraordinary visual aids in most situations, but in the landing phase, with no depth perception, they greatly limited a pilot's ability to properly judge the aircraft's rate of descent to touchdown. NGV landings could be considered good, bad, or "colorful." As the pilot set the aircraft down smoothly, wings level, the copilot reversed the propellers' pitch while the pilot mashed the toe brakes; the cargo airlifter decelerated quickly. Tonight's night landing was textbook perfect.

The loadmaster lowered the ramp just as the Hercules stopped in a cloud of dirt and dust. A pair of mechanics stepped off the trailing edge of the cargo ramp and pivoted three smaller ramps until they touched the ground, then they moved out of the way as the YO-3A was rolled out of its container, through the cargo door, and out onto the dirt runway. Duncan Hunter rode a small contraption on the side of the YO-3A and depressed a footbrake to control the matte black airplane's speed down the cargo ramp and onto the runway. As the Yo-Yo passed them, the mechanics raced into the container and helped the Bobs lift the wings from the wing cradles. When the Yo-Yo was well clear of the MC-130's tail, Hunter applied more pressure to the footbrake to stop the YO-3A. McGee watched Hunter uncouple the footbrake assembly, run back to the aircraft's opening and place the device on the cargo ramp. That was McGee's cue to get to their airplane, raise the canopy, and jump into the back seat. Following him were the two Bobs and the two mechanics hauling out the glider-like wings as quickly as they could carry them.

Hunter raced McGee to the smallest of Lockheed's spy planes. With the canopy opening on the pneumatic piston, the men scrambled up and over the side of the fuselage and stepped on the seat pan inside. Both men stepped down into the foot wells and hunkered in their seats as Hunter flipped on the battery switch. He connected his helmet's "pigtail," the communication cord for the interphone system, and their boom microphones. As electrical systems powered up, the men fastened their lap and shoulder belts. Hunter sped through his checklists to get airborne.

As the Bobs finished hanging the wings, the Air Force mechanics sprinted into the cargo area of the Hercules and into the YO-3A's container for cans of aviation gasoline. As each Bob connected the wing's aileron control cables to the fuselage's cable system, the specially-designed, NASCAR-inspired, fuel cans—capable of draining eight gallons in eight seconds—were dumped into the left and right wing tanks by the mechanics. In less than thirty seconds, thirty-two gallons sloshed in the wing tanks. With the wing tanks full of fuel, Bob and Bob, and the two mechanics peeled tape from the fuselage and taped all exposed joints and fuel access doors. The support crew's tasks were complete and they threw their thumbs into the air to signal, "We're clear," as they stepped away from the YO-3A.

Hunter set the aircraft for engine start as McGee monitored the men's progress. Flipping his night vision goggles over his eyes, Hunter looked out over to the edge of the wing and rocked the control stick from left to right, fore and aft as he verified the flight control cables were connected and the flight controls responded properly. With one final check to ensure the electrically-driven fuel pumps in the wings were running, Hunter engaged the starter.

The six-bladed propeller spun 720° before the engine lit off, sending a puff of white smoke through the complex muffler system before it was expelled well behind the cockpit. No one could hear the engine exhaust or the YO-3A's propeller over the C-130's four idling Allison turboprops. Hunter checked for rising oil and manifold air pressures before he programmed the throttle to takeoff power.

The two Bobs and the Air Force mechanics ran back into the Hercules and prepared the C-130 for an immediate departure—the loadmaster barked into his microphone "All Clear!" As the brakes were released on the cargo airplane, the loadmaster raised the ramp and closed the cargo door. Through the shrinking aperture of a rising ramp and a lowering cargo door, Bob and Bob watched their little black airplane disappear into the night, just as the ramp and ramp door came together. Sixty seconds after Hunter raised the YO-3A landing gear handle and the flaps, the C-130 executed a short field takeoff and was also airborne and heading south toward the coast. The MC-130 would take the circuitous route to their rendezvous point due west.

. . .

Seasoned international airline passengers know how it is when it's very late into the last phase of the flight. The cabin has been darkened for sleep and flight attendants begin to stir in the galleys to prepare the final meal before the airplane descends and lands. The dissimilar and discordant sounds of a compact commercial kitchen are heard right before the lamps in the cabin are switched on to flood the interior with bright light that the majority of passengers find unwanted and painful. For those not wearing a sleep mask or without a blanket pulled over their heads, the sudden fury of the cabin's intense floodlights immediately assaults the optic nerves like a visual alarm clock. Stabbing pain forces eyelids to slam shut as passengers fight against the rude and unnecessary measures used to awaken them. Frequent flying passengers wear earplugs or headphones to offset the susurration of white noise and the mechanical hiss of 600-mile per hour winds racing over the airframe. They also protect their ears against the cacophony of aluminum carts banging, oven doors slamming, and soda cans rattling in the galleys in the planned attempt to gently awaken the masses for their final meal of the flight.

Demetrius Eastwood lifted his sleep mask to confirm the noise that had penetrated his earplugs and awakened him was the flight attendants' movements in the cabin and galley; that it was time to rise, time to sit up, time to eat and prepare to get off the jet. Surprisingly, the cabin was still very dark with only a trace of light softly splashing from above the overhead compartments, and curiously, there was none of the expected tumult coming from the galley kitchen. The cabin was eerily quiet. Surprised it wasn't the usual clatter that had roused him from his slumber, Eastwood lifted his head from his lie-flat seat to determine what had disturbed the ambiance surrounding him. He peered over the armrest to see a hideous black handle protruding from the neck of the man sitting directly across the aisle. The sight of a knife grip, a blood drenched shirt, and an empty leather shoulder holster jolted Eastwood fully awake. As adrenaline spiked throughout his body, he froze in fear; his senses on full alert. His eyes remained fixed on the body of the dead air marshal as the man's torso and arms shuddered. *God, I hope this is a dream!*

Eastwood flashed back to Vietnam when he was an infantry officer during his first firefight. He turned in the direction of the call for help; a Marine had taken a bullet in the neck. He froze momentarily then, too, as a corpsman worked frantically to save the young man's life as blood and air escaped from gaping wounds so devastating....

When the unmistakable sound of a gunshot echoed from the front of the airplane, Eastwood snapped out of the past and spun back into his present. Upright in his seat, he stared forward; his eyes strained to see into the darkened passageway of lavatories, the galley, and cockpit entrance. *The cockpit was being attacked!*

In his periphery, dozens of heads sprang up from their beds as if they had been catapulted into stunned silence. Throughout the business class cabin there was a hush; the only sound was the constant drone of air friction over the aircraft's fuselage. Although they hadn't seen it, they heard the unambiguous sound of terrorism loose in their airplane. Unable to move or run, and with nowhere to go, they closed their gaping mouths and awaited their fate in stony silence.

Khalid arose confused; he stammered and muttered incomprehensively in Arabic and sought answers from Eastwood. But Eastwood wouldn't engage the Libyan sitting next to him and pushed him back down into his seat. Although Khalid was confused, he complied. As he returned to his pillow, he shook his head and whispered in disgust, "Moslems."

Ahead, Eastwood saw the impenetrable cockpit door open and the silhouette of a man with a pistol slip into the flight deck. Between the blinks of his eyes, the cockpit door closed again. Eastwood expected to hear the sound of multiple muffled pistol shots burst from the cockpit, but nothing came. Others had seen the man with a gun enter the flight deck; the passengers in the two premium classes were in a state of shock and disbelief at what they had heard and seen.

He again looked at the man with the black handle in his throat. *This can't be happening!* Long ago trained in the martial arts of timing his assault and balancing defensive actions with offensive attacks, Eastwood knew his opportunity to do something to prevent the takeover of the jet had passed when the shadow of a man with a raised weapon closed the cockpit door behind him. He had been asleep; he had heard something out of the ordinary but dismissed it as the routine of weary flight attendants. He was also out of position, a seat belt across his lap and without a weapon; he never had the chance to interrupt the plan. He admonished himself. If he had been awake would he have been able or ready to recognize the incremental signs of an attack? To interrupt a terrorist attack requires a sense, an instinct, a flicker of insight and nerves so quick that you act instantaneously. What did he see—nothing! He was asleep! He missed all the clues. The subtle shift of the terrorist's weight as the knife was thrust into the man's neck and through his spine had disturbed the atmosphere around him, but he had missed it. He missed the telltale glances of a murderous terrorist; glances that presaged the attack and set off the next chain of events. Yes, he had missed all the signs. He had gotten old, and the old man was fast asleep when his fellow passengers needed him the most. Other than Eastwood, no one had yet noticed the dead air marshal. Eastwood had heard death throes and dismissed them as background noise.

After a dozen hours airborne, the policemen on the upper and lower decks of the massive airplane had let their guards down. Passengers walked freely by them without notice or concern; it was a long flight and they had fallen asleep. A case study of complacency colliding with a case study of planning and scheduling. No one noticed a man walk to the lower deck to rendezvous with another and return with a backpack. No one noticed two men, one on the upper deck and one from the lower deck, as they waited for their smart telephones to vibrate at the synchronized time. No one noticed as the two men arose from their seats and quickly located and closed on their targets in the subdued lighting. No one noticed as they viciously jammed the composite material daggers into the throats of the sleeping undercover policemen. Three men on each deck had rendezvoused with a fourth to receive pistols. In seconds, three men patrolled the aisles with hidden pistols as they awaited their cue.

After quietly killing the air marshal in his seat and removing the policeman's weapon, the man pistol-whipped a flight attendant in the galley as he raced to the front of the jumbo jet. He placed the barrel of the air marshal's pistol against the exposed circular lock of the cockpit door and pulled the trigger.

The locking mechanism securing the cockpit door wasn't designed for a point-blank-range, high-powered weapon assault. The .45 caliber bullet slammed into the face of the lock, ripping the stainless steel bolt from its mounting. The force of the projectile blasted the lock into the cockpit where it struck one of the multifunction displays on the aircraft's instrument panel. The sound was deafening in the enclosed cockpit, and the pilot, copilot, and flight engineer instinctively moved to protect themselves from the compressed sonic shockwave in the enclosed space. Autopilot kept the aircraft on altitude and heading.

Instantly upon firing, the pistol was ripped from the terrorist's grip, and his ears were concussed from the pistol blast. He hadn't anticipated the recoil well. The concentrated blast and reaction of the slug slamming into the lock face nearly broke the man's hand as the recoil sent the gun flying. Time ticked away; he either entered the cockpit and subdued the crew or the whole plan was for naught. He quickly located and recovered the weapon from the floor and stepped into the cockpit.

He pointed the gun into the face of the stunned pilot and then the copilot. He was surprised to see another man in the communications center of the giant airplane. He backhanded the flight engineer with the butt of the pistol. The copilot reached to the IFF control panel to program 7500 into the system, the Identify Friend or Foe code for Hijack. The terrorist's voice crackled as he spoke; the weapon shook in his hands as he pointed it at the copilot, "Remove your hand from the control panel. *Do it!* Do not make me kill you. You will do exactly what I tell you." The terrorist leaned over the center console and checked that the transponder codes in the IFF didn't read 7500. The four digits read something else so he rotated the selector switch to OFF. As he had been trained, he said, "Now you'll pull the circuit breakers to turn off the transponders."

· · ·

Kelly Horne jumped at the sound of a bullet tearing into metal. It awoke everyone on the flight deck. The one hundred people in the first and business class areas sat up in their beds in shock and bewilderment. They stared in the direction of the cockpit, intuitively knowing it was under assault. Some people expected sudden cabin decompression, with loose articles and people flying dramatically through the cabin, and being sucked through holes in the fuselage. But the only sound was from a man who ran into the business class area and waving a pistol as he screamed, *"Lie down—do not move and don't talk or you'll be shot! Surrender your cell phones or you'll be shot!"*

While the terrorist was making demands and waving his gun around the cabin in a threatening manner, Kelly and her fellow passengers moved to comply. She extracted her BlackBerry from her backpack on the floor beside her seat. She assessed the situation to determine when she would have to surrender her communication device or if she had time to hide it. With all of the mayhem in the cabin, she knew she had a few minutes to do something. She awakened her device from its battery saving mode, drafted, and sent a text message as fast she could and pressed several buttons to kill the ringer. Then she wedged it between the seats in front of her, tried to recall her training from the Farm, as she waited for more instructions from the tyrant with a gun.

CHAPTER TWENTY-SEVEN

The YO-3A winged above the tops of date palms on an easterly heading. Its long thin wings sliced through the thick, high-humidity jungle air as the sharp nose cone of the six-bladed propeller pointed toward the first of three targets twenty miles away. With the autopilot engaged and programmed with the global positioning system coordinates of the suspected Boko Haram hideout, Hunter merely monitored the aircraft's track and engine performance. Since takeoff and crossing the Benin-Nigerian border, he and McGee had talked intermittently, telling stories and jokes and swapping lies between mission essential communications. As the aircraft approached the first suspected hideout, Hunter's tone and demeanor turned businesslike.

Takeoff and climb out were as routine as slipping on deck shoes; once done it was forgotten. Ingressing to the target was administrative; a multiplicity of disparate items to be accomplished for the relatively short haul to the target intercept point. Hunter had set aileron, elevator, and rudder trims shortly after they leveled off at 3,000 feel AGL. All engine instruments were "in the green;" oil pressures in the engine and reduction gearboxes were high but remained in the normal operating range. The tip of the needle of the airspeed indicator rested on the demarcation line between red and yellow, between danger and caution zones. Hunter trimmed the airplane to fly at its fastest design speed without entering the red zone of V_{NE} or never to exceed speed.

The mission was to get in and get out as fast as possible, but within the aircraft's engineering design parameters. Hunter didn't want to break a propeller by overstressing the rotating components or "over-temping" or "over-torquing" the engine or the gearbox. Smooth night air ensured the wings and the airframe wouldn't be unduly stressed from thermals.

As typically occurred when flying in Sub-Saharan Africa, the smooth air and high engine RPM had set up a low frequency vibration throughout the aircraft's fuselage which was pleasing and therapeutic, and at times, soporific. During a period of quietude when Hunter was busy navigating and the noise reduction headphones in the men's helmets cancelled any extraneous sound, a very relaxed McGee had closed his eyes momentarily. He awoke with a start when Hunter spoke into the interphone system. He was so astonished to have been asleep that he couldn't admit it to Hunter. He asked him to repeat what he had said. "Say again?"

"Ten miles; I'm going to throttle back and slow down and toss out the FLIR and the gun."

"Roger." McGee rubbed his eyes and stretched his neck before answering. "You did all this by yourself for how long? Dude, this shit is spooky."

"One of the reasons I need a partner. These are long slugs to get into position and it's hard to fall asleep when you're aviating, navigating, and communicating. The human factors term is crew coordination. Lynche would tell me just enough of a story—with him at the CIA doing something no one would ever believe or know about—and just when it'd start to get interesting he'd tell me he couldn't say any more. I probably heard the same partial story fifty times. I regaled him with new stuff from flying F-4s, or some racquetball tournament, or time when I had my Corvette on the race track. Any bullshit was fair game but we didn't talk politics in the air."

"He's a little liberal, if I recall."

"He is although not a true believer or a bomb thrower or anything like that. Just part of the early Agency and State Department culture where they ruled the roost and tried to keep their political leanings a secret; like they had to do that. I really didn't have any secrets—I couldn't tell you squat from the top secret red books from my old F-4 days on how this missile acted when fired or what that radar system did or didn't do. But I know everything he did at CIA was a secret; probably even when he had to crap. But talking kept us alert and alive. At least it did me."

"I can understand that. Keeping secrets, same with being a SEAL. We had our share of interesting missions, and we trained all the time. We couldn't talk about any of it. No one ever had a need to know the details or the outcomes."

Hunter flipped a switch on a panel underneath the instrument panel. He said, "10-4. FLIR coming out."

"It's easy to get lulled to sleep out here."

"I know. I don't think I told you I fell asleep not too long ago after a long mission and found myself heading out to sea. If it hadn't been for the autopilot and one of the Bobs calling me on the radio my stupidity would've killed me."

The center multifunction display on McGee's instrument panel came alive with the black and whites shades of FLIR imagery. The forward-looking infrared indicated a hot spot on the horizon; its bright white thermal image showing in the center of the display panel. McGee hurried to finish his story. "I can appreciate that now. Never knew sleep could kill you. When we had an opportunity to sleep, we did. Some of my best sleeps were in the back of C-130 after we had been extracted from a mission."

"I really don't know what you guys did. Saw some SEALs blowing up some things out in the Yuma desert once. Blissfully ignorant I guess. Gun coming out." Hunter used the coolie hat on the control stick to slew the FLIR ball to the left and right to check its range of motion. The only thermal image in the area was dead ahead. Hunter trimmed the aircraft and adjusted the throttle to compensate for the additional drag created by the infrared sensor and the suspended rifle. "My FLIR. Your gun, sir. Potential target twelve o'clock."

"Your FLIR; my gun. You're going to give me ranging info?" McGee gripped the joystick controlling the gun. He swung the weapon to the left and right to recall its feel and reaction times.

"I will. Laser rangefinder indicates five miles. Laser designator at the ready. We'll make a slow pass abeam of the target to see what's down there and what they're doing, if anything. The overheads and ISR products suggested an unusual level of activity had been occurring here. The analysts believe they're using this location as a rendezvous point." Hunter checked the center multifunction display; all systems were either on, or energized, or were in standby. He scanned the instrument panel for any abnormal engine or fuel quantity indications. Finding none, he flipped his night vision goggles over his eyes and began scanning the area for light sources. "I'm going to climb a bit and look-see if there's anything else in the area." Hunter disengaged the autopilot and took manual control of the YO-3A.

The little airplane zoomed to 5,000 AGL and leveled off. "Looks like a string of vehicles inbound, probably seven-to-ten miles. We'll check this camp—the satellite analysis suggested this part of the forest is the starting point. If we find dudes with weapons then this should be the right place. These guys have a way of giving themselves away. For me, it's their attitude and their weapons. I suppose you've seen every weapon there is; I think you can pick out what they are if these guys show up with ordnance."

"I'd be a crappy SEAL if I couldn't."

As McGee talked, Hunter's head rocked left and right, scanning the horizon, searching for any light source. The ANVIS-9's dual photomultiplier tubes captured all the light in the sky. A million stars which couldn't be seen under normal conditions were illuminated as green pixilated haze in the upper half of the ocular; in the lower half of the ocular, the well-defined leaves of date palms and other flora could be seen beneath the airplane.

In the night vision devices, the bonfire burned bright in lighter shades of green. Hunter flew closer to the light sources to determine human activity with crystal green granularity. There's a fire, but no one was outside, only a goat. Whoever started the fire must be inside the mud brick structure. If he couldn't find them with the NVGs, he should be able to with the FLIR.

McGee focused on the thermal images generated by the FLIR.

"Should be easy; nearly every weapon in Africa is an AK. I've probably field stripped and fired every weapon ever made; pistols from around the world, rifles, RPGs, and even MANPADS. We specialized in weapons and counterterrorism. We trained to recover a kidnapped president, board ships in high seas, disarm nukes...."

Hunter found McGee's last assertion odd and asked for clarification. His transmission stepped on McGee's. "Disarm nukes? No shit? Did you ever have to do that?"

"You know...If I told you...."

"You'd have to kill me. I'm familiar." Both man laughed into their microphones.

"Well, let's just say it's been a very long time since I had to do anything like that. Mostly forgot about that episode. Kind of like your F-4's red books."

"Ah."

"We killed the enemies of America. That was the real job."

Hunter rotated the NVGs away from his eyes and returned to the FLIR display. "10-4. Ok, Bill, the image on the nose looks like a bonfire but no welcoming committee that I can see. Still could be someone in the building. The vehicles heading this way is very unusual. No one travels in large groups in the jungle at these hours. These might be our guys. We'll check them out and see what they're all about. It might be nothing, or it might be something. If we're lucky, you're going to whack some terrorists."

The only signs of life in the immediate area captured in the heat signature of the thermal sensor were the bonfire and a goat, and in the distance the headlights, engine, and exhaust of several two and four-wheel vehicles. As Hunter steered the quiet airplane to intercept the lead trucks, McGee marveled at Hunter's ability to coordinate the zoom, pan and tilt, and motion controller of the gyroscopically stabilized FLIR system to achieve greater definition of the black and white images.

"Man, I love it when technology works!" said McGee.

"Ok, sir. I'm going to put the FLIR on the guys in the trucks. We want to see if they're friendlies or bad guys." Hunter turned the optics of the FLIR toward the line of vehicles and worked the zoom control to achieve greater definition of the men in or on the machines.

McGee recalled the information contained in the mission file. Facsimile newspaper clippings of pictures and articles of Boko Haram leaders as they tore through the northeastern part of Nigeria painted a picture of a growing terrorist movement. Every week the Associated Press news agency or Al-Jazeera reported a hundred or more people killed or kidnapped in Nigeria's northeast. Hundreds of buildings were razed, and hundreds of vehicles were destroyed by armed groups in the latest attack on agricultural and commercial towns.

The leader of the Boko Haram group warned leading Nigerian politicians and religious leaders that his fighters would target them for pursuing democracy and Western-style education. He had been known to say, "The reason I'll kill you is that you're infidels; you follow democracy, and whoever follows democracy is an infidel and my enemy." He remembered from the file in Lynche's office that Boko Haram's goal was to transform Nigeria into an Islamic state through intimidation and fear, even though half of Nigeria's 160 million citizens were Christians.

The file included intelligence collected from ISR and HUMINT sources that suggested Boko Haram leaders had gone on raiding parties, streaming across the northwestern part of the country leaving a wake of dismembered bodies, incinerated buildings and schools, and burned out vehicles. Government forces responded too slowly, sometimes arriving at the scenes of carnage days after a murderous spree. CIA analysts recorded their concerns that government responses could have been purposely slow. This was a sure sign of widespread fear in the Nigerian army, fear of confronting the al-Qaeda affiliate group.

Schools were attacked, Christian mothers and fathers were hacked to death for not being Muslim or being unable to recite the Sura Al-Fatiha, the first chapter of the Qur'an. During some murderous orgies, the soldiers and leaders took young girls as trophies. Few news agencies were permitted to enter the northern areas and those that were allowed in to interview the Boko Haram leaders recorded threats to the President and his army. They were warned not to come to the northern territories unless they wished to die as infidels. Over the years, several journalists reported that the goal of the unabashed terrorist group was to turn the country Muslim. Christians were no longer welcome, and if they decided to stay in Nigeria, it was at their own peril. Submit or die.

Other analyses and embassy dispatches in the DCI's file described means and methods the leaders used to recruit followers. There was grotesque anecdotal evidence of men who initially resisted the threat of amputation or death, but eventually converted to Islam, only to be forced to kill their families to prove their devotion to Allah. One article after another, one CIA analysis after another, one embassy dispatch after another painted a story of a charismatic Muslim man and his murderous followers on a rampage. CIA updates to the PDB, the President's Daily Brief, regarding the critical and deteriorating situation in Nigeria were discussed in the Oval Office. Cheap weapons flowed into the porous northern border areas from arms dealers in adjacent countries, gifts from anonymous donors from the Middle East.

A Deputy DCI memo relayed a discussion between the Nigerian President and the POTUS. The subject was the Boko Haram group and their hideous recruiting methods, as well as their surprise expansion into the northwestern territories. The memo indicated the Nigerian President had requested American unmanned systems to destroy the al-Qaeda sympathizers. DCI Lynche recommended the Boko Haram leaders moved to the top of the President's disposition matrix. Subsequently, a greater number of ISR flights from the south patrolled the north to try and locate the camps, the hideouts, and the Boko Haram command post. Usually a trail of dead and dismembered bodies or a village on fire indicated where the terrorist group had been. They left their signature calling cards—a string of body parts strewn in the streets with vultures congregating high over the devastated areas.

The actual horrors were greater than what was reported. In the beginning, some Nigerian media, newspaper correspondents mostly, reported accurately. Then the newspapers and their executives and editors were threatened, resulting in a virtual news blackout. Family members attacked in Lagos and Abuja ensured Boko Haram stories wouldn't be told. What remained was a thin network of informants—HUMINT—to gather intelligence, take photographs, and report the news of Boko Haram atrocities to U.S. Embassy personnel.

The Ambassador informed the Nigerian leader that the U.S. Government would provide more twin-engine ISR aircraft and other assets as they become available. U.S. military and intelligence officers flooded into Nigeria and moved into office buildings in the capital and Lagos. A joint task force was created between Nigerian and U.S. military and intelligence forces. Money flowed to informants. With satellite imagery and ISR products from numerous flights over the disputed areas, a picture began to emerge of who the Boko Haram leaders were, what specifically presaged an attack in the towns, and when and where the group could be expected to attack next. The Nigerian leaders were frustrated with the Americans' procedures and penchant for planning. The Americans relied on proven methods but the Nigerians expected more action and sought much more firepower.

McGee returned to the present when Hunter spoke, "Looks like these are our guys. I'm certain those are *youngsters*.... Yes, sir, those are girls in the back of the trucks. Over a dozen. *Damn!*"

McGee sucked a lungful of air as he stared at the images of frightened children. He had two girls at home and the thought of them in the hands of evil men focused his thoughts and resolve. He wouldn't feel any remorse. "They all have AKs."

Hunter said, "Tally ho! I would say the top dogs are in the lead vehicle. What do you think? Big Toyota SUV."

"I agree—they're in the nicer truck and the leaders aren't about to suck on dust for miles."

"Double checked, gun armed," said Hunter.

"Roger. You have the LD, I have the gun. I recommend we wait until they stop; we'll watch the behavior of the leaders, prioritize them, and then eliminate them. Then the other men."

"Sounds like a plan, sir."

"Duncan, I hope you brought enough bullets."

"We've got twenty."

"That might not be enough."

"I have faith in your expertise to kill scum," offered Hunter.

McGee lifted his eyes from the screen and turned his head, to the blackness of the night. Something was bothering him and he struggled to articulate his thoughts. After returning his gaze on the FLIR image, McGee asked, "Do we have to let one go?"

Hunter knew what McGee was intimating. The plan was to kill all the terrorists, all but one. One lucky bastard terrorist would live to tell the story of how his friends had died, ambushed by an unseen rival tribe or group. But in this case, there was an obvious solution. "No one needs to know, Bill, and besides, the girls will report it was something or someone unseen."

"They're stopping. Showtime."

Hunter placed the dot of the laser designator on the chest of the first man to step from the big Toyota. "You're cleared hot. I say kill them. Kill them all...*and* their pet goat. Let Allah sort them out."

• • •

The aircrew's eyes snapped to the green SATCOM light flashing on the instrument panel. A call bounced off a satellite had come through on the satellite telephone. The co-pilot reached over his shoulder to lift the yellow SATCOM receiver from its cradle on the bulkhead. A minute later, he had unbuckled his harness and extricated himself from the cockpit in search of the Director of Central Intelligence. In the darkened cabin, he was surprised to find the DCI asleep in a recliner instead of his sleeping berth at the rear of the jet. The shockingly beautiful brunette deputy director was nowhere to be seen.

Lynche awoke when the copilot nudged him and informed him of the call from the White House. He nodded as if the magic words

"Situation Room" could suddenly drain all the energy from him. In the diffused lighting, he sat for a couple of seconds before he folded the chair with a flick of a handle and walked to the back of the airplane.

He epitomized the look of having slept in his slacks for a week, tie loosened, top shirt button undone. His face was sallow with heavy dark bags under his eyes. Day-old grey beard. He paused for a moment as if he couldn't understand why he had been asleep in the cabin and not in the suite, but then barged inside. Dull light strips on the floor provided sufficient illumination in the berth so he wouldn't stumble over something. As the door had closed behind him he saw Nazy Cunningham was in the bed, and realized he'd awakened her. They were both surprised by the situation, but he waved her to "go back to sleep." Then he turned and slipped into the desk chair and inserted a crypto PC card into a slot in what appeared to be an ordinary high-end office desk telephone. Lifting the receiver of the remote Secure Terminal Equipment, he waited for the signal processor to read the chip on the printed circuit card and complete the connection. Lynche said little. He listened intently and stared at the wall while pretending to be invisible. After a few seconds, he extracted a pen and a small notebook from his shirt pocket and began to write.

In the subdued light, Nazy watched the man's demeanor and expression go from neutral and curious to defeat and anguish. She knew the person on the other end of the telephone was relaying extremely bad news. Executives were called at the most inopportune times when something bad occurred; leaders were never called in the middle of the night with good news. Good news could wait, but bad news never got better with time. As the DCI said, "Lynche copies all. Goodnight," Nazy monitored his actions and waited for him to initiate a conversation. After a minute of gently shaking his head, Nazy asked, "Are you ok, sir?"

Head shaking turned to head nodding as he slowly spun in the chair to face the woman in his bed. "There's been a hijacking. A Nigerian jumbo. Some unknown group demanded a billion dollars or they'll blow the jet from the sky."

"Did we have any intel to expect...this?"

"No; there were no known threats before the hijacking. Several dozen minor diplomats are aboard. The bad news, Kelly Horne and another intelligence officer are on board."

"Oh, my Lord. Are they sure?"

Lynche crossed his arms and nodded. "Not sure how this will play out. Terrorists in the past have been able to smuggle a bomb on a jet to target Agency personnel that are aboard, but our guys are too new, too junior. I can't believe that's the case here. There were no other demands—no release of KSM or the Taliban's top five from Gitmo— just money. The Nigerian president said they'll pay the ransom but they don't have the gold in the country."

"Why does gold keep popping up in our conversations?"

"Gold? I don't have an answer to that. The President authorized the transfer of some of our reserves, per the demands."

"Any...casualties aboard the airplane?"

Lynche hung his head slightly and talked to the floor. "You know what I know. Other than the aircraft was heading to Lagos, but we don't know anything else at this point. The FBI is investigating. That's another hijacking out of JFK."

"Another?"

"9/11 was the last. We're supposed to have eliminated those possibilities."

"Any chatter?"

"No. No hints, and MI5 and the Israelis were just as surprised as we were."

"Greg, didn't our source, MOOSE, say something about an airplane? Or was it an airport?"

Lynche's head shot up and he looked at Nazy. Energy returned to his eyes. The two spooks silently contemplated what the intelligence officer that escaped from Liberia had said during his debrief.

"Nazy, your memo said, I'm certain, airport. The Monrovia airport. I remember that because of all of our fond memories of the place." A brief smile punctuated Lynche's face as he recalled the highpoints of

343

his last trip to Monrovia.

"He also said he thought something was in process." Nazy moved to the edge of the mattress, sat up, and allowed her bare toes to touch the floor. "There may not be a connection."

"In our business, there's no such thing as a coincidence." A knock on the cabin door made Lynche and Nazy jump. Lynche was instantly embarrassed that he was alone in the cabin with Nazy; he mashed his eyelids together and excoriated himself. *Tongues will be wagging now for sure! At least she's dressed.* He opened and rolled his eyes at the situation and arose to open the door; he didn't expect to see the four bars on the epaulettes of the pilot.

"You have another call, Director."

Lynche nodded vigorously and returned to the STE on the desk and waited for the encrypted connection to be made. After a few seconds, Lynche responded, "Lynche copies all. Goodnight."

Nazy didn't know if the DCI would share the new information, but his body language and demeanor had definitely changed. Intrigue replaced concern; he looked at her and cocked his head slightly and said, "The jet landed in *Monrovia*."

Nazy wasn't surprised. "Something is definitely going on. What do you think?"

"I agree. No such thing as a coincidence. Special Operations Command is assembling an emergency response team that'll head to Liberia. Won't be there for at least twelve, maybe fourteen hours. A lot of bad can happen in twelve—fourteen hours."

"What are you going to do?"

"*We* can't do anything from here. *We* are going back to bed, if we can wind down. Get some sleep, Nazy. We have a full plate tomorrow, and maybe if the gold is delivered and everyone's happy, that jet will be on its way."

"You don't believe that do you?"

"No, but that's all I can do for now. Others with more capabilities than ours are en route to respond. Since Entebbe, SOCOM trains for these events and they have the dot; they have that mission." Lynche unconsciously began tapping his finger on the door. Nazy could see he was thinking about something and wasn't able to move until he resolved the thought.

Lynche nodded and moved to open the door. He was about to leave when Nazy asked, "What about Duncan?"

"What about Duncan?"

"Isn't he in Nigeria? Isn't he going to Liberia? *Monrovia?*"

"Yes, but we can't talk to him and even if we could, I don't know what we'd tell him. I'm inclined to remain comm-out while he's on mission. And, and...there's nothing he can do. He'll have to divert to the other airport. What's the name of that airport? The President of the country lives at one end of the runway—ah, yes, Spriggs Payne. But other than that, yeah, there's nothing he can do." He excoriated himself for allowing trivial information to escape his lips. He must be really tired.

"Can't he fly over the airport or something? It just seems...."

"Nazy, we can't break his cover. We need to let this play out. It'll work itself out if the ransom is paid. If not, SOCOM will have some SEALs or Delta on a jet, and they'll handle the situation. Get some rest. We have our own mission to complete." He yawned mightily and said, "We still have a few hours before we land. I'll see you shortly." As Lynche stepped through the door he said over his shoulder, "Good night, Nazy."

Nazy yawned and returned to her pillow. She lay thinking of Kelly being on that jet, terrified of the hijackers; it was a horrible situation and thinking about it just upset her. She pushed the evil thoughts aside and said aloud, "Really, what could Duncan do?"

CHAPTER TWENTY-EIGHT

"So what do we have, my brother?" The man from the Muslim Brotherhood was tired; his voice came across as mechanical and unemotional. He was ready to leave; for several hours he had been ready to leave the confines of the musty and sterile conference room and the torture of his uncomfortable chair. Only the *financier* wasn't about to let any of them go until Anjam, *the Stars*, was safely in Africa, and the American and Nigerian Presidents had responded favorably to their demands.

"It is done. The aircraft is on the ground. The Americans are pouring gold out of their Fort Knox. In a few hours we'll have what's rightfully ours." Dr. Bruce Rothwell tapped his hand to get the attention of his nurse, who brought a carafe of orange juice and refilled his glass. "It's a time to celebrate." Rothwell raised his newly filled glass and offered a toast, but words failed him and he trembled. He brought the glass to his chest and bowed in exhaustion. His breathing was forceful and rapid; hyperventilation was a real possibility. He tried again to toast his guests, but he was too emotional. The strain on his face was evident from the hollow cheeks, the ashen skin, and his bloodshot eye.

"You've done well, my brother," interjected the old man from al-Qaeda; he stood and nodded slightly in deference and raised a goblet. The words were silky smooth and severed the tension in the room. "Peace be upon you."

Rothwell recovered quickly; he lifted a heavy brow and said, "And, to you. Thank you, my brother. Your men did exceedingly well. Thank you. It's late. May we meet for breakfast to discuss the events of the evening?"

"That's a very good suggestion. This has been very stressful for all of us," offered the Muslim Brotherhood general. He stood as he couldn't wait to escape the room. He had a woman waiting for him in his room. He edged toward the door, caught between the no-man's land of rudeness and indifference. Rothwell wasn't entirely sympathetic.

"Mutually beneficial and rewarding. We'll see you in the morning, my brother. Ten o'clock?" asked the al-Qaeda leader as he moved closer to the door. Rothwell's nurse had courteously unlatched the door and held it open for the men to depart. As the al-Qaeda man approached the door, he recalled he had forgotten a sensitive topic, so he stopped, turned, and asked Rothwell, "What about the infidel, Hunter?"

"What about him?"

"We haven't heard anything?"

Rothwell cocked his head as he spoke, "No. He'll come out of hiding soon, and our Brothers will take care of him."

The man from al-Qaeda effeminately tossed back his *keffiyeh*, like a teenage girl unconsciously pushing her hair off her shoulder. He left the room, saying, "*Insha'allah, Insha'allah.*" Once free of the framing, he raced for the elevators; his white *dishdasha* and black *keffiyeh* flittered behind him.

· · ·

There was no more movement in the jungle compound. Pickup trucks idled in a half circle around the decrepit concrete structure as a makeshift security buffer between the old schoolhouse and the hidden terrors of the jungle. Bodies of men were scattered inside the safety zone which had been crudely designed to protect them. They had won their ground battle with the invisible enemy but lost the air war.

Hunter kept the aircraft in the right-handed turn and programmed the FLIR; he searched the building and the vehicles for any evidence of a hidden or an escaped man. Any game or domesticated animals in the area had run away from the gunfire. There were no active thermal signatures within a three-mile radius of the idling trucks. Finding only terrified little girls holding one another in the back of pickups, it was time to go.

The thermal image of the youngsters huddled in the beds of pickup trucks, shrieking and trembling in fear—but untouched—pleased McGee as he stared at the shrinking image on the monitor. Hunter interrupted the reverie in the cockpit when he leveled the wings and announced, "We're out of here." The FLIR image died instantly as Hunter threw switches to kill the power and stowed the sensor. The gyroscopically-stabilized FLIR ball rotated into the fuselage followed by the gun. Without the drag-inducing components in the airstream, the aircraft quickly picked up speed.

As Hunter accelerated the YO-3A to its maximum velocity, he engaged and programmed the autopilot for Roberts Field. McGee reflected on the carnage behind them. He observed that Hunter had been correct. Even when under fire, the men on the ground had been unable to discern the nature or the direction of the threat. They didn't look up but their worst nightmare: a sniper or an army must have hidden somewhere in the jungle, picking off the Boko Haram men one at a time. Almost twenty men returned fire into the darkness from behind the arc of Toyotas and abandoned motorcycles. As they fired their AK-47s on full automatic, white-hot lines filled and crisscrossed the FLIR scope from gun to jungle.

McGee and Hunter had watched the actions and deportment of those men who gave orders and those who followed directions. Three men were clearly shouting orders and instructions to the others. As the al-Qaeda sympathizers shredded the jungle with hundreds of bullets, Hunter laser designated the obvious leaders first as primary targets. McGee aimed and fired the monster-bore rifle under the airplane. Every five seconds another leader jerked and spun viciously before falling heavily on the ground. As the aircraft circled the semi-hidden building, Hunter laser-designated targets of opportunity who presented the best center-mass targets.

In their periphery, both young and old fighters noticed as their comrades jerked and dropped. They redoubled their efforts to protect the group and save themselves to no avail. As Hunter programmed the FLIR and aimed the laser designator "tagging" each target, McGee got into a rhythm of aiming and firing the gun, verifying that each target had been hit before acquiring Hunter's next laser-designated target. Even as men continued to drop around them, the Boko Haram men fought their invisible enemy to the death. They never once looked up. In less than two minutes, all was quiet in the compound and above.

Crossing the Benin-Nigeria border, Hunter checked his fuel and the destination programmed into the GPS. McGee had been quiet for a long time. He finally asked, "You did this by yourself?"

Hunter exhaled and nodded his helmeted head. He spoke into the microphone and said, "Yeah, onesies and twosies. Stationary targets. It would've been impossible to do what we did tonight solo. That's what teamwork can do. Do we have any saved rounds?"

"One."

"So I counted 19 for 19. We got into a rhythm quickly. Very impressive, Bullfrog."

"Teamwork, Maverick. They made it easy. No fire discipline. The gun on this airplane is an incredible capability. If someone had just used an unmanned platform and shot them with a Hellfire, those girls would be dead."

"I know. If you don't care about the innocent you can kill them all with a missile. We're surgical and precise; we only kill the bad guys. And with what they planned to do with those girls, they deserved to die. I won't lose any sleep." After a few minutes Duncan asked McGee if he wanted to fly the airplane.

"Sure—you'll have to watch me."

"It's all trimmed up; you don't have to do much. Autopilot is off."

The men talked little about the mission as they flew over Benin and Togo and into Ghana. A few lights in the blackness marked homes or vehicles on remote roads. The programmed route of flight skirted the major towns of Yendi and Sunyani in Ghana and Bouake, and Man in Cote D'Ivoire before making a direct approach into Monrovia's main but remote international airport. The equatorial easterly trade winds at eight degrees north of the equator, the same winds that pushed thunderstorms off the African continent and into the Atlantic to become tropical storms and hurricanes, added another twenty knots on the tail of the YO-YO. Hunter commented they were making good time with a surplus of gas and McGee was doing well maintaining altitude and heading. There wasn't a chance either would get sleepy.

Hunter fished his BlackBerry from a flight suit pocket. He noticed the tiny red flashing light, signaling either email or text messages had been received. At the altitude they were flying, receiving data from an in-range cell phone tower wasn't unexpected, even in Africa. With all of his international travels, Hunter paid the premiums for international cell phone service and data plans. In Africa though, it was sometimes a hit or miss proposition. He had read somewhere the fastest growing cell phone market on the planet was Africa, and cell phone towers were going up everywhere. Just as Hunter began to unlock the device with a password to access his messages, the radio came alive. The U.S. Air Force Special Operations MC-130 was calling. Breaking radio silence was done only for emergencies. McGee raised his head from the instruments and took notice. He was more focused on what came out of the radio than flying the airplane.

"Red Bull Four One, Red Bull Four Two."

"Red Bull Four Two, Four One—Go!" Hunter winced as he let go of the transmit switch.

"Roger Four One. Be advised Four Two diverting to the alternate. Copy?" The BlackBerry continued to flash its red light. Duncan Hunter scanned outside. The cell phone's pulsing red light reflected off the canopy.

"Roger Four Two, understand divert, alternate. Are there issues with the primary?" He adjusted the elevator trim to keep the aircraft level, overriding McGee's inattention.

"Red Bull Four One, tower reports the field is closed. We could see there's a jumbo in the middle of the runway. Tower apologizes and will dispatch a fuel truck to the alternate. Copy?"

Hunter wasn't happy with the change in plans. The whole purpose of flying across four tiny African countries in the early morning hours was for the Hercules to get fuel before the isolated airport shut down for the night so they would be able to recover the YO-3A under the cover of darkness. Mission planning had designated the alternate landing site, Spriggs Payne, as the default designated emergency divert field since there were no other secure and low-use airports in the area. Spriggs could handle the weight of the C-130 easily, and the runway was long enough for a safe departure. It's drawback was that it was situated in the middle of the bustling city of Monrovia, and the diminutive airport's surrounding area was heavily populated and well illuminated. Roberts Field by comparison was remote, thirty miles away from the main population center. Situated on 5,000 acres of flat scrubland abutting the Firestone Rubber Plantation and bordering the Farmington River, Roberts Field was the perfect airport for clandestine operations.

Roberts Field had a long and distinguished history in American and Liberian aviation and was endeavoring to return to its former glory after fifteen years of civil war. It had been the primary airfield for the U.S. Army when they attacked the *Desert Fox*, Nazi Field Marshal Erwin Rommel, in North Africa. The Army launched twin-engine bombers north across the Sahara to harry the entrenched Nazi's rear flank. Roberts Field had been a long-time Pan American Airways connector for Boeing 707s and 747s going to South Africa and the Middle East. Up until the time it ceased operations, Pan Am maintained a hotel on the beach for their aircrews. And because of its proximity to the equator, the Roberts Field runway had been lengthened and strengthened by the National Aeronautics and Space Administration as an emergency landing strip for the American Space Shuttle. During the civil war, the "Merchant of Death" Victor Bout operated IL-76s into and out of Roberts, running guns to the rebels while smuggling blood diamonds from Liberian mines. Even though other gun smugglers frequented the airport after the war, Roberts

Field was rarely used and was the perfect rendezvous point for *Noble Savage* missions in western Africa, especially at night after the remote airport was closed and all of its workers went home.

"That sucks," offered Hunter to McGee before he responded to the Air Force crew. As the mission commander, he anticipated the possible change of plans with contingency solutions such as pushing to the divert field in case of a Roberts Field closure. They were in Africa where the aircraft accident rate was astronomical. With African aircraft or airlines anything could happen at any time. The Special Operations aircrew were following the mission brief to the letter. Not being able to use Roberts Field could put the very low-profile mission in jeopardy. As he sucked air to give himself a moment to regain his composure before he replied to the MC-130, he punted to the red light flashing on the BlackBerry and decided it could no longer be ignored. He responded to the crew then turned his focus on the electronic device begging to be read. "Red Bull Four Two, roger copy all."

McGee returned to flying the airplane, head down and focused on the heading and attitude instruments, as Hunter keyed the password into the electronic device and tapped the email application icon. He saw nothing which required his immediate attention. Next he tapped the text message application icon. Three separate text messages from Kelly were in the Inbox:

hijacked. nigerian flt 3

landed not sure where

i'm ok

Hunter stared at the tiny backlit screen with the three individual bullet phrases. He reached for the control stick and depressed the radio switch to transmit, "Red Bull Four Two—can you ID the aircraft on the ground at the primary? Could you make out the airline livery?" Bill McGee became instantly alert and lifted his head from the instruments as he tried to peer over his instrument panel to see what Duncan was doing.

"Red Bull Four One, roger. It's an Airbus three eighty. Two rows of cabin lights. Unable to see the tail."

Hunter responded, "Red Bull Four Two, could you call the tower and ask which airline is clobbering their runway and see if there's an ETD, over?"

"Red Bull Four One, standby."

McGee allowed some time to pass before he asked, "What's going on, Maverick?" Hunter waited for the Special Operations aircrew to respond.

"Red Bull Four One, they report an aircraft declared an emergency. Unknown departure. Copy?"

"Roger, thank you, Sir. Good night Red Bull Four Two. See you soon."

"What's going on, Maverick?"

"Our ride home is going to our alternate rendezvous point. I think a hijacked jet is sitting in the middle of the runway at ROB. Roberts Field."

After several moments of silence, the big man in the back seat asked, "That a problem?"

Hunter glanced into the mirrors on the canopy bow and saw the reflection of a very curious, confused, and disturbed McGee. Hunter didn't know what to say. Each breath felt like knives were being stuck into his lungs. His brain fired signals through his cortex like a fireworks display on New Year's and when it stopped, he was left with the dull realization there was nothing he could do.

McGee didn't press the issue and continued flying the airplane. Hunter got his breathing under control after a few minutes. Scanning the horizon and the instrument panel, he spoke into the microphone. "I think my daughter is on that jet."

· · ·

The Air Force general led Greg Lynche and Nazy Cunningham through a gauntlet of heavily armed military policemen. With a head of steam and squared shoulders, Major General Volner returned the salute of the head of the security detail. She handed the Security Forces Chief Master Sergeant her line badge and vouched for the visitors in her group. The sentry took a quick glance at both sides before he returned it to his wing commander. Then he quickly opened the access door into the huge aircraft hangar for the distinguished visitors. The military police largely ignored the general in her flight suit and the man in a business suit, but their eyes followed the staggeringly beautiful woman in tennis shoes, khakis, and a long sleeve white collared shirt. The men with guns exchanged muddled looks; a woman like that was out of place on an Air Force Base. One MP realized he had been so distracted by the dark-haired woman that he couldn't give an adequate description of the old man with the commander.

Greeting the group on the white painted floor of the brightly lit expanse of the maintenance facility was a stooped, shriveled, nebbish octogenarian. His lab coat was heavily stained in browns, greens, and greys, but his wrinkled hands were clean. The old scientist didn't shake hands and didn't make eye contact with anyone but Lynche—some wordless ideations were exchanged and agreed to—but after a few moments, his gaze fell and lingered on the ankles of the woman in trainers. He nodded and muttered something incomprehensible to Lynche who joined in nodding synchronously. He then followed the bent man as he led the way out of the passageway into the expanse of the hangar, shuffling and wobbling the whole way. The two women glanced at each other, shrugged, and followed the men who were walking like Laurel and Hardy out for a stroll.

They could smell it before they saw it. The distinct aroma of mold and mildew and rotten wood filled the air. The floor of the hangar was filled with a labyrinth of free-standing partitions. Volner wondered if the odors assaulting her senses and wrinkling her nose were from the materials pulled up from the old Nazi chamber or indelicate emanations from the old man as he walked down the hall.

While he appeared weak and feeble, his voice was strong and firm. "We're still excavating, of course," offered Dr. Edgar Howell, gesticulating with a hand as if to emphasize some fine point. The Curator Emeritus at the Smithsonian Institution and on-call forensics expert for the CIAs' Science and Technology Directorate turned to face Lynche. He wasn't a happy man, and he would make his concerns known.

"Of course. Of course," offered a sympathetic Lynche. Nazy noticed the DCI was unusually agreeable. The old doctor seemed pissed at something, but he waited until he had an audience of his people nearby before he vented his spleen.

"We can't rush this excavation, as much as you demand and insist. We've *exhumed* almost a hundred pieces...."

"I indicated, Doctor Howell, that this would be a herculean effort. You have a hundred pieces. Do you have any idea of what remains?" Lynche acted as if he took the lead in questioning Dr. Howell. Nazy, her arms behind her, remained well out of the line of fire standing back with the Air Force woman, who clasped her hands tightly in front of her. It wasn't every day one witnessed old professionals sparring.

The women tried to listen to the men but were distracted with the other activities in the building. Nazy was calm and interested in the old artwork, but she was significantly jet-lagged and yawned from time to time. The general was interested in what was going on in her hangar that had been commandeered by the CIA. The Agency had been given free reign by direction of the Air Force Chief of Staff. She didn't want to get crosswise with her service's head four-star or the head of the CIA, but she was curious as to what the Agency people had removed from the underground bunker. She didn't see the aircraft from the underground facility that had really intrigued her, but the general held her position to hear some of the answers of the condition of the missing museum artwork which had been looted by the Nazis. Volner was keenly aware of the historic nature of the enterprise.

The wizened old man stopped and raised his head with a look of disgust. Lynche immediately thought he had said something improper until the man began relating what had been brought to the surface and what remained underground. Dr. Howell pointed a bent finger at

Lynche vigorously. "So far, two thousand containers have been identified. You told me a few hundred. The first one hundred are in here, in triage, if you will. Most are untouched; some are damaged. Many of the outside containers are in some state in between. Then there's the issue of the three missing Fabergé imperial eggs."

"You found the missing Fabergé imperial eggs in the cave too?" Lynche was rocked back on his heels.

Howell stole another glance at Nazy Cunningham and nodded salaciously. "Please try to keep up Director. Yes, three missing Fabergés and four others for which there are no records, pictures or designs." His eyes ran across Nazy's torso, stopped at her bosom, and said, "They're priceless."

Lynche refrained from kicking the old man in the shins but the lecher turned away and returned to business.

"They're a combination of unmatched craftsmanship, creativity, and elegance that will never be seen again. Pity. As I said, there are over two thousand items. The conditions to do proper archeology are insufficient."

Lynche was unconvinced. "Two *thousand?* We didn't see anything like that! Are you sure?"

"I can only say, *Director Lynche*, you must not have seen the entire trove. When my technicians and I arrived, we discovered there are more passageways and chambers down there than in King Tut's tomb. Rooms behind the doors of abandoned metalworking and carpentry shops were filled to the brim. That's where we found the Fabergés. We have no idea what is really down there and your notebook is woefully inadequate. There's five years' worth of work down there. I need more people."

"But it will take forever to get more workers cleared, and we don't have five years or five months."

"So you're stuck with us. I'll not be rushed. We're going to recover the artifacts *properly*." He hissed and wagged his bony, crooked finger at Lynche, "We'll do these recoveries per established art and archeological methods. I won't be badgered or hurried."

356

"Dr. Howell, if you've recovered a hundred specimens, I believe that'll be sufficient for my use, at least for the time being. I just need as many as you can display so an art expert can inspect them." The little man walked away, mumbling and waving frail hands and arms. Lynche, Nazy, and General Volner followed.

Lynche and Nazy exchanged glances and scanned the various work stations where recovery and restorative work was in progress. The ancient art archeologist suddenly stopped and dropped his eyes to again gaze at Nazy's feet for half a minute. Then he shook his head and turned away muttering. General Volner wasn't amused with the old codger but was intrigued with the activities within the hangar. Men and women in white lab coats and latex gloves gingerly handled the crumbling wood containers, the gilded frames, and the delicate statues.

Photographic equipment dominated one makeshift cubicle while a portable X-ray machine filled another. A different process was conducted in each of the many cubicle stations: uncrating, unwrapping, cataloging, and inspecting. Photographing, inspecting, and restoration stations culminated in a temporary display station. Nazy counted almost thirty workers who occasionally gawked at Lynche's group of intruders.

Lynche had seen enough. It would have to be enough. "You're doing an incredible job, Dr. Howell, and I want you to know I appreciate it. I'd like to get out of your hair; it's very late for you and your team, and we need to be back here at 10 o'clock in the morning."

"We'll be here," said the feisty old man. With his chin on his chest, he strained to be inconspicuous in sneaking another peak at Nazy. He leaned as he nodded, then muttered as he shuffled away.

Five minutes later, the general pulled her staff car to a stop at the distinguished visitors quarters complex. Nazy and Lynche said their thank yous and goodbyes to General Volner in the vehicle. The CIA executives walked to their rooms in silence.

Something had been bothering Nazy since they were in the hangar. Before they left CIA HQ, Lynche had indicated he was bringing Nazy

NO NEED TO KNOW

onto the Special Access Program BLUE SHOES. She had already been "read on" to the program designed to purchase man-portable tactical nuclear weapons from the former Soviet Union. She thought she should have been part of the discussions with the crusty Dr. Howell. When they stopped at her suite, she turned and asked Lynche, "I couldn't comprehend or hear what Doctor Howell had to say at the end. Could you understand him?"

The question caught Greg unawares, which caused him to cough violently. Nazy had seen the man's coughing fits before, but it was usually when Duncan said something humorous; she didn't think what she asked was funny. He worked to quiet the spasms and recover his breath, and just short of hyperventilating, he finally said, "I don't know if I should tell you, but he said he'd rather look at you than any of the stuff they'd removed from that hole. That you're living art."

The comment brought an embarrassed smile and a Cornish response. "Well, ah, that was *sweet*."

"Nazy. He's a dirty old man, and he couldn't keep his eyes off of you. I need him to do a job and not ogle my...my...."

"Assistant? *Daughter?*"

Lynche broke out in a massive smile, stuck his tongue deep in his cheek and nodded vigorously. He exhaled in embarrassment. "Yeah, you and Duncan are kind of like the kids I never had. It's hard not to view you as the daughter I wish I had. You really are an incredible woman and...."

Nazy positioned herself to look Lynche in the eye. "Greg, I appreciate your protecting me. Please know you're the father I...I *wish* I had. You've always been there for me and Duncan. Thank you." Nazy moved closer and hugged him.

"It may have been a mistake to bring you. Tongues are already wagging. Everyone knew Rothwell's predecessor was a flaming, well, you know, and Rothwell was a certified roué. Then I send you to the safe house before bringing you with me. So it only makes sense that some will think that the DCIs are some sort of...I don't know. You know what I mean."

The jet lag was catching up to her and sleep beckoned. Nazy yawned and nodded and said, "You've been thoroughly professional and have followed the protocols. I don't think you've been overly protective in your position. But I do think you've been as protective as I would expect a great father to be." She suddenly enjoyed playing the role of an adult daughter.

Lynche grinned; there was no arousal or thoughts of being that close to Nazy. Other men at the CIA were not so fortunate to be able to touch or take in her scent. Some shared their "Nazy Cunningham stories" of when they were able to work closely with her on a project— "There I was, sitting right across the table from her and looked into her eyes, probing to see if there's anything there, a hint or a smile, but she just wasn't interested." She crushed many a man's ideations without trying or even knowing. Lynche had moved past the easy, salacious thoughts and into the realm of proud father, watching his little girl grow up and take the world by the horns.

"That, I doubt. I was always gone, and Connie is my third wife. The Agency is hard on families as I'm sure you know; the hours and the separations are worst parts of the job. You and Duncan know that all too well." He wagged his finger at her playfully, "But anyone would be immensely proud to have you as a daughter. I'll see you in the morning. Hopefully, by then we'll have some good news on Kelly and Duncan."

She nodded and pinched her lips, suddenly thinking about Duncan and his daughter.

Lynche could see she was getting emotional. It was time to go. "Good night, Nazy."

Nazy pushed her sad thoughts away, and then she smiled and yawned. She leaned into Greg and hugged him again. All hugs from Nazy always felt slightly sexual, but not this one. There was huskiness to her voice. "I'm praying for both of them. I hope you know I would've been blessed to have been your daughter. Good night, Greg." She turned and entered her suite, leaving Lynche to grin and ponder the imponderables.

CHAPTER TWENTY-NINE

McGee railed at Hunter. "*You have a daughter?* Why am I always the last to know? And how do you know that?"

"I do, and I received a text message from her. We're low enough to catch a cell phone tower and slow enough for the service to forward my messages."

"Seriously, in Africa?"

"Yes, sir. International service is expensive as hell but...."

"In this case worth it. And it works in Africa? Who knew?"

"Yes, sir." Hunter slowly shook his head.

"So, what are you going to do?"

"What *can* I do? Worry, like any dad. I can't even believe this is happening. Yeah, I can worry....and pray."

Duncan told McGee how Kelly Horne had found him and given up her career in the Air Force to go into the CIA. "I think she had visions of doing what you're doing, being the guy in back paying her dues before moving into this front seat. And now, on her first assignment her jet gets hijacked. That's ugly luck, and there's nothing I can do about it."

"*This* is ugly work, Maverick. Not everyone can do this; whacking terrorists isn't for everybody. It'll put most folks on the shrink's couch. Can't see a woman doing it, even being the pilot. Killing the enemy—even snuffing out the Boko Haram trash—is more emotional than we like to admit. Don't let her do it. Just my two cents."

McGee could see Hunter's helmet shake gently in the reflection of the canopy. He figured Hunter was too focused on his daughter and her predicament to respond. There's nothing anyone could do; a

360

hijacking always had to play itself out. McGee sensed a distraction would be worthwhile. Time to talk shop.

"I'll tell you a little secret. My first assignment was to take down a couple of airline skyjackers—that's what they called them back then. I was with Team Three in Kuwait. It didn't go well." His deep crackling voice conveyed an ominous tone.

"You're doing a great job cheering me up." After a few quiet seconds, Hunter said, "I don't think any of them go well. Didn't they lose a bunch of civilians even in Entebbe?"

It almost sounded like the pragmatic Hunter was back, but now wasn't the time to quit. He still needed a little coaxing to come off the cliff. McGee continued, "At Entebbe, only three. Rescued over a hundred. A week of planning, a cast of hundreds all for a ninety minute operation. At an airport—they weren't even on the plane. The Israelis were lucky. No one had ever done anything so intricate; they fooled the hijackers. You have to remember, the hostages were taken off the jet and were being held in the terminal building. Every other terrorist organization learned from that op, and as a consequence, every other hijacking became exponentially more difficult. Future hijackers learned many lessons and would never again allow their passengers to leave the aircraft.

"Unless those pax didn't have any political leverage," said Hunter.

"That's right. Students take over the U.S. Embassy in Tehran and let the so-called oppressed groups leave; blacks and Hispanics were allowed to leave. Hijackers do the same thing for a number of reasons. If you can rid yourself of some dudes and are able to concentrate on a smaller number, a more manageable number of hostages, you're doing yourself a favor on so many levels. They also kill someone just to get everyone's attention; they mean business. Islamists do it time and time again."

"Yes, sir. Seen that. What was the Navy diver's name?"

"You're thinking of Robert Stethem. Seabee. Two Lebanese men smuggled pistols and grenades through the Athens airport; they beat him and shot him in the temple and dumped his body onto the ramp.

The point is, jets are virtually impossible to assault without a massive loss of life, and the bad guys don't care about living. They just blow up the airplane and themselves. Nine-eleven is the new normal."

"You're not cheering me up."

"Yeah, I know. It's different now. Is your daughter's…is Kelly on a 747?"

"Bigger. Airbus 380. Double decker."

"Oh, so that's what that meant. Anyway, with the terrorists' suicidal change in tactics, passengers have also changed tactics."

"What do you mean?" Hunter cocked his head to see McGee in the mirrors.

"After 9/11, American passengers will no longer tolerate hijackers with knives at the throat of stewardesses."

"Flight attendants—they have dudes now."

"I'm dating myself. You know, Maverick, I don't get out much anymore. This has been a real treat, I want you to know! But, I feel for you. No one saw this coming."

"Hey, I *take* you places! We're over the Ivory Coast or *Côte d'Ivoire*; my French isn't too good."

"As I said, those things don't end well."

Hunter resigned himself that Kelly's situation was far beyond his control and worrying about it wasn't going to help matters while they were still on the "back end" of the mission. He was trying to put a positive spin on their conversation to take his mind off of Kelly and hijackers, and he was aware that the usually laconic McGee was talking, stringing cogent perceptive sentences together without having to be prodded. Maybe the change in character was because of the severity of the situation or more likely, Bill finally had a topic he could relate to. There's no finer expert on terrorists and counterterrorism, and Hunter appreciated the diversion.

McGee had been the undergraduate student in the conversations about aviation, airplanes, and airborne sensors, but when the topic shifted to his area of expertise in special operations, counterterrorism activities, and killing the enemies of America, Hunter was the acknowledged neophyte and student. Hunter noticed McGee slipped unconsciously into instructor mode. While at the Naval War College, the top tier national security and strategic defense coursework thoroughly enthralled him. Although an accomplished instructor of all things aviation, he was a model and energetic student, and soaked up the course material like a dime store sponge. With the impossible situation in Liberia an hour ahead, Duncan also gathered as much information as the SEAL would offer. Counterterrorism wasn't Hunter's core competency. Learning more of the ways of the ninja-like SEALs took his mind off Kelly being a hostage on a hijacked jet.

McGee worried about Duncan. He had seen strong men break under the great stress of a loved one in grave danger. SEALs were a band of brothers; they would willingly give their life for a comrade in danger, throwing themselves onto grenades or shielding a wounded SEAL with their body.

He knew Hunter was in great pain but was hiding it well. He would be tremendously distracted until the hijacking came to a resolution. Although McGee trusted Hunter to fly the YO-3A, when it came time to land he needed to be sure Duncan's mind was clear and focused. Hunter was a professional pilot, but the fact he was living through a compressed period of hell had to adversely affect him. McGee would keep Hunter distracted from the hijacking until they landed. It wasn't his style to be loquacious, but the situation could be viewed as a teachable moment. He was an instructor. He could teach the old Marine a few things.

"They'd need a lot of help for a plane that size."

Hunter exhaled and nodded, "There's five, six, maybe seven hundred people on that jet. Yeah, the 9/11 turds had five to a jet, and those weren't even jumbos."

"That's my point; they'd need a bunch of people to stop a passenger uprising. Unless they have guns. If it was well orchestrated and they were able to get guns on the plane, then they might have been able to get away with six or eight. If that was the case they'd have to demonstrate they were serious and committed."

"What do you mean, serious and committed?" The ambiguous comment struck Hunter as odd. He thought he knew what McGee meant but maybe he didn't. He wasn't sure he was processing information very well because of all the distractions.

"They've probably already killed a few people to prove they're serious and committed. There's a point when the passengers just acquiesce and wait for the cavalry to come save them."

"Gotcha. Since it's on the ground, I think they had to have gotten access to the cockpit. The new cockpit doors are like vault doors, very hard to break in. I'll bet they were able to get into the cockpit. It's a must do." As the words left Hunter's mouth, some distant and obscure memory was clawing its way into his consciousness. He tilted his head like the Victrola dog, beseeching his brain to give him a little more information. McGee continued to talk but Hunter only caught the tail end of a comment while trying to squeeze the information from his brain.

"....no matter what they do or don't do, someone will sue them."

"Makes sense." The squirrel in Hunter's head was spinning the wheel faster.

"Bill, so how would SEALs do it, if they could get in?"

"Terrorists won't willingly open the door now, and the baggage compartments usually don't have access to the cabin. It's virtually impossible to get in. That's one of the many reasons airplane passengers make great hostages, especially when politics are in play."

"It's a pressure tube; the fuselage is a tube."

"Not many ways to get in," said the gravelly voice from the back seat.

It was an obvious statement, but Hunter could feel a piece of a mystery puzzle slip into its socket. He scanned the instruments hoping to find a clue to what was poking at his grey matter. Without thinking of the ridiculousness of the idea that had formed, he blurted out, "What if you could get in without them knowing?"

McGee thought Hunter wasn't listening. "You cannot get in unless they open a door and they'll never open the door for an assault team.

SWAT teams have tried in the past, disguised as caterers or baggage handlers. If Delta Forces had to break in the door then they would have to have major diversions. I'm not aware of any circumstances where a rescue team was able to get inside an airplane without the terrorists' knowledge." He'd keep Hunter entertained and distracted by answering his asinine and impossible questions. "But, if you could get inside without them knowing, the good guys would have a huge advantage. You'd negate their advantages and leverage your own. If you could get inside, undetected and unmolested, you should be able to take them out even if they're carrying guns. At least my guys would be able to do it."

"Wouldn't you need some other advantages?"

"Ideally, you'd want to do it when the cabin is completely dark. Delta would have NVGs to target them. Laser sights. You know...."

"Like what we did with the Boko Haram trash?"

"...mmm yes...but, that never happens. You can't get in and the aircraft is always lit up." McGee flicked his eyes to meet Hunter's in his cockpit mirrors. *He's always thinking.*

Hunter rolled scenarios in his head. "Probably demand external electrical power. Or maybe it'd be better for the assault team if the auxiliary power plant continued to run and powered the electrics and air conditioning." Hunter wiped sweat from his forehead and rubbed his eyes. *What am I missing? This is impossible. Academic exercise.*

"Yes, that would be even better. What are you thinking, Mav? I can understand you wanting to do something, but assaulting a jet is one of the hardest things a SWAT team or Delta can do. In fact, no one but the Israelis have ever done it without massive loss of life, and their strategy was to wait out the terrorists until their special ops guys gained an advantage. Additionally, it takes hours to prepare. If and when Delta gets on scene, their strategy will be to wait them out or give them what they want. If the bad guys get careless, they might be able to take one or two out with a sniper."

"Thanks, Bill." Hunter turned and stared out into the void of Africa. He understood and comprehended all—it made perfect sense.

He looked out over the nose to see the lights of Buchanan on the horizon at ten o'clock. Named for Thomas Buchanan, cousin of President James Buchanan, and first governor of Liberia. The third largest city in Liberia lay seventy miles from Monrovia. They'd be landing soon and would be on their way back to the Azores. Duncan decided he would fly over Roberts Field and take a look at the jet on the Space Shuttle's emergency runway for himself. He continued to think about the hijacked jet on the airport.

Nigerian Airways

Airbus 380.

I think...the 380 in the television was...Nigerian Airways.

Big jet, water cannon arch. Beautiful green and white monster.

A dude proudly flying the Nigerian flag from the top of the jet. Laughing about the water spray...chased the dude back inside. That was fun....

The water chased the dude with the flag back inside.

The dude with the flag back went back inside.

From the top of the jet. Well above the cockpit. How do you fly a flag from the top of the jet? Hunter blinked wildly. Phosphenes burst in his eyes. He tilted his head as if it'd give him a different perspective. His eyes were completely unfocused.

There has to be a door on top of the jet. New airliners have smooth windows. They don't have the drag-inducing sliding cockpit windows for escape hatches. Now have actual escape hatches for their long-distance relief crews. There's a door on top of the jet....

There's a door on top of the jet!

Hunter said, "There's a door on top of the jet."

"What?" asked McGee.

"There's a door on top of the jet. Some kind of maintenance hatch. Emergency hatch. All new jets have smooth fixed cockpit windows. These jets are huge—they need to carry more than one crew. This one, they must have built in emergency hatches."

"What are you talking about?" Duncan explained to him what they had seen on the TV before they left the room at Lajes. He told the story from start to finish, from the flag being flown at the top of the aircraft and the water cannon that drenched the dude and chased him back inside the Airbus.

"The Delta guys will have that info. Airline guys will work with them; tell them all that stuff." McGee sensed that Hunter's genius was back at work. He had seen in up close and personal when Duncan had conceived of a way to kill plants with light while reading a National Geographic. He was intrigued but not yet convinced. *So what? There's a door on top of the jet.*

"So if they get the brief that there's an emergency hatch, how will Delta get on top of the jet?" Hunter strained to sort out answers to the hundreds of questions now ricocheting in his cranium.

"Well, that's the trick. You have to have ladders, one of those mobile stairs. Catering truck with a lift. Like I said, it's impossible."

"What about parachuting onto the jet?"

McGee's head shot up and he met Hunter's eyes in the oblong mirrors on the canopy bow. *Oh my God!* He initially considered the maneuver as hair brained, upon instant introspection, it wasn't such a wild idea. "That's an option. I've not heard of that, but yes, in theory, that's an option. If there's a door on top of the jet, I have to tell you, Maverick, that would put a different light on things."

"Really?"

"If there's a...what did you call it?"

"Maintenance or emergency hatch."

"If there's a maintenance or emergency hatch, and they could parachute onto the top of the jet, and they could actually get in, then, yeah, they'd have an advantage. I'm afraid, *I guarantee you,* no one from Delta will parachute onto the aircraft. They'd load up with body armor and wait. And there're already airborne. They don't have chutes. Not standard procedures for a hijacking."

Hunter harrumphed and gazed out the town of Buchanan passing left, abeam. Evil thoughts leaked into his consciousness. Evil men often abuse women on hijacked jets. They have the weapons and they have the power, and they do to them whatever suits them. Sexual

NO NEED TO KNOW

assaults often occurred, rarely reported in the media. Kelly was young and beautiful. She couldn't hide her beauty or her innocence. She'd be the perfect target, and a terrorist would find time to abuse her, just like the Boko Haram trash dragged the youngsters away from their families. He was grateful for the distraction when McGee began to talk again.

Then McGee chortled, "Under that scenario, I could do it myself, at least one deck. If the lights were out."

"What do you mean?"

"There'd be chaos. All it takes is one spec op dude to get in. Those guys in the airplane don't have NVGs. It's inconceivable to think they could plan for that kind of contingency. The guy with NVGs and a laser sight could pick off the bad guys like one-two-three. It'd be over in seconds. In theory."

"Like we did with Boko Haram?"

"Yes, sir."

"But there's two decks. Wouldn't you need some help? One person to clear one level and someone else to clear the other?"

"With two levels, I'd definitely need your help. Yes."

"So, in theory, you and I could parachute onto the back of that jet...."

"In theory. I'm not sure what good you'd be since you suck at landings."

Hunter grinned and ignored the impolite dig at his parachuting skills. "In theory, we could open the maintenance hatch...get inside...."

"You'd have to do some of that pilot shit and turn out the lights."

"Of course, I'd have to turn out the lights."

"In theory." McGee continued to play, taking Hunter's mind off the problems his daughter was facing. "I don't know how you'd turn out the lights, but yes. In theory."

"...and with your NVGs and your .45 cal, with its laser sight, in theory...."

"*Our* NVGs; *our* .45s; our laser pointers. I couldn't do it myself if the jet is that big. You'd need one person for each deck. In theory, of course." McGee again looked up to see Hunter's reflection. He had a distant look.

"In theory, you could take out all the bad guys on one deck."

"On one deck. You'd take out all the bad guys on the other deck. All advantages shift to the attacker. The defender would be fixated in survival. At least that's how it'd go unless they detonated a bomb. It's all theory." McGee sat up straight in the aircraft seat and fixated on the reflection in the little mirrors. He tried to read Hunter's eyes in the soft red light as he met Hunter's curious but thoughtful expression. *What did he just say? In theory, I could take out all the bad guys. At least I could when I was a younger man.*

"Yeah, in theory." Hunter remained introspective and composed. He scanned the instrument panel then the horizon. *In theory, he could do it. However, that's not an emphatic, fait accompli. So close!*

The two men flew along for several quiet minutes. Glancing into the mirrors every few seconds, McGee found Hunter's expression hadn't changed. *What did he say? What am I missing? The logical progression of this line of reasoning is, all things being equal, assaulting a hijacked jet is still impossible. I could do it, in theory. But the gap between theory and execution is as wide and deep as the Rio Grande. We need to run the war game out to its conclusion.*

"In theory," began McGee, "how would we parachute out of this? It'd crash and burn, and alert the hijackers that something was up. We lose the element of surprise. The jig would be up. That would be the showstopper."

"In theory, that would be true. But, what if I said this airplane has an automatic takeoff and landing system? All the high-end unmanned aircraft have the hardware and software, and this has been upgraded to function as an optionally manned platform. I can program it to land at a designated runway, and it will land and shut down the engine."

"Seriously?" McGee furrowed his thick brows and frowned. *Under that scenario, you would have the element of surprise. We would have the element of surprise. Nothing's changed. A special operation avoids assaulting hijacked jets because it's impossible.*

"And it's more than theory. I've made several 'hands-off landings.' I know it works. The aircraft's survivability isn't the issue."

McGee sat in stony silence thinking, planning, considering. *We've avoided assaulting jets because it's impossible to get in. However, if there's a way in.... You'd have the element of surprise.* After running through myriad scenarios and recalling the lessons learned from similar operations, McGee concluded...*This one's different....* Several more minutes passed before McGee whispered into his boom microphone, "They'd never expect it...."

Hunter answered indifferently, "How could they?" There's no expectation the discussion was anything but an academic distraction and a diversion. He and McGee would let the *"what ifs"* play themselves out before they landed. Hunter chortled at the whole idea. It was preposterous, but his thoughts were caught in the no-man's land between inaction and action. Do nothing and hope for the best. Hope and pray Kelly is safe and everything will come out for the good. Do something that's ridiculous and insane, with no planning or full understanding of the situation on the ground, and you may as well just jump off the Golden Gate Bridge holding your nose on the way down. The discussion was just an interesting academic exercise. *Just two guys bullshitting. But....*

Two more quiet minutes passed before both men tried to talk into the interphone at the same time. Duncan acquiesced. "Sorry, sir; you first."

McGee asked, "Who said, 'Rapidity is the essence of war: take advantage of the enemy's unreadiness, make your way by unexpected routes, and attack unguarded spots?'"

"Not Clausewitz, for damn sure. Sun Tzu. You make an interesting point for a war college instructor. Sir."

"Former war college instructor. Can you send your little girl an email or a text to see if we can get some intel?"

"Like what?" *What are you thinking?*

"Number of assholes on the airplane, if they have guns and what type. Bomb threats. That sort of thing."

"I can try." *What are you thinking?*

"You'll put her in danger if she's caught."

"I don't know if it will go through. I know there are cell towers at the airport. We're low enough but may not be close enough yet to pick up a tower for a message to go through. So what are you thinking?"

"Maverick, it's a no brainer. It's like when you and Greg went after bin Laden—there's no one else that could do it but you. You were on scene; you had the jet and the connections. No matter how much I wanted to be a part of that, I couldn't. I had to let someone else do it. Now it is you and I. We're here; we have the right equipment, and we're on scene. If you're certain we could get in, I'm certain we can stop the bad guys. And...I'm up for it."

"Seriously. You up for it?"

"I am. SEALs rarely have such an opportunity. We're break down the door kind of guys. This is our forte. But we need a door to break down—in this case, just open the friggin' hatch. And then we need to be able to get the lights off."

"I think it's more than a little crazy. If we can get in, I'll turn the lights off."

"If anybody can, you can. I'll make an honorary SEAL out of you yet. What are you doing?"

"I'm checking what we have. What we have and don't have. No body armor. The Colts have silencers and laser sights. We have NVGs. Am I missing anything essential?"

"You gave me a first aid kit and a .45! You think of everything."

"I didn't think of this." Hunter's thumbs pressed buttons for a message and hit SEND. "Message away."

"Yes, you did. You just couldn't say it. We'll take advantage of their unreadiness; we'll have the element of surprise on our side. Make your way by unexpected routes—no one would ever think to parachute onto the aircraft. Attack unguarded spots. That's brilliant. There's no way they know of that emergency hatch. Now all you need to think of is how to get the lights off in the cabin. You follow my lead and we'll split the effort. One takes the top deck and other one takes the lower."

Hunter nodded and looked back at McGee in the canopy bow mirrors. The man was smiling like a Cheshire cat. "Duncan, I know you can do it. You just have to pay attention to the landing area and get set up for it. We'll jump high enough to have plenty of time to get set up for a coordinated approach and land along the length of the fuselage."

Hunter nodded and said, "I have the airplane."

McGee released his grip on the control stick and took his feet off the rudder pedals. He confirmed, "You have the airplane. What's the plan?"

"We have Roberts on the nose and there's the jet. I want to get a closer look at the airplane. We need to talk a little more about this. FLIR coming out. I don't want any surprises. I don't want to find the grounds are covered with bad guys and they can see us."

"Good point."

With the FLIR deployed and the YO-3A slowed and in quiet mode, Hunter controlled the thermal sensor as he and McGee scanned the area around the airplane and the airport. Hunter checked the windsock, which stood limp, meaning calm winds. At least for the present. After three circuits over the airfield, Duncan summarized, "Ok, all I see is a few people standing near the airport terminal. They're well out of the way and are no factor. I doubt they'll be able to see us. There are virtually no ramp lights—one of these days I'll tell you the reason for that."

"Tell me now!"

"The Firestone Rubber Plantation has a small hydroelectric plant and provides only so much electricity to the airport. At night the airport goes on generator power so only essential equipment is powered. Ramp lights aren't essential."

"So it'll be noisy as well?"

"The generator farm is near where those guys are standing, so yes, should be. Ok—the jet's engines are off. No external power cart so they're on aux power, which is burning brightly at the tail—see the heat plume? Lots of noisemakers on the field."

"What's the plan? How do we get....?"

"Standby. Red Bull Four Two, Red Bull Four One."

The U.S. Air Force Special Operations C-130 answered immediately. "Red Bull Four One, Four Two, Go."

"Red Bull Four Two, please pass to our playmates to recover the package as usual but not to leave until we arrive."

"Now, that was confusing." McGee's smile reflected in the mirrors.

Hunter could envision the confusion and concern in the Hercules cockpit between the aircrew and his crew. There was a very long pause before there was a response, "Red Bull Four One, Red Bull Four Two, Copy."

"Ok, Bullfrog, if we can't get in then they're not going to leave without us. I've inputted the GPS coordinates for the airport, and engaged and set the landing system for Spriggs Payne. Still no reply from Kelly—don't know whether that's good or bad. It is what it is. All I have to do is pull the canopy jettison handle and we have a convertible. That's the plan; that's how we get out of here."

"Roger."

"Ok. Lower your seat all the way now. Once the canopy is gone, it will be very difficult getting out of the cockpit. Seventy knot winds will buffet us for a moment. Try to hunker down to protect yourself from the wind. We need to get up and stand in the seat, and then we throw ourselves over the side. I'm ready to go. I'm sure we need to be at a specific altitude; I've no idea what that is. Am I missing anything?"

McGee specified the best altitude for being able to maneuver safely and indicated it'd be helpful if they knew the wind directions. Hunter said he wasn't going to ask the tower "for the winds," but he checked the wind direction from the "lighted T" on the field as he climbed to McGee's recommended altitude. McGee keyed the microphone and said, "I guess I don't have to worry about you landing this thing."

"You were worried about me?" *Seriously?*

"Yea, well, it was more for selfish reasons. I didn't want you crashing this because you were distracted—you know...."

"I guess that's touching, but I'm ok."

"I know you are, Maverick." McGee said,

"I'll go right, and you go left."

"Roger, I have the left," said McGee.

At two miles from the Airbus, Hunter said, "I can't believe we're doing this."

"What would you do if you came upon a car crash?"

"Render aid. Help."

"What would you do if you came upon a bank robbery?"

At a mile and a half from the Airbus, Hunter said, "I'd want to do the Dirty Harry thing and whack the bad guy. Is there another answer?"

"No. This is the same thing. We're on scene rendering aid. Moreover, we have guns, and some of us have the training. Are you ready for this, Maverick, leaving your perfectly good airplane? Just follow me."

"Sir, I'll follow you anywhere. I'll be right behind you when we land. Ok—make sure we haven't forgot anything. NVGs powered up, down and locked. Chute harness tight. Helmet chin strap tight. Lap belts unbuckled. Disconnect your pigtail and I'll blow the canopy. See you on the jet, Bullfrog. I'm ready. Hold on, it's going to get turbulent in here."

At four thousand feet altitude and a mile away, the YO-3A was on a trajectory to pass perpendicularly over the Nigerian jet. "This looks good, Maverick. Time to go."

Hunter and McGee squeezed the communication connectors at the back of their helmets to break the connection. Duncan yanked on the canopy jettison handle.

The shear wire holding the handle in place easily broke; levers forced the canopy up into the airstream that whisked it away faster than a blink. One second the smooth Plexiglas transparency was there; the next it was gone.

Simultaneously, both men jumped onto their cockpit seats into the buffeting winds and bailed out—McGee left, Hunter right—over the side of the perfectly good YO-3A.

CHAPTER THIRTY

The JFK airport policeman raced to the curb to intercept the driver of the vehicle who seemed to think he could park any damn place he wanted. In no uncertain terms he'd tell the damn idiot who stopped his car in the NO PARKING area that he couldn't park at the front of the airport, and that he had to leave. His arms pumped with every stride; his belt and holster wobbled on his narrow hips with every step. It had been a crappy day, and he wasn't about to put up with another scofflaw, especially one who so carelessly flaunted the law.

Assistant FBI Director in Charge, Joe Ianniello, stepped from the unmarked Crown Victoria to get his bearings. He was built like a fullback with shoulders as wide as eagle's wingspan. He had the remains of a pugilistic nose that looked like he had gone too many rounds with George Foreman. As he dragged his jacket from the rear seat, he scanned the area for a few seconds to take in the moment. He noticed people running to and from the departure level just as he expected. Ianniello knew all the trouble was inside. He slammed the door and pulled on the dark blue windbreaker emblazoned with foot-tall letters FBI on the back.

Before he took the next necessary lungful of air to excoriate the unnaturally large dumbass stepping from car, the traffic cop's eyes bulged at the three-letters on the man's jacket. He choked on his own spit and veered away from the collision of law enforcement agencies. He looked for an immediate face-saving diversion and quickly found another dolt who had parked along the departure curb of the international terminal. He pivoted 45° and never broke stride, grateful he hadn't gotten into a losing pissing contest over jurisdiction and parking permits. He ran to the new target and barked at him to leave.

The captain of the airport police and two FBI special agents hurried out of the airport building to escort the head of the FBI's Field Office into the airport. There were no handshakes or greetings. Ianniello was briefed an aircraft was hijacked en route to its destination. An investigation into a possible security breach was underway. The last time an aircraft had been hijacked from JFK was 9/11, and that didn't end well. With 700 hijacked passengers on one of the world's largest passenger aircraft, it wasn't a time for salutations.

"Whaddya have?" asked Ianniello, without breaking stride.

"Chief, you need to see this for yourself," answered one of the special agents who joined up with the burly and grey assistant director. The three men reversed course to match the direction and velocity of the senior FBI man and entered the terminal building, like Marines marching in step. The man in the FBI jacket and the airport captain walked side by side through the double automatic doors. The three men shotgunned the information they had and provided different situation reports as they hurried across polished granite floors to the escalator that took them upstairs to the Airport Security Operations Center.

"TSA was breached--infiltrated," said a special agent.

"The video record leaves no doubt the screener allowed weapons onto the sterile side of the concourse," said the other special agent.

"Muslim woman," offered the airport police captain.

Assistant Director Ianniello stopped and wagged his finger at the police officer. "I don't want politics or religions mentioned during this investigation. We have a suspect. Their beliefs are immaterial at this stage." He set off leaving the three men to exchange knowing glances.

The special agents caught up to their boss as the airport police captain brought up the rear. At a nondescript and unmarked door, the captain used his electronic access card to gain entry into the ASOC. The four men entered the heavily air-conditioned and dark, control room where several TSA agents monitored hundreds of screens mounted on the walls and workstations.

"Over here—we have something for your private viewing," suggested the airport captain, the sting of the FBI's agent's rebuke still fresh in his memory. The Lead Supervisory TSA Officer joined the men at the workstation.

Racks upon racks of stacked electronic devices recorded camera images from a thousand cameras strategically placed throughout the concourse. Cameras monitored passenger flow, entry control points and gate doors, as well as passengers entering the airport security checkpoint. Multiple cameras hidden in innocuous dark semispherical covers on ceiling tiles caught detailed images of passengers moving through security lanes. They took photographic-quality images of the faces and bodies and bags of passengers at their first stop in the process, the identification check. Cameras monitored every passenger as they placed their bags onto the x-ray machine conveyor belt and as they entered the magnetometers. They also monitored their actions after being cleared "onto the sterile side of the concourse," the area certified to be free of weapons and other hazardous materials. The screening process was captured by four separate cameras.

Camera 1 displayed the passengers with their bags as they approached the X-ray machine. Camera 2 displayed the contents of the plastic tubs on the conveyor belt for X-ray. Camera 3 displayed a full frontal "headshot" view of the passengers' face as they passed through the magnetometer. Camera 4 showed the X-ray image of what was screened.

"It took two hours of scanning to find the right date-time group, but this four-channel tells the story," offered the FBI special agent who sat at a desk with four monitors. He pounded the keyboard and worked the mouse to bring up the video. The four separate monitors displayed the four separate video feeds. "Here we go. Here's our guys in line. We have them talking with one another. Here they put their bags on the conveyor and go through the magnetometer. Then check this out...."

"Freeze it!" shouted Assistant Director Ianniello. The four men stared hard at the X-ray image on one screen and the image of the man passing through the metal detector. They noted the date-time group in the corner of the images. "Back it up to where he shows up in the queue."

The FBI special agent reversed the digital recording until they saw the image of the Middle Eastern man entering the security line. "Chief, notice the actions of the screener. She checked her watch and lifted her head." Watching the disparate actions on the four monitors synchronized in time was challenging but no one was in a hurry.

"She's on a timeline," uttered the police captain. The special agents silently nodded. The Supervisory TSA Officer frowned and squinted his eyes.

"Ok. Forward, normal speed." The men's eyes darted from monitor to monitor. The woman behind the X-ray monitor began to glance up and into the masses of passengers in line for security processing. A clean-shaven man passed through the initial TSA screening that matched boarding pass with passport identification. The Assistant Director asked the Supervisory TSA Officer, "We have the detail on the boarding pass and passport?"

"Yes, sir. Coming up." An image, tightly framed and focused on the lectern top clearly showed that the name on the passport and boarding pass were one and the same. A camera displayed the facial image of the man waiting to be processed at the lectern. He looked around casually before returning his eyes to the TSA agent behind the stout wooden lectern. Another camera displayed the man's backpack.

Ianniello asked, "Muhammad Yusef; can you print that out with his picture?" The special agent nodded and clicked the control mouse several times as the other special agent shuffled off to retrieve the printed images from some remote printer.

"Forward." They watched the man with the inconspicuous black backpack collect his documents and proceed past a TSA agent who directed him to use a designated screening station. Once "Muhammad Yusef" was behind the busy TSA agent directing traffic, he appeared to become momentarily confused.

"What's his problem," asked Ianniello. The men scrutinized the monitors, looking for a clue when Assistant Director Ianniello shouted, "He found her! He was looking for her. No other screener is wearing a headscarf, a *hijab*—look, he's guiding on to her like a beacon! Christ! That TSA officer just let him pick his X-ray machine. That's the game right there. Shit. Can you print out the images in the X-ray?"

"There's more, Chief," indicated the airport police chief.

"What's left?"

"The woman. If we fast forward the video she gets up from her chair and departs the airport. You might want her picture too. Her name is Abby Kesselring."

"That's not very...*Islamic*," suggested one of the special agents.

The airport police captain interjected, "Pretty sure she's a convert. She usually has lunch with a couple of other TSA officers that don't look like they were of Middle Eastern descent either—maybe one; they all wear headscarves. They've been interviewed and are cooperating. One of them provided the name of Kesselring's mosque."

Immediately after the reported hijacking, the airport police captain had watched the video with the FBI special agents and the Supervisory TSA Officer. He had identified TSO Kesselring instantly. His emotions had run the gamut from surprised to furious.

The FBI men then raced through the airport toward the concourse, confronted the lead TSA officer, demanding her personnel file. They retrieved information from Kesselring's emergency data card, her address and whom to notify in the case of an emergency. The FBI men entered an All-Points Bulletin into the instant messaging system for law enforcement and intelligence community officials for Abby Kesselring. Her name was automatically sent to the Terrorist Screening Center and was placed on both the No-Fly List and Terrorist Watch List. A pair of special agents had converged on Kesselring's apartment only to find it empty. Her parents were interviewed by another pair of special agents, but the distraught mother and father reported they hadn't seen or heard from her in weeks.

As the Special Agent in Charge returned from the printer with a sheaf of color prints, his cell phone began to warble. He handed the flimsies to the Assistant Director as he answered the electronic device. After several "uh huhs" and an "oh shit" he punched a button on the cell and turned to the FBI Assistant Director, nodding to the stack of photographs in his hand. "She's dead."

Assistant Director Ianniello raised his head to meet the man's eyes. He wasn't amused or surprised. "How?"

"Defenestrated. Eight floors. Don't know if she jumped or was pushed."

"Or was dead before she was tossed out the window," offered Ianniello.

"That too. We have a report she was last seen alive entering a mosque. Carrying a bag."

Assistant Director Ianniello said to the picture of Abby Kesselring, "Well, that's not going to make the Director very happy. Muslim outreach programs at mosques don't work very well when they're harboring *jihadis*."

· · ·

It was the moment they knew he had screwed up. The earsplitting report from the pistol reverberated throughout the cabin. Passengers reflexively jumped into a defensive posture at the sound, then sat stony faced and wide-eyed, wondering if they would be next. A faint puff of smoke leaked from the barrel of the Russian Makarov. No smell of cordite found its way into the aircraft's air conditioning system. No one moved and no one breathed.

At point blank range, the terrorist shot the African man in the face; the man who smugly challenged him with, "How do we know that gun is loaded?" Everyone in the premiere classes sat ramrod-straight in rapt attention. The demonstration of terrorism was complete and the captive masses were terrified. If there had been any doubt in their minds, every man and woman in the economy class section of the airliner had confirmed that the guns brandished were not props; the bullets were real. The *jihadis* had no compunction in using the weapons; these men were on a mission. In the sudden silence of the cabin, the terrorist waved his weapon from side to side and announced, "If you do exactly as I say, no one else will get hurt. Do not be a fool."

The man pointed the gun at Nigerian businessmen and excoriated Nigeria for crimes, economic crimes, social crimes, and crimes against Allah. He pointed his gun at the women and cursed them for dressing immodestly and for being immoral. As he walked up and down the aisles, his eyes scanned the eyes of passengers for any suggestion of threatening or non-compliant behaviors. Finding nothing but concern or terror in their faces, he shouted at a trembling flight attendant demanding she bring him "sacks." She had no "sacks" but struggled to find the words to ask for clarification. He berated her and jammed the pistol under her chin; he continued to scan the passengers to see if there were any heroes willing to stand up to him. The woman staggered into the galley and returned offering several transparent trashcan liners.

"Collect all watches, and monies, and passports—*GO!*" He pushed her toward the front of the airplane into the first class area.

. . .

The echo of the gunshot found its way onto the lower deck just as the pilots stepped from the cockpit closely followed by another jihadi with a gun. They were paraded through the first class and business class sections to the back of the aircraft. Walking down the aisle with slumped shoulders and fear in their eyes, the Nigerian aircrew struggled not to look into the eyes of their passengers. They were ashamed that they had failed to prevent the terrorists from entering the cockpit and had allowed them to commandeer the aircraft. With the aircrew removed from the cockpit, the passengers' hopes for a quick and peaceful resolution were crushed. The pilots' spirits were totally crushed; failing to protect their passengers, they staggered to the back of the airplane as if they were walking to their own hanging.

NO NEED TO KNOW

. . .

On the upper and lower decks, as flight attendants passed the "sack" to gather the passengers' belongings, the terrorist's eyes continually scanned the hundreds of passengers, looking for threats and targets. The eyes of the jihadi in the business class section kept returning to the young redheaded woman sitting in the rearmost seat. He'd had his eye on her since she entered the airplane; he envisioned having her if he was given the chance. *Insha'allah!*

During the earliest minutes of the hijacking, Kelly Horne anticipated that she and the other travelers would have their valuables removed at some point in the flight. Her hands shook as she removed her gold Rolex watch and slipped it into the arch of her tennis shoe. Strapped between her breasts, under her baggy sweatshirt, rested a hidden body pouch with her passport and most of her money. The man with the gun scrutinized all the belongings being spilled into the large clear plastic bags. The jihadi suddenly pistol-whipped a man for failing to remove a big gold watch from his wrist, and threatened to shoot him if he didn't comply and place it in the sack. The hijacker waved his pistol and repeated his demand that the passengers put all their valuables into the sack. He ordered the flight attendant to hurry.

Kelly took stock of the terrorist; he wasn't Asian or African, but his accented broken English suggested he might be from the Middle East. She'd had limited contact with Arabs and Muslims, and had ignored or rebuffed those she had met if they showed any interest in her. She was a Christian, and she wasn't interested in Muslim men. As the flight attendant and the man approached, she couldn't ignore him any longer. His leering look of interest demanded she look at him. When his eyes found hers, she quit analyzing the man to assess her situation and focus on survival. He might let her missing watch slide if he had noticed it, but he would expect her to contribute something to the bag. She was in business class and it was assumed that great wealth had been carried aboard even if the passengers wore ratty clothes and shoes.

During the Intelligence Officers' Course at the Farm, the instructors spoke of these types of situations, drawing from the experiences of countless other CIA employees who had survived embassies being overrun, having their cover blown in a hostile country, or being on an airplane and having their aircraft hijacked. Kelly vividly recalled the lecture, *"You must be prepared, and you must remain calm. You must keep your wits about you. You must have a plan to escape scrutiny, and you must have a plan to escape. You must take the most valuable thing you own—your U.S. diplomatic passport—and hide it; you must accept that everything else is disposable and may allow you live a little longer. You must realize your life is irreplaceable. You must be someone else and never be suspected of being a CIA officer."* When the plastic bag filled with wallets, watches, and cash was presented to her, Kelly dropped in the blue covered Canadian passport and few dollar bills. She turned her head in submission as the dark-skinned man glared at her.

Eastwood's ears still rang from the gunshot in the confined space. He had a front row seat to the man's ministrations and threats, and when the pistol was fired, like most of the passengers around him, he tried to curb the instinct to suck great quantities of air. He expected to smell the burnt acetone from the fired round and was surprised when he didn't. He thought, *Maybe when you're about to piss yourself, your nose stops working. Or maybe the smell of cordite from a single gunshot is a fantasy.* When the terrorist wasn't looking in his direction, he followed the man's eyes, as did most of the other passengers. It was obvious to Eastwood that the jihadi was infatuated with the attractive young woman in the back row. He had earlier dismissed the red headed woman as being a missionary worker, probably from a non-governmental organization, a volunteer or an employee for one of the many NGOs that supported a host of Christian activities in Africa. She wore a small gold cross around her neck and had that essence of innocence about her that screamed she was a good little Christian girl.

As the jihadi continually glanced at her, Eastwood was struck by the incongruity of her presence. He'd seen the young NGO employees and volunteers before in the field and on the airplanes. They travelled in groups, never alone, and they never flew in the business class section. So the little lady was an immediate enigma; she stuck out like a drop of blood on black paper. *And, in this situation, you don't want to bring attention to yourself. With that red hair girl you're going to be toast. Being a pretty young thing in this situation cannot be good. Nothing I can do to help you, young lady. Be smart and try to be inconspicuous!*

After the aircraft had landed and come to a halt, Eastwood had tried to assess their situation. He knew they had be in Africa, but Africa was a huge continent. However, the huge Airbus couldn't have landed at just any airport in Africa, he reasoned. He knew that airports interested in servicing the new jumbo jet, double-deck airliner had to upgrade their runways, taxiways, and ramps to handle the million-pound behemoth. It wouldn't be permitted to land, or more importantly use the taxiways or parking ramp, if their composition were not as strong as the runway landing area. The twin-deck Airbus would crush concrete and crumple asphalt designed to support the massive yet lighter Boeings. He recalled only a handful of airports in the world had done their due diligence and made the investment in their facilities to accommodate Airbus 380 flight operations. He and the other passengers strained to peer out the oversized windows to gain a hint to where they were, but there were no lights outside. Wherever they were, help would be a very long time coming, and it appeared they weren't leaving anytime soon, if ever.

CHAPTER THIRTY-ONE

Under the black canopies of high-performance, ram-air parachutes, Hunter trailed McGee by a hundred yards. He matched McGee's rate of descent and was about fifty feet higher. Their glide path into Roberts International Airport was smooth and coordinated. Hunter continually assessed the sight picture in his NVGs and worked the risers to steer the chute along the same trajectory as McGee's flight path. His head ratcheted up and down as he followed the big green image of McGee sailing onto the back of the big dark jet.

Like the professional parachutist he was, Bullfrog's boots touched down on the imaginary centerline of the jet, right where a line of blade antennas ran the length of the top of the fuselage. The SEAL landed perfectly; flaring his canopy at the precise moment to allow him to "walk onto" the back of the airplane.

Satisfied with his footing and that he was safe on top of the jet, McGee immediately collapsed and gathered his parachute. In one fluid motion, he unbuckled and stepped out of his harness, then turned toward the rear of the aircraft to locate Hunter in his NVGs. He was stunned at what he saw.

Hunter believed he was doing well in following McGee, but as he made his approach past the aircraft's tail, he recognized his situation had suddenly changed for the worse. He was drifting away from the airplane and realized he had no possibility of landing on top of the jet; he hadn't allowed for winds spilling up and over the side of the jet. The lack of depth perception in the NVGs compounded his inability to sense that he had been moving slightly away from the Airbus. It was too late to correct his position or to overfly the big jet and allow what little wind there was to bring him back to the top of the jet in a coordinated and natural maneuver. He was going to miss the airplane's broad back.

Intuitively, he yanked as hard as he dared on the left riser to get the parachute to turn more into the wind, trying to arrest the rightward drift and move more to the left toward the jet's surface. As the side of the airplane began to fill up his night vision goggles, he realized his corrective actions were too little and too late. He prepared to slam into the side of the jet and slide down the side of the three-story high fuselage. He braced his feet as they touched the aircraft ten feet from the top of the Airbus' centerline. Seeing that Hunter wasn't going to land properly, McGee sprinted down the spine of the A380 towards his friend.

With just enough air still in the parachute's canopy as he touched down, Hunter dug the toes of his boots into the side of the jet and tried to "run up" the side of the fuselage. His rubber-lug soles found some purchase with every step…until his chute began to collapse. With the instantaneous loss of tension between Hunter and his parachute, he lost what minute traction he had on the side of the airplane and he began to slip. He was going down.

At the last second, McGee grabbed the closest available shred of the quickly deflating parachute and pulled. The man's back and massive biceps flexed under the strain of the falling weight and the disappearing image of Hunter's helmet. The nylon canopy slipped in McGee's hands and raced through his fingers until he got his other hand on the material. He strained to stop the material from running out; he braced for the pain and fire that would surely come. With fingers the size of screwdriver handles, McGee crushed the material in his hands; the additional grippage stopped Hunter's trajectory over the side of the airplane. Hand over hand, McGee fought Hunter's dead weight and the parachute's natural silkiness. He wrapped the nylon over his arms and pulled Hunter up to the top of the jet, past the critical angle. Hunter regained some of his footing as McGee dragged him safely aboard. With Hunter on his back, an exhausted McGee sat down and leaned over to face an embarrassed and grinning Duncan Hunter.

Over the din of the auxiliary power unit's exhaust Hunter said, "Thank you, Sir. Nice catch." Then after a few breaths, "That was too close."

McGee had recovered from the spontaneous emergency outburst of exertion and stood up. In his low radio announcer voice, he boomed, "It wasn't *that* close. But you need to lose some weight. Let's go."

• • •

The man with the gun spat words at Kelly Horne, "You come with me!"

She shook her head. She stared at the man as he pointed his gun into her face. She could see he was furious and she expected him to shoot her.

If it's come to this, let it be. I will not submit!

The men and women in the business class section stared at the woman's act of defiance. They glared hate and venom at the lust-filled man. Demetrius Eastwood, several rows forward and on the other side of the cabin, shouted at the terrorist, "*Hey!*"

The *jihadi* was enraged at the interruption and immediately spun in the direction of the man's insolence. Men and women in their seats threw their heads down to their laps to get out of the line of fire. Eastwood remained upright and wondered if the last word he ever spoke was going to be, "Hey!"

The cabin was still and quiet as the jihadi turned back to Horne and reached for her. Kelly anticipated being struck or worse. When the man pressed the barrel of the pistol into her temple Kelly closed her eyes and said, "Yea, though I walk through the valley of the shadow of death, I will fear no evil, for thou *art* with me...."

Then the lights went out.

NO NEED TO KNOW

. . .

Hunter located the recessed, door-mounted handle and depressed the push-button. He and McGee dropped through the emergency hatch atop the jumbo jet. They left the high humidity of the Liberian jungle for the cold dry air in the enclosed space. Once inside the airplane, they found they were in the berthing area, the sleeping quarters for the relief aircrew. No one was home but a short stack of three single beds and a small kitchen dominated the small room. A spiral staircase connected the cockpit below to the room upstairs. With his silenced pistol at the ready, Hunter pointed the weapon down and gingerly descended the stairs to find the cockpit illuminated but empty.

He scanned the expansive cockpit and saw the cockpit door was closed. He noticed the round locking mechanism was missing. Assuming the Airbus cockpit controls and instruments were basically laid out like his Gulfstream business jet, he moved with the confidence of an experienced jet pilot and looked up to the overhead center panel to find the APU control panel. He flipped the NVGs over his eyes and powered them up just as he flicked the avionics master switch and shut down all the electrical and air conditioning systems on the jet. Hunter raised the silenced .45, and the green laser beam led the way out the door.

. . .

Hundreds of passengers shrieked in fear when the cabin went black and silent as the aircraft hydraulic and electrical systems ceased to operate. Women and children cried, parents comforted, and the terrorists screamed for quiet. There was some light from the emergency lighting strips marking the aisles. Each *jihadi* yelled for people to remain in their seats and to be quiet. They were fearful and very nervous, and they jumped at any sound. They spun around and pointed their weapons, demanding everyone sit and be quiet.

Kelly felt the pressure of the pistol removed from the side of her face as passengers screamed. She opened her eyes and the cabin was virtually pitch black, except for some faint light coming from the floor. She believed the man who had wanted her to go with him had stepped away from her, but she sensed he was still near. The distraction was immediately liberating and she impulsively kicked the man and felt her knee slide up between his legs into his groin. As she heard the man gasp for air; she jumped back into her seat and balled herself up in a defensive posture. Kelly shook in her seat as she thought she was going to be killed.

．　　．　　．

Eastwood saw a shadow race up the aisle, heard the distinctive report of a silenced weapon and its spent cartridge case "ringing" as it was ejected from a semi-automatic pistol. Following the sound of the spent brass were heavy footfalls running down the aisle toward the back of the jet. His mouth was agape with shock.

．　　．　　．

On the upper deck of the jumbo airliner, McGee shot men with guns. Each man brandishing a pistol received a bullet into the heart, just left of center of the sternum; where the laser dot stopped, a bullet entered. Four men down.

On the lower deck, Duncan Hunter raced out of the cockpit, with pistol leading and laser sight darting for targets of opportunity. Every fifty feet he slowed to target accurately and dropped a man with a gun. Center mass; he watched the bullets enter the men's torso in shades of green. After fifty adrenaline-spiked seconds, all the terrorists were down. Hunter stood near the rear of the jet and jammed fingers in his mouth and whistled as loud as he could.

He searched for the distinctive shoulder boards that pilots and copilot wear on their uniforms. Hunter yelled as loud as he could, "Help is here! Stay in your seats! Where's the crew?"

From the back of the jet, a dozen voices squealed in unison, "Here! Here!"

Some passengers sat quietly while others wept openly and tried to touch the shadow that had come to rescue them.

．　．　．

When the cabin lights suddenly illuminated and the air conditioning began to blow from tiny nozzles overhead, nearly every passenger and the flight attendant erupted in cheers and applause. Strangers hugged their seat neighbors. Some passengers got out of their seats to pummel the dead terrorists in the aisles. McGee and Hunter collected all the firearms and searched each corpse for any signs of life, additional weapons, or other dangerous items. The pilot announced over the public address system for everyone to strap in and prepare for an immediate departure.

．　．　．

With the lights on throughout the aircraft, Hunter ran down the aisle through the first and business class sections. He found McGee descending from a winding staircase, receiving congratulatory handshakes and hand-slaps as he moved through the business class section. With his NVGs still over his eyes, McGee still wielded his weapon as he approached with a grin.

Every passenger watched the two men in the black coveralls and helmets converge and exchange smiles. When Hunter heard a young woman's voice shout, *"Maverick!"* he moved quickly around other seated travelers to get to the woman who had raised her hand.

She stood as the man in black Nomex approached. He stepped on top of the dead terrorist to get to her. She stepped into the passageway and wrapped her arms around him. Every passenger in the business class section watched the man and woman embrace. With the release of pent up emotions, Kelly fought hard not to cry, but lost the battle.

After a few firm seconds, he pulled her away. He said, "I came as fast as I could. You okay?" She trembled in his arms.

"Yes, sir," Kelly said with a smile that beamed incredulity. Tears filled her eyes and ran down her cheeks. She couldn't believe her father was standing before her, holding her. There was so much she wanted to say, but under the circumstances, it wasn't the time or the place. Completely overwhelmed emotionally, she never thought to tell her father "their little secret" was out; that she and Nazy had met and that Nazy knew she was his daughter.

With an arm around her waist, he slipped his .45 into a pocket and cleared tears from her cheeks with his free hand. He fingered her chin to make her look at him in his helmet and NVGs. "I have to go. I'll talk with you later." Hunter's sense of urgency to leave quickly overtook his desire to comfort his daughter. He released her and again stepped on the chest of the corpse which emitted a ghoulishly wet burp. He turned to intercept McGee at the base of the staircase when he heard, *"Hey Maverick!"* His head snapped at the direction of the voice, surprised to find Colonel Eastwood on the other side of the jet. He approached the man still buckled in his seat.

A stunned Eastwood said, *"It's not possible!"* and burst out laughing as Hunter held out his hand with McGee close behind. The unmistakable low-frequency rumble under his feet and the sound of an engine starting caught Hunter's attention. He shook the old Marine's hand, dumped all the hijackers' weapons into Eastwood's lap, gave the old colonel an informal salute, turned and said to McGee, "We have to go—*now!*"

As Hunter and McGee raced up the spiral staircase between flight decks and hurried to the front of the jet, the men and women of the lower deck began to chant what they had heard regarding the man in black; they clapped and stomped their feet until it spread throughout the airliner, *"Yea, Maverick! Yea, Maverick! Yea, Maverick!"*

. . .

They raced to get off the jet. A second engine was started and brought up to idle while the external position lights were turned on, floodlights illuminated the six-story tail. Hunter envisioned the pilot and copilot tearing through their checklists to get the Airbus off the ground as soon as they could.

After closing the emergency hatch and gathering their parachutes, Hunter and McGee ran amidships and slid down the fuselage and onto the wing. The inboard engine was started and rumbled to life under their feet as they scrambled across the left wing. When they reached the end of the wing, Hunter and McGee strung their parachutes over the wingtip and rappelled to the ground, shimmying down their canopies and shroud lines until their feet touched the reinforced asphalt. A flick of the lines and the canopies pulled away from the wingtip and fell to earth. As they gathered their parachutes, the engine closest to them began its start sequence. Hunter and McGee ran for their lives as the massive engines spooled to high power. The engine closest to them could have easily sucked the men off their feet and into its twelve-foot wide intake had they lingered in its danger zone.

Well clear of the aircraft, Hunter and McGee slowed to a walk and continued side by side toward the terminal. After a few dozen steps, Hunter stopped and turned toward the unmistakable sound of four Rolls-Royce turbofan engines being programmed to takeoff thrust. McGee followed his lead and they watched the airliner lumber down the remaining length of the 11,000-foot runway. With a light fuel load and a gentle headwind, *The Nigerian Queen* quickly lifted off, retracted the gear, and turned to the east. A minute after liftoff, the airport was again quiet and dark. Standing on the taxiway between the airport terminal and the runway, it was hot and muggy, and peaceful. The lights of the Airbus quickly disappeared over the horizon. McGee and Hunter stood stone still and silent. They realized they were sweating profusely.

As Hunter realized what they had accomplished, he turned to his friend and then looked skyward. He saw clear skies and the dizzying Milky Way in all of its glory. McGee joined him in scanning the skies, and after several moments, turned and pounded Hunter's chest eagerly. With a broad smile and pride in his eyes he said, "I have to say, good sir, that was well done."

"Thanks, Bullfrog. Couldn't have done it without you." Hunter lowered his head and looked at the man. "We make a pretty damn good team."

McGee's fist turned to a pointed finger, poking him in the chest. "We do. But you suck as a skydiver." Hunter broke out in laughter and McGee joined him; Hunter nodded in agreement at his parachuting deficiencies. As they turned back toward the dimly lit terminal, a pair of headlights suddenly illuminated near the building. McGee's instincts spiked and he became increasingly concerned at what he couldn't see. They were out in the open, in the middle of an African airport; they were sitting-duck targets. He reached into his pocket and gripped his pistol.

The vehicle pulled away from the poorly illuminated building then turned toward the men, as if someone had seen them dismount the jumbo jet and walk toward the airport building. Hunter seemed unconcerned by the vehicle's movement toward them and McGee tried to gain a sense of comfort by asking, "Welcome crew?" He changed magazines in his pistol and racked a fresh cartridge into the chamber.

"Hopefully, it's just the airport manager."

McGee was struck by Hunter's laissez-faire, offhanded comment just as the vehicle's headlights momentarily raked across a distant derelict aircraft parked in high weeds before it straightened its course and bore down on them. He slipped the .45 behind his back. He didn't like being illuminated even for a second.

Then McGee pointed the pistol off in the direction of dark and asked, "I saw a jet over there…somewhere. Is that…*the jet?*"

Hunter looked over at his friend with a sly grin. "It is."

Again, the men burst out in laughter, sharing the secret. Hunter stopped walking. McGee returned the pistol to his back. "Yeah, that's the jet. Occasionally, I wonder what's left of him. Then I think; it doesn't matter. He's gone."

"You're evil." McGee grinned and turned his eyes toward the approaching vehicle. "It's a good evil."

"Been said before. My mama wouldn't like what's happened to her little boy."

The vehicle came upon the two men and slowed. Hunter removed his helmet and waited for the vehicle to stop. The driver stepped out into the lights as McGee nervously re-gripped his weapon. He stood still as Hunter approached. In the headlights, Hunter energetically hugged the man. McGee heard his partner ask, "Give a couple of vets a ride into town?"

McGee relaxed his grip on the .45 and approached the side of the vehicle. LeMarcus Leonard watched the big black man step from the headlights and come to the driver's side of the Toyota. Hunter made introductions, then the airport manager barked at him, ignoring McGee for the moment. He put his hands on his hips and said, "Dude! You appear out of the dark carrying parachutes, coming from a jet that had been hijacked. Then, the big jet suddenly leaves? And you just want a ride into town? *Oh, Hell no!* Bullshit. Give it up. Tell me what you did."

McGee sensed the man wasn't a threat but a friend; he harrumphed and changed his focus to the aircraft's outline off in the distance as he pocketed the .45. Hunter was initially taken aback by Leonard's tone and body language. He knew the airport manager wasn't serious and was about to respond when Leonard noticed McGee looking off in the direction of the final resting place of Osama bin Laden.

"I'll sell it to you cheap. Last one I have in inventory." Hunter frowned and was unimpressed with Leonard's diversion. They needed to get to their aircraft some thirty miles away.

"What is it?" asked McGee.

"Yak-40. It was the private coach of Viktor Bout until a bird took out the upper engine; no one's sure whether it happened during take-off or landing. He left it and never came back."

"Ah, the Merchant of Death. We used to call his airline 'Air Cesspool.' Like all of his aircraft, I'll bet it was Liberian registered." McGee smirked, not giving up on the idea he wanted to see the remains of Osama bin Laden, even if he was just a pile of rat droppings.

Hunter interjected, "After the fall of the Soviet Union, air force officers loaded their families aboard IL-76s and Yak-40s and Antanovs24s and flew them out of the country. Other enterprising KGB colonels emptied armories and weapons storage depots—some even stole MANPADS and...."

"Even suitcase nukes," suggested McGee.

"Yes, sir, whatever they could take so that they could barter with the U.S. or terrorists and become instant capitalists. Bout organized the Russian pilots to fly the aircraft, sold AK-47s and RPGs, and flooded Africa with them. That's one of the reasons the U.N. has been here for so long, trying to find the weapons that were used in 15-16 years of civil war. IL-76s were flying out of the USSR so fast they became expendable. LeMarcus, we really need to go."

Leonard ignored him. "I was thinking of moving it or dismantling it."

Before Leonard could finish his thought, Hunter turned to the airport manager and said, "Don't." Then, without saying anything else, Hunter tossed his parachute into the bed of the Toyota and got in. Leonard and McGee looked at each other questioningly, then over at the silhouette of the decrepit jet before following Hunter into the truck. McGee got in the back seat.

LeMarcus Leonard drove the Toyota HiLux with skill and caution through the little hamlet of Smell-No Taste along Airport Road. Dozens of Liberian men and women walked on narrow dirt paths along both sides of the road. As they left the hamlet in the rearview mirror, Hunter provided McGee with a running commentary. "During

World War Two, when Roberts Field was being built by the U.S. government as a staging area for aircraft to check the expansion of Axis powers in North Africa, Army cooks prepared meals around the clock for the pilots, mechanics, and support personnel. The Liberians lived in grass huts in this area, they smelled the food being prepared but couldn't get the soldiers to surrender samples or let them taste the strange, odiferous concoctions the airmen ate. Soon this area was called Smell-No Taste."

"Seriously?"

"Can't make that stuff up. LeMarcus has been the airport manager at Roberts for several years. Let's say we recruited him; Greg and me...."

"Mostly you," offered LeMarcus Leonard. Hunter patted the man on the shoulder. "They needed a dude to do this work."

"LeMarcus was also the last man to go through the Full Spectrum Training Center before Yoder passed away. Officially, he's the airport manager, but maybe since he's not working with me anymore, maybe he's working for Greg; non-official cover? Did I miss anything?"

Once clear of the congestion that was the jungle village of Smell-No Taste, LeMarcus sped down the blacktop. He asked, "Not really. You going to tell me how you happened to be on my airport? Those aren't exactly airline traveling clothes. You do know *Mr. Former Border Patrol*, all about 'illegal entry.' If there had been another airport manager, your ass would be off to jail in a microsecond. And no white boy wants to go to a Liberian jail." LeMarcus grinned a full set of teeth at Hunter, who nodded.

McGee's booming voice responded, "LeMarcus, I think it's best that you never saw us. This is going to get out—hell, the passengers were chanting *Maverick* as we left the airplane. There are some incredibly bad actors out there and their tentacles are everywhere. For that airplane to land here, there must be people on the ground that knew some details of the hijacking. If they think you have information, they will take it from you, and you won't be allowed to live."

LeMarcus turned to Hunter and said, "That's the same line you gave me the last time. I want to do some cool shit too."

"And what did I say the last time?" Hunter was serious.

"No need to know. You know boss, you're an asshole!"

The three men erupted in laughter and coughed until they could compose themselves.

"He can be pretty funny—sometimes," deadpanned McGee.

Leonard drove through the outskirts of Monrovia and related how he had discovered an unannounced jet on his airport. "I moved into the station master's house, finally. The field was closed for a couple of hours, everyone had gone home when I heard a big jet's thrust reversers. I didn't even hear it approach! I drove to the airport and saw this A-380 sitting in the middle of the runway. All the lights were off except the cabin lights. I drove up to the jet but the door never opened. I drove to the tower and talked to the crew who told me not to broadcast their position or who they were or they would throw women and children out the door. I called the Chief of Station and asked him if the world was missing a jumbo. A few men showed up from the village thinking there would be ground and baggage handling work, since the jet flew over their heads on approach, but I sent them home. A couple of hours later, the engines started, the external lights illuminated, and you came traipsing across the taxiway as it took off."

The men drove on as the airport manager highlighted all the new buildings, gas stations, and restaurants since Hunter's last visit. Hunter asked how the President was doing and got an answer that was more how the Director of Civil Aviation was doing. "She's fine; he should be in jail. I don't know why she doesn't put that crook in jail."

"Please give her my regards. You know what the answer is."

"Yeah, I know; I don't want to believe it. Nevertheless, she keeps me around and keeps him off my back, and you can use the airport when you or DOD need it. And you pay me very well. That was the deal."

"I know, LeMarcus. Politics suck." Hunter gave McGee a look that said he would explain it all later. He changed the subject. "So what have you been doing with yourself?"

NO NEED TO KNOW

"You mean before I was interrupted with a hijacked airplane on my airport?"

"Uh huh."

"Would you believe I hacked into my *buddy's* Escalade OnStar system? He's in Atlanta." Hunter immediately broke up with laughter and pounded his hands together loudly while McGee listened in confusion for more information. "So I find him and start to track him, then I hack into the Atlanta traffic grid and I give him red lights wherever he goes. *Long red lights.* I also put him on the TSA terrorist watch list, so it will be a while before he can convince the TSA that he shouldn't be on it. I had just reported his Caddy had been stolen when I heard the thrust reversers of the 380. I had these visions of him getting pulled over and arrested, but you dropping in was way more entertaining."

McGee snapped, "And, you call *Duncan* an asshole? Remind me not to piss you off!" Again, the truck erupted in riotous laughter. As the truck cabin returned to a normal level of quietude, McGee offered, "LeMarcus, I think Duncan's got an interesting cast of *brotha'* friends."

Leonard never took his eyes off the road but picked up the tone and puckish line of attack as he said, "I think he's a racist. He had me up on the plantation for years while he and Lynche played spook. I felt like I had been cast off to the Island of Misfit Toys."

Hunter frowned and paused before saying, "He's not being accurate. He lived on the Firestone Plantation while the airport manager's house was being refurbished. It's the most secure place in Liberia." Hunter frowned at the men and feigned hurt.

"Oh, in that case, that definitely makes him a Democrat." McGee turned to face Hunter, "You had him on a *plantation?* What are all your liberal friends going to think?"

Leonard spun in his seat, absolutely shocked. "*He's got liberal friends?* No way!" Leonard and McGee burst out in hearty laughter; Hunter screwed up his face and laughed along.

A pause in the levity allowed Hunter to say, "I was going to ask you if you've been doing any of that ethical hacking stuff but it seems like you've moved into the entertainment business."

McGee lightheartedly pointed at Hunter and shook his head; the man could take a joke as well as dish them out. LeMarcus continued, "The short answer is yes. The Madam has me sift through the bank records of everyone in the government. I find those who have questionable accounts and deposits. I let her know—they go to jail. *All but my buddy!* New guys come in and try to steal from the government or get their relatives on the payroll somewhere—something like that. I screw with the newspapers from time to time. It's so easy here; there's no real security. Hardly worth the effort. If I didn't screw with the director general, especially when he's out of the country, I'm afraid I'd lose my touch."

Hunter said, "You've lost your hair. I expected the cornrows. Bill, when we found LeMarcus, I told Yoder not to say anything about his hair or piss him off because he could empty his bank account in seconds."

"Still could. Not many opportunities lately to probe bank vaults. Too busy with the airport, and of course, the general director still wants to kill me. If he ever found out I was screwing with him, he would. I think the stress of this job has made me bald."

McGee rubbed his thinning grey hair and said, "Hanging out with Duncan will do that to you." The men laughed as the first street lights of the City of Monrovia came into view.

Leonard made good use of the light early morning traffic and sped through town. He turned off the main road and onto one of the side roads, stopped at the checkpoint at the guard shack, and entered the Spriggs Payne airport. He didn't need directions; the dark grey MC-130 dominated the parking ramp and started one of its outboard engines as the HiLux came to a stop, just clear of the wing and in sight of the passenger entry door. The men said their goodbyes and conveyed their gratitude; Hunter and McGee got out of the truck, grabbed their parachutes and helmets, and walked onto the cargo airplane. As the men stepped into the side door of the MC-130 and disappeared, Leonard shook his head, waved one last time, and drove off.

Hunter and McGee climbed into the cabin of the Hercules as their support crew, Bob and Bob, cheerfully waved at them and gave them two "thumbs up." The men tossed their bundled parachutes in the direction of the two septuagenarians, turned and stepped up and into the cockpit just as the number two engine started. As the aircraft gently shook and vibrated from the propellers turning out on the wing, the aircrew vigorously welcomed Hunter and McGee into the cockpit. Hunter shouted over the din, "Thanks for waiting for us."

The pilot turned in his seat, and with a look of awe and admiration, said, "Looks like you guys have been busy."

"Not sure what you're talking about." Hunter smiled impishly and overacted that he was confused. It was obvious the aircrew knew something Hunter didn't, and it wasn't a time to confirm or generate rumors.

"It's on the airways that Navy SEALs stormed the hijacked jet at Roberts; they killed the terrorists and got the plane back on its way."

Hunter smiled whimsically as he glanced at McGee.

"*SEALs!*" deadpanned McGee. "Even in the middle of Liberia?"

"Wow; they're everywhere!" shouted Hunter.

The pilot and copilot could tell the old guys in black Nomex with silenced pistols poking out of their flight vests were totally unserious and would never volunteer the truth. However, they knew. They knew the two men standing hunched over in the cockpit had somehow been involved in the rescue operation. They knew the quiet airplane landed without their pilots. Without being told the circumstantial evidence or details, they knew. And their admiration and respect for the grey haired men grew exponentially. But they also knew the drill; and their job was to get the men into and out of locations as quickly and as quietly as possible. They knew they didn't have a need to know anything else. An exchange of glances and grins conveyed the pilot and co-pilot weren't going to get specific answers voluntarily. It was best to drop the charade. They needed to leave Liberia and quit bullshitting.

Hunter knew the men in the Hercules cockpit would forever share the shadowy secret. Duncan patted the pilot and copilot on the shoulder and told them, "Thanks again for all of your help. You guys helped make *it* all possible, whatever the definition of 'it' is," and he left the cockpit. The aircrew immediately turned to the chore of getting airborne. As Hunter and McGee stepped down from the cockpit, the pilot keyed the interphone and said to the copilot, "I always thought ninjas were young kung fu dudes."

The reunion with Bob and Bob was filled with backslaps and handshakes. After checking on the status and condition of the YO-3A and answering some benign questions, which brought more smiles to the newly-energetic old guys, Hunter exclaimed "all this excitement" had worn him out and playfully indicated he needed a nap. McGee seconded the idea. Before the aircraft had even lined up on the runway for takeoff, Hunter and McGee unzipped their boots and flight suits, and the four men slipped into sleeping bags. They pulled sleep masks over their eyes and noise-cancelling headsets over their ears.

The C-130 took off and departed to the north. The aircrew monitored the commercial airline radio traffic that had come alive with other airlines flying the air routes crisscrossing West Africa. After reaching cruising altitude, the pilot depressed the interphone switch to speak with the co-pilot and flight engineer in the cockpit. "I think I know what I want to be when I grow up."

"What's that?" asked the co-pilot.

"Like our heroes in the back. Quietly doing amazing things that no one will ever know anything about."

CHAPTER THIRTY-TWO

Lynche woke with a start. Over the monotonous hum of the air conditioning unit, his BlackBerry rang and vibrated on the nightstand. Momentarily confused and lethargic from sleep, he jabbed at buttons to squelch the alarm. Four nines on the small screen indicated the White House was calling. He blinked several times to help comprehend what he was seeing. After he pushed the connect button he said, "Good morning, Mr. President."

"Greg, did I wake you?"

"I was just getting up, Sir."

"I need to know if one of your boys rescued the Nigerian airliner."

Greg came fully awake and swung his legs off the bed and onto the floor. "Sir, I've no idea what you're talking about. The last I heard we were moving assets per the demands. I know of no rescue effort. That's generally SOCOM's area of responsibility, I think Army Delta Forces; that's more their forte."

"SOCOM is disavowing any knowledge. They had assembled a rescue crew and weren't even on the runway when the news came through. So you haven't heard?"

"No, Sir. I take it someone...freed the airliner? Was it the passengers?" Lynche immediately assumed it was impossible for an external assault team to get inside an airliner. He had visions of a brave group of passengers, like the passengers aboard United Airlines Flight 93, who refused to be terrorized and took matters into their own hands to overwhelm the hijackers. *If Special Operations Command and the CIA's Special Activities Group weren't involved, who could it be?*

The President continued, "Greg, I received a call from the Nigerian

President that the aircraft had been taken to Monrovia, Liberia, that Navy SEALs killed all the hijackers, and that the transfer of assets needed to be suspended. So it wasn't your guys?"

"Monrovia?" Lynche started to get a bad feeling in the pit of his stomach. With his other hand, he grabbed the television remote control and stabbed at the big red button to energize the monitor.

The President continued, "Monrovia. Isn't that weird? Why would they take the jet to Liberia? Also, it seems one or both of the rescuers were called Maverick. I'm not sure...."

Lynche threw his head back and nearly fell back into the middle of the mattress as the President verified the sinking feeling in his belly. The sudden information completely disrupted his situational awareness and he nearly lost his grip on both devices. Once he recovered his grip on the cell phone he said, "Mr. President, Sir, I don't know how...but our boy from Texas was due to land in Monrovia. And, of course his call sign is...."

"...*Maverick*. Of course! *It was your guys!*" The receiver crackled as the President erupted in laughter on the other end of the telephone. Greg Lynche was hung up on the Cartesian coordinates of awe, pride and anger. He didn't know which to be, but knew that the man he recruited for unusual missions had again left him stunned and nearly speechless. He felt the pride of a father whose son had excelled beyond his wildest dreams and had far surpassed all of his highest expectations. *Duncan Hunter and his sidekick Bill McGee had somehow got inside the Airbus and eliminated the terrorists?* Lynche washed aside the applause for his prodigy and replaced it with disappointment and a growing sense of opprobrium. The bad news was that Hunter's little Houdini trick could mean the *Noble Savage* mission may have been completely compromised. Lynche's voice couldn't hide his concern. With the television on some news channel, he scrolled through channels looking for Al-Jazeera Africa.

"Sir, our Texan will likely check-in soon. I'll get validation as soon as I can and will send you a situation report." Lynche found the desired television channel with the buggy emblem in the corner and creepy crawler at the bottom of the screen just as a microphone was stuck under the nose of a jubilant airline passenger. The banner spelled out Hijacked Nigerian Airways freed by American Commandos.

"I don't think that'll be necessary, Greg. We know it was him— we'll let the world believe it was a SEAL rescue. SOCOM will continue to cite they don't discuss ongoing operations."

"SOCOM did provide the ride. Thank you, Mr. President." Lynche tried to read the lips of the woman being interviewed.

"How's your other project?"

"Due in about four hours. He would be a fool not to take the offer."

"Let's hope. It's been a very *interesting* evening. Let me know if you need anything. Good night, Greg."

Five time zones away, the President yawned in Lynche's ear; Lynche stifled his from being heard.

"Will do, Mr. President. Good night, Sir."

．　．　．

The man from al-Qaeda stormed into the room, his black *keffiyeh* flapped behind him as if caught in a wind tunnel. He was nearly volcanic from Rothwell's terse telephone call minutes earlier; he wouldn't be dissuaded from ripping into the former American intelligence chief for yet another failure. Discussions with other members of the council conveyed their dismay as well as a growing realization that the former CIA man's vision of very large rewards coming from very large risks wasn't working. Demonstrating unity and a sense of urgency not usually displayed by such a mature group of master terrorists, they faced one inescapable fact—they had nothing to show for any of their efforts.

As the last member of the council arrived at the secure conference room, the would-be second-in-command demanded answers, but all he could articulate were questions. He pointed toward the huge television monitor and glared at Bruce Rothwell. Then composing himself he said calmly, "Peace be upon you and the Mercy of Allah and His blessings." That said, he erupted in a fount of vitriol and spittle, and shouted, *"How is this possible?!"*

When Rothwell didn't move or blink, the grey-bearded man from Afghanistan became enraged. "We've nothing! *Nothing* to show for this effort! *Raqqa, how is this possible?"*

Rothwell sat transfixed, unblinking, eyes riveted to the huge television monitor in abject disbelief as passengers from an ill-fated Nigerian airliner were interviewed as they disembarked from the aircraft. He didn't acknowledge the man's presence with the expected courtesy and obeisance. He couldn't; he could barely focus on the center of the television. All noise and external distractions were processed through his brain as static.

The former Director of Central Intelligence sat and stared catatonically while gently trembling, as if afflicted by the early stages of Parkinson's disease. With no response from the man at the head of the table, the man from al-Qaeda wondered if the strain of defeat had been too much for the physically damaged Rothwell. The unresponsiveness and tremors suggested a stroke or a repressed neurodegenerative disorder brought about by the stress of yet another spectacular failure. The man had so much potential. He led them to dozens of spies who had or had tried to infiltrate the Brotherhood and al-Qaeda. He led them to other secrets that brought much-needed funds. It wasn't the time to lose him or kill him. There was much more information to glean from the man's mind. Al-Qaeda would allow Rothwell to think he was using the Brotherhood, but when it was time to kill Brother Raqqa, the greybeard would do it himself. He said softly, "Raqqa, can you hear me?"

Rothwell's eye remained focused on the television as the words scrolled across the bottom of the monitor. He sensed there were others in the room and slowly lifted his gaze from the TV to the man. Life had drained from the man's heavily bloodshot eye.

"Brother Mahmood...?

"Yes, brother...Raqqa," said the greybeard softly. "Can you hear me?" He couldn't tell if Rothwell was nodding or if another bout of the tremors was affecting him.

He turned his head away as if embarrassed. "Yes, I can hear you. This is very unfortunate."

"Brother Raqqa, how did this happen?"

"I don't know...yet. There's a...great...*disturbance.* I can feel it. These people getting off the airplane. I sense they know and will soon tell me, tell the world. They know." Rothwell lifted a quivering hand as an emaciated finger pointed at the monitor. "They know. They will tell us."

The man from al-Qaeda and the men from the Muslim Brotherhood looked at the monitor and back at Rothwell several times in an attempt to decipher the cryptic words. *How is this possible?* rang through the old Afghani's head. "It was impossible to find the aircraft—no one could find the aircraft. No radar over Africa. It couldn't be tracked by satellite. How did this happen?" He partitioned his attention between the TV monitor with new information streaming across the screen and a more responsive Rothwell.

Rothwell offered, "It was...impossible for any special operations groups to mount a rescue effort. Not enough time to form a plan and complete and execute a time-sensitive decision cycle. It was an unanticipated target. In the middle of Africa. There was no time...it was isolated...*purposely,* so that no one could respond quickly. It was a perfect plan!"

"But it happened!" shouted the al-Qaeda general. He shot-gunned questions hoping something would trigger a better response than, "They will tell us." He asked, "Did the passengers or those flying security guards overpower the mujahedeen?"

"No—one person was interviewed and said they only saw two men. Dressed in black with strange glasses over their eyes." Rothwell's eye remained on the screen as he spoke in hushed spurts.

"Two men? Men in black?" The man spat in disgust. It was simply unbelievable that two men could overpower eight of al-Qaeda's best clandestine warriors.

"That's what...was reported." Rothwell pointed and nodded more vigorously than usual, as if some growing awareness was casting light onto a dark patch of his mind.

"Could these strange glasses have been night vision?"

H shouted, "Immaterial! *How did they get on the aircraft in the middle of Africa?* How did they get on? If we can determine how they got onto the aircraft...."

The man from al-Qaeda noticed a new person being interviewed and pointed at the television. "What's that woman saying? Turn up the volume!"

As Rothwell stabbed an arthritic finger in the middle of the television remote control, increasing the volume emanating from the device on the wall, his cellular telephone rang and vibrated on the conference table. The woman on the monitor was singing as he removed his finger from one device, pressed the touch screen on the other to answer the cellphone. After a few seconds of listening to the voice from the handheld, Rothwell dropped it onto the table with a thud. The sound of the electronic device falling onto the table startled the men around the conference table. Rothwell heard something familiar coming from the television, from the singing woman. He turned an eye to the man whose eyes were begging for information, something good and positive. Rothwell sighed and said, "The American airplane...returned. The gold...is gone." He shook his head in disbelief as he became more aware of what the woman was saying in the distance, in her sing-song voice.

"That was expected, Brother Raqqa. *After that!*" The man furiously pointed to the monitor.

"It's confirmed. What's that bitch saying?" Rothwell dismissively waved his hand in the direction of the television.

"She described a white man in black coveralls and a helmet and strange small binoculars. She said the lights went out in the airplane and people screamed. They thought they were going to die. But an American voice—a *white* man's voice—said they were there to help them and to stay in their seats. After a few minutes the lights came back on. The white man joined with a black man with the same uniform, and they disappeared through the front of the airplane. The passengers were so afraid and then so thankful—then she said they were grateful for the Mavericks! What does that mean? *Grateful for the Mavericks?*"

Like sunrise to a vampire, Rothwell recoiled at the word. His eye rolled into the back of his head—he jumped in his chair as if he had been zapped with a cattle prod. The al-Qaeda man was the most concerned and believed the man was having a stroke or an epileptic fit, as hyperventilation racked Rothwell's damaged body.

As the shock of the word wore off and his senses struggled to return to normal, he recalled an increasingly clearer memory of accusing Duncan Hunter of being...a *maverick*, to disqualify him from participating in the President's special access program. And the memories of being embarrassed as Hunter told him—*lectured him*—that he might be a *maverick* but the retired Marine fighter pilot had earned the call sign *Maverick*; his friends often called him *Maverick*. The woman on the television could have uttered any other word in the English language and the enigma of who rescued *The Nigerian Queen* would have remained a mystery. However, to utter...to sing the praises of the *Mavericks*, he now knew who was responsible—for rescuing the airplane and releasing the President's file—but he couldn't comprehend how Hunter had done either one.

One of the Muslim Brotherhood men and the man from Afghanistan were about to rush out of the room to find the man's male nurse as Rothwell struggled to gain his composure and control his body. When he appeared calmer, the bearded al-Qaeda man took his seat but didn't take his eyes off Brother Raqqa.

Rothwell took a very long time before he could control his breathing and say, "I'm afraid...it means...the infidel...was behind the rescue."

Confused, the men around the table asked, "What infidel?"

Rothwell suddenly turned to the group as if they were imbeciles and summoned the last of his energy reserves to lift his remaining arm and slam down his distorted, scarred fist on the table. A new bout of spontaneous hyperventilation struck him; spittle flew as he forced out a primeval scream, *"Hunter!"*

The name sucked away all of Rothwell's energy and seemingly crushed his spirit, as he collapsed in his chair. With all of the dramatic flips in personality and speech, the al-Qaeda man wondered if he was witnessing a nervous breakdown or worse. He allowed a passing thought that Rothwell's every action was in response to something the infidel Hunter had done to him. Furthermore, it was remarkable he hadn't mentioned the woman. That Rothwell wanted bloody vengeance on Hunter wasn't a secret, but his plans to strip away the woman from the infidel were neither unobvious nor were they proving effective. His thoughts were interrupted when Rothwell began trembling and spoke again.

"We have to find the suitcase bombs. There must be someone who knows of their whereabouts."

"For that you need money. We...."

He turned to the man from Egypt. "Use our reserves. If we don't find them before the Americans are able to acquire them, our movement will crumble, and the Brotherhood and al-Qaeda will vanish in the desert winds. Do you not see?"

"What I see Brother Raqqa is that the Americans and Europeans have made it very difficult for us to raise sufficient money. Even the Saudi perfumed princes have been warned off. I do agree. If this plan fails...."

"Some traitorous Russians are holding them somewhere. We didn't know where. The CIA knew how many and even their serial numbers. What we need is greater human intelligence. Someone knows. Someone can be motivated to tell. They will tell us...."

"We must find the bombs. Brother Raqqa, do you not have a contact? I'm surprised you don't know someone in Russia."

"I know a few, my brother. However, I'm afraid that the man I know already has the bombs and is trying to barter them. He wouldn't sell them to me before. No money...no amount interested him. Only the Nazi artwork."

"Then our mission is defined for us. We must find the bombs; if that mission is unsuccessful, then we must find the location of their transfer and...."

Rothwell turned a beady eye toward the old terrorist and said, "And steal them."

The man from al-Qaeda stroked his greybeard. "*Insha'allah.* That would be best."

The man from the Muslim brotherhood offered, "*Bismillah ir-Rahman ir-Rahim.*"

Rothwell repeated the most frequent phrase in the Qur'an, "In the name of Allah, most Gracious, and most Compassionate. Go in Peace. We've much work to do."

When the men from al-Qaeda and the Muslim Brotherhood left the penthouse suite, Rothwell fingered the TV remote control to squelch the sound. As words of news programmed across the base of the monitor, he said, dejectedly, "Will my other plan also fail?"

CHAPTER THIRTY-THREE

The gold and red Boeing 747 popped out from under a dark thick cloud layer and into a thin diaphanous fog. Tiny vapor trails from the wingtips grew into long thick white ropes as the aircraft approached the military airport. Men and women in blue uniforms amassed on the flight line to view the distinctive aircraft with its bulbous nose cocked up at an angle and landing gear and flaps extended into the airstream. The massive aircraft looked like a ponderous beast wallowing in the haze, and growing in size with every second. How could anything so big fly slowly—so slow that those on the airfield watching the aircraft felt the 747 should fall from the sky.

As the jumbo continued its steady approach, what they witnessed was in reality, an optical illusion. Air Force personnel were accustomed to seeing the fury of the little aluminum lawn darts that were F-16 single-seat fighter aircraft roaring down the runway—with afterburners aflame—and shooting off the concrete into the wild blue yonder and quickly disappearing from view. When those same front-line fighters returned from their missions, the jets seemed to land with the same sense of urgency, landing one after another at very high speed. The visual incongruence of the very large aircraft, apparently taking its time in the air while the little jets hurried home, was disturbing and unsettling for some, as eyes and minds played tricks on the observers. The landing speeds for the two aircraft were essentially the same. They knew it, but their eyes didn't want to believe it.

As the Boeing touched down on the runway, the Air Force commander, Major General Volner, in a flight suit with a bevy of colorful, intricately embroidered patches, stepped from behind the wheel of a dark blue van. Greg Lynche and Nazy Cunningham exited the other doors. From the billeting office to the flight line, Lynche had briefed the plan to the commander but had left out specific details. The general didn't have a need to know some of the particulars. Nazy listened with a light ear.

"Boris Nastakovich is a former KGB colonel. There's a reason we call him *Nasty*. He was a master interrogator at Lubyanka prison. He's fluent in at least a dozen languages. In the years following the collapse of the Soviet Union, he disappeared, and when he reappeared, he materialized as an oil billionaire. How he acquired his wealth is the subject of much speculation. He's known to be sybarite with a penchant for tall beautiful women." Lynche strained not to glance at Nazy and remained focused on General Volner. "He's flashy with his money, hence the 747. His relationship with the Russian president is unknown however, we believe they are or were close. Of course, both men were KGB colonels, career intelligence officers."

The general raised her head toward Lynche. She was a little surprised the DCI would brief her informally on the man coming to the air base. But Lynche hadn't given away any secrets. Most of what he said was common knowledge from open sources; some information could be found on the internet. "Bonnie, I suspect you'll want him off the field as soon as practical, and so do I. This isn't a social call. I expect he'll want to see the recovery and restoration efforts, and I don't have any problem with that. To the greatest extent possible, I'd like his and my conversation to be private, so I would appreciate you ladies drifting back...."

"We'll be out of earshot," offered Nazy.

"I'm not sure what he'll say between the hangar and the excavation site. Bonnie, I'd appreciate it if you forget everything you hear from the man. Anyone with that kind of power and money is not to be trifled with. They have many friends and enemies that could do you great harm. Consequently, he could bring incredible danger to you and your family. Any other time, I wouldn't trust him, but under these conditions, I have to have a business conversation with him. This is a significant national security issue. The less you know the better."

The general gritted her teeth and nodded.

"Thank you." Lynche marshaled his thoughts for the next phase of the operation. "I'm not sure what to expect. Intelligence agents generally don't talk, and when they do, they phrase things to get you to open up and spill your guts. Which is exactly what I want him to do, but he's trained not to do that. So we could have a Mexican standoff in seconds, and that'll make for some very short conversations." Lynche turned to General Volner and grinned. She turned and nodded appreciatively.

Lynche continued, "I can't tell you what we're doing but your boss indicated you can keep a secret. Boris has something we want very badly. We'll see if we can make a deal."

High wind buffeted the three Americans on the aircraft ramp as the jet pulled up in front of the base operations building with engines roaring and billowing clouds of dust. The auxiliary power unit screamed from the rear of the airplane as the engines shut down. A double-wide airstair, built into the clamshell-style door of the aircraft, smoothly unfolded from the belly of Boeing's largest airplane. Lynche had seen the unique door configuration before from a guided tour of an Air Force 747 used as the National Alternate Operations Center aircraft. That aircraft was equipped with workstations and telephones in the event of a national emergency, such as a nuclear attack on the homeland. He was sure the Russian's jet was equipped with beds and sofas; some internet rumors indicated there were ceiling mirrors for entertaining clients and concubines for stratospheric debauchery. Once Russian oil billionaires determined they could buy anything, they usually did.

When the airstairs were fully lowered and rested just above the ground, a diminutive but stocky man descended the stairs. He watched the placement of his feet—he had a head of steam and immediately gave the impression he was a man in a hurry.

The six-foot two Lynche turned to five-ten Nazy and said into her ear, "I heard he was small but I didn't expect Lilliputian." She didn't react or respond. Lynche stepped off to greet the Russian, and the women, as briefed, followed a few paces behind.

With the APU wailing from the aircraft and the natural turbulent wind racing between the buildings and the hangars, it was impossible to hear what Lynche and Nastakovich said between them. The men greeted each other warmly. The beanpole Lynche towered over the barrel-chested, and much shorter, former intelligence chief from Moscow. Lynche crossed his arms as he talked, as if the wind chilled his chest, while Nastakovich's arms hung straight down as if he were indifferent to what the man from the CIA was saying. Lynche gestured toward the two women, and Nastakovich and Lynche moved to them. Introductions were made. The Russian's English was flawless Mid-western American, a product of years of KGB English training.

Major General Volner offered her hand and the old KGB colonel shook it as he would any other military officer. Nazy was introduced as Miss Lane; she offered her hand. The Russian clicked his heels and bowed slightly at the offered delicate hand with the huge diamond ring. He closed his eyes and softly kissed her fingers and said, "Enchanted." The gesture of courtesy and politeness was followed by more salacious thoughts as he mimicked her British accent, "A distinct pleasure to meet you, *Miss* Lane. Is it Miss *Lois* Lane?" He released her hand and smiled with smallish yellow teeth, stained from years of nicotine and caffeine.

The clumsy Lois Lane reference shot over the DCI's head like Superman heading to the Fortress of Solitude. Lynche's eyes flashed as the former denizen of the Lubyanka was already reaching into his bag of tricks, trying to elicit any information from every target. The DCI was proud of Nazy as she deflected the surreptitious request when she replied, "No, just Miss Lane."

"Do you want to see what we've recovered?" asked Lynche, trying to change Nastakovich's train of thought.

The old KGB colonel glanced at each of the three Americans before answering, this time with no accent. "I would like to see what you've recovered first, and then I would like to see where the art was hidden."

Lynche gestured for the Russian to walk with him toward the nearest aircraft hangar. The women brought up the rear.

The old spooks maintained a professional running commentary. Lynche gestured repeatedly and was politely animated while Nastakovich's arms hung limp, as if the old KBG spy were afflicted with a chronic stiff-arm disease.

As they entered the hangar, they met the very busy and stoic Dr. Edgar Howell, who was lovingly admiring a recently recovered and restored Raphael, *The Rising of Christ*. The man from the Smithsonian Institution lifted an eye to the approaching guests and said, "This is an unknown piece, possibly from an unknown *predella*. We think...well, it's been suggested this painting could predate the works of the Baronci altarpiece, Raphael's first recorded commission. This is priceless." He didn't even try to mask his contempt toward Lynche for allowing the Russian to take the artwork away. But when the dirty old man spied Nazy Cunningham standing inconspicuously behind the thin Lynche, he tried to surreptitiously move to get a better view of the woman and her legs. He was disappointed; she was in slacks and trainers again, so he returned his focus to the Raphael.

The three Americans and the Russian were confused by the ancient man's words and actions. Nastakovich's eyes wandered to the painting and offered, "Your Allen Dulles accused Comrade Stalin of holding the looted artworks in secret depositories...in Moscow and Saint Petersburg. Adolph Hitler was very effective in emptying museums and estates and engaging in a disinformation campaign that the Soviet Union always had the...lost artwork. There's more?"

The man from the Smithsonian spun away from the two men and placed the painting on an immaculately clean workbench. His disgust was obvious. The Russian ignored the affront.

Lynche wanted to kick the decrepit man for being an ass; he'd have words with him later. "This way," said Lynche, leaving Howell to split his admiration between the Italian Renaissance master and the exotic lady from the CIA.

The group walked through all of the different processing stations in the aircraft hangar. They watched as two crates were disassembled board by board revealing thick paper covers; the wrappings of a set of three unknown paintings and a lapis lazuli urn. The men leaned over the shoulders of a pair of women using solvents and cotton swabs to remove grime and dirt from another vaguely familiar but very large portrait of an elderly man with a bottle of wine and a slab of cheese.

Nastakovich moved from painting to painting like a rat scurrying through a labyrinth in search for dropped cheddar. The Americans followed silently behind the little Russian. When he spied a meter-high lapis lazuli urn with heavy gold filigree handles being removed from its rotten wood protection, he stopped in his tracks and shook his head in wonder. After scrutinizing several dozen individual pieces, he turned to Lynche. "I'm ready to see where these were stored."

Nastakovich insisted on sitting next to Nazy in the van. Lynche road shotgun and turned in his seat to engage the billionaire in business, but the Russian had other ideas. The general steered the van away from the base of the control tower and drove slowly. Sitting next to "Miss Lane," seemed to loosen the man's tongue as he relaxed on the hard bench seat and spontaneously started to tell a story. Lynche was immediately suspicious; Nazy was intrigued.

"That Raphael that your Doctor Howell found so fascinating is the property of the Soviet Union. I've been searching for that painting and others like it for over forty years. I doubt you know of what you possess. There's much history—much, much history. It is a story worth sharing." Nastakovich turned to look out the window of the van, either pausing for effect or deciding what to tell and how much. His voice had trailed off to almost a whisper, as if the finding of something so rare as the Raphael or Miss Lane overwhelmed his ability to concentrate and speak.

Lynche was taken aback; the conversation had taken a decidedly unexpected turn. KGB officers never offer anything and they never shared information. *This is very odd! Had the man's retirement from the KGB softened him?* "Boris, you may be correct. I'll acknowledge I don't know what's all in storage, but it seems you do. What do you mean the Raphael *is* the property of the...*former* Soviet Union?"

Nazy's brows furrowed with questions but she didn't have much time to wonder as the man from Moscow began speaking again.

"During the winter of 1916, before the February Revolution, Tsar Nickolas dispatched several trains to Paris. The trains carried the artworks from museums in Moscow, St. Petersburg, and Petrograd primarily.... The Raphael and hundreds of others had been in the hands of the Royal family and the wealthy. The Tsar sensed the Bolsheviks would be successful in 1917 and would defeat his Monarchy, and he was correct. Nickolas Romanov wouldn't allow Comrade Lenin to damage or destroy, or confiscate or sell the Motherland's major priceless artwork, so he moved them to safety."

"Lenin was furious to learn the art had been removed from the major cities, under the cover of darkness, and sent to Paris to be stored at the Louvre. He punished Nickolas Romanov in the most horrific way possible. The tsarina and the princesses were not executed *immediately,* as history has recorded. Let's say, for the sake of Miss Lane and the General, that the sexual deviancy and brutality of Saddam and his sons were amateurish by comparison to the Bolsheviks."

Nazy turned away from Nastakovich and exhaled deeply. Thoughts of a mother and her daughters being abused and viciously raped brought back her own horrors from Algeria. She wouldn't allow the man to see her uneasiness, so she turned back to face the man who would allow such despicable and evil words to escape his mouth. Despite his attempt to soften the image, some images couldn't be softened. She glanced at Lynche to affirm she was doing ok and for him not to worry.

Nastakovich ignored the visual communication between the CIA officers. He continued, "Comrades Lenin and Stalin struggled to have the artwork returned to the Soviet Union. A secret addendum to the Nazi-Soviet Non-Aggression Pact agreed to the orderly transfer of any and all Russian artwork held in Europe, but of course, Hitler...how do you say?"

"Reneged?" offered Nazy. She surprised herself at regaining her composure and was embarrassed by her quick interjection. Nastakovich smiled broadly and nodded.

"Hitler invaded France without a single piece returned to Moscow. He emptied the basement of the Louvre and scattered our historical artwork throughout Germany. Or so we thought."

He half-scowled at Lynche and returned to look out of the van window. The vehicle had negotiated rows of structures—warehouses, hangars, office buildings—before turning onto an unimproved road. The general didn't even look at the warning sign proscribing entry onto the perimeter road; she just continued to drive and listen.

"Soviet agents tracked the Nazi general in charge of logistics for Adolph Hitler's and Goering's special projects. We knew he had been responsible for finding and removing art from across Europe, he said, 'for safekeeping.' He traveled with a Gestapo security detail."

The old Nazi ranks and names rolled off the man's lips like he was a *stormtrooper*. Nazy noticed the man's Bavarian German was impeccable. Lynche knew the man's Deutsch was another product from the KGB's many schools of espionage.

"He had been carrying a satchel with national security secrets of the Third Reich. Canaris' diary. A comprehensive catalog of all artwork in safekeeping. Locations of Zionist gold. He didn't know the locations of the artwork, per se, but the key was in the satchel."

Lynche and Nazy suppressed any urge to blink or look away from the Russian. *The key was in the satchel? Did the Soviets interview the Nazi general?*

Nastakovich stared at Nazy as he spoke, "One night, as he stopped for some drinks in Lyon ... France, he claimed an American Marine Corps officer—*in uniform*—stole his satchel. Shot them all in the knee. Of course, the Nazis chased the Marine into Switzerland. Hitler dispatched dozens of *Abwehrkommando*, the Nazi's clandestine Special Forces, to find the thief. They operated in disguise, wearing American or Swiss uniforms. They reportedly saw the Marine with the satchel, but they never caught up to him." He turned to face Lynche, "We know the satchel was delivered to your Allen Dulles. Please accept we found it difficult to believe you didn't know what you were given."

Lynche indicated forcefully, "I understand the information contained therein was coded—you can appreciate that in Vichy France the Nazis used a variant of the Diffie-Hellman protocol, using what we now call elliptic-curve cryptography. They used a symmetric key cipher. That was cutting edge technology in 1944. Passé now."

"I chased the location of the art for many years. How did you find the location? Why now? How did you break the code?"

Lynche hesitated answering for a moment. He tossed to Boris the gold coin Hunter had given him. "A kid stumbled into one of the secret passages. He took several of these and told no one."

It was the first time Nazy had heard the story and she broadcast her megawatt smile. *Duncan. Luckiest man I know!*

Major General Volner announced, "We're here." An armed guard saluted the general's vehicle as she pulled to a stop.

Nastakovich helped Nazy out of the van and looked around the thinly wooded area but couldn't locate the entrance immediately, although a dozen military policemen stood guard in front of small hillock. Lynche said, "Let's see what the Nazis hid."

"You know what they stole, Director Lynche. I want it back."

The Director of Central Intelligence led the Russian to the well-disguised cave opening. The women stayed near the van and chatted aimlessly. Nastakovich raised his head to the stylized elongated eagle; its weathered outline had been drilled into the rock face with hundreds of half-inch-deep, uniformly spaced holes. The effect was striking, and cold. The ten-foot-wide eagle clutched a wreath in its talons. Perfectly centered inside the wreath was a swastika. The entrance to Hades couldn't have been more intimidating.

Nastakovich paused for a moment to scrutinize the old cold emblem of the Nazi party. He investigated the entrance surroundings; the concave concrete wall behind him that masked the entrance was cleverly constructed as a movable closure. It displayed all the hallmarks of German ingenuity and engineering. His forty-year quest lay before him. He directed his question to Lynche, "How much was damaged?"

"Surprisingly, very little. Nearly every piece, I understand, was well protected." Lynche gestured for the Russian to enter. The antechamber was well illuminated and had been cleared of all crated artwork. They walked in single file, past mounds of gold coins. Lynche had left orders that the gold was to remain in place until after the viewing.

Nastakovich nodded and said, "Not what I expected. I expected bullion, not coins."

"What we have here is the remains of six million people, the gold pried from their mouths, their jewelry. Crudely smelted into coins." Lynche exhaled forcefully.

The Russian followed Lynche through a garage-door sized opening into the deep cavernous workspace. None of the aircraft components and fixtures had been touched by the art recovery crews.

"Aircraft manufacturing facility? Incredible. What kind of aircraft is this?" Nastakovich screwed up his face at the strange large fuselage.

"I think it's a jet-powered glider."

"No more Gary Powers!" said Nastakovich smarmily. Lynche impassioned face indicated he wasn't amused. "I believe you. No one could orchestrate such an elaborate hoax. Not even the KGB."

Lynche ignored the slight, continued in his thoughts. He paused to point at the long aluminum aircraft components. "Maybe this was the Nazis' ultra-long range bomber that never got off the ground." Nastakovich ignored the airplane; Lynche gestured directions. "This way; the main trove is this way." As the men walked through a long undisturbed passageway, away from the women, Lynche stopped. His voice reverberated in the enclosed space. "I understand you have two devices. I want them both. I'm willing to give you one hundred paintings—your choice of artwork, for both devices." As they resumed walking, many dozens of dark wooden crates emerged from the darkness.

"When will you have all of this excavated?" The Russian accent had crept back into his speech.

"Boris, you can appreciate the recovery work is tedious—only a finite number of people have the skills and the clearances. I...."

"I no longer want the gold. 200 masters per device. My choice."

"I'm not going to quibble. I agree. I have a master list of the artwork. Our man from the Smithsonian believes there's five years' worth of work here. I want the devices as soon as possible."

The men stood nearly toe to toe amid hundreds of decaying crates and boxes. Both men demonstrated a serious mien, deep in thought, trying to anticipate the other's next move and offer. Lynche broke the momentary impasse. "I'd like to work out an exchange."

"What do you propose?"

"We will transfer to you the 100 pieces we've in process. You turn over the devices. If you would like to participate in the recovery, cataloging, and restoration, you may provide your own experts to help validate the authenticity of the art and assist in the restoration. You can catalog and prioritize the pieces you desire."

The Russian placed his chin in his hand.

"I showed you mine; you need to show me yours."

"What do you mean, show me yours?" The Russian wasn't familiar with the near-vulgar American allusion.

"This is a business transaction. We've showed you what we have. There needs to be some reciprocity."

"Explain."

"I propose we provide an expert that can vouch for the devices, to ensure they are what you say they are."

"You don't trust me?" Nastakovich feigned hurt and disappointment.

"Do you really want me to answer that? No, Boris, there have been numerous fakes and dummies on the black market, even inert casings some KGB colonels have tried to sell to al-Qaeda or Iran. I want someone to vouch for them. You must have anticipated I would...*ask*."

"Demand...." interjected the little man from Russia.

"We're gentlemen. Let's say, ask. As you may have a team assist in the recovery of the art in these rooms, to verify and validate their authenticity, I must insist on reciprocity. Trust, but verify. Once we agree, you receive the artwork in process as collateral and I receive the devices."

"Trust but verify?" Nastakovich acted as if he had been stabbed in the heart. Hearing the phrase coined by Ronald Reagan hurt deeply.

Lynche smiled and nodded. "Yes, sir. Trust but verify."

The ride back to the jumbo jet was made in intermittent silence. The general drove as fast as she dared, as if she was racing to the nearest facilities in order to relieve a full bladder. No stories being told; there was only the Russian's intermittent wheedling of Nazy. "So, Miss Lane, I could make you a very happy woman. I'm very rich."

"Thank you for the offer, Mr. Nastakovich. I'm already a very happy woman." She waved her hand to highlight a boulder of a diamond on the platinum band.

"Obviously, Mr. Lane is a very lucky man."

Lynche interjected, "I can vouch he is the luckiest guy on the planet."

The occupants of the van erupted in light laughter as the general drove straight onto the parking ramp to within fifty feet of the 747's stairs. Nastakovich said his goodbyes to the general and waved at Nazy. The Boeing's aircrew started the APU, flooding the flight line area with the high-pitched whine of a small turbojet. Lynche walked Nastakovich to the base of the aircraft's airstairs.

"Director Lynche, I accept your offer. Have your expert arrive at the Ashgabat airport in seventy-two hours. My men will pick him up...." He took one final long look at Nazy and then turned back to Lynche. "...so he may inspect the devices. I expect your expert will put a seal on the devices to annotate, to attest they are genuine."

Lynche jerked perceptibly, as if a chill pulsed through his body. "Yes, that's what I anticipated. An expert, a seal."

"He inspects; he affixes...your seal. We arrange transfer and you take delivery. We can do this in one week's time."

Lynche held out his hand and said, "You have a deal."

Nastakovich shook hands firmly. He nodded toward the women

standing outside the van and said, "She is very beautiful. I was unaware the CIA had such beautiful women."

The outboard starboard engine started and added significantly to the noise on the ramp. Lynche released the man's hand and lowered his head. "It's a blessing and a curse. Some asshole is always hitting on my...daughter."

The man from Russia lowered his stolid businessman façade and raised an eyebrow from the insult and embarrassment. "My apologies and congratulations, Director Lynche. My file isn't adequate on you. Mrs. Lynche must be a breathtaking woman." With a final glance toward the women, Nastakovich said, "No luggage for your man. You don't want him to go missing if he is found carrying a tracking device. Remember, trust but verify."

With kind eyes and a mischievous glint, Lynche grinned at the former Presidential axiom.

Before the Russian turned and started up the dozen steps of the airstairs he said, "You probably knew the history of Tsar Nicolas but not the context. He and his family would've been banished from Russia had he not ridiculed Lenin over the art. Many men and women have died trying to recover the artworks. I'll be in touch, *comrade Director*."

As Nastakovich ascended the aircraft stairs, Lynche scanned the bulk of the Boeing and noticed things he hadn't seen before when the great aircraft taxied into its position. The jet might have been a flying bedroom but it was also a flying boardroom and probably a command post. Having bought and overseen the installation of several highly specialized electronic systems and their conformal antennas for Agency aircraft as well as for the YO-3A, Lynche was surprised the 747 was outfitted and modeled in every way after Air Force One, the U. S. President's aircraft. He saw atop the aircraft the same types of aerodynamically smooth antennae for electronic countermeasures defense, systems to jam enemy radars. Built into the leading edge of the wing, to confuse infrared missile guidance systems, the latest mirror-ball defense technology was installed. Behind the wing of the big jet, Lynche could just barely make out the unmistakable shape of a pair of infrared countermeasures canisters—dispensers for flares and chaff to thwart surface-to-air missiles. Out of the corner of his eye, he could see that the Russian had stepped into the aircraft and had started to turn around.

The additional sound from a second engine being started and brought up to idle made speaking at a normal volume impossible. Over its high-pitched whine, Lynche shouted, *"Da! Spasiba!" Yes! Thank you.*

Nastakovich tossed his head back and waved, and said to himself, *"And, he speaks Russian too?"* The airstairs was raised into the jet. Lynche pivoted away from the aircraft and hurried across the tarmac.

By the time he returned to the van and the two women, the engines on the port wing had been started. The Boeing taxied off the parking ramp and turned to enter the taxiway. For a minute, the three Americans watched the big jet plod its way down the taxiway as its engine exhaust pushed away dust and debris on either side.

Lynche looked at Nazy and Volner and said, "General Volner, we need to get to the consulate."

"The bullet train is the fastest way to get there. I can take you to the station. If we leave now you might be able to catch the express; nonstop to Frankfurt."

Lynche unhesitatingly said, "Let's go," and raced the women into the van. As they drove off the air base, Lynche returned to what he saw on the jet and mused momentarily about the countermeasures systems aboard the 747. *The cagey Nasty thought of everything.*

CHAPTER THIRTY-FOUR

Immediately after landing, the Special Operations aircrew buttoned up the MC-130—placing the appropriate intake, exhaust, and pitot covers in their place—and inserted safety pins with their long red streamers—REMOVE BEFORE FLIGHT—into the landing gear. The six military men dragged their exhausted bodies into the passenger van for the trip to the Lajes Field lodging facility. Unlike their civilian passengers who had benefitted from six hours of uninterrupted sleep, each Air Force Airman looked forward to a shower and a very long sleep. Again, the receptionist at the Mid Atlantic Lodge didn't ask questions as she handed the flight engineer ten keys for ten VIP rooms.

Hunter rotated the diverter valve in the shower to OFF when he heard from his living room, "You're not going to believe this!" He stepped from the shower and quickly toweled off. Duncan pulled on a green T-shirt with WATERBOARDING INSTRUCTOR stenciled across his pectorals, and a pair of cargo shorts. He found McGee standing in front of the room's television with a remote control in one hand and a carton of juice in the other.

"It's on every channel," announced McGee with a gesture toward the monitor on the wall of the suite. "You're a hero." When he found the channel he was looking for, he sipped orange juice and stood transfixed on the monitor. The images on the TV suggested their cover had probably been blown. Hunter pinched the bridge of his nose in exasperation and defeat.

McGee frowned at the message on Hunter's shirt. He drained the carton and tossed it into the trash. "You may second guess that maybe it wasn't such a good idea. I submit, whatever comes, it was a great idea and was positively worth it."

"No one can attribute anything to us. I'm not worried." Hunter raked his hand through damp hair. His eyes were full of confidence and a mischievous glint.

"We kept our NOGs over our eyes—no one could ID us."

"That's about the only good thing that came out of that."

"Really? Dude, you saved your daughter and we freed 700 passengers and a jumbo jet. No one got hurt but a bunch of terrorists. Saving your little girl like that will always be something no other man will ever be able to top. She texts you and you come to the rescue. Fathers live for moments where they come to the rescue of their daughters."

Hunter grinned. He supposed he didn't do too bad for a dad.

"But we left some calling cards. Check that out." McGee gestured toward the monitor with the TV remote.

Hunter shifted his hands to his face and rubbed his eyes vigorously, as if he rubbed them hard enough the Al-Jazeera pictures and banners would be erased. When he stopped rubbing and looked at the screen as it scrolled across the bottom of the television, he couldn't believe what he saw: NAVY SEAL MAVERICKS RESCUED HIJACKED NIGERIAN AIRWAYS JET. He closed his eyes and shook his head in embarrassment.

Hunter jumped when his BlackBerry rang and vibrated. McGee turned a cautious eye to his partner. They were not supposed to get calls until they had returned to the United States. The tiny screen displayed UNKNOWN in the window with a series of zeros underneath. He knew the string of identical numbers meant the signal had been sent through a CIA switchboard; he inhaled with anxiety and punched the button to connect. He heard the hiss of the encryption software communicating with another secure telephone unit somewhere. He paused to allow the algorithms to scramble his voice and when the rustle in the background ceased, he asked, "Hello?"

The conspicuous noise suggested the signal originated from a submerged submarine; but the voice was unmistakable. "*Maverick*—nice job in Monrovia. I send you to do a job with the lowest possible visibility and the next thing I know you're on every friggin' channel from Al-Jazeera to Zee TV! You do know what covert ops are or did you just blow off all the security protocols like Bogotá?" Sarcasm dripped with every syllable. Lynche had to get his pound of flesh before Hunter could react with some excuse.

"Sir, I...."

"The President said, 'good job' as well. We believe we can contain the damage...of your little adventure. Navy SEALs will take the credit. Is Bullfrog there? I need to talk to him."

Hunter blinked wildly at the Director's spiel through castigation, approbation, and dismissal. He turned the little black device over to McGee. "It's for you."

McGee was surprised but not concerned. He couldn't fathom who would want to talk to him on Hunter's BlackBerry, but if he read Hunter's facial and body language correctly, he would probably be speaking with the Director of Central Intelligence. He answered, listened intently, and grunted or acknowledged in monosyllabic responses. Hunter tried to read the big man's body language, but huge sculpted muscles had a dialect all their own, and he gave up. After several minutes he said, "Thank you. I've some experience in that area although it's dated. I can do that, sir. I don't see any issues. Your CONOPS is solid. I'm in."

DCI Lynche said, "Thank you, Bill. I'll have a passport and briefing materials delivered to you inside of 24 hours. We'll make arrangements for you to leave Lajes via commercial air."

Lynche and Nazy Cunningham exchanged glances then continued to watch the news coverage of the Nigerian Airways dramatic aircraft rescue. On-scene interviews continued as they unfolded on one of several monitors inside the Frankfurt consulate communications center. Lynche held up a hand to stop the bevy of intelligence officers rotating in and out of the COMM Center cubicles bringing messages and cables from Headquarters, the White House, and the National

Security Agency. He didn't want anyone to hear what he had to say. What he wanted, once he was off the secure telephone, was an update on the whereabouts and safety of his two intelligence officers who were on the Nigerian jet.

Lynche articulated his assessment of the situation to McGee and his plan to get a trusted agent into country to prove the veracity of the small weapons of mass destruction. Nazy continued to monitor the scrolling banners along the bottom of the many simultaneous telecasts, but her eyes always returned to the one monitor at the lower left of the wall of monitors. She felt a growing pride that her Duncan stumbled onto the crisis at the Liberian airport and rescued the people on the hijacked aircraft, and hopefully that included Kelly Horne.

Her reverie was interrupted when Lynche said that it was a "damn shame, but not totally unexpected" that Al-Jazeera's reporting was so tightly focused on the rescuers. Lynche was concerned the next person paraded in front of a camera would give a jaw dropping description of Hunter or McGee, or worse, cellphone video and completely shred their cover.

Al-Jazeera had its usefulness as an intelligence resource. Some of their correspondents were obviously working for some local terrorist network, and the leadership worked furiously to identify and negate threats to al-Qaeda and the Muslim Brotherhood. Despite anfractuous ties to the terrorist underworld, Al-Jazeera was the undisputed leader in coverage of Muslim affairs in Africa and the Middle East. Their reporters could get into places Western reporters dare not go. This made Al-Jazeera a "must watch" for members of the intelligence community when they were in Europe, Africa, or the Middle East.

McGee offered, "I recall there were some fairly sophisticated safety interlocks and even booby traps. If you've someone who knows those systems, or whose expertise is more up to date on those, that would be helpful."

"I'll see what I can do. Thanks, Bill. It goes without saying, we'll make it worth it." Lynche smiled at Nazy and elevated his free thumb to signify Bill McGee had agreed to the plan. He knew he would.

428

McGee ran to the sound of gunfire.

"Thanks. You want to talk to the hero?" McGee winked at Hunter, who thought he might be allowed to talk to Nazy.

"Yeah...." McGee handed the device back to Hunter. Duncan didn't know what to make of the one-sided conversation he heard. It made little sense, but he had a long relationship with Lynche, and he anticipated the DCI had made his point and would soon replace piquant pokes with professional points.

"Yes, sir?"

"I think I know how you did it. The real question is the Yo-Yo airworthy and available for a pop up?"

Hunter's eyes shot to McGee, with questions, intrigue, and apprehension. A voice in his head said, "Run to the sound of the guns!" Between breaths, he answered, "We've a spare canopy and the airplane is in good shape. I don't see a problem. And we've enough fuel for several missions."

"Good. Bill has the CONOPS. Let's call this phase two. You need to be in Kabul in less than seventy hours or so. Enjoy your stay. Try not to get shot at, ok? Oh, and don't ever do anything like that again! Got it?" Lynche wagged his finger in the air on every syllable, for emphasis. He smiled when he said it and half-swiveled in his chair to see Nazy focused on the monitor tuned to Al-Jazeera. He pivoted back to the desk.

"You know me. Anything else? How's my best girl?"

"Busy. Maybe one of these days I'll let you see her again, but you'll have to do a lot better to overcome this latest screw-up. I'll let her know you're still alive...or something."

"You're all heart. You know you're acting like an overprotective father on prom night, or something."

"I think she's become my adopted daughter, and I'm against her dating *mavericks*! Talk with you later."

Hunter turned to McGee with a pained expression and said, "Now, what are we doing?" McGee pointed to a chair for Hunter to take a seat. Then he told him.

. . .

The Director of Central Intelligence hung up the handset and fingered through several dispatches before he tossed the papers into a burn bag. He turned to Nazy, and what he saw in her eyes and face shocked him. Color had drained from her face and lips, and her demeanor had changed remarkably from just seconds previously. He'd seen similar symptoms before in women who were about to faint. His eyes scanned the wall of monitors for a clue, but nothing he could see would account for her sudden fear. She held a trembling hand to her mouth as she sat unblinking, in stunned silence.

Lynche asked Nazy, his voice full of concern and compassion, "Nazy, are you ok? What's wrong?" His eyes darted from her to the monitor she seemed to be watching. He expected the worst, that somehow Al-Jazeera had discovered and reported the identities of his intelligence officers on the hijacked aircraft or had transmitted an image of Hunter or McGee.

Several seconds passed before Nazy regained her composure. She inhaled heavily and turned to Lynche. Her face didn't belie her anguish and introspection; she was hurt and confused. She lowered her eyes and hand as she struggled to say, "Al-Jazeera... the Royal Jordanian...Chief Justice. Collapsed. In critical condition. I think my...father...is dying."

. . .

Once the Airbus was safely airborne and on its way to Lagos, nearly every passenger aboard *The Nigerian Queen* retreated into his or her inner self. They sat quietly, most in a state of shock. Those who were lucid wondered myriad things and worried if the men in black who dispatched the hijackers had found and accounted for every terrorist. The co-pilot made several announcements and issued several directives. He said that flight attendants would barricade the cockpit door and wouldn't serve any food or refreshments for the remainder of the flight. Passengers would remain in their seats until police or the military released them. With little to do, a pair of flight attendants covered the dead with airline blankets to hide the horrific deaths of the innocent and conceal the mortal wounds of the cocky and evil terrorists. Plastic bags filled with passports, watches, wallets, money and other incidentals were passed so the passengers could retrieve their personal belongings.

Most of the men in business class glanced continually or circumspectly at the attractive redheaded woman sitting in the back row, the one who had shouted, "Maverick" when the rescuers entered their seating area. After being terrorized for hours, countless passengers had been astonished and speechless when they saw an obviously white man in a black jumpsuit—with a huge pistol tucked under his arm—emerge from the staircase and move about the cabin with supreme confidence and commanding presence. Many reacted with surprise when the white woman with the titian hair had embraced the rescuer.

Most passengers had talked among themselves to relieve the stress and terror of the last hours. But not the cymotrichous redhead. She sat quietly thinking how incredible it was that her father had answered her text messages, got aboard the airplane, and killed the terrorists. *How was that even possible?*

Demetrius Eastwood tried several times to catch the eye of the young woman on the opposite side of the aircraft. He wondered who she was that she had recognized, called out, and embraced the man who was obviously Duncan Hunter.

Kelly Horne gazed out the airplane's window. She admonished herself for calling out her father's call sign and remained curious about the man who shook her father's hand. She didn't want to meet him or discuss her spontaneous outburst. She had more important things to consider.

There had been some training at the Farm for these types of

situations, she recalled. After an in-flight hijack attempt, everyone on the aircraft would likely be interviewed and forced to give a statement and contact information before they'd be allowed to leave the airplane. She practiced what she would say so that she would be able to leave as expeditiously as possible while giving the least amount of information for the official record. She would use her diplomatic passport as leverage to get ahead of the crowds and out of the airport, and to get to the safety of the U.S. Embassy.

After landing, a hundred heavily armed police and military men rushed onto the airplane's upper and lower decks as if they were going to assault a phalanx of terrorists barricaded in the galleys or the restrooms. The pilot and co-pilot met with the leaders of the airport police and the military and explained that no one had seen what had happened because the cabin lights had been extinguished. All they knew was the white man had encouraged them to expedite their takeoff and set a heading for Lagos. So the aircrew were released to return to the cockpit.

After interviewing the passengers, the officials learned that two men, one white one black, had disabled the hijackers in the dark airplane. A few people had seen tiny flashes coming from what they believed to be weapons. The police chief asked, "No one saw anything else?" The passengers in business class responded with gentle shakes of their heads. When the police chief said, "Let them go," those in the first and business class sections gathered their bags and silently departed the airplane.

Kelly was closest to the aircraft door and was the first one off the Airbus. She ran as fast as she could through the air bridge and down the concourse to the Customs kiosk. Eastwood assembled his video and support crew as soon as they were off the jet and clear of the arrival gate. He had watched the red-haired woman jump out of her seat and hurry through the aircraft door when the police officer said, "...let them go." He cursed because he knew he'd never get the opportunity to ask her how she recognized Hunter as one of the rescuers.

On the other side of Customs' kiosk and departure turnstile, Kelly walked to the baggage claim area and spotted a man holding a sign that read "CHICKWEED." When she walked up to him he challenged her with, "Miss Sheel?" She responded, "Call me Norma Jean." She held out her hand which made him smile. The pretty woman would make him act like a fool if he wasn't careful.

"I'm Chad Oko. You're late and you must be exhausted. It's at least three hours to Abuja."

"We're driving?" asked Horne. She shifted her bag on her shoulder. After sixteen hours sitting on a jet, the thought of sitting in a car for several more was none too pleasing. But in the safety of the embassy car, she extracted her BlackBerry from her backpack and fired off emails to Nazy Cunningham and her father.

Oko continued to speak as the white woman fiddled with her electronic device. It seemed like with the advent of cell phones, those who had one always had their face planted in the tiny screens, as if they held some kind of magical device that could tell you things you never knew, like the news or the weather on the other side of the globe. He said, "Flying on an African airliner is taking your life in your hands. It's very unsafe."

"Tell me about it!" she said incredulously. She doubted the man was aware of her adventures in the country's newest airliner.

"We drive everywhere if you want arrive alive. I understand you're our new pilot."

Horne acknowledged with a nod and a smile.

"That's very good. You're greatly needed. Much turmoil in the north. The Boko Haram is spreading its influence rapidly." He turned to her. With an eerie and unsettled timber in his voice, he said, "The Islamists are completely out of control. They have massacred many Christians. We hope you'll be able to find them."

Kelly considered what the man said for several moments. She turned to look out the window and take in her surroundings. She had been briefed that Nigeria was the most populous country in Africa and that Lagos had the distinction of being the most densely populated city on the continent. She could see that hundreds of cars clogged the four-lanes leading into and out of the airport. Hundreds of people stood around the wide curving entrance of the airport. It reminded her of the teeming masses pouring from a professional football stadium. People were everywhere. As the sole white woman in view, she felt vulnerable and conspicuous as if a thousand eyes watched and scrutinized her every move.

The congestion of vehicles and people assaulted her sense of proportion and her nose. The Japanese-made cars were small, and the Nigerian men were generally tall and thin. The air was heavy and dank with the smell of automobiles and sweat. Traffic moved so slowly that Horne commented to the quiet driver, "If they added another dozen cars to the road, I think there'd be total gridlock."

Without taking his eyes off the road, Oko said, "There's some truth to that. Nigeria, like Angola, is awash in oil money, but there's no plan, no discipline, and no structure. They're putting up buildings that no one wants or can afford, and everyone's buying cell phones, cars, and consumables. It's positively mad."

Kelly was exhausted from all of the terror on the Airbus and from the excitement of landing in Nigeria with its hordes of people. She tried to relax. But thoughts of the airplane, the hijacker, and her father clouded her mind. She had recognized him in the black flight suit, even though he was hiding behind night vision goggles; she wanted him to know she was ok. Somehow he had received her message; somehow he was in Africa; somehow he got on the airplane.

She relived the terrifying moments right before the lights went out when she thought she was going to be raped or killed. She had been in the middle of a prayer when the terrorist threatened her. The next time she saw the hijacker was when her father stepped on his corpse to get to her.

Kelly reconciled that her father was justified in killing the terrorists. She felt no remorse for the evil, dead man, but felt conflicted and guilty that she hadn't said a prayer for the innocents who had lost their lives aboard the aircraft. As she finally wound down from the tempest of the evening, she closed her eyes and fell asleep. She didn't wake up until the vehicle entered the U.S. Embassy compound in Abuja, the capital of Nigeria.

. . .

Eastwood couldn't find the redheaded girl and let any notion that he would die on the vine; it wasn't meant to be. The rest of his video crew joined him as they walked in single file through the overcrowded concourse to Customs and baggage claim. As the video crew retrieved their equipment cases from the baggage-handling carousel, two Nigerian Army officers, resplendent in their dark green uniforms with colored buttons and badges, introduced themselves to the famous war correspondent.

Salutations and greetings among the men were boisterous, hearty, and welcome. The general officer politely gestured for the war correspondent to accompany him from the arrival hall of the airport. Eastwood accepted the offer. They departed the building engaged in innocuous discussions of his adventure on Nigeria's newest jet. Eastwood took a final glance around the expansive, high-ceilinged structure for a white woman, specifically one with red and curly hair. If there had been a white woman anywhere, she would've stuck out in the sea of Africans.

A half-hour later, the Nigerian general bid Eastwood adieu as a convoy of thirty military armored personnel carriers and a four-door Toyota HiLux pickup truck barreled north to Abuja. Embedded with the Nigerian Army, Eastwood graciously and continually thanked his benefactors for their assistance and the armed escort. And he quietly thanked his boss back at the network who made a few telephone calls to the Nigerian president. The President was intrigued that a major American network had expressed interest in their growing Islamist terrorism problem in the north. With Eastwood as the point man, the Nigerian head of state approved the concept and facilitated the mission.

The leader of the convoy, a broad-chested colonel named Emmanuel, delivered his view of the situation to Eastwood and his officers. "Boko Haram is the most effective and successful guerrilla group in Nigeria. Nowhere in Nigeria is safe from their bands of marauders. They have carried out attacks all across the country, primarily in the northeast. In one day, in a town close to the border with Cameroon, they killed almost four hundred people."

"Colonel Emmanuel, excuse me," said Eastwood, "This is the first I've heard of four hundred people being killed. Is this a state secret? The world does not know...."

"Colonel Eastwood, please understand the sensitivity of this intelligence. This information...would rarely be reported in Nigeria, let alone the outside world. I'll show you all of it! This is why we have thirty vehicles and two hundred men to escort you into the occupied territory; the President wants this story to be told. We need much help. We believe the Boko Haram is being provided money from the al-Qaeda. They're growing very fast. Very, very fast. You'll see abandoned villages, burned schools, destroyed towns. The local home guard tries to protect the towns and the schools. Armed with machetes and bows and arrows, they fight to their death. The Boko Haram massacres them like everyone who gets in their way. Village police are no match. Their fighters have stayed in the east; we believe the leaders will move into the west in a very short time. Your American intelligence service suggests they're moving into the west and this is where we shall go."

During the five-hour trip, two hours over poor roads, Eastwood returned to the Toyota where he and his video crew noticed and commented that the soldiers were both curious and fearful. They were curious why a group of predominately white men would want to get as close as possible to report on the Islamic splinter group. They were fearful that the indigenous and nefarious Boko Haram—which hated the white man and Christians—would be especially cruel and savage to anyone who would provide aid and comfort to them.

After passing through Abuja, the convoy headed to the northwest corner of the country where a new atrocity had recently been reported and the trail was still fresh. The fast moving terrorist group had kidnapped over twenty Christian girls from a school. Western media wouldn't pick up the story for fear of reporting on yet another barbaric Islamic travesty in Africa.

.   .   .

The cameramen slept in the back of the truck as Khalid drove in the middle of the army convoy of very large trucks. He found the changes in culture and surroundings stark and difficult to comprehend. Libya was a tribal nation built upon the sand. Once away from the city, Nigeria appeared to be a nation carved from towering jungle and savannahs with dual-track roads linking small, impoverished villages. He saw boys urinating on the side of the road and bare-chested women living in grass or mud huts. He expected elephants or lions to run across the roadbed; the possibilities were endless. He turned to say something to Eastwood in the passenger seat but found him staring blankly out the window; clearly, something was on the man's mind so he didn't interrupt him. There'd be time to talk.

Some of Eastwood's senses had been deadened by the road noise and the men vigorously snoring behind him. He hadn't known whether to expect chaos or mayhem, but he felt a little guilty for resisting the effort to investigate the murderous al-Qaeda-affiliated thugs terrorizing Nigeria. The head of the network had pulled more than a few strings to secure the services of the Nigerian army, and he felt secure in the company of fellow soldiers. He ran through several mental checklists in preparation for the next phase of investigative journalism, but when he got to the step of donning of body armor his thoughts were hijacked by images of the Nigerian Airways jet. Many questions seeped into his mind.

The rescue couldn't have been planned. It had to be a spontaneous, random event. Rescues take days of coordination and planning. How did Hunter and McGee get into the aircraft? Who was the Little Red Riding Hood and how did those two old gray wolves get there?

437

CHAPTER THIRTY-FIVE

"I haven't talked to my parents since coming to America. My father put a little money into an account after I left Jordan, and I never said thank you. After meeting Duncan and coming to Langley, I never even thought about going back or even looking back. But it's...unsettling...to discover your father is very ill. He may be dead for all I know. It's difficult to believe that information is *real*." Nazy held her hands together in her lap and spoke softly.

Lynche tried valiantly to console Nazy and at the same time pay attention to the information that raced across the bottom of a television monitor. He hadn't seen it all. His eyes bounced from Nazy to the monitor, hoping the network would run the information again for the world to see. After a couple of minutes of Nazy talking to the floor and Lynche distractedly patting her arm in a display of concern and compassion, the announcement ran again:

THE CHIEF JUSTICE OF THE ROYAL JORDANIAN COURT COLLAPSED REPORTED TO BE IN CRITICAL CONDITION.

Lynche fixated on the screen like a calf looking at a new gate. He got quiet and stopped patting Nazy's arm. Warning bells went off in his head. He snapped out of his trance when she noticed he had stopped comforting her. She raised her head. "Greg?"

He turned slightly in his chair; his expression concerned her. She had known him since her first days of being accepted by the CIA, and he had never acted in the fashion she witnessed now. Again, she cautiously asked, "Greg?"

438

His mind raced with dreadful and gruesome thoughts. He looked deeply into her eyes. "Nazy, I think you need to call your mother." His voice was low and monotone.

His brows furrowed and a distant expression telegraphed to her that he was thinking deeply about something. What he said made little sense. What did her mother have to do with this? Before she could ask what he meant, he seemed to snap out of his introspection. He shook his head as if he had seen a disturbing picture. In a way, he had.

"Nazy, you need to ask your mother if your father has been poisoned; specifically, radiation poisoning." He put his face in his hands and rubbed his eyes as if he could erase an unwanted sign. "Crap, I'm starting to act and sound like Duncan."

Like a switch being toggled on and off, Nazy smiled at the comment and then returned to being serious. "What? Radiation poisoning? What about acting like Duncan? I'm confused."

"That's how his mind works. He takes tiny discontinuous bits of information, discards distractors and false leads and uses raw logic that drives him to a solution."

"But why? I don't understand."

"Nazy, have you ever seen anything like that banner? It would have to be a slow news day for someone at Al-Jazeera to include a snippet that the chief justice of the Royal Jordanian court has collapsed and is reported to be in critical condition. Information like that is…*reserved* for heads of state or prime ministers, not judges or lawyers. What do the political parties do when they want a certain bit of information out in the public domain? They leak it. What do we do? If we need to get a story 'out there' we pay an editor or a reporter to put something into the papers or get something on a telecast. Rothwell was a master at manipulating the press, buying, and placing strategic leaks when there's a need. You say he's alive, and I say he's behind all of this. The best spooks, despite what's in novels, are old spooks."

"I don't understand the radiation poisoning angle."

"We've been talking a lot about KGB—Rothwell and his KGB ties. Boris is old KGB; Vladimir is old KGB. I can tell you the head of the Jordanian GID, the General Intelligence Department, the

Mukhabarat, was once suspected of being old KGB. I can't remember his name. What's the angle; where am I going?"

Nazy nodded. Having been an analyst for the Near East Division for the better part of a decade, she rarely had to consider Russian influences in the world of al-Qaeda or the Muslim Brotherhood. Their founders fought the Soviet Union in Afghanistan. At once, she saw where the KGB must have either had some double agents either inside the terrorist organizations or were trying to infiltrate. The Agency struggled to get a spy inside, but the only man to have successfully infiltrated both was the former DCI, Bruce Rothwell.

Lynche continued, "In 2006, the KGB surreptitiously poisoned Alexander Litvinenko. He suddenly fell ill, was hospitalized, and three weeks later, he died of a lethal dose of polonium-210."

"Rothwell's a master spy and knows every intelligence service and intelligence officer will be monitoring Al-Jazeera for intel on the hijacking. Somehow, he had to be involved in the hijacking of that jet as well as the attacks on you and Duncan. Duncan would reduce his logic tree to a single branch and say, 'Rothwell's been infatuated with you from day one; you've flown the coop from your house in Maryland and *Spindletop*. He's been after you since day one and he's sending a message to you.' It's not beyond the bounds of reason to think Rothwell has somehow got to your father to flush his quarry quickly and efficiently, to get you to break cover. He's checked your secret personnel file and knows you're the daughter of the Royal Jordanian court. You've dropped off the grid and that banner from Al-Jazeera is a single ping to get you to surface. It's a ploy and a trap. Nazy, I'm saying you need to find out what happened to your father and eliminate the possibility that he was poisoned."

"But...poisoning my father? That makes no sense."

"Nazy, please listen to me. It's not a question I can have the Station Chief ask at the hospital. Please call your mother and ask your father's doctor to check for acute radiation poisoning. No one would ever look for poisoning, specifically radiation poisoning. It's the one thing that can have an immediate effect with symptoms suggesting something other than radiation. If it's nothing, you can cart me off to St.

Elizabeth's. However, if he's ingested polonium or something like it, he might be able to be put on some drugs—potassium iodide or something. He might be saved. I don't think we've a lot of time to discuss it."

"I don't know...."

"I'm not one to give an order, Nazy, but call your mother and find out what has stricken your father. And start thinking about going to Amman; you need to make the call from the comm center. It's likely the call will be monitored so be careful what you say. While you're doing that, I need to make a couple of other calls."

"You're not thinking I should go see him! If it's a trap, I...don't think it's wise to go. But my heart tells me if he is grave, then maybe I should...before he passes away."

"Classic KGB. Play on your sensibilities and loyalties. This is a chess match played by a master. In chess, this is called a 'forced march,' and we're being manipulated. You're being forced to respond and act. You have to break cover and call."

Nazy frowned. "This is a dirty business. They're despicable. Rothwell is despicable." The DCI rose from his seat and took her hand. She was visibly distraught and conflicted; her knuckles were white with tension. She didn't want to make contact with her family. And she promised herself and Duncan that she would never return to the Middle East.

They had caught her once and had nearly killed her. The thought of returning to the land of Islam, even relatively quiet, terror-free Jordan was too much. It made sense that there was likely an active plan to draw her out into the open for the express purpose to capturing her. This was a bridge too far. She couldn't imagine any situation where Lynche could convince her to return to Jordan, the place of her birth, to see a father who had betrayed her. She couldn't comprehend going to a place where the man who was obviously obsessed with her and was likely in the arms of al-Qaeda and the Brotherhood could get to her. She looked up at Lynche with baleful and pleading eyes that said, "I don't think I can do it. Please don't make me do it." She continually shook her head in fear.

Lynche saw the pain and terror renewed in her eyes; she was trying to telegraph something she couldn't articulate. He squeezed her hand to reassure her. "I think I understand that woman's intuition thing has kicked in right about now. Okay. It's probably not a good idea for you to call your mom. Nazy, I think there's another way. And to do that means I've much to do."

She leaped at him, wrapping her arms around his neck as she sobbed. He wrapped his arms around her and patted her back until she stopped crying. Once he was sure she had calmed down, he returned to work, firing off messages and making telephone calls.

•   •   •

Rothwell walked unsteadily to the sliding glass door. His nurse kept an eye on him for fear his wobbling would result in a trip and a fall. With only one arm, his balance was already poor and breaking a fall could mean breaking a neck. He had come too far for that. He gazed out over the rolling hills of Amman, awash in white, multi-storied buildings and blue domed minarets. He knew that he was getting better; his strength was increasing; his sense of balance was improving. But overcoming his fear of the balcony and of heights was still a work in progress. He gingerly backed away from the door with his eyes focused on the stucco balustrade.

He had no recollection of the tiny suicidal helicopters or the explosions that had shattered the door of his room at the Amman Sheraton Hotel and had blown him out of the top-floor suite. The blast had been sufficient to blow him through the glass door and over the balcony's wrought iron balustrade. His arm had nearly been severed, but the shredded and fractured forearm had caught awkwardly in the metal safety railing. His body swung once before the arm could no longer sustain the dead weight. It separated from his shoulder and released his torso to fall fortuitously onto the balcony below. He awoke much later without an arm, without an eye, and with a shattered body.

Over the weeks of rest and rehabilitation, Rothwell concluded that somehow Duncan Hunter was responsible. Hunter was responsible for his loss of Nazy Cunningham; he was responsible for the loss of billions in gold coin the United States had paid a master terrorist to refrain from blowing up any more jet airliners, and he was responsible for the loss of his arm and his eye. Now he was convinced that Duncan Hunter was responsible for his coalition of al-Qaeda and Muslim Brotherhood officers losing the Nazi artwork, the Airbus, and the gold the U.S. President would surely pay. Hunter would pay; he would pay with the loss of the woman he loved, and he would pay with pain. Rothwell knew pain.

Rothwell returned to his chair at the head of the conference table. At the opposite end of the dark wood table the wide screen television continued to run clips of the Nigerian aircraft rescue. The news of the death of the hijackers and of the men who had apparently freed the airliner had been on several stations. He was bewildered that surprisingly little reporting came from Liberia. What the Liberian press reported was incidental—the hijacked aircraft made a stop believed to be in Monrovia, Liberia. Two men in black had disabled the hijackers and were seen crawling off the aircraft wing before the aircraft took off. Rothwell shook his head in disgust. *Two men? If Hunter is one of the men, who's the other?*

Rothwell pushed buttons on the remote to return to the Al-Jazeera channel just in time to see snippets of news scroll across the bottom of the screen. The conference room telephone rang in the background and interrupted his thoughts. Nizar brought *jaffa* orange juice and the phone, handed him the hand receiver, and left the room before Rothwell answered, "Yes?"

"Have they seen it?"

"Of course. It would've been impossible for them to miss it. We'll be ready for them. She'll come. The infidel will follow."

The connection was terminated. He returned the handset to its cradle and noticed his hand wasn't as shaky as it had been in the past. Rothwell smiled at his growing grip. After all the failures of the previous hours and days, things were finally looking up.

443

CHAPTER THIRTY-SIX

Kelly Horne entered the cockpit and strapped into the pilot seat of the Beechcraft King Air. The sensor operator closed and locked the door after she climbed inside the cabin. The copilot read off the start and before taxi-checklist items, and she responded to the challenges. After the engines were started and the Before Takeoff checklist was complete, she called Abuja International Airport departure control for takeoff clearance. The air traffic controller provided departure instructions and altimeter settings then directed the pilot to "read back."

Horne and the copilot adjusted their barometric altimeters to the reported setting and wrote down the clearance instructions. She fired them right back, as directed. She had done this countless times before in different multi-engine airplanes, but this was her first time in Africa, and this would be the first time she would pilot a King Air.

The copilot, Dick Osbourne, was impressed with her flight discipline and light touch on the yoke. The takeoff, departure, and climb out were by the numbers. Only when she leveled off at seven thousand feet did she engage the autopilot.

"That was great, Kelly. Where'd you learn to fly?" he asked. He fingered his handlebar moustache unconsciously.

"Primarily the Air Force—I got my private pilot license when I was 16; Air Force Academy and flew everything I could. I was a T-38 flight instructor before coming to the Agency. You?"

"Army Spec Ops." He said it like it was a separate service from the U.S. Army. "Helicopters. The 160th. Transitioned into turboprops as a contractor and flew some spooks around while in Afghanistan; they

444

liked what I did and helped me to come over to the dark side." He grinned at her and allowed her time to digest what it meant to be a special operations pilot in a war zone. Then he asked, "What do you know of Boko Haram?"

Horne glanced at the tall, muscular, and glabrous man then returned to scan the instrument panel. "Not much. Nothing recent in U.S. papers. The mission brief indicated they're an al-Qaeda offshoot. They have a history of horrific crimes across much of northeastern Nigeria. And they're spreading their influence."

"That's the general, politically correct version. So typical from State. What the security office didn't tell you—hell, the media won't report it either—Boko Haram is in the business of making final solutions. They roll into town and go door-to-door, house-to-house, school-to-school. They don't quit until all the Christians are dead. They take great pleasure in killing Christians, especially white preachers. And when they're done, they move to the next town and go on killing, usually kids. But not girls."

Kelly hadn't bargained for the drastic change in the cockpit discussion. But it happened so often she should have expected it. After the takeoff, climb out, and level off, aircrews had much free time on their hands. During the "administrative" period of flight, the straight, level, and boring phase of flight, pilots told jokes and talked; they talked about anything and everything. They would monitor the aircraft's instruments and the communication and navigation systems until they approached the mission area.

Osbourne would announce to the sensor operator when they arrived in the working area. After conducting a few hours of airborne surveillance to capture some intelligence on the terrorist group, they'd return to Abuja with Kelly landing the airplane.

She knew when she accepted this assignment that the missions would be classified and were very sensitive, politically and professionally. She didn't know what to expect flying with an older gentleman; there was always some professional friction between pilots. Pilots from pole to pole, from the Prime Meridian and back again, believed they were the second coming of Charles Lindbergh, Manfred von Richthofen, or Chuck Yeager—sometimes all rolled up into one. Egos ruled in the special operations, fighter and attack aircraft communities. In the early days of piloting commercial airliners, until the incorporation of Cockpit Voice Recorders and stringent safety measures to improve crew coordination in the cockpit, speech in the cockpit was dictated by the pilot in command. Now in aircraft where there were no cockpit voice recorders, chatter was unrestrained, usually a free flow of thoughts, concerns, and opinions.

What Kelly heard confused her. She wrinkled her nose and asked, "Why would they do that? If true, that's pure evil. That makes no sense. It's hard for me to believe that."

Osbourne looked out of his side window and said into the microphone, "You're not in Kansas anymore, Kelly; welcome to African politics. What makes no sense is that the U.S. has allowed a group like Boko Haram to fester, to spread. This happened because the liberals at State have prevented the U.S. government from listing them as a designated foreign terrorist organization. If you find anything in the papers, the media will only report that the murderous group is misunderstood, and that its actions have nothing to do with the teachings of Mohammad."

Horne continued to look at the man with disbelief. "Why does that make a difference—being designated a terrorist group?"

He smiled at her; he was enjoying the instructor role. "Well, being designated a terrorist organization turns on several aspects of U.S. laws. It's illegal for a terrorist organization to do business; it cuts off access to the U.S. financial system and anyone else associated with it. And it encourages others to stigmatize and isolate those foreign organizations. Of course, if you get on the list, al-Qaeda and the KGB will dump more money in your coffers."

"Wow. I had no idea."

"But you have to look at Boko Haram across its history. The previous administration wouldn't list it as a terror group, primarily because they embraced the Muslim Brotherhood and al-Qaeda. The other reason, Boko Haram's leaders are black, and their stated goals is the extermination of Christians and white men. That just so happens to be the unstated goals of the Democratic Party."

She changed her expression to one of skepticism and disbelief. She was appalled. *He must be one of those guys they call the hard right. Or maybe not.*

Osbourne had a captive audience and loved to hear the sound of his voice. "We're at the pointy end of the spear, Kelly. You'll see the unvarnished truth while you're here. Boko Haram took money from bin Laden after 9/11, got training from al-Qaeda, and is on the local channels espousing that they want to impose Sharia in Nigeria. And kill infidels. Do your homework and you'll see that the liberals and Democrats back home ignored their murderous actions. They won't even acknowledge that Boko Haram is a problem and a threat, even after a few thousands of people have been killed. Our new President declared that what was going on in Nigeria was an insane policy and...well, now we're here. There are now Agency airplanes and more IOs in the field. Liberals do nothing but work to stay in power and coddle terrorists. Conservatives go after terrorists. It's that simple."

Kelly's mind was filled with questions. She began to dismiss what the old guy said as balderdash, political hyperbole. But there was a strange element of truth to what he said and how he said it. He sounded a little like her father. She scanned the instrument panel then returned to listen to her copilot who was in the middle of a world-class rant.

"...but they will accuse and smear Republicans and say that it's grotesquely irresponsible to suggest that Boko Haram has anything to do with Islam. They attack the messenger and the message; they can't defend the truth. Here, you're exposed to all the nuances and the dynamics of this real world situation. You're going to see the aftermath of their murderous rampages. That's called ground truth."

She nodded and smiled, and returned to scanning her instrument panel. Kelly considered the advice and observations of her copilot. He was a lot like her dad and spoke of political realities in black and white terms. She chuckled to herself that the man must have thought she was, politically, like him for him to have opened up like that. How could he have known or sensed that was beyond her understanding. She turned to look out her window but then heard the barely detectable hiss that presaged someone in the airplane had keyed their microphone. From his workstation in the cabin the sensor operator said, "We've multiple targets, dead ahead. Five miles."

The copilot depressed his microphone switch twice—zippered the mic—to indicate the transmission was heard. He turned to Kelly and said, "Kelly, ground truth. Life is very cheap in Nigeria. It's not unusual to see human road kill. Boko Haram uses the shock effect of terrorism to spread their message by using a machete or an AK-47, or by stripping little girls from the arms of their parents and selling them into slavery. Or worse. They're positively barbaric, and in my humble opinion, they need to be stopped. If anyone deserves to die, it's this group. What they do is absolutely indefensible, and why liberals and Democrats wrap their arms around these guys cannot be understood by rational men; it's unreasonable and despicable."

Kelly nodded and smiled thinly. She clicked her microphone switch twice, which elicited a smile from the old man.

"We get to fly above the murder and mayhem being recorded in the back. I don't want to tell you what's likely going on down there. But it'll be captured for all to see. The good part of this job is that we actually see the analysis after all the tapes are downloaded. We're building a picture. Others will determine what to do with it."

Her skin prickled as if a cold breeze had entered the cockpit. She turned away from the impassioned man to hide her thoughts. *Jumping from the Air Force to the CIA may have been a mistake. What's a nice Catholic girl like me doing in a place like this?*

. . .

The headlights of the lead convoy truck suddenly illuminated a string of young girls, holding hands and walking down the center of the dual track road. All of the vehicles stopped; floodlights atop the armored personnel carrier (APC) flooded the road with light and blinded the girls. Hands and arms shielded eyes accustomed to the dark. The colonel in the lead vehicle leaned forward to get a better view of what they had stumbled upon.

A couple of dozen young girls, probably from eight to fifteen years old, huddled together, exhausted, unable to go any further and unable to comprehend what new hell had stopped them. Through shielded eyes, some of the older girls recognized the odd-looking vehicles; their captors had driven the tall-wheeled bulky military vehicles and trucks. They wondered if another group of the evil men had found them and would take them back. Dread and anguish overcame them, and they shook with fear.

Soldiers, assault weapons at the ready, poured out of the back of the APCs in anticipation of an ambush. More sweeping lamps atop the vehicles flooded the surrounding area with powerful beams of white light. The Nigerian colonel dismounted; a junior officer was given an order to investigate. All of the men from the APCs held their position as the junior officer approached the girls and called out, "We're here to help you!"

The girls from the village had heard that declaration before, right before being rounded up and forced to watch their relatives killed by men in uniform. They had no energy to run so they stood their ground.

The lack of movement from the young women concerned the leaders in the lead vehicle, and they remained wary. Nigerian soldiers had heard the Boko Haram was fond of the ambush and had used children several times to set up killing zones. Soldiers and children had died in the crossfire, and the Boko Haram acquired several military armored personnel carriers, trucks, and weapons for their treachery.

Eastwood jumped out of the truck and walked through a wall of soldiers; he unhesitatingly approached the girls. Marty Marceau filmed the spectacle from the lead vehicle; this was when Eastwood was at his best. The lieutenant turned and explained to Eastwood, "These girls have walked many miles to return to their village. They say another tribe killed the men that took them."

Eastwood glanced at the Nigerian colonel and then asked the lieutenant if any of the girls were injured. Twenty-four youngsters shook their heads at the white man's question. Eastwood smiled broadly and received two dozen smiles in return. "We need to get you home," said Eastwood, waving them to come with him, and not thinking they may no longer have a home.

Colonel Emmanuel ordered the last vehicle in the convoy to take the girls to their village. Eastwood observed one tall youngster who remained with the colonel in the lead APC. She pointed the way to where they had escaped from the Boko Haram camp. Eastwood got the girl's name, Ellen, and the convoy proceeded with her on board. After three hours on a poor road—a poor road in Nigeria actually means it's "virtually impassable" and that it's easier to walk through the ruts, washouts, and potholes than it is to drive—Ellen noticeably tensed and indicated the building, the vehicles, and the dead men were just ahead in the headlight beams. Again, floodlights were switched on to illuminate the entire area ahead and to the flanks. Everyone in the lead APC saw the pickup trucks and an APC parked in an arc, nose to tail, close to an old, mud brick structure. Eastwood recognized the defensive posture of the trucks; it reminded him of a circle of wagons from the frontier days of the old West. The building protected their rear flank.

Soldiers were ordered to dismount and set up a protective perimeter. The teenaged Ellen was confused by the scene in the headlights. "All the bad men killed. It is a sin to kill." She made the sign of the Cross and whispered the Trinitarian formula. Eastwood and Colonel Emmanuel glanced at each other. There were no men to be seen in the headlights of the vehicles.

Eastwood stepped from the APC and was joined by his crew. They followed several soldiers to the string of Boko Haram trucks. Some soldiers raced from vehicle to vehicle; some raced to the structure, and others spread out and laid on the ground with their AK-47 assault rifles with large banana-shaped magazines. Marty and the camera crew shot video of Eastwood interviewing the tallish, round-faced youngster and Colonel Emmanuel as they stood by the side of the terrorist's APC. Eastwood listened to the girl relate what the men did to the other tribe in the jungle. He asked, "Did you see the other tribesmen?"

"No," she said and shook her head vigorously.

Colonel Emmanuel sent Ellen back to their APC as he and Eastwood investigated. Khalid held a powerful spotlight for Marty, keeping the beam tightly focused on Eastwood who pointed at large pools of dried blood and hundreds of spent 7.62mm brass casings amid a number of AK-47s. Some were covered in blood. Eastwood immediately noticed that all of the weapons on the ground and all of the spent brass were on one side of the vehicles, those closest to the building.

The men were careful not to step in the pools of blood; their eyes fixated on the ground. As Eastwood pointed to the blood and the assault rifle brass for the cameraman, he noticed several peculiar holes in the ground, holes about the size of a man's finger. At first he thought nothing of the holes in the ground, but then asked the Nigerian commander, "Colonel Emmanuel, are there any bullet holes on the other side of these trucks? Looks like they were in a hell of a firefight...."

After several soldiers scrutinized the exteriors of the line of trucks, they returned at a jog, snapped to attention, saluted and reported, "There are no bullet holes in the vehicles, sir!"

Eastwood returned to the odd tiny tunnels, wondering if they could have been made by a tiny mole. As the floodlight swept across the ground, he noticed that the holes were uniform in size. *Moles would've pushed dirt up and out—these aren't mole holes! So what the Hell are they?* The insight caught him off guard as he looked at the finger-sized holes more closely. He waved for more light; soldiers concentrated torch beams near his feet. The holes were a couple of feet away from the main pools of dried blood and featured an angular displacement. They were not vertical but went off at an angle like tiny narrow cylinders of a V12 engine. Eastwood asked, "Colonel Emmanuel, what happened to the bodies? Ellen said there were about twenty men but where are they? There are about twenty AKs here. Also, are you aware of any animal that could make these holes? Snakes, for example?"

The mention of snakes sent a few of the soldiers with flashlights scurrying back to their APC. Colonel Emmanuel replied, "Lions are very rare in this part of Nigeria. These drag marks suggest hyenas or lions found the bodies and dragged them off into the bush." At the mention of lions, Khalid dropped his lamp, slithered away from the scene, and raced back to the safety of the American's Toyota.

Eastwood counted over a dozen holes and asked Marty Marceau to see if there were any others on the other side of the trucks. After a couple of minutes, Marty reported, "There's no blood, no bullet casings, and no holes. But the colonel is correct. There are multiple ground scars that suggest several somethings, heavy somethings, were dragged into the jungle."

"Like a body?" Eastwood raised his head to meet the man's eyes.

"No. Several bodies." Marty pointed the video camera's built-in floodlight at the holes in the ground. They were definitely strange.

The odd-angled holes now had Eastwood's full attention. He reached into the pocket of his cargo pants and dug out his well-worn and ubiquitous Leatherman multi-tool. He began to dig into one of the holes. Nigerian soldiers and the colonel stood and watched the crazy white man dig into the soil. They provided many beams of light as Eastwood carefully followed the hollow shaft of the hole. After several minutes and a depth of two feet, Eastwood struck something hard. He expanded his digging and energy as he clawed the ground with the screwdriver blade until he fully uncovered what he had hit. Eastwood brushed away loose dirt to get a better look. Marceau shined his flashlight beam into the excavation with the other lights.

Eastwood gently lifted his discovery into the light. He brought the three-quarter inch thick, four-inch long piece of heavy metal closer to his face. He brushed away more dirt and debris; his eyes got wide when he realized he was holding a bullet. He looked up at Marceau and the Nigerian colonel with questioning eyes, but no one had an answer. All eyes were riveted to the projectile. Eastwood didn't recognize the bullet or its composition. Nothing about the bullet was typical. Eastwood was aware of copper-clad, lead jacketed bullets, but this one was made of steel, polished steel. Its very large bore was striking, over twice the size of a normal, man-killing bullet. This was one-shot, one-kill ammunition, very unique and highly specialized ammo. He turned the bullet to look at the nose and wiped it off to find curved smooth glass, not a steel jacket or a polymer insert. *It's...a...glass...lens!* He muttered to himself, *That's...impossible!*

The lights from the APCs were insufficient for a detailed look, so Marceau brought his flashlight closer for a better inspection. Colonel Emmanuel shot a look at his soldiers that they interpreted as "stay back," then he leaned in to get a better look for himself.

The camera operator again raised the videorecorder to his shoulder to shed light and to record the bullet. Unable to get the camera lens close enough to get a sharp picture, Marceau aborted the attempt to film the projectile and said, "It looks like a...*rocket ship*. Are those really fins?"

Eastwood nodded and untucked the front of his white denim shirt to wipe down the tiny, rocket ship bullet until it was dirt-free. He noticed there was no cannelure, no discernable line where the casing would've been crimped to the bullet head. Finding that missing detail a bit odd, he turned the bullet over to wipe down and inspect the tail only to have a clod of dirt fall from a deep, precision-machined cavity. *It really is a rocket ship!* he thought and brought the butt-end of the bullet to his nose and sniffed. *That's what chemical rocket propellants smell like!*

Eastwood chuckled; he couldn't believe what he was holding. His eyes returned to the odd angle of holes in the ground. He considered the situation for a few moments as he formulated a plan. As Colonel Emmanuel, the soldiers, and his video crew looked on, Eastwood scanned the area until he found something suitable in a copse of green reeds near the decrepit building. He slipped the remarkable bullet into his shirt pocket and collapsed the screwdriver blade back into the handle of the multi-tool. He flipped open the long knife blade and cut a handful of five-foot long bamboo reeds. He trimmed the wrist-thick sheaf to a uniform length and handed a few of them to Marty. "Put one of these in each of these weird holes."

More curious soldiers gathered to watch Eastwood and his cameraman, still lugging his videocamera with one hand, insert the long reeds into the holes in the ground. The remaining men turned their flashlights onto the reeds. Marty began filming Eastwood's track and his actions. When he was done, the crowd of men hushed, not understanding what they saw or what they were supposed to see.

Colonel Emmanuel watched the spectacle as the white reporter chased an imaginary creature that made holes in the ground. He was no longer impressed with the distraction; he and his men were out in the open. He felt very exposed to danger and made the decision to leave. There was nothing more to see here and it was time to move on.

Before he could give the order to move out a soldier raced up to him and saluted smartly. The thin helmeted man whispered into the colonel's ear for a full minute before he was dismissed. Momentarily confused as to what to say, if anything, he deferred for a few seconds, then returned his gaze to Eastwood. It appeared the American was completing his impromptu experiment. It was as good a time as any to change the vector of the investigation so Colonel Emmanuel said, "There are several sets of...human remains at the edge of the jungle. Hyenas and lions are in the area." He crossed his arms across his chest and looked at Eastwood for a response, but the correspondent ignored the news.

Eastwood didn't hear the military man. He was solely focused on the reeds sticking out of the ground. There was no pattern on the ground; their position were so random they could have been made by a clown on a pogo stick. However, it struck Eastwood that all of the reeds highlighted a uniform angle, and generally, pointed in a uniform direction—off into the sky above the jungle. They were like bicycle spokes converging toward an imaginary hub arcing off in the distance. Eastwood fished the bullet from his pocket, rotated it between his fingers, and slowly raised his eyes to the heavens.

Marty Marceau asked his boss, "What does it mean, Dory?"

A thin smile formed as Eastwood shook his head. *It's not possible! It's not possible!* The last time he uttered that phrase he was standing on a hijacked jet as Duncan Hunter appeared out of nowhere wearing black Nomex and NVGs and shook his hand. Eastwood figured he now knew "who," and he surmised "why," but he didn't know "how." He looked around the circle of men who were awaiting a response. He realized Marty and the others didn't have a need to know, so he pinched his lips shut in response.

The Nigerian commander's patience was at its limit. Just as Colonel Emmanuel announced the convoy must leave, Eastwood raised his head and took in the full glory of the Milky Way. As he stepped off toward his vehicle, he thought he had solved the mystery. He whispered, "*Damn.*"

CHAPTER THIRTY-SEVEN

Syncopated footsteps echoed off the wooden portico of the Lajes Mid Atlantic Lodge announcing the approach of people. Hunter glanced at the wall clock inside the beige trimmed suite and guessed, "Men."

Without looking up McGee disagreed, "Your ears suck. Women." Sunlight and shadows flickered through wooden slats of the venetian blinds to reveal the speed of their guests' arrival. Hunter and McGee didn't know who was generating the footsteps but they knew who had sent them and where they were from. They were expected, and they were at the door.

Director Lynche had been busy. The CIA's ultimate decision maker commandeered the office of the Frankfurt consulate's security chief. He fired off an uninterrupted string of cables and conducted several secure conference calls. A dozen Intelligence Officers and the Chief of Station from the U.S. Embassy in Berlin relocated to the subordinate consulate 260 miles southwest. A steady flow of dispatches from embassies in Western Africa, the Middle East, and Europe were brought from the communications center to the DCI. Trays of food were ordered, delivered, and consumed; pots of coffee were filled and rapidly emptied. For 24 hours the temporary CIA command post in Frankfurt buzzed with activity as the DCI ran multiple and simultaneous operations.

A "Personal For—Urgent" cable was sent to the American Ambassador in Amman requesting a direct channel be established with the Jordanian king. Multiple cables to the Science and Technology Directorate galvanized teams of technicians and scientists to produce and deliver some tools of the espionage trade to the Azores, to

Turkmenistan, to Afghanistan, and to Germany. Watching him work without sleep, Nazy Cunningham thought Greg Lynche had aged ten years in the last 24 hours. The latest status report the DCI read had verified the special teams from S&T were on the ground in the Azores, Afghanistan, and in Amman.

Hunter jumped from his seat and opened the door to a young man with an Oakley backpack and an older woman with a Belting leather briefcase. He didn't recognize either one from S&T and was amused when the woman asked, "Do you have some ID?"

McGee chortled and stifled a desire to blurt out a request for their IDs as well. He and Hunter offered passports for inspection. Hunter inquired, "And you are...?"

"Miss S and he's Mr. T."

Hunter thought, *Seriously Lynche? Mr. T?*

Without an invitation, the man—Mr. T—barged past Hunter into the room and removed the black backpack. He extracted a black box with an antenna that resembled a stylized number sign. In one continuous motion he turned the device on and scanned the four corners of the room for listening devices. Hunter, McGee and Miss S watched dispassionately. After a minute, Mr. T clicked off the device and said, "Clear." He returned the scanner to the backpack and extracted a neon-green rubberized device that Hunter recognized as a signal and voice jammer, what Lynche called a Growler. Mr. T energized the device, placed it on the table, and left the room. He waited outside on the porch in an Adirondack chair, tapping a smart phone with both thumbs.

Miss S had short dark, dyed hair and wore dark glasses. She was all business as she tossed the briefcase onto the small patio table next to the Growler and said, "Mr. McGee, you're now Alan Hawthorn. You're the President of Business Development for Lockheed Martin—you do know they're a defense giant?"

McGee nonplussed, nodded. Miss S said, "Good. Customs may ask you a number of questions. You sell C-130 aircraft and are on a business trip." She removed several items from the briefcase and handed a U.S. tourist passport to McGee. "Please review the visas contained within. It provides a nine-year history of international travel. Once you're through customs, you'll probably be met by two or three men. You can expect to be searched, strip-searched, before you leave the airport. Be advised, there's no chip in this passport. If they find a tracking capability on you, the standard protocol is to kill you. You should know that. Here are two metal seals for your objectives; these are one-time use so don't insert anything into them until you're ready to affix them to the nuclear devices. Understand?"

"Yes, ma'am."

"Ok. You can expect them to provide a change of clothes; they're not going to let you have your clothes back—so don't take your lucky socks. I wouldn't be surprised if they scan to see if you have a chip—you don't have one in you do you?"

McGee was barely able to say, "No, not that I know of."

Hunter asked, "He'll be completely naked?"

"Electronically sterile is more accurate, Mr. Hunter, we're dealing with old school KGB. We know their tricks; they know ours. There's not much we can do. There are rules of engagement for these types of verification missions; no tricks or we'll never see Mr. Hawthorn again. The DCI was adamant. I did bring something that might be of benefit. Your choice."

"What's that?" McGee was interested but wary.

The little old lady reached into the briefcase and extracted a small glass vial and said, "Fingernail polish. It's clear; matte finish. Looks natural. Undetectable. Until it's activated."

"Then what?" Hunter found the idea of fingernail polish to be preposterous.

"Once activated, the polish will release enough photons to be seen with night vision systems out to a range of ten miles. I understand there may be a sensor in the operations area. Once activated, it's good for several hours."

"I'll think about it," said the newly minted Alan Hawthorn.

Miss S handed the other documents to McGee. "Mr. Hawthorn,

here are some business cards, a wallet with dollars, euros, and rubles, and first class round-trip tickets to Ashgabat, Turkmenistan. Once through customs, someone will meet you holding a Lockheed sign. You'll be challenged with, 'Welcome to Tashkent, Mr. Hawthorn.' You reply, 'This is not Uzbekistan, Mr. Powers.' Powers is a veiled reference to...."

"Gary Powers, U-2 pilot?" offered Hunter.

"Correct," said the S&T woman. "That information was provided through other means. We're not sure if there's a message in there or not. I continue. The man will correct himself and you shake hands. Any questions so far?"

Hunter looked at McGee who faked like he was going to shake his head. "Do you know what I am to look for? I've never actually handled any of the Soviet backpack devices."

Miss S said, "Mr. Hawthorn, I have a presentation. This should answer your questions and any concerns. Mr. Hunter, this presentation is 'eyes only' for Mr. Hawthorn; a strictly need to know basis." Duncan, knowing when he wasn't wanted, saluted McGee informally and left the room, joining Mr. T out on the patio overlooking the Atlantic Ocean.

Miss S energized the laptop computer within the briefcase. She and McGee discussed the inspection, arming and disarming procedures for the former Soviet Union's miniaturized nuclear weapons. The hour-long slide presentation included the location where the CIA believed the weapons were likely being held. He viewed detailed procedures to identify the three main types of portable tactical nuclear weapons—one, two, and five kiloton devices—and the major components from the RA-115 family of what the press euphemistically called "suitcase bombs." Ten of these weapons had gone missing after the fall of the Soviet Union. She slowly covered the detailed and multi-level procedures to disable the "Lightning" booby-traps; twenty slides accounted for nearly half of the hour-long audio and slide show. Miss S wrapped up the presentation by slamming the laptop shut and handing McGee a slip of graph paper with ten lines of numbers. "These are the serial numbers of the missing devices. Ten total. We really would like to get these off the street so they never make it to the black market. Any questions?"

McGee first shook his head then said, "How do you activate the polish?" The woman looked McGee in the eyes, de-energized the Growler and placed it inside the briefcase; she snapped it closed and stood. He followed her lead. Obviously, the meeting was over.

Miss S said with a grin, "Stick your fingers in your mouth." She held out her delicate hand and shook Bill McGee's. She didn't let go of his massive hand; it was as if his touch softened her hard and crusty demeanor in a snap. When she spoke, she was deferential; the business façade replaced with awe and respect. She had never before briefed a man who would most likely die in the performance of his duties. "Thank you for your service, Mr. Hawthorn. Good luck and Godspeed."

McGee's smile buoyed her. "Miss S, that was a very good brief. You were very thorough and your response time was phenomenal. Please accept my appreciation and thank your team for all their help."

The woman left the room and gestured for Mr. T to leave with her. As their footfalls drifted away, Hunter and McGee returned to the suite. McGee closed the door, and they looked at each other with grins. McGee facetiously stated, "Like I told you—women." Hunter wouldn't take the bait, shook his head, and asked if there was anything new or interesting in the woman's brief.

Not expecting McGee to share details of the brief, Hunter was very confused with the big man's two-word answer: *"Fingernail polish."*

Hunter, and to a lesser extent, McGee would have fingernail polish on their minds for days.

. . .

The two men sat behind the driver in silence and took in the many changing views of Lajes Field. Pulling to a stop at the military base operations complex, Hunter slid out of the military van then reached back inside and shook McGee's hand. "Bullfrog, take great care, good sir. See you on the other side."

"You too, Maverick." As Hunter turned and jogged to the awaiting Hercules, McGee instructed the driver to return to the lodge. It'd be several hours before he would take the shuttle to the commercial side of the airfield and catch a jet to Portugal, then to Moscow and Ashgabat. Over the next twenty hours of waiting and flying, he would replay, countless times, the complicated procedures to disable the booby-traps on the devices. He war-gamed several scenarios of what he would do if he was ambushed, captured, or injured. Not planning for the worst-case scenario would be a crime, and it would piss him off. He reminded himself there's nothing worse than having a pissed off U.S. Navy SEAL on your ass, even if it's your own ass.

A half-hour after Hunter and McGee said their goodbyes, the Special Operations MC-130 was airborne and heading west for the Strait of Gibraltar. The YO-3A had been repaired and fitted with the replacement canopy. The Hercules would stop in Amman, Jordan for a "gas and go" before continuing on to their final destination. Hunter bristled at the assignment. Kabul, Afghanistan was "a shit sandwich" for several reasons, none of which made any operational sense. Kabul International Airport, with intermittent commercial and non-stop military traffic, was too busy to conduct clandestine aircraft operations; there was no place to park a C-130, and there was no optimum place to hide the long-winged, special-purpose airplane. But he had been there before; the takeoff was as colorful as the landing—both of which nearly gave the stolid back-seater, Greg Lynche, a conniption.

As were their habits for the long flight legs, Hunter and the Bobs were asleep in their sleeping bags, sound suppressors over their ears and sleep masks over their eyes. He dreamed of Nazy...wearing nothing but a smile and red fingernail polish.

· · ·

The Saudi prince, his wife, and three bodyguards stepped from the airstairs of the white and blue-trimmed Gulfstream business jet. Onlookers in the exclusive executive terminal, well away from and opposite the bustle of the main terminal of the Queen Alia International Airport, recognized the man's wealth and status. The white silk *keffiyeh* and black and gold-laced shoulder coverings over the Nehru-collared, cream-colored *thobe* signified the man's status within the Saudi hierarchy. The solid gold Rolex President chronograph and the blistering new Gulfstream 550 indicated the man was an extremely wealthy mid-level son or grandson of the Saudi king. Those in the executive terminal knew a full prince, a brother of the king, would've arrived in a Boeing 757, 767, or even a 777. Wives rarely traveled with the Royal party. But the minor prince's spouse, in a black *burqa* with an eye slit, followed well behind her husband as he walked from the aircraft and across the tarmac.

The watchful eyes of the men from the Jordanian secret service monitored the customs processing—no prince or member of any of the Royal families would be expected to go through the Customs kiosk in the main arrival terminal at Queen Alia. Members of the Royal family were handled by a courteous wait staff and a deferential concierge at the luxurious lounge in the separate, spacious and isolated executive VIP terminal.

The concierge delivered the Islamic green-covered, gold-embossed passports of the Saudi prince and his spouse to the Customs official sitting in a side office out of view of the high-powered transient clientele. He took a cursory glance at the photograph inside the prince's passport and virtually ignored the spouse's passport; there was nothing to look at, just a photograph of a blob of black on a white background. The picture of the woman in a full black *burqa* looked more like a rejected Rorschach test than an image of a human. The Customs official stamped both documents and returned them to the concierge.

After the Royal group departed the airport, a Jordanian secret service agent casually checked the Customs computer screen against the international database and was happy with the processing of the Saudi Royalty. The man and woman were not the couple he was to be on the lookout for; no issues and no troubles indicated there was nothing to report to the Director of the Mukhabarat.

The heavy black Mercedes AMG left the airport and wound its way through downtown Amman to the Arab Medical Center. Two bodyguards remained with the bulletproof vehicle as the prince and his wife, her *burqa* billowing in the wind, stepped from the armored car and entered the hospital through the main entrance. A bodyguard in black sunglasses, a white *thobe* and *keffiyeh* followed behind the prince and his wife, continually scanning about and ahead for signs of trouble. Although they were in Jordan, the Switzerland of the Middle East, members and sympathizers of al-Qaeda were always on the lookout to kill or harass any of the despised Saudi Royals.

The elevator ride to the intensive care ward was made in silence; the woman rode in the rearmost portion of the elevator car. At the nurses' station the woman's voice from within the *burqa* asked for directions to the appropriate room. Accustomed to the steady stream of visitors to see the men and women at death's door on the floor, the nurses gave the polite woman in black an abrupt gesture to show the way.

She and the prince entered the room to see the man, old and frail. Monitors and IVs were hooked up to his hands and arms. Lights in the private room were dim and presaged the termination of visiting hours. The room was redolent with a pungent oil from a tin near the window. The woman softly closed the door behind her and trembled with anticipation as the prince remained in the shadows.

The man in the bed lifted a tired unfocused eye to see who had entered the room. He saw only the shapeless and foreboding shadow of a wraith moving closer...to take him away. When the deathly black shadow touched his arm with a hand decorated with red nail polish, he opened both eyes and was immediately confused to see a woman in a *burqa* in the room. No woman was permitted to be alone with him; it was not permitted, even in liberal Jordan. But too tired to protest, he exhaled forcefully and raised his eyes to meet the woman's gaze through the narrow slit of the *burqa*. As the woman stepped closer to his face, illumination from an over-the-shoulder bed light fell on platinum-green irises framed by kohl-rimmed eyelids. The man's recognition of the woman's eyes was instantaneous.

The old, grey-bearded man trembled with excitement and strained to reach for the woman's hand; he struggled to gain control of his emotions before he could say, "Marwa...my daughter...you've come."

Nazy Cunningham wept as she held her father's hand with both of hers. Her tears destroyed her heavy eye makeup. Greg Lynche watched the touching reconnection of father and daughter, and smiled from under the long grey theatrical beard.

. . .

The large number and diverse mix of well-wishers entering the hospital and taking the lift to the sixth floor kept the two short plump men in black and white checkerboard *keffiyehs* and white *dishdashas* busy in the reception area. They recorded and relayed the sometimes-specific information on anyone that used the main entrance of the hospital and took one of the elevators to the intensive care unit. It was near the end of visiting hours when the Saudi prince, his wife, and the ever-present bodyguards passed through the polished granite walkway to the elevator stack. One of the men relayed on a cellular telephone that a woman had come to visit the ICU. He commented, "A Saudi brought his black bag with him, but she didn't look like the woman in the picture." The speaker laughed at his witticism at the disparaging reference of a woman who wore the traditional *burqa*; the comment dripped with contempt, derision, and mockery.

The man on the other end of the telephone asked if any other women had come to call on the chief justice.

"No, just now. The prince and his bag." What the man said was amusing and he was surprised the sheikh on the other end of the telephone circuit couldn't see the humor in his comment.

"What did the prince look like?" Mild exasperation prefaced the tone of the question.

"Saudi...a Saudi prince. White keffiyeh, black and gold frock; white *thobe*. Beard. All Saudis look the same to me."

Bruce Rothwell terminated the connection and cursed under his breath. He dropped the cellular with a clatter and said to the two men around the conference table, the leaders from al-Qaeda and the Muslim Brotherhood, "the woman is in Amman." He pointed to the al-Qaeda general, "They pulled one of your tricks; came in through the front door with her in a *burqa* and no one thought anything of it." The former Director of Central Intelligence shook his head at the apparent stupidity of the men staked out at the medical center.

"Then, the infidel Hunter cannot be too far behind?" asked the Muslim Brotherhood leader.

"I want to know who she's with. Maybe the new DCI is with her—what's his name? Lynche. That's correct. That makes more sense than the infidel. But, my brother, you are correct. If he isn't already here, he will soon come to Amman."

"Is this Lynche vulnerable? Possible to take him?" asked the Muslim Brotherhood leader. Evil and curiosity filled his eyes.

Rothwell dismissed the idea of kidnapping Lynche with a wave of his hand. The words screamed in his head, *They still don't understand!* He flexed his hand as if it was swollen and arthritic before slamming it down on the table. "Impossible, if it is Lynche. We were successful getting the woman to come. Now we must focus on Hunter! You'll get him this time. You must be prepared!"

The two men in the different colored *keffiyehs* nodded and cupped their hands as they responded, "*Insha'allah*, my brother. We'll be ready."

CHAPTER THIRTY-EIGHT

The Nigerian Army was exhausted from traveling into what was tantamount to disputed territory—an undeclared war zone without fronts and flanks but marked with the bloody trail of bodies and burned-out buildings. Every man in the convoy expected to find a string of butchered Christians and a trail of young female bodies, discarded after being used and abused, hauled off into the bush for one of Boko Haram's signature blood orgies of murder, rape and forced conversion to Islam. To find the girls safe, relatively unharmed, and surprisingly unmolested was so shocking as to be unbelievable.

With the extraction of a single incredible projectile from the pools of dried blood and scattered spent bullet casings of Kalashnikovs, the civilian and military men of the mission struggled to make sense of the dichotomy between what was expected and what was actually found. They expected death and dismemberment, destruction and extermination, but found a couple of dozen live girls only a little worse for wear and the remains of the Boko Haram leaders dismembered, strewn about and consumed.

On the return trip, the convoy took a circuitous route and passed through several towns hit earlier by the al-Qaeda affiliate. There the men in the trucks met with their original expectations. They drove slowly through villages roughly connected by a tortuous, barely passable network of roads and single-track paths. Corpses and body parts lay asunder; vehicles were wrecked and torched, and school buildings were burned to the ground. Flies were so thick as to be a menace to breathing. No one from the Nigerian APCs had the courage to investigate the interior of the burnt-out schools. There was no expectation of finding anybody alive. No one could have survived the obvious inferno. Eastwood's crew filmed it all.

When they got to the colonel's APC, the bulky Colonel Emmanuel struggled to get out of the personnel carrier gracefully. He met Eastwood one last time with warmth and respect. He explained, "The atrocities of the Boko Haram aren't well known outside of Nigeria. My people wonder why America does not help fight the scourge of the north. You'll tell the story and the story of the girls. Not all Islam is bad, but terrorists like the Boko Haram are very, very bad."

Eastwood considered what he would say before he stated the obvious. "Colonel Emmanuel, I'm fond of saying the greatest power of the media is the power to ignore. You are correct, Sir, the American people are totally unaware of this problem, and that was the purpose of my mission: to investigate and tell the world and hopefully, galvanize enough of our politicians into action to help you in this fight. You and your men are heroes for confronting these devils and rescuing those girls."

The colonel lowered his head slightly. He had no words to tell Eastwood, and he would have few words to tell his superiors. He raised his head, shook Eastwood's hand, and returned to his vehicle. Eastwood and his crew stood on the side of the road at the entrance to the Abjua Sheraton Hotel and waved until the last APC drove past them.

After a shower and a meal, Eastwood met with Marty Marceau to shoot opening and closing comments before filing his report. Karl Mann facilitated the effort to bounce the signal off a satellite just nine degrees above the equator and parked in a geosynchronous orbit to the corporate offices of the network in New York City. Eastwood provided everything they had filmed and investigated to his producer but failed to mention the very special bullet or the video recording of reeds protruding from the ground. He decided that there were some things his CEO might have wanted in his special report, but he didn't have a need to know everything the team did and found; at least, not yet.

· · ·

After conducting a pair of familiarization flights of the King Air aircraft and the working area—the northern third of Nigeria, it was Dick Osbourne's turn to fly the left seat, so Kelly Horne moved into the co-pilot's position. Taxi, takeoff, and departure from Abuja International Airport were by the numbers; the mustachioed old codger maintained precise airspeed and altitude control, giving the youngster a goal to work towards. He acknowledged she was a "good stick" but still, not that good in the Beechcraft. However, it'd be only a matter of time before she would be outflying him, and both of them knew it. With a folded topographical chart in her lap, Horne crossed-checked their position with the GPS and pointed out several landmarks to verify they were on course.

The intelligence brief had indicated a large Nigerian convoy had penetrated into the northwestern area of concern. The Boko Haram group had left the safe confines of Cameroon and northeastern Nigeria and pushed west through the soft underbelly of the western Nigerian communities where Nigerian army units were scarce and towns were poorly protected by local militias. Dick Osbourne found it difficult to believe that the Boko Haram had, in one regard, changed their MO. In another, they had not—the kidnapping of girls from a little known Christian school may have been too much of a golden opportunity for them to ignore.

"Dick, so what we're really doing is building a case?" asked Kelly Horne.

"That's correct. Collect intel and process it; like turning over the pieces of a puzzle so you can make some sense of what you're seeing."

"I get that, but I guess I'm wondering the bigger question. Why?"

Osbourne checked the GPS to demonstrate he was paying attention to his scan. "Our target is ten minutes out."

"That's how I read it."

"Ok, I'll make this short and sweet. Why? My experience is the former President didn't give a rat's ass of what's going on in this part of the world. He didn't care and wrote off Africa for whatever reason. Now it's become a hotbed of terrorist activity. He didn't do anything to help the Nigerians squash Boko Haram when they were manageable, and what happened is what always happens, they filled the vacuum with bodies. I don't think I'm overly critical of the former POTUS, but what I see of our current President is that he puts what's right above politics. The Nigerian army can't deal with the situation, so we're here providing the necessary support and intel. We go and find them, report what we find, and hope the Embassy or State or the President does something with the intel. When there wasn't anyone here, no intel was captured and the Boko Haram flourished. They were able to operate in an area devoid of militias and army. Now that we're here...."

Horne nodded. "We capture the needed intel." They were flying over a particularly dark stretch of Nigerian jungle where they hadn't seen a single light from a house or the headlights of a vehicle for several minutes. She said, "We don't want to go down in this area."

"That's why we've two engines on this baby. Safety. If we were to lose a motor we could get back."

"Flying single engine in this area would have to be...."

"Scary. Only the really brave or certifiably crazy bastards fly the singles, the super-spook airplanes."

Horne snapped her head to the pilot in command. "What do you mean by 'super-spook?' I thought we're in the super-spook airplane."

Osbourne rattled his head and his moustache followed. "Several years ago, I saw what had to be an Agency operation. Really sensitive work, guys in Schweizers. Highly modified motorized gliders. Quiet, single-engine airplanes. High coolness factor. There's no telling what they were doing. I was curious but had no need to know; I knew when to keep my mouth shut."

Bells went off in Kelly head. *That's what Dad does! He said he flies quiet airplanes but never told me what kind. The model on his desk wasn't a Schweizer. I've flown their motor gliders at the Air Force Academy.*

Osbourne glanced over to his co-pilot to see she was in deep thought. Both aviators were interrupted when the sensor operator in

469

the cabin keyed his microphone and announced, "Tally Ho, on the nose. Got the building and the vehicles outlined in the brief. I wish you could see all the hot spots. No humans but there must be thirty hyenas and lions in the area. Big lions."

Kelly recovered from the distraction of her father and playfully patted the glare shield of the aircraft and said, "You be a nice girl and keep flying. We don't want to go down in this area."

Osbourne and the sensor operator said, in unison, "Amen to that!"

"Kelly, set up an orbit here. So we have lions, hyenas, and trucks, and a building but no humans? Zeke, what do you make of that?" asked Osbourne.

"The Nigerian Army indicated they suspected a rival tribe ambushed the Boko Haram at this location. The brief indicated they picked up twenty or so weapons. We've seen the telltale signs of a Boko Haram 'seize and destroy' operation, but it terminates out here in the bush? Wouldn't any rival group have taken the weapons and the vehicles? Hell, why wouldn't they?"

Horne offered, "There were twenty-something girls rescued as well. I'm not so naïve to think that a competitor group wouldn't have taken possession of the weapons and the vehicles *and the girls*? Isn't that more likely? What am I missing? This situation doesn't make any sense."

Osbourne lifted his head from his chest and asked, "If it wasn't another group, then how did that happen? It almost seems whoever took out the bad guys was beamed up to a spaceship."

"The girls said the men were shot. But what if they were shot from...the air?" Horne asked the two men over the microphone. It took several seconds before Osbourne responded.

"The only airplane that could do that is a gunship. I flew Apaches and there's no way, from the air, to differentiate between bad guys and good girls, to kill the former and not touch the latter. Impossible in close quarters. Or it might be better said that I'm unaware of any airborne capability that can deliver such precision firing. The state of technology is just not there yet."

"As far as you know?" Horne wasn't convinced the technology 'wasn't there yet' and had a flashback to a couple of men in black helmets and flight suits with NGVs on the upper deck of a hijacked jet. She thought about the impossibility of the scenario as Osbourne rolled the aircraft wings level and headed back to Abuja. She was in a faraway trance-like state for a few seconds, thinking, considering the art of the possible when the flash of insight struck her mute.

She turned and rummaged in her flight bag. She found a whiz-wheel flight calculator and her BlackBerry. She yanked a folded topographical map of western Africa from a map case onto her lap. From the little black telephone, she scrolled through her text message history and wrote down several numbers. Osbourne was amused by the curious and harried antics of his copilot. Horne asked, "Do you mind if I program the GPS for Monrovia? I'd like to check something."

With nothing to see in the blackness of the night, Osbourne punched in the Monrovia airport designator—ROB—into the GPS and instantly the device provided flight vector, statute miles, wind direction and speed, and estimated time of arrival. "You mean, like that? ETA less than three hours. You want to go to Liberia?"

She shook her head. *The state of technology isn't there yet. What if the state of technology was...there? Here? What else could it be?* She turned to look at the older man. He was confused by her actions but not concerned. *How could my father have been so close to be able to rescue the crew and airplane?* Then it hit her; she covered her mouth and unconsciously burst out, "Oh, my...."

CHAPTER THIRTY-NINE

The white and blue Aeroflot Ilyushin Il-96 set up for a left-hand approach over the city to the runway on the northern outskirts of Ashgabat, the City of White Marble. Passengers on the port side of the wide body airliner pressed faces and noses to the smallish windows to see the buildings, structures, mosques, and edifices of smooth polished white marble. It was as if the zoning laws excluded the grey striations of the Calacatta or Arabiscato marble but mandated the exclusive use of pure white Thassos. Blue-domed mosques, intricate masonry, and tall gold-topped buildings punctuated the spaces between black asphalt that ran laterally and longitudinally. Flying over the picturesque city, which was wedged between the Kopet Dag mountain range to the south and the Kara Kum desert to the north, provided a dramatic effect. McGee couldn't help but wonder if their wandering route over the city was to show the power, might, and skill of the Turkmen people or make the case that white marble was cheap and plentiful in the area.

The man traveling as Alan Hawthorn in one of the handful of first class seats on the Russian-manufactured jet had one of the few window seats. He stared lazily out the transparency as the jet started its turn to the runway of the Mehrabad Airport. The number of white marble structures surprised him; the diversity and magnificent architecture of the structures astonished him. He hadn't seen anything like it in the Muslim world before. His usual destinations in the Middle East were in the middle of a war zone where buildings were measured not in beauty but in "bombed into rubble" or "bombed out." He noticed a long boardwalk structure of lines and circles. He swore he had seen that specific design before on a Led Zeppelin album cover, the name of which escaped him.

Landing and disembarking from the airliner was smooth and quick, especially for Aeroflot's first class passengers who received head of the line privileges. The walk to the immigration holding area was stark and sterile with white walls and ceiling tiles and a polished white marble floor, but no restroom facilities to be seen. McGee would wait to pee.

"What's the purpose of your visit?" the indifferent and bored customs official asked of the man who presented himself for entry by surrendering his passport. Without looking up at the man, the Turkmen customs agent thumbed through the thick passport for the appropriate visa. Only then did he check the photograph inside the passport and look up to find a very large and very black gentlemen standing before him with the same dark eyes in the laminated picture staring back at him.

"Business," offered Alan Hawthorn, with a hint of a smile as he peered through tiny wire-rimmed glasses.

Customs officials profiled and classified the traveling public quickly. Hundreds of people passed through the kiosks daily. Religious people were pleasant and often tried to engage the officers in inane pleasantries, as if they might know where the best hotels and restaurants were located. Military men carried themselves with degrees of importance; the higher the rank, the puffier, and snottier they were. Business people were odd and new, especially those from America. The oddest business people of all were the black men, and there had been more and more African-Americans claiming to be businessmen and executives. The customs officials noticed that some Americans passing through the country carried themselves with the unmistakable confidence and deportment of an elite soldier even though they dressed in suits and ties. Their passports and entry documents were always perfect, unlike nearly everyone else who passed through the airport. The customs man stamped the entry time into Hawthorn's passport, initialed it, and handed it back to him.

Traveling in a business suit instead of in his comfortable cargo pants and loose fitting shirt wasn't as bad as it could have been. Having to buy a suit in the Azores on short notice had been an adventure—especially knowing it'd be confiscated and not returned. He found a suit maker with enough fabric to cover his half-acre of muscles but finding something that resembled dress shoes was nearly impossible. The only shoe available represented Europe's latest fashion, and it was a flop. It was like having a duckbill for toes—McGee could barely walk in them and running was out of the question. The shoes proved the feminization of European men was in full swing. When the Custom's man lowered his eyes, businessman Hawthorn knew his time was up at the booth, and it was time to look for a man with a sign.

After clearing Customs, McGee immediately picked out the man he would meet. Past and present special operations forces warriors across the military spectrum, carried themselves in a distinct and unambiguous way. Generally, they were bodybuilders with much muscle mass. In a crowd of small, diminutive, and undernourished people, massive pectorals and biceps separated the strong from the weak—the specially-trained from the barely-trained. And then there were the eyes: impassioned, hardened and menacing eyes that had seen the bloodiest battles and the worst wounds in the most horrible of hellholes over a lifetime of killing their country's enemies. The man with the A4-sized sign with blue lettering strained the seams of the white *dishdasha*, and his white *keffiyeh* was the size of a pup tent. The former enemy of America was as big as McGee but significantly older and fleshier and a little taller. *Probably old KGB* was McGee's first thought. His second thought was the same as the man holding the sign: *He's not going to be easy to kill.*

McGee exchanged the challenges and responses as briefed by the hyperactive Miss S, and allowed the man to lead him to the toilets. U.S. Navy SEAL, Bill McGee, was on high alert.

He wasn't surprised to find two other very large and thick men in traditional Arab dress in the stinky men's toilet, essentially holes in the floor. When told to remove his clothes, McGee did so without question while maintaining his grip on the A7-sized card and two long, embossed aluminum strips that the little fireball, Miss S, had given him in the Azores. The monster of a man who met him at the customs exit pulled a long black scanner, akin to an elongated paddleboard, out of a backpack and wanded the naked Hawthorn from head to toe. He watched his clothes and shoes get bundled and tossed into the toilet's refuse receptacle. He was handed a white *thobe*, a white *keffiyeh* and black *agal*, and a pair of oversized and well-worn sandals. Now the four men looked like natives, although McGee was definitely much darker than the others. When the three Russian men exchanged approving grunts, Hawthorn broke out in a short cough and once he recovered, asked, "Now can I take a piss?" He didn't wash his hands after he relieved himself; the three former KGB didn't question the black man's sanitary habits and didn't seem to mind.

They didn't drive through the City of White Marble but passed through the slums of Ashgabat on a dirt road that was surprisingly free of ruts instead of being a long continuous dirt washboard. After a couple of minutes, the ancient Land Rover five-door station wagon smoothly rolled onto the pavement of the highway and headed southeast. McGee was surprised and grateful he wasn't blindfolded. So far, the Russians had acted professionally; it was their job to get Alan Hawthorn to a location so he could verify the serial numbers of the missing devices and affix a seal. The selection of the faded green four-wheel-drive truck, with a spare tire lashed to the hood and a half-dozen jerry cans sitting atop a stout metal carrying cage affixed to the roof, suggested the road ahead would be long and arduous. McGee coughed a few times for good measure; the Russians glanced toward him whenever he did.

McGee awoke when the Land Rover left the smooth pavement for a much rougher road through a cut in some foothills. Through the windscreen he could make out the faint outline of a mountainous horizon. He cursed himself for falling asleep as now he had no idea where he was or how long he'd been out. He looked out his backseat window and saw nothing but stars and blackness. For the first time in a very long time the former Navy SEAL was concerned.

After an hour of climbing and descending a series of hills, the road leveled off into a gentle climb with ruts that weren't as severe. McGee felt the deceleration and turned to look forward. He saw that a heavily fortified fence and gate stood in their way. The man in the passenger seat slipped out the door, repositioned an AK-47 over his shoulder, and moved to the gate in front of the Land Rover's headlights. A huge chain with huge multiple locks secured the sturdy gate. The rusty gate looked like it had once been designed to thwart a platoon of Marines, but now it looked as if it wouldn't slow a casual interloper if he vigorously shook the chain link. The shackles of two large Master-style locks, the bodies of which were as big as McGee's fists, were linked together. One lock shined with newness; the other was dull, rusty, and antique. The man spun the wheels on the bottom of the new lock and pulled down on the shackle to unlatch it. He fed the heavy links of chain through the gate until it fell onto the ground and the gate swung wide, allowing the Land Rover's driver to enter.

"Now I blindfold you," said the man in the backseat with McGee.

In the faint light from the instrument panel, McGee coughed several times then looked at the man and nodded as he wordlessly complied.

• • •

It was highly unusual for the King of Jordan to visit the American Embassy without all the pomp, circumstance, and protocols associated with an official visit. It was more appropriate for the Ambassador to make an official call on the King at the Royal Palace, as he had done days earlier in response to the DCI's request to hand deliver a message. The King's visit wasn't an official or scheduled function, and the Embassy staff was in a high state of indignation while His Royal Highness met with the Director of Central Intelligence in the private office of the Ambassador. The Ambassador was left standing outside his own office door.

Lynche's ever-present Growler was energized and placed on the Ambassador's desk to crush any electronic eavesdropping. Greg Lynche wore a grey Brooks Brothers business suit. The 43rd-generation, direct descendant of the Prophet Mohammad, wore a finely tailored Saville Row black suit with chalk pinstripe. The men gripped hands and greeted each other warmly; they kissed cheeks in the Arab style three times to show their deep affection and respect. Lynche offered the expected salutations from the President and trusted the Queen and the Royal Family were well. Once the standing pleasantries were out of the way, he offered the King an overstuffed leather chair and didn't sit until His Majesty was seated. Tea wasn't served.

"Your Highness, I thank you for your understanding."

"I should be thanking you, Greg. I credit you for saving Omar's life." The Jordanian King's voice was strong; his flawless English was delivered with a taste of a New England accent from his days in the exclusive Deerfield Academy in Massachusetts. As the words left his lips, his demeanor shifted from that of a joyful and pleasant monarch to a deeply troubled and concerned friend. He leaned forward in his chair and listened intently.

"Your Highness, that's most generous, but I must confess I didn't know what we were dealing with; in many ways I still don't. Call it a hunch."

"A hunch? Well, the vaunted CIA director did well with...a hunch. You were correct; you're to be commended."

"Thank you, Your Excellency. This was a unique situation and a fast-moving one at that. I didn't know who else I could trust. This was a time-sensitive and very dangerous situation. What I didn't want to convey and couldn't convey until I had more evidence, is that if the chief justice was in fact poisoned, then I suspect your General Intelligence Department had a significant hand in the poisoning. Regrettably, there's an old link, recently uncovered, between my predecessor and your chief of intelligence."

The King's striking good looks and buoyant demeanor changed

quickly into the frown of an angry man; he looked from under heavy brows and stared at Lynche. "An old link? This is very disturbing, Director Lynche." He raised his hands as in a question before returning them to his lap. "I would appreciate knowing the background, your discovery, and who else knows. Major General Faisal has been a trusted advisor for many years and is a friend of the Royal family."

Lynche relayed the tiniest thread of the story about Dr. Bruce Rothwell. The former Director of Central Intelligence was trained in the communist tactics of concealment and deception by the Soviet Union at the Lumumba Friendship University, and was, in all likelihood, a highly placed KGB and sleeper agent. An even thinner thread implicated the head of the Jordanian Secret Police was possibly collaborating with Rothwell on a project. He reported that Rothwell disappeared from the United States before he could be called before Congress to testify, only to turn up later in Amman. He was photographed in the company of some very senior leaders with known al-Qaeda and Muslim Brotherhood ties. Lynche assured the King that the U.S. hadn't tried to assassinate Rothwell with a bomb, that the day the Agency discovered he was in Jordan was the day the Sheraton Hotel was bombed.

"Major General Faisal said the evidence of the bombing was clearly the work of the CIA."

"Your Excellency, I can assure you, unequivocally, the CIA had no part in the assassination attempt on Dr. Rothwell or the al-Qaeda general."

"I must tell you, Greg, General Faisal thought your President authorized a secret drone attack on both men. He was sure of it, but every hotel guest who was interviewed reported a deafening noise, like millions of honeybees, came from the elevator before the explosion. In the debris, we found small airplane parts, tiny motors and propellers. General Faisal was convinced your Agency was responsible. Maybe classic drones weren't used, but possibly tiny bombers were used. Something from your Science and Technology Directorate?"

"That's very interesting, Your Highness; I'm afraid not. Sir, if we had done it I would tell you, and you'd get a personal apology from the President. However, the facts are we don't know who attacked Rothwell; I'm a little embarrassed to say it took too long for us to discover the whereabouts of the former Director. A group of Navy SEALs reported to security that one of the most wanted terrorists had waltzed through the lobby of the Sheraton followed by the head of the Jordanian Secret Police, and later Dr. Rothwell in a *thobe* and a *keffiyeh*. The day we received that dispatch was the day of the bombing. We're investigating, but our FBI has been prevented from coming to Jordan to help with your investigation."

"I think you can see why General Faisal believed the CIA had conducted the operation and recommended no U.S. access to the crime scene or the country. I'll reverse that decision." The King nodded approvingly which encouraged Lynche to continue.

"Your Highness, one of our best analysts discovered the KGB link with Rothwell, even though Rothwell had been reported to be dead. Some old KGB let their guard down with the news of Rothwell's demise. Some internal assessments suggested that Rothwell was behind the bombing so he could disappear. For something like that he'd need a lot of help. In Amman. Several weeks after Rothwell was reported to be dead, we lost dozens of intelligence agents—virtually overnight—across Africa and the Middle East. One was killed on the beach at the Dead Sea Resort."

"That isn't sufficient to implicate Major General Faisal in any wrongdoing."

"No, Your Excellency. That thread is very thin, I grant you that, but my analyst has been systematically targeted for kidnapping or death. We have foiled their attempts on multiple fronts and have hidden her well. When Al-Jazeera announced the Jordanian Chief Justice had collapsed and was in critical condition, it was, for me, too coincidental—an overreach. The evidence and the intelligence derived by my analyst suggested Rothwell is alive, in Amman, and is probably staying at the Amman Marriott. Major General Faisal visited the

Marriott, and a few days later your chief justice is struck with an illness. All we have are threads, but in this business sometimes all it takes is just a few threads to weave the whole conspiracy tapestry."

The King of Jordan paused and reflected. The missing pieces of Lynche's puzzle troubled him; what he now knew troubled him. There were too many unanswered questions. He needed more information. "Greg, you are convinced your Dr. Rothwell is alive? And General Faisal is likely a collaborator?"

"Yes, Your Excellency."

"And you believe Major General Faisal poisoned Chief Justice Kamal?"

"Yes, Your Excellency. He or one of his trusted agents."

"Which is what was found when they pumped his stomach. Why would anyone do that? I don't understand how you suspected the poisoning of Omar." The King wasn't convinced and needed to hear more.

"Your Excellency, this is where the story takes a strange turn. I believe Rothwell tried to flush my analyst out of hiding, to get the daughter of the chief justice to come to Amman to either kill her or kidnap her. Or for some other purpose we haven't determined."

Shocked at the revelation, the King demanded an answer. "*Marwa...Kamal?* Explain this to me."

Lynche closed his eyes for a moment and considered what he would say. To be fully honest with the helpful monarch would be a breach of trust and poor politics. On the other hand, not saying anything or lying would likely get them thrown out of the country. He had to be careful; the King could be trusted with some secrets. "Your Excellency, Miss Kamal is now working for...me. She's the analyst."

The King sat back in the chair and tapped his fingertips together in a teepee. "Ah, that explains much." He allowed the information to swirl in his head, then he broke out in a mischievous smile. His bushy eyebrows shot up. "Have you seen her mother?"

"No, Your Excellency." Lynche wondered where the King was heading.

"A face...as if Michelangelo had painted a goddess. And the daughter was even more beautiful." He shook his head and smiled at the long faded memory; Lynche nodded because he understood. Some women were simply striking and unforgettable, and Nazy Cunningham, *née*, Marwa Kamal, was all that and more.

"All of this has been because of Marwa Kamal?"

He didn't want to talk about trading paintings for suitcase nukes, and he wouldn't. "Your Majesty, there's some history—I would say Rothwell is obsessed. Possibly insane. But put that aside for the moment. I think there's more. First, al-Qaeda and the Muslim Brotherhood are struggling financially. We believe Rothwell is selling secrets to whoever will buy them, and he knows how to extract billions from the U.S. treasury. The only scenario that makes much sense is that he's assumed a leadership position in one or both organizations and is working to secure greater operating funds. Most recently, they've tried to hijack a jumbo jet and hold it for ransom...."

"This latest hijacking? In Africa?"

"Yes, Your Excellency. We've reason to believe Rothwell was behind that. There was a demand, a billion dollars in gold. I don't have tangible evidence, but in this business, we rarely do."

"You've no direct evidence, but Miss Kamal strongly suggests that Faisal was behind the poisoning of her father."

Lynche nodded and smiled through pinched lips. He extracted a document from his suit coat pocket and handed it to the King. "Your Majesty, what you have there is a class roster from a Russian training facility. Miss Kamal was able to extract that from some classified documents that became available after the Soviet Union fell. A former soviet intelligence officer who ran a school house to train a variety of people—the Ayatollahs Khomeini and Khamenei for instance—also trained and dispatched our Dr. Rothwell and your General Faisal under their real names, not pseudonyms, in propaganda methods and special activities. One training course was 'unconventional means and methods' to assassinate a target. Using poisons and radioactive materials."

The King waved his hand in small circles as he talked. "I understand now, Mr. Lynche. I sense there's more to this situation than meets the eye. Your Rothwell is a very...*damaged* individual, emotionally and physically. It's apparent he lusts after the lovely Marwa Kamal. We could use some help in determining how the bomb blast occurred at the Sheraton hotel. If you know where your Dr. Rothwell is...."

"Your Excellency, he hasn't been seen for some time. We believe he's in the Amman Marriott. However, we don't have proof. An investigation needs to be conducted."

The King of Jordan stood up and said, "I want him found, and I want his al-Qaeda and Muslim Brotherhood friends out of Jordan. I'll deal with General Faisal. I'll call your President Hernandez and invite the FBI to assist with the immediate investigation of the hotel bombing. How more can I help you Mr. Lynche?" He held out a hand for goodbye.

"Your Highness, I think there's one more thing...."

The King raised his eyebrows nearly to this hairline at Lynche's suggestion.

CHAPTER FORTY

Dick Osbourne and Kelly Horne strolled into the Security Office of the U.S. Embassy for their flight brief. They were surprised to find the Chief of Station and the Ambassador, already there and engaged in a spirited discussion with the Security Chief. Horne heard "hideouts" and suspected the topic was the previous night's flight and sensor download.

Never one for political correctness, Osbourne interjected, "What's with the meeting of the minds?" He thought he was being funny but no one laughed. Horne was mortified and embarrassed. The Ambassador ignored the comment as did the COS who continued, "It's easy to find their hideouts—follow the trail of fire and destruction, and where it ends, like the pot of gold at the end of the rainbow, you'll find the bloody remains of Boko Haram."

The Ambassador crossed his arms over his scrawny chest and looked at Horne for answers. "What did you find, Miss Horne? Was there a trail of breadcrumbs leading to this group?"

"Yes, sir, if you mean a trail of bodies, burned-out vehicles, and buildings leading into and out of a town, then yes. Inside the Nigerian border and across. Seems like the tribal areas of Cameroon are being used as safe havens."

The COS shot back, "Could be. They're hell-bent on turning the northern area red with blood if the Christians don't leave or convert."

"That's their MO," said the Security Officer with a ring of confidence. Osbourne glanced at the woman who wore her hair long and stringy. She didn't impress him.

The Ambassador looked at the two pilots with curiosity and said,

"We've received a very good report this morning from a U.S. correspondent that found—essentially—the same thing as you did in the northwest corner of the country. We had no idea he was in country doing a special on Boko Haram for American television."

Osbourne mimicked the Ambassador, crossed his arms over his chest, and rested them on his paunch. "That's not going to go over well. No one gives a crap about Nigeria. Nigerians don't even give a crap about Nigeria."

"It's probably more accurate to say the American voter doesn't know anything about this country or their troubles. They think everyone here is living in mud huts, and the women run around topless like in an old National Geographic." The Ambassador uncrossed his arms to make his point and then slipped his hands in his pockets. Osbourne mimicked him much to the dismay of the COS.

"Uh...news flash. They do live in mud and reed huts and run around topless, at least in the jungles in the north." Osbourne smirked at his own cleverness.

The Chief of Station ignored the old pilot and interjected, "Colonel Eastwood followed the trail to the point of finding a couple of dozen of the most recently kidnapped girls—but no Boko Haram. Found their trucks and found the girls walking home, apparently frightened but unharmed. They said men wearing military fatigues and carrying weapons showed up in pickup trucks. The village leaders thought Nigerian soldiers had come to protect them from Boko Haram, but the soldiers rounded up everyone in the village. They separated the girls and then killed everyone else."

Kelly listened to the COS' narrative and noticed a discrepancy. She waited for the conversation to come back around to the missed topic. After internally debating with herself, she gave up and asked the obvious, "What happened to the men?"

"Lions and hyenas apparently dragged them into the bush," said the COS. There was an element of skepticism in his voice and it came through as his voice crackled.

"That makes no sense." The Ambassador unholstered his hands

from his pockets and again crossed his arms.

"The Nigerian Army suggested a rival group ambushed them." The security officer looked up from her notes and smiled. She wasn't wearing a bra; no one noticed and no one cared.

"Really?" barked Osbourne. For all of the time he had been flying over northern Nigeria, not once had he ever encountered another organized group in the bush or in the towns. "Anne, do we know of any organized group in the northwest? I haven't seen a hint that there's another armed tribal group. We've been all over that area. Individual huts, tiny villages—they're farmers or they fish from the rivers. No one was ever armed."

The security woman checked her notes and shook her flyaway hair. "No. There isn't one."

Osbourne was emphatic. "Boko Haram only wanders into those places for fresh pickings: new talent, unsuspecting children, banks, stores. Normally, tribal elders would make a stand if they knew the terrorists are coming. They know they're likely to get killed, but they still make a stand. They...."

The Chief of Station took a deep breath and alerted everyone in the room he was about to speak. "The Army and Eastwood reported widespread destruction in several towns. But there's a kicker." He pointed his finger into the imaginary circle of people like an old schoolmarm trying to make a point.

"What's that?" they asked in unison.

"When they found the Boko Haram vehicles, the ground was littered with brass, guns, and blood. Some of the girls said the bad men fired into the bush at an unseen enemy, but whoever was in the jungle shot the murderous bastards. The girls said during the firefight that one man fell every few seconds. The weird part was that the army didn't find a single spent casing in the tree line of the jungle, suggesting there wasn't anyone in the jungle. There may have been a sniper in hiding, but if there was a group then they must have had incredible discipline to pick up their brass and not leave a trace that they were there. The Army only found traces...remains of men after they were dragged into the tree line."

"Lion food," offered Osbourne. "That was exactly what we found when we flew over that area." The Ambassador, the COS, the Security Chief and Kelly were repulsed at the notion and disgusted with Osbourne's insistence on being crass.

"The Nigerian Army, understandably, is very superstitious. They told Eastwood they believed some jungle god or something took out the Boko Haram." The COS pursed his lips and nodded.

"One of the girls said it was God," said the Security Officer.

"What?" asked Osbourne and Horne simultaneously.

She continued, "Only one girl said, supposedly, that the stars flashed. Then when the stars stopped flashing the men stopped firing. They were dead on the ground. They crossed themselves believing that God had saved them, so they got out of the trucks and tried to run home."

Horne wasn't the only one in the room who drew the conclusion that stars knocking down bad men indicated something other than God was behind the Boko Haram men's demise. Osbourne shot her a look as they had just talked about a similar capability the night before. She asked, "Where're the reporters?"

"On their way home, I suppose." The Ambassador didn't know for sure and after gesturing he didn't know, his hands returned to his pockets.

"Who were these reporters again?" Everyone in the room was confused at Horne's question. The COS bailed her out. "Demetrius Eastwood: old war correspondent, retired Marine Corps colonel. The Marine Security Guards went crazy when he arrived. I suppose he's a rock star in the Marine Corps; he signed copies of his books and posed for pictures. Said getting out of Nigeria should be a lot easier than getting in. He and his crew had a hell of a trip flying to Lagos. Like you, he was on that hijacked jet."

All heads turned to Kelly Horne, who felt foolish being the new source of interest and scrutiny. The COS knew he would generate some unwanted interest with the remark, but he had a purpose.

"There's an investigation going on, so don't ask Kelly to comment—and that means not here or in the air. No one has a need to know until the investigation is complete. Got it?"

With that command, the meeting broke up. The Ambassador threw his hands up and left the room. The Security Officer ran her hands through her hair and put it into a wiry ponytail. Before leaving the room, the COS put a finger into the chest of Dick Osbourne and said, "That especially means you." He winked at Horne as he left.

"Are you ready for your mission brief?" asked the Security Officer.

Horne nodded and listened closely.

Osbourne heard nothing, he couldn't take his eyes off Horne. Mild fantasies were replaced with newfound respect. He'd been around long enough to know some people were "touched" with good luck, and being in the right place at the right time during a crisis or an emergency could make or break a career. Horne was young and on the uptick; he was old and on a downward glide path. His eyes returned to the Security Officer as he thought about what could have been as Kelly Horne focused on the brief, took mental and written notes, and listened.

. . .

Thick dark clouds hung low over the city and obscured the view of the Hindu Kush to the east. Unusually still moist air between the ground and the meteorological ceiling created a temperature inversion. The resulting acrid atmosphere—exacerbated by the suspended fecal particulate from centuries of burning animal dung for cooking and heat—cast a smelly residue over the city, like brown pollen that covered anything and everything outside. The indigenous population of three million was indifferent to the miasma, while visitors soon learned never to eat or rub one's eyes outdoors and prayed for thunderstorms to scrub the foul air clean. With no winds or rain in the forecast, any respite from the stifling feculent stench wouldn't be forthcoming.

Duncan Hunter tried in vain not to breathe the crappy airborne concoction and expedited his departure from the airport with his oxygen mask on. It was an advantage and a necessity since he would be flying over several tall mountains in the minor ranges of the Hindu Kush, the "teenagers," those mountains that were just thirteen, fourteen, and fifteen thousand feet high. To the east were the beginnings of the "twenty-somethings," the northwestern part of the Himalaya chain that stretched into Pakistan, India, China, and Nepal.

One hour after sunset, it was sufficiently dark on the airport to launch the YO-3A from the airport's northern-most hangar. Bob and Bob helped to keep the aircraft's wingtips from hitting the hangar's span as Hunter taxied out of the structure and turned left onto the taxiway. Seeing there were no other aircraft in the area, he pushed the throttle to the stops, and the YO-3A quickly lifted off, barely clearing the fence at the end of the taxiway. Bob and Bob exchanged, "He's crazy" after watching the aircraft power down the taxiway that was shorter and narrower than the runway and many times more dangerous. The two Bobs rolled their eyes and shuddered at the thought of Hunter's very short-field takeoff, where taxiways are very rarely used for takeoffs and landings, where such stunts usually end in a crash. However, Hunter was intimate with the capabilities and performance of the Yo-Yo, especially at the high altitude of Kabul. He wasn't about to call for and wait for takeoff clearance at the Hold Short Line of the runway for a secret mission. He was in a hurry and took what was available. When he barely cleared the chain link fence at the perimeter of the airport, he sucked his positive-feed oxygen mask dry thinking he might have screwed up.

The GPS and heading indicator showed the way to the secret city in Turkmenistan. He pointed the nose of the aircraft to the most direct route and retarded the throttle slightly from takeoff power to achieve near-redline airspeed. He felt he was late and eased the throttle forward to eke out a few more RPMs and flew the airplane near its "never to exceed" airspeed.

After two hours of slicing through hazy air, Hunter removed his oxygen mask as he crossed the border of Turkmenistan just east of the border of Iran. He recalled that the last time he and Lynche had gotten close to the Iranian border a missile defense battery launched a radar-guided missile at them. When the warning lights and tones in his headset had indicated a missile had been fired at them, Hunter rolled the YO-3A inverted and executed a descending half-loop. When the missile hit the ground behind them, Hunter and Lynche were just a few feet above the earth, in level flight, pointed in the opposite direction. He never forgave the Iranians for almost killing him and Lynche. Now he had ninety minutes to go before reaching his target. He hoped the secret city really was the hiding place of the suitcase devices; that they were not somewhere else.

Hunter was confident he would find McGee. He slowed the aircraft, deployed the FLIR, and began to search for any thermal images. He was supposed to be the luckiest guy he knew, and he was again pushing his luck to the limit.

CHAPTER FORTY-ONE

After thirty minutes of climbing and descending hills of varying gradient and slope, the stretched Land Rover found a stretch of flat road, giving the riders inside a much-needed respite from the potentially axle-breaking trip. As the truck rocked, rolled, and found the occasional pothole, eliciting grunts and yelps from the Russians, Bill McGee held on tight and remained silent as the super-stiff suspension components were stressed to their limits. Wedged in the corner with legs and arms braced to protect himself from flying around the inside the truck, he felt like he'd been tossed about like a ball bearing rattling around in a spray can. He had several opportunities to peek from under the poorly tied blindfold but refrained from cheating. Knowing that even through the course of tumbling inside the cabin of the truck, the three men had to be watching and looking for an excuse to terminate the operation, or him. When the Land Rover finally found flat purchase, the driver coordinated gearshift and clutch and urged the drivetrain to accelerate as the old truck raced into the night.

A series of turns on flat ground followed by a slow stop suggested to McGee they had arrived in the secret city.

The ancient Land Rover oscillated as men left the vehicle from either side, one left then one right. McGee hadn't been told to move; he understood he'd either be given the command to lift his blindfold or someone would help him from the vehicle.

Nearby, he heard the sound of a gasoline-powered motor as it chugged to life and struggled to find a steady state RPM. He assumed the noise was from a generator, that the men needed to power lights or equipment. With the cacophony of the motor in the background,

McGee was startled when his door opened and he was helped out of the truck. He coughed several times in the cool air.

The wind in his face felt refreshing, even with the blindfold in place. With a hand on each arm, he was led away from the vehicle across a surface as hard as concrete. They walked for dozens of steps until the men tugged on his arms to have him stop just as his feet crossed the threshold onto a wooden landing. He sensed a slightly unsteady floor under his feet that swayed marginally but perceptibly. *An elevator?*

The clattering of metal competed with the engine noise in the distance. McGee expected he would soon feel the free-falling sensation of an elevator descending and smiled internally when his senses proved him right. He envisioned an ancient industrial or hotel elevator cage with an expandable metal gate. He doubted the antique elevator was an elegant model with filigrees and swirls and contrasting paint. No, it was Russian and that meant a lowest cost and technically acceptable design: cheap, rusty, barely functional, worker utilitarian. The lack of acoustics didn't give away many clues.

Miss S, the woman from the Science and Technology Directorate, had described the old mining city, with one of the deepest open pit mines in the world, as a "closed city." On the satellite map the town was labeled, Ginibezogorsk. "Once a thriving multipurpose mining town of 40,000, Ginibezogorsk is now an official closed city, a place where no one is allowed to visit. Any trespassers that crossed the authorities would be tossed into the half-mile deep pit where a cesspool of chemicals would turn a corpse into gas and jelly in a matter of days. In its heyday, Ginibezogorsk featured high-rise apartments, restaurants, a sanitation system, a runway, a railroad, a smelter, and hundreds of trucks that brought up blocks of pure white granite as well as tons of uranium ore. Memorial plaques honoring famous Soviet physicists were bolted to the corners of each building."

McGee had scrutinized the satellite photographs. He had seen only the tops of buildings, streets, the remnants of a railroad, and an abandoned runway. He hadn't looked for anything specific but worked to memorize the layout of the city, so if he were forced to escape the city, he'd have some idea which way to turn and what to expect. He remembered looking up at Miss S as he waited for her to continue.

"Up until the city was closed, special permits were required to enter the main gate. We expect your escorts will avoid the checkpoints along the road and will likely sneak through the wall surrounding the city. There are traces of trails that have been used to gain entry. Ginibezogorsk was also known as G-23. Each secret city has a mysterious number attached to its name, like a cheap sci-fi thriller. We've no clue what to make of their numbering system; their numbering system makes no sense. But we know the KGB oversaw the operations," Miss S had said.

She then provided a sight picture of the city for McGee to visualize. With a gold slim line pen, she circumscribed the former 5000-acre base and indicated it was protected by three lines of fences and barbed wire, and numerous checkpoints and gates. She pointed out the administrative and residential centers, the special residences for the scientists, and laboratories used for developing the military-nuclear industry and extracting rare-earth minerals. The city remained secret until the collapse of the Soviet Union in 1991. "The scientists lived in prestigious internal exile. They received a steady supply of foreign foods and special privileges. Their children attended some of the best schools the old Soviet system could offer."

"With the fall of the USSR, the scientists and rocket specialists—the elite of the Russian army—all scrambled to find work or escape Russia and find freedom. Some were very entrepreneurial. Cargo pilots loaded up IL-76s and An-12s with their families and all their belongings and flew out of the chaotic crumbling country; some started airlines. Man-portable shoulder-launched weapons and tactical nuclear devices went missing by the planeload; we've tried to locate them and get them off the black market. Ten man-portable tactical nuclear devices remain unaccounted for."

"You can see that the abandoned facility looks like a set for a post-apocalyptic film. Historians and our sources say there is no documentation on whether the Soviets ever stored nuclear weapons here although if they did, they would have been stored on the northern side of the base, in a pair of bunkers protected by doors weighing more than six tons."

McGee asked Miss S what became of the people living in the city. He knew the answer before she spoke.

"You can probably guess, the KGB was given the task of neutralizing the physicists and scientists and others. Everyone but the elite were pushed out of the cities, like G-23, and resettled. KGB colonels shot the scientists and their families and disposed of their bodies in the pit mines. Any fears of having a Russian scientist or physicist appear in an American or British research facility or university was squelched."

When the elevator stopped, someone removed McGee's blindfold.

. . .

After ninety minutes of flying across vast stretches of hostile and austere land in Turkmenistan, the FLIR hadn't picked up a single source of life. No rabbits, no goats, no ibex, no snow leopards, and no man. Hunter had a passing thought that the device wasn't working properly, but he knew it was. The various thermal gradients of soil and plants were represented clearly, just no bright white contrast of heat against the cool dark high desert. As he climbed over a minor mountain range, a tiny white-hot thermal image suddenly popped into the FLIR scope off in the distance. Hunter shouted with glee and zoomed the optics to the maximum to find the heat signatures of a generator and the engine of a large truck near the edge of the rapidly improving view of a substantial open pit mine. With no humans present, Hunter slowed the aircraft and deployed the gun.

. . .

It took his eyes several seconds to adjust to the bright lights of the area he was standing in and the corridor that lay ahead. One of two fifteen-foot high, four-foot thick blast doors was open. He coughed hard, bringing up enough phlegm to spit, well away from where the men walked. One large Russian gestured for McGee to lead; another hand signal directed him to turn into a room, which looked suspiciously like an abandoned jail cell.

Upon entering, McGee found the man he had met first, ripping a dusty dark blanket off of two aluminum ice-chest-sized containers in the middle of the stark room. The big Russian motioned, "Here you are" with a wave of his hand and waited for McGee to inspect the devices and affix his seals.

McGee asked for a Geiger counter, a battery control unit (BCU), and a programmer. One man left the room and returned within a minute with the requested equipment. McGee walked to the first of the cases, bent over, flipped open latches, and removed a polyfoam insert from the inside. He checked the radiation levels before removing the surprisingly heavy ovoid-shaped bomb. A coughing fit struck him as he tightly cradled the thermonuclear device with one hand. His outburst of coughing, coupled with the cradling of the bomb, immediately frightened the Russians. He took notice of their reactions. Had the bombs been inert or fakes, he may have expected a different reaction from them.

When his cough subsided, he matched the serial number of the device with one of the serial numbers on his index card. He returned the bomb back into its container and repeated the process with the other lead-lined aluminum case. The three Russians watched intently as McGee methodically went through a series of diagnostic checks after inserting the battery control unit and powering up the bomb using the notebook-shaped programmer. After he was satisfied with the viability of the BCUs and the devices, McGee removed the BCUs and disconnected the programmer from each bomb before returning the bombs to their cases and snapping their closures shut. He placed one aluminum seal through each of the case's fastening mechanism.

The Russians' expressions changed from curious to smug when McGee said, "Thank you," to the men. But then he asked the bulky man if he could "see the others." He coughed hard again.

The Russians reacted to his request violently. One vehemently denied there were other bombs. Another acted as if he was shocked that the American knew there were other weapons. The third man looked up to the big man and asked, "What kind of bullshit is this?"

. . .

Hunter decelerated the aircraft as he arrived over the secret city. As he slipped the YO-3A into its "quiet" mode of flight and made minute adjustments to the throttle and established a gentle left-hand orbit. He was nearly fixated on the FLIR scope, wishing for a thermal signature of a human, of Bill McGee. He located the white-thermal image of a portable generator running near the football field-sized one-story building where the truck was parked. He could see that the vehicle's engine was cooling off. He'd scanned hundreds of vehicles in various stages of the infrared spectrum and knew from experience that the truck with the white-hot engine compartment looked to be an older Land Rover. When he couldn't find another thermal signature in the area, he placed the YO-3A on autopilot and checked the gun system. He flipped down his night vision goggles to inspect the area and was awed by the size of the abandoned city and the hole in the ground. He thought of Aztec and Mayan ruins and Cambodian abandoned cities and wondered if what he was seeing was just a new updated version. Why build them; why leave them?

. . .

"We're interested in all of the devices. I have ten numbers. I was told I'd be able to inspect all ten devices, that there wasn't any problem." McGee saw consternation in their faces. He hoped they couldn't see through his poker face. Even in the cool subterranean caverns, the altitude and thin air was affecting him. He was sweating like a post-race stallion from the Kentucky Derby. He offered the list to the man closest to him. "Ten devices—ten serial numbers. I certified the first two for immediate transfer and shipment. Please tell me you were briefed–this operation has been going so well. I can't believe you weren't briefed. If you cannot contact your supervisor, then I guess I'll have to come back another time."

The big man who did all of the gesturing and talking nodded to the man closest to the door; it looked like an approval.

In five minutes, McGee had entered four adjoining rooms and inspected eight more containers. He coughed hard as he entered every room, then recovered and thanked the man for his support and help. His mission was complete, his coughing appeared to be getting worse as he left the last of the rooms; he didn't look back as he heard the prison door close behind him. The Russians had much experience in dealing with prisoners with tuberculosis, and the black man's cough reminded them of the disease. They would try to keep as far away from him as possible.

As he entered the elevator cage McGee was again blindfolded. He memorized the position of each man in the elevator cab; he didn't hear anyone move or shift his position. Before the expandable metal gate closed, McGee was struck with another deep and hoarse coughing bout; it came and went. He recovered and stood quietly, with his arms down and his hands together. As the lift accelerated upwards, the Russians didn't respond to his latest bout. They had grown tired of McGee's acute coughing outbursts and ignored the diseased man.

McGee's next cough reflexively brought his hands to his mouth. In a single motion, he flexed and rippled his chest muscles with as much pent-up energy as he could muster. He drove his elbows into the throats of the two men standing on either side of him. The taller Russian had been facing the gate, but at the sound of crushed windpipes he turned to find an un-blindfolded McGee in full attack mode.

. . .

Hunter slewed the FLIR toward the landing strip and then returned the sensor ball's field of view back to the cooling engine of the Land Rover. He decided his NVGs gave him a better view of the condition of the runway if he needed to use it, or if an airborne special operations unit in Afghanistan might find it useful.

. . .

McGee karate-kicked the man operating the gate in the knee. One foot slammed into the patella, hyperextending it to the breaking point; his other foot crushed the Russian's testicles. He snapped the necks of the two men writhing in pain from their crushed larynxes, and then he pummeled the tall Russian with an elbow until he was dead. A bell sounded as the elevator had stopped; McGee's adrenaline had spiked so fast he didn't hear the tiny klaxon or feel the cab stop. Assured the three men were dead, he worked to control his emotions and heavy breathing. He wiped the sweat from his forehead with his sleeve, then gently dislodged his glasses from the bridge of his nose. After a few deep breaths, he opened the sliding gate. He stepped out of the dull light of the elevator cab and into the cool near-total darkness of G-23.

. . .

In the FLIR scope, Hunter jumped as the thermal image of a man appeared out of nowhere. The image in the screen wore a *dishdasha*. Hunter cursed and slewed the gun toward the "unfriendly." He activated the gun targeting system, selected ARMED on the multifunction display, and placed his thumb on the coolie-hat controller to drive the precision targeting software and placed the crosshairs of the device, center mass, on the man's torso. With his pinkie finger on the control stick, he depressed the laser designator switch to overlay the laser dot on the man's back.

· · ·

McGee took three steps away from the building, stopped, and immediately stuck his fingers in his mouth. He placed his palms together and raised his hands over his head. He hoped to God what little saliva he could muster would activate the CIA's special fingernail polish and release enough photons to be seen with night vision systems. The sudden outburst of energy had dried his throat, and as he tried to speak he could only come up with a very real, very dry cough. *"Don't shoot me, Maverick!"*

· · ·

Hunter assessed the situation on the ground before he pulled the trigger of the gun system. The man had his back to Hunter and wore the traditional Arabic garb, but no *keffiyeh*. *That's odd.* The aircraft was in a slow turn when the image raised his hands over his head and formed a teepee; the signal that McGee and Hunter agreed on if for some reason the CIA's amazing fingernail polish was a bust. *Well, I'll be…. Bullfrog, you made it!*

Hunter quickly took his hand off the aircraft's control stick and disarmed the gun system before he stowed the weapon. He changed the mode of the laser designator with a touch of a switch on the multi-function display panel. When Hunter looked back up and out of the cockpit, he could see McGee's fingernails begin to fluoresce in his NVGs. He used the touch-screen of the MFD to type a message and once he was satisfied with it, he depressed the switch at the base of his control stick to energize the laser designator. He put pressure on the coolie hat switch on top of the control stick to move the LD to the desired position on the ground, a few feet from McGee's location. A red laser traced out foot-tall letters, "YOU OK?"

. . .

McGee was instantly relieved to see the query in front of him. He raised a single thumb as he kept his head down; he didn't want to take any chance of his eyes being hit with the glint of the airborne laser and inadvertently blinding him. He then gestured with both arms in a downward motion. From some old memory, he remembered the hand and arm signals for helicopters but had no clue how to tell a fixed wing pilot to land.

. . .

The communication system developed on the fly seemed to be good enough; they could "talk" as long as Hunter typed out the questions, transmitted them on a laser beam, and received either approval or disapproval from McGee in the form of a hand and arm signal. When the old SEAL began to wave his arms up and down Hunter typed and transmitted, "YOU WANT ME TO LAND." Hunter smiled when McGee raised two thumbs up. He typed and the laser spelled out in a flickering red trace, "ON MY WAY TO RUNWAY." He jammed the throttle to the stop, climbed to 2,500 feet AGL, and scanned the area with the FLIR. The only hot spots in a twenty-five mile radius of the secret city were a cooling Land Rover and a humming generator. After sweeping the area with the sensor, Hunter stowed the FLIR, deployed the landing gear, and set up for a short-field landing.

Hunter shut down the engine and crawled from the cockpit before the propeller stopped turning. Under the sliver of an approaching new moon, Hunter walked to the rear of the airplane and embraced Bill McGee. When McGee released his grip on Hunter, he broke out in laughter and finally said; "Damn, you're a sight for sore eyes."

"No shit! When you stepped outside...."

"Don't tell me you put a pipper on my ass. My mouth was so dry I couldn't spit. I about shit myself, thinking the fingernail crap wasn't going to work, and you were going to shoot me."

"Not bloody likely!" Hunter turned back to the cockpit, reached over the side, brought out three bottles of water, and gave one to his partner.

McGee couldn't get the top off fast enough and literally poured the fluid down his throat. "You're a god!" Hunter handed him the other bottle and popped the top off his; the men shared a slow pull on the magical liquid.

"That fingernail stuff worked."

"You can't tell my girls."

"Understand that. No one has a need to know." The men banged half-empty bottles together to seal the deal.

After McGee finished his bottle of water he said, "There's ten suitcases. I'm not leaving without them."

In the faint moonlight Hunter could see he was dead serious. "How do you expect to get them out of here?"

"I was hoping you had some ideas. I could drive and you provide air cover, or something like that."

"Ok.... It's not like we're not spontaneous or anything. We got a truck and an airplane—with limited carrying capability. What does one of those suitcase things weigh?" A squirrel was let loose in Hunter's head.

"The WEPS are easily over a hundred-fifty pounds. The carrying cases another hundred; lead lined. They aren't really suitcases but more ice chest—beer cooler size."

Hunter pinched his eyes with his fingers. McGee wondered what Duncan was thinking. There was a sense of urgency to leave with the bombs and the logistics of making it to the Afghanistan border with ten thermonuclear devices of dubious stability was becoming more complex and difficult by the second. When Hunter next spoke, McGee couldn't believe what he heard and asked, "Say again?"

"What can you do with these suitcase devices?"

"I'm not sure I understand the question." He crossed his thick arms over his mighty pectorals. "What are you thinking?"

Hunter told him.

"You're insane! *Oh, hell no!* I cannot do that. It might sound okay on the surface, but I don't want to go to jail; I want to see my girls grow up. Duncan, this conversation never happened. We have to get the hell out of here and get to the border." McGee saw Hunter was still churning wild and worst-case scenarios or differential equations in his head. His idea was crazy.

Hunter asked, "Who said, 'Rapidity is the essence of war: take advantage of the enemy's unreadiness, make your way by unexpected routes, and attack unguarded spots?'"

"Don't give me that shit; that was different. No fucking way, Maverick." The big man shook his head, trying to exorcize the thought Hunter had planted between his ears.

Hunter stood his ground, then mirrored McGee's head pivoting on the skeletal axis. Both men shook their heads in disbelief.

It was impossible, criminal, insane. After a few moments of reflection, McGee began to see there was an element of...*genius* to it. "The answer to your question. It's a two-part process. You have to have a battery control unit for each and a control head—a programmer...for each. I only saw two BCUs and two control heads. Ten weapons total; one, two, and five kiloton."

"The control head, programmer, does what exactly?"

"It arms the weapon and allows you to program how it goes off. Timer, impact, booby trap." In the moonlight, McGee read Hunter's face and didn't like what he saw.

Hunter stared at McGee. It was instantly obvious they were at a crossroads in their relationship. McGee wasn't about to have any part of it.

"I can't be a part of that, Duncan. No way." He made motions to walk away from Hunter; he held his hands to his head as if to squeeze the poisonous thoughts out of his mind. Then McGee flipped around and jammed a finger in Hunter's chest. "Think about the person you are and who you want to be. *This* isn't you. *This* isn't the *man* I know, the guy who put his integrity on the line for me."

"Sir, I hear what you're saying. I think I just see our situation a little differently."

"Duncan, we don't kill women and children. I have no problems killing the enemies of America, but this I cannot do. I won't do it. I'm the only one that can arm those things and I won't do it. Dude, this boils down to your personal integrity. I can't think of a sadder moment in life than losing one's integrity. Everything you've worked for, everything we've worked for—you want to throw away, right out the door. For what?"

Hunter had little difficulty understanding the pushback. The issues between the United States and Iran were complex and many, but no one in government ever realistically considered dropping a bomb on Iran unless provoked or in retaliation to an attack. Strategic plans never involved the wholesale killing of civilians; that was the purview of terrorists. "Bill, this isn't the person I want to be but the situation screams out it...*should* be done. We're here for a reason."

McGee continued to shake his head, which telegraphed that he wouldn't help Hunter in his plan. Hunter didn't know how to arm the weapons, and McGee had drawn a line in the proverbial sand. He had the key to unlocking the bombs, and he wasn't about to give it to Hunter. The discussion was closed. It was time to move on and get the suitcases out of the country.

"Bill, I think I know a way."

"You've thirty seconds, and then we're getting out of here."

"What if we warned them? Gave them time to evacuate."

McGee stared at Hunter. Forty-five seconds passed before he blinked. Fifteen seconds later, McGee screwed shut his eyes and wished he hadn't ever said anything. "How do you plan to do that? We're in Turkmenistan. On a secret mission you know."

"Did your...escorts have cell phones?"

"There's a sat phone in the Land Rover."

"Well, that's even better. What do you say if we can get them to evacuate?"

"What's this 'we shit' *kemosabe*? I don't mind blowing up a bunch of fanatics in a hotel but I don't want any kids killed, even if they grow up to be tomorrow's terrorists."

"We give them several hours to evacuate. That should be enough time to get away."

"You can't be serious. Even that's impossible. I...cannot support that Duncan. I can't!" McGee hated Hunter at that moment, for allowing the genie in the bottle to escape, for allowing him to crack his integrity, for showing him there may be another way. If women and children could be safely evacuated, was that sufficient justification to reconsider initiating a world-altering event? He was close to hyperventilating. Reasons and excuses rattled around his cranium; he tried to find the magic words to put the genie back into the bottle. McGee put his hands on his hips and exhaled.

Hunter's eyes were calm but deadly serious.

"You're insane."

"I know."

"What's the plan?" As Hunter relayed his idea, it was McGee's turn to pinch his eyes with his fingers. "God help us. Make your call."

CHAPTER FORTY-TWO

Men and women jumped wide awake when the air raid sirens erupted in an ear-splitting, grating wail. Round and round the elongated horns spun atop telephone poles, sputtering 170 decibels of the deafening electronic-generated noise. Thousands of men and women sat up in their beds while children awoke and cried. Everyone waited for the sirens to stop the shrill screaming and listened for the spoken commands from the disaster alert system. They expected to hear, as they had heard for fifteen years, "This was a test of the emergency alert system," and then they would return to their pillows. This night was different. Never had the system gone off at such an hour.

What people heard galvanized them to leave the city. Traffic out of the city was chaotic with vehicles driving away from the heart of the complex, six cars abreast across the four-lane highway. Overloaded cars, buses, and trucks filled the roads.

The covert intelligence officer identified by the code name IRONMAN sent a burst transmission to an overhead satellite. He reported that the sirens had gone off at Natanz, Iran and the "giant voice" loudhailer system repeated, "Russian bombers are coming, Russian bombers are coming! Three hours! Three hours! This is not a test. This is not a test. Evacuate! Evacuate!" He signed off saying he wasn't taking any chances and was leaving the city with all of the other residents.

. . .

"I don't want to know! I don't want to know! I know I said I wanted to do cool shit, but now I don't want to know!" LeMarcus Leonard erupted from his computer desk and ran out of the back door into the night and flung his cellphone into the black waters of the Farmington River. When he came back inside the stationmaster's house, he went to bed and tried to sleep.

. . .

The satellite telephone buzzed, and the display screen illuminated. It displayed a meaningless number and four letters: DONE.

The word took his breath away. His heart began to pound in his chest. Hunter shared the message from the tiny display screen.

"Un-frickin' believable," snorted McGee, shaking his head.

In the glow of the illuminated sat phone screen, the men looked at each other. After several seconds of silence, Hunter asked, "You ready?" McGee continued to shake his head in disbelief. Hunter again stated the great Sun Tzu. "Take advantage of the enemy's unreadiness, make your way by unexpected routes, and attack unguarded spots."

"I can't imagine the unintended consequences of what you're contemplating. However, we're here for a reason and doing nothing seems to be the wrong answer. This might do something positive." He sucked another lungful of the thin night air and said, "Okay. I'm in, Maverick. Let's do it and get the hell out of here."

. . .

McGee rode the elevator down with his eyes closed. He knew which level to stop on by counting the number of seconds of his first ride. He entered the rooms with the suitcase nuclear devices and dragged them—two at a time—to the elevator. Ten devices, five trips to the elevator, two lifts to ground level; one exhausted, retired Navy SEAL.

Hunter dragged three very large stinking Russians to the edge of the open pit mine. Before he pushed them over the edge, he double checked the contents of their pockets and patted them down. He found a Makarov pistol strapped to the calf of the largest man. Hunter didn't hear anything when he pushed the men over the side, one at a time.

As he jogged back to the sound of the generator he thought of what McGee must have done to kill the men without a weapon. He didn't feel remorse for the dead men but did feel a level of pride and awe that the SEAL was on his side and was his friend. McGee teased him often about being an apex predator, but after seeing the man's work without a weapon, Hunter knew who was the real apex predator. When he arrived at the Land Rover, he found his equally spent partner resting across the hood of the truck and inhaling another bottle of water. Ten aluminum cases, reminiscent of oversized, high-end, aluminum video camera shipping containers, were neatly stacked in five columns of two. Hunter said, "You must have a T-Rex for a pet. You're an animal."

A physically diminished McGee grinned at Hunter and told him to drive. Hunter saluted smartly, just like a smart ass.

The men uncased two egg-shaped devices from their containers. Hunter used the lap belts and shoulder straps to secure the devices in the pilot and copilot seats of the YO-3A. McGee connected battery control units and controllers and armed both bombs for impact detonation.

Leaning over the side of the canopy rail, McGee said, "Just don't crash on takeoff, big boy." A part of him hoped the aircraft wouldn't start so they could abandon the idea. However, he thought of their experience in Liberia; when you are given an opportunity to do something for your country, you need to be a man, step up to the plate, and do it. Rescuing passengers from troglodyte terrorists was a no-brainer. He still wasn't sure about starting World War III.

Hunter stood by the side of the aircraft. He said, "Of the 4,000 men and women of our military killed in action in Afghanistan and Iraq, most were lost due to Iranian IEDs. For each American lost or maimed by Iranian IEDs, the ayatollahs and mullahs in charge deserve to be vaporized. They're hell bent to build nuclear weapons to launch an attack on U.S. soil or on our allies. If I could, I'd destroy all of their installations. If I could, I would lay Iran naked before its enemies for the next 500 years. Iran, under the mullahs, is an existential threat to the U.S. and the West. No one can or will do anything about it. What did Nathan Hale say, 'I only regret that I have but one life to give for my country.' If I go to jail, so be it. Only an idiot would stick around and not evacuate. Moms and dads will get their kids out of town."

"I hope you're right."

"You know the damned ayatollahs will give some terrorist group any bomb they build. What's been our mission on this program, to eliminate threats before they fester into something bad; something worse that 9/11? This has been our mission's charter."

It was a generally accepted premise across the world and in the intelligence community specifically, that once Teheran achieved the capability to make nuclear bombs they would use them. Iranian leaders continually threatened Israel, the "Little Satan," directly and by extension, the United States, the "Great Satan." The radical Iranian leaders lived for the day when they had a bomb to punish one of the "Satans." The Iranians were trying to develop or purchase a weapons delivery system, but with America's and Israeli anti-ballistic missile systems, the chances of an Iranian rocket reaching its designated target were poor. It was obvious to the intelligence community the ayatollahs would most likely rely on another delivery system. They would give any developed nuclear device to a terrorist group. The threat was real and was America's and Israel's greatest fear.

McGee's hopes of a mechanical problem aborting the impromptu mission were dashed when Hunter started the airplane. There was no going back.

Hunter programmed the Yo-Yo's flight computer and the aircraft's automatic takeoff and landing system. He knew where to send the airplane, to the Iranian city with the country's largest nuclear reactor and uranium processing and centrifuge complex. The YO-3A's satellite internet capability secured the coordinates of the target reactor. Programming the aircraft's route of flight for its one-way mission was accomplished in less than three minutes.

At idle RPM, Hunter was buffeted by the propeller wash as he closed the canopy and crawled off the wing. As he stepped away from the unmanned harbinger of death, he felt as if he was jumping onto a grenade to save some Marines in combat. *What doesn't kill you only makes you stronger. Maybe I'll only go to jail.*

Hunter dashed the negative thoughts and commented, "You have to love today's technology."

"When it works," offered a sarcastic and sorrowful McGee.

With the engine idling, tail wheel locked, and the aircraft pointed down the runway of the secret city, Hunter walked to the Land Rover. Holding bottles of water, McGee joined him at the front of the vehicle. Hunter pulled out his BlackBerry and tapped an icon to activate the line-of-sight program that activated the automatic takeoff and landing system. He tapped another button and dragged his finger across the small touch screen to advance the throttle to takeoff power. When the engine responded with the increased propeller noise, he didn't pause to reflect on what he was about to do. Two taps on the screen icon released the brakes; the aircraft accelerated down the runway, lifted off, and disappeared into the night.

· · ·

The Deputy Director of Operations had run out of his office, down the stairs from his seventh floor office, and into the Operations Center, which was already bustling with the fury of an anthill that had been kicked over. The initial message from the covert intelligence officer in Iran started a chain reaction of events—notifications at the highest levels of government and queries within the intelligence community— to determine the probability and veracity of the warning.

Previous warnings of a potential or pending nuclear incident had been the result of stalled disarmament talks, when the face-to-face discussions with the North Korean dictator would inevitably conclude with launching a missile over Japan's airspace. Trying to reason with the fat little tyrant was like playing chess with a pigeon that would knock over all the pieces, crap on the board, and then strut around Pyongyang like he'd won the World Chess Championships.

When dealing with the secretive and autocratic religious theocracy of Iran, it was like finding a new species of poisonous toad in a Peruvian rain forest—the small mullahs and ayatollahs looked harmless and peaceful in their cloaks and turbans, but they were mercurial and spiteful, and had an subtle lethality all their own. And they hated America.

A growing crescendo of landline telephones ringing, and senior Intelligence Officers barking questions or shouting directions into hand receivers lowered immediately when the portly DDO entered the Ops Center. Amid the chaos someone had mercifully squelched the ear-piercing alarm that indicated the entrance door had been open for more than a few seconds as a continuous stream of people entered or left the Ops Center. The most important of the group entered at a dead run; the less important walked out. Red strobe lights flashed along the ceiling to indicate top-secret materials and operational plans were out of their safes and being used at the fifty workstations. The men and women of the Crisis Action Team (CAT) had been through National Command Authority drills countless times with the on again, off again, nuclear tests or missile launches from North Korea. The rumor that the CAT had been activated for Iran and not Korea caused a sense of urgency and unease in their response. Iran was viewed to be many months away from deploying a mobile launcher and perfecting a warhead delivery system. If their collective analysis was off, this could be very bad.

When Corey Cook ascended the raised platform and center-most position in the auditorium-sized command center, the DDO said into the open microphone in the middle of his desk, "Let me have your attention!" The decreasing clamor and movement within the room were replaced by silence, stillness, and a sense of foreboding. Every person stopped what he or she was doing and turned to face Cook. He continued, "This is a real world event, not a drill. Here's the situation. The emergency warning system in Natanz, Iran was activated and their broadcast system transmitted that Russian bombers were inbound and that the warning wasn't a drill. They had three hours to evacuate. That's what we know at this moment. Your mission is to communicate, coordinate, and corroborate all relevant intel and analyses to this desk. My intention is to disseminate and direct that information to the National Command Authority and the White House Situation Room. Let me first have a roll call, and then I'll come to you for a SITREP."

A large rectangular electronic board continually updated the status of the agencies or offices that were present or on a secure line at a location other than the CIA Langley HQ. The DDO asked for all members of the intelligence community to check in—from the White House Situation Room to the Department of State. He informed those in the auditorium and on the telephones that he was the central authority for the National Intelligence Agency and the CIA. The DCI was deployed to the Middle East and would be coming up on the net soon. He also told the Intelligence Bureaus and Offices of the Departments of Homeland Security, Justice, and Treasury to stand down after the roll call; he went down the list of the other departments for their status and updates.

The DOD liaison was on the phone with the Pentagon, the DOD's Crisis Action Center was being flooded by generals, admirals, and dozens of colonels and Navy captains. As the office of prime responsibility for any U.S. response, the Secretary of Defense had implemented DEFCON 2 because the Russian military was the reported nuclear aggressor. The CIA and its subordinate intelligence offices were looking for the purported Russian bombers and other activities related to a nuclear attack.

DDO Cook called out, "Sit Room?"

A female voice from the White House Situation room calmly provided, "POTUS has spoken with the Israeli PM who reports that they have not—repeat, haven't launched any direct action. They also received notification that the evacuation order in the city of Natanz was preceded by 'Russian bombers were coming. No further information at this time."

"Thank you, Sit Room; NSA?"

"We back-traced the signals and commands that energized the emergency alert system and loudspeakers in the city. Preliminary findings, it looks like a bank in Teheran was the trigger point, but our analysts aren't convinced—first, it makes no sense and as such, it may be a hacker who knows how to cover his tracks."

"He or she use a loop?"

"First blush it does look like a Mobius Three Loop protocol; maybe one of ours but possibly European. Remote chance it could be a prank."

"Keep on it. NRO?" DDO Cook furiously scribbled notes.

"There's no evidence of any bombers or any airborne assets in the area. We've programmed an asset for a flyby. We'll bump it into the correct orbit for a close look in 20 minutes. We don't know what the weather looks like over the target as yet. Give me a minute!"

The DDO mashed his lips, grateful that the NRO would reprogram their most secret satellite for the crisis action team, even if the CAT event turned out to be a bust. Familiar with the capabilities of the very special purpose asset, he knew the NRO would be scrambling to repurpose the satellite and would be sure to check the weather over the target. If the skies were overcast, the mission would likely be scrubbed. The satellite's sensors could look through clouds, but for this flyby, they would need the high-resolution camera to provide a clear picture of the warned target. Cook yelled across the room, "NRO! Where's that weather brief?"

The African-American woman from the NRO raised her hand and said, "Cloud cover minimal—no factor for a flyby. Break, Break! Iranian missile batteries along the Turkmenistan border reported a single momentary radar hit twenty-five minutes after the hour. The direction, track, and transitory nature of the radar contact suggested a stealthy, radar-evasive type UAV, probably a single but possible multiple UAVs. They're of unknown origin. Our early warning system didn't register any low flying aircraft leaving Turkmenistan airspace and penetrating Iran from the north."

A rotund man who served as liaison from the National Security Agency raised his hand and spoke into the microphone. DDO Cook recognized the hand and told the man to report. "NSA confirms that a missile battery reported the radar ghost. The field commander stepped outside of his trailer just as an aircraft flew directly over his position. The officer reported he *felt then saw* a shadow of an airplane but didn't hear its motor. He insisted the aircraft was on course to penetrate the off-limits nuclear area in Natanz. The confirmed incursion crashed the switchboards in Tehran and Qom."

"Do we have that tape; can we analyze their data? Are we sure it's a drone?" The DDO looked about the command center for someone to provide him answers. Again, the NRO woman came to the rescue.

"We've a partial; the size of the signature suggested slow-flying drone, not a cruise missile, and not a full sized bomber. I'll flip it to you if you give me a destination."

"Got it. NSA, you've an update?"

"The country is in lockdown. The city has been evacuated. The head ayatollah called the Russian president and complained. Pilots were directed to scramble to their jets to intercept, but so far, nothing has launched; apparently pilots chose to evacuate with their families rather than attack the intruder. We're getting a steady stream of information and intelligence, much of it on open channels. Their telecommunications system has crashed. Updates coming. More to follow in three minutes."

The man from the NRO looked for an opening to speak and blurted out, "NRO can verify, no aircraft launches anywhere in Iran nor from Israel. Russia is likewise quiet."

The man from Office of Terrorism and Financial Intelligence at the Department of Treasury raised his hand. DDO Cook jerked his head to suggest the man come to him.

"I said you could stand down."

"You did, but I have a piece of information that might be relevant. I have a report there was an EFT between the Bank of Tehran and the Bank of Moscow for one billion U.S. dollars. It was pushed into an account for a Boris Nastakovich. It was just a strange...."

"That's probably worth the interruption. Thanks for the update." As he ran the Treasury information around his head—did it mean anything or not—a flash of insight hit DDO Cook. He asked the group, "Are we sure Russia is clean? Near East, who else would be capable of launching an aircraft; a stealthy aircraft from Turkmenistan? Are we sure the Russians have clean hands?"

The DIA woman raised her hand at her workstation. "I think I can answer both interrogatives. There has been no additional or spurious activity at any Israeli facility over the past forty-eight hours—nothing other than their normal patrol aircraft. At this moment, it looks like only the Russian air force could launch an aircraft from one of their bases—there's an unused secret city not too far from the Iranian border. And, it has an 8,000-foot runway." Dozens of people snapped their heads up to look at the attractive woman with the interesting observation. Then their heads went back down to computer monitors as they queried databases.

"That's very good and may be key. Someone get me a picture and a map of that secret city and put it up on the screen. Where's that missile battery in relation to that location? Are any ops underway in those local areas, and please confirm all of our IOs and U.S. personnel have been evacuated or notified." The DDO nodded replies to several who indicated their IOs were both notified and moving to safe havens or were at a location that wasn't likely to be impacted. He asked, "Are we positive only Natanz generated a warning; no others?"

Several men and women in the room responded loudly and in unison, "Only Natanz."

With one hand holding a telephone to his ear, a big gruff-looking U.S. Army colonel raised his free hand and announced, "SOCOM received a request for immediate airlift assistance at the Turkmenistan-Afghanistan border. Used an Agency code word. The 160th SOAR is inbound." The colonel knew the evening was going to get more interesting by the second.

DDO Corey Cook was shocked at the information and screamed over the din of activity, "Whose guy is that!? *Who's running that op!?*" As he scanned the hall of men and women with telephones to their ears or their eyes on a computer monitor, seeking an answer to his directive, he noticed immediately the line on the status board indicating "DCI" had changed from red to green. With no one confessing to having an IO in the area, he frowned and instinctively reached down and punched the button on his telephone system. He spoke directly and deferentially to the Director of Central Intelligence. After the DDO provided a lengthy brief and status update, to include the bizarre electronic funds transfer to the Russian billionaire, DCI Lynche thanked Corey Cook for his good work and asked to be patched to the White House.

"Belay my last! I've been informed the correct response to my questions is 'no need to know' so please refrain from any further references or speculation to any op in that area. The DCI is up on the grid, briefed, and updated. Let me go around the room again for your SITREPs." Cook was livid the DCI had withheld an operation from him, but he had an emergency to run.

In the command center, the fifty people from across the intelligence community and DOD panned their eyes to the big screens on the wall showing multiple images—satellite, topographical, climatic, physical, road, and several thematic maps of the Turkmenistan-Afghanistan-Iranian border area. It was human nature to wonder who could be involved in the clandestine operation and how that operation was related to the current crisis at hand. Just as the DDO was about to snap at the distracted men and women in the room, the U.S. Air Force officer from the NRO left his workstation and stopped in front of the DDO.

"Sir, ten minutes we'll have eyes on the target."

The NRO officer received a 'thumbs up' from the DDO. "Live video? That's exceptional. Feed it through for our board and make sure the White House is connected."

The DDO realized he had been standing the whole time, so fully engaged in the reporting and assimilation of intelligence gathering, analyses, and dissemination that he had lost awareness of his own body. He was standing; his feet hurt, and his mouth was dry from non-stop talking and shouting over people and machine noise. Images were continually being displayed on the many large monitors in the room. The shuffling of the pictures would probably have given a few of the older IOs a good case of vertigo had they not been heads-down, undistractedly doing their work, running their checklists during the crisis. For Corey Cook, a picture formed not on the wall of monitors but in his mind, and it puzzled him. The little voice in his head screamed, *If I had no need to know, then what the hell is going on? Is the DCI actually running his own operation? With the White House?*

CHAPTER FORTY-THREE

The only aerodynamically shaped satellite in the U.S. intelligence community inventory got a gentle nudge as it approached the North Pole. The culmination of the imagination of a long dead World War II Nazi space scientist and a band of American aerospace engineers, before the days when liberal environmentalists and other Luddites invaded NASA, the KH-10 reconnaissance satellite on its polar orbit obeyed the commands of its controller and reported its position. A puff of argon gas sent through steering nozzles altered the trajectory of the National Reconnaissance Office's most secret spacecraft design as it headed for a rendezvous overhead the Islamic Republic of Iran and the secret nuclear facilities of Natanz. All camera systems were activated for the specially programmed one-time pass.

As envisioned by its creator and as built by a consortium of aerospace firms, the *waverider* would subtly maintain its established orbit just above the exosphere 1,000km above the surface of the Earth until it was called upon to execute a "flyby." Supercomputers were programmed to "push" the odd-shaped spacecraft with stubby winglets out of its stable orbit to penetrate the thermosphere and ride waves of charged ions to an altitude of 100km, skimming along the Kármán Line for a series of high-stability, low-angle, precision panoramic video and photographs. Once the mission was complete, a small rocket engine would boost the waverider back to its orbit into the interstitial boundary between the Earth's atmosphere and outer space.

For Adolph Hitler, the waverider was a coveted unmanned spacecraft designed to deliver a single atomic weapon on New York City and Washington, DC. For John F. Kennedy, the waverider was a proof of concept design to carry cameras for closer looks at Russian launch sites, strategic airfields, and their secret cities. The KH-10 was very old, very complicated, and very labor intensive; but when you were dealing with the worst of the worst terrorists, America sometimes had to bring out the old stuff. When the intelligence community desired real-time intel, there wasn't a finer responsive resource in the NRO inventory.

Colonel Bong entered the National Reconnaissance Office's Operations Complex and asked for the location and status of the KH-10. A satellite controller sitting in a basement operations office clicked a few buttons on her monitor and responded into a microphone, "Penetration successful, approaching Kármán and the target."

"Status?"

Rising internal core temperatures during deorbit again indicated a potential problem. The controller had seen the phenomena the last time the waverider was activated. She crosschecked her twin monitors when, like before, the internal temperature indications began to decrease. The G-meter recorded a rough transition as the spacecraft passed through the Kármán Line. The electronic voice of the female controller announced, "More turbulence than expected. All systems up and programmed for multispectral view of the target. Camera doors confirmed open. On course and on altitude to intercept the target in five minutes."

The tall dark-haired colonel crossed his arms over his chest, his blue shirt festooned with dozens of ribbons, badges, and insignia. He knew standard satellites could only provide God's-eye views of targets—directly down from space. One could see the tops of houses, automobiles, buildings, and ships, but not what was under an awning, in a window, who was in the driver's seat of a car, or what was on the hangar deck of an aircraft carrier. The beauty of the KH-10 was that it flew so low and with its Hubble-like optics that it took pictures at a very depressed slant angle so that analysts could take, with acceptable granularity, the pictures the conspiracy theorists claimed the NRO possessed. How else could one read a license plate from space? The satellite had been used to try to get a picture of Osama bin Laden in his Pakistani villa, but the timing was always off. The NRO didn't bring the KH-10 out of hibernation unless it was an emergency.

The colonel jumped when the satellite controller barked, "Target locked on for flyby. Harmonic cameras and all sensors focused and running; decreasing slant range, five-mile swath. Sir, your pictures are on the screen."

Colonel Bong depressed the microphone key at his fingertips. "CIA Command Center, approach is from the north; target center position, full five mile resolution; main camera and all side lobe recorders active. Natanz reactor, center screen. Do you copy?"

. . .

In the CIA Operations Center, every monitor on every wall and desk displayed images of a large, brightly illuminated industrial complex of what appeared to be an operational oil refinery. The video camera focused on the largest structure on the compound. The unmistakable shape of a nuclear reactor containment building grew in size with every second. The Deputy Director of Operations keyed his microphone, "Roger. Contact; buildings but no people. Looks deserted...."

Then a microsecond later, every screen reverted to an electronic white picture. People all around the room blinked their eyes forcefully to get a different picture than the blank one they were seeing.

The expectation, from those with need to know access, was stunning live video as the satellite raced toward the nuclear complex. When the billboard-sized screen filled with white electronic noise, no one spoke in the NRO Operations Complex, the CIA Operations Center, or at the White House Situation Room. Eight thousand miles away, at the U.S. Embassy in Amman, DCI Lynche didn't have a monitor with an image and was concerned by the quiet on the other end of the secure telephone. He yelled into the telephone, "What happened?"

518

The long distance interrogatory snapped the suddenly silent men and women of the intelligence community out of their shock. They knew what had happened but were unable to articulate a single word. They believed they had witnessed the opening salvo of a new world war; one where thermonuclear devices would be exchanged. The DDO shook his head to reset his mind; he recovered his train of thought and, for the moment, ignored his boss. He mashed the transmit button and demanded answers of the colonel at the NRO. "NRO, what happened?"

Colonel Bong stared at the huge overhead screen as the southbound satellite displayed the ever-increasing aspect of the north face of the ever-increasing large reactor dome. He blinked, and then a white flash blotted out the image. Unable to comprehend what he saw or thought he saw, the colonel stood dumb and mute, disbelieving what was on the screen. The voice from the remote satellite controller announced, "Possible breakup of the asset. Right before we lost telemetry, there was a sudden spike in the temperature of the asset, and it's no longer responsive. Over."

Across the conference table two men exclaimed their dismay, which jolted Bong back to the present. He fired off several interrogatives and after thirty long seconds, he spoke into his microphone, "NRO's investigating; possible breakup of the asset. The asset is no longer responsive. I thought we may have had a surface EMP which knocked out the asset but that's impossible. I'm getting confirmations that we've lost all steerage of the asset; telemetry and imagery dead. Predict reentry and impact in the Indian Ocean. If that was EMP, I expect reports of GEOSATS affected. When I know more, I'll report. NRO out."

The DDO lifted his telephone receiver and spoke to the DCI. "Did you get that?"

Lynche, stunned, replied, "I did. So we don't know if anything was sent into Iran, or if it hit the facility?"

"I didn't see anything hit the reactor. There may have been something, but the low-level camera was just about to show us the other side of the reactor when it exploded into white. All we have here are blank screens. The NRO is getting other assets to feed data and overheads, and to see if EMP was the culprit."

Lynche asked uneasily, "Did anyone see an aircraft approach or hit the facility?"

"Sir, an Iranian missile battery near Turkmenistan border reported a single radar hit. Our analysts suggest it could have been a single or even multiple stealthy UAVs. Up until the asset broke up, we couldn't tell. The imagery was outstanding with optimum granularity, and complete analysis of the video is underway. They should have analysts looking at the tape. If we find anything I'll send you a response under separate cover."

"Thanks, Corey. That'll work. I'm going to sign off and call the President."

"Hold one, Greg. I'm getting a report of a major seismic event in Iran. U.S. Geological Survey is reporting a significant seismic spike in the middle of Iran; more details to follow."

"U.S.G.S. says there was an event?" Lynche was crestfallen.

"That's what our Interior liaison is reporting, but no specificity. There may have been a breakup of the satellite and there may have been a detonation on the ground. We'll know more in a few minutes. I'll maintain the CAT; we probably have another emergency to deal with. I expect DOD to go DEFCON One." Cook was exhausted and wasn't ready for the increase in threat condition. DCIs had a way of being out of town when the shit hit the fan.

Lynche said, "You can handle it. I'll give you a call soon. Thanks."

"Yes, sir."

. . .

President Javier Hernandez left the Situation Room and ignored his personal secretary's announcements as he entered the Oval Office, shaking his head, breathing deeply. He glared at the top of the Resolute Desk where both of his telephones were ringing. He sat down, read the screens, killed the ringers, and took the call from his CIA Director.

The President's dark-brown eyes were sad under his distinguished, perfectly combed, salt-and-pepper hair. The former reporter for a San Antonio television station was photogenic on screen, a bulldog in the field, and fearless in reporting. He made a name for himself investigating and reporting on the challenges the U.S. Border Patrol faced doing their jobs when the Democratic Party leaders, from the President on down, did everything possible to prevent Border Patrol Agents from upholding immigration laws. He ran for Congress and won the seat as the first Republican ever to represent his district. He was quickly elevated to the position of Speaker of the House. Under the threat of impeachment, the former President resigned and Congressman Javier Hernandez became the 45th President of the United States. Now he was on the spot, afraid a program to exchange Russian oil paintings for Russian nuclear bombs may have blown up in his face.

He sat quietly, his hands together, fingers touching in a point, and listened to the DCI without interrupting the old spook. Lights continually flashed on the telephone with new calls. The President of the United States noticed the red line—The Hot Line—from Moscow. The President of Russia was at the other end. He could wait.

"Greg, so now we've accounted for *all* the missing suitcase bombs?"

"Yes, Mr. President. Confirmed eight devices safe in Afghanistan, and our guys report two were neutralized. The Geological Survey suggests there has been an event in Iran; my deputy wouldn't say it, but it was likely consistent with a nuclear detonation. I believe we know where those other two went. I don't know exactly how it was done but I have an idea. I'll probably kill Duncan when I see him."

"Don't be too hard on him. Yet. He may have done us all a great favor."

Greg Lynche closed his eyes and slowly shook his head. He would kill Hunter later. "And, then there's the odd EFT of a billion dollars U.S. to Boris Nastakovich from the Bank of Tehran. I wouldn't have said anything about that, but since we were dealing with him it may be relevant."

The President pounded a pen on a tablet as he listened. "EFT?"

"Electronic funds transfer. Treasury reports it went to the Bank of Moscow."

"I don't know what to make of that either, but I think that's very interesting. Overall, Greg, I think that's fantastic news. If the city was evacuated and no one was hurt this may turn out to be a pretty good night after all."

Hernandez thanked Director Lynche for his update and signed off. The President touched the red button on the multi-button device, transferring the waiting call to his handset.

He said softly, "Good evening, Vladimir. Are you missing a drone, or is Boris Nastakovich trying to start World War Three?"

CHAPTER FORTY-FOUR

The upper deck of the Boeing 747 rocked with the electronic sounds of *Cream* blaring from hidden speakers. Disco lights reflecting off a rotating mirrored ball drew multicolored designs across the parquet floor, small tables, and overstuffed cushions. The dusty remains of lines of cocaine on small mirrors danced to the low frequency vibrations of repeated playing of *White Room*. Four semi-naked women writhed suggestively or twerked each other on the small dance floor.

Nastakovich felt like celebrating. He had negotiated what he considered the deal of the century. With very little investment, he had secured hundreds of pieces of priceless artwork. The KGB colonel that offered to sell him the tactical nuclear devices for a thousand Krugerrands was surprised to be paid in lead. It made Nastakovich smile to recall the look on the man's face when he shot the drunkard in the knees, dragged him to the edge of the mining pit, and pushed him over the side. He chuckled anew that he didn't have to move the devices or find another hiding place. And he had played the CIA brilliantly, getting them to reveal the location of the artwork and making the deal. He would exchange the other bombs for the rest of the art. All in due time. It was time to celebrate and enjoy the fruits of his labor.

He loved the beat of the old time American rock and roll. He envied the carefree sex of the American hippy and lusted after the bountifully augmented bosoms of the American women dancing merrily on the upper deck of his airliner. He partied nearly every night in his jet with his little harem of adventuresome women from New York City and Los Angeles. He banged hips with one topless longhaired beauty before stopping to take a drink, spilling over his naked chest the best vodka Russia could produce. The cool liquid made him laugh aloud, and his massive wet belly shook with sweat, booze, and spittle. As he leaned against the granite-topped bar in the middle of the jet, he smiled lewdly as a pair of bent-over blonde women ran lines of cocaine up their noses as fast as a third could scrape together the fine powder in a long shallow mound, reminiscent of the hump of a shallow grave. Another dark-haired beauty, clad in a red thong, spun around in circles and danced by herself in the middle of the floor.

Nastakovich was ready to move the party to a different level of debauchery when he noticed the red light flashing from his smart telephone sitting on the bar top. At first he ignored the device; he was having too good a time to be interrupted. However, curiosity got the better of him, and he leaned over to check the number. Through the alcohol and the drugs, he found enough functioning brain cells to remember the only people who had his number on that telephone were his friends from the Kremlin. It took several poorly aimed stabs with a very inebriated finger to activate the device and determine who was calling—his mentor from his days in the Lubyanka, now the President of Russia.

He shouted at the women to "quiet down" but they ignored him and another round of *White Room* reverberated throughout the aircraft. Nastakovich pressed the connect button to talk to his former comrade intelligence officer as he staggered down the winding stairs to find a quieter place from which to speak to his President. The connection went through halfway down the steps as he shouted a friendly but slurred, "*Da? Vladimir!*"

Several seconds went by but there was no voice, no answer, nothing other than the natural side-tone to indicate the connection was completed on the other end. He looked at the device and again asked, "Da? Vladimir, speak up. You've taken me away from a wonderful party." He slammed a fist on his chest. "You ride horses; I ride American models!"

The line clicked off; gone was the side tone in the tiny speaker. He slowly checked the touch screen and verified the call had ended. Nastakovich swayed and wondered what Vladimir...*the President* wanted with him. He started back up the spiral staircase, wobbling with every step. If *the President* wanted to talk with him, the old colonel would have to call him back.

The music crescendoed with every step up the stairs. At the landing, Nastakovich first looked at his bare feet and then found his three blonde buxom women, arms around each other's waists, singing at the top of their lungs in the center of the dance floor. Their naked pendulous breasts swayed side to side in an off tempo, "*At the party she was kindness in the hard crowd....*"

He eyed the women salaciously and staggered to a sofa near a bank of windows to ogle them, to arouse him, to admire the perfect flesh, and the handiwork of the best plastic surgeons of America's medical schools. His brain reconnected with the lyrics playing in the background as he looked away from the skinny white flesh in thongs and high heels before he glanced casually out one of the airliner's windows. His head bobbed to the beat; he patted his hand on the bulkhead to "*Yellow tigers crouched in jungles in her dark eyes....*"

Through the fog of bottles of vodka, there was a delayed reaction to what he saw outside the fence of the Kazan International Airport. Nastakovich was first amused then slowly taken aback as several vehicles drove up to the airport's perimeter fence adjacent to the small terminal building and shut off their headlights. He could barely comprehend what he was seeing. Was it odd or not? He laughed at the mechanical tigers crouching in the jungle of buildings and hangars, now with their dark eyes. *Were they watching?* He struggled with his own eyes; he blinked wildly and willed them to focus better on the darkened fence line. *Why did the tiger's eyes go out?* He laughed at his cleverness.

A steady stream of vehicles joined the others, drove to the face of the fence, and parked side-by-side. Headlights were extinguished when the vehicles stopped moving. Disparate thoughts congealed; Nastakovich sat still in his stupor and tried to make some sense of the activity at the airport's edge. The call from the President started to bother him. He hadn't seen this kind of activity outside an airport before, and it confused him. The President hadn't called him before when he was known to be partying. Like *Vladimir*, the Wild Horseman from Leningrad, Boris had dumped his mare of a wife and had a new filly to ride. Nastakovich again peered into the darkness. *Who's out there?*

Suddenly from a deep recessed spark of consciousness born from his survival training of forty years, he felt cold from his fingers to his large, bulbous, ruddy nose, and he shivered. A shot of epinephrine tried to burrow through his alcohol-soaked brain to trigger the hyper-arousal reaction response to the first hint of a perceived threat, but it was met with a firewall of bottles of Green Label vodka.

Are the tigers a threat? "*I'm safe in my jet!*" he boasted and tossed his arms to his side. He blinked spasmodically to help clear his vision and his thoughts. Between blinks, more vehicles arrived and lined the fence. He stared out the window, trying to comprehend. *What...is out there?*

The lone brunette with the pixie haircut unsteadily stumbled to the sofa and juggled her ponderous breasts in front of Nastakovich's small face to get his attention. He could barely hear her as she squealed, "Pay 'tention to me!" He shoved her away and ran in a drunken arc to the other side of the jet to another sofa and more windows. He mashed his face against the plastic transparent barrier to see more vehicles' headlights lining up on the other side of the airport before killing their lamps. Eric Clapton sang again, "*Tigers crouched in jungles, with their dark eyes....*" Tigers were watching him.

Something was happening—surrounding him—he sensed a growing danger, and he ran as well as a drunk could run without falling.

Nastakovich barreled through two nearly naked women as if they were a split of bowling pins and stumbled down the stairs to the lower deck of the 747. A minute later Nastakovich returned to the lounge with the pilots, pushing and screaming at them to get the aircraft airborne.

. . .

As the second engine of the 747 started, the Russian Army colonel tossed his cigarette to the ground and mashed it with a heavy boot. He radioed his commander that "as expected, the bird was about to flee its nest." The general at the other end of the radio stoically confirmed, "An enemy of the State cannot be allowed to leave. You have your orders."

Orders spread around the airport perimeter fence to prepare for an immediate aircraft launch. As the jumbo jet started its other engines and taxied to the runway, men dismounted from armored personnel carriers and offloaded thin wooden shipping containers. One by one, men extracted dozens of man-portable, infrared-homing, surface-to-air missiles from the containers. Officers passed out battery control units to each of the shooters; those that received the charging devices from their superiors jammed the BCUs into the handle of the weapons and energized the homing and firing circuitry. The shooters took up positions behind their vehicles and waited for the order to fire.

. . .

The Boeing's engines screamed at maximum power as the massive aircraft quickly picked up speed down the runway. After accelerating past the 4,000 foot marker, the pilots rotated the nose wheels off the runway and retracted the main landing gear just as the weight came off the main landing gear wheels. Feeling they were safely airborne, the pilot and copilot stared out of their windows, not sure what they were looking for. The pilot suggested the boss had too much to drink and the old paranoias were getting to him.

. . .

The takeoff lights of the aircraft extinguished as the 747 jumped off the runway and tried to climb as quickly as possible. The command from the colonel rippled down the line of vehicles lining the fence; the order to "fire" was given, confirmed, and repeated. In seconds, as the heat-seeking circuitry in a dozen SAMs acquired the thermal signature of the jet's engines, a cascade of surface-to-air missiles sought to overtake the slow flying silhouette of the Boeing as it strained to put as much distance between them and the ground as quickly as possible.

The multiple instantaneous flashes of solid rocket motors igniting stunned the pilot and copilot. Nastakovich realized they were being attacked as a barrage of missiles was released from the perimeter of the airport. The men in the cockpit mashed an oversized button in the middle of the center console as dozens of infrared countermeasures, magnesium flares, ejected from their canisters mounted in the empennage at the rear of the aircraft. As the jet ran the gauntlet of shoulder-launched SAMs, another dozen were launched and chased the white-hot decoys which fell below and behind the 747. The area surrounding the end of the runway was brilliantly lit up from the magnesium flares as the burning metal and exploding warheads turned night to day.

As more missiles were fired, more flares were ejected from the getaway jet. Boris was transfixed at the window and urged the big jet to go faster to escape the onslaught of the rockets with warheads. Cream was about to replay *White Room*.

When the Boeing's countermeasures ejector canisters were emptied, another wave of missiles chased the fleeing airliner's exhaust and struck the engines on both sides of the aircraft. A fourth wave of SAMs shot from the ground like bottle rockets and guided onto the red-hot engines now streaming fire from ruptured fuel lines. Several missiles ignited fuel leaking from the wings and with the suddenness of a balloon popping, the aircraft burst in an arcing white-hot inferno. A single shock wave crushed the airframe like giant hands smashing an aluminum can, and the fiery, twisted wreckage fell from the sky and crashed a mile from the runway, evoking another huge explosion as fuselage tanks literally added new fuel to the fire.

The colonel pounded out another foreign cigarette from a box and lit it. He radioed his general that the emergency response mission to prevent a bourgeois traitor from escaping justice was an unqualified success.

CHAPTER FORTY-FIVE

The video crew set up the room for a broadcast. The producer in New York City wanted a field report as soon as possible, preferably Eastwood's firsthand experience during the hijacking. Then she wanted a report on his findings in northern Nigeria and the status of the Boko Haram terrorists. Thin, tall, and gregarious, Karl Mann worked to establish a satellite connection with a collapsible dish clipped to a rail on the room's balcony. Light rain began to fall and he mumbled under his breath about probably losing the signal if the weather worsened. He tried to find comfort knowing they were on the lee side of the hotel; maybe it'd provide enough of a barrier to hold off the freshening winds which could rip their dish off the balcony.

Marty Marceau, Eastwood's long-time camera operator of multiple campaigns in Iraq and Afghanistan, set up backdrops and microphones and connected his earpiece to the mixer box. Khalid watched as Marceau set up a laptop computer from which Eastwood would read. News information, via email, was coming in from several subscriptions services in every quadrant of the globe. News of an Iranian reactor explosion hit all the major news services and threatened to kick Eastwood's hijacking and terrorism stories out of the news cycle, hence the sense of urgency to get his story on the wire before it was overcome by other worldly events.

A wall of the room was used as a backdrop. No one watching the telecast would see the bed and furniture piled in a corner to make room for Eastwood to be seen without distractions.

Mann stepped from the night of the balcony and into the bright floodlights of the room. Eastwood took his position. Marceau had the camera on a tripod and confirmed that the image was transmitting to the satellite nearly directly overhead in a geostationary orbit. Mann acknowledged they were receiving audio and data from the corporate offices; it was displayed on the laptop and synched with New York City network with only a three-second delay. Eastwood was experienced in the procedures for transmitting with the delay.

Colonel Eastwood entered the cleared space with makeup troweled onto his face to make him look "natural." He was in his field uniform of cargo pants and denim shirt. Marceau helped run the earpiece wire up the back of Eastwood's shirt and wedged the receiver into his ear. Mann counted down the seconds for the audio and video feeds; he snapped his finger and pointed at Eastwood. The video camera was rolling; they were live and transmitting.

Eastwood heard the question in the earpiece and responded to the late-night anchor in New York. She asked several questions about the harrowing ordeal on the airliner, and Eastwood fired back answers that were short and pithy. He played down any hint of heroism. When asked if U.S. Navy SEALs had boarded the aircraft and neutralized the terrorists, Eastwood responded, "Well, they certainly looked like SEALs—I've seen probably a few hundred over my career. One second they were there, and the next they were gone, scrambling off the wing."

"Were you able to ascertain how they got aboard the aircraft?"

"Can't help you there, Morghan. I'm just glad they were able to free the passengers and crew allowing us to continue to our destination. After they neutralized the terrorists there was so much excitement that it precipitated a spontaneous celebration aboard the aircraft."

"Thank you for that report, Dory. We're glad you and your crew are safe. Let's talk about the terrorist group, Boko Haram. Were you able to make contact, and what did you find?"

The audio delay was noticeable as he waited for the network's complete transmission before responding with the lines he had rehearsed for the previous hour. "We were escorted by the Nigerian army to the northwestern part of Nigeria where a number of villages had recently been devastated. The terrorist group had reportedly kidnapped several dozen young girls. While we were on the trail, we found some of the girls alone and walking home—but no Boko Haram. They told a harrowing story of their kidnapping—being forced into trucks by men wearing military uniforms and carrying weapons. They thought the men were Nigerian soldiers who had come to protect them from Boko Haram."

"But that wasn't who they were?" asked the late night anchor.

"Definitely not. One brave girl named Ellen explained that the soldiers gathered everyone in the center of the village where they separated the girls and then killed everyone else. When we found the girls, they told their story. Apparently, a rival tribe ambushed the Boko Haram and rescued them. When the firing stopped, the girls ran away."

"That's incredible, Dory. So the girls hadn't been... molested?" The question was tentative; a streak of fear in the woman's voice resonated as if she expected the worst but hoped for the best.

"I don't think so. The girls mentioned the men threatened to convert them to Islam and marry them, but someone intervened, and I understand from the one brave young lady the terrorists weren't able to consummate their nefarious plans." Eastwood subconsciously slipped his hand into his pants pocket to touch the bullet he had dug up; he fondled it like a talisman. He chuffed and thought, *Yes, someone intervened! And, I think I know who!*

He signed off with his customary informal salute to the camera and said, "Thank you, Morghan. Goodnight." Eastwood held his smile until Marceau terminated the transmission and drew his fingers across his throat to signal the video feed had been cut.

. . .

The television monitor switched from the image of a smiling Eastwood and instantly filled with the image of the perky blonde late-night news host in New York City. High power lights made the woman's eyes, earrings, and red lips sparkle, as if a star filter was mounted on the camera lens. "Thank you for the late night report, Dory. We'll look forward to your next report. We now have a special report from Washington, DC. We go to the White House where the President is set to deliver an address to the nation."

. . .

As thunderstorms moved into northern Nigeria and were racing westward toward Benin, Togo, and Ghana, flying for the night was out of the question. The embassy was closed, and the only place of refuge was her apartment on the compound. Kelly Horne still wore her flight suit, believing there might be a chance the weather would clear so she and Osbourne could conduct their scheduled surveillance missions. With thunder booming every few seconds, she was grateful the electricity was still on and the air conditioning was still running. Nigeria was hot and humid, and it was taking a long time for Kelly to acclimate. Her years in Southwest Texas acquainted her with heat, but not the stifling humidity.

She paused for a moment instead of clicking off the television she had been watching. She shook her head in wonder. *That was the man that shook Dad's hand on the jet. He's a reporter! And he's here in Abuja?* She returned her gaze to the TV to see the President of the United States at his desk in the Oval Office looking concerned and Presidential. She reclined against the armrest of the sofa and crossed her legs. She turned up the volume to hear what the leader of the free world had to say at such a late hour.

She sat up straight when the President said a nuclear incident had occurred in Iran. She turned up the volume again to hear the former Texas congressman say, "The world knows our deep concern about the Republic of Iran building a nuclear weapon and their stated objectives to eradicate the Jewish people from the face of the earth. Approximately two hours ago, a nuclear reactor exploded in Natanz, Iran. I've consulted with the Prime Minister of Israel and the President of Russia. The Israeli Prime Minister assured me that no Israeli aircraft

NO NEED TO KNOW

or personnel were involved in this incident. The President of Russia and I verified through our strategic assets that there were no aircraft in the area before the reactor exploded, suggesting the Natanz reactor suffered an internal failure. The United States has offered the government of Iran the use of unmanned heavy-lift helicopters to entomb the remains of the exposed reactor with concrete, and Americans stand at the ready to provide additional assistance. Since this incident explicitly appears to be an internal problem, the Russian President and I have agreed not to put our armed forces on alert. There will be more information in the coming days. The Iranian people will need our prayers as the Iranian government and the United Nations conduct investigations into this mishap."

Kelly muted the audio from the television with the remote control. In the sudden silence she became aware of the increase in the intensity of the monsoon rains outside her apartment as it pummeled the tile roof above and the concrete landing below. The rain wouldn't be an issue in falling asleep, and she was about to turn off the TV when an information banner scrolled across the bottom of the screen:

RUSSIAN BILLIONAIRE BORIS NASTAKOVICH'S PRIVATE JET PLUNGED TO THE GROUND IN REPUBLIC OF TATARSTAN. RUSSIAN AUTHORITIES INVESTIGATING.

The information meant nothing to her so Kelly got out of her flying boots and flight suit, turned off the television, and went to bed.

• • •

A furious storm raged outside the hotel as Dory Eastwood and crew huddled around the small computer monitor and watched the American President's address to the Nation. Marceau broke the silence in the room and asked, "What does it all mean, if anything?"

Eastwood answered, "It's more than a little unusual for the President to get so far out in front of a potential crisis. The fact that he talked to both the Israelis and the Russians tells me it was an accident and not direct action from the Israelis, who would've been viewed as the usual suspect. They didn't bomb the Iranian reactor. I would say I don't see that there's a story here, but I was under the impression reactors can't just blow up—I thought they melt down. Oh, well. I say it's late and time for us to pack our trash and get ready to leave in the morning."

Head nods all round approved the plan. Eastwood tossed the heavy bullet he had dug up into the air as he walked out of the makeshift broadcast room. The members of his team returned their equipment to their cases while Khalid returned the room's furniture back to its original setting.

. . .

Colonel Bong turned from the television monitor in his office to the computer monitor on his desktop. His fingers rested on his keyboard, positioned to type a series of commands to shut down his computer, call it a night, and go home. In the excitement of the waverider satellite being killed by an internal failure and not the result of the electromagnetic pulse of an atomic blast, he knew there was something he had forgotten to consider: all of the data collected from the flyby. The distraction of pushing—and then terminating—the real-time video to the CIA operations center was minor. The senior intelligence executives in McLean liked the video and liked to show clips and snippets of operations to members of Congress and the White House.

Bong rubbed his eyes and yawned; the action seemed to break the mental logjam in his head. *The President said it was an accident, but why was there a warning. I suppose the public doesn't have a need to know. An accident would've been spontaneous and would've killed the entire population of the city and the surrounding area. And then there's the issue of the blast. Reactors don't explode, because they're not bombs. Only a thermonuclear device could have destroyed the facility. There had to have been a bomb! It had to be! I can't be the only one to figure out the obvious!*

He scanned his office walls looking at the pictures of family and friends and memorable events, tens of "Attaboy" plaques from former assignments, the trophies, and the artifacts of an outstanding career coming to a close.

Bong was tired but knew he hadn't completed his work. He shook the computer mouse to wake up his sleeping computer. He inserted his blue-badge into the slot on the keyboard and logged on. As he accessed the NRO's intranet and called up the KH-10 Waverider files, he excoriated himself and whispered his guilt, "I didn't review the output of the other sensors."

As he waited for the files to load into his computer, he reviewed the destruction analysis report of the KH-10: Ever increasing heat, presumably from a puncture of the satellite's hull, burned through the outer heat shield to the electronics and then the fuel tank exploded. The timing was coincidental; not EMP. He shook his head. He wanted to retire with one last remarkable mission. It wasn't to be.

He reviewed the video file up to the point of the blast. He enlarged the final five frames before the explosion; he confirmed there was nothing odd or unexpected in any of the frames. He returned the video file to the shared folder and extracted the infrared file taken by the low-level satellite as it raced across the sky toward the reactor in Natanz. He reviewed the thermal imagery up to the point of the blast but stopped when he saw the white-hot image of a long-winged airplane approach the hotter white image of the nuclear reactor. Bong rocked back in his chair and stared, agape, at the single frame. The ghostly glider-like visage stunned him.

"What the hell is that?" The Air Force colonel ran long fingers through thick black hair. He'd seen that shape before; he called up another file from the last time the waverider had been deployed. He compared images and pounded his fingers nervously on his desk. With a click of the mouse, the images on the screen increased in size and decreased in clarity. He clicked the mouse like a madman with commands to send the images to his private printer. He held the papers with both hands for several seconds before he folded them in quarters and tucked them into his shirt pocket. Two more clicks of the computer mouse and the infrared files were deleted from the folders.

. . .

Bong drove through the NRO's main gate and waved at the gate guard as he always did. The passenger seat and the useless rear area were filled with the pictures and tokens from his office walls. He habitually pointed the nose of the pea-green Porsche 911 Turbo one last time toward Manassas, and for the first time since he acquired the 1985 "whale tail," drove under the speed limit.

CHAPTER FORTY-SIX

"*Sahib*, we must go!" The Jordanian nurse rustled Dr. Rothwell in his bed and again whispered, "*Sahib*, we must go!" Rothwell's remaining eye shot open with venom flashing from a deeply furrowed brow before relaxing and transitioning to concern, then compliance. It took two seconds for the former DCI to fully awaken and realize he was in danger. There wasn't time to debate or ask questions how the nurse knew they needed to evacuate their hideout atop the Marriott. Hopefully, there'd be time for that in the car.

It would take a harrowing two minutes to leave the comfort and safety of the executive suite, ride the elevator to the lobby, and walk through the portico to an awaiting car. Nizar half-carried the crippled man as they flew down the stairwell.

. . .

The taxi offloaded the four Americans in front of the hotel. The YO-3A's maintenance experts, Bob and Bob, carped and struggled to get out of the back of the van; seventy-year old backs and legs were stiff from the long ride from the Marka Air Base to the Amman Marriott. McGee stepped from the passenger seat and thanked the nearly terrified driver for the lift; the man had never seen such a muscular black man before. Jordanian men, by comparison, were thin and could have been snapped in two by the powerful man with the tiny glasses. Duncan handed the man behind the wheel—who jumped when Hunter nudged him—a wad of Jordanian dinars and then stepped from the vehicle. Once Hunter closed the door and was clear of the taxi, the driver sped away from the hotel entrance.

"I think you scared him," offered Hunter.

McGee responded with a half-hearted grin, followed by a long and energetic yawn. "He had plenty to say about the Israelis bombing Iran."

Bob and Bob stood quietly and listened to the men's exchange, hoping for a sliver of new information to answer the myriad questions running through their heads. When Hunter and McGee had suddenly appeared back at the airport in Kabul without the YO-3A, the septuagenarians sensed it wasn't a good time to ask where the airplane was. And when rumors swept through the MC-130 cockpit and cabin that a nuclear accident had occurred in Iran, the two old mechanics sat up and took notice of any gesture or signal from Hunter that would confirm what they were thinking. Hunter and McGee never showed any interest in the news coming across the airwaves. The Bobs had been with Hunter long enough to know that when something unusual was reported in the local press or the regional media, there must be a connection with Hunter and the quiet airplane. If Duncan didn't say anything, they weren't going to ask. They were paid to maintain the aircraft and keep the project a secret, not ask questions. But the loss of the aircraft meant their employment could be in jeopardy.

"He shouldn't believe everything he reads on Al Gore's amazing internet." Hunter smirked and chuckled. Bob and Bob couldn't discern if their boss was just being playfully sarcastic or was playing with words or *double entendres*.

McGee shook his head in amazement at what they had been through. Hunter, McGee and crew were exhausted from the previous twenty-four hours. After driving across unimproved roads and the open high desert of Turkmenistan, crossing into Afghanistan with an octet of miniaturized thermonuclear devices, Hunter and McGee were met by contingent of four black helicopters from the U.S. Army's 160th Special Operations Aviation Regiment—and a CIA officer.

Several aircrew offloaded the ice-chest-sized containers and loaded them aboard a pair of MH-60 Blackhawks. Another group of Army aircrewmen removed the spare fuel cans and rolled the Land Rover onto a cargo net and fastened the metal ends of the netting to a "long wire" external cargo pendant. In less than ninety seconds, the weapons were positioned and secured so Hunter and McGee had climbed aboard and buckled in. Soon they were airborne, with the trailing helicopter carrying the antique Land Rover slung forty feet underneath.

Once they arrived at the Kabul airport, the CIA man took responsibility for the containers while Hunter and McGee ran from the special operations helicopter to their waiting MC-130. In five minutes, the Hercules was airborne. Hunter and McGee changed into matching cargo pants and black long sleeve T-shirts. Soon they were fast asleep on the troop seats, leaving Bob and Bob bewildered and saddened that there was no discussion and no Yo-Yo to take home.

The Special Operations MC-130 departed to the south across the barren spit of Pakistan toward the Indian Ocean, avoiding Iran, and flying direct to Jordan across Kuwait and Iraq. Upon landing at the small Marka Air Base in Amman, the YO-3A's container was offloaded for sea shipment to the United States while the Hercules was rolled into a Royal Jordanian Air Force (RJAF) hangar for some maintenance by the onboard AFSOC mechanics—primarily a tire and brake change—followed by an aircraft wash. The dirt and grime accumulated from flying, virtually nonstop, from the U.S. to Africa to Afghanistan and to Jordan had been significant, and the added drag affected the performance of the big airplane. Once the aircrew and Hunter's team offloaded their gear, a hundred men from the RJAF swarmed over the aircraft from nose to tail to fix minor discrepancies, swap some parts, and scrub the airframe.

Bob Jones and Bob Smith interrupted a moment of silence to say that they would take advantage of the break in action to sightsee in Jordan; they looked forward going to Mount Nebo and Jaresh, and the iconic Petra. Bill McGee announced that after a steak, a beer, and a long sleep in a real bed, he planned to take the first jet to the U.S to return to his family.

Duncan Hunter was flabbergasted to learn Nazy was in Amman. He indicated to McGee and the Bobs that he didn't know how long he would be staying. There was an unstated sense of urgency and importance to maintain secure communication discipline; to thwart government eavesdropping software, they wouldn't make telephone calls. He exchanged abbreviated text messages with Nazy saying he would meet her at the Arab Medical Center after the crew stopped at the hotel.

Nazy had sworn she would never return to Islamic lands, and he was immeasurably curious to find out why she was in the Middle East and why the rendezvous point was a hospital.

As the van drove off, Hunter informed the hotel doorman he would need a taxi. Duncan shook the hands of both Bobs and McGee, and told them he'd see them soon. The Bobs sensed they weren't going to get any answers to their main question—*what happened to our airplane*—so they went inside the hotel and left Hunter and McGee alone under the expansive awning of the hotel. The two men stood, virtually toe-to-toe, and said nothing, but their facial expressions told a thousand stories.

McGee stretched and yawned. Hunter wiped a little perspiration from his forehead. "I'm not sure what's going on, but I'm headed to the Arab Medical Center. Nazy's there, and I don't know why."

"If you need a hand, anything, let me know," offered McGee. "Whatever I can do; you know...."

"I do, Bill. I think I can handle it from here. Thanks. And thanks for everything." Over McGee's bulky trapezoidal shoulders Hunter saw an approaching Arab couple, he in traditional dress and she in a black *burqa*. Knowing the sensitivity of the situation, Hunter turned his eyes and body away so as not to look at the woman.

With a flick of his wrist to wave goodbye, McGee turned toward the glass doors to enter the hotel's lobby and nearly collided with a huge Arab, as big and wide but much taller than him. The man wore a dull *thobe*, ratty sandals, and a white *keffiyeh* that covered much of his face as he led an asymmetric, slow-walking woman wearing the long flowing *burqa* out to the curb of the hotel. McGee offered several apologies to the man, hurried to get well out of the way of the trailing woman, who at one point, stumbled slightly and very nearly fell; the billowy black material of the *burqa* got in the way of her black trainers and impeded a quick recovery.

The Arab scowled at McGee, which McGee largely ignored; it'd take much more than a bulky scowling Middle Eastern man to intimidate the former Navy SEAL. As the woman in the *burqa* recovered from her near tumble, the man in the *thobe* continued to an awaiting BMW and opened the door.

Something struck McGee as odd; he stopped and casually observed the man and his woman, who seemed to be in a hurry to get away from him and into the safety of the large black car. He stood just inside the sliding glass doors, backpack and helmet bag in his hands, and watched the now curious and somewhat expedited actions of the Arab and his wife.

Hunter remained at the curb and turned to surreptitiously admire the coachwork of the Seven-series BMW that had pulled up to the curb. He recognized the tiny details of an armored car with a bulletproof windshield and steel deflector plates behind the grille to protect its occupants from small arms and possibly small-bore rifles. He smugly thought the quality of the workmanship was nowhere near as good as what his men and women produced in Texas. He heard the slap of leather on the tile sidewalk as the Arab and his wife approached. Hunter innocuously wondered who required such a car in the relatively terrorism-free country of Jordan. Hunter picked up on the flash of black material in the corner of his eye and, by the deference exhibited by her huge companion, knew immediately it was the Arab woman in a full body covering who merited the protection. Knowing the sensitivities of the Arab male and his possessions, Duncan turned away to avoid looking in the direction of the woman in black.

It struck McGee as odd that the woman under the *burqa* seemed to be staring at Hunter as she staggered by him and stumbled into the

542

rear of the big black car. That she was apparently fixated on Hunter's profile wasn't too surprising. Hunter was a good-looking man, and McGee had seen other women at the war college turn their head to watch a younger Hunter walk by before embarrassingly stumbling or colliding into something. Since Hunter took no notice of the odd events occurring around him, McGee shrugged. But he noticed the frail woman under the *burqa* had big feet as he turned and entered the hotel.

.   .   .

It took every ounce of energy not to scream or lunge at the man at the curb waiting for a taxi. Rothwell's good eye could see clearly through the *burqa*'s eye mesh, that his nemesis was standing only a few feet away from him. Bodyguards from al-Qaeda and the Muslim Brotherhood brought the BMW up to the entrance of the hotel. The nurse led the procession and Rothwell, still shocked to see Duncan Hunter in such close proximity, stumbled as he entered the vehicle. Once the door closed, the big black car drove away. As if the movement had been coordinated, a string of Jordanian police cars with light bars flashing, passed the BMW and turned into the hotel entrance just as the big, long, black car passed through the discharge security gate and departed the hotel property. As a decade of police cars rolled up to the hotel entrance, several tens of policemen poured out of their vehicles and ran into the Marriott.

.   .   .

Hunter momentarily thought the police were coming for him, but when they blew right by him, he moved out of their way to give them unfettered access to the hotel lobby doors. For two minutes, armed policemen in uniform, some with military assault rifles, rushed into the hotel or took up positions outside.

The doorman and Hunter were curious bystanders until a man walked up to the doorman. After some arm waving and shoulders shrugging, the doorman informed Hunter his taxi had arrived, but with the hotel entrance congested with police vehicles, he'd have to walk to the road to catch it.

.   .   .

Nazy Cunningham sat in the back of the embassy car nearly bouncing in the seat with anticipation of seeing Duncan. He had texted her that he would see her soon. She thought she would surprise him at the Marriott; Duncan always stayed at Marriotts. Minutes after leaving the hospital, she was concerned she might miss him if he didn't check into the hotel, or take a shower, or worse, took a taxi directly to the medical center. To ensure she would be able to surprise him, she had to find him. So she logged in to a special application on her BlackBerry—Find My BlackBerry. Ideations of finding Duncan in his room, preparing for a shower urged her fingers to work a little faster.

Once the program was activated, the software sent a signal—a "ping" to pinpoint Hunter's device. Three cell phone towers found the interrogated BlackBerry and triangulated its position in less than ninety seconds. Inside of two minutes, the onscreen messages indicated the targeted BlackBerry had been found and the map on the tiny screen displayed its current location—the Amman Marriott. Inside a half-mile to the hotel she felt confident she would intercept him at the hotel—maybe wrapped in a towel, maybe he'd be naked in his room—and cancelled the tracking program. She put her BlackBerry in the pocket of her *burqa*.

What she didn't expect to see was police vehicles flooding the Marriott's parking area. It would take several minutes for the driver to be allowed entry into the hotel's parking area, so she got out, raced up the slight hill, and entered the lobby. Amid dozens of uniformed police and military men, she saw Bill McGee sitting in the open-air restaurant, nursing a long-necked beer. She raced up the stairs and shouted, "Bill!"

The last thing McGee expected to see or hear was his name being uttered from a woman in a *burqa*. It created quite a scene when he realized it was Nazy; he stood just in time for her to wrap her arms around him. Police and military standing in the lobby frowned at the black man and the covered woman embracing; such a public display of affection from a covered woman was wholly unexpected and, in the eyes of a few of the policemen, illegal. In Saudi Arabia, someone would've gone directly to jail.

McGee avoided the obvious question—why are you wearing a *burqa*—and moved to break her heart when he said, "You just missed him! He took a taxi to the hospital to see you. If you texted him, he would've stayed and waited for you."

It was incongruous talking to Nazy through the material's eye slit. Her silver-green eyes were unobscured by the tiny slit of the head covering, and they were striking. Several times he tried to turn away, intuitively knowing she was in a *burqa* for a reason, and that reason, had to be to maintain cover. Now she was blowing her cover.

"I wanted to surprise him!"

"Well, text him—call him—and tell him to come back."

She nodded. She threw communication discipline to the side. Nazy tried Duncan's number but it just rang in her ear until it switched to voice mail. Even through the eye slit of the *burqa*, McGee could tell her emotions ran from being crushed to confused.

· · ·

As soon as the taxi cleared the hotel security gate, Hunter asked the driver if they could stop somewhere and get some flowers. The driver's English was good, and he was apparently agreeable when he said, "Of course" several times. The pleasant driver, nodding and gesturing with a free hand, hadn't driven very far from the hotel when he turned down a narrow road.

Hunter was unsure if the man was taking him to a flower shop or hadn't understood the request when the taxi driver swerved hard and smashed the brakes; another vehicle had cut them off and the driver's mongoose-like reflexes prevented a collision. Pinched to a stop, the driver mashed the horn button and began to rail at the other driver for his imbecilic maneuver on such a narrow street.

Duncan was thrown to the side of the taxi. He recovered from the sudden stoppage, steadied himself in the rear of the taxi, and assessed the situation; no paint had been traded between the vehicles and the taxi driver did what all drivers do when they're cut off in the middle of the road. He leaned on the horn, gestured like a hyperactive monkey, and screamed Arabic epithets.

When two men burst from the car in front of the taxi, Hunter realized the near collision was intentional and that he was the target. Adrenaline spiked his system and he instinctively shot to the opposite side of the taxi away from danger. He was reaching for the door handle to get out of the taxi when both of the rear side windows exploded. Hunter's momentum and attempt to escape was negated as he instinctively covered his head and face from the flying glass. He never saw the Taser darts as they slammed into his torso, one in his chest and one in his back. The suddenness of 50,000 volts discharging through his body involuntarily stiffened him; a primal guttural scream erupted from clenched jaws. As the first dart immobilized him, the second Taser dart—so closely after the first—nearly rendered him unconscious as his body again froze him in place. The electrical signals to his heart were disrupted and aortic valves, caught between pulses, were unable to move. When the men yanked Hunter from the back of the taxi, he shuddered uncontrollably as his heart struggled to return to normal rhythm. Two quick punches to his face finished what the Taser started, and Hunter fell limp and lifeless.

. . .

Nazy explained why she and Greg Lynche were in Amman, why they were operating in costume, and why her father was hospitalized.

McGee nodded and moved closer as he asked Nazy to try Duncan's number again. The relative calm and silence of the lobby and restaurant was shattered as policemen with rifles ran from the elevators and mustered in the lobby.

"Do you know why they're here?" asked Nazy, nodding her head in the direction of the reception desk where a collar of policemen milled about, waiting for their next assignment. Uneasiness crept over her. McGee sensed something ominous too.

They were in the intelligence community and sensed something significant was occurring in the wide-open lobby, but they had no indications why police would feel the need to invade the hotel. They did know it was totally unlike Hunter to be unreachable. He always checked his BlackBerry and never turned off the ringer or the vibrator, even when he taught class. McGee used his cell phone to try to reach Hunter; he became more worried than before when Duncan didn't answer his phone. Then he said, "He's on his way to the hospital. We need to go. You have a driver?"

Nazy nodded then, in a flash of inspiration, she said, "I had Duncan's location here at the Marriott before he left. I should be able to find him again. Track him to the hospital." She flashed her BlackBerry to emphasize her plan and started pressing buttons.

She explained the "app" on her BlackBerry, that it was a thumbnail bit of software designed to find missing smart phones when they've been lost or stolen. "I know it works; it had Duncan here at the hotel. I'm calling it now." She placed the device on the table and watched the layers of maps of Amman be replaced with another with more details, such as street names and the direction of the device. "I really did just miss him. This shows his BlackBerry is actually moving away from the hotel...."

"And...?"

McGee watched her shoulders slump under the slick material of the *burqa*. With her knowledge of her hometown, it was obvious the green dot on the screen wasn't moving where Nazy had expected it to be heading.

"Um, Bill, it's...it's stopped and it's well away from the medical center."

"That cannot be good. Let's get out of here."

Virtually every policeman and hotel staffer's head turned to watch the black man and the woman in the black *burqa* rush out of the hotel side-by-side, so un-Islamic. Like lab rats negotiating the labyrinth of vehicles and military trucks, they found the embassy vehicle. They jumped in the back and Nazy directed the driver to the address the GPS had indicated as the location of Duncan Hunter's BlackBerry.

• • •

Bruce Rothwell removed the *burqa* and watched the brawny Nizar strip the physically exhausted Hunter and haul him up to a crudely hewn wooden stock. Bright red circles marked where the Taser darts had slammed into Duncan's chest and back.

The Jordanian roughly inserted the American's limp arms into the recesses of the ancient torture device and slammed closed the heavy length of timber, trapping Hunter's arms and exposing his hands and wrists. He kicked the infidel's legs into place as if he were kneeling before the old bloodied stock. The big man viciously removed the stainless and gold Rolex watch from the prisoner's wrist and kicked the nude man's clothes out of his way as he left the room.

Hunter's BlackBerry rocketed out of his trousers pocket as his clothes flew across the room. Rothwell caught the arc of the device in the corner of his eye and retrieved it. He removed the battery to ensure the device was unusable and tossed the components onto a large table with numerous implements of torture.

As the door closed behind the nurse, Rothwell found the energy to viciously backhanded Hunter to rouse him. He poured a bucket of ice over the semi-conscious man's head and testicles and waited for the hyperventilating Hunter to gather his senses. What he had to do and say would require the Texan's undivided attention.

When Hunter was able to claw through the fog of pain, he spit out a mouth full of blood. Once he was able to focus on his surroundings, he despaired at what he saw. He glimpsed the tools of torture which lined one wall: chains, swords, knives, shackles, braces, awls, hammers, saws and pliers. All were hung from crude hooks made from coat hangers and rebar. Two black flags with white script hung on an adjacent wall; an old wooden chair sat between the flag's display. Hunter couldn't read Arabic but knew what the writing spelled out: There is no God but God, and Muhammad is His messenger. He closed his eyes in defeat. He was in a room where beheading videos were recorded.

Rothwell punished Hunter when he closed his eyes by kicking his exposed scrotum. Hunter vomited from the blows and that elicited another assault from Rothwell's only hand.

· · ·

As Nazy removed the *burqa*, the embassy driver drove through the upscale part of Amman per her directions. They stopped short of a cul-de-sac near Shara Street and the Prince Faisal bin al-Hussein Square where tourists and U.S., British, and Australian embassy personnel frequented the Western nightclubs and the McDonald's restaurant. Nazy whispered, "I once lived in the area, only a block away. We're close."

With Nazy occupied with her smart phone and the constantly updating tracking application, McGee resolved to be very quiet as he tried to think through what could have happened to his friend and partner. He assumed the worst; that somehow Hunter had been captured and taken somewhere against his will. Members of the military and the intelligence community were always told to be forever vigilant when in the Middle East, to travel in groups and avoid becoming a target. He assured himself Duncan was too good, too seasoned, and too circumspect to allow himself to be taken without a fight. But he allowed the creeping thought that it could still happen if the conditions were favorable. Even though the icon in Nazy's

BlackBerry demonstrated Hunter's phone had moved across town, it didn't suggest whether Hunter was dead or alive. He replayed in his mind every minor deviation from normal activity from the time they landed up until he left Hunter at the curb of the hotel. Policemen and militia rushing into the hotel was very odd, and the embassy driver knew from monitoring the police's radio channel that the Jordanians were mobilizing to capture some major terrorists reported to be hiding in plain sight at the hotel.

It may have been strange that the policemen in the lobby were either dejected or relieved, but there was no apparent proof that they had cornered or captured their quarry. There wasn't anything truly odd about the Arab husband and the *burqa*-wearing wife leaving the hotel...but there was something unusual in the way she stumbled, the way she reacted when she saw Hunter. *Why would she do that?*

It came to McGee as an epiphany—the woman in the *burqa* wasn't a woman but a man, and likely the terrorist the Jordanian police were after. Why and how would a terrorist have recognized Duncan Hunter? He wouldn't suggest the terrorist that snuck out of the hotel might be the former CIA director, and he wouldn't share his analysis with Nazy, at least not yet. He told Nazy to stay put as he got out of the car.

With worried eyes she said, "I've lost the signal."

McGee nodded and raced away from the car. He peered around a wall to get his first view of the buildings in the cul-de-sac. He scanned the target building for signs of watchers. He didn't like the area—lines of departure were too narrow and the field of view too wide—and deemed a frontal approach was too risky. The three-story house was too well-protected with a tall wall, and unlike the other compounds in the cul-de-sac, painted wrought iron pikes stuck high atop the concrete fence were prominently displayed to dissuade interlopers from scaling the brick and spike-topped barrier. McGee returned to the vehicle and quietly asked Nazy to put the *burqa* back on and wander into the cul-de-sac as if she were looking for a friend. He told the embassy driver, "Give me your sidearm."

The driver was incredulous. He turned to look at McGee and then Nazy and said with a hint of sarcasm, "I don't think so."

Through the open car window, McGee smashed the man's jaw and took the disoriented man's pistol from a shoulder holster. It was unlikely the driver heard, "That wasn't a request!"

. . .

Unable to lift Hunter's head for an unimpeded attack, Rothwell crushed Duncan's unprotected face with one of the items from the wall of torture tools, a set of unpolished brass knuckles. His aim was poor. The metal tore into the semi-unconscious man's cheek; the tissue around his eye was damaged and immediately turned puffy. Rothwell placed a hand on his hip and lectured Hunter for ruining his life and stealing his woman. "I wanted to see your face as I screwed your precious Nazy Cunningham and made her beg me to release you."

Hunter spat blood and slurred, "You couldn't keep your dick in your pants and you blame me? Typical liberal trash. Aren't you a Muslim? I thought you hated women and liked boys. Or are you into camels?"

Rothwell became enraged and again kicked Hunter in the groin. Hunter cried out from the spike in pain but didn't lose consciousness as he had hoped. Rothwell again pounded Hunter's face with his brass-knuckled fist until the solid metal device fell from his exhausted hand and clattered to the floor of the torture room. He was breathing hard, nearly hyperventilating with hate. He was pleased with his work. After a few quiet minutes of rest, Rothwell sidled up to the bloodied wooden stock and whispered, conspiratorially, "I know you released the President's file. Your whore gave it to you."

Hunter spat blood through loose teeth, "Fuck you." He was exhausted and couldn't raise his head.

Rothwell laughed sinisterly, "It's time, *Maverick*, you thief."

He pushed off from the bloodied Marine pilot. Rothwell staggered across the room and around the narrow worktable with a fiery Bunsen burner in the middle. He retrieved a sword from the wall. His strength grew with every new drop of adrenaline flooding his system; he felt the vestiges of an erection coming on. Rothwell overacted as he checked the weapon's weight and feel in his hand; its heft and balance excited him more each second. As he moved back toward Hunter in the stock with hands exposed, Rothwell recited from the Qur'an. "As for the thief, amputate their hands in recompense for what they committed as a deterrent from Allah. Allah is exalted in might and wise. *It's time to punish this infidel!*"

The words rang in his ears like claxons. Hunter hoped to be unconscious when the blow came. As blood dribbled from his mouth and cheeks, he regretted his failure. He closed his eyes and waited for the killing blow.

. . .

McGee instructed Nazy to wail for her cheating husband as she entered the cul-de-sac. He ran around to the rear of the compound and scaled a corner of the back wall. When he dropped inside the brick fence, he could hear Nazy screech, "*Waleeeeed! Waleeeeed!*" He hoped she would be enough of a distraction to bring any watchful eyes from the rear of the building into the cul-de-sac. Finding a control panel to open the garage atop an L-shaped pole, he pressed the solitary button and the roll-up door of the garage began to rise. With the Glock leading his way, he cautiously descended and entered the underground garage.

He had slipped the safety off the pistol and his senses were immediately hypersensitive. He smelled gas, cigarettes, and soap when he entered. There were luxury cars on both sides of the garage. He checked the hood of a familiar BMW 750 for heat and confirmed it was still hot to the touch. Across the expanse of the garage, over the clicking and clacking sounds of the cooling BMW engine, he thought he heard a muffled cry followed by a voice. He moved toward the sounds and passed an open area with a drain. A rolled up hose hung on a peg and several buckets, brushes, and containers of soap sat around it. After a few more steps, McGee jumped when the compressor of a commercial icemaker kicked to life. He surmised someone washed the cars of the building in the basement garage, and the water source used to wash vehicles also supplied the icemaker for the building's residents. For a second he wondered if he had entered the correct building but the warmth of the BMW reminded him he had to be correct.

In the darkest and deepest part of the garage, he found a door and tried the knob. Locked. He placed his ear to the door and could hear a man speaking, reciting from the Qur'an. McGee didn't recognize the words but knew he had to act. He stepped away from the door and rammed it with all of the strength in his body, leading with his left shoulder and followed with the Glock in his right hand. The hinges held but not the latch; the door flung open with the fury of a small explosion of shattered wood. When McGee recovered, his eyes were instantly drawn to the center of the room. As in a slow motion movie, he saw Hunter's hand being severed by a downward slashing sword. Both hand and sword fell to the ground. With wide eyes he saw, two perfectly sliced white bones, the ulna and the radius, before the meaty stump spurted blood all over the stock and onto the floor.

A shocked Bruce Rothwell staggered from the exertion of cutting off the hand of the thief and turned toward the sound of the door being ripped from its latch. McGee raised the Glock and shot the bent-over man in his good eye three times with three rapid pulls of the trigger. As Rothwell's lifeless body fell over, his trephinated skull smashed apart on the concrete floor.

Moving as a man possessed, as the life of his friend spilled onto the floor, McGee pocketed the weapon and pushed out the pin holding the upper part of the stock in place. He grabbed Hunter's bloodied arm and with a powerful grip, crushed the stump to stop the bleeding. With his other hand, he ripped off his belt and wrapped it tightly around the truncated forearm as a tourniquet. Once the unconscious Hunter was freed, McGee tossed him onto his back as if he were a child's backpack. His heart pounded like a jackhammer as he reached down and retrieved his friend's hand, the fingers limp, and the wrist leaking blood. The hand was grey and lifeless.

Before McGee stepped out of the torture chamber and into the garage, he recovered Hunter's watch and BlackBerry and slid them into a pocket. With Hunter on his back, he kicked a wash bucket toward the icemaker and filled the bottom of the container with ice cubes. He placed Hunter's severed hand atop the ice and then shoveled two more scoops of ice to top off the bucket. He ran up and out of the subterranean garage, the pistol leading the way.

McGee pressed the button on a gate opener just outside the garage, and the tall wide gate swung open to the cul-de-sac. He dashed to the corner where the embassy car was waiting.

Nazy first heard, then saw the compound's gate opening. From the light of a single streetlamp, she saw McGee emerge from the swinging gate with a naked man on his back. She lifted up the sides of her *burqa* with both hands and ran after him. As she converged on the two men and the embassy car, Bill McGee barked at her, "*Get in, get in!*"

CHAPTER FORTY-SEVEN

Duncan Hunter was barely conscious, wobbling on the edge between being fully alert and dropping back into the deep sleep of anesthesia. He chose to drift back into more sleep. The recovery nurse wouldn't have it. It was time for him to awake up and show her he was out from under the influence of the sleep-inducing drugs. She shook him and patted his bruised and sutured face with a cool terrycloth. "I'm awake," he slurred. He wasn't happy to leave his happy sleepy place. His mouth was dry and sore as if something hard and nasty had been shoved down his throat. He didn't want to wake up; he didn't want to face the nightmare awaiting him.

Hunter wasn't like most men coming out of anesthesia. He wasn't belligerent or vituperative or combative. He just wanted to get the hell out of the hospital. When asked later, he couldn't remember any conversation in the post-surgery recovery room or even being moved to a room. After sixteen hours of surgery, he'd be impaired a little while longer.

He grew more aware of his surroundings. Soft murmurs of electronics and hydraulics, beeps and pumps, scurried in and out of earshot. His chin remained rooted on his right shoulder, as if his subconscious commanded the somatic cortex to ensure he couldn't see the damage on his left. At first, the noises seemed random ambiguous and capricious, but then he noticed incremental increases in clarity. Olfactory glands suddenly picked up the scents of astringents and alcohol; a growing current of cinnamon reminded him of Nazy. He remembered passing an airport Cinnabon shop and thinking of her. The spice's aroma always made him think of her, and that always made his knees weak. As best as he could muster in his weakened capacity, he took in a lungful of the glorious aroma.

Then he heard. People. Maybe...people. Maybe...talking. Maybe people...walking. He sensed he wasn't alone but didn't recognize any of the background sounds. He was used to the cacophony of jets and airplanes, of turbofans and turboprops, but not hospital noise. He began to decipher words, and then voices; one of the voices confirmed his suspicions. Maybe he could remain asleep, hide and listen. He caught his breath when he thought her voice was near, that *sezy* British voice. She was with him. *What will she say?*

He struggled to open heavy eyes. He tried to move; he felt cramped and stiff, and it was difficult to take a full breath. It felt as if Bill McGee was sitting on his chest. His mouth was dry and thick; he tried to swallow. His throat was sore, and he didn't know why. Then he heard Nazy...Nazy's voice. He felt pressure on his fingers and hoped it really was her.

When he opened an eye, things were blurry, as if waxed paper covered his pupil. More movement and sounds filled his ears. He tried to respond to the sultry British voice. He sighed and croaked through dry lips, "That...must...have...hurt...."

Those surrounding the hospital bed glanced nervously at each other. Their collective inhalations of breath nearly sucked all of the available air out of the room. No one could speak; no one dared to say what was on their minds.

Another crusty eye tried to open through lids puffy from Rothwell's brass-knuckled blows. Nazy's blurred face hovered over him as her smile improved by the millisecond. He blinked away the gritty membrane covering his eyes. It was getting easier to breathe and move and see. He struggled to finish, "...when you... fell from heaven."

Her pinched smile turned to a clenched jaw as Nazy wept.

Bill McGee patted Hunter's feet; he chuckled and said, "He'll be ok."

Greg Lynche, arms crossed, shook his head in disbelief. "What he is, is incorrigible."

Nazy Cunningham wiped a flood of tears away with her sleeves.

Hunter gained strength and clarity with every breath. "Kiss me. I need therapy. Systematic doses, repeated several times a day. And, some water." He still wouldn't look left and chose to focus on the people to his right.

Nazy kissed him ferociously said, "Hey, Baby, I love you."

He closed his eyes with a feeble attempt at a grin. "You better." When he opened them again, he asked, "Where am I?"

"Arab Medical Center," said Lynche. McGee smiled broadly as he stood with arms crossed across his chest like a proud father.

"Please...tell me...I'm in the Hand Clinic."

McGee and Lynche exchanged confused glances. Nazy smiled broadly and nodded vigorously. She remembered his story. She cried. "Yes, Baby. You're in the Hand Clinic."

"So I take it I still have a hand?"

"Yes. Bill saved your ass and saved your hand," said Lynche. He didn't know whether to scowl or be happy.

Hunter slowly moved a heavy head to see the beer keg-sized bandage and clear tubes attached to his arm. He turned away and said, "Thank you, Sir, Bill. You're amazing." Hunter raised a hand, heavily taped with IV tubes, to take and shake McGee's. Tears pooled in Hunter's eyes.

McGee's rich voice boomed, "Gave me a scare, Maverick."

"I didn't think anything could scare you." Hunter re-gripped the big man's thick fingers. He mouthed, *Thank you* as McGee smiled, pulled away, and stepped back to allow Nazy and Lynche to have some time with Hunter.

As Nazy took Hunter's good hand, McGee couldn't say what he was thinking, so he let the compliment dissolve on its own accord. *I almost saw you bleed out; die right in front of my eyes. We were very lucky; very, very lucky. It wasn't your time to die, my friend. And, you weren't going to die on my watch.*

Lynche sensed it'd be a good time to change the subject. He had so much pent up frustration because of Hunter that he wanted to scold

NO NEED TO KNOW

him and yell at him. The unauthorized rescue of the jumbo jet could be excused, mitigated, and he could close the case file on that effort with a medal and possibly a reward. Sending thermonuclear devices into Iran was the last straw.

Duncan, the Maverick, had become lawless; he was judge and jury unto himself. He had morphed into a renegade, *a maverick*, and his actions over the past month were clearly out of bounds. He would have his clearances pulled and have him kicked off the program; but those actions would wait until they returned to the United States. It'd be unseemly to unload his total dissatisfaction and disappointment with him in this condition. Lynche tried to offer something positive to shunt the negative feelings he was dealing with. "You're lucky, Duncan. I understand your micro-surgeons were trained at Harvard."

Nazy brightened and concurred, "The Hand Clinic has the finest hand surgeons in the region." She nodded and sought reciprocation from Duncan. He could barely take his eyes off her.

At first, Duncan didn't respond, as if he hadn't heard or was thinking of something else. Finally, he asked, "I hope those Harvard-educated doctors put the thing on right—are you sure they have the thumb going the right way?"

McGee grinned; Nazy largely ignored the comment and touched Duncan's face. Lynche had had enough; it wasn't the time or place to pop off at him, but he had one more thing he wanted to say.

"You definitely know how to win friends and influence people. I understand they dumped a half-dozen units of blood in your ass. I think you can now say you have the blood of the Prophet Mohammed running through your veins. What do you think of that?"

McGee and Nazy looked at Lynche with confusion and concern and then at Hunter as they awaited his response. Several introspective seconds passed before Duncan asked, "*Allahu Akbar?*"

McGee chuckled and Nazy frowned while the Director of Central Intelligence reached for Hunter's good hand and squeezed. "Maverick, you're too damn much. I'm glad you're okay. I have to return home—somehow a reactor blew up. The President wants you home as soon as you're able to travel. Bill and Nazy can stay here until you are released." He looked at Nazy and continued, "I think it's extremely dangerous for all of us to be here. There may be another attempt, and if they think Nazy is here as well, well..., you get my drift. The King has his personal security detail in the hospital, just for us. Try not to embarrass me; I'm out of favors."

"Thank you, Greg."

"If you were able to travel now, we'd be on a jet. The doc said a day or two. Nazy needs to be with you. Bill can take care of himself. Obviously." Lynche released Hunter's hand and pointed at him. "We'll debrief when you're able. Get some rest."

Bill McGee came around the bed, gripped Hunter's hand, and gave it a little shake just as the nurse entered the room and announced the patient must sleep. McGee released Hunter's hand, reached into a pocket of his cargo pants, and said, "Oh, I almost forgot, I think these belong to you."

Nazy and Lynche turned to look at the McGee. He tossed Duncan's BlackBerry and Rolex watch at the foot of the bed. McGee touched his fingers to his brow in a salute.

Hunter nodded and shifted his eyes to the nurse and followed her as she moved around to the left side of the bed to his elevated and heavily bandaged arm. He focused on the tips of his fingers poking out from thick cotton with oxygen sensors affixed to confirm circulation.

A suppressed and garbled thought bubbled up past the last of the anesthesia. As Lynche and McGee turned to leave, Hunter's voice stopped them. "You need to find the nurse."

Lynche stopped, turned, and blinked. "What do you mean? Your nurse is right here."

Hunter's voice croaked. "Not my nurse. Rothwell's nurse. He would've been with Rothwell during the entire time. He probably knows about all of the plans and Rothwell's playmates. Maybe even the release of the file." Lynche, McGee, and Nazy exchanged concerned glances; would he blurt out other secrets? Duncan continued, "You need to get to him before someone else catches up with him."

Lynche added, "There wasn't anyone home when the police raided the safe house."

Hunter nodded in understanding as Lynche and McGee turned and left the room. The nurse injected a syringe of clear liquid into an access port on the IV tubing. "This will make you sleep." After she checked Hunter's bandages, monitor connections, and blanket, she left.

Nazy held his hand tight and leaned in close, their noses almost touched. "I was so afraid I lost you," she whispered. Sensing she would lose him to sleep, she talked quickly. "I also know about Kelly; I think I know why you couldn't tell me. She doesn't know about this, but I'm going to tell her you're okay."

"Baby, I'm sorry…I just couldn't say anything. You'll have to tell me how you met."

"I will." He held her hand tight. The shame of not being able to tell her he had a daughter rose up like a tsunami and crashed in an outburst of tears. For several seconds, Nazy patted his hand lovingly until he calmed.

Hunter's breathing started to be affected by the drugs injected into his IV. He struggled to maintain his awareness. He wasn't ready to go. He had so many questions to ask. "Baby. Why are you here? In Amman?"

"My father was poisoned, and Greg thought I needed to be here. Greg saved his life."

"You're incredible. Very brave…."

"I know." Tears welled in both eyes. "Bill was the real incredible one."

"I thought…I wouldn't see you…again. I thought…I thought I was dead." He closed his eyes and took large breaths. She could tell he was about to shut down.

"I love you, Baby," she said, holding his good hand tight.

"I love…you…Nazy…*Cunning…hammm….*"

EPILOGUE

July 4, 2013
Fredericksburg, Texas

Nazy slipped from the bed and padded to the bathroom leaving Hunter flat on his back and grinning like an old fool, just as she had found him. He insisted he'd be okay; she wasn't convinced it was safe and was afraid she'd hurt him. In the end, she was correct in her assessments, but he wasn't about to admit the limits of his discomfort.

He rolled his head to the side to watch her nakedness disappear around the corner of the bedroom to start the shower. The master bedroom's ceiling fan had nearly succeeded in dissipating the scent of their sex, and he took one last lungful before it completely vaporized. Hunter let his eyes drift back to the source of his discomfiture and sighed.

The Army hospital in San Antonio had built an apparatus, like a truncated bicycle frame, with two rigid tubes attached to his hip to elevate and stabilize his reattached hand. Hoses, needles, and electrodes were attached to various parts of his arm, hand, and fingers, pumping drugs and sending stimulating voltages to speed healing and expedite the recovery and usefulness of his hand. Quietly and privately, he joked that he knew what Frankenstein had gone through and what it felt like to be put back together, although he didn't recall the monster having a girlfriend who would ride him despite looking like he had been in a severe bicycle accident. *What doesn't kill you makes you stronger.*

Hunter was getting stronger, and he smiled thinly at the thought of how far he had come. He still had a long way to go, but there was significant progress according to the medical staff. He had surprised his physical therapists by moving his fingers and thumb slowly but fully. He was months away from having a grip. They promised him that would come with time.

He sat up and swung his feet off the bed. He checked his fingertips through the splint. Once a dull grey, the coloring in his hand had nearly returned to his usual pale shade of mahogany. The wrist, the site of the attack, still hurt like hell, but under the splint, some feeling was returning to his palm. The pain wasn't bad so Hunter had stopped taking the painkillers.

He could hear Nazy singing *sotto voce* in the shower. He disconnected the electrodes from his hand and moved to the edge of the bed with the bicycle contraption still strapped to his waist, in anticipation of Nazy coming to get him for his shower.

Hunter recalled the life changing events of the previous month. His continual introspection into how he could have been ambushed without seeing any of the warning signs forced him to face a series of uncomfortable truths. He had been so distracted and desirous of seeing Nazy that he had simply missed the warning and danger signs, even when they were right in front of his face. It was much like a homeowner who can no longer see that their garage is full of crap. They simply ignore the clutter. He ignored the subtle signs.

At first, he wanted to believe that he couldn't have done anything differently. However, the answer was right in front of him. When you're in the intelligence community, you have to stay true to the intelligence protocols; play it straight and never let your guard down. If or when you do, it's only a matter of time before your stupidity kills you. And, if you're acting like a dog in heat, or you think you can skirt the law by going outside the boundaries set by the mission planners or by breaking the long established protocols, you should consider yourself lucky you only lost a hand, albeit, temporarily. After working so hard to get to that unique place of "special trust and confidence" reserved for the best of the intelligence community, he had wandered off the reservation by sending weapons of mass destruction into Iran. He was partly ashamed, not proud, of what he had done. He nearly lost his life for his arrogance. After having some time for reflection, Hunter was sure his next bed would be in the basement of the Federal Penitentiary at Fort Leavenworth. He felt he deserved nothing less.

He had been surprised at not waking up in a federal prison. He was also surprised at the number of people who had visited him at Walter Reed National Medical Center. Just hours after leaving Jordan, when he wasn't in any shape or mood to have visitors, a troop of severely wounded soldiers, largely amputees from Iraq and Afghanistan visited him. Hollywood and country music stars and a spate of conservative politicians popped their heads in his room and offered their encouragement. They all thanked him for his service. Most remarked he was the oldest wounded warrior they had ever seen. Some visitors wondered why there was no name on the Intensive Care Ward door; why he wasn't introduced. For some it didn't matter. It was understood he was "one of those guys," one of the special operators from the Agency or SOCOM; one of the guys "at the pointy end of the spear." A dude with a clearance, special trust and confidence, and all that James Bond stuff. They needed encouragement and support too.

Leading the pack of well-wishers was the President of the United States. He visited injured troops in the many wards and detoured for several minutes to spend time with Hunter. After kicking the Secret Service out but leaving the Director of Central Intelligence in the room with his ever-present "Growler" anti-eavesdropping device, President Hernandez shook Hunter's good hand. He commended Duncan for finding the lost Russian art and Nazi gold, for rescuing the passengers of the Nigerian jumbo jet, and for recovering the missing suitcase nuclear weapons. The President wouldn't let go of Hunter's free hand which was hooked up to an IV and monitor cables. With an unvarnished politician's smile he said, as if it were a compliment, "Duncan, you look like hell. Some men in this world are born to do unpleasant jobs for the rest of us. You are one of those guys, someone who has been places and done things no one will ever know about. The Iranian 'accident' has set their plans back for decades. For that effort alone, the American people will be forever in your debt. Please know I'm very grateful knowing you're going to be okay."

Although lightly sedated, Hunter got emotional as he thanked the Chief Executive.

The President informed him of the unintended consequences of the reactor incident in Iran. The reported accident had been the catalyst for the overthrow of the mullahs and ayatollahs by the more moderate elements of the population. "Elections are scheduled and there's a promise of greater women's rights. Their nuclear program will be dismantled; Iran will get out of the terrorism business and seek greater peace with their neighbors. Iran's on trajectory to becoming a new state. You succeeded in doing something that was thought impossible in foreign affairs. I intend to reward you for your...let's call it, *initiative and heroism.* I've authorized the Distinguished Intelligence Cross for you and Captain McGee. Congratulations, *Maverick!* Well done." The President finally released his grip with Hunter.

"Thank you, Sir."

"After today, we'll never again talk about it. I don't have to tell you, no one has a need to know."

The Director of Central Intelligence offered, "Mr. President, you're just going to encourage him. He's like a one-man wrecking ball, and he's constantly losing airplanes."

Banter ricocheted around the room. The President offered, "Director Lynche, Duncan saved one airplane; the other gave its life for our country. A great patriot—his name escapes me—once said, 'I have too much admiration for those who fight evil, whether their choice of ends and means be right or wrong.' No one got hurt. I have to give him something more than a medal. Greg, how do you reward a guy who has everything and a pair of Distinguished Intelligence Crosses?" When the DCI failed to come up with an immediate answer, the President turned to Hunter and asked, "Any ideas, Duncan?" The President was in an ebullient mood; he threw his hands up and wide with the questioning gesture.

Hunter knew he had already been overcompensated and handsomely rewarded for his mission to Algeria. He felt he didn't need another reward for himself, so he gestured for the President to come closer. He whispered in his ear. After the Leader of the Free World leaned over to hear what Duncan had to say, he rose smiling, nodding vigorously, and agreed. "I don't think that's unreasonable. I'll see what I can do. That'll be my pleasure. Get some rest, Duncan. When you are up to it, I plan to have you, Greg, Captain McGee, *and Miss Cunningham* at the White House. When you're ready."

Lynche, mildly agitated, shook his head before he said, "Mr. President, we still don't know how the alarm was sounded to evacuate Natanz. Would you care to enlighten us, Maverick?"

The two men turned to look at Hunter for an answer. He returned a look of incredulity; the puffiness around bloodshot eyes had turned to a swirling spectrum of greens, blues, and violets. Hunter demurred for several seconds before he told them his co-conspirator was the Monrovia airport manager. "I wouldn't have mailed the package unless LeMarcus Leonard had been successful. It was all my idea. Bill McGee wasn't responsible in any way."

Lynche knew Duncan was telling the truth and appreciated the complex thinking needed to conceive such a plan and then carry it out. One person can make a difference. "That was an incredible risk but also a good plan. Therefore, I take it LeMarcus also sent a billion dollars to Nastakovich's account. To take the focus off the suitcase transfer. To put a spotlight on Nasty. To help make it look like an accident or that he had a hand in it."

A very tired Hunter nodded slightly. President Hernandez smiled. Lynche still wasn't happy with his former partner, but he couldn't show it in front of the President.

"In hindsight, that was probably a touch of genius. Like the Iranians, the Russians want to reestablish the Russian Empire, and there was an internal struggle for power. Their president blamed Nastakovich for trying to start a world war. We've an idea how they'll respond." Lynche gripped the Growler and considered what he would say. He settled on, "Nasty is no longer with us." Lynche's last line dripped with sarcasm. The President of the United States nodded. Hunter was confused.

The Secret Service knocked on the door. The President knew it was time to go. He squeezed Hunter's hand one last time and left the room.

After the door closed behind the President, Hunter asked, "What happened to the Russian?" Surely, Lynche would tell him.

Lynche paused to ponder the Embassy dispatch that had reported on the Russian weapons used against the civilian aircraft. The report provided that the surface-to-air missile, known as the SA-24 "*Grinch*" by NATO, had been fielded by the Russian Army since 2004. The DCI wasn't amused by the coincidence that dozens of *Grinches* were used to shoot down the Russian billionaire, and he wasn't about to tell Hunter. He was still quietly furious with Hunter, and he needed to get out of the room before he said something he would regret.

A smirking Lynche turned off the Growler and slipped it into his suit pocket. He replied, "Duncan, I know you're familiar with the principle of need to know. You have no need to know! This conversation is over. Keep that hand elevated. You need your rest. That's an order! I'll talk with you later."

.   .   .

Nazy walked into the bedroom rolling her hair in a bun as she pinned it up. "Are you ready? You sure you can do this? I can just as easily get a washcloth and wash you in bed."

He felt like half a monkey with his arm suspended up and away from his body by the carbon-fiber fixture. As he sat on the edge of the bed, large nipples and dark areolae danced in front of his face as she fussed over his damaged hand.

"I think you'd like that." He stifled a grin; he wasn't ready for the view to change.

"Well, I'd probably get all excited again, and I'm sure another go would likely kill you. I know you'll never tell me if I hurt you." She dragged a finger across his chin. "So how can I help?"

"We need to wrap my hand in some plastic so these electrodes and the IV port don't get wet." A trash can liner and duct tape proved to be sufficient protection against stray water.

Large earth-toned tiles spread across the floor and up the walls of the shower which was large enough to handle a thoroughbred. Turquoise cut-tile mosaics were woven into an intricate pattern behind a clear glass door. Nazy entered first, turned on the water, and aimed a hand wand at him. Hunter entered, assumed the position like a criminal being arrested—hands up—and Nazy got to work.

While she scrubbed him, she asked if he'd been reading or watching anything interesting. Hunter watched her create loads of lather and gingerly clean him with soapy hands. He talked about what had happened to him while she was at work in Langley. "I've watched a lot of television. I found the Eastwood specials on the terrorist groups in Nigeria. He reported on how the mosques in America are havens for the homegrown jihadis, but the FBI is unlikely to do anything about it. I also didn't tell you Eastwood visited me in Bethesda right before I returned home; he thanked me for dropping out of the sky and rescuing him and his fellow passengers. He wanted to know what happened to me, but I used Greg's favorite line that 'he didn't have a need to know.' The Colonel was interviewed on what it was like to have terrorists hijack your aircraft and to have Navy SEALs rescue you. He didn't say anything that would've blown our cover."

Nazy made gestures for him to turn around. She may have been listening, but didn't reply. He saw all the telltale signs that she was more interested in treating him like a patient instead of her therapist, lover, and fiancé.

"A couple of days ago, he came here for an interview but with another gentleman in tow. Imagine my surprise when he tossed me a bullet he dug from the ground in northern Nigeria. He introduced the other guy as Colonel David Bong."

"That's an unusual name," she said.

"Maybe. There's a famous Bong—Richard Bong. World War 2 fighter ace and Medal of Honor winner. Bong handed me a piece of paper. You'll never guess what he had."

"What?"

"It was an overhead. A picture of the thermal image of the YO-3A one-frame before it impacted the reactor building."

Nazy stopped soaping him, looked up, and frowned. "That's not good and absolutely illegal."

Hunter said, "Democrats do it all the time. There's a dude that took classified documents out of the National Archives—stuffed them in his pants, walked right out the building, and nothing ever happened to him. It's good to be a democrat."

"Baby, rules are different for political appointees. So is this Bong a democrat?"

"Bong's no democrat."

She moved from his shoulders and back and began to scrub his ass slowly and thoroughly, as if his buttocks were the dirtiest parts of his body and that more rubbing would somehow make it cleaner; like polishing an apple before you bit into it. She shook her head in disgust. "That's still smuggling classified documents."

Hunter couldn't tell if she was disgusted at his butt or Bong's treachery. But if he didn't start talking again, he knew her slow slick hands on his ass would likely get him aroused again, and that was fraught with peril. "Said the kettle to the pot…. I asked them, 'What do you want?' And they said, 'To put direct pressure on al-Qaeda or the Muslim Brotherhood requires a commitment the west isn't willing to make. So Jews and Christians will vanish from the region, as will the Yazidi or Shia or Kurds. We don't see any attention or action from the rest of the world, with the possible exception of you. These monsters must be stopped, but killing Christians and Jews and other Muslims in the name of radical Islam will never be a newsworthy item for the mainstream media. Someone must stand up to the real aspect of terrorism, the extermination of Jews and Christians.' They deduced I'm in the business and said, 'We want to help.'"

Nazy paused and tried to understand the unknown American kettle-pot idiom. She let it go, stopped cleaning Hunter's caboose, and came around to look at him. She didn't know if the information was good or bad. "So what did you tell them?"

"I said I had been thinking about starting a geopolitical intelligence and consulting firm, with an emphasis on helping clients identify threats and opportunities, make strategic decisions, and manage political and security risks by using quiet airplanes and other quiet technologies. I told them there's a lot of competition, like that big firm in Austin. There's a need to report what the press won't report. Blogs are only so effective. We would develop and provide open-source intelligence and report the atrocities. We would even report on how the closet commie liberals work in and against America. Eastwood said if we're going to pretend communists haven't infiltrated every branch of the government, he guessed we're also going to pretend terrorism doesn't originate in Muslim countries."

"I've seen the files. It's worse than anyone can imagine."

"I believe that, Baby. Anyway, they said to sign them up."

Nazy was still engaged absentmindedly soaping Duncan's body but killed any possible arousal by suddenly discussing his daughter. "I talk with Kelly on a daily basis—email, that is. At first it was the best way to tell her you were in the hospital and were doing well. I didn't tell her what happened, but the expectation was you'd make a full and speedy recovery. She probably thinks you had a vasectomy."

Hunter grinned and interjected, "Do you think Greg purposely assigned Kelly to your security detail? Since I was too afraid to tell you I had a daughter, he thought he'd have a go at it?"

"I haven't asked. He'll never tell. It's Greg. You know he does things, I think you call it, 'on the sly.' I wasn't mad or disappointed with you. I understood why you kept it a secret."

"How'd you figure it out?"

"Things she said and she has *a watch like mine*. New officers don't have gold Rolexes. For that matter, old officers don't have gold Rolexes either. Rolexes and Jaguar cars are a sign of spying."

"That was that traitorous Aldrich Ames. Another democrat."

She frowned and tried to bring the subject back to his daughter. "What about Kelly?"

"Oh. I've talked to her a little bit a couple of days ago. The connection is always crappy. She did say she was flying one of the new Nigerian quiet airplanes, and they were rooting out the remaining Boko Haram elements in the north. She said that the airplane was so much better than what she had been flying and that she can find those bad guys that don't want to be found. I sense she's making a name for herself. Hey, do you know what happened to KGB Boris, the billionaire?"

"The official word is that his airplane suffered an internal fuel cell problem. Apparently, 747s have a problem in that area."

"They don't. In other words, it was shot down."

"I don't know; Greg was curiously silent on the topic. I suppose I've no need to know that either. Sorry, Baby."

"Nazy, how's your father?"

She frowned for a moment. "Back at work. Mother and I are talking again. She wants to meet you. You'll get to see what I'll look like when I'm old and grey."

"No matter what, you'll still be the most beautiful thing on the planet."

"Thank you, Baby." She stood and rinsed Duncan from head to toe and avoided splashing water onto his raised, protected arm. The black structure attached to his hip and arm were impervious to water. She reached and touched the raised scars from the brass knuckles on his cheeks before lathering his face with thick white foam. He closed his eyes as she slowly shaved his face.

"Greg ever tell you who was responsible or how they did it?"

"He thought it was his counterpart in the Mukhabarat. The general and Rothwell were both old, school-trained KGB. We found some of the still classified Venona files, as well as some that were acquired through other means. We think they spiked his tea with polonium. Greg asked the King to have the hospital check for radiation poisoning. Saved his life. They caught General Faisal trying to leave the country." Nazy explained how she saw the banner on television and how Lynche deduced it was a message to her.

Hunter said, "That's incredible. Greg's a veritable Sherlock Holmes. Your father's very lucky. And Lynche did that all by himself?"

Nazy nodded and said, "He did. He also gave me credit for finding the gold and artwork. He and the President said someone had to take responsibility for finding it, and it wasn't a good idea for a contractor to get all the credit."

"I've always said you do good work, Miss Cunningham."

She flashed her gigawatt smile for several seconds in appreciation of the compliment. She said, "Of course, I've been allowed back into the house, but there's a security detail at both ends of the street. I thought my cover had been blown. Greg thinks Rothwell's infatuation with me and his use of proxies to get at me may have done so. We'll have to see what tomorrow brings. Once your cover is blown, you've become worthless to the Agency. I think, eventually, I'm going to have to move or…go into a witness protection program. Or something."

Hunter wondered if the comment was a hint of a coming change their relationship. He thought about nodding but she was still wielding a razor. He wondered about the ramifications of the new normal with Nazy being in DC. Lynche would ensure she was protected, but for how long? Would she be forced to leave the operations side of the business and move into administration, take a desk job, or even leave? Would that be bad? Would that be the catalyst for her to say she was done, take that final walk across the big granite seal at headquarters, and never return? Without moving his head, he took a long glance at her substructure, from her toes to her nose. Then it hit him. *Is she ready to get married? We've been engaged—it seems like forever!* He looked at her, seeking an answer but she ignored him. She was concentrating on not nicking his neck.

Nazy had him turn around to rinse the soap off his face; she moved into him and inadvertently raked her nipples across his arms and chest.

This titillated him, however, she was too busy to notice. "How's Bill and his family? They getting settled?" With the water wand shut off, Nazy pinched Duncan's shaven chin and turned him right and left to admire her work. She toweled him dry with delicate pats of terrycloth.

"They are. He's having the problem I assume all fathers have when boys start to hang around his house. He can't kill them for wanting to see his daughters. I think it's kind of funny. Anyway, he brought the girls over for a few minutes. You know what they told me? Told me they could kick my butt on the racquetball court!"

She feigned hurt for Duncan. "Did that hurt your feelings?"

"No. They giggled as they left the room. Have to give them credit for knowing when to kick a man when he's down."

Nazy and Hunter laughed aloud. He put his good arm around her and pulled her close for a hug. "Thanks for helping me. I don't think my ass has ever been cleaned like that."

When he released her, she said, with arms akimbo knuckles on hips, "It was exceptionally dirty."

"Obviously."

Impishly, she asked, "I'm getting hungry. Do you need help getting dressed? How *do you get dressed* with that thing?"

Hunter was afraid there was another double entendre imbedded in her question. She had nearly killed him earlier. It was better to punt and live another day. He offered a way out. "I'm sure Theresa has cooked up one of her specials." Hunter reflected that as soon as he got out of the hospital in San Antonio, he wanted some real Mexican food, and Theresa Yazzie was more than happy to provide. Three squares every day and coffee Häagen-Dazs ice cream whenever he wanted, which was often.

As they dressed, he was afraid to say he was surprised there hadn't been another attempt on his or Nazy's life. There hadn't been a single clue of unusual activity in Hunter's house. The Border Patrol installed seismic sensors around Hunter's ranch, and the State Highway Patrol added more cars to patrol the roads. Troopers visited the ranch for fresh coffee and sometimes breakfast. It was hard to believe there was

no one out there. There had been nothing, absolutely nothing. Hunter, Nazy, and Lynche knew Islamists don't give up. They were not off the grid, and it was only a matter of time before there was another attempt. Rothwell had said he knew Hunter had released the President's file. If he knew, who else knew?

Hunter dressed himself with one hand. Theresa Yazzie had modified several white dress shirts with cutouts and Velcro closures to accommodate the truncated bike frame. A couple of pair of shorts also got the Velcro treatment. He slipped his bare feet into deck shoes. When Nazy emerged from the bathroom, her hair was parted down the middle and slicked back behind her ears. She wore smoky eye shadow, a dab of makeup, and a Mona Lisa smile. Smooth tanned legs that wouldn't stop for streetlights caught his eye. She was an inferno. A year ago, she was a mess.

Hunter had done everything he could to help her recover from the aftermath of her mission in Algeria. He worried about losing her as she struggled not to lose her mind. Nazy had lost her baby; she had been gang raped, but Bill McGee had interrupted the savages who had begun to mutilate her.

Now there was role reversal. She couldn't do enough for him as he recovered from his surgery. As he had worried about her, she worried about his hand and his mind. She knew what it was like to be damaged physically and mentally, only Duncan hadn't pressed her for sex. For a moment, she felt guilty for telling him she had missed him terribly and wondering aloud if he were able. *I can do all the work!* she had suggested. Her train of thought was broken when she looked up to find him staring at her.

Hunter couldn't take his eyes off hers. Those green eyes would do that to him when he least expected it. She pushed her guilty thoughts out of her head and took him by his good hand to lead him out of the bedroom as he dragged his IV stand.

Lunch was on the veranda. There were candles on the table, and candles lined the porch rail. The setting was about as intimate as was possible on a Texas ranch. The Yazzies brought out food and drinks, then repaired to the kitchen to leave the lovers alone. Nazy rubbed her leg against his, as she had always done since their first dinner in Newport. While Duncan reciprocated with a smile and a hand atop Nazy's, he was distracted, still thirsty for news. He had more questions. Being unplugged from the CIA Headquarters building for a month would do that to a political junkie like Hunter.

"Baby, when the President came by the hospital, he said I helped find the long lost Russian art. I didn't know there was lost Russian art; I thought it was Nazi art and Nazi gold. Do you know something—anything—about all that? I'm confused."

Nazy related the story of how Tsar Nickolas dispatched several trains to Paris. The trains carried the artwork from across the country, from museums, the Royal family, and Russia's aristocrats and wealthy. "The purpose of moving the artwork was to keep it from falling into the hands of the Bolsheviks. When Lenin learned the art had been removed he was furious at Nickolas Romanov. Nastakovich made a point to say the Tsar, his wife, and the princesses were not immediately executed but tortured in the most evil way possible."

"So that was the artwork in the cave?"

"Yes. As far as we know."

"That's incredible. What are they going to do with the gold?"

"Probably go to the Holocaust Museum. I don't think a decision has been made on that." She paused for effect. "But I hear you're going to get one of the airplanes in the cave."

"Really!" He played coy.

"And a portrait."

"*Really?*" He was actually surprised.

"I heard you asked the President. You wanted an airplane? And a painting?" She feigned confusion.

"It's a Bugatti!"

"The airplane or the painting? I don't recognize those Italian names; they confuse me. I don't know what a Bugatti is." Nazy thought Duncan was making little sense and that wasn't like him. Maybe he was making fun of her. Maybe it was time for more medication.

"I'm sorry, Baby. Bugatti built amazing custom cars in the 20s and 30s. He tried his hands at airplanes with the same styling flourishes. Anyway, it's a long lost airplane that few know anything about. One was supposedly built for a race, and the serial number of the one in the cave indicates it was likely built as a military demonstrator."

"Only you would ask for an airplane no one knows anything about."

"It's what I do, Baby. Fly an airplane no one knows anything about." Nazy smiled at him and shook her head in amusement.

"And a painting?"

"I understand they have more than they can handle. I told the President, 'Maybe they have one with a beautiful dark-haired woman with green eyes. Like Miss Cunningham.' I can't imagine anybody could paint something as beautiful as you."

She took the compliment coquettishly. "Beggars can't be choosy." She brightened his demeanor when she smiled at him.

"Nazy, something has intrigued me from the very beginning—the location of the cave was in an encrypted document?"

"Yes, all the hidden locations were. Part of the Ortiz file."

"Who cracked the code, and how did they do it?"

She flashed a huge smile as she leaned over the table, revealing a valley of cleavage. Nazy wanted to touch him, to push his buttons, to extend revealing the answer until he could no longer stand the suspense. She backed away from the table and shrugged her shoulders, flashed the inside of her wrists, and massaged her neck.

Hunter was about to pop. He knew the answer was going to be impressive and unexpected.

"NSA of course. I understand they couldn't immediately break the code. We exchanged some emails. I guessed what I thought might be the missing cipher key. Then an analyst went to their National Cryptologic Museum. She accessed a codebook from the museum's archives and used one of the museum's Nazi Enigma machines that was on display. Five minutes later she broke the code. The document was a list of grid coordinates. I know what grid coordinates are now."

She smiled at finding the missing cipher code: *17 Nails*.

Hunter laughed heartily for a minute. "They have to use the old stuff too! Just like me." He was quiet for a few seconds then asked, "What's the boss doing these days? I know he's busy; he's always busy. Haven't heard from him in a couple of weeks. He won't return my calls."

Sometimes, what a woman doesn't say signals what she is thinking. Hunter read Nazy's body language and prepared for an oblique hazing. Her demeanor turned cool and serious. She lowered her head and talked without looking at him, a little ashamed at what she had to say. "He was so mad at you, Baby—he was furious. He just knew you blew your cover and all that you two worked on for so long. He thought you may have put yourself in too much danger rescuing the aircraft in Liberia. Don't get me wrong, Greg was proud of what you did…but he turned a livid shade of crimson because you risked your life and exposed the mission. I think there's a part of him that still cannot believe you and Bill were able to do what others thought impossible."

"Then the Iranian…*issue* pushed him over the top…. I think you hurt him when you…didn't *consult* him. I know, if you told him he wouldn't have approved. He could excuse some of your heroics, but Iran was, I think, just…*too much*. When he and I were in Amman, it seemed like the trajectory of your Iranian solution would work out. Eventually. He called it a stupid *stunt*. Maybe some of the pressure was taken off him by the President. I felt so bad that your relationship with Greg was probably broken. But if it wasn't, I thought it'd be a very long time before he forgave you."

Her eyes darted to his hand in the black plastic cast. She flicked her hair back as she raised her eyes to meet him. "But when you got…hurt, he may have thought you'd been punished enough. I don't really know. I think he's getting over it, because he wanted to know when you're going to be well enough to go to the White House and to start flying again."

Hunter was saddened by her soliloquy. However, with the reference to flying again he was immediately buoyed. He sat up and asked for validation, "Seriously?"

"I know he's not himself. I think he misses you. Being the DCI is a lonely job, and he talked with you like no one else at Langley. You're the only one he really trusted. You two have so much history. I don't think he'll immediately admit it. In some ways, by extension, it's also affected my relationship with him."

"I'm sorry, Baby. I never thought about what this would do to you."

"It's gotten better. And I think there's a reason. You told Greg you suspected someone from CTC was in Algeria when we were there."

"I did." Hunter smiled quizzically.

"Your suspicions proved to be true. Three senior officers were in Algiers. They left the day after the embassy was evacuated. Rothwell signed their orders. I tried to interview them but they wouldn't cooperate. They resigned the day I visited them."

"I knew it had to be something like that."

Nazy grew more introspective discussing what she thought were tough subjects. It was about to get tougher. She almost whispered, "When Greg ascertained what you did in Iran, I swear I died inside. If it was true you released hell on the mullahs, I didn't see any way for you not to be...sent to prison. The government could never cover up something as dramatic as that. The President, apparently, threatened the Russians and Greg's demeanor completely changed. Greg could see why you did it. He said he could never have done it. Personally or professionally."

"I have to tell you, Bill refused to go through with it unless he was assured no one would get hurt. The killer of America's enemies doesn't kill innocents—that what terrorists do. LeMarcus Leonard was a magician and made the impossible possible. I couldn't have done it without him, and I couldn't have done Liberia or Iran without Bill McGee. They were not one-man-shows."

"For as long as I've known you and Greg, I get the sense he has always wanted to do what you've done. I know he loves you like a son, and he treats me like the daughter he never had. Maybe he's a little jealous of what 'the son' has accomplished. Before I left Washington, he reminded me to tell you, 'There's many more terrorists to kill before this war is over.'"

Hunter said sanguinely, "There will always be a never-ending supply of bad guys." He then turned contrite. "I need to apologize to him. And I should stop poking at his liberal leanings."

Nazy smiled, nodded, and said, "Anyway, he has to go to Indiana...tomorrow. A small town, I believe. Ah, *Evans...ville?*"

Hunter smiled at an old memory. "That's where my dad grew up. Now, what could the DCI be doing in Indiana?" There were few reasons for the Director of Central Intelligence to leave Washington DC for a trip to Middle America. Hunter knew of one.

Nazy smiled back. "I think you should go and ask him."

"I think *we* should. But to do that, I need a lot of help. And for that I need to get out of this superstructure."

She looked at him curiously. "How do you plan to do that?"

. . .

A new, sparkling white and blue-trimmed Gulfstream G-550 taxied to its assigned parking spot, stopped, and shut down next to an older Gulfstream G-IVSP. Through the corporate jet's window, the Director of Central Intelligence recognized the other aircraft by its dullish white and red-trimmed paint and by its N-number. He was very surprised to see the jet belonging to Quiet Aero Systems on the parking ramp.

Few knew of the Director's travel plans. The itinerary of the head of the CIA was a carefully guarded secret. Obviously another security breach. Or maybe it was just Nazy Cunningham strategically leaking classified information, again. He closed his eyes and shook his head. He repeated to himself, "*It's not possible! It's not possible!*"

Lynche planted his face against the aircraft window and watched Duncan Hunter with a shiny black cast on his arm walk off the twenty-year old Gulfstream. He held it up as if he were Geronimo greeting another Apache warrior.

Lynche about burst a carotid. *I thought he had to have his arm elevated in some rigid tubular structure! I swear I'm going to kill him.*

Hunter ambled to the rear of the older jet and watched the CIA jet taxi into position and stop. He was free of the contraption that held his damaged hand in an elevated and fixed position; however, he retained the black plastic cast on his forearm with its electronic stimulation circuitry and battery pack.

As the DCI's turbines shutdown, he reflected on what it had taken to untangle himself from the stiff carbon-fiber structure used to keep his arm elevated. He was reminded of what the great test pilot, Chuck Yeager, did to ensure he would be the first pilot to crack the sound barrier. On the day before the historic flight in the experimental jet, Yeager had fallen off a horse and broken two ribs. He was in such pain that he couldn't close the aircraft's hatch by himself. A friend rigged up a segment of a broom handle for Yeager to seal the hatch of the X-1. Nazy Cunningham and Carlos Yazzie used a hacksaw and dykes to cut the bracing from Hunter's hip and chest to free his damaged arm. He wouldn't have been able to get into the cockpit of the G-IVSP, and he certainly wouldn't have been able to fly the jet looking like he needed to be strung up in hospital rigging and scaffolding. Nazy flipped switches, turned knobs, and performed other copilot duties that Hunter couldn't do with his bad arm braced in the jet's window.

At the sight of his former partner, Lynche worked himself up into a full lather. His business suit flecked and streaked with spittle as his blood pressure rose with every heartbeat. He couldn't wait to get off the jet, and he pushed the security men aside. Long arthritic legs raced down the airstairs and onto the tarmac. As Hunter approached the jet, much to the chagrin of the Director's security detail still on the aircraft, Lynche barked, *"Tell me you didn't fly that all by yourself!"* Hunter ignored the directive and assumed a position of contrition. Lynche demanded, "I cannot believe you! What the hell are you doing here?"

In a monotone, Hunter offered, "Sir. First, I came to apologize for being a world class asshole. I broke most, if not all, of Allen Dulles' 72

Rules of Spycraft. If you can see your way to forgive me, I would appreciate another chance." He pinched his lips together and waited for another round of invective.

The CIA security guards were ready to take down the man who had just walked up their boss, even if he looked like he couldn't fight his way out of wet paper bag.

The security guards could hear the emotional swing from pissed off to proud as Lynche, striving to contain his surprise, burst into laughter. Having Hunter apologize was cathartic, but he answered sarcastically, "I'll think about it...*Maverick*. It's going to be a long time—know that!" Lynche growled at him as he pointed his finger at Hunter. He sucked Indiana air and said, "As far as breaking all the rules, you *were* an egregious asshole. Dulles is probably rolling over in his grave. Just know that I'm glad you are alive." Lynche held out his hand, and Hunter responded with a hearty shake and reciprocal smile. The two-man CIA protection force relaxed. The pilot and copilot filed down the airstairs and walked passed the two men.

"Did you stop it?" asked Hunter.

Lynche didn't know if he wanted the discussion on the tarmac. It wouldn't be harmful to give up a little info. He said, "Only time will tell. POTUS ordered State to undergo polys."

"Will there be anyone left?" Hunter was more than sarcastic.

"Probably not. Congress is pushing back. It's going to be bloody. We're having some resignations too. Somewhat unexpectedly. I cannot predict how the left will respond." Lynche demeanor shifted from serious to unperturbed. "Oh yeah, you probably heard of that Iranian incident. Changed the whole dynamic in the Middle East. I may have been wrong about that."

"Sounds like moving day." Hunter grinned.

Lynche sucked air. "I suppose moving to the right is not all bad."

"Welcome to the fight, Director Lynche."

The CIA Director smiled and checked Hunter's cast. He asked, "Know why I'm here?"

Nazy watched from the window of the white and red jet. Her hand held to her mouth as tears ran down her cheeks.

Hunter replied, "It's hard not to see you had engine trouble or something, and had to land at this airport. I was lucky to get a parking spot before they open the doors for their annual airshow. You were lucky to find a place like this. Look around, there's lots of interesting aircraft to look at while your, ahem, aircraft gets fixed."

The man was incorrigible. Lynche said, "I'll ask again. Please tell me you didn't fly that all by yourself!"

"If it makes you feel better, I had help." He wiggled his fingers like a guitarist warming up his fingers. "See, all the ligaments are connected. No grip, of course."

"Who? How? What?" Lynche was completely confused.

As Nazy stepped off the old Gulfstream and walked around to the rear of the jet, Hunter answered as he swept his good hand toward all the airshow aircraft parked on the tarmac, "A *rara avis* among all these other rare birds. She makes a good copilot." Nazy smiled and waved at her boss as she walked to the two most important men in her life. She and Lynche embraced; she kissed him on the cheek as if she were his daughter. The security men had seen the Deputy Director of Counterintelligence before, but not in jeans or running shoes. They envied the old man as the woman crushed her breasts against his chest and pecked his cheek.

Before Lynche could completely uncouple from Nazy, a squad of four men in blue flight suits flanked by a Marine Corps Captain with a khaki colored "piss cutter" on his head and a Blue Angel patch on his flying coveralls approached the CIA jet. Hunter and Nazy stepped out of the way. The officer saluted the CIA Director and asked, "Are you ready, Director Lynche?"

Lynche returned the salute with an informal touch of the brow and offered his hand. "I am." The old spook shot a look that made the old Marine with the bum arm grin like a buffoon.

· · ·

Hunter and Nazy stood in the shadow of the Quiet Aero Systems jet and watched two men in blue flight suits and yellow helmets walk across the parking apron to a waiting aircraft. He said to no one in particular, "I love it when a plan comes together."

Nazy was confused. "Duncan, darling. What do you mean?" She tried to read his face and body language as Hunter hugged her, seemingly pleased with himself for something. Then he said, "There are some things you just don't miss. After that jet takes off, I think we need to go somewhere."

Something in the lilt of his voice was familiar. "Where?" she asked.

An impish grin offered, "Nowhere special."

She remembered the old line. They had played this game before and she was ready to play. "Well, I've *always* wanted to go *there*." She gripped his good arm and sensually pressed against him. Her green eyes sparkled in the sunlight. He couldn't look away.

"Where?" He had an idea. He tried to play dumb. It wasn't working.

She said, "Nowhere special. Actually, anyplace with you'll be special."

"Where would we go? Do you have any ideas?"

"I do, and I think…it's time, Mister Hunter." He looked at her for validation. In the distance, the unmistakable sound of a military jet engine started to spool up. The noise on the airport increased with every second.

She ignored the airplane and raised her eyebrows in surprise. In her best sexual British voice, she said, "I do. It's past time. I'm ready…I want to take that walk." He brought her close and kissed her passionately; he lifted her off her feet. They remained locked in love until a roaring jet taxied behind them, then they climbed into the Gulfstream. Hunter raised the airstairs and locked the door. From the cockpit, he and Nazy watched a twin-tailed aircraft taxi to the runway. He started the APU and began the start engines checklist.

The shiny blue and yellow, two-seat, U. S. Navy F/A-18D taxied past dozens of airshow aircraft, large and small, fixed-wing and helicopters, military airplanes, private and corporate aircraft. After a minute taxiing, the pilot took the runway and lined up on the centerline. He switched the radio to the assigned frequency and transmitted, "Evansville Tower, Angels Seven has Foxtrot; ready for departure." He checked the flight controls one last time—rudder pedals moved the twin rudders left and right, the control stick cycled through the ailerons and the stabilator, moving the flight controls up and down. He glanced in the canopy mirror at the man in the back seat in the blue flight suit and yellow helmet. The man's call sign emblazoned in blue letters above the dark grey visor. A boom microphone over his lips.

"All set, Grinch?"

The black and yellow ejection seat handle loomed large between his legs, at his crotch. Multi-function displays with scores of buttons stared back at him. Fifty years of wishing to ride in the seat of a high performance jet was about to come true. He was anxious but calm. He could have bounced around in the seat like a kid on Christmas morning, but heavy lap belts and shoulder straps held his ass firmly in the ejection seat. His heart raced. The anticipation was about to kill him as a gallon of adrenaline spiked his circulatory system. Through a massive grin, Greg Lynche said, "All set, Spock."

Instantly, the brakes released and the throttles were slammed to the stops, into MAX, engaging the afterburner. The big jet jumped from a standing start and compressed the men in their seats as the mighty turbofans behind them lit off with thirty-five-foot cones of fire, delivering 35,000 pounds of thrust. Lynche strained to utter, "Oh...my...God!"

The jet propelled down the runway accelerating the fighter to 200 knots in seconds. The pilot quickly raised the gear as the jet closely hugged the runway. With the landing gear and flaps up, at ten feet off the deck, the Hornet shot to the end of the runway like a bullet. At 450 knots, the pilot yanked the control stick back into his lap, snapping the nose of the jet straight up in a seven-G pull. Lynche's vision narrowed to the size of a basketball. He nearly blacked out, but the G-suit suddenly inflated against his abdomen and compressed his legs into twigs. His newly-learned straining maneuver prevented him from fully blacking out as the jet continued to accelerate in the vertical. The Grinch strained, grunted, and screamed against the G-forces as the aircraft punched through 20,000 feet in less than a minute from their standing start.

When the pilot slammed the throttles to idle and snapped-rolled the jet onto its back, he deftly programmed the jet's nose to touch the horizon. Then he snap-spun the aircraft upright and relaxed the pressure on the control stick, slapped the throttles forward and powered up and leveled off the aircraft. He allowed the man in the back seat a moment to recover from the prolonged anti-G straining maneuver. He was trying to give the DCI the ride of his life and it was working. The pilot took his hands off the flight controls and said, "Your jet, Grinch! Fly it like you stole it!"

Lynche's legs felt like they had been crushed, but he didn't care. He replied breathlessly, "My jet!" He gripped the throttles and control stick and placed his feet on the rudder pedals. He pointed the Number Seven aircraft of the *Blue Angels* Flight Demonstration Team toward the nearest cloud, jammed the throttles into afterburner, and said to himself, "*All is forgiven Maverick.*"

· · ·

The parking ramp was chock full of jets and general aviation airplanes. A single, older turbine-powered transport could get lost among the other airplanes of the rich and famous. But there's always room for one more, even if the aircraft was parked on an inactive taxiway. Jackson Hole wasn't a place where you would expect to find a mosque, an organized group of aircraft tail watchers, or Islamists on motorcycles carrying Uzis. This resort town was a place where, even at midnight, one could get anything, for a price, even discretion and anonymity.

The clock struck midnight at the Rusty Parrot Lodge. The desk clerk's pocket was filled with ten American Gold Eagles, payment for keeping the customer's name off the register and out of the computer. She had also been paid for making a series of telephone calls. She held the door for the pastor who scurried away into the night with her purse heavy with a score of gold coins.

At the rear of the resort, in a small and dark ballroom, an old disc jockey played a selection of romantic music requested by the man on the dance floor. Bobby Hatfield belted out the high notes of *Unchained Melody*. The couple slow-danced in a tight circle in the middle of a meager wooden dance floor.

She was more striking, sensual, and exotic than any women he had seen since coming to Wyoming. A white dress hugged every curve; the low-cut bodice emphasized her square shoulders and her high firm breasts. Her hair flowed easily across her shoulders and down her back.

The DJ wondered who the man and the green-eyed goddess on his arm could be. The man looked like an exhausted and battered Steve McQueen after a car race with a memorable finish line girl on one arm. His tuxedo looked good, although the sleeve was cut to accommodate a funny looking cast. The black crocodile boots were well worn, probably Lucchese. Somewhere on the floor was a red bow tie. The bride had untied it and let it fall from her fingers.

The man was probably the luckiest guy on the planet, obviously winning the trifecta of life—good looking, rich, and now sporting an imponderably beautiful trophy wife. With a pocketful of gold coins, the DJ knew better than to ask questions.

From the center of the miniature wooden dance floor, the groom said, "Play *Unforgettable*, Sam." The DJ cycled in the steamy belly-rubbing music as directed and observed the slow moving lovers. He had witnessed countless dancers over the years. This pair was uniquely electric. They were pressed together like interlocking puzzle pieces, fitting perfectly in the correct position. Her delicate hands and long fingers hung loosely over his shoulders. His arms, one of dubious functionality encumbered with a glossy black spider web splint, surrounded her back in an odd embrace.

The old DJ couldn't look away. Every movement had a purpose.

Noses touched delicately and suggestively with every sway of their bodies. Round and around they danced. She rubbed his knees to signal she was ready to go. A flick of his tongue across her lips was a tease. She pressed against him with a sense of urgency; she was on the verge of moaning and trembling in his arms.

He slightly eased the pressure against her back and she was grateful. They cooed at each other. He whispered in her ear, "I think you've been taking…dancing lessons…*Mrs. Hunter*." She breathlessly nodded, her forehead against his and jammed her lips into his with abandon. With his good hand, he raked fingernails across the fabric over an erect nipple, and she shuddered. He took her hand and kissed it. It was time. He held his bad arm up high and put his good arm around his wife's waist. They sauntered toward the exit as one, ignoring the DJ as if the man had never been in the room.

That must be the end, the DJ reasoned. He shut down the computer and disassembled his equipment. He hauled his kit through the lobby of the hotel, out to the parking lot, and loaded up an old 21-window VW Microbus. As he slipped behind the steering wheel of the Volkswagen, he reflected on how much of an impression the woman had left on him. Maybe he would learn who she was from the papers, the television, or the movies.

He fired up the van. It was late. He yawned as he fingered a handful of large coins, several months' worth of work for him. All for a handful of songs. He put the heavy coins away and put the rattletrap into gear. The promise of being paid in gold—*off-the-grid money*—the impromptu job spurred more than excitement. He was curious who would want a DJ at midnight, one who wouldn't ask any questions. Forget that the couple had ever been there. The bride was definitely unforgettable; the husband wasn't even a memory.

The VW put-putted away from the resort. The event had passed. It wasn't worth the time or the effort to find out who they were. As curious as he once was, a dozen $50 gold pieces jingled in his pocket, and he lost the need to know.

ACRONYMS/ABBREVIATIONS

A	Attack Aircraft
A380	Airbus jumbo double-deck aircraft model 380
AAFES	Army & Air Force Exchange Service
ACP	Automatic Colt Pistol
ADOC	Air Defense Operations Center
AFSOC	Air Force Special Operations Center
AG	Attorney General
AGL	Above Ground Level
AK	Automatic Kalashnikov
ANVIS	Aviator Night Vision
APU	Auxiliary Power Unit
AQ	Al-Qaeda
ATLS	Automating Takeoff and Landing System
BF	Bull Frog
BND	Bundesnachrichtendienst: The German Federal Intelligence Service
C	Cargo aircraft
CAT	Crisis Action Team
C/B	Chemical/Biological
CH	Cargo Helicopter
CIA	Central Intelligence Agency
CEO	Chief Executive Officer
COS	Chief Of Station
CPU	Central Processing Unit
CTC	Counter Terrorism Center, Short for NCTC
CV	Cargo Vertical; tilt rotor aircraft
CVR	Cockpit Voice Recorder
C-4	Composition C-4; a variety of plastic explosive
DC	District of Colombia
DC	Douglas Aircraft Company
DCI	Director of Central Intelligence
DEVGRU	Naval Special Warfare Development Group
DHS	Department of Homeland Security
DIA	Defense Intelligence Agency
DNA	Deoxyribonuleic Acid

DO	Director of Operations
DOD	Department of Defense
DOJ	Department of Justice
DOS	Secretary of State
EMP	Electromagnetic Pulse
ETA	Estimated Time of Arrival
F	Fighter aircraft
F/A	Fighter/Attack Aircraft
FARC	Fuerzas Armadas Revolucionarias de Colombia; the Revolutionary Armed Forces of Columbia
FBI	Federal Bureau of Investigation
FBO	Fixed Based Operator
FLIR	Forward Looking Infra-Red
FSB	Federal'naya Sluzba Benzopasnosti; the foreign intelligence and domestic security agency of the Russian Republic
FSTC	Full Spectrum Training Center
G	Gram
G	Gravity
G-IVSP	Gulfstream Model 4, Special Purpose
G-550	Gulfstream Model 550
GI	Government Issue
GPS	Global Positioning System
GS	General Schedule
H	Helicopter
HQ	Headquarters
HUMINT	Human Intelligence
ID	Identify/Identity/Identification
IED	Improvised Explosive Device
IC	Intelligence Community
ICU	Intensive Care Unit
IL	Ilyushin Design Bureau
IO	Indian Ocean
IO	Intelligence Officer
IARPA	Intelligence Advanced Research Projects Activity
IRS	Internal Revenue Service
JAC	Jordanian Aerospace Company
JFK	John F. Kennedy International Airport, airport three letter designation
JSOC	Joist Special Operations Command
JTF	Joint Task Force
JW	John Willard, for JW Marriott
KGB	Komitet Goshudarstyennoy Bezomanosti; the foreign intelligence and domestic security agency of the Soviet Union
KH	Key Hole; reconnaissance satellites designation
LD	Laser Designator
LZ	Landing Zone
MAC-10	Military Armament Corporation Model 10

MANPADS	Man-Portable Air-Defense Systems
MFD	Multi-Function Display
MI5	Military Intelligence, Section 5; the domestic counter-intelligence and security agency of the United Kingdom
MI6	Military Intelligence, Section 6; the secret intelligence service of the United Kingdom
MO	Modus Operendi
MPH	Miles per Hour
M-4	Carbine version of the longer barreled M16
NASA	National Aeronautics and Space Administration
NATO	North Atlantic Treaty Organization
NCS	National Clandestine Service
NCTC	National Counter Terrorism Center
NE	Near East Division
NOFORN	Not Releasable to Foreign Nationals
NRO	National Reconnaissance Office
NSA	National Security Agency
O	Observation aircraft
OCONUS	Outside the Continental United States
OSS	Office of Strategic Services
PDB	President's Daily Brief
PhD	Doctor of Philosophy
POTUS	President of the United States
POW	Prisoner of War
PPR	Prior Permission Required
PVS	Panoramic Vision System
QD	Quick Disconnect
RIO	Radio Intercept Officer
RM	Reichsmark
ROB	Roberts Field; airport three letter designation
RPG	Rocket Propelled Grenade
RPM	Revolutions per Minute
RRT	Rapid Response Team
R-11	Refueling Truck Model 11
S&T	Science and Technology
SAM	Surface to Air Missile
SAP	Special Access Program
SATCOM	Satellite Communications
SCI	Sensitive Compartmented Information
SCIF	Sensitive Compartmented Information Facility
SEAL	Sea, Air and Land
SERE	Survival, Escape, Resistance, and Evasion
SIS	Senior Intelligence Service
SOAR	Special Operations Airborne Regiment
SOC	Special Operations Command
SOF	Special Operations Forces
SR	Surveillance Reconnaissance aircraft; SR-71

SS	Schutzstaffel; the Nazi Party's "Protective Squadron"
SST	Super Sonic Transport
STE	Secure Terminal Equipment
SUV	Sport Utility Vehicle
SWAT	Special Weapons and Tactics
TS	Top Secret
TSA	Transportation Security Administration
TS/SCI	Top Secret/Sensitive Compartmented Information
TSO	Transportation Security Officer
TV	Television
10-4	Message Received, from Ten Code
UAV	Unmanned Aerial Vehicle
U.K.	United Kingdom
UPI	United Press International
UPS	United Parcel Service
U.S.	United States
U.S.G.S.	United States Geological Survey
U.S.S.	United States Ship
UV	Ultra Violet
VIP	Very Important Person
VNE	Velocity; Never to Exceed Speed
VP	Vice President
VW	Volkswagen
V12	V-type engine with twelve cylinders
WEPS	Weapons
WMD	Weapon(s) of Mass Destruction
Y	Prototype aircraft
YAK	Yakovlev Aircraft Corporation
YO-3A	Prototype Observation aircraft, model 3, series A
XKE	Jaguar E-Type

Purchase other Black Rose Writing titles at www.blackrosewriting.com/books
and use promo code PRINT to receive a 20% discount.

BLACK🌹ROSE
writing™

Made in United States
Orlando, FL
01 May 2024

46386074R10322